The First Aurora Teagarden Omnibus

Real Murders
A Bone to Pick
Three Bedrooms, One Corpse
The Julius House

Charlaine Harris

GOLLANCZ
LONDON

First published in Great Britain in 2010 by Gollancz
An imprint of the Orion Publishing Group
Orion House, 5 Upper St Martin's Lane,
London WC2H 9EA
An Hachette UK Company

A CIP catalogue record for this book
is available from the British Library

ISBN 978 0 575 09646 2 (Cased)
ISBN 978 0 575 09647 9 (Export Trade Paperback)

3 5 7 9 10 8 6 4

Typeset at The Spartan Press Ltd,
Lymington, Hants

Printed in Great Britain by Clays Ltd,
St Ives plc

The Orion Publishing Group's policy is to use papers that are natural, renewable and recyclable products and made from wood grown in sustainable forests. The logging and manufacturing processes are expected to conform to the environmental regulations of the country of origin.

www.charlaineharris.com
www.orionbooks.co.uk

Real Murders

'An ingenious plot and sufficient flow of blood keep the pages flying in Harris' novel . . . Harris draws the guilty and the innocent into an engrossing tale while inventing a heroine as capable and potentially complex as P. D. James' *Cordelia Gray*' *Publishers Weekly*

'*Real Murders* is the first adventure for Harris' perceptive protagonist and I eagerly look forward to the second . . . Harris' story alternately charms and chills, a difficult combination she manages with aplomb and brilliance'
Carolyn Hart, award-winning author of *Set Sail for Murder*

A Bone to Pick

'Entertaining' *Booklist*

'Pleasant reading . . . Heartily recommended' *Pen & Dagger*

Three Bedrooms, One Corpse

'Delightful . . . Clearly focused plot, animated description of character and real estate and sparkling prose commend this breath of fresh air to all collections' *Library Journal*

The Julius House

'In the best of the series to date . . . the author's brisk, upbeat style keeps tension simmering' *Publishers Weekly*

Also by Charlaine Harris from Gollancz:

SOOKIE STACKHOUSE

Dead Until Dark

Living Dead in Dallas

Club Dead

Dead to the World

Dead as a Doornail

Definitely Dead

All Together Dead

From Dead to Worse

Dead and Gone

A Touch of Dead

Dead in the Family

True Blood Omnibus

True Blood Omnibus II

HARPER CONNELLY

Grave Sight

Grave Surprise

An Ice Cold Grave

Grave Secret

The First Aurora Teagarden Omnibus

The Lily Bard Mysteries Omnibus

Real Murders

To Mother and Father

Chapter One

'Tonight I want to tell you about that most fascinating of murder mysteries, the Wallace case,' I told my mirror Enthusiastically.

I tried Sincere after that; then Earnest.

My brush caught in a tangle. 'Shoot!' I said, and tried again.

'I think the Wallace case can easily fill our whole program tonight,' I said Firmly.

We had twelve regular members, which worked out well with twelve programs a year. Not all cases could fill up a two-hour program, of course. Then the member responsible for presenting the Murder of the Month, as we jokingly called it, would have a guest speaker – someone from the police department in the city, or a psychologist who treated criminals, or the director of the local rape crisis center. Once or twice, we'd watched a movie.

But I'd come up lucky in the draw. There was more than enough material on the Wallace case, yet not so much that I'd be compelled to hurry over it. We'd allocated two meetings for Jack the Ripper. Jane Engle had taken one for the victims and the circumstances surrounding the crimes and Arthur Smith had taken another on the police investigation and the suspects. You can't skimp Jack.

'The elements of the Wallace case are these,' I continued. 'A man who called himself Qualtrough, a chess tournament, an apparently inoffensive woman named Julia Wallace, and of course the accused, her husband, William Herbert Wallace himself.' I gathered all my hair into a brown switch and debated whether to put it in a roll on the back of my head, braid it, or just fasten a band around it to keep it off my face. The braid. It made me feel artsy and intellectual. As I divided my hair into clumps, my eyes fell on the framed studio portrait of my mother she'd given me on my last birthday with an offhand, 'You said you wanted one.' My mother, who looks a lot like Lauren Bacall, is at least five-foot six, elegant to her fingertips, and has built her own small real estate empire. I am four-foot eleven, wear big round tortoise-rimmed glasses, and have fulfilled my childhood dream by becoming a librarian. And she named me Aurora, though to a woman herself baptized Aida, Aurora may not have seemed so outrageous.

Amazingly, I love my mother.

I sighed, as I often do when I think of her, and finished braiding my hair with practiced speed. I checked my reflection in the big mirror; brown hair, brown glasses, brown eyes, pink cheeks (artificial), and good skin (real). Since it was, after all, Friday night, I'd shucked my work clothes, a plain blouse and skirt, and opted for a snug white knit top and black slacks. Deciding I wasn't festive enough for William Herbert Wallace, I tied a yellow ribbon around the top of my braid and pulled on a yellow sweater.

A look at the clock told me it was finally time to go. I slapped on some lipstick, grabbed my purse, and bounded down the stairs. I glanced around the big den/dining/kitchen area that took up the back half of the ground floor of the townhouse. It was neat; I hate to come home to a messy place. I tracked down my notebook and located my keys, muttering facts about the Wallace case all the while. I had thought about xeroxing the indistinct old pictures of Julia Wallace's body and passing them out to show the murder scene, but I decided that would perhaps be ghoulish and certainly disrespectful to Mrs Wallace.

A club like Real Murders seemed odd enough to people who didn't share our enthusiasms, without adding the charge of ghoulishness. We kept a low profile.

I flipped on the outside light as I shut the door. It was already dark this early in spring; we hadn't switched to daylight savings time yet. In the excellent light over the back door, my patio with its high privacy fence looked swept and clean, the rose trees in their big tubs just coming into bud.

'Heigh ho, heigh ho, it's off to crime I go,' I hummed tunelessly, shutting the gate behind me. Each of the four townhouses 'owns' two parking spaces: there are extra ones on the other side of the lot for company. My neighbor two doors down, Bankston Waites, was getting into his car, too.

'I'll see you there,' he called. 'I've got to pick up Melanie first.'

'Okay, Bankston. Wallace tonight!'

'I know. We've been looking forward to it.'

I started up my car, courteously letting Bankston leave the lot first on his way to pick up his lady fair. It did cross my mind to feel sorry for myself that Melanie Clark had a date and I always arrived at Real Murders by myself, but I didn't want to get all gloomy. I would see my friends and have as good a Friday night as I usually had. Maybe better.

As I backed up I noticed that the townhouse next to mine had bright windows and an unfamiliar car was parked in one of its assigned spaces. So that was what Mother's message taped to my back door had meant.

She'd been urging me to get an answering machine, since the townhouse tenants (her tenants) might need to leave me (the resident manager) messages while I was at work at the library. Actually, I believe my mother just wanted to know she could talk to me while I wasn't even home.

I'd had the townhouse next door cleaned after the last tenants left. It had been in perfect condition to show, I reassured myself. I'd go meet the new neighbor tomorrow, since it was my Saturday off.

I drove up Parson Road far enough to pass the library where I worked, then turned left to get to the area of small shops and filling stations where the VFW Hall was. I was mentally rehearsing all the way.

But I might as well have left my notes at home.

Chapter Two

Real Murders met in the VFW Hall and paid the Veterans a small fee for the privilege. The fee went into a fund for the annual VFW Christmas party, so everyone was pleased with our arrangement. Of course the building was much larger than a little group like Real Murders needed, but we did like the privacy.

A VFW officer would meet a club member at the building thirty minutes before the meeting and unlock it. That club member was responsible for restoring the room to the way we'd found it and returning the key after the meeting. This year the 'opening' member was Mamie Wright, since she was vice president. She would arrange the chairs in a semicircle in front of the podium and set up the refreshments table. We rotated bringing the refreshments.

I got there early that evening. I get almost everywhere early.

There were already two cars in the parking lot, which was tucked behind the small building and had a landscaped screening of crepe myrtles, still grotesquely bare in the early spring. The arc lamps in the lot had come on automatically at dusk. I parked my Chevette under the glow of the lamp nearest the back door. Murder buffs are all too aware of the dangers of this world.

As I stepped into the hall, the heavy metal door clanged shut behind me. There were only five rooms in the building; the single door in the middle of the wall to my left opened into the big main room, where we held our meetings. The four doors to my right led into a small conference room, then the men's, the ladies', and, at the end of the corridor, a small kitchen. All the doors were shut, as usual, since propping them open required more tenacity than any of us were able to summon. The VFW Hall had been constructed to withstand enemy attack, we had decided, and those heavy doors kept the little building very quiet. Even now, when I knew from the cars outside that there were at least two people here, I heard nothing.

The effect of all those shut doors in that blank corridor was also unnerving. It was like a little beige tunnel, interrupted only by the pay phone mounted on the wall. I recalled once telling Bankston Waites that if that phone rang, I'd expect Rod Serling to be on the other end, telling me I had now entered the 'Twilight Zone.' I half smiled at the idea and turned to grasp the knob of the door to the big meeting room.

The phone rang.

I swung around and took two hesitant steps toward it, my heart banging against my chest. Still nothing moved in the silent building.

The phone rang again. My hand closed around it reluctantly.

'Hello?' I said softly, and then cleared my throat and tried again. 'Hello,' I said firmly.

'May I speak to Julia Wallace, please?' The voice was a whisper.

My scalp crawled. 'What?' I said shakily.

'Julia . . .' whispered the caller.

The other phone was hung up.

I was still standing holding the receiver when the door to the women's room opened and Sally Allison came out.

I shrieked.

'God almighty, Roe, I don't look that bad, do I?' Sally said in amazement.

'No, no, it's the phone call . . .' I was very close to crying, and I was embarrassed about that. Sally was a reporter for the Lawrenceton paper, and she was a good reporter, a tough and intelligent woman in her late forties. Sally was the veteran of a runaway teenage marriage that had ended when the resulting baby was born. I'd gone to high school with that baby, named Perry, and now I worked with him at the library. I loathed Perry; but I liked Sally a lot, even if sometimes her relentless questioning made me squirm. Sally was one of the reasons I was so well prepared for my Wallace lecture.

Now she elicited all the facts about the phone call from me in a series of concise questions that led to a sensible conclusion; the call was a prank perpetrated by a club member, or maybe the child of a club member, since it seemed almost juvenile when Sally put it in her framework.

I felt somehow cheated, but also relieved.

Sally retrieved a tray and a couple of boxes of cookies from the small conference room. She'd deposited them there, she explained, when she entered and suddenly felt the urgency of the two cups of coffee she'd had after supper.

'I didn't even think I could make it across the hall into the big room,' she said with a roll of her tan eyes.

'How's life at the newspaper?' I asked, just to keep Sally talking while I got over my shock.

I couldn't dismiss the phone call as lightly and logically as Sally. As I trailed after her into the big meeting room, half listening to her account of a fight she'd had with the new publisher, I could still taste the metallic surge of adrenaline in my mouth. My arms had goosepimples, and I pulled my sweater tightly around me.

As she arranged the cookies on her tray, Sally began telling me about the election that would be held to select someone to fill out the term of our unexpectedly deceased mayor. 'He keeled over right in his office, according to his secretary,' she said casually as she realigned a row of Oreos. 'And after having been mayor only a month! He'd just gotten a new desk.' She shook her head, regretting the loss of the mayor or the waste of the desk, I wasn't sure which.

'Sally,' I said before I knew I was going to, 'where's Mamie?'

'Who cares?' Sally asked frankly. She cocked one surprised eyebrow at me.

I knew I should laugh, since Sally and I had discussed our mutual distaste of Mamie before, but I didn't bother. I was beginning to be irritated with Sally, standing there looking sensible and attractive in her curly bronze permanent, her well-worn expensive suit, and her well-worn expensive shoes.

'When I pulled in the parking lot,' I said quite evenly, 'there were two cars, yours and Mamie's. I recognized Mamie's, because she's got a Chevette like mine, but white instead of blue. So you are here and I am here, but where is Mamie?'

'She's set the chairs up right and made the coffee,' Sally said after looking around. 'But I don't see her purse. Maybe she ran home for something.'

'How'd she get past us?'

'Oh, I don't know.' Sally was beginning to sound irritated with me, too. 'She'll show up. She always does!'

And we both laughed a little, trying to lose our displeasure with each other in our amusement at Mamie Wright's determination to go to everything her husband attended, be in every club he joined, share his life to the fullest.

Bankston Waites and his light of love, Melanie Clark, came in as I put my notebook on the podium and slid my purse underneath it. Melanie was a clerk at Mamie's husband's insurance office, and Bankston was a loan officer at Associated Second Bank. They'd been dating about a year, having become interested in each other at Real Murders meetings, though they'd gone through Lawrenceton High School together a few years ahead of me without striking any sparks.

Bankston's mother had told me last week in the grocery store that she was expecting an interesting announcement from the couple any day. She made a particular point of telling me that, since I'd gone out with Bankston a few times over a year ago, and she wanted me to know he was going to be out of circulation. If she was waiting in suspense for that interesting announcement, she was the only one. There wasn't anyone in Lawrenceton Bankston and Melanie's age left for them to marry, except each other. Bankston was thirty-two, Melanie a year or two older. Bankston had scanty blond hair, a pleasant round face, and mild blue eyes; he was Mr Average. Or at least he had been; I noticed for the first time that his shoulder and arm muscles were bulging underneath his shirt sleeves.

'Have you been lifting weights, Bankston?' I asked in some amazement. I might have been more interested if he'd shown that much initiative when I'd dated him.

He looked embarrassed but pleased. 'Yeah, can you tell a difference?'

'I certainly can,' I said with genuine admiration. It was hard to credit Melanie Clark with being the motivation for such a revolutionary change in Bankston's sedentary life, but undoubtedly she was. Perhaps her absorption in him could be all the more complete since she had no family to claim her devotion. Her parents, both 'only' children, had been dead for years – her mother from cancer, her father hit by a drunk driver.

Right now Melanie the motivator was looking miffed.

'What do you think about all this, Melanie?' I asked hastily.

Melanie visibly relaxed when I acknowledged her proprietorship. I made a mental note to speak carefully around her, since Bankston lived in one of 'my' townhouses. Melanie must surely know Bankston and I had gone out together and it would be too easy for her to build something incorrect out of a landlady-tenant relationship.

'Working out's done wonders for Bankston,' she said neutrally. But there was an unmistakable cast to her words. Melanie wanted me to get a specific message, that she and Bankston were having sex. I was a little shocked at her wanting me to know that. There was a gleam in her eyes that made me realize Melanie had banked fires under her sedate exterior. Under the straight dark hair conservatively cut, under the plain dress, Melanie was definitely feeling her oats. Her hips and bosom were heavy, but suddenly I saw them as Bankston must, as fertility symbols instead of liabilities. And I had a further revelation; not only were Bankston and Melanie having sex, they were having it often and exotically.

I looked at Melanie with more respect. Anyone who could pull the wool over the collective eye of Lawrenceton as effectively as Melanie had earned it.

'There was a phone call before you got here,' I began, and they focused on me with interest. But before I could tell them about it, I heard a luscious ripple of laughter from the opening door. My friend Lizanne Buckley came in, accompanied by a very tall red-haired man. Seeing Lizanne here was a surprise. Lizanne didn't read a book from one year to the next, and her hobbies, if she had any, did not include crime.

'What on earth is she doing here?' Melanie said. She seemed really put out, and I decided we had here another Mamie Wright in the making.

Lizanne (Elizabeth Anna) Buckley was the most beautiful woman in Lawrenceton. Without Lizanne exerting herself in the slightest (and she never did) men would throw themselves on the floor for her to saunter on; and saunter she would, calm and smiling, never looking down. She was kind, in her passive, lazy way; and she was conscientious, so long as not too much was demanded of her. Her job as receptionist and phone answerer at the Power and Light Company was just perfect for her – and for the utility company. Men paid their bills promptly and smilingly, and anyone who got huffy over the telephone was immediately passed to someone higher on the totem pole. No one ever sustained a huff in person. It was simply impossible for ninety percent of the population to remain angry in Lizanne's presence.

But she required constant entertainment from her dates, and the tall red-haired man with the beaky nose and wire-rimmed glasses seemed to be making heavy weather of it.

'Do you know who he is, the man with Lizanne?' I asked Melanie.

'You don't recognize him?' Melanie's surprise was a shade overdone.

So I was supposed to know him. I re-examined the newcomer. He was wearing slacks and a sport coat in light brown, and a plain white shirt; he had huge hands and feet, and his longish hair flew around his head in a copper nimbus. I had to shake my head.

'He's Robin Crusoe, the mystery writer,' Melanie said triumphantly.

The insurance clerk beats the librarian in her own bailiwick.

'He looks different without the pipe in his mouth,' John Queensland said from behind my right shoulder. John, our wealthy real-estate-rich president, was immaculate as usual; an expensive suit, a white shirt, his creamy white hair smooth and the part sharp as an arrow. John had become more interesting to me when he'd started dating my mother. I felt there must be substance below the stuffed-shirt exterior. After all, he was a Lizzie Borden expert . . . and he believed she was innocent! A true romantic, though he hid it well.

'So what's he doing here?' I asked practically. 'With Lizanne.'

'I'll find out,' said John promptly. 'I should greet him anyway, as club president. Of course visitors are welcome, though I don't believe we've ever had any before.'

'Wait, I need to tell you about this phone call,' I said quickly. The newcomer had distracted me. 'When I came in a few minutes ago—'

But Lizanne had spotted me and was swaying over to our little group, her semi-famous escort in tow.

'Roe, I brought you all some company tonight,' Lizanne said with her agreeable smile. And she introduced us all around with facility, since Lizanne knows everyone in Lawrenceton. My hand was engulfed in the writer's huge boney one, and he really shook it, too. I liked that; I hate it when people just kind of press your hand and let it drop. I looked up and up at his crinkly mouth and little hazel eyes, and I just liked him altogether.

'Roe, this is Robin Crusoe, who just moved to Lawrenceton,' Lizanne said. 'Robin, this is Roe Teagarden.'

He gave me an appreciative smile but he was with Lizanne, so I realistically built nothing on that.

'I thought Robin Crusoe was a pseudonym,' Bankston murmured in my ear.

'I did too,' I whispered, 'but apparently not.'

'Poor guy, his parents must have been nuts,' Bankston said with a snigger, until he remembered from my raised eyebrows that he was talking to a woman named Aurora Teagarden.

'I met Robin when he came in to get his utilities turned on,' Lizanne was telling John Queensland. John was saying all the proper things to Robin Crusoe, glad to have such a well-known name in our little town, hope you stay a while, ta-dah ta-dah ta-dah. John edged Robin over to meet Sally Allison, who was chatting with our newest member, a police officer named Arthur Smith. If Robin was built tall and lanky, Arthur was short and solid, with coarse curly pale hair and the flat confrontive stare of the bull who knows he has nothing to fear because he is the toughest male on the farm.

'You're lucky to have met such a well-known writer,' I said enviously to Lizanne. I still wanted to tell someone about the phone call, but Lizanne was hardly the person. She sure didn't know who Julia Wallace was. And she didn't know who Robin Crusoe was either, as it turned out.

'Writer?' she said indifferently. 'I'm kind of bored.'

I stared at her incredulously. Bored by Robin Crusoe?

One afternoon when I'd been at the Power and Light Company paying my bill, she'd told me, 'I don't know what it is, but even when I pretty much like a man, after I date him a while, he gets to seem kind of tiresome. I just can't be bothered to act interested anymore, and then finally I tell him I don't want to go out anymore. They always get upset,' she'd added, with a philosophical shake of her shining dark hair. Lovely Lizanne had never been married, and lived in a tiny apartment close to her job, and went home to her parents' house for lunch every day.

Robin Crusoe, desirable writer, was striking out with Lizanne even now. She looked – sleepy.

He reappeared at her side.

'Where do you live in Lawrenceton?' I asked, because the newcomer seemed dolefully aware he wasn't making the grade with our local siren.

'Parson Road. A townhouse. I'm camping there until my furniture comes, which it should do tomorrow. The rent here is so much less for a nicer place than I could find anywhere in the city close to the college.'

Suddenly I felt quite cheerful. I said, 'I'm your landlady,' but after we'd talked about the coincidence for a moment, a glance at my watch unsettled me. John Queensland was making a significant face at me over Arthur Smith's shoulder. Since he was president, he had to open the meeting, and he was ready to start.

I glanced around, counting heads. Jane Engle and LeMaster Cane had come in on each other's heels and were chatting while preparing their coffee cups. Jane was a retired school librarian who substituted at both the school and the public libraries, a surprisingly sophisticated spinster who specialized in Victorian murders. She wore her silver hair in a chignon, and never, never wore slacks. Jane looked sweet and fragile as aged lace, but after thirty years of school children she was tough as a marine sergeant. Jane's idol was Madeleine Smith, the highly sexed young Scottish poisoner, which sometimes made me wonder about Jane's past. LeMaster was our only black member, a stout middle-aged bearded man with huge brown eyes who owned a dry cleaning business. LeMaster was most interested in the racially motivated murders of the sixties and early seventies, the Zebra murders in San Francisco and the Jones-Piagentini shooting in New York, for example.

Sally's son, Perry Allison, had come in, too, and had taken a seat without speaking to anyone. Perry had not actually joined Real Murders, but he had come to the past two meetings, to my dismay. I saw quite enough of him at work. Perry showed a rather unnerving knowledge of modern serial murderers like the Hillside Stranglers and the Green River killer, in which the motivation was clearly sexual.

Gifford Doakes was standing by himself. Unless Gifford brought his friend Reynaldo, this was a pretty common situation, since Gifford was openly interested in massacres – St Valentine's Day, the Holocaust, it didn't make any difference to Gifford Doakes. He liked piled bodies. Most of us were involved in Real Murders for reasons that would probably bear the light of day; gosh, who doesn't read the articles about murders in the newspaper? But Gifford was another story. Maybe he'd joined our club with the idea that we swapped some sickening sort of bloody pornography, and he was only sticking with the club in the hope that soon we'd trust him enough to share with him. When he brought Reynaldo, we didn't know how to treat him. Was Reynaldo a guest, or Gifford's date? A shade of difference there, and one which had us all a little anxious, especially John Queensland, who felt it his duty as president to speak to everyone in the club.

And Mamie Wright wasn't anywhere in the room.

If Mamie had been here long enough to set up the chairs and make the coffee, and her car was still in the parking lot, then she must be here somewhere. Though I didn't like Mamie, her non-appearance was beginning to seem so strange that I felt obliged to pin down her whereabouts.

Just as I reached the door, Mamie's husband, Gerald, came in. He had his briefcase under his arm and he looked angry. Because he looked so irate, and because I felt stupid for being uneasy, I did a strange thing; though I was searching for his wife, I let him pass without speaking.

The hall seemed very quiet after the heavy door shut off the hum of conversation. The white-with-speckles linoleum and beige paint almost sparkled with cleanliness under the harsh fluorescent lights. I was praying the phone wouldn't ring again as I looked at the four doors on the other side of the hall. With a fleeting, absurd image of 'The Lady or the Tiger' I went to my right to open the door to the small conference room. Sally had told me she'd already been in the room, but just to temporarily park the tray of cookies, so I checked the room carefully. Since there was practically nothing to examine except a table and chairs, that took seconds.

I opened the next door in the hall, the women's room, even though Sally had also been in there. Since there were only two stalls, she'd have been pretty sure to know of Mamie's presence. But I bent over to look under the doors. No feet. I opened both doors. Nothing.

I didn't quite have the guts to check the adjoining men's room, but since Arthur Smith entered it while I hesitated, I figured I'd hear about it soon if Mamie was in there.

I moved on, and out of all the glaring beigeness I caught a little glimpse of something different, so I looked down at the base of the door and saw a smear. It was red-brown.

The separate sources of my uneasiness suddenly coalesced into horror. I was holding my breath when my hand reached out to open that door to the last room, the little kitchen used for fixing the refreshments . . .

. . . and saw an empty turquoise shoe upright on its ridiculous high heel, right inside the door.

And then I saw the blood spattered everywhere on the shining beige enamel of the stove and refrigerator.

And the raincoat.

Finally I made myself look at Mamie. She was so dead. Her head was the wrong shape entirely. Her dyed black hair was matted with clots of her blood. I thought, the human body is supposed to be ninety percent water, not ninety percent blood. Then my ears were buzzing and I felt very weak, and though I knew I was alone in the hall, I felt the presence of something horrible in that kitchen, something to dread. And it was not poor Mamie Wright.

I heard a door swoosh shut in the hall. I heard Arthur Smith's voice say, 'Miss Teagarden? Anything wrong?'

'It's Mamie,' I whispered, though I'd intended a normal voice. 'It's Mrs Wright.' I ruined the effect of all this formality by simply folding onto the floor. My knees seemed to have turned to faulty hinges.

He was behind me in an instant. He half bent to help me up but was frozen by what he saw over my head.

'Are you sure that's Mamie Wright?' he asked.

The working part of my brain told me Arthur Smith was quite right to ask. Perhaps coming on this unsuspicious, I would have wondered too. Her eye – oh my God, her eye.

'She's missing from the big room, but her car is outside. And that's her shoe.' I managed to say that with my fingers pressed to my mouth.

When Mamie had first worn them, I'd thought those shoes the most poisonous footwear I'd ever seen. I hate turquoise anyway. I let myself enjoy thinking about hating turquoise. It was a lot more pleasing than thinking about what was right in front of me.

The policeman stepped over me very carefully and squatted

with even more care by the body. He put his fingers against her neck. I felt bile rise up in my throat – no pulse, of course. How ridiculous! Mamie was so dead.

'Can you stand up?' he asked after a moment. He dusted his fingers together as he rose.

'If you help.'

Without further ado, Arthur Smith hauled me to my feet and out the doorway in one motion. He was very strong. He kept one arm around me while he shut the door. He leaned me against that door. Deep blue eyes looked at me consideringly. 'You're very light,' he said. 'You'll be all right for a few seconds. I'm going to use the phone right here on the wall.'

'Okay.' My voice sounded weird; light, tinny. I'd always wondered if I could keep my head if I found a body, and here I was, keeping my head, I told myself insanely as I watched him go down the hall to the pay phone. I was glad he didn't have to leave my sight. I might not be so level if I were standing in that hall alone, with a body behind me.

While Arthur muttered into the phone I kept my eyes on the door to the large room across the hall where John Queensland must be itching to open the meeting. I thought about what I'd just seen. I wasn't thinking about Mamie being dead, about the reality and finality of her death. I was thinking about the scene that had been staged, starring Mamie Wright as *the corpse*. The casting of the corpse had been deliberate, but the role of *the finder of the body* had by chance been taken by me. The whole thing was a scene deliberately staged by someone, and suddenly I knew what had been biting at me underneath the horror.

I thought faster than I'd ever thought before. I didn't feel sick anymore.

Arthur crossed the hall to the door of the large room and pushed it open just enough to insert his head in the gap. I could hear him address the other members of the club.

'Uh, folks, folks?' The voices stilled. 'There's been an accident,' he said with no emphasis. 'I'm going to have to ask you all to stay in this room for a little while, until we can get things under control out here.'

The situation, as far as I could see, was completely under control.

'Where's Roe Teagarden?' John Queensland's voice demanded.

Good old John. I'd have to tell Mother about that, she'd be touched.

'She's fine. I'll be back with you in a minute.'

Gerald Wright's thin voice. 'Where's my wife, Mr Smith?'

'I'll get back with all of you in a few minutes,' repeated the policeman firmly, and shut the door behind him. He stood lost in thought. I wondered if this detective had ever been the first on the scene of a murder investigation. He seemed to be ticking steps off mentally, from the way he was waggling his fingers and staring into space.

I waited. Then my legs started trembling and I thought I might fold again. 'Arthur,' I said sharply. 'Detective Smith.'

He jumped; he'd forgotten me. He took my arm solicitously.

I whacked at him with my free hand out of sheer aggravation. 'I'm not trying to get you to help me, I want to tell you something!'

He steered me into a chair in the little conference room and put on a waiting face.

'I was supposed to lecture tonight on the Wallace case, you remember? William Herbert Wallace and his wife, Julia, England, 1931?'

He nodded his curly pale head and I could see he was a million miles away. I felt like slapping him again. I knew I sounded like an idiot, but I was coming to the point. 'I don't know how much you remember about the Wallace case – if you don't know anything, I can fill you in later.' I waved my hands to show that was inconsequential, here came the real meat. 'What I want to tell you, what's important, is that Mamie Wright's been killed exactly like Julia Wallace. She's been *arranged*.'

Bingo! That blue gaze was almost frighteningly intense now. I felt like a bug impaled on a pin. This was not a lightweight man.

'Point out a few comparisons before the lab guys get here, so I can have them photographed.'

I blew out a breath of relief. 'The raincoat under Mamie. It hasn't rained here in days. A raincoat was found under Julia Wallace. And Mamie's been placed by the little oven. Mrs Wallace was found by a gas fire. She was bludgeoned to death. Like Mamie, I think. Mr Wallace was an insurance salesman. So is Gerald Wright. I'll bet there's more I haven't thought of yet. Mamie's about the same age as Julia Wallace . . . There are just so many parallels I don't think I could've imagined them.'

Arthur stared at me thoughtfully for a few long seconds. 'Are there any photographs of the Wallace murder scene?' he asked.

The xeroxed pictures would have come in handy now, I thought.

'Yes, I've seen one, there may be more.'

'Was the husband, Wallace, arrested?'

'Yes, and convicted. But later the sentence was overturned somehow or other, and he was freed.'

'Okay. Come with me.'

'One more thing,' I said urgently. 'The phone rang when I got here tonight and it was someone asking for Julia Wallace.'

Chapter Three

The silent hall was not silent anymore. As we left the conference room, the law came in the back door. It was represented by a heavy-set man in a plaid jacket who was taller and older than Arthur, and two men in uniform. As I stood back against the wall, temporarily forgotten, Arthur led them down the hall and opened the door to the kitchen. They crowded around the door looking in. They were all silent for a moment. The youngest man in uniform winced and then wrenched his face straight. The other uniformed man shook his head once and then stared in at Mamie with a disgusted expression. What disgusted him, I wondered? The mess that had been made with the body of a human being? The waste of a life? The fact that someone living in the town he had to protect had seen fit to do this terrible thing?

I realized the man in the plaid jacket was the sergeant of detectives; I'd seen his picture in the paper when he'd arrested a drug pusher. Now he pursed his mouth briefly and said, 'Damn,' with little expression.

Arthur began telling them things, going swiftly and in a low voice. I could tell what point in his narrative he'd reached when their heads swung toward me simultaneously. I didn't know whether to nod or what. I just stared back at them and felt a thousand years old. Their faces turned back to Arthur and he continued his briefing.

The two men in uniform left the building while Arthur and the sergeant continued their discussion. Arthur seemed to be enumerating things, while the sergeant nodded his head in approval and occasionally interjected some comment. Arthur had a little notebook out and was jotting in it as they spoke.

Another memory about the sergeant stirred.

His name was Jack Burns. He'd bought his house from my mother. He was married to a school teacher and had two kids in college. Now Jack Burns gave Arthur a sharp nod, as clear as a starting gun. Arthur went to the door to the meeting room and pushed it open.

'Mr Wright, could you come here for a minute, please?' Detective Arthur Smith asked, in a voice so devoid of expression that it was a warning in itself.

Gerald Wright came into the hall hesitantly. No one in the big room could fail to know by now that something was drastically wrong, and I wondered what they'd been saying. Gerald took a step toward me, but Arthur took his arm quite firmly and guided Gerald into the little conference room. I knew he was about to tell Gerald that his wife was dead, and I found myself wondering how Gerald would take it. Then I was ashamed.

At moments I understood in decent human terms what had happened to a woman I knew, and at moments I seemed to be thinking of Mamie's death as one of our club's study cases.

'Miss Teagarden,' said Jack Burns's good-old-boy drawl, 'you must be Aida Teagarden's child.'

Well, I had a father, too: but he'd committed the dreadful sin of coming in from foreign parts (Texas) to work on our local Georgia paper, marrying my mother, begetting me, and then leaving and divorcing Lawrenceton's own Aida Brattle Teagarden. I said, 'Yes.'

'I'm mighty sorry you had to see something like that,' Jack Burns said, shaking his heavy head mournfully.

It was almost like a burlesque of regret, it was laid on so heavily; was he being sarcastic? I looked down, and for once said nothing. I didn't need this right now; I was shaken and confused.

'It just seems so strange to me that a sweet young woman like you would come to a club like this,' Jack Burns went on slowly, his tone expressing stunned bewilderment. 'Could you just kind of clarify for me what the purpose of this – organization – is?'

I had to answer a direct question. But why was he asking me? His own detective belonged to the same club. I wished this middle-aged man with his plaid suit and his cowboy boots would melt through the floor. As slightly as I knew Arthur, I wanted him back. This man was scary. I pushed my glasses back up my nose with shaking fingers.

'We meet once a month,' I said in an uneven voice. 'And we talk about a famous murder case, usually a pretty old one.'

The sergeant apparently gave this deep thought. 'Talk about it—?' he inquired gently.

'Ah . . . sometimes just learn about it, who was killed and how and why and by whom.' Our members favored different *w*'s.

I was most interested in the victim.

'Or sometimes,' I stumbled on, 'depending on the case, we decide if the police arrested the right person. Or if the murder was unsolved, we talk about who may have been guilty. Sometimes we watch a movie.'

'Movie?' Raised beetly brows, a gentle inquiring shake of the head.

'Like *The Thin Blue Line*. Or a fictionalized movie based on a real case. *In Cold Blood* . . .'

'But not ever,' he asked delicately, 'what you would call a – snuff movie?'

'Oh my God,' I said sickly. 'Oh my God, no.' In my naivete, I said, 'How could you think that?'

'Well, Miss Teagarden, this here is a real murder, and we have to ask real questions.' And his face was not nice at all. Our club had offended something in Jack Burns. How would Arthur fare, a policeman who was actually a member? But it seemed he would be working on the investigation in some capacity.

'Now, Miss Teagarden,' Jack Burns went on, his mask back in place, his voice as buttery as a waffle, 'I am going to head up this investigation, and my two homicide detectives will work on this, and Arthur Smith will assist us, since he knows all you people. I know you'll cooperate to the fullest with him. He tells me you know a little more about this than the others, that you got some kind of phone call and you found the body. We may have to talk to you a few times about this, but you just have patience with us.'

And I knew from his face I had better be willing to turn over my every waking minute, if that was required of me.

By this time I felt that Arthur Smith was my oldest and dearest friend, so much safer did he seem than this terrifying man with his terrifying questions. And he stepped out from behind his sergeant now, his face blank and his eyes cautious. He'd heard at least some of this conversation, which would have sounded almost routine without Burns's menacing manner.

'Miss Teagarden,' Arthur said brusquely, 'will you go into the room with the others now? Please don't discuss with them what's happened out here. And thanks.' With Gerald presumably grieving in the small conference room and Mamie dead in the kitchen, I had to join the others unless he wanted me to stand in the bathroom.

With a medley of feelings, relief predominating, I was pushing open the door when I felt a hand on my arm. 'Sorry,' murmured Arthur. Over his shoulder, I saw the plaid back of Sergeant Burns's jacket as he held open the back door to admit uniformed policemen loaded down with equipment. 'If you don't mind, I'll come to see you tomorrow morning about this Wallace thing. Will you be at work?'

'Tomorrow's my day off,' I said. 'I can be at home tomorrow morning.'

'Nine o'clock too early?'

'No, that's fine.'

As I went in the larger room where my fellow club members were clustered anxiously, I thought about the intelligence pitted against Arthur Smith's. Someone was painstaking and artistic in a debased and imaginative way. Someone had issued a challenge to whoever cared to take it up. 'Figure out who I am if you can, you amateur students of crime. I've graduated to the real thing. Here is my work.'

I felt an instinctive urge to hide what I was thinking. I wiped my mind clean of my nasty thoughts and tried not to meet the eyes of any of my fellow club members, who were all waiting tensely for me in the big room. But Sally Allison was a pro at catching reluctant eyes, and I saw her mouth open when she caught mine. I knew beyond a doubt she was going to ask me if I'd found Mamie Wright. Sally was no fool. I shook my head firmly, and she came no closer.

'Are you all right, child?' John Queensland asked, advancing with the dignity that was the keystone of his character. 'Your mother will be terribly upset when she hears . . .' But since John, who was after all a wee mite pompous, realized he had no idea what my mother was going to hear, he had to trail off into silence. He asked me a question with a look.

'I'm sorry,' I said in a tiny squeak. I shook my head in irritation. 'I'm sorry,' I said more strongly, 'I don't think Detective Smith wants me to talk until he talks to you.' I gave John a small smile and went to sit by myself in a chair by the coffee urn, trying to ignore the indignant looks and mutters of dissatisfaction cast in my direction. Gifford Doakes was walking back and forth as if he were pacing a cage. The policemen outside seemed to be making him extremely nervous. The novelist Robin Crusoe was looking eager and curious; Lizanne just looked bored. LeMaster Cane, Melanie and Bankston, and Jane Engle were talking together in low voices. For the first time, I realized another club member, Benjamin Greer, was missing. Benjamin's attendance was erratic, like his life in general, so I didn't put any particular weight on that. Sally was sitting by her son Perry, whose thin slash of a mouth was twisted into a very peculiar smile. Perry's elevator did not stop at every floor.

I poured myself a cup of coffee, wishing it were a shot of bourbon. I thought of Mamie getting to the meeting early, setting everything up, making this very coffee so we wouldn't have to drink Sally's dreadful brew . . . I burst into tears, and slopped coffee all down my yellow sweater.

Those awful turquoise shoes. I kept seeing that empty shoe sitting upright in the middle of the floor.

I heard a soft sweet soothing murmur and knew Lizanne Buckley had come to my aid. Lizanne generously blocked me from the view of the room with an uncomfortable hunch of her tall body. I heard the scrape of a chair and saw a pair of long thin trousered legs. Her escort, the red-headed novelist, was helping her out, and then he tactfully moved away. Lizanne lowered herself into the chair and hitched it closer to me. Her manicured hand stuffed a handkerchief into my stubby one.

'Let's just think about something else,' Lizanne said in a low, even voice. She seemed quite sure I could think about something else. 'Stupid ole me,' said Lizanne charmingly. 'I just can't get interested in the things this Robin Crusoe likes, like people getting murdered. So if you like him, you're welcome to him. I think maybe you and him would suit each other. Nothing wrong with him,' she added hastily, in case I should assume she was offering me something shoddy. 'He'd just be happier with you, I think. Don't you?' she asked persuasively. She just knew a man would make me feel better.

'Lizanne,' I said, with a few gasps and sobs interposed here and there, 'you're wonderful. I don't know anyone to top you. There aren't too many single men our age in Lawrenceton to date, are there?'

Lizanne looked puzzled. She'd obviously noticed no lack of single men to date. I wondered where all her men came from. Probably drove from as far away as two hundred miles. 'Thanks, Lizanne,' I said helplessly.

Sergeant Burns appeared in the doorway and scanned the room. I had no doubt he was memorizing each and every face. I could tell by his scowl when he saw her that he knew Sally Allison was a reporter. He looked even angrier when he saw Gifford Doakes, who stopped his pacing and stared back at Burns with a sneering face.

'Okay, folks,' he said peremptorily, eyeing us as if we were rather degenerate strangers caught half-dressed, 'we've had a death here.'

That could hardly have been a bombshell – after all, the people in this group were adept at picking up clues. But there was a shocked-sounding buzz of conversation in the wake of Burns's announcement. A few reactions were marked. Perry Allison got a strange smirk on his face, and I was even more strongly reminded that in the past Perry had had what people called 'nervous problems,' though he did his work at the library well enough. His mother Sally was watching his face with obvious anxiety. The red-haired writer's face lit with excitement, though he decently tried to tone it down. None of this could touch him personally, of course. He was new in town, had barely met a soul, and this was his first visit to Real Murders.

I envied him.

He saw me watching him, observing his excitement, and he turned red.

Burns said clearly, 'I'm going to take you out of the room one by one, to the smaller room across the hall, and one of our uniformed officers will take your statement. Then I'm going to let you go home, though we'll need to talk to you all again later, I imagine. I'll start with Miss Teagarden, since she's had a shock.'

Lizanne pressed my hand when I got up to leave. As I crossed the hall, I saw the building was teeming with police. I hadn't known Lawrenceton had that many in uniform. I was learning a lot tonight, one way or another.

The business of having my statement taken would have been interesting if I hadn't been so upset and tired. After all, I'd read about police procedure for years, about police questioning all available witnesses to a crime, and here I was, being questioned by a real policeman about a real crime. But the only lasting impression I carried away with me was that of thoroughness. Every question was asked twice, in different ways. The phone call, of course, came in for a great deal of attention. The pity of it was that I could say so little about it. I was faintly worried when Jack Burns stepped in and asked me very persistently about Sally Allison and her movements and demeanor; but I had to face the fact that since Sally and I were first on the scene (though we didn't know it at the time) we would be questioned most intensely.

I had my fingerprints taken, too, which would have been very interesting under other circumstances. As I left the room I glanced toward the kitchen without wanting to. Mamie Wright, housewife and wearer of high heels, was being processed as the *murder victim*. I didn't know where Gerald Wright was; since the small conference room had been free, he must have been driven home or even to the police station. Of course he would be the most suspected, and I knew chances were he'd probably done it, but I could find no relief in the thought.

I didn't believe Gerald had done it. I thought the person, man or woman, who'd called the VFW Hall had done it, and I didn't believe Gerald Wright would have resorted to such elaborate means if he'd wanted to kill Mamie. He might have buried her in his cellar, like Crippen, but he would not have killed her at the VFW and then called to alert the rest of the club members to his actions. Actually, Gerald didn't seem to have enough sense of fun, if that was what you wanted to term it. This murder had a kind of bizarre playfulness about it. Mamie'd been arranged like a doll, and the phone call was like a childish 'Nyah, nyah, you can't catch me.'

As I went out to my car very slowly, I was mulling over that phone call. It was a red flag, surely, to alert the club to the near certainty that this murder had been planned and executed by a club member. Mamie Wright, wife of an insurance salesman in Lawrenceton, Georgia, had been battered to death and arranged after death to copy the murder of the wife of an insurance company employee in Liverpool, England. This had been done on the premises where the club met, on the night it met to discuss that very case. It was possible someone outside the club had a grudge against us, though I couldn't imagine why. No, someone had decided to have his own kind of fun with us. And that someone was almost surely someone I knew, almost surely a member of Real Murders.

I could scarcely believe I had to walk out to my car by myself, drive it home by myself, enter my dark home – by myself. But then I realized that all the members of Real Murders, alive or dead, with the exception of Benjamin Greer, were under police scrutiny at this very moment.

I was the safest person in Lawrenceton.

I drove slowly, double-checked myself at stop signs, and used my turn signals long before I needed to. I was so completely tired I was afraid I'd look drunk to any passing patrol officers . . . if there were any left on the streets. I was so glad to turn the car into my familiar slot, put my key in my own lock, and plod into my own territory. Functioning through a woolly fog of fatigue, I dialed Mother's number. When she answered I told her that no matter what she heard, I was just fine and nothing awful had happened to me. I cut off her questions, left the phone off the hook, and saw by the kitchen clock that it was only 9:30. Amazing.

I trudged up the stairs, pulling off my sweater and shirt as I went. I just managed to shuck the rest of my clothes, pull on my nightgown, and crawl into bed before sleep hit me.

At 3 A.M. I woke in a cold sweat. My dream had been one big close-up of Mamie Wright's head.

Someone was crazy; or someone was unbelievably vicious.

Or both.

Chapter Four

I turned the water on full force, let it get good and hot, and stepped into the shower. It was 7 A.M. on a cool, crisp spring morning, and my first conscious thought was: I don't have to go to work today. The next thought was: my life has changed forever.

Not much had ever really happened to me; not big things, either wonderful or horrible. My parents getting divorced was bad, but even I had been able to see it was better for them. I had already gotten my driver's license by then, so they didn't need to shuttle me back and forth. Maybe the divorce had made me cautious, but caution is not a bad thing. I had a neat and tidy life in a messy world, and if sometimes I suspected I was trying to fulfill the stereotype of a small-town librarian, well, I had yearnings to play other roles, too. In the movies, sometimes those dry librarians with their hair in buns suddenly let their juices gush, shook their hair loose, threw off their glasses, and did a tango.

Maybe I would. But in the meantime, I could have a small pride in myself. I had done okay the night before, not great but okay. I had gotten through it.

I went through the tedious business of drying my mass of hair and pulled on some old jeans and a sweater. I padded downstairs in my moccasins and brewed some coffee, a big pot. I'd gotten my lawn chairs and table set up on the patio a week before, when I'd decided it was going to stay spring for good, so after getting my papers from the little-used front doorstep, I carried my first cup out to the patio. It was possible to feel alone there, though of course the Crandalls on one side and Robin Crusoe on the other could see my patio from their second floor back bedroom. The back bedroom was small and I knew everyone used it as a guest room, so the chances were good that no one was looking.

Sally hadn't managed to get the story in the local paper. I was sure that had been printed before the meeting even started. But the local man employed by the city paper had had better luck. 'Lawrenceton Woman Murdered' ran the uninspired headline in the City and State section. A picture of Mamie accompanied the article, and I was impressed by the stringer's industry. I scanned the story quickly. It was necessarily short, and had little in it I didn't know, except that the police hadn't found Mamie's purse. I frowned at that. It didn't seem to fit somehow. There was no hint of this murder being like any other murder. I wondered if the police had requested that fact be withheld. But it would be all over Lawrenceton soon, I was sure. Lawrenceton, despite its new population of commuters to Atlanta, was still a small town at heart. My name was included: *'Ms Teagarden, anxious at Mrs Wright's continued absence, searched the building and found Mrs Wright's body in the kitchen.'* I shivered. It sounded so simple in print.

I'd put the phone back on the hook, and now it rang. Mother, of course, I thought, and went back into the kitchen. I picked up the receiver as I poured more coffee.

'Are you all right?' she asked immediately. 'John Queensland came over last night after the police let him go, and he told me all about it.'

John Queensland was certainly making a determined effort to endear himself to Mother. Well, she'd been on her own (but not always alone) for a long time.

'I'm pretty much all right,' I said cautiously.

'Was it awful?'

'Yes,' I said, and I meant it. It had been horrible, but exciting, and the more hours separated me from the event, the more exciting and bearable it was becoming. I didn't want to lose the horror; that was what kept you civilized.

'I'm sorry,' she said helplessly. Neither of us knew what to say next. 'Your father called me,' she blurted out. 'You must have had your phone off the hook?'

'Uh-huh.'

'He was worried, too. About you. And he said you were going to keep Phillip next weekend? He wondered if you would be able; he said if you didn't feel like it, just give him a call, he'd change his plans.' Mother was doing her best not to call her ex-husband a selfish bastard for mentioning such a thing at a time like this.

I had a half-brother, Phillip, six, a scary and wonderful boy whom I could stand for whole weekends occasionally without my nerves completely shattering. I'd completely forgotten that Dad and his second wife, Betty Jo, (quite a reaction to an Aida Teagarden) were leaving for a convention in Chattanooga in a few days.

'No, that'll be okay, I'll give him a call later today,' I said.

'Well. You will call me if you need me to do anything? I can bring you some lunch, or you can come stay with me.'

'No, I'm fine.' A slight exaggeration, but close enough to the truth. I suddenly wanted to say something real, something indelible, to my mother. But the only thing I could think of wouldn't bear uttering. I wanted to say I felt more alive than I had in years; that finally something bigger than myself had happened to me. Now, instead of reading about an old murder, seeing passion and desperation and evil in print on a page, I knew these things to be possessed by people around me. And I said, 'Really, I'm okay. And the police are coming by this morning; I'd better go get ready.'

'All right, Aurora. But call me if you get scared. And you can always stay here.'

I had a sudden flood of nervous energy after I hung up. I looked around me, and decided to put it to good use picking up. First my den/dining room/kitchen right off the patio, then the formal front room that I seldom used. I checked the little downstairs bathroom for toilet paper, and ran up the stairs to make my bed and straighten up. The guest bedroom was pristine, as usual. I gathered up my dirty clothes and trotted downstairs with the bundle, tossing it unceremoniously down the basement stairs to land in front of the washer. Lawrenceton is on high enough ground for basements to be feasible.

When I looked at the clock and saw I had fifteen minutes left before Arthur Smith was due to come, I checked the coffee level and went back upstairs to put on some makeup. That was simple enough, since I wore little, and I hardly had to look in the mirror to do it. But out of habit I did, and I didn't look any more interesting or experienced than I had the day before. My face was still pale and round, my nose short and straight and suitable for holding up my glasses, my eyes magnified behind those glasses and round and brown. My hair unbound flew all around my head in a waving brown mass halfway down my back, and for once I let it be. It would get in my way and stick to the corners of my mouth and get caught in the hinges of my glasses, but what the hell! Then I heard the double ring of the front doorbell and flew downstairs.

People almost always came to the back door instead of the front, but Arthur had parked on the street instead of in the parking area behind the apartments. Under the fresh suit, shaved jaw, and curling pale hair still damp from the shower, he looked tired.

'Are you all right this morning?' he asked.

'Yes, pretty much. Come in.'

He looked all around him, openly, when he passed through the living room, missing nothing. He paused at the big room where I really lived. 'Nice,' he said, sounding impressed. The sunny room with the big window overlooking the patio with its rose trees did look attractive. Exposed brick walls and all the books make an intelligent-looking room, anyway, I thought, and I waved him onto the tan suede love seat as I asked him if he wanted coffee.

'Yes, black,' he said fervently. 'I was up most of the night.'

When I bent over to put his cup on the low table in front of him, I realized with some embarrassment that his eyes weren't on the coffee cup.

I settled opposite him in my favorite chair, low enough that my feet can touch the floor, wide enough to curl up inside, with a little table beside it just big enough to hold a book and a coffee cup.

Arthur took a sip of his coffee, eyed me again as he told me it was good, and got down to business.

'You were right, the body was definitely moved after death to the position it was in when you found it,' he said directly. 'She was killed there in the kitchen. Jack Burns is having a hard time swallowing this theory, that she was deliberately killed to mimic the Wallace murder, but I'm going to try to convince him. He's in charge though; I'm assisting on this one since I know all the people involved, but I'm really a burglary detective.'

Some questions flew through my head, but I decided it wouldn't be polite to ask them. Sort of like asking a doctor about your own symptoms at a party. 'Why is Jack Burns so scary?' I asked abruptly. 'Why does he make an effort to intimidate you? What's the point?'

At least Arthur didn't have to ask me what I meant. He knew exactly what Jack Burns was like.

'Jack doesn't care if people like him or not,' Arthur said simply. 'That's a big advantage, especially to a cop. He doesn't even care if other cops like him. He just wants cases solved as soon as possible, he wants witnesses to tell him everything they know, and he wants the guilty punished. He wants the world to go his way, and he doesn't care what he has to do to make it happen.'

That sounded pretty frightening to me. 'At least you know where you are with him,' I said weakly. Arthur nodded matter-of-factly.

'Tell me everything you know about the Wallace case,' he said.

'Well, I'm up on it of course, since it was supposed to be the topic last night,' I explained. 'I wonder if – whoever killed Mamie – picked it for that reason?'

I was actually kind of glad I'd finally get to deliver part of my laboriously prepared lecture. And to a fellow aficionado, a professional at that.

'The ultimate murder mystery, according to several eminent crime writers,' I began. 'William Herbert Wallace, Liverpool insurance salesman,' I raised a finger to indicate one point of similarity, 'and married with no children,' I raised a second finger. Then I thought Arthur could probably do without me telling him his job. 'Wallace and his wife Julia were middle aged and hadn't much money, but did have intellectual leanings. They played duets together in the evening. They didn't entertain much or have many friends. They weren't known to quarrel.

'Wallace had a regular schedule for collecting insurance payments from subscribers to his particular company, and he'd bring the money home with him for one night, Tuesday. Wallace played chess, too, and was entered in a tournament at a local club. There was a play-off chart establishing when he'd be playing, posted on the wall at the club. Anyone who came in could see it.' I raised my eyebrows at Arthur to make sure he marked that important point. He nodded.

'Okay. Wallace didn't have a phone at home. He got a call at the chess club right before he arrived there one day. Another member took the message. The caller identified himself as "Qualtrough." The caller said that he wanted to take out a policy on his daughter and asked that Wallace be given a message to come around to Qualtrough's house the next evening, Tuesday.

'Now, the bad thing about this call, from Wallace's point of view,' I explained, warming to my subject, 'is that it came to the club when Wallace wasn't there. And there was a telephone booth Wallace could have used, close to his home, if he himself placed the "Qualtrough" call.'

Arthur scribbled in a little leather notepad he produced from somewhere.

'Now – Wallace comes in very soon after Qualtrough has called the club. Wallace talks about this message to the other chess players. Maybe he means to impress it on their memory? Either he is a murderer and is setting up his alibi, or the real murderer is making sure Wallace will be out of the house Tuesday evening. And this dual possibility, that almost hanged Wallace, runs throughout the case.' Could any writer have imagined anything as interesting as this? I wanted to ask.

But instead I plunged back in. 'So on the appointed night Wallace goes looking for this man Qualtrough who wants to take out some insurance. Granted, he was a man who needed all the business he could get, and granted, we know what insurance salesmen are still like today, but even so, Wallace went to extreme lengths to find this potential customer. The address Qualtrough left at the chess club was in Menlove Gardens East. There's a Menlove Gardens North, South, and West, but no Menlove Gardens East; so it was a clever false address to give. Wallace asks many people he meets – even a policeman! – if they know where he can find this address. He may be stubborn, or he may be determined to fix himself in the memories of as many people as possible.

'Since there simply was no such address, he went home.'

I paused to take a long drink of my tepid coffee.

'She was already dead?' Arthur asked astutely.

'Right, that's the point. If Wallace killed her, he had to have done it before he left on this wild goose chase. If so, what I'm about to tell you was all acting.

'He gets home and tries to open his front door, he later says. His key won't work. He thinks Julia has bolted the front door and for some reason can't hear him knock. Whatever was the case, a couple who live next door leave their house and see Wallace at his back door, apparently in distress. He tells them about the front door being bolted. Either his distress is genuine, or he's been hanging around in the back alley waiting for someone else to witness his entrance.'

Arthur's blond head shook slowly from side to side as he contemplated the twists and turns of this classic. I imagined the Liverpool police force in 1931 sitting and shaking their heads in exactly the same way. Or perhaps not; they'd been convinced early on that they had their man.

'Was Wallace friendly with those neighbors?' he asked.

'Not particularly. Good, but impersonal, relationship.'

'So he could count on their being accepted as impartial witnesses,' Arthur observed.

'If he did it. Incidentally, the upshot of all this about the front door lock, which Wallace said resisted his key, turned out to be a major point in the trial, but the testimony was pretty murky. Also iffy was the evidence of a child who knocked on the door with the day's milk, or a newspaper or something. Mrs Wallace answered the door, alive and well; and if it could have been proved Wallace had already left, he would have been cleared. But it couldn't be.' I took a deep breath. Here came the crucial scene. 'Be that as it may. Wallace and the couple *do* enter the house, *do* see a few things out of place in the kitchen and another room, I think, but no major ransacking. The box where Wallace kept the insurance money had been rifled. Of course, this was a Tuesday, when there should've been a lot of money.

'The neighbors by this time are scared. Then Wallace calls them into the front room, a parlor, rarely used.

'Julia Wallace is there, lying in front of the gas fire, with a raincoat under her. The raincoat, partially burned, is not hers. She's been beaten to death, with extreme brutality, unnecessary force. She has not been raped.' I stopped suddenly. 'I assume Mamie wasn't?' I said finally, frightened of the answer.

'Doesn't look like it right now,' Arthur said absently, still taking notes.

I blew my breath out. 'Well, Wallace theorizes that "Qualtrough," who of course must be the murderer if Wallace is innocent, called at the house after Wallace left. He was evidently someone Julia didn't know well, or at all, because she showed him into the company parlor.' Just like I would an insurance salesman, I thought. 'The raincoat, an old one of Wallace's, she perhaps threw over her shoulders because the disused room was cold until the gas fire, which she apparently lit, had had a chance to heat it. The money that had been taken hadn't actually been much, since Wallace had been ill that week and hadn't been able to collect everything he was supposed to. But no one else would have known that, presumably.

'Julia certainly hadn't been having an affair, and had never personally offended anyone that the police could discover.

'And that's the Wallace case.'

Arthur sat lost in thought, his blue eyes fixed intently on some internal point. 'Wobbly, either way,' he said finally.

'Right,' I agreed. 'There's no real case against Wallace, except that he was her husband, the only person who seemed to know her well enough to kill her. Everything he said could've been true . . . in which case, he was tried for killing the one person in the world he loved, while all the time the real killer went free.'

'So Wallace was arrested?'

'And convicted. But after he spent some time in prison, he was released by a unique ruling in British law. I think a higher court simply ruled that there hadn't been enough evidence for a jury to convict Wallace, no matter what the jury said. But prison and the whole experience had broken Wallace, and he died two or three years later, still saying he was innocent. He said he suspected who Qualtrough was, but he had no proof.'

'I'd have gone for Wallace, too, on the basis of that evidence,' Arthur said unhesitatingly. 'The probability is with Wallace, as you said, because it's usually the husband who wants his wife out of the way . . . yet since there's no clear-cut evidence either way, I'm almost surprised the state chose to prosecute.'

'Probably,' I said without thinking, 'the police were under a lot of pressure to make an arrest.'

Arthur looked so tired and gloomy that I tried to change the subject. 'Why'd you join Real Murders?' I asked. 'Isn't that a little strange for a policeman?'

'Not this policeman,' he said a little sharply. I shrank in my chair.

'Listen, Roe, I wanted to go to law school, but there wasn't enough money.' Arthur's family was pretty humble, I recalled. I thought I'd gone to high school with one of his sisters. Arthur must be three or four years older than I. 'I made it through two years of college before I realized I couldn't make it financially, because I just couldn't work and carry a full course load. School bored me then, too. So I decided to go into law from another angle. Policemen aren't all alike, you know.'

I could tell he'd given this lecture before.

'Some cops are right out of Joseph Wambaugh's books, because he was a cop and he writes pretty good books. Loud, drinkers, macho, mostly uneducated, sometimes brutal. There are a few nuts, like there are in any line of work, and there are a few Birchers.

There aren't many Liberals with a capital 'L', and not too many college graduates. But within those rough lines, we've got all kinds of people. Some of my friends – some cops – watch every cop show on television they can catch, so they'll know how to act. Some of them – not many – read Dostoevsky.' He smiled, and it looked almost strange on him. 'I just like to study old crimes, figure out how the police thought on the case, pick apart their procedure – ever read about the June Anne Devaney case, Blackburn, England, oh, about late 1930's?'

'A child murder, right?'

'Right. You know the police persuaded every adult male in Blackburn to have his fingerprints taken?' Arthur's face practically shone with enthusiasm. 'That's how they caught Peter Griffiths. By comparing thousands of fingerprints with the ones Griffiths left on the scene.' He was lost in admiration for a moment. 'That's why I joined Real Murders,' he said. 'But what could a woman like Mamie Wright get out of studying the Wallace case?'

'Oh, a chaperoned husband!' I said with a grin, and then felt a sharp pang of dismay as Arthur reopened his little notebook.

Almost gently, Arthur said, 'Now, this murder is real. It's a new murder.'

'I know,' I said, and I saw Mamie again.

'Did they quarrel much, Gerald and Mamie?'

'Never, that I saw or heard,' I said firmly and truthfully. I'd always believed Wallace was innocent. 'She just seemed to be keeping an eye on him around other women.'

'Do you think her suspicions were correct?'

'It never occurred to me they could be. Gerald is just so stuffy and . . . Arthur? Could Gerald have done this?' I didn't mean emotionally, I meant practically, and Arthur realized it.

'Do you know why Gerald says he was late to the meeting, why Mamie came on her own instead of riding with him? He got a call from a man he didn't know, asking Gerald to talk with him about some insurance for his daughter.'

I know my mouth was hanging open. I slowly shut it, but feared I looked no more intelligent.

'Someone's really slapping us in the face, Arthur,' I said slowly. 'Maybe especially challenging you. Mamie wasn't even killed because she was *Mamie.*' That was especially horrible. 'It was just because she was an insurance salesman's wife.'

'But you'd figured it out last night. You know that.'

'But what if there are more? What if he copies the June Anne Devaney murder, and kills a three-year-old? What if he copies the Ripper murders? Or kills people like Ed Gein did, to eat?'

'Don't go imagining nightmares,' Arthur said briskly. He was so matter of fact I knew he'd already thought of the possibility himself. 'Now, I've got to write down everything you did yesterday, starting from when you left work.'

If he meant to jolt me out of the horrors, he succeeded. Even if only on paper, I was someone who had to account for her movements; not exactly a suspect, but a possibility. Then too, my arrival time at the meeting would help pinpoint the time of death. Though I'd gone over this all the night before, once more I carefully related my trivial doings.

'Do you have a good account of the Wallace killing I could borrow?' he asked, rising from the couch reluctantly. He looked even more worn, as if relaxing for a while hadn't helped, just made him feel his exhaustion. 'And I need a list of club members, too.'

'I can help you with the Wallace killing,' I said. 'But you'll have to get the list from Jane Engle. She's the club secretary.' I had the book on hand I'd used to prepare my lecture. I checked to make sure my name was written inside, told Arthur I'd have him arrested if he didn't return it, and walked with him to the front door.

To my surprise, he put his hands on my shoulders and gripped them with no mean pressure.

'Don't look so dismal,' he said. The wide blue eyes caught mine. I felt a jolt tingle up my spine. 'You caught something last night most people wouldn't have. You were tough and smart and quick-thinking.' He caught a loose strand of my hair and rolled it between his fingers. 'I'll talk to you soon,' he said. 'Maybe tomorrow.'

As it turned out, we spoke somewhat sooner than that.

Chapter Five

I'd noticed a moving van parked in front of Robin Crusoe's apartment when I let Arthur out. Out of sheer curiosity, when the phone began to ring, I decided to take my calls on my bedside phone, which had a long cord, so I could stare out the front windows at the unloading. And the phone was ringing nonstop, as the news about Mamie Wright's murder spread among friends and co-workers. Just when I was about to dial his number, my father called. He seemed about equally concerned with my emotional health and with whether or not I still felt I could keep Phillip.

'Are you okay?' Phillip himself said softly. He is a shrieker in person, but unaccountably soft-spoken over the telephone.

'Yes, brother, I'm okay,' I answered.

''Cause I really want to come see you. Can I?'

'Sure.'

'Are you going to make pecan pie?'

'I might, if I was asked nicely.'

'Please, please, please?'

'That's pretty nice. Count on the pie.'

'Yahoo!'

'Do you feel I'm blackmailing you?' Father asked when Phillip relinquished the phone.

'Well, yes.'

'Okay, okay, I feel guilty. But Betty Jo really wants to go to this convention. Her best friend from college married a newspaperman, too, and they're going to be there.'

'Tell her I'll still keep him.' I loved Phillip, though at first I'd been terrified to even hold him, having no experience whatsoever with babies. To give Betty Jo credit, she's always been all for Phillip's getting to know his big sister.

After I'd hung up, the rest of the day gaped ahead of me like a black cave. Since it was my day off I tried to do day-off things; I paid bills, did my laundry.

My best friend, Amina Day, had just moved to Houston to take such a good job that I couldn't grudge her the move; but I missed her, and I'd felt very much an unadventurous village bumpkin before I'd stepped into the VFW kitchen. Amina wasn't going to believe I'd had a bona fide shocking experience right in Lawrenceton. I decided to call her that night, and the prospect cheered me.

Now that the first shock of last night had worn off, it all seemed curiously unreal, like a book. I'd read so many books, both fiction and nonfiction, in which a young woman walked into a room (across a field, down the stairs, in an alley) and found *the body*. I could distance myself from the reality of a dead Mamie by thinking of the situation, rather than the person.

I picked out all these distinctions while eating a nutritious lunch of Cheezits and tuna fish. All this thinking led me back to the depressing conclusion that so little had happened in my life for so long, that when something did I had to pick at it over and over. No moment was going to sneak by *me* unobserved and unanalyzed.

Clearly, some action was called for.

With the taste of lunch in my mouth it was easy to decide that that action should take the form of going to the grocery store. I made one of my methodical little lists and gathered up my coupons.

Of course the store was extra crowded on Saturday, and I saw several people who knew what had happened the night before. I found myself reluctant to talk about it to people who hadn't been there. I hadn't been asked to avoid mentioning the murder's connection to an old murder case, but I didn't see any sense in having to explain it to ten people in a row, either. Even the minimal responses I made slowed me down considerably, and forty minutes later I was only halfway through my list. As I stood at the meat counter debating between 'lean' and 'extra lean' hamburger, I heard a tapping noise. It grew more and more imperative, until I looked up. Benjamin Greer, the only member of Real Murders who hadn't been at the meeting the night before, was tapping on the clear glass that separated the butchers from the refrigerated meat counter. Behind him, gleaming steel machines were doing their job, and another butcher in a bloodstained apron like Benjamin's was packing roasts.

Benjamin was stout with wispy blond hair that he swept up and over his premature bald spot. He'd tried to grow a mustache to augment his missing scalp hair, but it had given the impression that his upper lip was dirty, and I was glad to see he'd shaved the thing off. He wasn't very tall, and he wasn't very bright, and he tried to make up for these factors with a puppylike friendliness and willingness to do whatever one asked. On the down side, if his help was not needed, no matter how tactfully you expressed it, he turned sullen and self-pitying. Benjamin was a difficult person, one of those people who make you feel ashamed of yourself if you dislike him, while making it almost impossible to like him.

I disliked him, of course. He'd asked me out three times, and every time, feeling deeply ashamed of myself, I'd told him no. Even as desperate for a date as I was, I couldn't stomach the thought of going out with Benjamin.

He'd tried a fundamentalist church, he'd tried coaching Little League, and now he was trying Real Murders.

I smiled at him falsely and damned the hamburger meat that had led me into his sight.

He hurried through the swinging door to the right of the meat. I steeled myself to be nice.

'The police came to my apartment last night,' he said breathlessly. 'They wanted to know why I hadn't come to the meeting.'

'What did you say?' I asked bluntly. The bloodstained apron was making me feel unwell. Suddenly hamburger seemed quite distasteful.

'Oh, I hated to miss your presentation,' he assured me, as if I'd been worried, 'but I had something else I had to do.' Put that in your pipe and smoke it, his expression said. Benjamin's words were as mild and apologetic and his voice was as abased as usual, but his face was another matter.

I looked inquiring and waited. Definitely not the hamburger. Maybe no red meat at all.

'I'm in politics,' Benjamin told me, his voice modest but his face triumphant.

'The mayoral race?' I guessed.

'Right. I'm helping out Morrison Pettigrue. I'm his campaign manager.' And Benjamin's voice quivered with pride.

Whoever Morrison Pettigrue was, he was sure to lose. The name rang a faint bell, but I wasn't willing to stand there waiting to recall what I knew.

'I wish you luck,' I said with as good a smile as I could scrape together.

'Would you like to go to a rally with me next week?'

My God, he *wanted* me to kick him in the face. That was the only explanation. I looked at him and thought, you pathetic person. Then I felt ashamed, of course, and that made me angry at myself, and him.

'No, Benjamin,' I said with finality. I could not offer an excuse. I did not want this to happen again.

'Okay,' he said, with martyrdom in his voice. 'Well . . . I'll be seeing you.' The hurt quivered dramatically just under his brave smile.

The old reply came to the tip of my tongue, and I bit it back. But as I wheeled my cart away, I whispered, 'Not if I see you first.' As I slowed down to stare at the dog food bags, just so he wouldn't look out the window and see me speeding away as fast as I could move, I realized there were a couple of funny things about our conversation.

He hadn't asked any questions about last night. He hadn't asked who had been at the meeting, he hadn't said how strange it was that the only night he'd missed was the night something extraordinary happened. He hadn't even asked how it felt to discover Mamie's body, something everyone I'd seen today had been trying to ask me in roundabout ways.

I puzzled over it while I selected shampoo, and then decided not to worry about Benjamin Greer. Instead, I would get mad at the shelf stockers. Naturally, every kind of heavily sugared cereal based on a cartoon show was at my eye level, while cereal bought by grown-ups was stacked way above my head. I could reach them, but then the stockers had laid other boxes down on top of the row of upright boxes. If I pulled out the one I could reach, the others on top of it would come toppling down, making lots of noise and attracting lots of attention. You can tell I know from experience.

I turned sideways to maximize my stretch and stood on my tiptoes. No go. I was just going to have to switch brands or start eating cereal that tasted like bubble gum. That horrible thought galvanized me into another attempt.

'Here, young lady, let me get that for you,' said an unbearably patronizing voice from somewhere above me. A huge hand reached over my head, grasped the box easily, and like a crane lowered the box into my cart.

I gripped the cart handle as if it were my temper. I breathed out once deeply, and then in again. I slowly turned to face my benefactor. I looked up – and up – into a comically dismayed face topped by a thatch of longish red hair.

'Oh, gosh, I'm sorry,' said Robin Crusoe. Hazel eyes blinked at me anxiously from behind his wire-rims. 'I thought – from the back, you know, you look about twelve. But certainly not from the *front*.'

He realized what he'd just said, and his eyes closed in horror.

I was beginning to enjoy this.

A fleeting image crossed my mind of us in an intimate situation, and I wondered if it would work at all. I couldn't help it; I began to smile.

He smiled back, relieved, and I saw his charm instantly. He had a crooked smile, a little shy.

'I don't think we should talk like this,' he said, indicating the difference in our heights. 'Why don't I come over after I get my groceries put up? You live right by me, I think you said last night? You make me want to pick you up so I can see you better.'

That so closely matched a certain image crossing my mind that I could feel my face turning red. 'Please do come over. I'm sure you have a lot of questions after last night,' I said.

'That would be great. My place is in such a mess that I need a break from looking at boxes.'

'Okay, then. About an hour?'

'Sure, see you then – your name's really Roe?'

'Short for Aurora,' I explained. 'Aurora Teagarden.'

He didn't seem to think my name was unusual at all.

'Coffee? Soft drink? Orange juice?' I offered.

'Beer?' he countered.

'Wine.'

'Okay. I don't usually drink at this hour, but if anything will drive you to drink, it's moving.'

Feeling naughty at having a drink before five in the afternoon, I filled two glasses and joined him in the living room. I sat in the same chair I'd taken that morning when Arthur had been there, and felt incredibly female and powerful at entertaining two men in my home on the same day.

Robin, like Arthur, was impressed with the room. 'I hope mine looks half this good when I've finished unpacking. I have no talent at all for making things look nice.'

My friend Amina would have said I didn't either. 'Are you settled in?' I asked politely.

'I got my bed put together while the moving men were unloading the rest of the van, and I've hung my clothes in the closet. At least I had a chair for the detective to sit in this morning. They carried it in right as he walked to the door.'

'Arthur Smith?' I was surprised. He hadn't told me he was going to interview Robin after he left my place. I'd shut the door assuming he'd get in his car and drive off. He must have left Robin's apartment before I started spying out the front upstairs window.

'Yes, he was checking up on the way I happened to come to the club meeting—'

'How *did* you know about it?' I interrupted with intense curiosity.

'Well,' he said with reddening face, 'when I went to the utility company, I got to talking with Lizanne, and when she found out I write mysteries, she remembered the club. Evidently you told her about it one time.' I hadn't imagined Lizanne was listening. She'd looked, as usual, bored. 'So Lizanne called John Queensland, who said Real Murders was meeting that very night and visitors could come, so I asked her . . .'

'Just wondered,' I said neutrally.

'That Sergeant Burns, he's a grim kind of man,' Robin said thoughtfully. 'And Detective Smith is no lightweight.'

'You didn't even know Mamie, it's out of the question you could be suspected.'

'Well, I guess I could have known her before. But I didn't, and I think Smith believes that. But I bet he'll check. That's a guy I wouldn't like to have on my trail.'

'Mamie wouldn't have gotten there before 7:00,' I said thoughtfully. 'And I have no alibi for 7:00 to 7:30. She had to meet the VFW president at the VFW Hall to get the key. And I think after every meeting she had to run by his house to return the key.'

'Nope. Yesterday she dropped by the president's house and picked up the key. She told them she needed to get in early, she had some kind of appointment to meet someone there before the meeting.'

'How'd you know that?' I was agog and indignant.

'The detective asked to use the phone to call the station and I pieced that together from listening to his end of the conversation,' he said frankly. Aha, another person who was curious by nature.

'Oh. So,' I said slowly, thinking as I went, 'whoever killed her actually had plenty of time to fix everything up. He got her to come early somehow, so he'd have buckets of time to kill her and arrange her and go home to clean up.' I drained my glass and shuddered.

Robin said hastily, 'Tell me about the other club members.'

I decided that question was the real purpose of his visit. I felt disappointed, but philosophical.

'Jane Engle, the white-haired older lady,' I began. 'She's retired but works from time to time substitute teaching or substituting at the library. She's an expert on Victorian murders.' And then I ran down the list on my fingers: Gifford Doakes, Melanie Clark, Bankston Waites, John Queensland, LeMaster Cane, Arthur Smith, Mamie and Gerald Wright, Perry Allison, Sally Allison, Benjamin Greer. 'But Perry's only just started coming,' I explained. 'I guess he's not really a member.'

Robin nodded, and his red hair fell across his eyes. He brushed it back absently.

That absorption in his face and the small gesture did something to me.

'What about you?' he asked. 'Give me a little biography.'

'Not much to tell. I went to high school here, went to a small private college, did some graduate work at the university in library science and came home and got a job at the local library.'

Robin looked disconcerted.

'All right, it never occurred to me not to come back,' I said after a moment. 'What about you?'

'Oh, I'm going to teach a course at the university. The writer they had lined up had a heart attack . . . Do you ever do impulsive things?' Robin asked suddenly.

One of the strongest impulses I'd ever felt urged me to put down my wineglass, walk over to Robin Crusoe, a writer I'd known only a few hours, sit on his lap, and kiss him until he fainted.

'Almost never,' I said with real regret. 'Why?'

'Have you ever experienced . . .'

My doorbell chimed twice.

'Excuse me,' I said with even deeper regret, and answered the front door.

Mr Windham, my mail carrier, handed me a brown-wrapped package. 'I couldn't fit this in your box,' he explained.

I glanced at the mailing label. 'Oh, it's not to me, it's to Mother,' I said, puzzled.

'Well, we have to deliver by addresses, so I had to bring it here,' Mr Windham said righteously.

Of course, he was right; my address was on the package. The return address was my father's home in the city. The label itself was typed, as usual for Father. He's gotten a new typewriter, I thought, surprised. His old Smith-Corona had been the only typewriter he'd ever used. 'Maybe he'd mailed it to Mother from his office and used a typewriter there? Then I noticed the date.

'Six days?' I said incredulously. 'It took six days for this to travel thirty miles?'

Mr Windham shrugged defensively.

My father hadn't said a word about mailing us anything. As I shut the front door, I reflected that Father hadn't sent Mother a package in my memory, certainly never since the divorce. I was eaten up with curiosity. I stopped at the kitchen phone on my way back to the living room. She was in her office, and said she'd stop by on her way to show a house. She was as puzzled as I was, and I hated to hear that little thread of excitement in her voice.

Robin seemed to be dozing in his chair, so I quietly picked up our wineglasses and washed them so I could put them away before Mother got there. I didn't need her arching her eyebrows at me. Actually, I was glad to have a breather. I'd almost done something radical earlier, and it was almost as much fun to think about nearly having done it as it would have been (maybe) to do it.

When Mother came through the gate, Robin woke up – if he'd really been asleep – and I introduced them.

Robin stood courteously, shook hands properly, and admired Mother as she was used to being admired, from her perfectly frosted hair to her slim elegant legs. Mother was wearing one of her very expensive suits, this one in a champagne color, and she looked like a million-dollar saleswoman. Which she was, several times over.

'So nice to see you again, Mr Crusoe,' she said in her husky voice. 'I'm sorry you had such a bad experience your first evening in our little town. Really, Lawrenceton is a lovely place, and I'm sure you won't regret living here and commuting to the city.'

I handed her the box. She looked at the return address sharply, then began ripping open the wrapping while she kept up an idle conversation with Robin.

'Mrs See's!' we exclaimed simultaneously when we saw the white and black box.

'Candy?' Robin said uncertainly. He sat back down when I did.

'Very good candy,' Mother said happily. 'They sell it out west, and in the Midwest too, but you can't get it down here. I used to have a cousin in St Louis who'd send me a box every Christmas, but she passed away last year. So Roe and I were thinking we'd never get a box of Mrs See's again!'

'I want the chocolate-almond clusters!' I reminded her.

'They're yours,' Mother assured me. 'You know I only like the creams . . . hum. No note. That's odd.'

'I guess Dad just remembered how much you liked them,' I offered, but it was a weak offering. Somehow the gesture just wasn't like my father; it was an impulse gift, since Mother's birthday was months away, and he hadn't been giving her a birthday present since they divorced, anyway. So, a nice impulse. But my father never did impulsive things; I came by my caution honestly.

Mother had offered the box to Robin, who shook his head. She settled down to the delightful task of choosing her first piece of Mrs See's. It was one of our favorite little Christmas rituals, and the spring weather felt all wrong suddenly.

'It's been so long,' she mused. She finally sighed and lifted a piece. 'Aurora, isn't this the one with caramel filling?'

I peered at the chocolate in question. I was sitting down, Mother was standing up, so I could see what she hadn't. There was a hole in the bottom of the chocolate.

It had gotten banged around in shipment?

Abruptly I leaned forward and pulled another chocolate out of its paper frill. It was a nut cluster and it was pristine. I breathed out a sigh of relief. Just in case, I picked up another cream. It had a hole in the bottom, too.

'Mom. Put the candy down.'

'Is this a piece you wanted?' she asked, eyebrows raised at my tone.

'Put it *down.*'

She did, and looked at me angrily.

'There's something wrong with it, Mom. Robin, look.' I poked at the piece she'd relinquished with my finger.

Robin lifted the chocolate delicately with his long fingers and peered at the bottom. He put it down and looked at several more. My mother looked cross and frightened.

'Surely this is ridiculous,' she said.

'I don't think so, Mrs Teagarden,' Robin answered finally. 'I think someone's tried to poison you, and maybe Roe, too.'

Chapter Six

So Arthur came to my apartment on official business twice in one day, and he brought another detective with him this time, or maybe she brought him. Lynn Liggett was a homicide detective, and she was as tall as Arthur, which made her tall for a woman.

I can't say I was afraid right then. I was confused at the label apparently addressed by my father, I was indignant that someone had tried to trick us into eating something unhealthy, but I was sure that with poisons being so hard to obtain, whatever was in the candy would prove to be something that might have caused us to have a few bad hours, but simply couldn't have killed Mother or me.

Arthur seemed pretty grim about the whole thing, and Lynn Liggett asked us questions. And more questions. I could see the lapel pin on Mother's jacket heave. When Detective Liggett bagged the candy and carried it out to Arthur's car, Mother said to me in a furious whisper, 'She acts like we are people who don't live decent lives!'

'She doesn't know us, Mother,' I said soothingly, though to tell the truth I was a little peeved with Detective Liggett myself. Questions like, 'Have you recently finished a relationship that left someone bitter with you, Mrs Teagarden?' and 'Miss Teagarden, how long have you known Mr Crusoe?' had not left a good taste in my mouth either. I'd never before been able to understand why good citizens didn't cooperate with the police – after all, they had their job to do, they didn't know you personally, to them all citizens should be treated alike, blah blah blah, right?

Now I could understand. Jack Burns looking at me like I was a day-old catfish corpse had been one thing, an isolated incident maybe. I wanted to say, Liggett, romantic relationships don't figure in this, some maniac mailed this candy to Mother and dragged me into it by addressing it to me! But I knew Lynn Liggett was obliged to ask us these questions and I was bound to answer them. And still I resented it.

Maybe it wouldn't have bothered me if Lynn Liggett hadn't been a woman.

Not that I didn't think women should be detectives. I certainly did think women should be detectives, and I thought many women I knew would be great detectives – you should see some of my fellow librarians tracking down an overdue book, and I'm not being facetious.

But Lynn Liggett seemed to be evaluating me as a fellow woman, and she found me wanting. She looked down at me and found me smaller than her 'every whichaways,' as I remembered my grandmother saying. I conjectured that since being tall must have given Detective Liggett problems, she automatically assumed I felt superior to her as a woman, since I was so short and therefore more 'feminine.' Since she couldn't compete with me on that level, Liggett figured she'd be tougher, more suspicious, coldly professional. A strong frontier woman as opposed to me, the namby-pamby, useless stay-back-in-the-effete-east toy woman.

I know a lot about role-playing, and she couldn't pull that bull on me. I was tempted to burst into tears, pull out a lace handkerchief – if I had possessed such a useless thing – and say, 'Ar-thur! Little ole me is just so scared!' Because I could see that this had little to do with me, but much to do with Arthur.

Getting right down to the nitty-gritty, Homicide Detective Liggett had the hots for Burglary Detective Smith, and as Detective Liggett saw it, Detective Smith had the hots for me.

It's taken me a long time to spell out what I sensed in a matter of minutes. I was disappointed in Lynn Liggett, because I would have liked to be her friend and listen to her stories about her job. I hoped she was a more subtle detective than she was a woman. And I had to answer the damn questions anyway, even though I knew, Mother knew, and I believe Arthur knew, that they were a waste of time.

Robin stayed the whole time, though his presence was not absolutely necessary once he'd told his simple story to the detectives. 'I ran into Roe Teagarden in the grocery, and asked her if I could come over here to relax a little since my place is such a mess. When the candy came, she seemed quite surprised, yes. I also saw the hole in the bottom of the piece of candy when Mrs Teagarden held it up. No, I didn't know either Roe or Mrs Teagarden until the last two days. I met Mrs Teagarden briefly when I went by her real estate office to rendezvous with the lady who was going to show me the apartment next door, and I didn't meet Roe until the Real Murders meeting last night.'

'And you've been here since when?' Arthur asked quietly. He was standing in the kitchen talking to Robin, while Detective Liggett questioned Mother and me as we sat on the couch and she crouched on the love seat.

'Oh, I've been here about an hour and a half,' Robin said with a slight edge.

Arthur's voice had had absolutely no overtone whatsoever (Liggett was not quite that good), but I had the distinct feeling that everyone here was following his or her own agenda, except possibly my mother. She was certainly no dummy when a sexual element entered the air, however, and in fact she suddenly gave me one of her dazzling smiles of approval, which I could have done without since Detective Liggett seemed to intercept it and interpret it as some kind of reflection on her.

My mother rose and swept up her purse and terminated the interview. 'My daughter is fine and I am fine, and I cannot imagine that my former husband sent this candy or ever intended to hurt either of us,' she said decisively. 'He adores Aurora, and he and I have a civil relationship. Our little family habits are no secret to anyone. I don't imagine our little Christmas custom of a box of candy has gone unremarked. Probably, I've bored people many times by talking about it. We'll be interested to hear, of course, when you all find out what is actually in the candy – if anything. Maybe the holes in the bottom are just to alarm us, and this is some practical joke. Thanks for coming, and I have to be getting back to the office.' I stood up too, and Lynn Liggett felt forced to walk to the door with us.

My mother got into her car first, while Arthur and Lynn conferred together on the patio. Robin was clearly undecided about what he should do. Arthur throwing out his male challenge, in however subdued a way, had struck Robin by surprise, and he was squinting thoughtfully at my stove without seeing it. He was probably wondering what he'd gotten into, and if this murder investigation was going to be as much fun as he'd anticipated.

I was abruptly sick of all of them. Maybe I hadn't been a big dating success because I was a boring person, but possibly it had been because I had limited tolerance for all this preliminary maneuvering and signal reading. My friend Amina Day loved all this stuff and was practically a professional at it. I missed Amina suddenly and desperately.

'Come have lunch with me in the city Monday,' Robin suggested, having reached some internal decision.

I thought a moment. 'Okay,' I agreed. 'I covered for another librarian when she took her kid to the orthodontist last week, so I don't have to go in Monday until two o'clock.'

'Are you familiar with the university campus? Oh, sure, you went there. Well, meet me at Tarkington Hall, the English building. I'll be finishing up a writer's workshop at 11:45 on the third floor in Room 36. We'll just leave from there, if that suits you.'

'That'll be fine. See you then.'

'If you need me for anything, I'll be at home all day tomorrow getting ready for my classes.'

'Thanks.'

The phone rang inside and I turned to get it as Robin sauntered out my gate, waving a casual hand to the two detectives. An excited male voice asked for Arthur, and I called him to the phone. Lynn Liggett had recovered her cool, and when I called, 'Arthur! Phone!' her mouth only twitched a little. Oops, silly me. Should have said Detective Smith.

I watered my rose trees while Arthur talked inside. Lynn regarded me thoughtfully. The silence between us was pretty fragile, and I felt small talk was not a good idea, but I tried anyway.

'How long have you been on the force here?' I asked.

'About three years. I came here as a patrol officer, then got promoted.'

Maybe Detective Liggett and I would have become bosom buddies in a few more minutes, but Arthur came out of the apartment then with electricity crackling in every step.

'The purse has been found,' he said to his co-worker.

'No shit! 'Where?'

'Stuffed under the front seat of a car.'

Well, say which one! I almost said indignantly.

But Arthur didn't, of course, and he and his confrere were out the gate with nary a word for me. And I'll give this to Lynn Liggett, she was too involved in her work to look back at me in triumph.

To keep my hands busy while my mind roamed around, I began refinishing an old wooden two-drawer chest that I'd had in my guest bedroom for months waiting for just such a moment. After I wrestled it down the stairs and out onto the patio, the sanding turned out to be just the thing I needed.

Naturally I thought about the candy incident, and wondered if the police had called my father yet. I couldn't imagine what he'd think of all this. As I scrubbed my hands under the kitchen sink after finishing, I had a new thought, one I should have had before. Did sending the candy to Mother imitate another crime? I went to my shelves and began searching through all my 'true murder' books. I couldn't find anything, so this incident wasn't patterned after one of the better-known murders. Jane Engle, my fellow librarian, had a larger personal collection than I, so I called her and told her what had happened.

'That rings a faint bell . . . it's an American murder, I think,' Jane said interestedly. 'Isn't this bizarre, Roe? That such things could happen in Lawrenceton? To us? Because I really begin to think this is happening to us, to the members of our little club.

Did you hear that Mamie's purse has been found under the seat in Melanie Clark's car?'

'Melanie! Oh, I can't believe it!'

'The police may be taking that seriously, but Roe, you and I know that's ridiculous. I mean, Melanie Clark. It's a plant.'

'Huh?'

'A club member was killed, and another club member is being used to divert suspicion.'

'You think whoever killed Mamie took her purse and deliberately planted it under Melanie's car seat,' I said slowly.

'Oh, yes.' I could picture Jane standing in her tiny house full of her mother's furniture, Jane's silver chignon gleaming amid bookcases full of gory death.

'But Melanie and Gerald Wright could have had something going,' I protested weakly. 'Melanie could really have done it.'

'Aurora, you know she's absolutely head over heels about Bankston Waites. The little house she rents is just down the street from mine and I can't help but notice his car is there a great deal.' Jane tactfully didn't specify whether that included overnight.

'Her car is here a lot too,' I admitted.

'So,' Jane said persuasively, 'I am sure that this candy thing is another old murder case revisited, and maybe the police will find the poison in another club member's kitchen!'

'Maybe,' I said slowly. 'Then none of us are safe.'

'No,' Jane said. 'Not really.'

'Who could have it in for us that bad?'

'My dear, I haven't the slightest. But you can bet I'll be thinking about it, and I'm going to start looking for a case like yours right this moment.'

'Thanks, Jane,' I said, and I hung up with much to think about, myself.

I had nothing special to do that night, as my Saturday nights had tended to run the past couple of years. Right after I ate my Saturday splurge of pizza and salad, I remembered my resolution to call Amina in Houston.

Miraculously, she was in. Amina hadn't been in on a Saturday night in twelve years, and she was going out later, she said immediately, but her date was a department store manager who worked late on Saturday.

'How is Houston?' I asked wistfully.

'Oh, it's great! So much to do! And everyone at work is so friendly.' Amina was a first-rate legal secretary.

People almost always were friendly to Amina. She was a slender brown-eyed freckle-faced extrovert almost exactly my age, and I'd grown up with her and remained best friends with her through college. Amina had married and divorced childlessly, the only interruption in her long, exhaustive dating career. She was not really pretty, but she was irresistible – a laughing, chattering live wire, never at a loss for a word. She had a great talent for enjoying life and for maximizing every asset she'd been born with or acquired (her hair was not exactly naturally blond). My mother should have had Amina for a daughter, I thought suddenly.

After Amina finished telling me about her job, I dropped my bombshell.

'You found a body! Oh, yick! Who was it?' Amina shrieked. 'Are you okay? Are you having bad dreams? Was the chocolate really poisoned?'

Amina being my best friend, I told her the truth. 'I don't know yet if the chocolate was poisoned. Yes, I'm having bad dreams, but this is really exciting at the same time.'

'Are you safe, do you think?' she asked anxiously. 'Do you want to come stay with me until this is all over? I can't believe this is happening to you! You're so nice!'

'Well, nice or not,' I retorted grimly, 'it's happening. Thanks for asking me, Amina, and I will come to see you soon. But I have to stay here for now. I don't think I'm in any more danger. This was my turn to be targeted, I guess, and I came out okay.' I skipped my speculation with Arthur that maybe the killer would go on killing, and Jane Engle's conjecture that maybe we would all be drawn in, and cut right to Amina's area of expertise.

'I have a situation here,' I began, and at once had her undivided attention. The nuances and dosey-does between the sexes were

Amina's bread and butter. I hadn't had anything like this to tell Amina since we were in high school. It was hard to credit that grown people still engaged in all this – foreplay.

'So,' Amina said when I'd finished. 'Arthur is a little resentful that this Robin spent the afternoon at your place, and Robin's trying to decide whether he likes you well enough to keep up the beginning of your relationship in view of Arthur's slight proprietary air. Though Arthur is not the proprietor of anything yet, right?'

'Right.'

'And you haven't actually had a date with either of these bozos, right?'

'Right.'

'But Robin has asked you to lunch in the city for Monday.'

'Uh-huh.'

'And you're supposed to meet him at the classroom.'

'Yep.'

'And Lizanne has definitely discarded this Robin.' Amina and Lizanne had always had a curious relationship. Amina operated on personality and Lizanne on looks, but they'd both run through the male population of Lawrenceton and surrounding towns at an amazing rate.

'Lizanne formally bequeathed him to me,' I told Amina.

'She's not greedy,' Amina conceded. 'If she doesn't want 'em, she lets 'em know, and she lets 'em go. Now, if you're going to meet him at the university, you realize he's going to be sitting in a classroom full of little chickies just panting to hop in bed with a famous writer. He's not ugly, right?'

'He's not conventionally handsome,' I said. 'He has charm.'

'Well, don't wear one of those blouse and skirt combinations you're always wearing to work!'

'What do you suggest I wear?' I inquired coldly.

'Listen, you called me for advice,' Amina reminded me. 'Okay, I'm giving it to you. You've had an awful time. Nothing makes you feel better than a few new clothes, and you can afford it. So go to my mom's shop tomorrow when it opens, and get something new. Maybe a classic town 'n country type dress. Stick to little earrings, since you're so short, and maybe a few gold chains.' (A few? I was lucky to have one my mother had given me for Christmas. Amina's boyfriends gave her gold chains for every occasion, in whatever length or thickness they could afford. She probably had twenty.) 'That should be fine for a casual lunch in the city,' Amina concluded.

'You think he'll notice me as a woman, not just a fellow murder buff?'

'If you want him to notice you as a woman, just lust after him.'

'Huh?'

'I don't mean lick your lips or pant. Keep conversation normal. Don't do anything obvious. You have to keep it so you don't lose anything if he decides he's not interested.' Amina was interested in saving face.

'So what do I do?'

'Just *lust*. Keep everything going like normal, but sort of concentrate on the area below your waist and above your knees, right? And send out *waves*. You can do it. It's like the Kegel exercise. You can't show anyone how to do it, but if you describe it to a woman, she can pick it up.'

'I'll try,' I said doubtfully.

'Don't worry, it'll come naturally,' Amina told me. 'I have to hang up, the doorbell is ringing. Call me again and tell me how it goes, okay? The only thing wrong with Houston is that you aren't here.'

'I miss you,' I said.

'Yeah, and I miss you, but you needed me to leave,' Amina said, and then she did hang up.

And after a moment's disbelief, I knew she was right. Her departure had freed me from the role of the most popular woman's best friend, a role that required I not attempt to make the most of myself because even the best of me could not compete with Amina. I almost had to be the intellectual drab one.

I was sitting thinking about what Amina had said when the phone rang while my hand was still resting on it. I jumped a mile.

'It's me again,' Amina said rapidly. 'Listen, Franklin is waiting for me in the living room, but I ran back here to my other phone to tell you this. You said Perry Allison was in that club with you? You watch out for Perry. When he was in college with me, he and I took a lot of the same courses our freshman year. But he would have these mood swings. He'd be hyper-excited and follow me around just jabbering, then he'd be all quiet and sullen and just stare at me. Finally the college called his mother.'

'Poor Sally,' I said involuntarily.

'She came and got him and I think committed him, not just because of me but because he was skipping classes and no one would room with him because his habits got so strange.'

'I think he's beginning to repeat that pattern, Amina. He's still holding together at the library, but I see Sally looking worried these days.'

'You just watch out for him. He never hurt anyone that I know of, though he made a bunch of people nervous. But if he's involved in this murder thing, you watch out!'

'Thanks, Amina.'

'Sure, 'bye now.'

And she was gone again to enjoy herself with Franklin.

Chapter Seven

Sunday dawned warm and rainy. A breeze swooped over the fence and rustled my rose trees. It was not a morning to eat breakfast on the patio. I fried bacon and ate my bakery sweet roll while listening to a local radio broadcast. The mayoral candidates were answering questions on this morning's talk show. The election promised more interest than the usual Democratic shoo-in, since not only was there a Republican candidate who actually had a slim chance, there was a candidate from the – gasp – Communist Party! Of course, this was the candidate whose campaign Benjamin Greer was managing. Poor miserable Benjamin, hoping that the Communist Party and politics would be his salvation. Of course the Communist, Morrison Pettigrue, was one of the New People, one of those who'd fled the city but wanted to stay close to it.

At least this would be a unifying election for Lawrenceton. None of the candidates was black, which always made for a tense campaign and a divisive one. The Republican and Democrat were having the time of their political lives, giving sane, sober answers to banal questions, and thoroughly enjoying Pettigrue's fiery responses that sometimes bordered on the irrational.

Bless his heart, I thought sadly, not only is he a Communist but he's also very unappealing. I'd made a point of looking for Pettigrue's campaign posters on the way back from the grocery store the day before. They said nothing about the Communist Party (just 'Elect Morrison Pettigrue, the People's Choice, for Mayor') and they showed him to be a grim-featured swarthy man who had obviously suffered badly from acne.

I listened while I ate breakfast, but then I switched to some country and western music for my dishwashing. Domestic chores always went faster when you could sing about drinkin' and cheatin'.

It was such a nice little morning I decided to go to church. I often did. I sometimes enjoyed it and felt better for going, but I felt no spiritual compulsion. I went because I hoped I'd 'catch it,' like deliberately exposing myself to the chicken pox. Sometimes I even wore a hat and gloves, though that was bordering on parody and gloves were not so easy to find anymore. It wasn't a hat-and-gloves day, today, too dark and rainy, and I wasn't in a role-playing mood, anyway.

As I pulled into the Presbyterian parking lot, I wondered if I'd see Melanie Clark, who sometimes attended. Had she been arrested? I couldn't believe stolid Melanie truly was in danger of being charged with Mamie Wright's murder. The only possible motive anyone could attribute to Melanie was an affair with Gerald Wright. Someone . . . some murderer, I reminded myself . . . was playing an awful joke on Melanie.

I drifted through the service, thinking about God and Mamie. I felt horrible when I thought of what another human being had done to Mamie; yet I had to face it, when she had been alive the predominant feeling I'd had for her had been contempt. Now Mamie's soul, and I believe we do all have one, was facing God, as I would one day too. This was too close to the bone for me, and I buried that thought so I could dig it up later when I wasn't so vulnerable.

I made my way out of church, speaking with most of the congregation along my way. All the talk I heard was about Melanie and her predicament, and the latest information appeared to be that Melanie had had to go down to the police station for a while, but on Bankston's vehement vouching for her every move on the evening of Mamie Wright's death, she'd been allowed to go home and (the feeling went) was thus exonerated.

Melanie herself was an orphan, but Bankston's mother was a Presbyterian. Today of course she was the center of an attentive group on the church steps. Mrs Waites was as blond and blue-eyed as her son, and ordinarily just as phlegmatic. But this Sunday she was an angry woman and didn't care who knew it. She was mad at the police for suspecting 'that sweet Melanie' for one single minute. As if a girl like that was going to beat a fly to death, much less a grown woman! And those police suggesting that maybe things weren't as they should be between Melanie and Mr Wright! As if wild horses could drag Melanie and Bankston away from each other! At least this awful thing had gone and gotten Bankston to speak his mind. He and Melanie were going to be married in two months. No, a date hadn't been set, but they were going to decide about one today, and Melanie was going to go down to Millie's Gifts this week and pick out china and silver patterns.

This was a triumphant moment for Mrs Waites, who had been trying to marry off Bankston for years. Her other children were settled, and Bankston's apparent willingness to wait for the right woman to come to him, instead of actively searching himself, had tried Mrs Waites to the limit.

I would have to go pick out a fork or salad plate. I'd given lots of similar gifts in a hundred different patterns. I sighed, and tried hard not to feel sorry for myself as I drove to Mother's. I always ate Sunday lunch with her, unless she was off on one of the myriad real estate conventions she attended or out showing houses.

Mother (who had spent a rare Sunday morning at home) was in fine spirits because she'd sold a $200,000 house the day before, after she'd left my apartment. Not too many women can get poisoned chocolates, be interrogated by the police, and sell expensive properties in the same day.

'I'm trying to get John to let me list his house,' she told me over the pot roast.

'What? Why would he sell his house? It's beautiful.'

'His wife has been dead several years now, and all the children are gone, and he doesn't need a big house to rattle around in,' my mother said.

'You've been divorced for twelve years, your child is gone, and you don't need a big house to rattle around in either,' I pointed out. I had been wondering why my mother didn't unload the 'four by two-storey brick w/frpl and 3 baths' I'd grown up in.

'Well, there's a possibility John will have somewhere else to live soon,' Mother said too casually. 'We may get married.'

God, everyone was doing it!

I pulled myself together and looked happy for Mother's sake. I managed to say the right things, and I meant them, and she seemed pleased.

What on earth could I get them for a wedding present?

'Since John doesn't seem to want to talk about his involvement with Real Murders right now,' Mother said suddenly, 'why don't you just tell me about this club?'

'John's an expert on Lizzie Borden,' I explained.

'If you really want to know about his main interest, apart from golf and you, it's Lizzie. You ought to read Victoria Lincoln's *A Private Disgrace*. That's one of the best books about the Borden case I've read.'

'Um, Aurora . . . who was Lizzie Borden?'

I gaped at my mother. 'That's like asking a baseball fan who Mickey Mantle was,' I said finally. 'I didn't know that a person could not know who Lizzie Borden was. Just ask John. He'll talk your ear off. But if you read the book first, he'll appreciate it.'

Mother actually wrote the title in her little notebook. She really meant it about John Queensland, she was really serious about getting married. I couldn't decide how I felt; I only knew how I ought to feel. At least acting that out made my mother happy.

'Really, Aurora, I want you to tell me about the club in general, though I do want to discuss John's particular interest intelligently, of course. Now that you and he are both tied in with this horrible murder, and you and I got sent that candy, I want to know what the background on these crimes is.'

'Mother, I can't remember when Real Murders started . . . about three years ago, I guess. There was a book signing at Thy Sting, the mystery book store in the city. And all of us now in Real Murders turned up for the signing, which was being held for a book about a real murder. It was such a funny coincidence, all us

Lawrenceton people showing up, interested in the same thing, that we sort of agreed to call each other and start something up we could all come to in our own town. So we began meeting every month, and the format for the meetings just evolved – a lecture and discussion on a real murder most months, a related topic other months.' I shrugged. I was getting tired of explaining Real Murders. I expected Mother to change the subject now, as she always had before when I'd tried to talk about my interest in the club.

'You told me earlier that you believe Mamie Wright's murder was patterned on the Wallace murder,' Mother said instead. 'And you said that Jane Engle believes that the candy being sent to us is also patterned like another crime – she's trying to look it up?'

I nodded.

'You're in danger,' my mother said flatly. 'I want you to leave Lawrenceton until this is all over. There's no way you can be implicated, like poor Melanie was with that purse hidden in her car, if you're out of town.'

'Well, that would be great, Mom,' I said, knowing she hated to be called 'Mom,' 'but I happen to have a job. I'm supposed to just go to my boss and tell him my mother is scared something might happen to me, so I have to get out of town for an indefinite period of time? Just hold my job, Mr Clerrick?'

'Aren't you scared?' she asked furiously.

'Yes, yes! If you had seen what this killer can do, if you had seen Mamie Wright's head, or what was left of it, you'd be scared too! But I can't leave! I have a life!'

My mother didn't say anything, but her unguarded response, which showed clearly in those amazing eyebrows, was 'Since when?'

I went home with a plateful of leftovers for supper, as usual, and decided to have a Sunday afternoon and evening of self-pity. Sunday afternoons are good for that. I took off my pretty dress (no matter what Amina says, I do have some pretty and flattering clothes) and put on my nastiest sweats. I stopped short of washing off my makeup and messing up my hair, but I felt that way.

What I hated to do most was wash windows, so I decided today was the day. The clouds had lightened a little and I no longer expected rain, so I collected all the window washing paraphernalia and did the downstairs, grimly spraying and wiping and then repeating the process. I carried around my step stool, even with its boost barely reaching the top panes. When they were shining clearly, I trudged upstairs with my cleaning rag and spray bottle and began on the guest bedroom. It overlooked the parking lot, so I had a great view of the elderly couple next door, the Crandalls, coming home in their Sunday best. Perhaps they'd been to a married child's for lunch . . . they had several children here in town, and I recalled Teentsy Crandall mentioning at least eight grandchildren. Teentsy and her husband, Jed, were laughing together, and he patted her on the shoulder as he held open the gate. No sooner were they inside than Bankston's blue car entered the lot and he and Melanie emerged holding hands and smoldering at each other. Even to me, and I am not really experienced, it was apparent that they could hardly wait until they got inside.

As a crowning touch to a feel-sorry-for-yourself afternoon, it could hardly be beat. What did I have to look forward to? I asked myself rhetorically. *60 Minutes* and heated-up pot roast.

I decided I'd take Amina's advice after all. I'd be there when her mom's shop opened at 10:00 the next morning. With luck and my charge card, I could be ready for my trip to the city to have lunch with Robin Crusoe.

Then I decided that there was, after all, something I could do with my evening. I picked up my personal phone book and began dialing.

Chapter Eight

By 8:00 they were all there. It was crowded in my apartment, with Jane, Gerald, and Sally given the best seats and the others perched on chairs from the dinette set or sitting on the floor, like the lovebirds, Melanie and Bankston. I hadn't called Robin, because he had only been to Real Murders one time; one disastrous time. LeMaster Cane was sitting apart from everyone else, speaking to no one, his dark face deliberately blank. Gifford had brought Reynaldo, and they were huddled together with their backs pressed against the wall, looking sullen. Gerald still looked shocked, his pouchy face white and strained. Benjamin Greer was trying to be buddies with Perry Allison, who was openly sneering. Sally was trying not to watch her son, and carrying on a sporadic conversation with Arthur, who looked exhausted. John's creamy white head was bent toward Jane, who was talking quietly.

Even under the circumstances, I was sorely tempted to stand and say, 'I guess you're wondering why I called you all here,' but I didn't quite have the nerve. And after all, they knew why they were here.

I had assumed John would take the lead, since he was the president of our club. But he was looking at me expectantly, and I realized that it was up to me to start.

'Friends,' I said loudly, and the little rags of conversation stopped as though they'd been trimmed off with a knife. I paused for a minute, trying to marshall my thoughts, and Gifford said, 'Stand up so we can see ya.'

I saw several nods, so I stood. 'First,' I resumed, 'I want to tell Gerald we're all sorry, grieved, about Mamie.' Gerald looked around listlessly, acknowledging the murmur of sympathy with a nod of his head.

'Then,' I went on, 'I think we need to talk about what's happening to us.' I had everyone's undivided attention. 'I guess you all know about the tampered-with candy sent to me and my mother. I can't say poisoned, because we don't know for sure it was; so I can't be sure the intent was to kill. But I suppose we can assume that.' I looked around to see if anyone would disagree. No one did. 'And of course you all also know that Mamie's purse was put in Melanie's car.'

Melanie looked down in embarrassment, her straight dark hair swinging forward to hide her face. Bankston put his arm around her and held her close. 'As if Melanie would do such a thing,' he said hotly.

'Well, we all know that,' I said.

'Of course,' Jane chimed indignantly.

'I know,' I went on very, very carefully, 'that Sally and Arthur are in a delicate position tonight. Sally might want to report to the paper that we met, and Arthur will have to tell the police that he was here and what happened. I can see that. But I hope that Sally will agree that tonight is off the record.'

Everyone looked at Sally, who threw back her bronze head and glared at us all. 'The police want me not to print that the murder was a copy,' she said in exasperation. 'But everyone in Real Murders has been telling other people anyway. I'm losing the best story I ever had. Now you all want me to not be a reporter tonight. It's like asking Arthur not to be a policeman for a couple of hours.'

'Then you won't keep this off the record?' Gifford said unexpectedly. ''Cause if this isn't off the record, I'm out the door.' He stared at Sally, and smoothed back his long hair.

'Oh, all right,' Sally said. Her tan eyes snapped as she glared around the room. 'But I'm telling you all, this is the last time anything said to me about these murders is off the record!'

That reduced us all to speechlessness for a moment.

'Just what did you want us here for, dear?' Jane asked.

Good question. I took the plunge.

'It's probably one of us, right?' I said nervously.

No one moved. No one turned to look at the person beside him.

A presence in the room gathered power in that silence. That presence was fear, of course. We were all afraid, or getting there.

'But it may be an enemy of someone here,' said Arthur finally.

'So, who has enemies?' I inquired. 'I know that sounds naive, but for God's sake, we have to think, or we'll be mired in this until someone else dies.'

'I think you're overstating this,' said Melanie. She actually had a little social smile on her lips.

'How, Melanie?' asked Perry suddenly. 'How could Roe possibly be overstating this? We all know what's happened. We sure don't have to be geniuses to figure out that Mamie's murder was meant to be like Julia Wallace's. One of us is nuts. And we all know from reading so much about it, that a psychotic murderer can be as nice as pie on the outside and a screaming loony inside. What about Ted Bundy?'

'I just meant—' Melanie began uncertainly, 'I just meant that maybe, I don't know, someone we don't know is doing this, and it really isn't tied in to us at all. Maybe the presence of a group like ours sparked all this in someone's mind.'

'Maybe pigs can fly,' muttered Reynaldo, and Gifford laughed.

It wasn't a normal laugh, and the presence was bumping and flopping around the room like a blind thing, ready to grab the first person it lit on. Everyone was getting more and more nervous. I had made a mistake, and we were accomplishing nothing.

'If any one of you does have an enemy, someone who knows about your membership in Real Murders, someone who, maybe, has been reading your club handouts or reading your books, getting interested in what we study, now is the time for you to think of that person,' I said. 'If we can't come up with someone like that, then this is the last meeting of Real Murders.'

This brought another silence, that of shocked realization.

'Of course,' breathed Jane Engle. 'This is the end of us.'

'It may be the end, literally, of more of us if we can't figure this out,' Sally said bluntly. 'Whoever this is, is going to go on. Can any of you see this stopping? It isn't in the picture. Someone's having a great time, and I'd put my money on it being someone in this room.'

'I for one have better things to do than sit in a room with all these accusations going around,' Benjamin said. 'I'm in politics now, and I would have quit Real Murders anyway. Don't anyone come trying to kill me, that's all, because I'll be waiting for him.'

He left amid uneasy whispering, and before he was quite out my back door, Gifford said audibly, 'Benjamin isn't worth killing. What an asshole.'

We were all feeling some permutation on that theme, I imagine.

'I'm sorry,' I said to everyone. 'I thought I could accomplish something. I thought if we were all together, we could remember something that would help solve this horrible murder.'

Everyone began to shift slightly, preparing to gather up whatever or whoever they'd come with.

John Queensland exhibited an unexpected sense of drama.

'The last meeting of Real Murders is now adjourned,' he said formally.

Chapter Nine

I looked wonderful. Amina's mom had nodded thoughtfully when I told her I needed something new to wear to lunch in the city, and it had to be something I could wear to work too. Amina hadn't told me to add that, but Amina wasn't paying the bill. Mrs Day flicked the laden hangers with a professional hand. She glanced from blouses to me with narrowed eyes, while I tried not to look as silly (or as hopeful) as I felt.

She extracted an ivory blouse with dark green vines twining up it, and a dark green bow ('At your age, honey, you don't need a bright one, too young') that nestled in the wild waves of my hair with definite femininity. I got khaki-colored pants with a wide belt and extravagant pleats, and shoes, too. I slipped them on to wear away from the store. Mrs Day clucked over my lipstick (not dark enough), but I stuck by my guns. I hated dark lipstick.

This was not a showy outfit, but it was a definite change for me. I felt great, and as I drove the mile out of town that got me to the interstate circling the city, I felt quite confident Robin would be impressed.

I felt less certain when I peeked through the one glass pane in the classroom door. As Amina had predicted, there were lots of cute college 'chickies' in Robin's creative writing workshop. I was willing to bet seven out of nine wrote poetry that dealt with world hunger and bitter endings to relationships. At least five weren't wearing bras. The four men in the workshop were of the serious and scraggly variety. They probably wrote existential plays. Or poetry about bitter endings to relationships.

When the rest rose to leave, two of the cute chickies lingered to fascinate Robin. I was smiling, thinking of Amina as I went into the classroom.

Robin naturally thought the grin was for him. He beamed back. 'Glad you found the room okay,' he said, and the young women – I reminded myself they were not girls – turned to stare at me. 'Lisa, Kimberly, this is Aurora Teagarden.' Oh, I hadn't seen that one coming. Robin and his good manners. The brunette looked incredulous, and the streaky blond sniggered before she could stop herself.

'Are you ready for lunch?' Robin asked, and their faces straightened in a jiffy.

Thanks, Robin. 'Yes, let's go,' I said clearly, smiling all the while.

'Sure. Well, I'll see you in class Wednesday,' he told Lisa and Kimberly. They sauntered out with their armfuls of books, and Robin tossed a couple of anthologies into his briefcase. 'Let me just stow this in my office,' he said. His office was right across the hall, and was full of books and papers, but not his, Robin explained. 'James Artis was supposed to teach three writers' workshops and one class on the history of the mystery novel. But when he had a heart attack, he recommended me.'

'Why'd you take it?' I asked. We strolled across campus companionably, heading for a salad and sandwich restaurant just down the street.

'I needed a change,' he said. 'I was tired of being shut up in a room writing all day. I'd written three books in a row with little or no break in between, I had no exciting ideas for my next book, and teaching just sounded interesting. James recommended Lawrenceton as a place where I wouldn't have to go broke paying rent, and after I'd been staying in a vacant visitor's room in one of the men's dorms for a couple of weeks, I was grateful to find the townhouse.'

'Are you planning on staying for any length of time?' I asked delicately.

'That depends on the success of the workshops and the class,' he said, 'and James's health. Even if I leave the university, I might stay in the area. So far I like it here just as well as the place I was living before. I don't really have ties anywhere anymore.

My parents have retired to Florida, so I don't have a reason to go back to my home town . . . St Louis,' he said in answer to my unspoken question.

He held open the door to the restaurant. It was a ferny place, with waiters and waitresses in matching aprons and blue jeans. Our waiter's name was Don, and he was happy to serve us today. A local 'mellow' rock listening station was being piped in for all us old rockers, who ranged in age from twenty-eight to forty-two. As we were looking at the menus, I decided to start lusting, as per Amina's instructions. While we ordered, I seemed to get it misdirected, for Don got pretty red in the face and kept trying to look down my blouse. Robin seemed to be receiving the brunt of it though. He rather hesitantly (high noon, public place, had to teach a class that afternoon) took my hand across the table.

I never knew how to react to that. My thoughts always ran, Wow, he took my hand, does that mean he wants to go to bed with me, or date me more, or what? And I never knew where to look. Into his eyes? Too challenging. At his hand? Pretty stupid. And was I supposed to move my hand to clasp his? Uncomfortable. I never *was* much good at this.

Our salads arrived, so we unhitched hands and picked up our forks with some relief. I was wondering whether I should try to keep on lusting while I ate, when I realized James Taylor had trailed to an end and the news was starting. The name of my town always made me pay attention. A neutral woman's voice was saying, 'In other news, Lawrenceton mayoral candidate Morrison Pettigrue was found slain today. Pettigrue, thirty-five, was campaigning as the candidate of the Communist Party. His campaign manager, Benjamin Greer, found Pettigrue dead of stab wounds in the bathtub of his Lawrenceton home. Sheets of paper were floating in the water, but police would not say whether any of those sheets contained a suicide note. Police have no suspects in the slaying, and declined to speculate on whether the killing was, as Greer claims, a political assassination.'

Our forks poised in midair, Robin and I stared at each other like stricken loonies, and not in lust either.

'In the tub,' Robin said.

'With a knife. And the paper clinches it.'

'Marat,' we said in unison.

'Poor Benjamin,' I said on my own. He'd rejected us, launched on his own new direction, and gotten kicked in the nuts.

'Smith would recognize it, right?' Robin asked me after some fruitless speculation on our part.

'I think so,' I said confidently. 'Arthur's smart and well-read.'

'Did you ever find out if the chocolates fit a pattern?'

'It rang a bell with Jane Engle,' I told him, and then had to explain who she was and why her memory was reliable. He'd only met the members of Real Murders once. 'She's looking for the right case.'

'Do you think she'll know by tomorrow night?' he asked.

'Well, I may see her today. Maybe she will have found something by then.'

'Is there a nice restaurant in Lawrenceton?'

'Well, there's the Carriage House.' It was a real carriage house, and required a reservation; the only place in Lawrenceton that had the pretensions to do so. I offered the names of a few more places, but the Carriage House had struck his fancy.

'This lunch is a washout, we haven't eaten half our salad,' he pointed out. 'Let me take you out tomorrow night, and we'll have time to talk and eat.'

'Why, thanks. Okay. The Carriage House is a dressy place,' I added, and wondered if the hint offended him.

'Thanks for warning me,' Robin said to my relief. 'I'll walk you back to your car.'

When I glanced at my watch, I saw he was right. All this walking, lusting, and speculation had used up as much time as I had, and I'd just make it to work on time.

'If you don't mind making our reservation, I'll pick you up tomorrow at 7:00,' Robin said as we reached my car.

Well, we had another date, though I didn't think it was strictly a social date. Robin had a professional interest in these murders, I figured, and I was the local who could interpret the scene for him.

But he gave me a peck on the cheek as I eased into my car, and I drove back to Lawrenceton singing James Taylor.

That was much nicer than picturing dark, scowling, acne-scarred Morrison Pettigrue turning the bath water scarlet with his blood.

Chapter Ten

'Cordelia Botkin, 1898,' Jane hissed triumphantly.

She'd come up behind me as I was reshelving books that had been checked in. I was at the end of a stack close to the wall, about to wheel my cart around the end and onto the next row. I drew in a breath down low in my chest, shut my eyes, and prayed to forgive her. Tuesday morning had been going so well.

'Roe, I'm so sorry! I thought you must have heard me coming.'

I shook my head. I tried not to lean on the cart so obviously.

'Cordelia who?' I finally managed to say.

'Botkin. It's close enough. It doesn't actually fit, but it's close enough. This was so sloppy that I think it was an afterthought, or maybe this was even supposed to come off before Mamie Wright was killed.'

'You're probably right, Jane. The box of candy took six days to get here, and it was mailed from the city, so whoever sent it probably thought I'd get it in two or three days.'

I glanced around to see if anyone was in earshot. Lillian Schmidt, another librarian, was shelving books a few stacks away, but she wasn't actually within hearing distance.

'How does it fit, Jane?'

Jane flipped open the notebook she always seemed to have with her. 'Cordelia Botkin lived in San Francisco. She became the mistress of the Associated Press bureau chief, John Dunning. He'd left a wife back in . . .' Jane scanned her notes, '. . . Dover, Delaware. Botkin mailed the wife several anonymous letters first, did your mother get any?'

I nodded. With a very stiff upper lip, Mother had told Lynn Liggett something she'd never thought significant enough to tell me: she'd gotten an incomprehensible and largely nasty anonymous letter in the mail a few days before the candy came. She'd thought the incident so ugly and meaningless that she hadn't wanted to 'upset' me with it. She had thrown it away, of course, but it had been typed.

I was willing to bet it had been typed on the same machine that had typed the mailing label on the package.

'Anyway,' Jane continued after checking her notes, 'Cordelia finally decided Dunning was going back to his wife, so she poisoned some bonbons and mailed them to Dunning's wife. The wife and a friend of hers died.'

'Died,' I said slowly.

Jane nodded, tactfully keeping her eyes on her notes. 'Your father is still in newspapers, isn't he, Roe?'

'Yes, he's not a reporter, but he's head of the advertising department.'

'And he's living with his new wife, which could be said to represent "another woman".'

'Well, yes.'

'So obviously the murderer saw the outline was roughly the same and seized the opportunity.'

'Did you tell Arthur Smith about this?'

'I thought I had better,' Jane said, with a wise nod of her head.

'What did he say?' I asked.

'He wanted to know which book I'd gotten my information from, wrote that down, thanked me, looked harassed, and told me goodbye. I got the impression he's having trouble convincing his superiors about the significance of these murders. What was in the candy, do you know yet?'

'No, they took the box to the state lab for analysis. Arthur warned us that some of the tests take quite a while.'

Lillian was moving closer and looking curious, a chronic state with Lillian. But all my co-workers were regarding me with more than normal interest. A quiet librarian finds a body at the meeting of a pretty odd club on Friday night, gets a box of doctored chocolates in the mail on Saturday, turns up dressed in all new and uncharacteristic clothes on Monday, has a whispered conference with an excited woman on Tuesday.

'I'd better go. I'm disturbing you at work,' Jane whispered. She knew Lillian quite well. 'But I was so excited when I tracked down the pattern, I just had to run down here and tell you. Of course, the Communist man's murder was patterned after the Marat assassination. Poor Benjamin Greer! He found the body, the newscast said.'

'Jane, I appreciate your researching this for me,' I hissed back. 'I'll take you out to lunch next week to thank you.' The last thing I wanted to talk about was Morrison Petrigrue's murder.

'Oh, my goodness, that's not necessary. You gave me something to do for a while. Substituting at the school and filling in here are interesting, but nothing has been as much fun in a long time as tracking down the right murder. However, I suspect I will have to get a new hobby. All these deaths, all this fear. This is getting too close to the bone for me.' And Jane sighed, though whether over the deaths of Mamie Wright and Morrison Pettigrue, or because she had to find a new hobby, I could not tell.

I was on the second floor of the library, which is a large gallery running around three walls and overlooking the ground floor, where the children's books, periodicals, and circulation desk are located. I was watching Jane stride out the front door and thinking about Cordelia Botkin when I recognized someone else who was exiting. It was Detective Lynn Liggett. The library director, Sam Clerrick, seemed to be walking her to the door. This struck me unpleasantly. I could only suppose that Lynn Liggett had been at the library asking questions about me. Maybe she had wanted to know my work hours? More about my character? How long I had been at work that day?

Filled with uneasy speculation, I rounded the corner of the next stack. I began shelving books automatically, still brooding over Detective Liggett's visit to the library. There was nothing bad Sam Clerrick could tell her about me, I reasoned. I was a conscientious employee. I was always on time, and I almost never got sick. I had never yelled at a member of the public, no matter how I'd been tempted – especially by parents who dumped their children at the library in the summer with instructions to amuse themselves for a couple of hours while mommy and daddy went shopping.

So why was I worried? I lectured myself. I was just seeing the down side of being involved in a criminal investigation. It was practically my civic duty not to mind being the object of police scrutiny.

I wondered if I could reasonably be considered a suspect in Mamie's murder. I could have done it, of course. I'd been home unobserved for at least an hour or more before I left for the meeting. Maybe one of the other tenants could vouch for my car being in its accustomed place, though that wouldn't be conclusive proof. And I supposed if I could have found a place that sold Mrs See's, I could have mailed myself the candy. I could have typed the label on one of the library typewriters. Maybe Detective Liggett had been getting typing samples from all the machines! Though if the samples did match the label, it wouldn't be proof that I typed it myself. And if the sample didn't match, I could have used another machine – maybe one in my mother's office?

Now the murder of Morrison Pettigrue was another kettle of fish entirely. I had never met Mr Pettigrue, and now never would. I hadn't known where he lived until one of the other librarians had told me, but I couldn't prove either of those things, now that I came to think about it. Ignorance is hard to prove. Besides, if he'd been killed late Sunday night after the abortive last meeting of Real Murders, I had no alibi at all. I'd been home alone feeling sorry for myself.

However, if by some miracle the killing could be proved to have occurred during the hour we were all together, we'd all be cleared! That would be too good to be true.

I was so busy trying to imagine all the pros and cons of arresting me that I bumped into Sally Allison, literally. She was looking at the books on needlework, of which the library had scores, Lawrenceton being a hell of a town for needlework.

I murmured an apology. Sally murmured back, 'Don't think about it,' but then she stayed glued to her spot, her eyes all too pointedly on the titles in front of her. The past couple of months, Sally has been a frequent patron of the library, even during what I supposed were her working hours. I didn't think she came to check out books, though she did leave with some every time. I was convinced she was checking on Perry. I wasn't surprised after what Amina had told me. Sometimes Sally didn't even speak to her son, I'd noticed, but eyed him from a distance, as if watching for some sign of trouble.

'How's your mother, Roe?' Sally asked.

'Just fine, thank you.'

'Gotten over your scare about the candy? I didn't get to ask you last night.'

Sally had called both Mother and me for an interview when she'd read the police blotter after the candy incident. Mother and I separately had been as brief as was congruent with courtesy, we discovered later when we compared notes. I thought my name had been in the paper enough recently, and Mother thought the whole incident too sordid to discuss. (Mother also, in her career-woman mode, thought an attempted poisoning would be bad for business.)

'Sally, I wasn't scared, because I didn't know then and I don't know now that someone was actually trying to hurt me or my mother. I'm going to say frankly, Sally, that you're my friend and you're a reporter, and I'm not sure recently just who I'm talking to.'

Sally turned to face me. She was not angry, but she was determined. 'Being a reporter on a small newspaper doesn't mean I'm not a real reporter, Roe. You're a Teagarden, so what happens to you is doubly news. Your mother is a very prominent woman in this town, and your father is a well-known man. The owner of our newspaper will not keep this police gag order agreement much longer. Does that answer your question? Lillian's coming. Have you read this book on bargello?'

I blinked and recovered. 'Now, Sally, I can't sew on a button. You'd have to ask Mother if you want to know about needlework.

Or Lillian,' I added brilliantly, as my co-worker wheeled her own cart past the other end of the stack.

Lillian, whose ears are as fine-tuned as a bat's, heard her own name and turned in, and right away she and Sally were embroiled in an incomprehensible conversation about French knots and candlewicking. A little sadly, I returned to my shelving. When I was no longer news, I wondered whether Sally would decide she was just a friend again.

When I looked at my watch and discovered it was four o'clock and I was due to get off at six, I realized I'd better think about what I was going to wear to the Carriage House with Robin. He had mentioned picking me up at seven, which gave me a scant hour to get home, shower, redo my makeup, and dress. Reservations had been no problem; Tuesday was not a heavy night at the Carriage House, and I'd told them 7:15. Now I had to decide what to wear. My dark blue silk was back from the cleaner's. Had I ever taken the matching sandals to be repaired after I noticed the strap coming loose? Desperately I wished I had bought the black heels I'd seen at Amina's mom's shop that morning. They'd had bows on the back of the heel, and I'd thought they were ravishing. Would I have time to run by and get them?

Gradually I became aware that someone was humming on the other side of my stack with a droning, bee-like monotony. It could only be Lillian. Sure enough, when I pulled out a veterinarian's 'humorous look at life with animals in and out of the house' which had been thrown in with the 364's, Lillian's round face was visible through the gap.

'I think we should be earning more money,' Lillian said sulkily, 'and I think we should be asked before being scheduled to work nights, and I think they should never have hired that new head librarian.'

'Sam Clerrick? Nights?' I said foolishly, not knowing where to begin with my questions. Lillian had been a big Sam Clerrick fan before this moment, to the best of my knowledge. Mr Clerrick seemed intelligent and tough to me, but I was reserving judgment on his ability to manage people.

'Oh, you haven't heard,' Lillian said with pleasure. 'What with all the excitement in your life lately, I guess you haven't had too much time to pay attention to ordinary everyday stuff.'

I rolled my eyes to the ceiling. 'Lillian, what?'

Lillian wriggled her heavy shoulders in anticipation. 'You know, the Board of Trustees met two nights ago? Of course, Sam Clerrick was there, and he told them that in his view staying open at night hadn't been tried sufficiently four years ago, when it was such a flop – you remember? He wants to reinstate it for a time, with the present staff. So instead of being open one night a week we'll be open three, for a four-month trial.'

Four years ago Lawrenceton had been a smaller town, and remaining open more than one night a week past six o'clock had only resulted in a higher electric bill and some bored librarians. Our one late night was a token bow to people who worked odd hours and couldn't get to the library any other time. Business had been picking up on that night, I thought fairly, and in view of Lawrenceton's recent population boom, another try at night opening was reasonable. Still, I felt mildly perturbed at the change in my schedule.

On the other hand, it was hard to regard my job as the most important thing in my life lately.

'How's he going to do it without increasing staff?' I asked without much interest.

'Instead of being on two librarians at a time, we'll be on in terms of librarian and volunteer on an open night.'

The volunteers were a mixed bunch. Mostly they tended to be older men and middle-aged to elderly women who really enjoyed books and felt at home in a library. Once they'd been trained, they were a god-send, except the very small percentage who'd taken the job to see their friends and gossip. That small percentage soon got bored and quit the program, anyway.

'I'm game,' I told Lillian.

'We're going to find out more about it officially today,' Lillian went on, looking disappointed at my mild reaction. 'There's a staff meeting at 5:30, so Perry Allison's going to relieve you at the circulation desk. Hey,' and Lillian looked at her watch obviously, 'isn't it time for you to get down there now?'

'Yes, Lillian, I see that it is,' I said with elaborate patience, 'and I am going.' We took turns on circulation as we did on almost every job, since the staff was too small for much specialization but definitely full of individuals who didn't hesitate to make their preferences known. I was darned if I was going to scurry downstairs because Lillian had looked at her watch, so I continued, 'I'm willing to give night hours another shot. More time off during the day might be nice, too.' *Since my night social calendar is not exactly crowded*, but I didn't feel it necessary to share that thought with Lillian.

I was relieved that the meeting wasn't going to be after the official library closing at 6:00. I suddenly recalled for sure that the sandals that went with the blue silk dress had a broken strap. 'Crumbs,' I muttered, shelving the last book on my cart with such force that one on the opposite side shot out and landed on the floor.

'My goodness,' said Lillian triumphantly as she bent to retrieve it. 'What's put us in such a snit, huh?'

I said something besides 'crumbs,' but I only moved my lips.

I usually enjoyed my tour in Circulation. I got to stand at the big desk to one side of the main entrance. I answered questions and accepted the books, taking the fines if the books were overdue, sliding their cards back in and putting them on book carts for transportation back to their shelves. Or I checked the books out. If there was a lot of traffic, I got a helper.

Today was a slow day, which was good since my mind wouldn't stay on my work but meandered down its own path. How close my mother had come to eating a piece of that candy. How Mamie's head had looked from the back. How glad I was I hadn't seen the front. Whether the importance of being the *finder of the body* had given Benjamin a new lease on life after the death of his political ambitions. How pleased I was about going out with Robin that night. How exciting I found Arthur Smith's blue eyes.

I yanked my thoughts away from this half-pleasant half-frightening stream of thought to exchange desultory conversation with the volunteer sitting with me at the checkout desk: Lizanne Buckley's father Arnie, a 66-year-old white-haired retiree with a mind like a steel trap. Once Mr Buckley grew interested in a subject, he read everything he could find about it, and he forgot precious little of what he read. When he was through with that subject, he was through for good, but he remained a semi-authority on it. Mr Buckley confessed on this warmish sleepy afternoon that he was beginning to find it difficult to find a new subject to research. I asked him how he'd found them before, and he said it had always happened naturally.

'For example, I see a bee on my roses. I say to myself, Gee! Isn't that bee smaller than the one over on that rose? Are they the same kind of bee? Does this kind only get pollen from roses? Why aren't there more roses growing wild if bees carry rose pollen all over? So I read up on bees, and maybe roses. But lately, I don't know, nothing seems to jump out and grab me.'

I sympathized and suggested now that warmer weather would permit him to take more walks, a new subject would present itself.

'In view of what's been happening in this town recently,' Mr Buckley commented, 'I thought it might be interesting to research murderers.'

I looked at him sharply, but he wasn't trying to hint about the involvement of Real Murders members in the series of crimes.

'Why don't you do that?' I asked after a minute.

'The books are all checked out,' he said.

'What?'

'Almost all the nonfiction books about murder and murderers are out,' he elaborated patiently.

That wasn't so startling, once I had time to mull it over. All the members of Real Murders – all the former members of Real Murders – were undoubtedly boning up and preparing themselves however they could for what might happen.

But someone might be boning up to make the happening occur.

That was sickening. I looked it in the face for a second, then had to turn away. I could not visualize, did not dare to visualize, someone I knew poring over books, trying to select what old murder to imitate next, what terrible act to re-create on the body of someone he knew.

Perry came to the desk to relieve me so I could attend the meeting, which seemed so irrelevant I almost picked up my sweater and walked out the front door instead. I had a date tonight, too. Suddenly my pleasure in that date was ashes in my mouth. At least part of my bleak mood could be written up to Perry; he was definitely in the throes of one of his downswings. His lips were set in a sullen line, the parentheses from nose to mouth deeper.

I felt sorry for Perry suddenly, and said, 'Hi, see you later,' as warmly as I could as I passed him on my way to the conference room. I regretted the warmth as he smiled in return. I wished he had stayed sullen. His smile was as vicious and meaningless as a shark's. I could imagine Perry as the Victorian poseur Neal Cream, giving prostitutes poison pills and then hanging around, hoping to watch them swallow.

'Go along to the meeting now,' he said nastily.

I gladly left as Arnie Buckley began the uphill battle of making conversation with Perry.

With no enthusiasm at all, I slumped in a dreadful metal chair in the library conference room and heard the news that was already stale. Mr Clerrick, with his usual efficiency and lack of knowledge of the human race, had already prepared the new duty charts and he distributed them on the spot, instead of giving everyone the chance to digest and discuss the new schedule.

I was down for Thursday night from six to nine, with Mr Buckley penciled in tentatively as my volunteer; the volunteers hadn't yet been asked individually if they were willing to work nights, though the volunteer president had agreed in principle. Mr Clerrick was going to put an advertisement in the newspaper telling our patrons the exciting news. (He actually said that.)

'Going out with our new resident writer tonight?' Perry inquired smoothly when I returned to the check-in desk.

He took me by surprise; my mind had been firmly on work, for once.

'Yes,' I said bluntly, without thought. 'Why?'

I'd let my distaste show; a mistake. I should have kept the surface of things amiable.

'Oh, no reason,' Perry said airily, but he began to smile, a smile so false and disagreeable that for the first time I felt a little afraid.

'I'll take the desk now,' I said. 'You can go back to your work.' I didn't smile and my voice was flat; it was too late now to patch it up. For an awful minute I didn't think he'd go, that the terrible gloom in Perry's head made him utterly reckless of keeping the surface of his life sewn together.

'See you later,' Perry said, with no smile at all.

I watched him go with goose bumps on my arms.

'Did he say something nasty to you, Roe?' asked Mr Buckley. He looked as pugnacious as a tiny old man with white hair can look.

'Not really. It's the way he said it,' I answered, wanting to be truthful but not wanting to upset Lizanne's father.

'That boy's got snakes in his head,' Mr Buckley pronounced.

'I think you must be right. Now about this new schedule . . .'

We were soon busy again, and the surface of things was restored; but I thought Perry Allison did indeed have snakes in his head, and that his mother's frequent calls at the library were monitoring visits. Sally Allison was aware of the snakes, frightened they might slither through the widening holes in Perry's mental state.

Mr Buckley and I were kept busy until closing time, with a spate of 'patrons' of all ages, coming in to do schoolwork, returning books after they'd left work. Being busy made me feel more like myself again, more like there was a point to what I was doing.

Arthur Smith was waiting by my car. I was so intent on getting home to get ready, and was so short on time, that I was more miffed than glad to see him at first.

'I hated to interrupt you at work unless I had to,' he said in his serious way.

'It's all right, Arthur. Do you have any news for me?' I thought perhaps the lab had analyzed whatever was in the chocolates.

'No, the lab work hasn't come back yet. Do you have any time?'

'Um . . . well, a few minutes.'

To my pleasure, he didn't look surprised at my lack of time.

'Well, come sit in my car, or walk with me down the block.'

I elected to walk, not wanting Lillian Schmidt to see me in a car with a man in the parking lot, for some reason. So we strolled down the sidewalk in the cooling of the evening. I can't keep up with some men since my legs are so short that they have to slow considerably but Arthur seemed to adapt well.

'What did you expect of that meeting Sunday night?' he asked abruptly.

'I don't know what I expected. A miracle. I wanted someone to have an idea that would make the whole nightmare go away. Instead, someone went out and killed Morrison Pettigrue. My meeting really worked, huh?'

'That death was planned before the meeting. What bites me is that I sat there in the same room with whoever killed that man, hours before he did it, and I didn't feel a thing. Even knowing a murderer was in that room . . .' He stopped, shook his head violently, and kept walking.

'Do the other police believe what you do, that one person is doing all this?'

'I'm having a hard time convincing some of the other detectives about the similarities of these two cases to old murders. And since the Pettigrue murder, they're even less inclined to listen, even though when I saw the scene I told them myself it was like the assassination of Jean-Paul Marat. They almost laughed. There are so many right-wing loonies who might want to kill an avowed Communist, only one or two of the other detectives are willing to accept that all these incidents are related.'

'I saw Lynn Liggett at the library today. I guess she was checking up on me.'

'We're checking up on anyone remotely involved,' Arthur said flatly. 'Liggett's just doing her job. I'm supposed to find out where you were Sunday night.'

'After the meeting?'

He nodded.

'At home. In bed. Alone. You know I didn't have anything to do with Mamie's death, or the chocolates, or Morrison Pettigrue's murder.'

'I know. I saw you when you found Mrs Wright's body.'

I felt a ridiculous flood of warmth and gratitude at being believed.

It was already late, and I did have to get ready, so I ventured, 'Is there anything else you wanted to see me about?'

'I'm a divorced man without any children,' Arthur said abruptly.

Taken aback, I nodded. I tried to look intelligently inquiring.

'One of the reasons I got divorced . . . my wife couldn't stand the fact that in police work, sometimes things came up and I couldn't make it on time for something we'd planned. Even in Lawrenceton, which is not New York or even Atlanta, right?'

He paused for a response, so I said, 'Right,' uncertainly.

'So, I want to go out with you.' Those hard blue eyes turned on me with devastating effect, 'But things will come up, and sometimes you'll be disappointed. You'd have to understand beforehand, if you want to go out with me too. I don't know if you do, but I wanted to get this all out front.'

I thought: (a) this was admirably frank, (b) did this guy have an ego, or what?, (c) since he had said, 'I don't know if you do,' there was hope for him, though it had probably been just a sop thrown in my direction, and (d) I did want to go out with him, but not from a position of weakness. Arthur was a strength-respecter.

It took me a few moments to work this through. A few days before, I would have said, 'Okay,' meekly, but since then I had weathered a few storms and it seemed to me I could manage better for myself.

I watched my feet pacing along the sidewalk as I said, 'If you're saying you want to go out with me, but that anything you're doing is more important than plans we might make, I can't agree to abide by such a lopsided – understanding.' I watched my feet move steadily. Arthur's shoes were shiny and black and would last maybe twenty years. 'Now, if you're saying the police department has priority in a crisis, I can see that. If you're not just providing a blanket excuse in advance to cover any time you just might feel like not showing up.' I took a deep breath. So far those shoes had not marched off in another direction. 'Okay. Also, this is sounding very – exclusive, since we haven't even been out yet. I would like to handle this one date at a time.'

I'd underestimated Arthur.

'I must have sounded too egotistical to swallow,' he said. 'I'm sorry. Will you go out with me one time?'

'Okay,' I said. Then I didn't know what to do. I looked sideways at him and he was smiling. 'What did I say "okay" to?' I asked.

'Unless I get assigned something I have to do, you have to remember this department is in the middle of a murder investigation . . .' As if I was going to forget! '. . . Saturday night? I've got a popcorn popper and a VCR.'

No first dates at a man's apartment. By God, he could take me out someplace the first time. I didn't feel like wrestling right away. My experience was limited, but I knew that much. Besides, with Arthur I might not wrestle, and I didn't want to start a relationship that way.

'I want to go roller skating,' I said out of the blue.

Arthur couldn't have looked more stunned if I'd told him I wanted to jump off the library roof. Why had I said that? I hadn't gone skating in years. I'd be black and blue and make a klutz of myself in the bargain.

But maybe he would too.

'That's original,' Arthur said slowly. 'You really want to do that?'

Stuck with it, I nodded grimly.

'Okay,' he said firmly. 'I'll pick you up at six, Saturday night. If that's all right. Then after we harm ourselves enough, we can go out to eat. All this is assuming I can have an evening off in the middle of three investigations. But maybe we'll have it wrapped up by then.'

'Fine,' I said. I could accept that.

We'd circled the block, so we parted at our respective cars. I watched Arthur pull out of the parking lot, and saw he was shaking his head to himself. I laughed out loud.

I hated being late and I was late for my date with Robin. I had to ask him to wait downstairs while I put on the finishing touches.

I'd bought the shoes and I was enchanted with myself. Robin didn't seem surprised or put out at having to wait; but I felt rude and at a disadvantage, as if I should have something better to show as the end result of all this preparation. However, as I looked in my full-length mirror before going down, I saw I hadn't turned out badly. There hadn't been time to put up my hair, so I wore it loose with the front held back with a cloisonné butterfly comb. The blue silk dress was sober but at least did emphasize my visible assets.

I felt very unsure before I went down the stairs, very self-conscious when I saw Robin look up. But he seemed pleased, and said, 'I like your dress.' In his gray suit he didn't seem like the companionable person who'd drunk my wine, or the college professor I'd pelvically lusted after at the restaurant, but more like the fairly famous writer he really was.

We discussed the Pettigrue murder at our table at the Carriage House, where the hostess seemed to recognize Robin's name vaguely. Though maybe she was thinking of the book character. She pronounced it 'Cur-so' and gave us a good table.

I asked him to tell me about his job at the university and how it would jibe with his writing time, both questions he seemed to have answered before. I realized this man was used to being interviewed, used to being recognized. I only felt better when I recalled that Lizanne had 'bequeathed' him to me, and right on the tail of that thought, Lizanne's parents, Arnie and Elsa, were seated at the table opposite ours. The Crandalls, who had the townhouse to the right of mine, sat down with them.

I had a social obligation here, so I identified them to Robin and went over to their table.

Arnie Buckley jumped right up, and pumped Robin's hand enthusiastically. 'Our Lizanne told us all about you!' he said. 'We're proud a famous writer like you has come to live in Lawrenceton. Do you like it?' Mr Buckley had always been a Chamber of Commerce member and unashamed Lawrenceton booster.

'It's an exciting place,' said Robin honestly.

'Well, well, you'll have to come by the library. Not as sophisticated as what you'll find in the city, but we like it! Elsa and I are both volunteers. Got to give our time to something now that we're retired!'

'I mostly just help with the book sale,' Elsa said modestly.

Elsa was Lizanne's stepmother, but she had been as pretty as Lizanne's mother must have been. Arnie Buckley was a lucky man when it came to pretty women. Now gray-haired and wrinkled, Elsa was still pleasant to look at and be with.

I hadn't known the Buckleys were friends of the Crandalls, but I could see where the attraction would lie. Jed Crandall, like Mr Buckley, was no chair-bound retiree, but a pepper pot of a man, easily angered and easily appeased. His wife had always been called Teentsy, and was still, though now she certainly outweighed her husband by forty pounds or more.

Teentsy and Jed now said the proper things to Robin about their being neighbors, asking him to drop in, Teentsy saying since he was a poor bachelor (and here she shot me a sly look) he might run short of food sometime, and if he did, just to knock on their door, they had a-plenty, as he could look at her and tell!

'Are you at all interested in guns?' Jed asked eagerly.

'Mr Jed has quite a collection,' I told Robin hastily, thinking he might need to be forewarned.

'Well, sometimes, from a professional standpoint. I'm a mystery writer,' he explained when the Crandalls looked blank, though the Buckleys were nodding with vigor, bless their hearts.

'Come by then, don't be a stranger!' Jed Crandall urged.

'Thank you, nice meeting you,' Robin said to the table in general, and in a chorus of 'see you soon's' and 'nice to've met you's' we retired to our table.

The meeting nudged Robin's voracious curiosity, and in telling him about the Crandalls and the Buckleys I began to feel more comfortable. We talked about Robin's new job, and then our food came, and by the time we began eating, I was ready to talk about the murders.

'Jane Engle came by the library today with a pretty solid theory,' I began, and told Robin about the likeness of 'our' case to that of Cordelia Botkin. He was intrigued.

'I've never heard of anything quite like this,' he said after our salad had been served. 'What a book this would make! Maybe I'll write about it myself, my first nonfiction book.' He had more distance from the case; new in town, he didn't know the victims personally (unless you could term Mother a victim) and probably he didn't know the perpetrator either. I was surprised that the crimes were so exciting to him, until he said after he'd swallowed a mouthful of tomato, 'You know, Roe, writing about crime doesn't mean you have direct experience. This is the closest I've ever come to a real murder.'

I could have said the same thing as a reader. I'd been an avid fan of both real and fictional crime for years, but this was my closest brush with violent death.

'I hope I never come any closer,' I said abruptly.

He reached across the table and took my hand. 'It doesn't seem too likely,' he said cautiously. 'I know the poisoned candy – well, we don't know yet if it was really poisoned or not, do we? That was scary. But it was impersonal, too, wasn't it? Your mother's situation vaguely fit the Botkin case, even if not as well as Mamie Wright fit Julia Wallace's profile. That was why she was picked.'

'But it was sent to *my address*,' I said, suddenly letting a fear overwhelm me that I thought I'd suppressed. 'That was to involve me. My mother fit the pattern; though that wouldn't have been any consolation to me if she'd died,' I added sharply. 'But sending it to my place. That was a deliberate attempt to make me – die. Or at least a witness to my mother's dying, or getting sick, depending on what was in the chocolates. That doesn't fit any pattern. That's about as personal as you can get.'

'What kind of person could *do* that?' Robin asked.

I met his eyes. 'That's the core, isn't it,' I said. 'That's one reason we like old murders so much. At a safe remove, we can think about the kind of person who can "do that" without remorse. Almost anyone could kill another person. I guess I could, if it came to being cornered. But I'm sure, I have to be sure, that not many people could sit back and plan other people dying as part of a game the killer decided to play. I have to believe that.'

'I do too,' he said.

'This really is someone who isn't acting for any of the famous motives Tennyson Jessie wrote about,' I continued. 'It must be someone acting out something he's always wanted to do. For some reason, now he's able to actually do it.'

'A member of your club.'

'A former member,' I said sadly, and told Robin about the Sunday night meeting.

We had to talk about something else; didn't we have anything to discuss besides murders? Robin, bless him, seemed to see I couldn't take any more, and began telling me about his agent, and about the process of getting a book published. He kept me laughing with anecdotes about book signings he'd endured and I responded with stories about people that came to the library and some of the wilder questions they'd asked. We actually had a cheerful evening, and we were still at our table when the Crandalls and the Buckleys paid their bill and left.

Since the Carriage House was at the south end of town, we had to pass in front of our townhouses to turn into the driveway on the side. There was a man standing in front of the row of townhouses, on the sidewalk. As we went by, he turned his white face to us and by the light of the streetlamp, I thought I recognized Perry.

I was distracted though by the kiss Robin gave me at my back door. It was unexpected and delicious, and the disparity in our heights was overcome quite satisfactorily. Maybe his asking me out hadn't been quite so impersonal as I'd supposed; his side of the kiss was delivered with great enthusiasm.

I went upstairs humming to myself and feeling very attractive; and when I slipped into my dark bedroom and peered out the window, the street was empty.

That night it rained. I was wakened by the drops pelting against my window. I could see the lightning flicker through my curtains.

I crept downstairs and rechecked my locks. I listened, and heard only the rain. I looked out all the windows and saw only the rain. By the streetlamp out front, I saw the water racing down the slight slope to the storm drain at the end of the block. Nothing else stirred.

Chapter Eleven

Getting up and going to work the next morning wasn't too easy, but it was reassuring. I caught myself humming in the shower and I put on more eye shadow than usual, but my denim skirt, striped blouse, and braided hair felt like a comforting uniform. Lillian and I were mending books in a windowless back room all morning. We managed to get along by swapping recipes or discussing the academic prowess of Lillian's seven-year-old. Though my part of this discussion consisted only of saying 'Oh, my goodness,' or 'Ooh,' at the appropriate moments, that suited me. I might have children myself one day – maybe stocky blond ones? Or big-nosed giants with flaming hair? And I would certainly tell everyone I met how wonderful they were.

It was good to get up from the work table and stretch before going home for lunch. I'd been so slow getting up I'd had a scanty breakfast, so I was pretty hungry and trying to visualize what was in my refrigerator as I twisted my key in the lock. When a voice boomed out from behind me, I wasn't frightened, just aggravated that I wasn't going to get to eat.

'Roe! Teentsy said you'd be coming in about now! Listen, we got a little problem in our place,' old Mr Crandall was saying.

I turned around, resigned to postponing food. 'What's the little problem, Mr Crandall?'

Mr Crandall was not eloquent about anything but guns, and finally I realized that if I was to understand the problem Teentsy was having with the washer, I'd better go along with him.

It wasn't right to feel put-upon; after all, this was my job. But I had been looking forward to eating without Lillian's voice droning in my ears, and since it was Wednesday, there should be a new

Time in my mailbox. I sighed quietly, and trudged across the patio in Mr Crandall's wake.

The Crandalls' washer and dryer were in the basement, of course, as they were in all four units. There was a straight flight of rather steep stairs down to the basement, open on one side except for a railing. I clopped down the Crandalls' stairs, Teentsy Crandall right behind me telling me about the washer catastrophe in minute detail. When I reached the bottom, I saw a spreading water stain. With a sinking feeling of doom and dismay, I knew I'd have to spend my lunch hour tracking down a plumber.

Despite all the odds against it, I struck gold with my first phone call. The Crandalls watched admiringly as I talked Ace Plumbing into paying my tenants a call in the next hour. Since Ace was one of the two plumbing firms my mother used for all her properties, perhaps it wasn't totally amazing to find them willing; but to actually get them to commit themselves to coming right away – now that was amazing! When I was off the phone and Teentsy put a plate with country fried steak, potatoes, and green beans in front of me, I suddenly saw the bright side of being a resident manager. 'Oh, you don't need to do that,' I said weakly, and dug in. Calories and cholesterol did not factor in Teentsy's cooking, so her food was absolutely delicious with that added spice of guilt.

Teentsy and Jed Crandall seemed delighted to have someone to talk to. They were quite a pair, Teentsy with her bountiful bosom and childish voice and gray curls, and Jed with his hard-as-a-rock seamed face.

While I ate, Teentsy frosted a cake and Mr Crandall – I couldn't bring myself to call him Jed – talked about his farm, which he'd sold the year before, and about how convenient it was for them to live in town where all their doctors and kinfolk and grandchildren were. He sounded unconvinced though, and I could tell he was spoiling for something to do.

'That sure was a nice young man we saw you with last night,' Teentsy said archly. 'Did you two have a good time?'

I was willing to bet Teentsy knew exactly when Robin had

brought me home. 'Oh, yes, it was fine,' I said in as noncommittal a voice as I could summon.

I glanced around their den and kitchen area. Mine was lined with books; Mr Crandall's was lined with guns. I knew next to nothing about firearms, and was fervently content to keep it that way, but even I could tell these guns were of all different ages and types. I started wondering about their value, and from there it was a natural leap to being concerned about my mother's insurance coverage of these units; what would her responsibility be in case of theft, for example? Though it would take a foolhardy burglar to attempt to take anything away from Jed Crandall.

Thinking of hazards and security in general led my thoughts in another direction. I looked at the Crandalls' back door. Sure enough, they'd added two extra locks.

I laid down my fork. 'Mr Jed, I have to talk to you about those extra locks,' I said gently.

Yes, he *had* read his lease agreement carefully. His tough old face went sheepish in an instant.

'Oh, Jed,' chided Teentsy, 'I told you you needed to speak to Roe about those locks.'

'Well, Roe,' her husband said, 'you can see this gun collection needs more protection than one lock on the back door.'

'I can appreciate how you feel, and I even agree,' I said carefully, 'but you know that if you do put on extra locks, you must give me a key, and you have to leave the locks in and give me all the keys if you ever decide to move. Of course I hope you never will, but you do have to give me an extra set of keys now.'

While Mr Crandall grumbled on about a man's home being his castle, and it going against the grain to give anyone else keys to that castle – even a nice gal like me – Teentsy was on her feet and rummaging through a drawer in the kitchen. She came up with a handful of keys immediately, and began sorting through them with a troubled look on her face.

'Now I've been promising myself I'd go through these and throw away the old ones we didn't need, and since we're retired I should have all the time in the world, but still I haven't done it,' she told me. 'Well, here are two that I'm sure are the spares for these locks . . . here, Jed, try them and make sure.'

While her husband tested the keys in the locks, she stirred the others around with a helpless finger. 'That looks like the key to that old trunk . . . I don't know about this one . . . you know, Roe, now that I think about it, one of these keys is to that apartment next door that that Mr Waites rents now. I know you remember Edith Warnstein, she had it before him. She gave us an extra key because she said she was always locking herself out and it was always when you were at work.'

'Well, when you find it, just bring it over sometime,' I said. Mr Crandall handed me his extra keys, which had proved to be the right ones, and I thanked Teentsy for the delicious lunch, feeling even more guilty that they'd fed me and then I'd 'invaded their castle.' It was hell being conscientious, sometimes. I felt much better when my departure coincided with the arrival of the plumber. Judging solely by his appearance – two-day beard stubble, bandanna over long ringlets of black hair, and Day-Glo overalls – I wouldn't have trusted him with *my* washer, but he hefted his tool bag in an authoritative way and actually wrote it down when I told him to bill my mother's company for the repairs, so I left feeling I'd performed a service.

I almost literally ran into Bankston on my way out the Crandalls' patio gate. He was hefting his golf bag, and looked shining clean, right out of the shower. He'd obviously been out at the country club having a few rounds. He looked surprised to see me. 'The Crandalls having plumbing problems?' he asked, nodding toward the plumber's truck.

'Yes,' I said distractedly, after glancing at my watch. 'Your washer and dryer okay?'

'Oh, sure. Listen, how are you doing after your troubles of the past few days?'

Bankston was being nice and polite, but I didn't have the time or the inclination to chitchat.

'Pretty well, thanks. I was glad to hear that you and Melanie are getting married,' I added, remembering that I did owe something to courtesy. 'I didn't have the chance to say anything the other night when we met at my place. Congratulations.'

'Thanks, Roe,' he said, in his deliberate way. 'We were lucky to finally really get to know each other.' His clear eyes were glowing, and it was apparent to me that he returned Melanie's strong feeling. I was a little envious, to tell the truth, and bitchily wondered what two such stolid people could have to 'really get to know.' I was also late.

'Congratulations,' I repeated sunnily, and pretty much meant it. 'I've got to run.' I rabbited away to my place to put the keys to the Crandalls' apartment on my official key ring, and though I needed to hurry back to the library, I took an extra minute to label them.

I would've been late anyway.

I drove north on Parson Road to get back to the library. The Buckleys' house was along the way, to my left.

By sheer coincidence, out of all the people who could have been driving by when Lizanne came out that front door, it was I. I just glanced to my left to admire the flowers in the Buckleys' front yard, and the front door opened, and a figure stumbled out. I knew it was Lizanne by the color of her hair and her figure and because her parents owned the house, but nothing about her posture and attitude was like Lizanne. She slumped on the front doorstep, clinging to the black iron railing that ran down the red-brick steps.

God forgive me, half of me wanted to continue on my route to the library and go back to work, in blessed ignorance; but the half that said my friend needed help seemed to control the car. I pulled in and crossed the street and then the lawn, dreading to reach Lizanne and find out why her face was so contorted and why there were stains on her hose, especially at the knees.

She didn't know I was there. Her long fingers with their beautifully manicured nails were ripping at her skirt, and her breath tore in and out of her lungs with a horrible wheeze. There were tear stains on her face, though no tears were coming now.

From her smell she had vomited recently. The slow, sweet, casual beauty had vanished.

I put my arm around her and tried to forget the sour smell, but it made my own stomach begin to lurch uneasily. The Crandalls' delicious lunch threatened to come right back up. I shut my eyes for a second. When I opened them she was looking at me and her fingers were clenched instead of restless.

'They're both dead, Roe,' she said clearly and terribly. 'My mama and my daddy are both dead. I knelt down to make sure, and I have my own daddy's blood on my clothes.'

Then she fell silent and stared at her skirt, and knowing I was inadequate, could not rise to this ghastly situation, I let my thoughts trace what they were good at: the pattern, the terrible impersonal pattern that real people were being forced to fit. This time it was Lizanne plus dead stepmother and father plus broad daylight plus bloody demise.

I wondered where the hatchet was.

'I just walked to the back door to eat lunch with them like I do every day,' she said suddenly. 'And when the door was locked, and they wouldn't answer, I unlocked the front here – this is the only key I have. They were – there was blood on the walls.'

'The walls?' I murmured stupidly, having no idea what I was going to say until it came out.

'Yes,' she said seriously, asserting an incredible truth, 'the *walls*. Daddy is on the sofa in there, Roe, the one where he sits to watch television, and he's just all . . . he's . . . and Mama is upstairs in the guest bedroom on the floor by the bed.'

I held her as tightly as I could and she bent and clung to me.

'I shouldn't have had to see them like that,' she whispered.

'No.'

Then she lapsed into silence.

I had to call the police.

I stood up like an old woman, and I felt like one. I turned to face the door Lizanne had shut behind her, and reached out like someone in a dream and opened it.

There was blood everywhere, sprayed in trails across the wall.

Lizanne was right; blood on the walls. And the ceilings. And the television set.

Arnie Buckley was visible from the front door, which opened opposite the doorway into the den. I supposed it was Arnie. It was the right size and was lying in Arnie's house, on his couch. His face had been obliterated.

I wanted to scream until someone knocked me out with a good strong shot. Nothing would get me to set one foot further into this house. More than I ever wanted anything, I wanted to walk back across the street, get in my car, and leave without looking back. It seemed I was always opening doors to look at dead people, hacked people, beaten people. I managed to shut this door, this white-painted suburban front door with the brass knocker, and as I plodded across the Buckleys' lawn to the nearest neighbors, I looked longingly at my Chevette.

I couldn't face calling myself, and I can't remember what I said to the lady next door. I only know that I plodded back to sit by Lizanne on the steps.

She spoke once, asking me in bewilderment why her folks had been killed. I told her, honestly, that they'd been killed by the same person who'd killed Mamie Wright. I hoped she wouldn't ask me why it had to be her parents. Her parents had been picked because she had been named Elizabeth, because she was unmarried, because her 'Mama' was not really her mama by blood. This was the pattern of Lizanne's life that loosely fit the Fall River, Massachusetts, murders; the murders committed in 1893 in an ugly, inconvenient, atmospherically tense home in a middle-class neighborhood, almost certainly committed by Mr Andrew Borden's younger daughter, Lizzie.

But I didn't think Lizanne ever heard anything I said, and that's just as well. I kept my arm around her so something human and warm would be there, and the smell continued to sicken me. I continued to do it because it was all I could do.

Jack Burns got out of the squad car that pulled up on the lawn. He actually had a doctor with him, a local surgeon, and I found out later that they'd been having lunch together when the call came. The doctor looked at Lizanne, at me, and hesitated, but Jack Burns stepped around us and gestured his friend into the house. The sergeant of detectives looked inside and then looked down at me with burning eyes. I was not the object of this look, just in its path. But it scorched me, the fury in those dark eyes.

'Don't touch anything! Be careful how you walk!' he ordered the doctor.

'Well, of course, he's dead,' came the doctor's voice. 'If you just need me to pronounce him dead, I can sure do that.'

'Any more?' Burns spat at me. He could see Lizanne wouldn't answer, I suppose.

'She said her stepmother is dead, upstairs,' I told him very quietly, though I don't think Lizanne would have heard me if I'd screamed it.

'Upstairs, Doc!' he ordered.

The doctor probably trotted right up, but I wouldn't have gone with him if a gun had been at my head.

'Dead up here, too,' he called down the stairs.

'Then get your ass out of there and let us go over this house,' Burns said violently.

The doctor trotted out the door and after thinking for a moment, simply walked down the street. He was not about to ask Jack Burns for a ride back to the restaurant. Burns went inside but I could not hear him walking over the wooden floor. He must be standing, looking. At least he pushed the door partly closed behind him so there was something between me and the horror.

Police cars were pulling up behind Burns's, the routine about to begin. Lynn Liggett got out of the first one. She immediately began giving orders to the uniformed men who spilled out of the next car.

'How did you happen to be here?' Lynn asked without any preliminaries.

'Did you call an ambulance yet for Lizanne?' I asked. I was beginning to shake off my lethargy, my odd dreaminess.

'Yes, there's one on the way.'

'Okay, I was just driving to work. She came out of the front door like this. She spoke to me a little and then I opened the door and looked in. I went next door to call the police.'

Lynn Liggett pushed open the door and looked in. I kept my eyes resolutely forward. Her fair skin took on a greenish tinge and her lips pressed together so hard they whitened.

The ambulance pulled up then, and I was glad to see it, because Lizanne's face was even waxier, and her hands were losing coordination. Her breathing seemed irregular and shallow. She was leaning on me heavily by the time the stretcher came up to the front steps, and she didn't acknowledge the presence of the ambulance drivers. They loaded her on the stretcher with quick efficiency. I walked by her down to the street, holding her hand, but she didn't know I was there, and by the time the stretcher was pushed into the back of the ambulance she seemed unconscious.

I watched the orange and white ambulance pull away from the curb. I didn't suppose I could leave. I rested on the hood of Lynn's car for what seemed like a long time, staring aimlessly ahead and thinking of as little as possible. Then I became aware Lynn Liggett was beside me.

'There's no question of Lizanne being blamed, is there?' I asked finally. I fully expected the detective to tell me to get lost and it was none of my business, but something had mellowed the woman since last I'd seen her. We had shared something terrible.

'No,' Detective Liggett said. 'Her neighbor says she heard Lizanne hammer on the back door and then she saw her walk around to the front and unlock the house, something so unusual that the neighbor already considered calling the police. It would take more than seven minutes to do that and clean up afterward. And it's fairly easy to see that her folks had already been dead about an hour by the time she got there.'

'Mr Buckley was due to come in to work at the library today at two, and we were going to share night duty tomorrow night,' I said.

'Yes, it's written on the calendar in the kitchen in the house.'

For some reason that gave me the cold shudders. Her job

included looking at dead people's calendars while they lay right there in their own blood. Appointments that would never be kept. I revised my attitude about Lynn Liggett right then and there.

'You know what this is just like.'

'The Borden case.'

I jerked my head around to look at her in surprise.

'Arthur's inside,' she explained. 'He told me about it.'

Arthur came out of the house then, with that same whitey-green pinched look Liggett had had. He nodded at me, not questioning my presence.

'John Queensland – from Real Murders?' I said. Arthur nodded. 'Well, he's a Borden expert.'

'I remembered. I'll get in touch with him this afternoon.'

I thought about the sweet old couple I'd seen having a good time at the restaurant the night before. I thought about having to tell the Crandalls their best friends had been hacked to death. Then I realized I should tell the detectives where I'd seen the Buckleys last night, in case for some reason it was important. After I'd explained to Arthur and Lynn, and Lynn had written down the Crandalls' names and the time I'd seen them the previous evening, I wanted to reach over to Arthur, pat or hug him, establish warm living contact with him. But I couldn't.

'It's the worst thing I hope I ever see. They really don't look much like people anymore,' Arthur said suddenly. He shoved his hands in his pockets. It was up to his fellow detectives to help him over this one, I realized. I was excluded from this bad moment, and truly, I was thankful.

I thought of a lot of things to say, but they were futile things. It was time for me to go. I got in my car and without considering what I was doing, I drove to work. I went to tell Mr Clerrick that our volunteer wouldn't be coming in that afternoon.

The rest of the afternoon just passed. Later, I couldn't remember a single thing I'd done after I returned to work. I remembered I'd felt good when I'd gotten up that morning and I couldn't believe it. I just wanted one day with nothing happening, nothing bad, nothing good. No excitement. Just a nice dull day like I'd had almost every day until recently.

Close to closing time, I saw one of the detectives whom I didn't know personally coming into the library. He went to Sam Clerrick's office on the ground floor, emerged in a matter of moments, and made a beeline to Lillian as she stood behind the circulation desk. The detective asked Lillian a couple of questions, and she answered eagerly. He wrote a few things down on his notepad, and left with a nod to her.

Lillian looked up to the second floor where I was again shelving books, and our eyes met. She looked excited, and more than that, turning quickly away. Soon when another librarian was in earshot, Lillian called her over. Their heads tilted close together, and after that the other librarian hurried to the periodicals room, where yet another librarian would be stationed. If the police kept coming here asking about me, I realized with a sick feeling, Mr Clerrick might let me go. I could tell myself I'd done nothing, but I suddenly knew it wouldn't make any difference. This wasn't just happening to me, I reminded myself. Probably members of Real Murders all over Lawrenceton were being similarly inconvenienced, and many other people whose lives these murders had touched, no matter how tangentially.

It was the old stone-in-the-pond effect. Instead of stones, bodies were being thrown into the pool of the community, and the resulting waves of misery, fear, and suspicion would brush more and more people until the crimes came to an end.

Chapter Twelve

Though I didn't know it until I left work, that afternoon had been a busy one for the news media, as well as the police.

Mamie's death had not aroused much interest in the city, though it had been front-page news in Lawrenceton. The box of candy had rated a couple of paragraphs on an inside page locally, and had failed to register at all in the city. But the murder of Morrison Pettigrue was news; the strange and offbeat murder of a strange and offbeat man, spiced with Benjamin's charge of political assassination. Benjamin may have been a local butcher who very obviously desired attention of any kind in the worst way, but he did deserve the title 'campaign manager' and he was quotable. The two local stringers for the city papers enjoyed a couple of days of unprecedented importance.

As Sally had told us so indignantly at the meeting at my place, she'd been asked by the police to keep the Julia Wallace speculations out of the paper. An account of the Julia Wallace murder would have little appeal for twentieth-century American newspaper readers, the police told Sally and her boss. And it would hinder their investigation. Sally was on an inside track with the Wright murder, no doubt about it, being a club member and actually present when the body was found, so she was furious to see her exclusive knowledge stay exclusive. But her boss, Macon Turner, agreed with the local police chief that it should be withheld for 'a few days.' It was from Macon Turner I pieced all this together later; he'd been wooing my mother for some months before John Queensland gained ascendancy, and we'd become friends.

Sally became frantic after the Pettigrue murder; the minute she'd learned from her police sources that there had been paper scattered on the surface of the bathwater, and that Pettigrue had been placed in the tub after death, she mentally scrolled through the assassinations of radicals and easily came up with Charlotte Corday's stabbing of Jean-Paul Marat in revolutionary France. Corday had gained entrance to Marat's house by pretending she would give him a list of traitors in her province. Then she killed Marat while he sat in the bath to alleviate a skin disease.

After Sally had thought it through, she exploded into Macon Turner's office and demanded to report the full story. She knew it would be the biggest story of her career. Turner, a friend of the police chief, hesitated a fatal couple of days. Then the Buckleys were slaughtered, and Sally, instantly drawing the obvious conclusion, prepared her story with full disclosure of the 'parallel' theory, as it became called.

Turner could no longer resist the biggest, best story that had come along since he'd bought the Lawrenceton *Sentinel*. By chance, the two stringers were not acquainted with any Real Murders members, who at any rate had not been doing a lot of talking about Mamie Wright's murder especially since the Sunday night meeting at my apartment. For example, LeMaster Cane told me later he'd decided even before the meeting that the murders in Lawrenceton were too much like old murders for it to be coincidental. But as a black man, he'd been too scared of being implicated to come forward. He'd already found by that time, too, that his hammer – with initials burned into the haft – was missing. He figured it had been used to kill Mamie.

The same afternoon the Buckleys were found slaughtered, the state lab phoned the local police to say that though the report was in the mail, they wanted Arthur and Lynn to know that what was in the candy my mother had received was a product called 'Ratkill.' If my mother had swallowed the candy without noticing the taste in time to spit it out, she would have been very sick. If by some wild chance her tastebuds had been jaded enough for her to eat three chocolates, she might have died. But the Ratkill had a strong odor and flavor by design, to prevent just such a thing happening; so the poisoning attempt seemed halfhearted and amateurish.

Then Lynn Liggett found the open box of Ratkill in Arthur's car.

The officer who had taken the telephone message from the state crime lab to relay to the detectives was a man named Paul Allison, and he was the brother of the man Sally'd been married to years before. He was a friend of Sally's, and he didn't care for Arthur. Paul Allison was standing in the police station parking lot when Lynn, reaching in Arthur's car to retrieve her forgotten notebook, found an open box of Ratkill under it. Lynn assumed that Arthur had gotten a sample for some reason, and lifted it up where Paul Allison could see it, before she sensed something was wrong and instinctively tried to conceal it.

After Paul Allison had seen the Ratkill, there was no possible way to conceal its finding, and Arthur had a lot of explaining to do; so did Lynn, who had been riding with Arthur off and on.

Paul Allison decided to do his own explaining – to Sally. He called her an hour later, and her full story was in print the next morning.

Sally's story created a sensation, which it fully deserved. Sally Allison, middle-aged newswoman, had finally gotten the story she'd hankered for all her life, and she went for it, no holds barred.

The stringers had not known about the 'parallel theory,' but they did know something strange was happening in Lawrenceton, which normally had a very low murder rate. When the Buckleys were killed, one of the stringers was listening to her police band scanner. While the police cars converged on the Buckley house, she was loading her camera. She stopped at the gas station to fill up her car, then drove slowly up Parson until she spotted the house. In front of the house was slumped a tall, lovely woman with blood on her legs, and sitting with her arm around the tall, lovely woman was a little librarian with big round glasses and a grim expression. I had been trying to ignore the heave of my stomach, because Lizanne smelled of vomit.

Her picture of us appeared on the front page of the Metro/State section of the evening city paper. Her sources in the police department had not been silent in the meantime, and the caption read: 'Elizabeth Buckley sits stunned on the steps of her parents' home after she discovered their bodies. She is being comforted by Aurora Teagarden, who discovered the body of Mrs Gerald Wright Friday night.'

So that afternoon while I worked in a daze at the library, newspeople were watching my apartment and my mother's office. It didn't occur to anyone that I might just go on to work after 'comforting' Lizanne. Of course, the paper was not yet out and I had not yet seen the picture, but by the time I got back to my apartment after leaving work, a television news crew was parked in my slot in the parking lot. They'd gotten early wind of the story, and since Lizanne was incommunicado in the hospital and Arthur and Lynn were embroiled in the Ratkill discovery at the police station, my mother and I were among the few remaining targets.

That is, until the news crew spotted Robin, who was arriving home from the university. The newsman was an avid mystery buff who recognized Robin, having read of his stepping in for the stricken writer who'd had the heart attack. The camera was trained on him in a flash, and the newsman came up with some hasty questions. Robin, used to being interviewed, handled it well. He was agreeable, without giving them much information. I saw him that night on the news.

Unfortunately, they weren't looking hard enough at Robin to prevent one of them spotting me when I got home. I might think it my duty to talk to the police, but I didn't have to talk to these people. One of them was holding an early copy of the paper, and as I got hesitantly out of my car, stupidly determined on going into my apartment and taking the longest, hottest bath on record, he held it out to me. He said something, I didn't know what, because I was so appalled at seeing the picture of poor Lizanne I couldn't listen. I felt surrounded, and I was, though the three men of the news team were in my mind magnified to thirty.

I was just worn out and couldn't deal with it.

'I don't want to say anything,' I said nervously, and I could tell the camera was running. The newsman was a looker with a beautiful smile, and I wanted him out of my way more than I'd ever wanted anything. I felt I was teetering dangerously on the brink of hysteria.

Robin decided to rescue me. He loomed up behind them, and motioned me to just walk between them. I wondered for a moment if they'd let me, but they parted and I scuttled by straight for Robin. He wrapped his arm around me and we turned our backs on the news team and headed for the patio gate.

I knew the camera was running still (the mystery novelist and his librarian landlady have adjacent apartments) and I had a flash of sense and a jolt of guts. I swiveled to face the camera.

'This is private property. It belongs to my mother and I am her representative here,' I said ominously. 'You do not have my permission to be on it. This is against the law.' I said that like it was a magic charm. And indeed, it seemed to be. For they did pile in their van, and leave! I was incredibly pleased with myself, and I was surprised on looking up to see Robin beaming like a fond daddy.

'Go get 'em, Aurora,' he said admiringly.

'I appreciate your sheltering me out there in the parking lot, Robin,' I said, 'but dammit, don't you patronize me!' I did a little independent swiveling and got in my back door without bursting into tears.

That night Arthur called me, to tell me the gloomy story of the Ratkill. 'Whoever this asshole is, he's playing games and he just went too far,' Arthur said savagely.

I would have thought murdering the Buckleys was going too far, myself.

After I'd commiserated as much as I decently could, I told him about the media problems I was having. I'd gotten several phone calls during my wonderful hot bath, effectively ruining it. Only the chance someone I might want to hear from would call me was keeping me from taking the phone off the hook. For the first time in my life, I was wishing I had an answering machine.

'I'm getting calls, too,' Arthur said gloomily. 'I'm not used to being the direct subject of all this news attention.'

'Neither am I,' I said. 'I hate it. I'm glad librarians don't have to have press conferences as part of their job. Do you think you're clear now of any suspicion?'

'Yes, I'm not on suspension or anything like that. At least I've built up enough respect here for that.'

'I'm glad.' And I was. I felt like I had someone on my side in the police force as long as Arthur was there. If he'd been suspended, not only would I have felt bad for his sake, I would have felt powerless.

'Go on and take the phone off the hook,' Arthur advised me now. 'But first call your mom and get her to put a big sign at the entrance to your parking lot that says in great big letters, "Private Property, Trespassers will be Prosecuted".'

'Good idea. Thanks.'

We said goodnight uneasily. We were both wondering what would happen next, and who it would happen to.

My mother woke her handyman up with a phone call that night and told him she'd pay him triple if he had the sign in the parking lot by 7:00 the next morning. She begged me to leave town, or come to stay with her, until somehow this situation ended. She'd known the Buckleys, and was horrified by the sheer terror they must have experienced before they died; the Buckleys were her age, her acquaintances.

'John had to go in to talk to the police,' she said. 'If he can help them, that's wonderful, but I hated for him to go. I wish you'd never joined that damn group, Aurora. But there's no point talking about it now. Won't you come stay over here?'

'Are you going to defend me, Mother?' I asked with a weary smile.

'With my last breath,' she said simply.

Suddenly I felt my mother was safer if I stayed away from her.

'I'll manage,' I told her. 'Thanks for taking care of the sign.'

Chapter Thirteen

I had a bad night.

I dreamed that men with cameras were coming into the bathroom while I was dressing and that one of them was the murderer. I swam up from a deep sleep to find rain was patting lightly against my bedroom window. I slept again.

When finally I woke up groggy I peered out the upstairs windows from behind my curtains to make sure no one was lying in wait for me. All the cars in the parking lot belonged there. No one was parked out front. There was a large unmistakable sign at the entrance to the parking lot. I padded down the stairs to get my coffee, but took it back up to my room. Mug in hand, I watched Robin leave for work in the city. I saw Bankston go out and get his papers, Teentsy's car pulled out. She must have needed something for breakfast, for she was back within ten minutes. The shower the night before had not amounted to much, not like the rain of two nights ago; the little puddles were already gone.

By the time Teentsy returned, I'd worked up enough courage to get my own papers. They were having a screaming field day. There was a picture of Arthur, a picture of Mamie and Gerald at their wedding, a picture of the Buckleys and Lizanne when the Buckleys had celebrated their twenty-fifth wedding anniversary, and a picture of Morrison Pettigrue taken when he'd announced he was running for mayor, with Benjamin beaming in the background like a proud father.

At least no one seemed to believe that Melanie and Arthur were guilty of anything but being the butt of ghastly practical jokes. I wondered where the hatchet that had killed the Buckleys would turn up, or the knife that had killed Morrison Pettigrue. How could the murderer sustain such a frenzy of activity? Surely there must be an enormous output of physical and emotional energy involved. Surely he must stop.

I managed to dab on some makeup so I wouldn't look like I was going to keel over and yanked my hair back into a ponytail. I pulled on a red turtleneck and navy blue skirt and cardigan. I looked like hell on wheels.

My only goal was to get to the library without anyone noticing me, and find out if there was any chance of putting in a normal day's work. To my utter relief, there were no strange cars in the library parking lot. The interest in me seemed to have ebbed. The day began to look possible.

I found out at work that Benjamin Greer had called a press conference that morning to announce another candidate would run for the Communist Party in the Lawrenceton mayoral election. The candidate proved to be Benjamin himself, who seemed to be the only other Communist resident of Lawrenceton. I didn't believe for a minute that Benjamin had any coherent political philosophy. He was getting as much publicity as he could while the attention of the media was still on our town. I wondered what would happen to Benjamin after the election. Would butchering at the grocery store ever be enough again?

Lillian Schmidt told me about Benjamin, and altogether covered herself with unexpected glory that morning. She worked side by side with me as though nothing at all had happened, with the exception of describing his press conference. I wanted to ask her why she was being so decent, but couldn't think of a way to phrase it that wasn't offensive. (Why are you being nice to me, when we don't like each other much? Why is a tactless person like you suddenly being the soul of tact?)

I was pulling on my sweater to leave for lunch, when Lillian said, 'I know you don't have anything to do with this mess, and I don't think it's fair that all this has happened to you. That policeman coming to ask me yesterday if you were really mending books with me all morning – I just decided last night that was ridiculous. Enough is enough.'

For once we agreed on something. 'Thanks, Lillian,' I said.

I felt a little better as I drove home. I took another route so I didn't have to pass the Buckleys' house. Over lunch I watched the news and saw Benjamin having his minutes of fame.

I was off Thursday afternoon since I was scheduled to work Thursday night. I'd been wise to make the effort to go to work in the morning, I found once I was home alone. Though I liked work, usually I liked my time off even more. Today was an exception. After I'd changed into jeans and sneakers, I couldn't settle on any one project. I did a little laundry, a little reading. I tried a new hairdo, but tore it apart before I was half through. Then my hair was tangled, and I had to brush it through so much to get out the snarls that it crackled around my head in a brown cloud of electric waves. I looked like I'd been contacted by Mars.

I called the hospital to see if I could visit Lizanne, but the nurse on her wing said Lizanne was only receiving visits from family. Then I thought of ordering flowers for the funeral, and called Sally Allison at the newspaper to find out when it would be. For the first time, the receptionist at the *Sentinel* asked my name before ringing Sally. She was riding the crest of the story, that was clear.

'What can I do for you, Roe?' she asked briskly. I felt she was only talking to me because I was still semi-newsworthy at the moment. I had been hot yesterday, but I was cooling off. The lack of excitement in Sally's voice was like a shot of adrenaline to me.

'I just wanted to know when the Buckleys' funeral would be, Sally.'

'Well, the bodies have gone for autopsy, and I don't know when they'll be released. So according to Lizanne's aunt, they just haven't been able to make any firm funeral plans yet.'

'Oh. Well . . .'

'Listen, while I've got you on the line . . . one of the cops said you were on the scene yesterday.' I knew Sally had seen the picture of me with Lizanne in the city paper. She was getting too full of herself. 'You want to tell me what happened while you were there?' she asked coaxingly. 'Is it true that Arnie was dismembered?'

'I wonder if you're really the right person to have on this story, Sally,' I said after a long pause during which I thought furiously.

Sally gasped as if her pet sheep had turned and bitten her.

'After all, you're in the club, and I guess we're all really involved, somehow or other, right?' And Sally had a son who was also a member, who could not exactly be called normal.

'I think I can keep my objectivity,' Sally said coldly. 'And I don't think being a member of Real Murders means you're automatically – involved.'

At least she wasn't asking me questions anymore.

My doorbell rang.

'I've got to go, Sally,' I said gently. And hung up.

I felt mildly ashamed of myself as I went to the door. Sally was doing her job. But I had a hard time accepting her switch from friend to reporter, my changing role from friend to source. It seemed like lately people 'doing their jobs' meant I got my life turned around.

I did remember to check my security spy hole. My visitor was Arthur. He looked as ghastly as I had earlier. The lines in his face looked deeper, making him appear at least ten years older.

'Have you had anything to eat?' I asked.

'No,' he admitted, after some thought. 'Not since five this morning. That's when I got up and went down to the station.' I pulled out a chair at my kitchen table and he sat down automatically.

It's hard to perform like Hannah Housewife when you've had no warning, but I microwaved a frozen ham and cheese sandwich, poured some potato chips out of a bag, and scraped together a rather depressing salad. However, Arthur seemed glad to see the plate, and ate it all after a silent prayer.

'Eat in peace,' I said and busied myself making coffee and wiping down the kitchen counter. It was an oddly domestic little interval. I felt more myself, less hunted, than I had since stopping to help Lizanne. It was possible work tonight would be entirely normal. And I would come home and sleep, hours and hours, in a clean nightgown.

After he ate, Arthur looked better. When I came to remove his empty plate, he took my wrist and pulled me into his lap, and kissed me. It was long, thorough, and intense. I really liked it very much. But maybe this was a little too fast for me. When by silent mutual accord we unclenched, I wiggled off his lap and tried to slow down my breathing.

'I just wanted to do something I would *enjoy*,' he said.

'Quite all right,' I said a little unsteadily, and poured him a cup of coffee while gesturing him to the couch. I sat a careful but not marked distance away.

'It's not going well?' I asked tentatively.

'Oh, it's going, now that I've got the Ratkill thing behind me. Of course our fingerprint guy had to go all over my car, and now I've got to get all that stuff off. I'm sure it won't turn up anything. Melanie Clark's car was clean as a whistle. We've completed the Buckley house search, and a neighborhood canvas to see if anyone saw anything. The only thing the house search turned up was a long hair, which may just be one of Lizanne's . . . we have to get a sample from her for comparison. And that's for your ears only. The murder weapon hasn't turned up yet, but it was a hatchet or something like that, of course.'

'You're really not a suspect?'

'Well, if I ever was, I'm not now. While the Buckleys were being murdered I was going door to door with another detective asking questions about the Wright murder. And come to think of it, right before the last meeting, when Mamie Wright was done in, I was booking a DWI at the station. I drove to the meeting directly from there. And Lynn was able to swear for me that the Ratkill hadn't been in the car all morning while we were riding around knocking on doors.'

'Good,' I said. 'Someone's got to be out of the running.'

'And thank God it's me, since the department needs every warm body it can get on this one. I've got to go.' He heaved himself to his feet, looking tired again.

'Arthur . . . what about me? Does anyone think I did it?'

'No, honey. Not since Pettigrue, anyway. His old house had one of those claw-footed tubs, way off the floor, and he was a tall man, maybe six-three. You couldn't have gotten him in that tub alone, no way. And around Lawrenceton enough people would know if you were steadily seeing some guy who'd help you move the body. No, I think Pettigrue definitely let you off the hook in just about everyone's mind.'

It was unnerving to think that my name had been spoken by men and women I didn't know, men and women who seriously considered I might have killed people in brutal and bloody ways. But all in all, after I'd talked to Arthur, I felt much better.

I saw him off with a light squeeze of his hand, and sat down to think a little. It was about time I thought instead of felt. I had crammed more feelings into the past week than I had in a year, I estimated.

The hair the police had found was probably brown, since it might be Lizanne's and hers was a rich chestnut. Who else could have shed that hair?

Well, I was a member of Real Murders who had long brown hair. Luckily for me, I'd been repairing books with Lillian Schmidt all morning. Melanie Clark had medium-length dull brown hair, and Sally, though her hair was shorter and lighter, could also be a contender. (Wouldn't it be something if Sally had committed all these murders so she could report them? A dazzling idea. Then I told myself to get back on the track.) Jane Engle's hair was definitely gray . . . then I thought of Gifford Doakes, whose hair was long and smoothly moussed into a pageboy or sometimes gathered in a ponytail, to John Queensland's disgust. Gifford was a scary person, and he was so interested in massacres . . . and his friend Reynaldo would probably do anything Gifford wanted.

But surely someone as flamboyant as Gifford would have been noticed going into the Buckleys' house?

Well, discarding the possible clue of the hair for the moment, how had the murderer gotten in and left? A neighbor had seen Lizanne enter, too soon before I'd arrived to have done everything that had been done to the Buckleys. So someone was in a position to view the front of the Buckley house at least part of the morning. I considered other approaches and tried to imagine an aerial view of the lot, but I am not good at geography at all, much less aerial geography.

I sat a while longer and thought some more, and found myself wandering to the patio gate several times to see if Robin was home yet from the university. It was going to rain later, and the day was cooling off rapidly. The sky was a dull uniform gray.

I pulled on my jacket finally and was heading out on my own when his big car pulled in. Robin unfolded from it with an armful of papers. Why doesn't he carry a briefcase? I wondered.

'Listen, change your shoes and come with me,' I suggested.

He looked down his beaky nose at my feet. 'Okay,' he said agreeably. 'Let me drop these papers inside. Someone stole my briefcase,' he said over his shoulder.

I pattered after him. 'Here?' I said, startled.

'Well, since I moved to Lawrenceton, and I'm fairly sure from here in the parking lot,' he said as he unlocked his back door.

I followed him in. Boxes were everywhere, and the only thing set in order was a computer table suitably laden with computer, disc drives, and printer. Robin dumped the papers and bounded upstairs, returning in a few seconds with some huge sneakers.

'What are we going to do?' he asked as he laced them up.

'I've been thinking. How did the murderer get into the Buckleys' house? It wasn't broken into, right? At least the papers this morning said not. So maybe the Buckleys left it unlocked and the killer just walked in and surprised them, or the killer rang the doorbell and the Buckleys let him – or her – in. But anyway, how did the killer approach the house? I just want to walk up that way and see. It had to be from the back, I think.'

'So we're going to see if we can do it ourselves?'

'That's what I thought.' But as we were leaving Robin's I had misgivings. 'Oh, maybe we better not. What if someone sees us and calls the police?'

'Then we'll just tell them what we're doing,' said Robin

reasonably, making it sound very simple. Of course, *his* mother wasn't the most prominent real estate dealer in town and a society leader to boot, I reflected.

But I had to go. It had been my idea.

So out of the parking lot we went, Robin striding ahead and me trailing behind, until he looked back and shortened his stride. The parking lot let out in the middle of the street that ran beside Robin's end apartment. Robin had turned right so I did, too, and at the corner we turned north to walk the two blocks up Parson to the Buckleys'. Perhaps as I'd driven past the Buckleys' on my way home to lunch the day before, the Buckleys were being slaughtered. I caught up with Robin at the next corner, shivering inside my light jacket. The house was on this next block.

Robin looked up the street, thinking. I looked down the side street; no houses faced the road. 'Of course, the trash alley,' I said, disgusted with myself.

'Huh?'

'This is one of the old areas, and this block hasn't been rebuilt in ages,' I explained. 'There's an alley between the houses facing Parson Road and the houses feeing Chestnut, which runs parallel to Parson. The same with this block we're standing on. But when you get south to our block, it's been rebuilt, with our apartments for one thing, and garbage collection is on the street.'

Under the gray sky we crossed the side street and came to the alley entrance. I'd felt so pursued and viewed yesterday, it was almost eerie how invisible I felt now. No houses facing this side street, little traffic. When we walked down the graveled alley, it was easy to see how the murderer had reached the house without being observed.

'And almost all these yards are fenced, which blocks the view of the alley,' Robin remarked, 'and of the Buckleys' back yard.'

The Buckleys' yard was one of the few unfenced ones. The ones on either side had five-foot privacy fences. We stopped at the very back of the yard by the garbage cans, with a clear view of the back door of the house. The yard was planted with the camellias and roses that Mrs Buckley had loved. In their garbage can – what an eerie thought – was probably a tissue she'd blotted her lipstick with, grounds from the coffee they'd drunk on their last morning, detritus of lives that no longer existed.

Yes, their garbage was surely still there . . . every one on Parson Road had garbage pickup on Monday. They'd been killed on Wednesday. I shuddered. 'Let's go,' I said. My mood had changed. I wasn't Delilah Detective anymore.

Robin turned slowly. 'So what would you do?' he said. 'If you didn't want to be observed, you'd have parked your car – where? Where we came into the alley?'

'No. That's a narrow street, and someone might remember having to pull out and around to get past your car.'

'What about at the north end of the alley?'

'No. There's a service station right across the street there, it's real busy.'

'So,' said Robin, striding ahead purposefully, 'we go back this way, the way we came. If you had an ax, where would you put it?'

'Oh, Robin,' I said nervously. 'Let's just go.' We were leaving the alley as unobserved as we had entered, as far as I could tell, and I was glad of it.

'I,' continued Robin, 'would drop it in one of these garbage cans waiting to be emptied.'

That was why Robin was a very good mystery writer.

'I'm sure the police have searched them,' I said firmly. 'I am not going to stand here and go through everyone's garbage. Then someone really would call the police.' Or would they? Apparently no one had spotted us so far.

We'd reached the end of the alley, at the spot we'd entered.

'If you wouldn't park here, you might just cross the street and go through the next alley,' he said thoughtfully. 'Park even farther away, be even less likely to be seen and connected.'

So we slipped across the narrow street into the next alley. This one had been widened a little when some apartments had been built. Their parking was in the back, and in the construction process a drainage ditch had been put in the alley to keep the parking lots clear. There were culverts to provide entrances and exits to the lots. I thought, I would put the ax in one of the culverts. And I wondered if the police had searched this block.

This alley too was silent and lifeless, and I began to have the unsettling feeling that maybe Robin and I were the only people left in Lawrenceton. The sun came out briefly and Robin took my hand, so I tried hard to feel better. But when he crouched to retie his shoe, I began looking in the ditches.

Certainly the culvert right by us hadn't been disturbed. The water oak leaves that half-blocked the opening were almost smoothly aligned, pointing in the same direction, by the heavy rain of the night before last. But the next one down . . . someone had been in that ditch, no doubt about it. The leaves had been shoved up around the opening so forcefully that the mud underneath had been uncovered. Perhaps the police had searched, but of course none of them were as short as I was, so they weren't at an angle to see a little gleam from inside the culvert, a gleam sparked by the unexpected and short-lived sunshine. And their arms weren't as long as Robin's so they couldn't have reached in and pulled out . . .

'My briefcase?' Robin said in shock and amazement. 'What's it doing here?' His fingers pried the gold-tone locks.

'Don't open it!' I shrieked, as Robin opened it, and out fell a bloodstained hatchet, to land with a thud on the packed leaves in the ditch.

Chapter Fourteen

While Robin stood guard over the horrible thing in the alley, I knocked on the door of one of the apartments. I could hear a baby screaming inside, so I knew someone was awake.

The exhausted young woman who answered the door was still in her nightgown. She was trusting enough to open the door to a stranger, and tired enough to accept my need to use her telephone incuriously. The baby screamed while I looked up the number of the police station, and kept it up while I dialed and talked to the desk officer, who had some trouble understanding what I was trying to tell him. When I hung up and thanked the young woman, the baby was still crying, though it had ebbed to a whimper.

'Poor baby,' I said tentatively.

'It's colic,' she explained. 'The doctor says the worst should be over soon.'

Aside from occasionally babysitting my half-brother Phillip when he was small, I knew nothing about babies. So I was glad to hear that the child had a specific complaint. By the time I thanked her and she shut the door behind me, I could hear the child starting to cry again.

I trudged back to the alley where Robin was sitting glumly, his back propped against the fence on the side opposite the apartments.

'Me and my great ideas,' I said bitterly, plopping down beside him.

He let that pass in a gentlemanly manner.

'Cover it up,' I suggested. 'I can't stand it.'

'How, without getting fingerprints on it? More fingerprints, that is.'

We solved that problem as a mist began to dampen my hair against my cheeks. I found a stick and Robin stuck it under the edge of the briefcase, lifting it and dragging it over the hatchet with its dreadful stains. We settled back against the fence, able now to hear the sirens approaching. I felt oddly calm.

'I wonder if I'll ever get my briefcase back,' Robin said. 'Someone came in our parking lot and reached in my car, and took my briefcase, so he could use it for hiding a murder weapon. I'd been thinking, Roe, when this case is all over, if it ever is, that I might try my hand at nonfiction. I'm here, I'm involved through knowing some of the people. I even met the Buckleys the very night before they were killed. I was there when you and your mother opened the chocolates. Now I'm here finding a murder weapon in *my* briefcase, and I'm telling you, I don't like this much anymore. I don't think I even want the damn briefcase as a memento, now that I think of it.' But after sitting for a moment in silence, he murmured, 'Wait till I tell my agent.'

The surface of his glasses began to be speckled with tiny drops of moisture. I took my own off and wiped them with a Kleenex. 'I've got to admire your lack of fear, Robin,' I said.

'Lack of fear?'

'You think they're not going to want to ask you a few questions?' I said pointedly.

He had only seconds to absorb this and look dismayed before an unmarked car pulled in the alley, with a patrol car right behind it. For some reason, we stood up.

And God bless me, who should emerge from the unmarked car but my friend Lynn Liggett, and she was mad as a wet hen.

'You're everywhere!' she said to me. 'I know you didn't do these murders, but I swear every time I turn around you're right in front of me!' She shook her head, as if trying to shake me out of it. Then words seemed to fail her. Her glance fell on the overturned open briefcase, with the handle of the hatchet protruding slightly from underneath.

'Who covered it up?' she said next. After we told her, and she lifted the briefcase from the bloody hatchet with the same stick, all her attention was on the murder weapon.

Yet another car appeared behind the patrol car. My heart sank even deeper as Jack Burns heaved himself out and strolled toward us. His body language said he was out for a casual amble in a pleasant neighborhood but his dark eyes snapped with anger and menace.

He stopped at the patrolmen, apparently the ones who had conducted the original alley search the day before and blistered them up and down in language I had only seen in print. Robin and I watched with interest as they began to search the alley for anything that might have been left by the murderer. I was willing to bet that if he'd left any other trace in the alley, this time it would be found.

People began to emerge from the apartments, and the alley that had seemed so silent and deserted began to be positively crowded. I saw the curtain move at the apartment of the young mother, and hoped the baby had calmed down by now. It occurred to me that this woman was the most likely to have seen something the previous day, since she was probably up almost all the time. I started to suggest this to Detective Liggett, but I reconsidered in time to save my head from being bitten off.

The hatchet and briefcase bagged, the policewoman turned back to us.

'Did you touch the briefcase, Miss Teagarden?' she asked me directly.

I shook my head.

'So you did,' she said to Robin, who nodded meekly. 'You're someone else who turns up everywhere.'

Finally Robin began to look worried.

'You need to go down to the station and have your fingerprints taken,' Lynn said brusquely.

'I had them made the other night,' Robin reminded her. 'Everyone at the Real Murders meeting had his or her prints taken.'

This reminder did not endear him to the detective.

'Whose idea was this stroll through the alley?' Lynn counter-attacked.

We looked at each other.

'Well,' I began, 'I started wondering how the Buckleys' murderer had reached their house without being seen . . .'

'But it was definitely me that wanted to go through this alley as well as the one behind the Buckley house,' Robin said manfully.

'Listen, you two,' Lynn said with an assumed calm, 'you don't seem to understand the real world very well.'

Robin and I didn't care for that accusation. I felt him stiffen beside me, and I drew myself up and narrowed my eyes.

'We are the police, and *we* are paid too damn little to investigate murders, but that's what we do. We don't sit and read about them, we solve them. We find clues, and we track down leads, and we knock on doors.' She paused and took a deep breath. I had found several flaws in her speech so far, but I wasn't about to point out to her that Arthur read a lot about murders and that the police so far hadn't solved a thing and that the clue of the hatchet would still be in the damn ditch if Robin and I hadn't unearthed it.

I had enough sense of self-preservation not to say those things. When Robin cleared his throat, I stepped on his toes.

I was sorry I'd stopped him a moment later when Lynn really began questioning him. I wouldn't have stood to her questioning as well as he, and I had to admire his composure. I could see that it did look peculiar; Robin arrives in town, the murders start. But I knew that Mamie Wright's murder had been planned before Robin came to live in Lawrenceton, and the chocolates had been sent to Mother even earlier. The officer pointed out, though, that Robin had been present at the discovery of Mamie Wright's body, having invited himself to a Real Murders meeting on his first night in town. And he'd been at my house when I'd received the chocolate box.

Lynn was certainly not the only detective who thought Robin's presence at so many key scenes was fishy. And perhaps I was not as clear and free of suspicion as Arthur had assured me, because when Jack Burns took up the questioning he was looking from

Robin to me with some significance. Here, he seemed to be thinking, is someone big who could have helped this woman get Pettigrue's body in the bathtub.

'I have to go to work in an hour and a half,' I said quietly to him, when I'd had all I could take.

He stopped in mid-sentence.

'Sure,' he said, seeming abruptly exhausted. 'Sure you do.' His fuel, it seemed, had been his exasperation with his own men missing the hatchet, and he'd run out of it. I liked him a lot better all of a sudden.

When Burns had taken over the role of castigator, Lynn had started knocking door to door at the apartments asking questions. Finally she reached the apartment where I'd used the phone, and the young woman, now in jeans and a sweater – she'd undoubtedly seen the police going door to door – answered in a flash. Lynn was obviously running through her list of questions, but I noticed after about the third one, she came to point like a bird dog. The young woman had said something Lynn was interested in hearing.

'Jack,' Lynn yelled, 'come here.'

'Go home,' Burns told us simply. 'We know where you are if we need you.' And he hurried over to Lynn.

Robin and I blew out a breath of relief simultaneously, and almost slunk out of the alley, trying as hard as we possibly could to attract no more official attention. Once we were out into the street, Robin went flying along home and dragged me with him by the hand.

When we reached our parking lot we finally stopped for breath. Robin hugged me and dropped a quick kiss on the top of my head, the most convenient spot for him. 'That was really interesting,' he commented, and I began laughing until my sides hurt. Robin's red eyebrows flew up, and his glasses slid down, and then he began laughing, too. I looked at my watch while I was thinking how long it had been since I'd really whooped like that, and when I saw what the time was, I told Robin I had to go change clothes. At least for a few hours, I had forgotten to be afraid about working at the library alone that night.

It had not been noticed until the last moment that no one had been scheduled to take Mr Buckley's place on the roster. None of the other librarians would now admit to having the evening free, and all the volunteers had been scheduled for other nights.

I told Robin this hurriedly, and he said, 'I'm sure the police patrols have been stepped up. But maybe I'll stop in on you tonight. If you need me, call me. I'll be here.' He went in his gate and I went in mine.

As I pulled on the same blue skirt and red turtleneck I'd worn that morning, I was doing my best not to think of the hatchet. It had been unspeakable. On my drive to work I hoped that the library would be flooded with patrons so I wouldn't have time to think.

I was taking over the checkout desk from Jane Engle, who had been substituting for one of the librarians whose child had the flu. Jane looked the same, with her perfectly neat gray hair, her perfectly clean wire-rimmed glasses, and her anonymous gray suit. But inside, I could see she was no longer a sophisticated and curious witness to the Lawrenceton murders, but a terrified woman. And she was glad to get out of the library. 'All the others left at five, not a single patron's come in since then,' she told me in a shaky voice. 'And frankly, Aurora, I've been delighted. I'm scared to be alone with anyone anymore, no matter how well I think I know them.'

I patted Jane on the arm awkwardly. Though at times we'd eaten lunch together, mostly on days after club meetings when we wanted to discuss the program, Jane and I had had a friendly, but never intimate, relationship.

'Other people are interested in our little club for the first time,' Jane went on, 'and I've had to answer a lot of questions no one ever bothered to ask me before. People think I'm a little strange for having belonged to Real Murders.' Jane was definitely a woman who would hate to be thought strange.

'Well,' I said hesitantly, 'just because we had a different sort of hobby—' Come to think of it, maybe we *were* a little strange, all of us Real Murderers, as we had sometimes called ourselves laughingly.

Ho-ho.

'One of us really is a murderer, you know,' Jane chimed in eerily. I felt my thoughts were becoming visible in a balloon over my head. 'It's gone beyond an academic interest in death and gore and psychology. I could feel it that night we met in your apartment.'

'Who do you think it is, Jane?' I said impulsively, as she tied her scarf and extracted her keys from her purse.

'I am sure it's someone in our club, of course, or possibly a near connection of some sort to a club member. I don't know if this person has always been disturbed, or if he's just now decided to play a ghastly series of tricks on his fellow members. Or maybe there is more than one murderer and they're acting together.'

'It doesn't have to be someone in Real Murders, Jane, just someone who doesn't like one of us, someone who wants us to be in trouble.' She was standing by the front door by then, and I wanted her to stay as much as she wanted to go.

She shrugged, not willing to argue. 'It's frightening to me,' she said quietly, 'to imagine what case I fit. I go over my books, checking out cases, to see what elderly woman living alone I resemble. What old murder victim.'

I stared at her with my mouth open. I was appalled to realize what Jane had been going through, because of her active and probably accurate mind.

Then a mother trailing two reluctant toddlers came through the door, and Jane slipped out to go home to her waiting house, to leaf through her true crime books in search of the pattern she would fit.

Thank God other people were in the library when Gifford Doakes came in, or I might have shrieked and run. Gifford, massacre enthusiast, had always sounded the warning bell in my brain that cautions me to pick and choose my conversation topics. Though I really didn't know too much about him, I'd always kept my distance from Gifford and limited my contact with him to the bare bones of courtesy.

You wanted to be polite to Gifford. You were a little scared not to be.

I had no idea what Gifford did for a living, but he dressed like a *Miami Vice* drug lord, in extremely stylish clothes and with his long brown hair carefully arranged. I wouldn't have been surprised to see a shoulder holster under his jacket.

Maybe Gifford *was* a drug lord.

And here he came now, gliding over to the checkout desk. I glanced around; that dynamic twosome, Melanie Clark and Bankston Waites, had come in a few minutes previously, their heads close together and laughing, and I could now see Bankston upstairs in the biography section, while Melanie was flipping through *Good Housekeeping* in the magazine area on the ground floor. Probably looking for a new meatloaf recipe. But bless her, she was there within call.

Gifford was right across the desk from me, and my hand closed over the nearest thing, which proved to be the stapler. A really effective deterrent, I told myself bitterly. I could see his shadow, Reynaldo, standing outside the double glass doors, pacing around in the near dark of the parking lot. He would pass through a pool of light from the arc lamps that provided safety for the lot – theoretically – and then vanish into the gloom, reappearing seconds later.

'How ya doing, Roe?' Gifford asked perfunctorily.

'Um. Okay.'

'Listen, I hear you and that writer found the murder weapon in the Buckley case today.'

The Buckley case? I had a sudden vision of an anthology of accounts of the decade's most notable murders, and of Lizanne's parents' slaughter being included. Other people would read about their deaths, and speculate, as I had speculated about other unsolved cases. Could it have been the Daughter? Or the Policeman who also belonged to the Real Murders Club? I realized that these murders would be made into a book . . . maybe by Joe McGuinniss or Joan Barthel or Robin, if his taste for it revived . . . and I would be in it, because of the chocolates. Maybe just 'when the candy arrived at the home of Mrs Teagarden's daughter Aurora . . .'

For a minute I was very confused. Was I in a book about old murders that I was reading, or was this all happening to me now? It would be nice to have the distance a book would give me. But Gifford's one earring was all too real, and the leopard-like pacing of Reynaldo – in the prosaic library parking lot! – was all too real, too.

'Tell me about the ax,' Gifford was demanding.

'It was a hatchet, Gifford. An ax wouldn't fit in a briefcase.' I was immediately furious with myself for contradicting a scary guy like Gifford; but then I consciously realized what my unconscious must have noted. Gifford Doakes was a man with a mission, and he was not interested in sidetracks.

'This long?' He held his hands apart.

'Yes, about.' Standard hatchet size.

'Wood handle with black tape wrapped around the grip?'

'Yes,' I agreed. I had forgotten the tape until he mentioned it.

'Damn,' he hissed, and then he said a few other things, and his dark eyes blinked rapidly. Gifford Doakes was a frightened man and a furious one. I was scared as hell, too, not only of the murderer but more immediately of Gifford. Who was maybe also the murderer.

I gripped the stapler even harder, and felt like a fool planning to battle a crazy man with a stapler that even, I suddenly remembered, contained no staples. Well, strike that line of defense.

'Now I have to go to the police station,' Gifford said unexpectedly. 'That's my hatchet, I'm almost positive. Reynaldo found out it was missing yesterday.'

I laid down the stapler very gently on my desk, glanced upward and saw Bankston looking over the second-floor railing. He raised his eyebrows in a silent query. I shook my head. I didn't think I needed help anymore. I thought Gifford was just as nervous as the rest of us, and for good reason. At this moment, sophisticated pageboy and sharp clothes notwithstanding, Gifford was chewing on his thumbnail like a five-year-old facing a difficult world.

'You'd better go to the police now,' I said to him carefully. And he wheeled and was out the door before I could catch my breath.

Gifford's hatchet, Robin's briefcase. Those not cast as victims were being cast as murderers, to provide even more fun for the killer.

I wondered which category was scheduled for me. Surely finder-of-the-body would suffice.

I was still pondering this and other unpleasant related topics thirty minutes later when Perry Allison came in. I could hardly believe my luck at seeing Gifford and Perry in one evening. Two great guys. At least while Gifford had been here, so had a few other people, but in the intervening half hour Bankston and Melanie and the two other patrons had trickled out the door.

This time I quietly opened a drawer and slid out a pair of scissors. I checked my watch; only fifteen minutes to go till closing time.

'Roe!' he babbled. 'Qué pasa?' His hands beat a manic tattoo on the desk.

I felt a stirring of dismay. This wasn't even the familiar unpleasant Perry, who had perhaps skipped some prescribed medication. Perry was on drugs no doctor had ever given him. The appeal of 'recreational' drugs had completely passed me by, but I wasn't totally naive.

'Nothing much, Perry,' I said cautiously.

'How can you say that? Things here are just *hopping*,' he told me, his eyebrows flying all over his narrow face. 'A murder a day, practically. Your honey, the cop, was at my place this afternoon. Asking questions. Making insinuations. About me! I couldn't hurt a fly!'

And Perry laughed and came around the desk in a few quick steps.

'Scissors?' He whooped. 'Sssssscissssors?' He experimented with hissing. I was so taken aback by his quick moves and jerky head movements, so unlike the Perry I worked with, that it took me by surprise when his hand shot out to grasp the wrist of my hand that was holding the scissors. He gripped with manic pressure.

'That hurts, Perry,' I said sharply. 'Let go.'

But Perry laughed and laughed, never relaxing his grip. I knew in a minute I would drop the scissors and I could not imagine what would happen after that.

Abruptly, he turned enraged. 'You were going to stab me,' he shouted furiously. 'Not one of you wants me to make it! Not one of you knows what that hospital was like!'

He was right, and under other circumstances I would have listened with some sympathy. But I was in pain and terrified.

I could just barely feel the scissors still gripped in my numbing fingers.

In a day filled with strange incidents, this crazed man screaming at me, his emotional intensity spilling over me in this quiet and civilized building where people came to pick out nice quiet civilized books.

Then he began shaking me to get me to listen, his other hand gripping my shoulder like a vise, and he never stopped talking, angry, sad, full of pain and self-pity.

I began to get angry myself, and suddenly something in me just snapped. I raised my foot and stomped on his instep with every ounce of force I could summon. With a wail of pain, he let go of me, and in that instant I turned and raced for the front door.

I ran smack into Sally Allison.

'Oh my God,' she said hoarsely. 'Are you all right? He didn't hurt you?' Without waiting for an answer she shouted at her son over my head, 'Perry, what in God's name has gotten into you?'

'Oh, Mom,' he said hopelessly and began to cry.

'He's on drugs, Sally,' I said raggedly. She held me away from her and scanned me for injuries, letting loose a visible sigh of relief when she saw no blood. She saw the scissors still in my hand and looked horrified. 'You weren't going to hurt him?' she asked incredulously.

'Sally, only a mother could say that,' I said. 'Now, you get him out of here and take him home.'

'Listen to me, please, Roe,' Sally pleaded. I was still frightened, but I was acutely uncomfortable, too. I had never had anybody beg me, as Sally unmistakably was begging me now. 'Listen, he didn't take his medicine today. He's okay when he takes his medicine, really. You know he can come to work and perform his job, no one's complained about that, right? So please, please don't tell anyone about this.'

'About what?' asked a quiet voice above my head, and I realized Robin had come in quietly. I looked up to his craggy face, his now-serious crinkly mouth, and I was so glad to see him I could have wept. 'I came to check up on you,' he said to me. 'Mrs Allison, I think I met you at the club meeting.'

'Yes,' Sally said, trying hard to pull herself together. 'Perry! Come on!'

He walked over to her, his wet face blank and tired, his shoulders slumped.

'Let's go home,' his mother suggested. 'We have to talk about our agreement, about the promise you made me.'

Without looking at me or saying a word, Perry followed his mother out the door. I collapsed against Robin and cried a little, still holding the stupid scissors. His huge hand smoothed my hair. When the worst was over, I said, 'I have to lock up, I'm closing now. I don't care if Santa Claus comes to check out a book. This library is closed.'

'Going to tell me what happened?'

'You bet I am, but first I want to get out of this place.' I hated detaching myself from the comfortable chest and enfolding arms; it had been nice to feel protected by a big strong man for a few seconds. But I wanted to leave that building and go home more than I wanted anything else, and with luck, we could repeat the scene at my place with amenities handy.

Chapter Fifteen

'Maybe,' Robin speculated between bites of a pretzel stick, 'there's more than one murderer.'

If we ever spent a night together, it wasn't going to be tonight. The mood had faded.

'Oh, Robin! I can't believe that for a minute. There couldn't be two people that evil in Lawrenceton at the same time, doing the same thing!' One was bad enough; two would get us in the history books for sure.

He waved the pretzel stick at me emphatically. 'Why not, Roe? A copycat killer. Maybe someone, for example, wanted the Buckleys out of the way for some reason, and after Mamie got killed he saw his chance. Or maybe someone wanted to do in Pettigrue, and killed Mamie and the Buckleys to cloud the issue.'

There was a certain amount of precedent for that, but more often in mystery novels than in real life, I thought.

'I guess it's possible,' I conceded. 'But Robin, I just don't want to believe it.'

'Maybe, then, there's more than one killer. I mean, a team of murderers.'

'Jane Engle said the same thing,' I recalled belatedly. 'Two people? How could you look at anyone who knew you had done that, Robin?' I could truly not imagine saying, 'Hey, buddy, look at the way I socked Mamie!' I felt almost nauseated. That two people could agree on such a plan, and mutually carry it out . . .

'Hillside Stranglers,' Robin reminded me. 'Burke and Hare.'

'But the Hillside Stranglers were sex murderers,' I objected, 'and Burke and Hare wanted to sell the bodies to medical schools.'

'Well, true. These killings are apparently just for fun. Just to tease.'

I thought of Gifford and his hatchet. The killer was teasing in more than one way. 'Wait till you hear this!' I exclaimed.

Robin felt better when I'd told him he and Melanie and Arthur had company in the category of Implicated Innocent. 'Though it would be clever of this Gifford,' Robin cautioned, 'to use his own ax, and then claim its use proved him innocent.'

'I wonder if Gifford is that clever,' I said. 'Gifford is crafty, I think, but I believe he's pretty limited in imagination.'

'And how well do you know him?' asked Robin, with a tiny edge to his voice.

'Not well,' I admitted. 'Just through seeing him at Real Murders. He's been coming about a year, I think. And he brings a *friend* named Reynaldo. Who apparently doesn't have a last name . . .'

The phone rang, and I reached out to pick it up, surprised at getting such a late call. People in Lawrenceton do not make phone calls after 10:00 P.M. At least, not the people I know. Robin tactfully took the occasion to go into the bathroom.

'Oh, God, I just looked at my watch, were you in bed?' Arthur asked.

'No,' I said, feeling ridiculously awkward with Robin in my place. Why should I? I asked myself. I could see two men at one time if I chose.

'I just finished work and got back to my place. I don't suppose there's any chance you want to come over?'

The idea sent a certain tingle down my spine, but all the conditions that had applied to Robin were still valid; plus, Robin was showing no signs of budging. In fact, he'd just gone to the refrigerator and refreshed his drink.

'I have to work tomorrow,' I said neutrally.

'Oh. Okay. I get the message. Roller skating or nothing.'

Ohmygosh. I had almost forgotten. Well, I had some pretty good reasons for not thinking about a Saturday night date.

'You think you will be able to get off?' I asked cautiously.

'I think so. I have some amazing news for you. You sitting down?'

Arthur sounded strange. Like someone who was trying to be excited and happy and just couldn't manage. And he hadn't mentioned the discovery of the hatchet and briefcase.

'Yes, I'm sitting. What?'

'Benjamin Greer just confessed to all the murders.'

'What? He what?'

'He confessed to killing Mamie Wright, Morrison Pettigrue, and the Buckleys.'

'But what about the box of candy? Why did he do that? Mother doesn't know him at all.'

'He says Morrison did that, because your mother is an example of what is worst about capitalism.'

'My mom – Morrison Pettigrue? I don't believe it,' I sputtered disconnectedly.

'You don't want this case to be over?'

'Yes, yes! But I don't believe he did it. I wish I did.'

'He's convinced a lot of the guys down here.'

'Did he know where the hatchet was hidden?'

'Everyone in town knows that now.'

'Did he know what it was in?'

'Pretty much everyone knows that, too.'

'Okay, who'd he steal the hatchet from, that he used to kill the Buckleys?'

'He hasn't said yet.'

'Gifford Doakes told me tonight that it was his hatchet.'

'He did?' And for the first time Arthur's voice showed some life and enthusiasm. 'Gifford hasn't been in here yet. As far as I know.'

'Well, he told me tonight at the library that his hatchet had been missing, and he asked me about that tape around the handle. I didn't bring it up, in fact I'd forgotten about it.'

'I'll pass that on to the men who are questioning Greer,' Arthur promised. 'That can be one of our test questions. But for some reason, Roe, this guy is convincing. He believes it, I think. And we have a witness.'

Robin had abandoned being polite and was beside himself to know what I was talking about. His eyebrows were winging around his face in interrogation. I kept waving my hand to keep him quiet.

'A witness to the murder.'

'No, a witness who saw him leave the hatchet in the alley.'

I remembered Lynn's excitement when she'd talked to the young mother in the apartments. I was willing to bet that that was the witness.

'So what did she see?' I asked sharply.

'Listen, this is police business that I can't tell you about in detail,' Arthur said flatly.

'I'm sorry if I'm trespassing, but I'm deeply involved in this, up to my neck, according to Lynn Liggett and your boss Jack Burns.'

'Well. You're off the hook now.'

'This is hard to soak in. I can't believe it's all over.'

'I'm going to sleep,' Arthur said, and the exhaustion made his voice slur. 'I'm going to sleep and sleep and sleep. And when I get up, we're going to talk about going roller skating.'

'Okay,' I said slowly. 'Listen, I just remembered that my little brother, Phillip, is coming tomorrow and spending the weekend.'

'Then we'll take him with us,' Arthur said smoothly, scarcely missing a beat.

'Okay. Talk to you later.' I was smiling as I hung up; I couldn't help it. 'It may be over, Robin,' I said, almost crying.

His mouth fell open. 'You mean, we don't have to worry anymore?' he asked.

'So it seems. An eyewitness places Benjamin Greer, the member of Real Murders who wasn't there the night Mamie got killed, depositing the briefcase in the culvert. And he has confessed to everything, except sending the candy, which he says Morrison Pettigrue did before he killed him. I'll have to call Mother. Pettigrue thought Mother was a terrible capitalist.'

We discussed this truly stunning development up and down and sideways and forwards, until I began to yawn and feel drowsy.

'Did I hear you mention that your brother is coming?' Robin asked tactfully.

'Yes, his name is Phillip, he's six. From my father's remarriage.

Dad and his wife are going to a convention in Chattanooga this weekend, and I've been scheduled for a long time to keep Phillip. Things were getting so grim here I was thinking about calling Dad and canceling or going to keep Phillip at their house, but now I guess it'll be okay to have him here.'

'You two get along? What do you do when he's visiting?'

'Oh, we play games. We go to the movies. He watches television. I read to him, things he can't read himself yet. One time we went bowling. That was a real disaster, but fun, too. Sometimes he brings his ball and glove and we play catch in the parking lot. I'm not very good at that, though. Phillip is a real baseball freak, he brings his cards every time he comes and we go through them, while I try not to yawn.'

'I like kids,' said Robin, and I could tell he was sincere. 'Maybe Saturday we can all go to the state park and have a picnic and hike one of the trails.'

That would be an hour drive to and from, plus allow maybe three hours for the hike and picnic, I figured rapidly. I could be back in time for roller skating, but Phillip would probably be exhausted from the park, and I might be, too. 'Maybe playing – is it called goofy golf? – would be better. I noticed a new place out on the highway into the city when I drove in Monday.' That felt years ago now.

'I saw that, too,' Robin said. 'Maybe Saturday afternoon?'

'Okay, he'll love it. Come meet him tomorrow night,' I offered. 'I promised to make pecan pie – that's Phillip's favorite. What about 7:00?'

'Great,' said Robin agreeably. He leaned over to give me a casual kiss. 'I'll see you then.' He seemed preoccupied as he left.

I locked the back door after Robin left, and checked my front door, though I seldom used it. If this whole imbroglio had had one effect, it was to make me permanently security conscious.

It had been a busy day even without the constant strain of living with a murderer in close proximity. Today we'd found the hatchet in Robin's briefcase, I'd had the weird confrontation with Gifford Doakes and the eerie scene in the library with Perry. I wondered if

Sally was right in her optimistic belief that no one at work besides me had noticed that Perry was unraveling. I hadn't exactly been in the current of office gossip the past week, being mostly the subject of it, I was sure.

Then Arthur had called with the bombshell about Benjamin.

Benjamin the loser. Benjamin the murderer?

As I made up the bed in the guest room for Phillip – though he usually ended up getting spooked at spending the night in a strange place and came in my room – I realized anew how abnormal the week had been. Usually, when I knew Phillip was going to make one of his four or five annual weekend visits, I spent several days preparing. I stocked all his favorite foods, planned lots of activities, checked out an armful of children's books, consulted the local movie schedules. I overdid it.

This was probably the appropriate amount of preparation for a six-year-old's visit; I made a bed for him, checked to see if I had the ingredients for his favorite dessert, and decided to take him to his favorite fast-food place for lunch on Saturday. And I looked forward to seeing him, this unexpected brother I had acquired after I'd become an adult. In the middle of the awfulness I'd seen lately, and the anxiety I'd suffered in so many unprecedented situations, having Phillip to visit seemed like a welcome return to normality.

Benjamin Greer.

I tried to believe it.

Chapter Sixteen

I woke up smiling. It took me a second to remember why, but when I remembered, I grinned all over. The murders were at an end. I had convinced myself in my sleep that Benjamin was confessing because he had done it and wanted the attention and infamy, not because he hadn't done it but wanted the attention and infamy anyway. After all, he had announced his candidacy for mayor, that should have given him enough fuel to run on for a while. It was Friday, I didn't have to work this weekend, Phillip was coming, I was interested in two men and what's more they were both interested in me. What more could a twenty-eight-year-old librarian ask for?

I made myself up with great care, had some fun with my eye shadow, and picked my brightest skirt and blouse to wear. It was a definitely springy set, white with yellow flowers scattered all over, and I let my hair hang loose with a yellow band to hold it back.

I had a large breakfast, cereal and toast and even a banana, and sang on my way out to my car.

'You're chipper this morning,' said Bankston, who was dressed in a very sober suit befitting a banker. He was smiling himself, and I remembered I'd seen Melanie's car pull out of the parking lot very early this morning.

'Oh, I have reason to be! You may not have heard yet, but someone admitted to the murders.'

'Who?' Bankston said after staring at me for a moment.

'Benjamin Greer.' Then I wondered belatedly if I was betraying a confidence. But my assurance returned when I remembered Arthur hadn't asked me to keep it quiet, and I hadn't told him I would. Also, I'd already told Robin, who would have throttled the news out of me if I'd hung up from my conversation with

Arthur and refused to tell him. Wait; I wasn't even going to say exaggerated things like that to myself anymore.

Bankston was thunderstruck. 'But he was just in to see me last week to get a loan for his candidate's campaign! Sorry, I shouldn't have mentioned that. It was a private transaction, bank business. But I'm just so – flabbergasted.'

'I was too,' I assured him.

'Well, well, I'll have to stop by Melanie's and tell her,' he said after a moment of thought. 'This will be such a relief to her. She's had a hard time since Mrs Wright's purse was found in her car.'

Right. Being pronounced a martyr at church and getting a marriage proposal was really a hard time. But I felt too cheerful to envy Melanie; I'd gone out with Bankston twice and wouldn't have him on a silver platter, as my mother always said.

Mother. That was someone who should hear the good news, too. I'd call her today. She was going to love being termed 'what was worst about capitalism.' That was a hard line to take after all Mother's hard work and struggle during the first few years with her business, though then she'd had my father's presence to give her renewed strength. He hadn't left until she was well on the road to success. I was trailing off into unpleasant thoughts, and snapped myself back quickly. Joy was the keynote of the day.

At work, all the librarians and volunteers seemed to have heard the good news, and I was back in the fold. Lillian went back to being her bitchy self, which was almost comforting. Sam Clerrick ventured forth from his charts and graphs and budgets to pat me on the shoulder in passing. I poked book cards in the stamper vigorously, took overdue money with a smile instead of expressionless disapproval, shelved with precision. The morning didn't just hurry by, it hopped, skipped, and jumped by.

The telephone rang twice while I was eating my microwaved egg rolls and browsing through an encyclopedia of twentieth-century murderers. I'd had that familiar irritating feeling that someone, sometime, had said something interesting that I wanted to pursue, mentioned some names I wanted to mull over, and I'd thought flipping through the book would help. But the phone destroyed even this wisp of idea.

The first caller was my father, who always opened with, 'How's my Doll?'

He hated calling me 'Roe' and I hated him calling me 'Doll'. We hadn't come up with anything neutral. 'I'm okay, Dad,' I said.

'Is it still okay with you if Phillip comes?' he asked anxiously. 'You know, if you are upset about the situation in Lawrenceton, we can stay home.'

In the background I could hear Phillip piping anxiously, 'Can I go, Daddy? Can I go?'

'The crisis seems to be over,' I said happily.

'They arrest someone?'

'They got a confession. I'm sure everything's going to be okay now,' I said. Maybe I wasn't all that sure. But I *was* pretty sure that I was going to be okay now. And I wanted to see my little brother.

'Well, I'll be bringing him about five o'clock, then,' Dad said. 'Betty Jo sends her love. We really appreciate this.'

I wasn't so sure about Betty Jo's love, but I was sure she did appreciate having a free, reliable babysitter for a whole weekend.

The next call was from my mother, of course. She still had some sort of psychic link to Dad, and if he called me she nearly always rang within the hour. If she was like Lauren Bacall, he was like Humphrey Bogart; an ugly guy with charisma coming out his ears. And bless his heart, he seemed quite unaware of it. But that charisma was still sending out alpha waves or something to my mother.

I knew that she must already have heard of Benjamin's confession, and sure enough, she had. She'd also heard he'd said Morrison Pettigrue had mailed her the chocolates. She was skeptical.

'How would Morrison Pettigrue hear about Mrs See's?' she asked. 'How would he know I always eat the creams?'

'He didn't have to know you always eat the creams,' I pointed out. 'There's just no way to get rat poison in the nut-filled ones.'

'That's true,' she admitted. 'I still have a hard time believing that one. I barely knew the man. I'd met him at some Chamber of Commerce meeting once and if I remember correctly, we talked about the need for new sidewalks downtown. It was a cordial conversation and he certainly gave no sign then that he thought I was some kind of leech living off the masses, or whatever.'

But if Benjamin was lying about the chocolates, he could also be lying about other things. And I wanted him to be telling the truth and nothing but the truth.

'Let's just shelve this until we find out more about it,' I suggested. 'Maybe he'll say something that'll make sense out of the whole thing.'

'Is – your brother – still staying with you this weekend?' Mother asked, in one of her lightning turns of thought.

I sighed silently. 'Yes, Mother. Dad's bringing Phillip by around five, and he'll be here until Sunday evening.' It would have been beneath Mother's dignity to avoid the sight of Phillip, but having made a point of talking to him once or twice, she usually stayed away while he was at my place.

'Well, I'll be talking to you again,' she was saying now. I could bet on that. I asked her about her business, and she chatted about that for a few minutes.

'Are you and John still thinking about getting married?' I asked.

'Well, we're discussing it.' There was a smile in her voice. 'I promise you'll be the first to know when we definitely decide.'

'As long as I'm the first,' I said. 'I really am happy for you.'

'I hear you have a new beau,' Mother said, which was a logical progression when you think about it.

'Which one have you heard about?' I asked, because I simply couldn't resist.

In someone less grand than my mother, I would've called the sound she made a delighted cackle. We hung up with mutual warmth, and I returned to work with the distinct feeling life was on the up and up for me.

My mother's 'beau', John Queensland, came into the library that afternoon while I was on the circulation desk. I realized he was practically the opposite of my father: handsome in an elder-statesman way, and overtly as dignified and reserved as Mother. He had been a widower for some time and still lived in the big two-story house he'd shared with his wife and their two children, both of whom had children of their own now. My contemporaries, I reminded myself gloomily.

As John was checking out two staid biographies of worthy people, he mentioned that his garage had been broken into some time within the last three weeks.

'I never use it anymore, I just park behind the house. The garage is so full of the boys' old stuff – I can't seem to get them to decide what to do with all their junk.' He sounded fond rather than complaining. 'But anyway, I went to track down my golf clubs since I intended scheduling a game with Bankston in this warmer weather, and the darned thing had been broken into and my golf clubs were gone.'

Since John was a Real Murderer, I was sure that this theft meant something. I told John about Gifford Doakes and his hatchet – amazingly, he hadn't heard – and left him to draw his own conclusions.

'I know Benjamin Greer has confessed,' I told John, 'but that's a bit of evidence the police might need. Just a confession isn't enough, I gather.'

'I think I'll go by the police station on my way back to the office,' John said thoughtfully. 'Those clubs had better be reported. The whole bag was taken, and it was a pretty distinctive set. Every time my kids went somewhere, they got a bumper sticker and put it on my golf bag, just a family joke . . .' And trailing off with unheard-of abstraction, John left the library. I thought of Arthur and sighed. I wondered if he'd appreciate being handed another out-of-the-blue fact.

Golf clubs. Maybe they'd already been used. Maybe they'd been used on Mamie. The weapon in that case had never been found, that I knew of. Maybe Benjamin would tell the police where the clubs were.

I let this nag at me until I got home and saw my father's car waiting at my apartment. As I greeted my father and hugged my half-brother, I made a resolution not to think about these killings for a couple of days. I wanted to enjoy Phillip's company.

Phillip is in the first grade and he can be very funny and very exasperating. He will eat about five things with any enthusiasm – five nutritious things, that is. (Anything with no nutritional value whatsoever is always acceptable to Phillip.) Luckily for me, one of those things is spaghetti sauce and another is pecan pie, not that either is exactly a health food.

'Roe! Are we having spaghetti tonight?' he asked eagerly.

'Sure,' I said, and smiled at him. I bent and kissed him before he could say, 'Yuck! No kisses!' He gave me a quick kiss back, then scrambled to get his suitcase and (much more important) a plastic garbage bag full of essential toys. 'I'm going to put these in my room,' he told Father, who was beaming at him with unadulterated pride.

'Son, I've got to go now,' Father told him. 'Your mom is anxious to get where we're going. You be good for your big sister, now, and do what she says to do without giving her any trouble.'

Phillip, half listened, mumbled, 'Sure, Dad,' and lugged his paraphernalia into my place.

'Well, Doll, this sure is nice of you,' my father said to me when Phillip had vanished.

'I like Phillip,' I said honestly. 'I like having him stay here.'

'Here are the phone numbers where we'll be staying,' Father said and fumbled a sheet of note-paper out of his pocket. 'If anything goes wrong, anything at all, call us straight away.'

'Okay, okay,' I reassured him. 'Don't worry. Have a good time. I'll see you Sunday night?'

'Yes, we should be here about five or six. If we're going to be any later than that, we'll call you. Don't forget to remind him about his prayers. Oh – if he runs a fever or anything, here's a box of chewable children's aspirin. He gets three. And he needs to have a glass of water by the bed at night.'

'I'll remember.' We hugged, and he got in his car with a lopsided smile and half-wave that I could see a woman would have a hard time forgetting. I watched Father drive out of the parking lot, and then heard Phillip shouting from the kitchen, 'Roe! You got any cookies?'

I supplied Phillip with two awful sandwich cookies that he'd told me were his favorites. Very pleased, he bounced outside with his garbage bag of toys, having dumped the 'inside' ones in the middle of my den. 'I bet you have to cook, so I'm going to be out here playing,' he said seriously.

I could take a hint. I got busy with the spaghetti sauce.

The next time I glanced out the window to check, I saw through my open patio gate that Phillip had already commandeered Bankston into playing baseball in the parking lot. Phillip had great scorn for my baseball playing ability, but Bankston had his approval. Bankston had taken off his suit coat and his tie immediately, and seemed not nearly so stuffy as he pitched the baseball to Phillip's waiting bat. They'd played before when Phillip had visited, and Bankston didn't seem to consider it an imposition.

Then Robin was drawn into the game when he got home, and he was acting as Phillip's catcher when I called from the patio gate that supper was ready.

'Yahoo!' Phillip shrieked, and propped his bat against the patio wall. I smiled and shrugged at his abandoned playmates and whispered to Phillip, 'Thank Bankston and Robin for a good game.' 'Thank you,' Phillip said obediently and dashed in to scramble into his chair at my small dining table. I glimpsed the top of Melanie's head in Bankston's open door as he went in, and Robin said, 'See you later, for pecan pie. I like your little brother,' as he strolled through the gate to his patio. I felt warm and flushed with pride at having such a cute brother – and a little warm, too, at Robin's smile, which had definitely been of the personal variety.

For the next twenty minutes I was occupied in seeing that Phillip used his napkin and said his prayer and ate at least a little serving of vegetables. I looked fondly at his perpetually tousled light brown hair and his startlingly blue eyes, so different from mine. Between bites of spaghetti and garlic bread, Phillip was telling me a long involved story about a fight on the school playground, involving a boy whose brother really knew karate and another boy who really had all the G.I. Joe attack vehicles. I listened with half an ear, the other part of my mind being increasingly occupied by the niggling feeling that I was supposed to know something. Or remember something. Or had I seen something? Whatever this 'something' was, I needed to call it to mind.

'My baseball!' shrieked Phillip suddenly.

He had my full attention. The shriek, which had sprung with no warning from his throat while he was telling me what the principal had done to the playground combatants, had scared the whosis out of me.

'But Phillip, it's dark,' I protested, as he catapulted out of his chair and dashed to the back door. I tried to remember if I'd ever seen him walk, and decided that I had, once, when he was about twelve months old. 'Here, at least take my flashlight!'

I managed to stuff it in his hand only because he was so partial to flashlights that he slowed down long enough for me to pull it from the kitchen cabinet.

'And try to remember where you last saw the ball!' I bellowed after him.

I'd finished my meal while Phillip was relating his long story, so I scraped my plate and put it in the dishwasher (Robin was due in a few minutes, and I wanted the place to look neat). The dessert plates were out, everything else was ready, so while I waited for a triumphant Phillip to return with his baseball, I idly looked at my shelves, putting a few books back in place that were out of order. I stared at the titles of all those books about bad or crazy or crazed people, men and women whose lives had crossed the faint line that demarks those who could but haven't from those who can and have.

Phillip had been gone a long time; I couldn't hear him out in the parking lot.

The phone rang.

'Yes?' I said abruptly into the receiver.

'Roe, it's Sally Allison.'

'What . . .'

'Have you seen Perry?'

'What? No!'

'Has he been . . . following you anymore?'

'No . . . at least, I haven't noticed if he has.'

'He . . .' Sally trailed off.

'Come on, Sally! What's the matter?' I asked roughly. I stared out through the kitchen window, hoping to see the beam of the flashlight bobbing around through the slats in the patio fence. I remembered the night Perry'd been across the street in the dark waiting for Robin to bring me home. I was terrified.

'He didn't take his medicine today. He didn't go to work. I don't know where he is. Maybe he took some more pills.'

'Call the police, then. Get them looking for him, Sally! What if he's here? My little brother's out alone in the dark!' I hung up the phone with a hysterical bang. I grabbed up my huge key ring, with some idea of taking my car around the block for a search, and I pulled out the second flashlight I kept ready.

It was my fault. The thing in the dark had gotten my little brother, a six-year-old child, and it was *my fault*. Oh Lord God, heavenly King, protect the child.

I left the back door wide open, the welcome light spilling into the deep dusk. The patio gate was already open, Phillip never remembered to close it. His bat was propped beside it as he'd left it coming in to supper.

'Phillip!' I screamed. Then I thought, maybe I should be quiet and creep. In a frenzy of indecision, I swung the flashlight to and fro. A few yards away, a car started up and pulled out of its space. As it went by, I saw it was Melanie in Bankston's car. She smiled and waved. I gaped after her. How could she not have heard me yell?

But I couldn't reason, I just kept walking and sweeping the ground with that beam of light, seeing nothing, nothing.

'Roe, what's wrong? I was just on my way over to your place!' Robin loomed above me in the dark.

'Phillip's gone, someone's got him! He left to get his baseball, he ran out the back door, he didn't come back!'

'I'll get a flashlight,' Robin said instantly. He turned to go to his telephone, 'listen—' he half turned back but kept moving, 'he wouldn't think it was funny to hide, would he?'

'I don't think so,' I said. I would have loved to have thought Phillip was giggling behind a bush somewhere, but I knew he wasn't. He couldn't have stayed hidden this long in the dark. He'd have jumped out long before, screaming 'boo,' his grin of triumph making his face shine. 'Listen, Robin, go ask the Crandalls if they've seen Phillip, and call the police. Perry Allison's mom just called and he's loose somewhere. She may not call the police. I'm going to work my way around to search the front yard.'

'Right,' Robin said briefly, and vanished into his place.

I walked quickly through the dark (and it was full dark now), the beam of the flashlight on the sidewalk before me. I'd pause, and swing the flashlight, and step on. I passed the Crandalls' gate, and had found nothing. I opened Bankston's gate. The flashlight beam caught something on Bankston's patio.

Phillip's baseball.

Oh, God, it had been here all the time, no wonder Phillip couldn't find it. Bankston had probably picked it up out of the parking lot to keep it to give Phillip tomorrow morning.

I lifted my hand to knock on Bankston's back door and my hand froze in midair. I thought about Melanie pulling out of the parking lot so strangely – she must have heard me scream.

And I'd told Phillip to think of where he'd seen it last. He'd seen it last in Bankston's hands.

Had Bankston been lying down in that car? Had he been lying on top of Phillip, to keep him quiet?

A long brown hair had been found in the Buckleys' house. Benjamin didn't have long brown hair. He had thinning blond hair. Like Bankston. He was medium height, like Bankston, and he had a round face. Like Bankston. It was Bankston the young mother had seen in the alley, not Benjamin Greer.

Melanie had long brown hair. *Together*. They had done the killings together.

And then I remembered that niggly little thing that had been bothering me. When John Queensland had described his golf bag, he'd said it had stickers all over it. That had been the golf bag Bankston was carrying into his place on Wednesday, so long after my lunch hour he hadn't expected me to be around at all, much less popping out of the Crandalls' gate. Bankston had stolen them from John Queensland.

Had Phillip been in Bankston's townhouse? I turned my flashlight on my key ring. You couldn't call it breaking and entering, I told myself hysterically. I had a key. I was the landlady. I turned it in the keyhole, opened the door as quietly as I could, and stepped inside.

I didn't call out. I left the back door open.

The kitchen light was on, and the kitchen/living room was a mess, but an ordinary mess. A library book was lying open on the counter, a book I had in my own personal library, Emlyn Williams's *Beyond Belief*. I felt sick, and had to bend over.

This time they were patterning themselves after Myra Hindley and Ian Brady, the 'Moors Murderers.' They were going to kill a child. They were going to kill my brother. The monster was not sitting in a jail cell in the Lawrenceton City Jail. The monsters lived here.

Hindley and Brady had tortured the children for a few hours first, so Phillip might be alive. If he'd been in the car, if they'd taken him to Melanie's place, wherever that was – right, the same street where Jane Engle lived – he might have left some trace.

Abandoning silence, I raced up the stairs. No one. In the larger bedroom there was a king-sized bed with a coil of rope beside it, and a camera was on the dresser.

Hindley and Brady, two low-level office workers who'd met on the job, had tape-recorded and photographed their victims.

The extra bedroom was full of exercise equipment: the source of Bankston's newly bulging muscles. There was a file box with its lid hanging back, key still in the lock. Anything he locked up, I wanted to see. I knocked it over and the magazines inside spilled out like a trail of slime. I looked at an open one in horror. I did not know it was possible to buy pictures of women being treated like that. When I had heard of the anti-pornography movement, I'd thought of the usual pictures of women who at least were apparently willing, being paid, and still healthy when the photo session was over.

I ran back downstairs, glanced into the living room, opened the closets. Nothing. I opened the door to the basement. The light was off, so the steps were dark from halfway down to the bottom. But something white was on one of the lower steps, just visible in the light spilling down from the kitchen.

I went down the stairs and crouched to pick it up. It was a baseball card.

I heard a muffled noise, and had time to think, Phillip! But then I felt a terrible pain across my shoulder and neck, and I was falling forward, my arms and legs tangled, my face scraping the edge of the steps. The next thing I knew I was on the floor of the basement and looking up at Bankston's face, stolid no more in the dim light but grinning like a gargoyle, and he had a golf club in his hand.

There was another switch at the bottom of the steps, and he turned it on. I heard the noise again, and with great pain turned my head to see Phillip, gagged and with his hands tied, sitting on a straight chair by the dryer. His face was wet with tears and his whole little body was curled into as tight a ball as he could manage in that chair. His feet could not touch the floor.

My heart broke.

I'd heard people say that all my life; their heart had broken because their love had deserted them, their heart had broken because their cat had died, their heart had broken because they'd dropped Grandma's vase.

I was going to die and I had cost my little brother his life, and my heart broke for what he would endure before they finally tired of him and killed him.

'We heard you come in,' Bankston said, smiling. 'We were down here waiting for you, weren't we, Phillip?'

Incredible, Bankston the banker. Bankston with the matching almond-tone washer and dryer. Bankston arranging a loan for a businessman in the afternoon and smashing Mamie Wright's face in the evening. Melanie the secretary, filling up her idle time while her boss was out of town by slaughtering the Buckleys with a hatchet. The perfect couple.

Phillip was crying hopelessly. 'Shut up, Phillip,' said the man who'd played baseball with him that afternoon. 'Every time you cry, I'll hit your sister. Won't I, sis?' And the golf club whistled through the air and Bankston broke my collarbone. My shriek must have covered Melanie's steps, because suddenly she was there looking down at me with pleasure.

'When I pulled in, the Scarecrow was searching the parking lot,' she said to Bankston. 'Here's the tape recorder. I can't believe we forgot it!'

Gee, what a madcap couple. She sounded for all the world like a housewife who'd remembered the potato salad in the fridge just as the family was leaving on its picnic.

I decided, when the pain had ebbed enough for me to think, that 'the Scarecrow' was Robin. I managed to look at Phillip again. God bless him, he was trying so hard not to make sounds, so Bankston wouldn't hit me again. I tried to push the pain away so I could look reassuring, but I could only stare at him and try not to scream myself. If I screamed, Bankston would hit me quite a lot.

Or maybe he would hit Phillip.

'What do you think?' Bankston asked her.

'No way we can get them out of here now,' Melanie said matter-of-factly. 'He said he'd called the police. One of us better go up soon and offer to help search. If we don't the police will want to look in here, I guess, get suspicious. We can't have that, can we?' and she smiled archly, and poked my leg with her foot, as if I were a piece of naughtiness that they had to conceal for convention's sake. She saw me looking at her. 'Get up and get over there by the kid,' she said, and then she kicked me. I moaned. 'I've always wanted to do that,' she said to Bankston with a smile.

It was not only the fall and the blows that made it hard to move, but the shock. I was in this most prosaic basement with these most prosaic people, and they were monsters that were going to kill me, me and my brother. I had read and marveled for years at people living cheek by jowl with psychopaths and not suspecting. And here I was, trying desperately to crawl across a concrete floor in a building my mother owned while friends looked for my brother outside, because I had never, never thought it could happen to me. I got to Phillip's side in a few moments, though the young woman I'd known all my life and gone to church with did kick me a few times on the journey. I grabbed the edge of the seat and dragged myself to my knees, and clumsily draped my good arm around Phillip. I wished Phillip would faint. His face was more than I could stand, and I had no consolation for him. We were looking at the faces of demons, and all the rules of kindness and courtesy that Phillip and I had been taught so carefully did not apply. No reward for good behavior.

'I got the tape recorder, but now we can't use it,' Melanie was pouting. 'I think that's when she got suspicious, when she saw me pull out of the parking lot. I didn't want to have to help her look, so I had to act like I didn't hear her. I don't guess we'll get to have any fun tonight.'

'I didn't think this through,' Bankston agreed. 'Now they'll be out there looking for the boy and her all night, and we'll have to go volunteer, too. At least now we've got her keys, they can't use the master set to come in here.' He held them up. I must have dropped them when I fell.

'You think they might insist on searching all the apartments?' Melanie asked anxiously. 'We can't turn them down if they ask.'

Bankston pondered. They were at the foot of the steps still. I could not get by them. I could not see any weapons besides the golf club, but even if I did attack them with my one good arm and my little remaining energy, the two of them could easily overcome me and the noise would not be heard by anyone . . . unless the Crandalls had decided to spend the evening in their basement. 'We'll just have to wing it,' Bankston said finally.

The baseball! Maybe Robin would see it, like I had.

'Did you talk to anyone when you pulled in?' Bankston was asking.

'Just what I told you before. Robin asked me if I had seen the boy, and I said no, but that I'd be glad to help look,' Melanie said with no irony whatsoever. 'Roe left the back door open, so I closed and relocked it. And I picked up the kid's baseball, it was still out on the patio.'

That was our death warrant, I reckoned.

Bankston cursed. 'How did it end up out there? I was sure I'd brought it in.'

'Don't worry about it,' Melanie said. 'Even if they did find it, you could just have said you'd been keeping it for him but he didn't ever show up looking for it.'

'You're right,' Bankston said fondly. 'What shall we do with those two? If we leave them tied up down here while we go help to search, they might somehow get loose. If we kill them right now, we lose our fun with the boy.' He strolled over to us and Melanie followed.

'You acted on impulse when you grabbed him,' Melanie observed. 'We should just go on and take care of them now, and hide them down here good. Then when the search dies down, we'll see if we can get them out to the car and dump them. Next time, no impulses, we'll do what we planned and nothing extra.'

'Are you criticizing me?' Bankston asked sharply. His voice was low and dangerous.

Her posture changed. I had never seen anything like it. She cringed and folded and became another person. 'No, never,' she whimpered, and she bent and licked his hand. I saw her eyes, and she was role-playing and it excited her immensely.

I was nauseated. I hoped I was blocking Phillip's view sufficiently. I huddled closer to him, though the pain from my collarbone was becoming more insistent. Phillip was shaking and he had wet himself. His breath was getting more and more ragged, and muffled sobs and whimpers broke out from time to time.

Melanie and Bankston were giving each other a kiss, and Bankston bent and bit her shoulder. She held him to her as though they would use each other right there, but then they unclenched and she said, 'We'd better do it now. Why run any more risks?'

'You're right,' Bankston agreed. He gave her the golf club, and she swung it through the air experimentally while he searched his pockets. In her black slacks and green sweater and knotted scarf she looked ready to tee off at the country club. In that small area the club whistled past me with no room to spare, and I started to protest, when I realized yet again that Melanie absolutely could not care less. Old assumptions die hard.

I saw a foot on the stairs behind them.

'Give me your scarf, Mel,' Bankston said suddenly. Melanie unknotted it instantly. 'This would be less messy, and I've never done it before,' he observed cheerfully. They never looked at me or at Phillip, except in passing, and I could tell to them we were not people like they were.

The foot was joined by a matching foot, and silently took another step down.

'Maybe I should tape this,' Melanie said brightly. 'It won't be what we had planned, but it might be interesting.'

The next step squeaked, and I screamed, 'God damn you to hell! How can you do this to me? How can you do this to a little boy?'

They were as shocked as though a chair had spoken. Melanie swung the club instantly with both hands. My body was covering Phillip's on the chair, but the blow was so strong the chair was rocked. It was easy to shriek as loud as a freight train. I saw the feet descend all the way in a rush.

'Shut up, bitch!' Melanie said furiously.

'Naw, you shut up,' a flat voice advised her.

It was old Mr Crandall, and he was carrying a very large gun.

The only sound in the basement was the sobbing coming from me, as I struggled to control myself. Phillip raised his bound wrists to loop his arms over my head. I wished more than ever that he'd faint.

'You're not going to shoot,' Bankston said. 'You old idiot. With this concrete floor, it'll ricochet and hit them.'

'I'd rather shoot them directly than leave them to you,' Mr Crandall said simply.

'Which one of us will you shoot first?' Melanie asked furiously. She'd been sidling away from Bankston a little at a time. 'You can't get us both, old man.'

'But I can,' said Robin from higher on the stairs, and he wasn't nearly as calm as Mr Crandall. I managed to look up. I saw Robin descending with a shotgun. 'Now I don't know as much about guns as Mr Crandall, but he loaded this, for me, and if I point it and fire, I am real sure I will hit something.'

If they tried anything desperate it would be now. I could feel the turmoil pouring from them. They looked at each other. I could only stare through a haze of pain at the green silk scarf in Bankston's hand. Oh, surely they must see it was over, over.

Suddenly the fight oozed out of them. They looked like what they used to be, for a moment: a bank loan officer and a secretary, who could not remember where they were or how they had come to be there. The scarf fell from Bankston's hand. Melanie lay down the golf club. They did not look at each other anymore.

There was a gust of people noise, and Arthur and Lynn Liggett came pelting down the stairs to be stopped short by the tableau.

Phillip's breath came out from behind the gag in a deep sigh, and he fainted. It seemed like such a good idea that I did it, too.

Chapter Seventeen

'If I'd had my Dynamite Man Particle Blaster they wouldn't have hurt us,' Phillip whispered. He simply would not be parted from me while I was being patched up. He held on to my hand or my leg or my torso; though many kind people offered to take him and rock him, or buy him an ice cream cone, or color with him, my little brother would not be separated from me. This definitely made it harder on me, but I tried to have so much sympathy for Phillip that the pain would not seem important. I'm afraid I found that to me, pain is very important, no matter who else has been hurt.

Now he was actually in the hospital bed with me, huddling as close to me as he could get, his eyes still wide and staring, but beginning to glaze over. I thought he'd had some kind of mild tranquilizer; I thought I remembered saying that was okay. My father and stepmother were driving back from Chattanooga; Robin, bless him, had found their phone number and called, miraculously catching them in their motel room.

'Phillip, if I hadn't had you to hold on to, I would have gone nuts,' I assured him. 'You were so brave. I know you were scared inside, like I was, but you were brave as a lion to hold yourself together.'

'I was thinking about escaping all the time. I was just waiting for a chance,' he informed me. There, he was beginning to sound more like Phillip. Then, less certainly, 'Roe, would they really have killed us?'

What was I supposed to say? I glanced over at Robin, who shrugged in an it's-up-to-you gesture. Why was I asking Robin what I should say to my little brother?

'Yes,' I said, and took a deep breath. 'Yes, they were really bad people. They were rotten apples. They were nice on the outside but full of worms on the inside.'

'But they're locked up in jail now?'

'You bet.' I thought about lawyers and bail and I shivered. Surely not. 'They can't ever get you again. They can't ever hurt anybody again. They're far away and all locked up, and your mom and dad will carry you home even farther away from them.'

'When are they gonna get here?' he asked desolately.

'Soon, soon, as fast as their car can come,' I said as soothingly as I could, perhaps for the fiftieth time, and thank God at that moment my father did come in, Betty Jo right behind him and under rigid control.

'Mama!' said Phillip, and all his hard-held toughness left him. He became an instant soggy puddle of little boy. Betty Jo swept him out of the hospital bed and into her arms and held him as tightly as he held her. 'Where can I take him?' she asked the nurse who'd followed them in. The nurse told her about an empty waiting room two doors down, and Betty Jo vanished with her precious armful. I was so glad to see Betty Jo take him I could have cried. There is no substitute for a real mother. At least I am no substitute for a real mother. The past few hours had certainly taught me that, if I'd ever doubted it.

My father bent and kissed me. 'I hear you saved his life,' he said, and tears trickled down his face. I had never seen my father cry. 'I am so thankful you are both safe, I prayed in the car all the way here. I could have lost both of you in one night.' Overwhelmed, he sank into the guest chair Robin had quietly vacated. Robin stood back in the shadows, the dim room light glinted off his red hair. I would never forget how he'd looked with the shotgun in his hands.

I was just too tired to appreciate my father's emotion. It was late, so late. I had almost been strangled by a bank loan officer with a green silk scarf. I had been hit by a secretary with a golf club. I had been terrified out of my mind for myself and my little brother. I had looked into the face of evil. Strong words, I told myself hazily, but true. The face of evil.

Finally, my dear father dried his eyes, told me he'd see me very soon, and said they were taking Phillip home that very night. 'We'll have to see about treatment for him,' he said apprehensively. 'I don't know how to help him.'

'I'll see you,' I mumbled.

'Thanks, Aurora,' he said. 'If you need help yourself, you know how to reach us.' But they were dying to get Phillip away, and his voice verged on perfunctory. I was a grown-up, right? I could take care of myself. Or my mother would take care of me. I let myself have a flash of bitterness, and made myself swallow it. He was not being careful of me, but he was right.

I drifted off to sleep for a second. Robin was holding my hand when I woke up. I think he had kissed me.

'That felt good,' I said. So he did it again. It felt even better.

'They were stupid really,' I said a little later.

'When you think about it, yes,' Robin agreed. 'I don't think they ever realized it wasn't a game when they began patterning the deaths after old murders. Bankston snatched Phillip on impulse when they should have waited and picked a victim from at least across town . . . If he'd really been intelligent, he would have known taking Phillip from the same place he himself lived, then keeping him in the townhouse instead of getting him out to Melanie's place . . . Well, maybe they would've smuggled him out, but you started looking too soon, and they didn't even consider you having keys.'

'How did you know where we were?' I asked. It had never occurred to me to question our last-minute rescue.

'When I saw Melanie pull back in, she acted strange,' he began. 'I had started to wonder where you'd disappeared, too, and her coming back after she'd just left a few minutes before seemed peculiar. She'd gone home to get her tape recorder, you know,' he said, and looked away into the shadows of the room. 'I ran around front, saw you weren't there searching, and decided there was only one place you could be. Really, I was just guessing,' he said frankly. 'You had disappeared as suddenly as Phillip, there were no strange cars around, Melanie tried to act concerned about

Phillip being missing but she wasn't, and she had that damn tape recorder. Perry Allison is very strange and maybe dangerous, but he's also obvious.' Robin reached down to take my hand. 'I had to persuade Mr Crandall in a hurry that we had to raid Bankston's place, but he was game. Even if I had made a mistake, he said, if Bankston was any kind of a man he would realize when a child and woman are missing, anything goes. Jed's a frontier kind of guy.'

'How'd you get in? Didn't Melanie lock the door behind her?'

'Yes, but Mrs Crandall had a key, the key she'd been meaning to bring over to you – I think she kept it because the former tenant used to lock herself out a lot.'

I would have laughed if my side hadn't hurt so much. The emergency room doctor said I'd be able to go home in the next day or two, but my collarbone and two ribs were broken, and I was bruised all over from tumbling down the stairs. There was a spectacularly ugly combination of bruise and scrape covering one cheek.

My mother wanted me to come home with her, but I was going to tell her I'd rather be in my own place, I decided, depending on how sore I was in the morning. Mother had flown into the hospital with every eyelash in place but a wild look in those fine eyes. We had hugged and talked for a while, and she had even shed a few tears (certainly atypical), but when she learned that as far as I knew my apartment was sitting wide open and, for that matter, Bankston's as well since the police were still searching it, she decided I was well enough to leave and flew off to see to safeguarding my property and the disposition of Bankston's.

My mother was a friend of Bankston's mother, and she was terrified of seeing Mrs Waites again. 'That poor woman,' Mother said. 'How can she live with having raised a monster like that? The other Waites children are fine people. What happened? He's known you all your life, Aurora! How could he hurt you? How could he think of hurting a child?'

'Who knows?' I said wearily. 'He was having a great time, the time of his life.' I had no sympathy to spare for Bankston's mother, right now. I had no extra emotion of any kind to throw around. I was drained, exhausted, and in pain. I had bruises and bandages galore. Even Robin's kiss didn't make me feel lecherous, just raised the possibility that someday I might feel that way. He was picking up his jacket now, getting ready to go.

'Robin,' I murmured. I seemed to be drifting down into sleep. He turned, and I realized that he was spent, too. His tall shoulders were stooped, the crinkly mouth drooping down at the corners. Even his flaming hair looked limp.

'You saved me,' I said.

'Nah, Jed Crandall saved you,' he said with an attempt at being off-hand. 'I was just back-up muscle.'

'You saved me. Thank you.' And then I drifted down a long spiral into sleep.

When I woke up again; the clock said 3:30 A.M. Someone else was sitting in the guest chair, someone short and stocky and blond and fast asleep. Arthur's head was slumped forward on his chest and he was snoring a little. I'd have to remember that.

My mouth was dry and my throat sore, so I reached for the cup of water on the bedside table. Naturally, it was just out of reach. I wiggled painfully sideways, still stretching, but then Arthur handed it to me.

'I didn't want to wake you up,' I told him.

'I was just dozing,' he said quietly.

'What happened?'

'Well, we found a box of – mementoes – at Melanie Clark's little rented house.'

'Mementoes?' I asked with dread.

'Yes. Pictures.'

I shook my head. I didn't want to hear more.

He nodded. 'Pretty awful. They photographed Mamie and the Buckleys after they died. And Morrison Pettigrue. Melanie made advances to him, it turns out, and she got him to get undressed that way. Then she killed him, and let Bankston in, and they arranged him.'

'So they confessed?'

'Well, Bankston did. He was proud.'

'So they weren't like Hindley and Brady in the end.'

'No. Melanie tried to kill herself.'

'Oh,' I said after a moment. 'Oh, no.'

'We had a watch on them both, so we caught her fairly quickly. She had taken off her bra and was trying to hang herself with it.'

So grotesque, but at least it showed human feeling.

'She was sorry,' I said softly.

'No,' Arthur said definitely. Sharply. 'She didn't want to be separated from Bankston.'

There seemed to be nothing to say. I handed my cup back to Arthur, who put it on the beside table and automatically refilled it.

'They were mad we hadn't found the weapon Bankston used to kill Mamie Wright. They were sure they'd planted it where we couldn't help but find it. It was a hammer they'd stolen from LeMaster Cane's garage, and it had his initials on it. But as it turns out, some kids had picked it up the same night they killed her, and the kids only got scared and turned it in tonight. Evidently Melanie and Bankston were going to use the golf clubs in the future. After you saw Bankston carrying them into his place – he'd just showered over at Melanie's after killing the Buckleys, and he was going to get the clubs out of his car at a time when he thought no one would be out and about at the apartments – he got scared and ditched the bag, the only distinctive thing about the set, the next dark night. But he kept one or two of the clubs on the off-chance he might need a weapon. Then you and Crusoe found the briefcase . . . We fell down on that one. I don't mind telling you, we wondered about Crusoe for a while after that. Tonight I was ready to shoot him when I saw him charging into Waites's place with a shotgun, but Jed Crandall's wife was running out of her gate saying, "My husband and Mr Crusoe have gone down in Bankston Waites's basement to catch the murderer!" I was half expecting to see Perry Allison down in that basement, standing over Waites's body, and yours, and Phillip's.'

'Where is Perry? Does anyone know?' It was Sally's call that had sent me running out in the dark soon enough to raise the alarm so Bankston and Melanie hadn't a chance to get Phillip away.

'He's checked himself into a mental hospital in the city,' Arthur said.

That was undoubtedly the place for him, but it would be hard on Sally.

'Benjamin?'

'We're sending him to State Psychiatric for evaluation. He also confessed to several other murders we'd definitely solved. Somehow finding Pettigrue's body unhinged him.'

'Oh, Arthur,' I said wearily, and began to cry for so many different reasons I couldn't count them. Arthur stuffed tissues in my hand, and after a while brought over a wet washrag and wiped my face very carefully.

'I guess roller skating tomorrow night is off?' Arthur asked seriously.

I gaped at him in shock until I realized that Arthur – of all people! – was making a joke. I couldn't help smiling. It slid all around my face, but it was a smile.

'I've got to go back to the station, Roe. They're still sorting through the stuff they found in the search, and there's a lot we don't know yet. How Bankston got Mamie Wright to come to the meeting early. Why he let Melanie mail you that candy. He'd bought it for her and brought it back from some convention in St Louis. But she had it in for you in a big way, and she thought you were the one who liked chocolate creams. That was the stupidest crime, since the typewriter's sitting in Gerald Wright's insurance office. We need to ask more questions, so we can back up these confessions with some solid evidence. Bankston has waived his right to have a lawyer present, but sooner or later he's gonna regret it and that'll be the end of the confession. Back to work for me.'

'Okay, Arthur. I was glad to see you come down the stairs tonight.'

'I was glad to see you alive.'

'It was close.'

'I know.' Then he bent over and kissed me, and I thought I was getting to be quite a hussy.

'I'll be back tomorrow,' he promised, and then he was gone, and for the first time in forever I was alone. I was exhausted to the bone, but I could not sleep. I was afraid to close my eyes.

I turned on the television to CNN, to find that I was on it. They were using a picture I'd had made when I joined the library staff. I looked impossibly sweet and young.

I was on the news. I'd be in the books when this case joined others in accounts of true murder cases. I had seen real murderers and I had almost been really murdered. That was something to ponder. I flicked the remote control to off.

I thought of Bankston and Melanie coming into the VFW Hall that night, disappointed to see me, maybe, since they expected I would have received and eaten the chocolate by that time. And I could see them waiting, waiting, for someone there to go looking for Mamie Wright. I remembered how fresh from the shower Bankston had looked when he was carrying in the stolen golf bag the day the Buckleys had been slaughtered. He'd been so shiny and clean . . . I had never, never suspected him. I heard Melanie's voice as she'd said, 'I've always wanted to do this,' and kicked me.

It was too close, too recent, I'd been frightened too deeply.

Of course, this hadn't turned out to be a real puzzler, like the 1928 intrafamilial poisonings in Croyden, England, unsolved to this day. Was Mrs Duff guilty? – Or could it have been . . . I drifted away in sleep.

A Bone to Pick

For Patrick, Timothy, and Julia

Chapter One

In less than a year, I went to three weddings and one funeral. By late May (at the second wedding but before the funeral) I had decided it was going to be the worst year of my life.

The second wedding was actually a happy one from my point of view, but my smile muscles ached all the next day from the anxious grin I'd forced to my lips. Being the daughter of the bride felt pretty peculiar.

My mother and her fiancé strolled between the folding chairs arranged in her living room, ended up before the handsome Episcopalian priest, and Aida Brattle Teagarden became Mrs John Queensland.

In the oddest way, I felt my parents had left home while I had stayed. My father and his second wife, with my half-brother, Phillip, had moved across the country to California in the past year. Now my mother, though she'd still be living in the same town, would definitely have new priorities.

That would be a relief.

So I beamed at John Queensland's married sons and their spouses. One of the wives was pregnant – my mother would be a stepgrandmother! I smiled graciously at Lawrenceton's new Episcopal priest, Aubrey Scott. I oozed goodwill at the real estate salespeople from my mother's business. I grinned at my best friend, Amina Day, until she told me to relax.

'You don't have to smile every second,' she whispered from one corner of her mouth, while the rest of her face paid respectful attention to the cake-cutting ceremony. I instantly rearranged my face into more sober lines, thankful beyond expression that Amina had been able to get a few days off from her job in Houston as a legal secretary. But later, at the reception, she told me my mother's wedding wasn't her only reason for coming back to Lawrenceton for the weekend.

'I'm getting married,' she said shyly, when we found a corner to ourselves. 'I told Mamma and Daddy last night.'

'To – which one?' I said, stunned.

'You haven't been listening to a word I said when I called you!'

Maybe I *had* let the specifics roll over me like a river. Amina had dated so many men. Since she'd reached fourteen, her incredible dating career had only been interrupted by one brief marriage.

'The department store manager?' I pushed my glasses back up on my nose the better to peer up at Amina, who is a very nice five feet, five inches. On good days I say I am five feet.

'No, Roe,' Amina said with a sigh. 'It's the lawyer from the firm across the hall from the place I work. Hugh Price.' Her face went all gooey.

So I asked the obligatory questions: how he'd asked her, how long they'd dated, if his mother was tolerable . . . and the date and location of the ceremony. Amina, a traditionalist, would finally be married in Lawrenceton, and they were going to wait a few months, which I thought was an excellent idea. Her first wedding had been an elopement with myself and the groom's best friend as incompatible attendants.

I was going to be a bridesmaid again. Amina was not the only friend I'd 'stood up' for, but she was the only one I'd stood up for twice. How many times could you be bridesmaid to the same bride? I wondered if the last time I came down the aisle ahead of Amina I would have to use a walker.

Then my mother and John made their dignified exit, John's white hair and white teeth gleaming, and my mother looking as glamorous as usual. They were going to honeymoon for three weeks in the Bahamas.

My mother's wedding day.

I got dressed for the first wedding, the January one, as though I was putting on armor to go into battle. I braided my bushy, wavy brown hair into a sophisticated (I hoped) pattern on the back of my head, put on the bra that maximized my most visible assets, and slid a brand-new gold-and-blue dress with padded shoulders over my head. The heels I was going to wear were ones I'd gotten to go with a dress I'd worn on a date with Robin Crusoe, and I sighed heavily as I slid my feet into them. It had been months since I'd seen Robin, and the day was depressing enough without thinking of him. At least the heels probably hiked me up to five foot two. I put on my makeup with my face as close to the illuminated mirror as I could manage, since without my glasses I can't make out my reflection very well. I put on as much makeup as I felt comfortable with, and then a little more. My round brown eyes got rounder, my lashes got longer, and then I covered them up with my big, round tortoise-shell glasses.

Sliding a precautionary handkerchief into my purse, I eyed myself in the mirror, hoped I looked dignified and unconcerned, and went down the stairs to the kitchen of my town-house apartment to gather up my keys and good coat before sallying forth to that most wretched of obligatory events, the Wedding of a Recent Former Boyfriend.

Arthur Smith and I had met through a club we both attended, Real Murders. He'd helped on the homicide investigation that had followed the murder of one of the club members, and the string of deaths that followed this initial murder. I'd dated Arthur for months after the investigation was over, and our relationship had been my only experience of a red-hot romance. We sizzled together we became something more than a nearly thirty librarian and a divorced policeman.

And then, as suddenly as the fire had flared, it died out, but on his side of the hearth first. I had finally gotten the message – 'I'm continuing this relationship until I can figure out a way to get out without a scene' – and with an immense effort I'd gathered my dignity together and ended our relationship without causing that scene. But it had taken all my emotional energy and willpower, and for maybe six months I'd been crying into my pillow.

Just when I was feeling better and hadn't driven past the police station in a week, I saw the engagement announcement in the *Sentinel*.

I saw green for envy, I saw red for rage, I saw blue for depression. I would never get married, I decided, I would just go to other people's weddings the rest of my life. Maybe I could arrange to be out of town the weekend of the wedding so I wouldn't be tempted to drive past the church.

Then the invitation came in the mail.

Lynn Liggett, Arthur's fiancée and fellow detective, had thrown down the gauntlet. Or at least that's how I interpreted the invitation.

Now, in my blue-and-gold and my fancy hairdo, I had grasped it. I'd picked out an impersonal and expensive plate in Lynn's pattern at the department store and left my card on it, and now I was going to the wedding.

The usher was a policeman I knew from the time I dated Arthur.

'Good to see you,' he said doubtfully. 'You look great, Roe.' He looked stiff and uncomfortable in his tux, but he offered his arm properly. 'Friend of the bride, or friend of the groom?' he asked automatically, and then flushed as red as a beet.

'Let's say friend of the groom,' I suggested gently, and gave myself high marks. Poor Detective Henske marched me down the aisle to an empty seat and dumped me with obvious relief.

I glanced around as little as possible, putting all my energy into looking relaxed and nonchalant, sort of as if I'd just happened to be appropriately dressed and just happened to see the wedding invitation on my way out the door, and decided I'd just drop in. It was all right to look at Arthur when he entered, everyone else was. His pale blond hair was crisp and curly and short, his blue eyes as direct and engaging as ever. He was wearing a gray tux and he looked great. It didn't hurt *quite* as much as I'd thought it would.

When the 'Wedding March' began, everyone rose for the entrance of the bride, and I gritted my teeth in anticipation. I was pretty sure my fixed smile looked more like a snarl. I turned reluctantly to watch Lynn make her entrance. Here she came, swathed in white, veiled, as tall as Arthur, her straight, short hair curled for the occasion. Lynn was almost a foot taller than I, something that had obviously bothered her, but I guessed it wasn't going to bother her anymore.

Then Lynn passed me, and when I saw her in profile I gasped. Lynn was clearly pregnant.

It would be hard to say why this was such a blow; I certainly hadn't wanted to become pregnant while I was dating Arthur, and would have been horrified if I'd been faced with the situation. But I had often thought of marrying him, and I had occasionally thought about babies; most women my age, if they do want to get married, do think about babies. Somehow, just for a little while, it seemed to me that I had been robbed of something.

I spoke to enough people on the way out of the church to be sure my attendance registered and would be reported to the happy couple, and then I skipped the reception. There was no point in putting myself through that. I thought it was pretty stupid of me to have come at all; not gallant, not brave, just dumb.

The funeral came third, a few days after my mother's wedding, and, as funerals go, it was pretty decent. Though it was in early June, the day Jane Engle was buried was not insufferably hot, and it was not raining. The little Episcopal church held a reasonable number of people – I won't say mourners, because Jane's passing was more a time to be marked than a tragic occasion. Jane had been old, and, as it turned out, very ill, though she had told no one. The people in the pews had gone to church with Jane, or remembered her from her years working in the high school library, but she had no family besides one aging cousin, Parnell Engle, who was himself too ill that day to come. Aubrey Scott, the Episcopal priest, whom I hadn't seen since my mother's wedding, was eloquent about Jane's inoffensive life and her charm and intelligence; Jane had certainly had her tart side, too, but the Reverend Mr Scott tactfully included that under 'colorful.' It was not an adjective I would have chosen for silver-haired Jane, never married – like me, I reminded myself miserably, and wondered if this many people would come to my funeral. My eyes wandered over the faces in the pews, all more or less familiar. Besides me, there was one other attendee from Real Murders, the disbanded club in which Jane and I had become friends – LeMaster Cane, a black businessman. He was sitting at the back in a pew by himself.

I made a point of standing by LeMaster at the graveside, so he wouldn't look so lonely. When I murmured that it was good to see him, he replied, 'Jane was the only white person who ever looked at me like she couldn't tell what color I am.' Which effectively shut me up.

I realized that I hadn't known Jane as well as I thought I had. For the first time, I really felt I would miss her.

I thought of her little, neat house, crammed with her mother's furniture and Jane's own books. I remembered Jane had liked cats, and I wondered if anyone had taken over the care of her gold tabby, Madeleine. (The cat had been named for the nineteenth-century Scottish poisoner Madeleine Smith, a favorite murderer of Jane's. Maybe Jane had been more 'colorful' than I'd realized. Not many little old ladies I knew had favorite murderers. Maybe I was 'colorful,' too.)

As I walked slowly to my car, leaving Jane Engle forever in Shady Rest Cemetery – I thought – I heard someone calling my name behind me.

'Miss Teagarden!' panted the man who was hurrying to catch up. I waited, wondering what on earth he could want. His round, red face topped by thinning light brown hair was familiar, but I couldn't recall his name.

'Bubba Sewell,' he introduced himself, giving my hand a quick shake. He had the thickest southern accent I'd heard in a long time. 'I was Miss Engle's lawyer. You are Aurora Teagarden, right?'

'Yes, excuse me,' I said. 'I was just so surprised.' I remembered now that I'd seen Bubba Sewell at the hospital during Jane's last illness.

'Well, it's fortunate you came today,' Bubba Sewell said. He'd caught his breath, and I saw him now as he undoubtedly wanted to present himself: an expensively suited, sophisticated but down-home man in the know. A college-educated good ole boy. His small brown eyes watched me sharply and curiously. 'Miss Engle had a clause in her will that is significant to you,' he said significantly.

'Oh?' I could feel my heels sinking into the soft turf and wondered if I'd have to step out of my shoes and pull them up by hand. It was warm enough for my face to feel damp; of course, my glasses began to slide down my nose. I poked them back up with my forefinger.

'Maybe you have a minute now to come by my office and talk about it?'

I glanced automatically at my watch. 'Yes, I have time,' I said judiciously after a moment's pause. This was pure bluff, so Mr Sewell wouldn't think I was a woman with nothing to do.

Actually, I very nearly was. A cutback in funding meant that, for the library to stay open the same number of hours, some staff had to go part-time. I hoped it was because I was the most recently hired that the first one to feel the ax was me. I was only working eighteen to twenty hours a week now. If I hadn't been living rent free and receiving a small salary as resident manager of one of Mother's apartment buildings (actually a row of four town houses), my situation would have been bleak in the extreme.

Mr Sewell gave me such elaborate directions to his office that I couldn't have gotten lost if I'd tried, and he furthermore insisted I follow him there. The whole way he gave turn signals so far in advance that I almost made the wrong left once. In addition he would wave and point into his rearview mirror, waiting to see me nod every time in acknowledgment. Since I'd lived in Lawrenceton my whole life, this was unnecessary and intensely irritating. Only my curiosity about what he was going to tell me kept me from ramming his rear, and then apologizing picturesquely with tears and a handkerchief.

'Wasn't too hard to find, was it!' he said encouragingly when I got out of my car in the parking lot of the Jasper Building, one of the oldest office buildings in our town and a familiar landmark to me from childhood.

'No,' I said briefly, not trusting myself to speak further.

'I'm up on the third floor,' Lawyer Sewell announced, I guess in case I got lost between the parking lot and the front door. I bit the inside of my lip and boarded the elevator in silence, while Sewell kept up a patter of small talk about the attendance at the funeral, how Jane's loss would affect many, many people, the weather, and why he liked having an office in the Jasper Building (atmosphere . . . much better than one of those prefabricated buildings).

By the time he opened his office door, I was wondering how sharp-tongued Jane could have endured Bubba Sewell. When I saw that he had three employees in his smallish office, I realized he must be more intelligent than he seemed, and there were other unmistakable signs of prosperity – knickknacks from the Sharper Image catalog, superior prints on the walls and leather upholstery on the chairs, and so on. I looked around Sewell's office while he gave some rapid instructions to the well-dressed red-haired secretary who was his first line of defense. She didn't seem like a fool, and she treated him with a kind of friendly respect.

'Well, well, now, let's see about you, Miss Teagarden,' the lawyer said jovially when we were alone.

'Where's that file? Gosh-a-Moses, it's somewhere in this mess here!'

Much rummaging among the papers on his desk. By now I was not deceived. Bubba Sewell for some reason found this Lord Peter Wimsey-like pretense of foolishness useful, but he was not foolish, not a bit.

'Here we are, it was right there all the time!' He flourished the file as though its existence had been in doubt.

I folded my hands in my lap and tried not to sigh obviously. I might have lots of time, but that didn't mean I wanted to spend it as an unwilling audience to a one-man performance.

'Hoo-wee, I'm sure glad you managed to turn it up,' I said.

Bubba Sewell's hands stilled, and he shot me an extremely sharp look from under his bushy eyebrows.

'Miss Teagarden,' he said, dropping his previous good-ole-boy manner completely, 'Miss Engle left you everything.'

*

Those are certainly some of the most thrilling words in the English language, but I wasn't going to let my jaw hit the floor. My hands, which had been clasped loosely in my lap, gripped convulsively for a minute, and I let out a long, silent breath.

'What's everything?' I asked.

Bubba Sewell told me that everything was Jane's house, its contents, and most of her bank account. She'd left her car and five thousand dollars to her cousin Parnell and his wife, Leah, on condition they took Madeleine the cat to live with them. I was relieved. I had never had a pet, and wouldn't have known what to do with the creature.

I had no idea what I should be saying or doing. I was so stunned I couldn't think what would be most seemly. I had done my mild grieving for Jane when I'd heard she'd gone, and at the graveside. I could tell that in a few minutes I was going to feel raw jubilation, since money problems had been troubling me. But at the moment mostly I was stunned.

'Why on earth did she do this?' I asked Bubba Sewell. 'Do you know?'

'When she came in to make her will, last year when there was all that trouble with the club you two were in, she said that this was the best way she knew to make sure someone never forgot her. She didn't want her name up on a building somewhere. She wasn't a' – the lawyer searched for the right words – 'philanthropist. Not a public person. She wanted to leave her money to an individual, not a cause, and I don't think she ever got along well with Parnell and Leah – do you know them?'

As a matter of fact, I am something rare in the South – a church hopper. I had met Jane's cousin and his wife at one of the churches I attended, I couldn't remember which one, though I thought it was one of Lawrenceton's more fundamentalist houses of worship. When they'd introduced themselves I'd asked if they were related to Jane, and Parnell had admitted he was a cousin, though with no great warmth. Leah had stared at me and said perhaps three words during the whole conversation.

'I've met them,' I told Sewell.

'They're old and they haven't had any children,' Sewell told me. 'Jane felt they wouldn't outlast her long and would probably leave all her money to their church, which she didn't want. So she thought and thought and settled on you.'

I thought and thought myself for a little bit. I looked up to find the lawyer eyeing me with speculation and some slight, impersonal disapproval. I figured he thought Jane should have left her money to cancer research or the SPCA or the orphanage.

'How much is in the account?' I asked briskly.

'Oh, in the checking account, maybe three thousand,' he said. 'I have the latest statements in this file. Of course, there are a few bills yet to come from Jane's last stay in the hospital, but her insurance will pick up most of that.'

Three thousand! That was nice. I could finish paying for my car, which would help my monthly bill situation a lot.

'You said "checking account",' I said, after I'd thought for a moment. 'Is there another account?'

'Oh, you bet,' said Sewell, with a return of his former bonhomie. 'Yes, ma'am! Miss Jane had a savings account she hardly ever touched. I tried a couple of times to interest her in investing it or at least buying a CD or a bond, but she said no, she liked her cash in her bank.' Sewell shook his receding hairline several times over this and tilted back in his chair.

I had a vicious moment of hoping it would go all the way over with him in it.

'Could you please tell me how much is in the savings account?' I asked through teeth that were not quite clenched.

Bubba Sewell lit up. I had finally asked the right question. He catapulted forward in his chair to a mighty squeal of springs, pounced on the file, and extracted another bank statement.

'Wel-l-l-l,' he drawled, puffing on the slit envelope and pulling out the paper inside, 'as of last month, that account had in it – let's see – right, about five hundred and fifty thousand dollars.'

Maybe this wasn't the worst year of my life after all.

Chapter Two

I floated out of Bubba Sewell's office, trying not to look as gleeful as I felt. He walked with me to the elevator, looking down at me as if he couldn't figure me out. Well, it was mutual, but I wasn't caring right now, no sirree.

'She inherited it from her mother,' Sewell said. 'Most of it. Also, when her mother died, Miss Engle sold her mother's house, which was very large and brought a great price, and she split the money from that with her brother. Then her brother died and left her his nearly intact share of the house money, plus his estate, which she turned into cash. He was a banker in Atlanta.'

I had money. I had a *lot* of money.

'I'll meet you at Jane's house tomorrow, and we'll have a look around at the contents, and I'll have a few things for you to sign. Would nine-thirty be convenient?'

I nodded with my lips pressed together so I wouldn't grin at him.

'And you know where it is?'

'Yes,' I breathed, thankful the elevator had come at last and the doors were opening.

'Well, I'll see you tomorrow morning, Miss Teagarden,' the lawyer said, setting his black glasses back on his nose and turning away as the doors closed with me inside.

I thought a scream of joy would echo up the elevator shaft, so I quietly but ecstatically said, 'Heehee-heeheehee,' all the way down and did a little jig before the doors opened on the marble lobby.

I managed to get home to the town house on Parson Road without hitting another car, and pulled into my parking place planning how I could celebrate. The young married couple who'd taken Robin's town house, to the left of mine, waved back hesitantly in answer to my beaming hello. The Crandalls' parking space to the right was empty; they were visiting a married son in another town. The woman who'd finally rented Bankston Waite's town house was at work, as always. There was a strange car parked in the second space allotted to my apartment, but since I didn't see anyone I assumed it was a guest of one of the other tenants who didn't know how to read.

I opened my patio gate singing to myself and hopping around happily (I am not much of a dancer) and surprised a strange man in black sticking a note to my back door.

It was a toss-up as to which of us was the more startled.

It took me a moment of staring to figure out who the man was. I finally recognized him as the Episcopal priest who'd performed Mother's wedding and Jane Engle's funeral. I'd talked to him at the wedding reception, but not at this morning's funeral. He was a couple of inches over six feet, probably in his late thirties, with dark hair beginning to gray to the color of his eyes, a neat mustache, and a clerical collar.

'Miss Teagarden, I was just leaving you a note,' he said, recovering neatly from his surprise at my singing, dancing entrance.

'Father Scott,' I said firmly, his name popping into my head at the last second. 'Good to see you.'

'You seem happy today,' he said, showing excellent teeth in a cautious smile. Maybe he thought I was drunk.

'Well, you know I was at Jane's funeral,' I began, but when his eyebrows flew up I realized I'd started at the wrong end.

'Please come in, Father, and I'll tell you why I'm so cheerful when it might seem . . . inappropriate.'

'Well, if you have a minute, I'll come in. Maybe I caught you at a bad time? And please call me Aubrey.'

'No, this is fine. And call me Aurora. Or Roe, most people just call me Roe.' Actually, I'd wanted a little alone time to get used to the idea of being rich, but telling someone would be fun, too. I tried to remember how messy the place was. 'Please come in, I'll make some coffee.' And I just laughed.

He surely thought I was crazy as a loon, but he had to come in now.

'I haven't seen you to talk to since my mother got married,' I babbled, as I twisted my key in the lock and flung open the door into the kitchen and living area. Good, it was quite neat.

'John's a wonderful man and a staunch member of the congregation,' he said, having to look down at me quite sharply now that I was close. Why didn't I ever meet short men? I was doomed to go through life with a crick in my neck. 'John and your mother are still on their honeymoon?'

'Yes, they're having such a good time I wouldn't be surprised if they stayed longer. My mother hasn't taken a vacation in at least six years. You know she owns a real estate business.'

'That's what John told me,' Aubrey Scott said politely. He was still standing right inside the door.

'Oh, I forgot my manners! Please come have a seat!' I tossed my purse on the counter and waved at the matching tan suede love seat and chair in the 'living area,' which lay beyond the 'kitchen area.'

The chair was clearly my special chair, from the brass lamp behind it for reading light to the small table loaded with my current book, a stained coffee mug, and a few magazines. Aubrey Scott wisely chose one end of the love seat.

'Listen,' I said, perching opposite him on the edge of my chair, 'I've got to tell you why I'm so giddy today. Normally I'm not like this at all.' Which was true, more's the pity. 'Jane Engle just left me a bunch of money, and, even though it may sound greedy, I've got to tell you I'm happy as a clam about it.'

'I don't blame you,' he said sincerely. I have noticed that, if there is one thing ministers are good at projecting, it is sincerity. 'If someone had left me a bunch of money, I'd be dancing, too. I had no idea Jane was a – that Jane had a lot to leave anyone.'

'Me either. She never lived like she had money. Let me get you a drink. Coffee? Or maybe a real drink?' I figured I could ask that, him being Episcopal. If he'd been, say, Parnell and Leah Engle's pastor, that question would have earned me a stiff lecture.

'If by real drink you mean one with alcohol, I wouldn't turn one down. It's after five o'clock, and conducting a funeral always drains me. What do you have? Any Seagram's, by any chance?'

'As a matter of fact, yes. What about a seven and seven?'

'Sounds great.'

As I mixed the Seagram's 7 with the 7 Up, added ice, and even produced cocktail napkins and nuts, it finally struck me as odd that the Episcopal priest would come to call. I couldn't exactly say, 'What are you doing here?' but I was curious. Well, he'd get around to it. Most of the preachers in Lawrenceton had had a go at roping me in at one time or another. I am a fairly regular churchgoer, but I seldom go to the same church twice in a row.

It would have been nice to run upstairs to change from my hot black funeral dress to something less formal, but I figured he would run out the back door if I proposed to slip into something comfortable.

I did take off my heels, caked with mud from the cemetery, after I sat down.

'So tell me about your inheritance,' he suggested after an awkward pause.

I couldn't recapture my initial excitement, but I could feel a grin turning up my lips as I told him about my friendship with Jane Engle and Bubba Sewell's approach after the service was over.

'That's amazing,' he murmured. 'You've been blessed.'

'Yes, I have,' I agreed wholeheartedly.

'And you say you weren't a particular friend of Jane's?'

'No. We were friends, but at times a month would go by without our seeing each other. And not thinking anything about it, either.'

'I don't suppose you've had enough time to plan anything to do with this unexpected legacy.'

'No.' And if he suggested some worthy cause, I would really resent it. I just wanted to be in proud ownership of a little house and a big (to me, anyway) fortune, at least for a while.

'I'm glad for you,' he said, and there was another awkward pause.

'Was there anything I could do to help you, did your note say . . . ? ' I trailed off. I tried to manage a look of intelligent expectancy.

'Well,' he said with an embarrassed laugh, 'actually, I . . . this is so stupid, I'm acting like I was in high school again. Actually . . . I just wanted to ask you out. On a date.'

'A date,' I repeated blankly.

I saw instantly that my astonishment was hurting him.

'No, it's not that that's peculiar,' I said hastily. 'I just wasn't expecting it.'

'Because I'm a minister.'

'Well – yes.'

He heaved a sigh and opened his mouth with a resigned expression.

'No, no!' I said, throwing my hands up. 'Don't make an "I'm only human" speech, if you were going to! I was gauche, I admit it! Of course I'll go out with you!'

I felt like I owed it to him now.

'You're not involved in another relationship at the moment?' he asked carefully.

I wondered if he had to wear the collar on dates.

'No, not for a while. In fact, I went to the wedding of my last relationship a few months ago.'

Suddenly Aubrey Scott smiled, and his big gray eyes crinkled up at the corners, and he looked good enough to eat.

'What would you like to do? The movies?'

I hadn't had a date since Arthur and I had split. Anything sounded good to me.

'Okay,' I said.

'Maybe we can go to the early show and go out to eat afterward.'

'Fine. When?'

'Tomorrow night?'

'Okay. The early show usually starts at five if we go to the triplex. Anything special you want to see?'

'Let's get there and decide.'

There could easily be three movies I did not want to see showing at one time, but the chances were at least one of them would be tolerable.

'Okay,' I said again. 'But if you're taking me out to supper, I want to treat you to the movie.'

He looked doubtful. 'I'm kind of a traditional guy,' he said. 'But if you want to do it that way, that'll be a new experience for me.' He sounded rather courageous about it.

After he left, I slowly finished my drink. I wondered if the rules for dating clergymen were different from the rules for dating regular guys. I told myself sternly that clergymen *are* regular guys, just regular guys who professionally relate to God. I knew I was being naive in thinking I had to act differently with Aubrey Scott than I would with another date. If I was so malicious or off-color or just plain wrongheaded that I had to constantly censor my conversation with a minister, then I needed the experience anyway. Perhaps it would be like dating a psychiatrist; you would always worry about what he spotted about you that you didn't know. Well, this date would be a 'learning experience' for me.

What a day! I shook my head as I plodded up the stairs to my bedroom. From being a poor, worried, spurned librarian I'd become a wealthy, secure, datable heiress.

The impulse to share my new status was almost irresistible. But Amina was back in Houston and preoccupied by her upcoming marriage, my mother was on her honeymoon (boy, would I enjoy telling *her*), my coworker Lillian Schmidt would find some way to make me feel guilty about it, and my sort-of-friend Sally Allison would want to put it in the paper. I'd really like to tell Robin Crusoe, my mystery writer friend, but he was in the big city of Atlanta, having decided the commute from Lawrenceton to his teaching position there was too much to handle – or at least that was the reason he'd given me. Unless I could tell him face-to-face, I wouldn't enjoy it. His face was one of my favorites.

Maybe some celebrations are just meant to be private. A big wahoo would have been out of line anyway, since Jane had had to die in order for this celebration to be held. I took off the black dress and put on a bathrobe and went downstairs to watch an old movie and eat half a bag of pretzels and then half a quart of chocolate fudge ripple ice cream.

Heiresses can do anything.

It was raining the next morning, a short summer shower that promised a steamy afternoon. The thunderclaps were sharp and scary, and I found myself jumping at each one as I drank my coffee. After I retrieved the paper (only a little wet) from the otherwise unused front doorstep that faced Parson Road, it began to slow down. By the time I'd had my shower and was dressed and ready for my appointment with Bubba Sewell, the sun had come out and mist began to rise from the puddles in the parking lot beyond the patio. I watched CNN for a while – heiresses need to be well informed – fidgeted with my makeup, ate a banana, and scrubbed the kitchen sink, and then finally it was time to go.

I couldn't figure out why I was so excited. The money wasn't going to be piled in the middle of the floor. I'd have to wait roughly two months to actually be able to spend it, Sewell had said. I'd been in Jane's little house before, and there was nothing so special about it.

Of course, now I owned it. I'd never owned something that big before.

I was independent of my mother, too. I could've made it by myself on my librarian's salary, though it would have been hard, but having the resident manager's job and therefore a free place to live and a little extra salary had certainly made a big difference.

I'd woken several times during the night and thought about living in Jane's house. My house. Or after probate I could sell it and buy elsewhere.

That morning, starting up my car to drive to Honor Street, the world was so full of possibilities it was just plain terrifying, in a happy roller-coaster way.

Jane's house was in one of the older residential neighborhoods. The streets were named for virtues. One reached Honor by way of Faith. Honor was a dead end, and Jane's house was the second from the corner on the right side. The houses in this neighborhood tended to be small – two or three bedrooms – with meticulously kept little yards dominated by large trees circled with flower beds. Jane's front yard was half filled by a live oak on the right side that shaded the bay window in the living room. The driveway ran in on the left, and there was a deep single-car carport attached to the house. A door in the rear of the carport told me there was some kind of storage room there. The kitchen door opened onto the carport, or you could (as I'd done as a visitor) park in the driveway and take the curving sidewalk to the front door. The house was white, like all the others on the street, and there were azalea bushes planted all around the foundation; it would be lovely in spring.

The marigolds Jane had planted around her mailbox had died from lack of water, I saw as I got out of the car. Somehow that little detail sobered me up completely. The hands that had planted those withered yellow flowers were now six feet underground and idle forever.

I was a bit early, so I took the time to look around at my new neighborhood. The corner house, to the right of Jane's as I faced it, had beautiful big climbing rosebushes around the front porch. The one to the left had had a lot added on, so that the original simple lines of the house were obscured. It had been bricked in, a garage with an apartment on top had been connected to the house by a roofed walk, a deck had been tacked on the back. The result was not happy. The last house on the street was next to that, and I remembered that the newspaper editor, Macon Turner, who had once dated my mother, lived there. The house directly across the street from Jane's, a pretty little house with canary yellow shutters, had a realtor's sign up with a big red SOLD slapped across it. The corner house on that side of the street was the one Melanie Clark, another member of the defunct Real Murders club, had rented for a while: now a Big Wheel parked in the driveway indicated children on the premises. One house took up the last two lots on that side, a rather dilapidated place with only one tree in a large yard. It sat blank-faced, the yellowing shades pulled down. A wheelchair ramp had been built on.

At this hour on a summer morning, the quiet was peaceful. But, behind the houses on Jane's side of the street, there was the large parking lot for the junior high school, with the school's own high fence keeping trash from being pitched in Jane's yard and students from using it as a shortcut. I was sure there would be more noise during the school year, but now that parking lot sat empty. By and by, a woman from the corner house on the other side of the street started up a lawn mower and that wonderful summer sound made me feel relaxed.

You planned for this, Jane, I thought. You wanted me to go in your house. You know me and you picked me for this.

Bubba Sewell's BMW pulled up to the curb, and I took a deep breath and walked toward it.

He handed me the keys. My hand closed over them. It felt like a formal investiture. 'There's no problem with you going on and working in this house now, clearing it out or preparing it for sale or whatever you want to do, it belongs to you and no one says different. I've advertised for anyone with claims on the estate to come forward, and so far no one has. But of course we can't spend any of the money,' he admonished me with a wagging finger. 'The house bills are still coming to me as executor, and they will until probate is settled.'

This was like being a week away from your birthday when you were six.

'This one,' he said, pointing to one key, 'opens the dead bolt on the front door. This one opens the punch lock on the front door. This little one is to Jane's safe deposit box at Eastern National, there's a little jewelry and a few papers in it, nothing much.'

I unlocked the door and we stepped in.

'Shit,' said Bubba Sewell in an unlawyerly way.

There was a heap of cushions from the living room chairs

thrown around. I could look through the living room into the kitchen and see similar disorder there.

Someone had broken in.

One of the rear windows, the one in the back bedroom, had been broken. It had been a pristine little room with chaste twin beds covered in white chenille. The wallpaper was floral and unobtrusive, and the glass was easy to sweep up on the hardwood floor. The first things I found in my new house were the dustpan and the broom, lying on the floor by the tall broom closet in the kitchen.

'I don't think anything's gone,' Sewell said with a good deal of surprise, 'but I'll call the police anyway. These people, they read the obituaries in the paper and go around breaking into the houses that are empty.'

I stood holding a dustpan full of glass. 'So why isn't anything missing?' I asked. 'The TV is still in the living room. The clock radio is still in here, and there's a microwave in the kitchen.'

'Maybe you're just plain lucky,' Sewell said, his eyes resting on me thoughtfully. He polished his glasses on a gleaming white handkerchief. 'Or maybe the kids were so young that just breaking in was enough thrill. Maybe they got scared halfway through. Who knows.'

'Tell me a few things.' I sat on one of the white beds and he sat down opposite me. The broken window (the storm this morning had soaked the curtains) made the room anything but intimate. I propped the broom against my knee and put the dustpan on the floor. 'What happened with this house after Jane died? Who came in here? Who has keys?'

'Jane died in the hospital, of course,' Sewell began. 'When she first went in, she still thought she might come home, so she had me hire a maid to come in and clean . . . empty the garbage, clear the perishables out of the refrigerator, and so on. Jane's neighbor to the side, Torrance Rideout – you know him? – he offered to keep her yard mowed for her, so he has a key to the tool and storage room, that's the door at the back of the carport.'

I nodded.

'But that's the only key he had,' the lawyer said, getting back on target. 'Then a few days later, when Jane learned – she wasn't coming home . . .'

'I visited her in the hospital, and she never said a word to me,' I murmured.

'She didn't like to talk about it. What was there to say? she asked me. I think she was right. But anyway . . . I kept the electricity and gas – the heat is gas, everything else is electric – hooked up, but I came over here and unplugged everything but the freezer – it's in the toolroom and it has food in it – and I stopped the papers and started having Jane's mail kept at the post office, then I'd pick it up and take it to her, it wasn't any trouble to me, my mail goes to the post office, too . . .'

Sewell had taken care of everything for Jane. Was this the care of a lawyer for a good client or the devotion of a friend?

'So,' he was saying briskly, 'the little bitty operating expenses for this house will come out of the estate, but I trust you won't mind, we kept it at a minimum. You know when you completely turn off the air or heat into a house, the house just seems to go downhill almost immediately, and there was always the slight chance Jane might make it and come home.'

'No, of course I don't mind paying the electric bill. Do Parnell and Leah have a key?'

'No, Jane was firm about that. Parnell came to me and offered to go through and get Jane's clothes and things packed away, but of course I told him no.'

'Oh?'

'They're yours,' he said simply. 'Everything' – and he gave that some emphasis, or was it only my imagination – 'everything in this house is yours. Parnell and Leah know about their five thousand, and Jane herself handed him the keys to her car two days before she died and let him take it from this carport, but, other than that, *whatever* is in this house' – and suddenly I was alert and very nearly scared – 'is yours to deal with however you see fit.'

My eyes narrowed with concentration. What was he saying that he wasn't really saying?

Somewhere, somewhere in this house, lurked a problem. For some reason, Jane's legacy wasn't entirely benevolent.

After calling the police about the break-in and calling the glass people to come to fix the window, Bubba Sewell took his departure.

'I don't think the police will even show up here since I couldn't tell them anything was missing. I'll stop by the station on my way back to the office, though,' he said on his way out the door.

I was relieved to hear that. I'd met most of the local policemen when I dated Arthur; policemen really stick together. 'There's no point in turning on the air conditioner until that back bedroom window is fixed,' Sewell added, 'but the thermostat is in the hall, when you need it.'

He was being mighty chary with my money. Now that I was so rich, I could fling open the windows and doors and set the thermostat on forty, if I wanted to do something so foolish and wasteful.

'If you have any problems, run into anything you can't handle, you just call me,' Sewell said again. He'd expressed that sentiment several times, in several different ways. But just once he had said, 'Miss Jane had a high opinion of you, that you could tackle any problem that came your way and make a success of it.'

I got the picture. By now I was so apprehensive, I heartily wanted Sewell to leave. Finally he was out the front door, and I knelt on the window seat in the bay window and partially opened the sectioned blinds surrounding it to watch his car pull away. When I was sure he was gone, I opened all the blinds and turned around to survey my new territory. The living room was carpeted, the only room in the house that was, and when Jane had had this done she'd run the carpet right up onto the window seat so that it was seamlessly covered, side, top, and all. There were some hand-embroidered pillows arranged on it, and the effect was very pretty. The carpet Jane had been so partial to was a muted rose with a tiny blue pattern, and her living room furniture (a sofa and two armchairs) picked up that shade of blue, while the lamp shades were white or rose. There was a small color television arranged for easy viewing from Jane's favorite chair. The antique table beside that chair was still stacked with magazines, a strange assortment that summed up Jane – *Southern Living, Mystery Scene, Lear's*, and a publication from the church.

The walls of this small room were lined with freestanding shelves overflowing with books. My mouth watered when I looked at them. One thing I knew Jane and I had shared: we loved books, we especially loved mysteries, and more than anything we loved books about real murders. Jane's collection had always been my envy.

At the rear of the living room was a dining area, with a beautiful table and chairs I believed Jane had inherited from her mother. I knew nothing about antiques and cared less, but the table and chairs were gleaming under a light coating of dust, and, as I straightened the cushions and pushed the couch back to its place against the wall (why would anyone move a couch when he broke into a house?), I was already worried about caring for the set.

At least all the books hadn't been thrown on the floor. Straightening this room actually took only a few moments.

I moved into the kitchen. I was avoiding Jane's bedroom. It could wait.

The kitchen had a large double window that looked onto the backyard, and a tiny table with two chairs was set right in front of the window. Here was where Jane and I had had coffee when I'd visited her, if she hadn't taken me into the living room.

The disorder in the kitchen was just as puzzling. The shallow upper cabinets were fine, had not been touched, but the deeper bottom cabinets had been emptied carelessly. Nothing had been poured out of its container or wantonly vandalized, but the contents had been moved as though the cabinet itself were the object of the search, not possible loot that could be taken away. And the broom closet, tall and thin, had received special attention.

I flipped on the kitchen light and stared at the wall in the back of the closet. It was marred with ' . . . knife gouges, sure as shooting,' I mumbled. While I stooped to reload the cabinet shelves with pots and pans, I thought about those gouges. The breaker-in had wanted to see if there was something fake about the back of the closet; that was the only interpretation I could put on the holes. And only the large bottom cabinets had been disturbed; only the large pieces of furniture in the living room.

So, Miss Genius, he was looking for something large. Okay, 'he' could be a woman, but I wasn't going to the trouble of thinking 'he or she.' 'He' would do very well for now. What large thing could Jane Engle have concealed in her house that anyone could possibly want enough to break in for? Unanswerable until I knew more, and I definitely had the feeling I would know more.

I finished picking up the kitchen and returned to the guest bedroom. The only disturbance there, now I'd cleared up the glass, was to the two single closets, which had been opened and emptied. There again, no attempt had been made to destroy or mutilate the items that had been taken from the closets; they'd just been emptied swiftly and thoroughly. Jane had stored her luggage in one closet, and the larger suitcases had been opened. Out-of-season clothes, boxes of pictures and mementos, a portable sewing machine, two boxes of Christmas decorations . . . all things I had to check through and decide on, but for now it was enough to shovel them all back in. As I hung up a heavy coat, I noticed the walls in these closets had been treated the same way as the broom closet in the kitchen.

The attic stairs pulled down in the little hall that had a bedroom door at each end and the bathroom door in the middle. A broad archway led from this hall back into the living room. This house actually was smaller than my town house by quite a few square feet, I realized. If I moved I would have less room but more independence.

It was going to be hot up in the attic, but it would certainly be much hotter by the afternoon. I gripped the cord and pulled down. I unfolded the stairs and stared at them doubtfully. They didn't look any too sturdy.

Jane hadn't liked to use them either, I found, after I'd eased my way up the creaking wooden stairs. There was very little in the attic but dust and disturbed insulation; the searcher had been up here, too, and an itchy time he must have had of it. A leftover strip of the living room carpet had been unrolled, a chest had its drawers halfway pulled out. I closed up the attic with some relief and washed my dusty hands and face in the bathroom sink. The bathroom was a good size, with a large linen cabinet below which was a half door that opened onto a wide space suitable for a laundry basket to hold dirty clothes. This half closet had received the same attention as the ones in the kitchen and guest bedroom.

The searcher was trying to find a secret hiding place for something that could be put in a drawer but not hidden behind books . . . something that couldn't be hidden between sheets and towels but could be hidden in a large pot. I tried to imagine Jane hiding – a suitcase full of money? What else? A box of – documents revealing a terrible secret? I opened the top half of the closet to look at Jane's neatly folded sheets and towels without actually seeing them. I should be grateful those hadn't been dumped out, too, I mused with half of my brain, since Jane had been a champion folder; the towels were neater than I'd ever get them, and the sheets appeared to have been ironed, something I hadn't seen since I was a child.

Not money or documents; those could have been divided to fit into the spaces that the searcher had ignored.

The doorbell rang, making me jump a foot.

It was only the glass repair people, a husband and wife team I'd called when window problems arose at my mother's apartments. They accepted me being at this address without any questions, and the woman commented when she saw the back window that lots of houses were getting broken into these days, though it had been a rarity when she'd been 'a kid'.

'Those people coming out from the city,' she told me seriously, raising her heavily penciled eyebrows.

'Reckon so?' I asked, to establish my goodwill.

'Oh sure, honey. They come out here to get away from the city, but they bring their city habits with 'em.'

Lawrenceton loved the commuters' money without actually trusting or loving the commuters.

While they tackled removing the broken glass and replacing it, I went into Jane's front bedroom. Somehow entering it was easier with someone else in the house. I am not superstitious, at least not consciously, but it seemed to me that Jane's presence was strongest in her bedroom, and having people busy in another room in the house made my entering her room less . . . personal.

It was a large bedroom, and Jane had a queen-sized four-poster with one bed table, a substantial chest of drawers, and a vanity table with a large mirror comfortably arranged. In the now-familiar way, the double closet was open and the contents tossed out simply to get them out of the way. There were built-in shelves on either side of the closet, and the shoes and purses had been swept from these, too.

There's not much as depressing as someone else's old shoes, when you have the job of disposing of them. Jane had not cared to put her money into her clothes and personal accessories. I could not ever recall Jane wearing anything I noticed particularly, or even anything I could definitely say was brand new. Her shoes were not expensive and were all well worn. It seemed to me Jane had not enjoyed her money at all; she'd lived in her little house with her Penney's and Sears wardrobe, buying books as her only extravagance. And she'd always struck me as content; she'd worked until she'd had to retire, and then come back to substitute at the library. Somehow this all seemed melancholy, and I had to shake myself to pull out of the blues.

What I needed, I told myself briskly, was to return with some large cartons, pack all Jane's clothing away, and haul the cartons over to the Goodwill. Jane had been a little taller than I, and thicker, too; nothing would fit or be suitable. I piled all the flung-down clothes and tossed the shoes on the bed; no point in loading them back into the closet when I knew I didn't need or want them. When that was done, I spent a few minutes pressing and poking and tapping in the closet myself.

It just sounded and felt like a closet to me.

I gave up and perched on the end of the bed, thinking of all the pots and pans, towels and sheets, magazines and books, sewing kits and Christmas ornaments, bobby pins and hair nets, handkerchiefs, that were now mine and my responsibility to do something with. Just thinking of it was tiring. I listened idly to the voices of the couple working in the back bedroom. You would have thought that since they lived together twenty-four hours a day they would've said all they could think of to say, but I could hear one offer the other a comment every now and then. This calm, intermittent dialogue seemed companionable, and I went into kind of a trance sitting on the end of that bed.

I had to be at work that afternoon for three hours, from one to four. I'd have just time to get home and get ready for my date with Aubrey Scott . . . did I really need to shower and change before we went to the movies? After going up in the attic, it would be a good idea. Today was much hotter than yesterday. Cartons . . . where to get some sturdy ones? Maybe the Dumpster behind Wal-Mart? The liquor store had good cartons, but they were too small for clothes packing. Would Jane's bookshelves look okay standing by my bookshelves? Should I move my books here? I could make the guest bedroom into a study. The only person I'd ever had as an overnight guest who didn't actually sleep with me, my half-brother Phillip, lived out in California now.

'We're through, Miss Teagarden,' called the husband half of the team.

I shook myself out of my stupor.

'Send the bill to Bubba Sewell in the Jasper Building. Here's the address,' and I ripped a piece of paper off a tablet Jane had left by the telephone. The telephone! Was it hooked up? No, I found after the repair team had left. Sewell had deemed it an unnecessary expense. Should I have it hooked back up? Under what name? Would I have two phone numbers, one here and one at the town house?

I'd had my fill of my inheritance for one day. Just as I locked the front door, I heard footsteps rustling through the grass and turned to see a barrel-chested man of about forty-five coming from the house to my left.

'Hi,' he said quickly. 'You're our new neighbor, I take it.'

'You must be Torrance Rideout. Thanks for taking such good care of the lawn.'

'Well, that's what I wanted to ask about.' Close up, Torrance Rideout looked like a man who'd once been handsome and still wasn't without the old sex appeal. His hair was muddy brown with only a few flecks of gray, and he looked like his beard would be heavy enough to shave twice a day. He had a craggy face, brown eyes surrounded by what I thought of as sun wrinkles, a dark tan, and he was wearing a green golf shirt and navy shorts. 'My wife, Marcia, and I were real sorry about Jane. She was a real good neighbor and we were sure sorry about her passing.'

I didn't feel like I was the right person to accept condolences, but I wasn't about to explain I'd inherited Jane's house not because we were the best of friends but because Jane wanted someone who could remember her for a good long while. So I just nodded, and hoped that would do.

Torrance Rideout seemed to accept that. 'Well, I've been mowing the yard, and I was wondering if you wanted me to do it one more week until you get your own yardman or mow it yourself, or just whatever you want to do. I'll be glad to do it.'

'You've already been to so much trouble . . .'

'Nope, no trouble. I told Jane when she went in the hospital not to worry about the yard, I'd take care of it. I've got a riding mower, I just ride it on over when I do my yard, and there ain't that much weed eating to do, just around a couple of flower beds. I did get Jane's mower out to do the tight places the riding mower can't get. But what I did want to tell you, someone dug a little in the backyard.'

We'd walked over to my car while Torrance talked, and I'd pulled out my keys. Now I stopped with my fingers on the car door handle. 'Dug up the backyard?' I echoed incredulously.

Come to think of it, that wasn't so surprising. I thought about it for a moment. Okay, something that could be kept in a hole in the ground as well as hidden in a house.

'I filled the holes back in,' Torrance went on, 'and Marcia's been keeping a special lookout since she's home during the day.'

I told Torrance someone had entered the house, and he expressed the expected astonishment and disgust. He hadn't seen the broken window when he'd last mowed the backyard two days before, he told me.

'I do thank you,' I said again. 'You've done so much.'

'No, no,' he protested quickly. 'We were kind of wondering if you were going to put the house on the market, or live in it yourself . . . Jane was our neighbor for so long, we kind of worry about breaking in a new one!'

'I haven't made up my mind,' I said, and left it at that, which seemed to stump Torrance Rideout.

'Well, see, we rent out that room over our garage,' he explained, 'and we have for a good long while. This area is not exactly zoned for rental units, but Jane never minded and our neighbor on the other side, Macon Turner, runs the paper, you know him? Macon never has cared. But new people in Jane's house, well, we didn't know . . .'

'I'll tell you the minute I make up my mind,' I said in as agreeable a way as I could.

'Well, well. We appreciate it, and if you need anything, just come ask me or Marcia. I'm out of town off and on most weeks, selling office supplies believe it or not, but then I'm home every weekend and some afternoons, and, like I said, Marcia's home and she'd love to help if she could.'

'Thank you for offering,' I said. 'And I'm sure I'll be talking to you soon. Thanks for all you've done with the yard.'

And finally I got to leave. I stopped at Burger King for lunch, regretting that I hadn't grabbed one of Jane's books to read while I ate. But I had plenty to think about: the emptied closets, the holes in the backyard, the hint Bubba Sewell had given me that Jane had left me a problem to solve. The sheer physical task of clearing the house of what I didn't want, and then the decision about what to do with the house itself. At least all these thoughts were preferable to thinking of myself yet again as the jilted lover, brooding over the upcoming Smith baby . . . feeling some how cheated by Lynn's pregnancy. It was much nicer to have decisions within my power to make, instead of having them made for me.

Now! I told myself briskly, to ward off the melancholy, as I dumped my cup and wrapper in the trash bin and left the restaurant. Now to work, then home, then out on a real date, and tomorrow get out early in the morning to find those boxes!

I should have remembered that my plans seldom work out.

Chapter Three

Work that afternoon more or less drifted by. I was on the check-out/check-in desk for three hours, making idle conversation with the patrons. I knew most of them by name, and had known them all my life. I could have made their day by telling each and every one of them, including my fellow librarians, about my good fortune, but somehow it seemed immodest. And it wasn't like my mother had died, which would have been an understandable transfer of fortune. Jane's legacy, which was beginning to make me (almost) more anxious than glad, was so inexplicable that it embarrassed me to talk about it. Everyone would find out about it sooner or later . . . mentioning it now would be much more understandable than keeping silent. The other librarians were talking about Jane anyway; she had substituted here after her retirement from the school system and had been a great reader for years. I'd seen several of my co-workers at the funeral.

But I couldn't think of any casual way to drop Jane's legacy into the conversation. I could already picture the eyebrows flying up, the looks that would pass when my back was turned. In ways not yet realized, Jane had made my life much easier. In ways I was just beginning to perceive, Jane had made my life extremely complicated. I decided, in the end, just to keep my mouth shut and take what the local gossip mill had to dish out.

Lillian Schmidt almost shook my resolution when she observed that she'd seen Bubba Sewell, the lawyer, call to me at the cemetery.

'What did he want?' Lillian asked directly, as she pulled the front of her blouse together to make the gap between the buttons temporarily disappear.

I just smiled.

'Oh! Well, he is single – *now* – but you know Bubba's been

married twice,' she told me with relish. The buttons were already straining again.

'Who to?' I asked ungrammatically, to steer her off my own conversation with the lawyer.

'First to Carey Osland. I don't know if you know her, she lives right by Jane . . . you remember what happened to Carey later on, her second husband? Mike Osland? Went out for diapers one night right after Carey'd had that little girl, and never came back? Carey had them search everywhere for that man, she just could not believe he would walk out on her like that, but he must have.'

'But before Mike Osland, Carey was married to Bubba Sewell?'

'Oh, right. Yes, for a little while, no children. Then after a year, Bubba married some girl from Atlanta, her daddy was some big lawyer, everyone thought it would be a good thing for his career.' Lillian did not bother to remember the name since the girl was not a Lawrenceton native and the marriage had not lasted. 'But that didn't work out, she cheated on him.'

I made vague regretful noises so that Lillian would continue.

'Then – hope you enjoy these, Miz Darwell, have a nice day – he started dating your friend Lizanne Buckley.'

'He's dating Lizanne?' I said in some surprise. 'I haven't seen her in quite a while. I've been mailing in my bill instead of taking it by, like I used to.'

Lizanne was the receptionist at the utility company. Lizanne was beautiful and agreeable, slow-witted but sure, like honey making its inexorable progress across a buttered pancake. Her parents had died the year before, and for a while that had put a crease across the perfect forehead and tear marks down the magnolia white cheeks, but gradually Lizanne's precious routine had encompassed this terrible change in her life and she had willed herself to forget the awfulness of it. She had sold her parents' house, bought herself one just like it with the proceeds, and resumed breaking hearts. Bubba Sewell must have been an optimist and a man who worshiped beauty to date the notoriously untouchable Lizanne. I wouldn't have thought it of him.

'So maybe he and Lizanne have broken up, he wants to take you out?' Lillian always got back on the track eventually.

'No, I'm going out with Aubrey Scott tonight,' I said, having thought of this evasion during her recital of Bubba Sewell's marital woes. 'The Episcopal priest. We met at my mother's wedding.'

It worked, and Lillian's high pleasure at knowing this exclusive fact put her in a good humor the rest of the afternoon.

I didn't realize how many Episcopalians there were in Lawrenceton until I went out with their priest.

Waiting in line for the movies I met at least five members of Aubrey's congregation. I tried to radiate respectability and wholesomeness, and kept wishing my wavy bunch of hair had been more cooperative when I'd tried to tame it before he picked me up. It flew in a warm cloud around my head, and for the hundredth time I thought of having it all cut off. At least my navy slacks and bright yellow shirt were neat and new, and my plain gold chain and earrings were good but – plain. Aubrey was in mufti, which definitely helped me to relax. He was disconcertingly attractive in his jeans and shirt; I had some definitely secular thoughts.

The movie we picked was a comedy, and we laughed at the same places, which was heartening. Our compatibility extended through dinner, where a mention of my mother's wedding prompted some reminiscences from Aubrey about weddings that had gone disastrously wrong. 'And the flower girl threw up at my own wedding,' he concluded.

'You've been married?' I said brilliantly. But he'd brought it up on purpose, of course, so I was doing the right thing.

'I'm a widower. She died three years ago of cancer,' he said simply.

I looked at my plate real hard.

'I haven't dated too much since then,' he went on. 'I feel like I'm pretty – inept at it.'

'You're doing fine so far,' I told him.

He smiled, and it was a very attractive smile.

'From what the teenagers in my congregation tell me, dating's changed a lot in the last twenty years, since last I went out on a date. I don't want – I just want to clear the air. You seem a little nervous from time to time about being out with a minister.'

'Well – yes.'

'Okay. I'm not perfect, and I don't expect you to be perfect. Everyone has attitudes and opinions that are not exactly toeing the line spiritually; we're all trying, and it'll take our whole lives to get there. That's what I believe. I also don't believe in premarital sex; I'm waiting for something to change my mind on that issue, but so far it hasn't happened. Did you want to know any of that?'

'As a matter of fact, yes. That's just about exactly what I did want to know.' What surprised me was the amount of relief I felt at the certainty that Aubrey would not try to get me to go to bed with him. Most dates I'd had in the past ten years, I'd spent half the time worried about what would happen when the guy took me home. Especially now, after my passionate involvement with Arthur, it was a load off my mind that Aubrey wouldn't expect me to make a decision about whether or not to go to bed with him. I brightened up and really began to enjoy myself. He didn't discuss his wife again, and I knew I would not introduce the subject.

Aubrey's ban on premarital sex did not include a ban on premarital kissing, I discovered when he walked me to my back door.

'Maybe we can go out again?'

'Give me a call,' I said with a smile.

'Thanks for this evening.'

'Thank *you*.'

We parted with mutual goodwill, and as I scrubbed my face and pulled on my nightgown the next day didn't seem so daunting. I wasn't scheduled to work at the library, so I could work at Jane's house. My house. I couldn't get used to the ownership.

But thinking of the house led to worrying about the break-in, about the holes in the backyard I hadn't yet seen, about the object of this strange search. It must be an object too big to be in the safe deposit box Bubba Sewell had mentioned; besides, he had told me there was nothing much in the box, implying he had seen the contents already.

I drifted off to sleep thinking, Something that couldn't be divided, something that couldn't be flattened . . .

When I woke up in the morning I knew where that something must be hidden.

I felt like I was on a secret mission. After I scrambled into some jeans and a T-shirt and ate some toast, I checked the sketchy contents of my tool drawer. I wasn't sure what I would need. Probably Jane had these same basic things, but I didn't feel like rummaging around until I found them. I ended up with a claw hammer and two screwdrivers, and after a little thought I added a broad-bladed putty knife. I managed to stuff all these in my purse except the hammer, and finally I managed that; but the haft stuck up from the draw-stringed gather. That wouldn't be too obvious, I told myself. I brushed my teeth hastily but didn't bother with makeup, so before eight o'clock I was pulling into the driveway on Honor.

I brought the car right up into the carport and entered through the kitchen door. The house was silent and stuffy. I found the thermostat in the little hall and pushed the switch to 'cool.' The central air hummed into life. I glanced through the rooms hastily; nothing seemed to have been disturbed during the night. I was sweating a little, and my hair kept sticking to my face, so I did track down a rubber band and pull it all back on my neck. I blew out a deep breath, braced my shoulders, and marched into the living room. I raised the blinds around the window seat to get as much light as possible, took out my tools, and began.

Whatever it was, it was in the window seat.

Jane had had it carpeted over, so no one would think of it as a container, but only as a feature of the room, a nice place to put a plant or some pretty pillows or a flower arrangement. The installer had done a good job, and I had a hell of a time prizing up the carpet. I saw Torrance Rideout pull out of his driveway, glance at the house, and drive away to work. A pretty, plump woman walked a fat dachshund down to the end of the street and back, letting the dog perform on my yard, I noticed indignantly. I recognized her, after I thought of it awhile, as I pried and pulled at the rose-colored carpet with its little blue figure. She was Carey Osland, once married to Bubba Sewell, once married to Mike Osland, the man who had decamped in such a spectacularly callous way. Carey Osland must live in the corner house with the big climbing roses by the front porch.

I plugged away, trying not to speculate about what was in the window seat, and finally I loosened enough carpet to grab an edge with both hands and yank.

The bay window really did contain a window seat with a hinged lid. I had been right. So why didn't I feel triumphant?

Whatever was in the house was my problem, Bubba Sewell had said.

Taking a deep breath, I raised the lid and peered into the window seat. The sun streamed down into the seat, bathing its contents with a gentle morning glow. There was a rather yellow pillowcase inside, a pillowcase with something round in it.

I reached in and pulled at the corner of the pillowcase, gingerly working it back and forth, trying not to disturb its contents. But finally I had to pull it off altogether, and the thing that had been in the pillowcase rolled onto its side.

A skull grinned up at me.

'Oh my God,' I said, slamming the lid down and sitting on the seat, covering my face with both trembling hands. The next minute I was in frantic action, lowering those blinds and shutting them, checking to make sure the front door was locked, finding the light switch, and flipping on the overhead light in the suddenly darkened room.

I opened the window seat again, hoping its contents had miraculously changed.

The skull still lay there with its slack-jawed grin.

Then the doorbell rang.

I jumped and squeaked. For a moment I stood indecisively. Then I tossed the tools into the seat with the thing, shut the lid, and yanked the loose carpet back up. It wouldn't settle back into place very well, having been removed so inexpertly, but I did the best I could and then heaped the fancy pillows around the edges to conceal the damage. But the carpet still sagged out a little. I pushed it into place, weighted it down with my purse. It still pouched. I grabbed some books from the shelves and stacked them on the window seat, too. Much better. The carpet stayed in place. The doorbell rang again. I stood for a moment composing my face.

Carey Osland, minus the dachshund, smiled at me in a friendly way when I finally opened the door. Her dark chestnut hair was lightly threaded with gray, but her round, pretty face was unlined. She was wearing a dress that was one step up from a bathrobe, and scuffed loafers.

'Hi, neighbor,' she said cheerfully. 'Aurora Teagarden, isn't it?'

'Yes,' I said, making a huge effort to sound casual and calm.

'I'm Carey Osland, I live in the house with the roses, on the corner,' and she pointed.

'I remember meeting you before, Carey, at a bridal shower, I think.'

'That's right – a long time ago. Whose was it?'

'Come in, come on in . . . Wasn't it Amina's shower, after she eloped?'

'Well, it must have been, 'cause that was when I was working at her mother's dress shop, that's why I got invited. I work at Marcus Hatfield now.'

Marcus Hatfield was the Lord & Taylor of Lawrenceton.

'That's why I'm such a slob now,' Carey went on smilingly. 'I get so tired of being dressed up.'

'Your nails look great,' I said admiringly. I am always impressed by someone who can wear long nails and keep them polished. I was also trying very hard not to think about the window seat, not to even glance in that direction. I had waved Carey to the couch so she'd have her back partially to it when she half-turned to talk to me as I sat in the armchair.

'Oh, honey, they're not real,' Carey said warmly. 'I never could keep my nails from chipping and getting broken . . . So, you and Jane must have been good friends?'

The unexpected change of subject and Carey's very understandable curiosity took me by surprise. My neighbors were definitely not of the big city impersonal variety.

'She left me the house,' I stated, figuring that settled that.

And it did. Carey couldn't think of a single way to get around that one to inquire as to our exact relationship.

I was beginning to wonder about our relationship, myself. Considering the little problem Jane had left me to deal with.

'So, do you plan on living here?' Carey had rallied and was counterattacking with even more directness.

'I don't know.' And I didn't add or explain. I liked Carey Osland, but I needed to be by myself with the thing in the window seat.

'Well' – Carey took a deep breath and released it – 'I guess I'd better be getting ready for work.'

'Thanks for coming by,' I said as warmly as I could. 'I'm sure I'll be seeing you again when I have things more settled here.'

'Like I said, I'm right next door, so if you need me, come on over. My little girl is away at summer camp till this weekend, so I'm all on my own.'

'Thanks so much, I may be taking you up on that,' I said, trying to beam goodwill and neighborliness enough to soften the fact that I did not want a prolonged conversation and I wanted her gone, things I was afraid I'd made offensively obvious.

My sigh of relief was so loud after I'd shut and locked the door behind her that I hoped she wouldn't hear it.

I sank down into the chair again and covered my face with my hands, preparing to think.

Sweet, fragile, silver-haired Jane Engle, school librarian and churchgoer, had murdered someone and put the victim's skull in her window seat. Then she'd had the window seat carpeted over so no one would think to look there for anything. The carpet was in excellent condition, but not new. Jane had lived in that house with a skull in her living room for some years.

That alone would take some hard getting used to.

I should call the police. My hand actually picked up the receiver before I remembered that the phone was disconnected and that I owed Jane Engle. I owed her big-time.

Jane had left me the house and the money and the skull.

I could not call the police and expose Jane to the world as a murderess. She had counted on that.

Drawn irresistibly, I went to the window seat and opened it again.

'Who the hell are you?' I asked the skull. With considerable squeamishness, I lifted it out with both hands. It wasn't white like bones looked in the movies, but brownish. I didn't know if it was a man's or a woman's skull, but the cause of death seemed apparent; there was a hole in the back of the skull, a hole with jagged edges.

How on earth had elderly Jane managed to deliver such a blow? Who could this be? Perhaps a visitor had fallen and bashed the back of his head on something, and Jane had been afraid she'd be accused of killing the person? That was a familiar and almost comforting plot to a regular mystery reader. Then I thought in a muddled way of *Arsenic and Old Lace*. Perhaps this was a homeless person, or a solitary old man with no family? But Lawrenceton was not large enough for a missing person to go unnoticed, I thought. At least I couldn't recall such a case for years.

Not since Carey Osland's husband had left to pick up diapers and had never returned.

I almost dropped the skull. Oh my Lord! Was this Mike Osland? I put the skull down on Jane's coffee table carefully, as if I might hurt it if I wasn't gentle. And what would I do with it now? I couldn't put it back in the window seat, now that I'd loosened the carpet and made the place conspicuous, and there was no way I could get the carpet to look as smooth as it had been. Maybe now that the house had been burgled, I could hide the skull in one of the places the searcher had already looked?

That raised a whole new slew of questions. Was this skull the thing the searcher had been looking for? If Jane had killed someone, how did anyone else know about it? Why come looking now? Why not just go to the police and say, 'Jane Engle has a skull in her house somewhere, I'm certain.' No matter how crazy they'd sound, that was what most people would do. Why had this person done otherwise?

This added up to more questions than I answered at the library in a month. Plus, those questions were a lot easier to answer. 'Can you recommend a good mystery without any, you know, sex, for my mother?' was a lot easier to answer than 'Whose skull is sitting on my coffee table?'

Okay, first things first. Hide the skull. I felt removing it from the house would be safest. (I say 'felt' because I was pretty much beyond reasoning.)

I got a brown Kroger bag from the kitchen and eased the skull into it. I put a can of coffee in another bag, figuring two bags were less conspicuous than one. After rearranging the window seat as best I could, I looked at my watch. It was ten o'clock, and Carey Osland should be at work. I'd seen Torrance Rideout leaving, but, according to what he'd told me the day before, his wife should be at home unless she was running errands.

I peeked through the blinds. The house across from Torrance Rideout's was as still as it had been the day before. The one across from Carey Osland's had two small children playing in the side yard next to Faith Street, a good distance away. All clear. But, even as I watched, a you-do-it moving van pulled up in front of the house across the street.

'Oh, great,' I muttered. 'Just great.' After a moment, though, I decided that the moving van would be far more interesting than my departure if anyone was watching. So, before I could worry about it, I grabbed up my purse and my two paper bags and went out the kitchen door into the carport.

'Aurora?' called a voice incredulously.

With a strong feeling that fate was dealing harshly with me, I turned to the people climbing out of the moving van, to see that my former lover, burglary detective Arthur Smith, and his bride, homicide detective Lynn Liggett, were moving in across the street.

Chapter Four

From being bizarre and upsetting, my day had moved into surrealistic. I walked on legs that didn't feel like my own toward two police detectives, my purse slung on my shoulder, a can of coffee in the bag in my right hand, a perforated skull in the bag in my left. My hands began sweating. I tried to force a pleasant expression on my face, but had no idea what I had achieved.

Next they're going to say, I thought, they're going to say – *What's in the bag?*

The only plus to meeting up with the very pregnant Mrs Smith at this moment was that I was so worried about the skull I was not concerned about the awkward personal situation I'd landed in. But I *was* aware – acutely – that I had on no makeup and my hair was restrained with a rubber band.

Arthur's fair skin flushed red, which it did when he was embarrassed, or angry, or – well, no, don't think about that. Arthur was too tough to embarrass easily, but he was embarrassed now.

'Are you visiting here?' Lynn asked hopefully.

'Jane Engle died,' I began to explain. 'Arthur, you remember Jane?'

He nodded. 'The Madeleine Smith expert.'

'Jane left me her house,' I said, and a childish part of me wanted to add, 'and lots and lots of money.' But a more mature part of my mind vetoed it, not only because I was carrying a skull in a bag and didn't want to prolong this encounter, but because money was not a legitimate score over Lynn acquiring Arthur. My modern brain told me that a married woman had no edge over an unmarried woman, but my primitive heart knew I would never be 'even' with Lynn until I married, myself.

It was a fragmented day in Chez Teagarden.

The Smiths looked dismayed, as well they might. Moving into their little dream home, baby on the way – baby very much on the way – and then the Old Girlfriend appears right across the street.

'I'm not sure whether or not I'll live here,' I said before they could ask me. 'But I'll be in and out the next week or two getting things straightened out.' Could I ever possibly straighten this out?

Lynn sighed. I looked up at her, really seeing her for the first time. Lynn's short brown hair looked lifeless, and, far from glowing with pregnancy, as I'd heard women did, Lynn's skin looked blotchy. But when she turned and looked back at the house, she looked very happy.

'How are you feeling, Lynn?' I asked politely.

'Pretty good. The ultrasound showed the baby is a lot further along than we thought, maybe by seven weeks, so we kind of rushed through buying the house to be sure we got in here and got everything settled before the baby comes.'

Just then, thank goodness, a car pulled up behind the van and some men piled out. I recognized them as police pals of Arthur's and Lynn's; they'd come to help unload the van.

Then I realized the man driving the car, the burly man about ten years older than Arthur, was Jack Burns, a detective sergeant, and one of the few people in the world I truly feared.

Here were at least seven policemen, including Jack Burns, and here I was with . . . I was scared to even think it with Jack Burns around. His zeal for dealing out punishment to wrongdoers was so sharp, his inner rage burned with such a flame, I felt he could smell concealment and falsehood. My legs began shaking. I was afraid someone would notice. How on earth did his two teenagers manage a private life?

'Good to have seen you,' I said abruptly. 'I hope your moving day goes as well as they ever do.'

They were relieved the encounter was over, too. Arthur gave me a casual wave as a shout from one of his buddies who had opened the back of the van summoned him to work.

'Come see us when we get settled in,' Lynn told me insincerely as I said good-bye and turned to leave.

'Take it easy, Lynn,' I called over my shoulder, as I crossed the street to my car on rubbery legs.

I put the bags carefully in the front seat and slid in myself. I wanted to sit and shake for a while, but I also wanted to get the hell out of there, so I turned the key in the ignition, turned on the air-conditioning full blast, and occupied a few moments buckling my seat belt, patting my face (which was streaming with sweat) with my handkerchief, anything to give me a little time to calm down before I had to drive. I backed out with great care, the unfamiliar driveway, the moving van parked right across the street, and the people milling around it making the process even more hazardous.

I managed to throw a casual wave in the direction of the moving crew, and some of them waved back. Jack Burns just stared; I wondered again about his wife and children, living with that burning stare that seemed to see all your secrets. Maybe he could switch it off at home? Sometimes even the men under his command seemed leery of him, I'd learned while I was dating Arthur.

I drove around aimlessly for a while, wondering what to do with the skull. I hated to take it to my own home; there was no good hiding place. I couldn't throw it away until I'd decided what to do with it. My safe deposit box at the bank wasn't big enough, and probably Jane's wasn't either: otherwise, surely she would have put the skull there originally. Anyway, the thought of carrying the paper bag into the bank was enough to make me giggle hysterically. I sure couldn't keep it in the trunk of my car. I checked with a glance to make sure my inspection sticker was up-to-date; yes, thank God. But I could be stopped for some traffic violation at any time; I never had been before, but, the way things were going today, it seemed likely.

I had a key to my mother's house, and she was gone.

No sooner had the thought crossed my mind than I turned at the next corner to head there. I wasn't happy about using

Mother's house for such a purpose, but it seemed the best thing to do at the time.

The air was dead and hot inside Mother's big home on Plantation Drive. I dashed up the stairs to my old room without thinking, then stood panting in the doorway trying to think of a good hiding place. I kept almost nothing here anymore, and this was really another guest bedroom now, but there might be something up in the closet.

There was: a zippered, pink plastic blanket bag in which Mother always stored the blue blankets for the twin beds in this room. No one would need to get blankets down in this weather. I pulled over the stool from the vanity table, climbed up on it, and unzipped the plastic bag. I took my Kroger bag, with its gruesome contents, and inserted it between the blankets. The bag would no longer zip with the extra bulk.

This was getting grotesque. Well, more grotesque.

I took out one of the blankets and doubled up the other one in half the blanket bag, leaving the other half for the skull. The bag zipped, and it didn't look too lumpy, I decided. I pushed it to the back of the shelf.

Now all I had to dispose of was a blanket. The chest of drawers was only partially full of odds and ends; Mother kept two drawers empty for guests. I stuffed the blanket in one, slammed it shut, then pulled it right back open. She might need the drawer. John was moving all his stuff in when they got back from their honeymoon. I felt like sitting on the floor and bursting into tears. I stood holding the damn blanket indecisively, thinking wildly of burning it or taking it home with me. I'd rather have the blanket than the skull.

The bed, of course. The best place to hide a blanket is on a bed.

I stripped the bedspread off, pitched the pillow on the floor, and fitted the blanket smoothly on the mattress. In a few more minutes, the bed looked exactly like it had before.

I dragged myself out of Mother's house and drove over to my own place. It seemed as though I'd gone two days without sleep, when in fact it was only now getting close to lunchtime. At least I didn't have to go to work this afternoon.

I poured myself a glass of iced tea and for once loaded it with sugar. I sat in my favorite chair and sipped it slowly. It was time to think.

Fact One. Jane Engle had left a skull concealed in her house. She might not have told Bubba Sewell what she'd done, but she'd hinted to him that all was not well – but that I would handle it.

Question: How had the skull gotten in Jane's house? Had she murdered its – owner? occupant?

Question: Where was the rest of the skeleton?

Question: How long ago had the head been placed in the window seat?

Fact Two. Someone else knew or suspected that the skull was in Jane's house. I could infer that this someone else was basically law-abiding since the searcher hadn't taken the chance to steal anything or vandalize the house to any degree. The broken window was small potatoes compared with what could have been wreaked on Jane's unoccupied house. So the skull was almost certainly the sole object of the search. Unless Jane had – horrible thought – something else hidden in her house?

Question: Would the searcher try again, or was he perhaps persuaded that the skull was no longer there? The yard had been searched, too, according to Torrance Rideout. I reminded myself to go in the backyard the next time I went to the house and see what had been done there.

Fact Three. I was in a jam. I could keep silent forever, throw the skull in a river, and try to forget I ever saw it; that approach had lots of appeal right now. Or I could take it to the police and tell them what I'd done. I could already feel myself shiver at the thought of Jack Burns's face, to say nothing of the incredulity on Arthur's. I heard myself stammer, 'Well, I hid it at my mother's house.' What kind of excuse could I offer for my strange actions? Even I could not understand exactly why I'd done what I'd done, except that I'd acted out of some kind of loyalty to Jane, influenced to some extent by all the money she'd left me.

Then and there, I pretty much ruled out going to the police unless something else turned up. I had no idea what my legal position was, but I couldn't imagine what I'd done so far was so very bad legally. Morally was another question.

But I definitely had a problem on my hands.

At this inopportune moment the doorbell rang. It was a day of unwelcome interruptions. I sighed and went to answer it, hoping it was someone I wanted to see. Aubrey?

But the day continued its apparently inexorable downhill slide. Parnell Engle and his wife, Leah, were at my front door, the door no one ever uses because they'd have to park in the back – ten feet from my back door – and then walk all the way around the whole row of town houses to the front to ring the bell. Of course, that was what Parnell and Leah had done.

'Mr Engle, Mrs Engle,' I said. 'Please come in.'

Parnell opened fire immediately. 'What did we do to Jane, Miss Teagarden? Did she tell you what we did to her that offended her so much she left everything to you?'

I didn't need this.

'Don't you start, Mr Engle,' I said sharply. 'Just don't you start. This is *not a good day*. You got a car, you got some money, you got Madeleine the cat. Just be glad of it and leave me alone.'

'We were Jane's own blood kin—'

'Don't start that with me,' I snapped. I was simply beyond trying to be polite. 'I don't know why she left everything to me, but it doesn't make me feel very lucky right now, believe me.'

'We realize,' he said with less whine and more dignity, 'that Jane did express her true wishes in her will. We know that she was in her good senses up until the end and that she made her choice knowing what she was doing. We're not going to contest the will. We just don't understand it.'

'Well, Mr Engle, neither do I.' Parnell would have had that skull at the police station in less time than it takes to talk about it. But it was good news that they weren't small-minded enough to contest the will and thereby cause me endless trouble and heartache. I knew Lawrenceton. Pretty soon people would start saying, Well, why *did* Jane Engle leave everything to a young woman she didn't even know very well? And speculation would run rampant; I couldn't even imagine the things people would make up to explain Jane's inexplicable legacy. People were going to talk anyway, but any dispute about the will would put a nasty twist on that speculation.

Looking at Parnell Engle and his silent wife, with their dowdy clothes and grievances, I suddenly wondered if I'd gotten the money to pay me for the inconvenience of the skull. What Jane had told Bubba Sewell might have been just a smoke screen. She may have read my character thoroughly, almost supematurally thoroughly, and known I would keep her secret.

'Good-bye,' I said to them gently, and closed my front door slowly, so they couldn't say I'd slammed it on them. I locked it carefully, and marched to my telephone. I looked up Bubba Sewell's number and dialed. He was in and available, to my surprise.

'How's things going, Miss Teagarden?' he drawled.

'Kind of bumpy, Mr Sewell.'

'Sorry to hear that. How can I be of assistance?'

'Did Jane leave me a letter?'

'What?'

'A letter, Mr Sewell. Did she leave me a letter, something I'm supposed to get after I've had the house a month, or something?'

'No, Miss Teagarden,'

'Not a cassette? No tape of any kind?'

'No, ma'am.'

'Did you see anything like that in the safe deposit box?'

'No, no, can't say as I did. Actually, I just rented that box after Jane became so ill, to put her good jewelry in.'

'And she didn't tell you what was in the house?' I asked carefully.

'Miss Teagarden, I have no idea what's in Miss Engle's house,' he said definitely. Very definitely.

I stopped, baffled. Bubba Sewell didn't want to know. If I told him, he might have to do something about it, and I hadn't yet decided what should be done.

'Thanks,' I said hopelessly. 'Oh, by the way . . .' And I told him about Parnell and Leah's visit.

'He said for sure they weren't going to contest?'

'He said they knew that Jane was in her right mind when she made her will, that they just wanted to know why she left everything the way she did.'

'But he didn't talk about going to court or getting his own lawyer?'

'No.'

'Let's just hope he meant it when he said he knew Jane was in her right mind when she made her will.'

On that happy note we told each other good-bye.

I returned to my chair and tried to pick up the thread of my reasoning. Soon I realized I'd gone as far as I could go.

It seemed to me that if I could find out who the skull had belonged to, I'd have a clearer course to follow. I could start by finding out how long the skull had been in the window seat. If Jane had kept the bill from the carpet layers, that would give me a definite date, because the skull had for sure been in the window seat when the carpet was installed over it. And it hadn't been disturbed since.

That meant I had to go back to Jane's house.

I sighed deeply.

I might as well have some lunch, collect some boxes, and go to work at the house this afternoon as I'd planned originally.

This time yesterday I'd been a woman with a happy future; now I was a woman with a secret, and it was such a strange, macabre secret that I felt I had GUILTY KNOWLEDGE written on my forehead.

The unloading across the street was still going on. I saw a large carton labeled with a picture of a baby crib being carried in, and almost wept. But I had other things to do today than beat myself over the head with losing Arthur. That grief had a stale, preoccupied feel to it.

The disorder in Jane's bedroom had to be cleared away before I could think about finding her papers. I carried in my boxes, found the coffeepot, and started the coffee (which I'd brought back, since I had carried it away in the morning) to perking. The house was so cool and so quiet that it almost made me drowsy. I turned on Jane's bedside radio; yuck, it was on the easy listening station. I found the public radio station after a second's search, and began to pack clothes to Beethoven. I searched each garment as I packed, just on the off chance I would find something that would explain the hidden skull. I just could not believe Jane would leave me this problem with no explanation.

Maybe she'd thought I'd never find it?

No, Jane had thought I'd find it sooner or later. Maybe not this soon. But sometime. Perhaps, if it hadn't been for the break-in and the holes in the backyard (and here I reminded myself again to check them), I wouldn't have worried about a thing, no matter how mysterious some of Bubba Sewell's statements had been.

Suddenly I thought of the old saw 'You don't look a gift horse in the mouth.' I recalled the skull's grin all too clearly, and I began laughing.

I had to laugh at something.

It didn't take quite as long as I expected to pack Jane's clothes. If something had struck my fancy, it wouldn't have bothered me to keep it; Jane had been a down-to-earth woman, and in some ways I supposed I was, too. But I saw nothing I wanted to keep except a cardigan or two, so anonymous that I wouldn't be constantly thinking, I am wearing Jane's clothes. So all the dresses and blouses, coats and shoes and skirts that had been in the closet were neatly boxed and ready to go to the Goodwill, with the vexing exception of a robe that slipped from its hanger to the floor. Every box was full to the brim, so I just left it where it fell. I loaded the boxes into my car trunk, then decided to take a break by strolling into the backyard and seeing what damage had been done there.

Jane's backyard was laid out neatly. There were two concrete benches, too hot to sit on in the June sun, placed on either side of a concrete birdbath surrounded by monkey grass. The monkey grass was getting out of hand, I noticed. Someone else had thought so, too; a big chunk of it had been uprooted. I'd dealt with monkey grass before and admired the unknown gardener's persistence. Then it came to me that this was one of the 'dug up' spots that Torrance Rideout had filled in for me. Looking around me more carefully, I saw a few more; all were around bushes, or under the two benches. None were out in the middle of the grass, which was a relief. I had to just shake my head over this; someone had seriously thought Jane had dug a hole out in her yard and stuck the skull in it? A pretty futile search after all this time Jane had had the skull.

That was a sobering thought. Desperate people are not gentle.

As I mooched around the neat little yard, counting the holes around the bushes that had screened the unattractive school fence from Jane's view, I became aware of movement in the Rideouts' backyard. Minimal movement. A woman was sunbathing on the huge sun deck in a lounge chair, a woman with a long, slim body already deeply browned and semiclad in a fire engine red bikini. Her chin-length, dyed, pale blond hair was held back by a matching band, and even her fingernails seemed to be the same shade of red. She was awfully turned out for sunbathing on her own deck, presuming this was Marcia Rideout.

'How are you, new neighbor?' she called languidly, a slim brown arm raising a glass of iced tea to her lips. This was the movement I'd glimpsed.

'Fine,' I lied automatically. 'And you?'

'Getting along, getting by.' She beckoned with a lazy wave. 'Come talk for a minute.'

When I was settled in a chair beside her, she extended a thin hand and said, 'Marcia Rideout.'

'Aurora Teagarden,' I murmured as I shook her hand, and the amusement flitted across her face and vanished. She pulled off her opaque sunglasses and gave me a direct look. Her eyes were dark blue, and she was drunk, or at least on her way there. Maybe she saw something in my face, because she popped the sunglasses right back on. I tried not to peer at her drink; I suspected it was not tea at all, but bourbon.

'Would you like something to drink?' Marcia Rideout offered.

'No thanks,' I said hastily.

'So you inherited the house. Think you'll like living there?'

'I don't know if I will live there,' I told her, watching her fingers run up and down the dripping glass. She took another sip.

'I drink sometimes,' she told me frankly.

I really couldn't think of anything to say.

'But only when Torrance isn't coming home. He has to spend the night on the road sometimes, maybe once every two weeks or so. And those days he's not coming home to spend the night, I drink. Very slowly.'

'I expect you get lonely,' I offered uncertainly.

She nodded. 'I expect I do. Now, Carey Osland on the other side of you, and Macon Turner on the other side of me, *they* don't get lonely. Macon sneaks over there through the backyards, some nights.'

'He must be an old-fashioned guy.' There was nothing to prevent Macon and Carey from enjoying each other's company. Macon was divorced and Carey was, too, presumably, unless Mike Osland was dead . . . and that reminded me of the skull, which I had enjoyed forgetting for a moment.

My comment struck Marcia Rideout as funny. As I watched her laugh, I saw she had more wrinkles than I'd figured, and I upped her age by maybe seven years. But from her body you sure couldn't tell it.

'I didn't used to have such a problem with being lonely,' Marcia said slowly, her amusement over. 'We used to have people renting this apartment.' She waved in the direction of the garage with its little room on top. 'One time it was a high school teacher, I liked her. Then she got another job and moved. Then it was Ben Greer, that jerk that works at the grocery chopping meat – you know him?'

'Yeah. He is a jerk.'

'So I was glad when he moved. Then we had a housepainter, Mark Kaplan . . .' She seemed to be drifting off, and I thought her eyes closed behind the dark glasses.

'What happened to him?' I asked politely.

'Oh. He was the only one who ever left in the night without paying the rent.'

'Gosh. Just skipped out? Bag and baggage?' Maybe another candidate for the skull?

'Yep. Well, he took some of his stuff. He never came back for the rest. You sure you don't want a drink? I have some real tea, you know.'

Unexpectedly, Marcia smiled, and I smiled back.

'No, thanks. You were saying about your tenant?'

'He ran out. And we haven't had anyone since. Torrance just doesn't want to fool with it. The past couple of years, he's gotten like that. I tell him he must be middle-aged. He and Jane and their big fight over that tree!'

I followed Marcia's pointing red-tipped finger. There was a tree just about midway between the houses. It had a curiously lopsided appearance, viewed from the Rideouts' deck.

'It's just about straddling the property line,' Marcia said. She had a slow, deep voice, very attractive. 'You won't believe, if you've got any sense, that people could fight about a tree.'

'People can fight about anything. I've been managing some apartments, and the tizzy people get into if someone uses their parking space!'

'Really, I can believe it. Well, as you can see, the tree is a little closer to Jane's house . . . your house.' Marcia took another sip from her drink. 'But Torrance didn't like those leaves, he got sick of raking them. So he talked to Jane about taking the tree down. It wasn't shading either house, really. Well, Jane had a fit. She really got hot. So Torrance just cut the branches that were over our property line. Ooo, Jane stomped over here the next day, and she said, "Now, Torrance Rideout, that was petty. I have a bone to pick with you." I wonder what the origin of that saying is? You happen to know?'

I shook my head, fascinated with the little story and Marcia's digression.

'There wasn't any putting the branches back, they were cut to hell,' said Marcia flatly, her southern accent roughening. 'And somehow Torrance got Jane calmed down. But things never were the same after that, between Torrance and Jane. But Jane and I still spoke, and we were on the board of the orphans' home together. I liked her.'

I had a hard time picturing Jane that angry. Jane had been a pleasant person, even sweet occasionally, always polite; but she was also extremely conscious of personal property, rather like my mother. Jane didn't have or want much in the way of things, but what she had was hers absolutely, not to be touched by other hands without proper permission being asked and granted. I saw from Marcia's little story how far that sense of property went. I was learning a lot about Jane now that it was too late. I hadn't known she'd been on the board of the orphans' home, actually and less bluntly named Mortimer House.

'Well,' Marcia continued slowly, 'at least the past couple of years they'd been getting along fine, Jane and Torrance . . . she forgave him, I guess. I'm sleepy now.'

'I'm sorry you had the trouble with Jane,' I said, feeling that somehow I should apologize for my benefactress. 'She was always such an intelligent, interesting person.' I stood to leave; Marcia's eyes were closed behind her sunglasses, I thought.

'Shoot, the fight she had with Torrance was nothin', you should have heard her and Carey go to it.'

'When was that?' I asked, trying to sound indifferent.

But Marcia Rideout was asleep, her hand still wrapped around her drink.

I trudged back to my task, sweating in the sun, worried about Marcia burning since she'd fallen asleep on the lounge. But she'd been slathered with oil. I made a mental note to look out the back from time to time to see if she was still there.

It was hard for me to picture Jane being furious with anyone and marching over to tell him about it. Of course, I'd never owned property. Maybe I would be the same way now. Neighbors could get very upset over things uninvolved people would laugh about. I remembered my mother, a cool and elegant Lauren Bacall type, telling me she was going to buy a rifle and shoot her neighbor's dog if it woke her up with its barking again. She had gone to the police instead and gotten a court order against the dog's owner after the police chief, an old friend, had come to her house and sat in the dark listening to the dog yapping one night. The dog's owner hadn't spoken to Mother since, and in fact had been transferred to another city, without the slightest sign of their mutual disgust slackening.

I wondered what Jane had fought with Carey about. It was hard to see how this could relate to my immediate problem, the skull; it sure wasn't the skull of Carey Osland or Torrance Rideout. I couldn't imagine Jane killing the Rideouts' tenant, Mark whatever-his-name-was, but at least I had the name of another person who might be The Skull.

Back in my house once again – I was practicing saying 'my house' – I began to search for Jane's papers. Everyone has some cache of canceled checks, old receipts, car papers, and tax stuff. I found Jane's in the guest bedroom, sorted into floral-patterned cardboard boxes by year. Jane kept everything, and she kept all those papers for seven years, I discovered. I sighed, swore, and opened the first box.

Chapter Five

I plugged in Jane's television and listened to the news with one ear while I went through Jane's papers. Apparently all the papers to do with the car had already been handed over to Parnell Engle, for there were no old inspection receipts or anything like that. It would have helped if Jane had kept all these papers in some kind of category, I told myself grumpily, trying not to think of my own jumble of papers in shoe boxes in my closet.

I'd started with the earliest box, dated seven years ago. Jane had kept receipts that surely could be thrown away now: dresses she'd bought, visits by the bug-spray man, the purchase of a telephone. I began sorting as I looked, the pile of definite discards getting higher and higher.

There's a certain pleasure in throwing things away. I was concentrating contentedly, so it took me awhile to realize I was hearing some kind of sound from outside. Someone seemed to be doing something to the screen door in the kitchen. I sat hunched on the living room floor, listening with every molecule. I reached over and switched off the television. Gradually I relaxed. Whatever was being done, it wasn't being done surreptitiously. Whatever the sound was, it escalated.

I stiffened my spine and went to investigate. I opened the wooden door cautiously, just as the noise repeated. Hanging spread-eagled on the screen door was a very large, very fat orange cat. This seemed to explain the funny snags I'd noticed on the screen when I went in the backyard earlier.

'Madeleine?' I said in amazement.

The cat gave a dismal yowl and dropped from the screen to the top step. Unthinkingly, I opened the door, and Madeleine was in in a flash.

'You wouldn't think a cat so fat could move so fast,' I said.

Madeleine was busy stalking through her house, sniffing and rubbing her side against the door frames.

To say I was in a snit would be putting it mildly. This cat was now Parnell and Leah's. Jane knew I was not partial to pets, not at all. My mother had never let me have one, and gradually her convictions about pet hygiene and inconvenience had influenced me. Now I would have to call Parnell, talk with him again, either take the cat to him or get him to come get the cat . . . she would probably scratch me if I tried to put her in my car . . . another complication in my life. I sank into one of the kitchen chairs and rested my head on my hands dismally.

Madeleine completed her house tour and came and sat in front of me, her front paws neatly covered by her plumy tail. She looked up at me expectantly. Her eyes were round and gold and had a kind of stare that reminded me of Arthur Smith's. That stare said, 'I am the toughest and the baddest, don't mess with me.' I found myself giving a halfhearted chuckle at Madeleine's machisma. Suddenly she crouched, and in one fluid movement shifted her bulk from the floor to the table – where Jane *ate*! I thought, horrified.

She could stare at me more effectively there. Growing impatient at my stupidity, Madeleine butted her golden head against my hand. I patted her uncertainly. She still seemed to be waiting for something. I tried to picture Jane with the cat, and I seemed to recall she'd scratched the animal behind the ears. I tried that. A deep rumble percolated somewhere in Madeleine's insides. The cat's eyes half-closed with pleasure. Encouraged by this response, I kept scratching her gently behind the ears, then switched to the area under her chin. This, too, was popular.

I grew tired of this after a while and stopped. Madeleine stretched, yawned, and jumped heavily down from the table. She walked over to one of the cabinets and sat in front of it, casting a significant look over her shoulder at me. Fool that I am, it took me a few minutes to get the message. Madeleine gave a soprano yowl. I opened the bottom cabinet, and saw only the pots and pans I'd reloaded the day before. Madeleine kept her stare steady. She seemed to feel I was a slow learner. I looked in the cabinets above the counter and found some canned cat food. I looked down at Madeleine and said brightly, 'This what you wanted?' She yowled again and began to pace back and forth, her eyes never leaving the black and green can. I hunted down the electric can opener, plugged it in, and used it. With a flourish, I set the can down on the floor. After a moment's dubious pause – she clearly wasn't used to eating from a can – Madeleine dived in. After a little more searching, I filled a plastic bowl with water and put it down by the can. This, too, met with the cat's approval.

I went to the phone to call Parnell, my feet dragging reluctantly. But of course I hadn't had the phone hooked up. I reminded myself again I'd have to do something about that, and looked at the cat, now grooming herself with great concentration. 'What am I going to do with you?' I muttered. I decided I'd leave her here for the night and call Parnell from my place. He could come get her in the morning. Somehow I hated to put her outside; she was an inside cat for the most part, I seemed to remember Jane telling me . . . though frankly I'd often tuned out when Jane chatted about the cat. Pet owners could be such bores. Madeleine would need a litter box; Jane had had one tucked away beside the refrigerator. It wasn't there now. Maybe it had been taken to the vet's where Madeleine had been boarded during Jane's illness. It was probably sitting uselessly at the Engles' house now.

I poked around in the trash left in Jane's room from my cleaning out the closet. Sure enough, there was a box of the appropriate size and shape. I put it in the corner by the refrigerator in the kitchen, and as Madeleine watched with keen attention I opened cabinets until I found a half-full bag of cat litter.

I felt rather proud of myself at handling the little problem the cat presented so quickly; though, when I considered, it seemed Madeleine had done all the handling. She had gotten back to her old home, gained entrance, been fed and watered, and had a toilet provided her, and now she jumped up on Jane's armchair in the living room, curled into a striped orange ball, and went to sleep. I watched her for a moment enviously, then I sighed and began sorting papers again.

In the fourth box I found what I wanted. The carpet had been installed three years ago. So the skull had become a skull sometime before that. Suddenly I realized what should have been obvious. Of course Jane had not killed someone and put his head in the window seat fresh, so to speak. The skull had already been a skull, not a head, before Jane had sealed it up. I was willing to concede that Jane obviously had a side unknown to me, or to anyone, though whoever had searched the house must at least suspect it. But I could not believe that Jane would live in a house with a decomposing head in the window seat. Jane had not been a monster.

What had Jane been? I pulled up my knees and wrapped my arms around them. Behind me, Madeleine, who had observed Jane longer than anyone, yawned and rearranged herself.

Jane had been a woman in her late seventies with silver hair almost always done up in a regal chignon. She had never worn slacks, always dresses. She had had a lively mind – an intelligent mind – and good manners. She had been interested in true crime, at a safe distance; her favorite cases were all Victorian or earlier. She had had a mother who was wealthy and who had held a prominent place in Lawrenceton society, and Jane had behaved as though she herself had neither. She had inherited from somewhere, though, a strong sense of property. But as far as the liberation of women went – well, Jane and I had had some discussions on that. Jane was a traditionalist, and though as a working woman she had believed in equal pay for equal work, some of the other tenets of the women's movement were lost on her. 'Women don't have to confront men, honey,' she'd told me one time. 'Women can always think their way around them.' Jane had not been a forgiving person, either; if she got really angry and did not receive an adequate apology, she held a grudge a good long while. She was not even aware of grudge holding, I'd observed; if she had been, she would have fought it, like she'd fought other traits in herself she didn't think were Christian. What else had Jane been? Conventionally moral, dependable, and she'd had an unexpectedly sly sense of humor.

In fact, wherever Jane was now, I was willing to bet she was looking at me and laughing. Me, with Jane's money and Jane's house and Jane's cat and Jane's skull.

After sorting more papers (I might as well finish what I've begun, I thought), I got up to stretch. It was raining outside, I discovered to my surprise. As I sat on the window seat and looked out the blinds, the rain got heavier and heavier and the thunder started to boom. The lights came on across the street in the little white house with yellow shutters, and through the front window I could see Lynn unpacking boxes, moving slowly and awkwardly. I wondered how having a baby felt, wondered if I would ever know. Finally, for no reason that I could discern, my feelings for Arthur ended, and the pain drained away. Tired of poring over receipts left from a life that was over, I thought about my own life. Living by myself was sometimes fun, but I didn't want to do it forever, as Jane had. I thought of Robin Crusoe, the mystery writer, who had left town when my romance with Arthur had heated up. I thought of Aubrey Scott. I was tired of being alone with my bizarre problem. I was tired of being alone, period.

I told myself to switch mental tracks in a hurry. There was something undeniably pleasant about being in my own house watching the rain come down outside, knowing I didn't have to go anywhere if I didn't want to. I was surrounded by books in a pretty room, I could occupy myself however I chose. Come on, I asked myself bravely, what do you choose to do? I almost chose to start crying, but instead I jumped up, found Jane's Soft Scrub, and cleaned the bathroom. A place isn't really yours until you clean it. Jane's place became mine, however temporarily, that afternoon. I cleaned and sorted and threw away and inventoried. I opened a can of soup and heated it in my saucepan on my stove. I ate it with my spoon. Madeleine came into the kitchen when she heard me bustling around and jumped up to watch me eat. This time I was not horrified. I looked over the book I'd pulled from Jane's shelves and addressed a few remarks to Madeleine while I ate.

It was still raining after I'd washed the pot and the spoon and the bowl, so I sat in Jane's chair in the living room, watching the rain and wondering what to do next. After a moment, the cat heaved herself up onto my lap. I wasn't quite sure how I felt about this liberty on the cat's part, but I decided I'd give it a try. I stroked the smooth fur tentatively and heard the deep percolation start up. What I needed, I decided, was to talk to someone who knew Lawrenceton in depth, someone who knew about Carey Osland's husband and the Rideouts' tenant. I'd been assuming the skull came from someone who lived close by, and suddenly I realized I'd better challenge that assumption.

Why had I thought that? There had to be a reason. Okay – Jane couldn't transport a body any distance. I just didn't think she'd been strong enough. But I remembered the hole in the skull and shuddered, feeling distinctly queasy for a moment. She'd been strong enough to do that. Had Jane herself cut off the head? I couldn't even picture it. Granted, Jane's bookshelves, like mine, were full of accounts about people who had done horrible things and gone unsuspected for long periods of time, but I just couldn't admit Jane might be like that. Something wasn't adding up.

It just might be my own dearly held assumptions and preconceptions. Jane, after all, was a Little Old Lady.

I was worn out physically and mentally. It was time to go back to my place. I unseated the cat, to her disgust, and filled her water dish, while making a mental note to call Parnell. I stuffed my car full of things to throw or give away, locked up, and left.

For Christmas, my mother had given me an answering machine, and its light was blinking when I let myself into my kitchen. I leaned against the counter while I punched the button to hear my messages.

'Roe, this is Aubrey. Sorry I didn't catch you in. I'll talk to you later. See you at church tomorrow?'

Ah oh. Tomorrow was Sunday. Maybe I should go to the Episcopal church. But since I didn't always go there, wouldn't it look a little pointed to show up right after I'd had a date with the pastor? On the other hand, here he was inviting me personally, and I'd hurt his feelings if I didn't show . . . oh hell.

'Hi, honey! We're having such a good time John and I decided to stay for a few more days! Stop by the office and make sure everyone's busy, okay? I'll be calling Eileen, but I think it would impress everyone if you went yourself. Talk to you later! Wait till you see my tan!'

Everyone at Mother's office knew that I was strictly an underling, and that I didn't know jack about the real estate business, though it wasn't uninteresting. I just didn't want to work full-time for Mother. Well, I was glad she was having a great time on her second (literally) honeymoon, and I was glad she'd finally taken a vacation of any sort. Eileen Norris, her second-in-command, was probably ready for Mother to come back. Mother's force of character and charm really smoothed things over.

'Roe, this is Robin.' I caught my breath and practically hugged the answering machine so I wouldn't miss a word. 'I'm leaving tonight for maybe three weeks in Europe, traveling cheap and with no reservations, so I don't know where I'll be when. I won't be working at the university next year. James Artis is over his heart attack. So I'm not sure what I'll be doing. I'll get in touch when I come back. Are you doing okay? How's Arthur?'

'He's married,' I said to the machine. 'He married someone else.'

I rummaged in my junk drawer frantically. 'Where's the address book? Where's the damn book?' I muttered. My scrabbling fingers finally found it, I searched through it, got the right page, punched in numbers frantically.

Ring. Ring. 'Hello?' a man said.

'Robin?'

'No, this is Phil. I'm subleasing Robin's apartment. He's left for Europe.'

'Oh, no,' I wailed.

'Can I take a message?' the voice asked, tactfully ignoring my distress.

'So he's going to be coming back to that apartment when he returns? For sure?'

'Yep, his stuff is all here.'

'Are you reliable? Can you give him a message in three weeks, or whenever he comes back?'

'I'll try,' the voice said with some amusement.

'This is important,' I warned him. 'To me, anyway.'

'Okay, shoot. I've got a pencil and paper right here.'

'Tell Robin,' I said, thinking as I spoke, 'that Roe, R-O-E, is fine.'

'Roe is fine,' repeated the voice obediently.

'Also say,' I continued, 'that Arthur married Lynn.'

'Okay, got it . . . anything else?'

'No, no thank you. That's all. Just as long as he knows that.'

'Well, this is a fresh legal pad, and I've labeled it "Robin's Messages," and I'll keep it here by the phone until he comes back,' said Phil's voice reassuringly.

'I'm sorry to sound so – well, like I think you'll throw it in the wastebasket – but this is the only way I have to get in touch with him.'

'Oh, I understand,' said Phil politely. 'And really, he will get this.'

'Thanks,' I said weakly. 'I appreciate it.'

'Good-bye,' said Phil.

'Parnell? This is Aurora Teagarden.'

'Oh. Well, what can I do for you?'

'Madeleine showed up at Jane's house today.'

'That dang cat! We've been looking for her high and low. We missed her two days ago, and we were feeling real bad, since Jane was so crazy about that durn animal.'

'Well, she came home.'

'We sure got a problem. She won't stay here, Aurora. We've caught up with her twice when she started off, but we can't keep chasing after her. As a matter of fact, we're leaving town to-morrow for two weeks, going to our summer place at Beaufort,

South Carolina, and we were going to check her back in the vet's, just to make sure everything went okay. Though animals mostly take care of themselves.'

Take care of themselves? The Engles expected pampered Madeleine to catch her own fish and mice for two weeks?

'Is that right?' I said, letting incredulity drip from my voice. 'No, I expect she can stay at the house for that two weeks. I can feed her when I go over there and empty her litter box.'

'Well,' said Parnell doubtfully, 'her time's almost up.'

The cat was dying? Oh my Lord. 'That's what the vet said?' I asked in amazement.

'Yes, ma'am,' Parnell said, sounding equally amazed.

'She sure looks fat for a cat that sick,' I said doubtfully.

I could not understand why Parnell Engle suddenly began laughing. His laugh was a little hoarse and rusty, but it was from the belly.

'Yes, ma'am,' he agreed with a little wheeze of joy, 'Madeleine is fat for a cat that's so sick.'

'I'll keep her then,' I said uncertainly.

'Oh, yes, Miss Teagarden, thanks. We'll see you when we come back.'

He was still barely controlling his chuckles when he hung up. I put down the receiver and shook my head. There was just no accounting for some people.

Chapter Six

As I retrieved my Sunday paper from my seldom-used front doorstep, I could tell it was already at least 83 degrees. The paper predicted 98 for the day, and I thought its forecast was modest. My central air was already humming. I showered and reluctantly put my hair up in hot curlers, trying to bring order to chaos. I poured my coffee and ate breakfast (a microwaved sweet roll) while I burrowed through the news. I love Sunday mornings, if I get up early enough to really enjoy my paper. Though I have my limits: I will only read the society section if I think my mother will be in it, and I will not read anything about next season's fashions. Amina Day's mom owned a women's clothing shop she had named Great Day, and I pretty much let her tell me what to buy. Under Mrs Day's influence I'd begun to weed out my librarian clothes, my solid-color interchangeable blouses and skirts. My wardrobe was a bit more diverse now.

The paper exhausted, I padded up the stairs and washed my glasses in the sink. While they dried, I squinted myopically into my closet. What was suitable for the girlfriend of the minister? Long sleeves sounded mandatory, but it was just too hot. I scooted hangers along the bar, humming tunelessly to myself. Shouldn't the girlfriend of the minister be perky but modest? Though perhaps, at nearly thirty, I was a bit old to be perky.

For a dizzying moment I imagined all the clothes I could buy with my inheritance. I had to give myself a little shake to come back to reality and review my wardrobe of the here and now. Here we go! A sleeveless navy blue shirtwaist with big white flowers printed on it. It had a full skirt and a white collar and belt. Just the thing, with my white purse and sandals.

All dressed, with my makeup on, I popped on my glasses and

surveyed the result. My hair had calmed down enough to be conventional, and the sandals made my legs look longer. They were hell to walk in, though, and my tolerance time for the high heels would expire right after church.

I walked as quickly as I safely could from my back door across the patio, out the gate in the fence around it, to the car under the long roof that sheltered all tenants' cars. I unlocked the driver's door and flung it open to let the heat blast escape. After a minute I climbed in, and the air conditioner came on one second after the motor. I had worked too hard on my appearance to arrive at the Episcopal church with sweat running down my face.

I accepted a bulletin from an usher and seated myself a carefully calculated distance from the pulpit. The middle-aged couple on the other end of the pew eyed me with open interest and gave me welcoming smiles. I smiled back before becoming immersed in figuring out the hymn and prayer book directions. A loud chord signaled the entrance of the priest, acolyte, lay reader, and choir, and I rose with the rest of the congregation.

Aubrey was just beautiful in his vestments. I drifted into an intoxicating daydream of myself as a minister's wife. It felt very odd to have kissed the man conducting the service. Then I got too involved in managing the prayer book to think about Aubrey for a while. One thing about the Episcopalians, they can't go to sleep during the service unless they're catnappers. You have to get up and down too often, and shake people's hands, and respond, and go up to the altar rail for communion. It's a busy service, not a spectator sport like in some churches. And I believed I had been to every church in Lawrenceton, except maybe one or two of the black ones.

I tried to listen with great attention to Aubrey's sermon, since I would surely have to make an intelligent comment later. To my pleasure, it was an excellent sermon, with some solid points about people's business relationships and how they should conform to religious teachings, too, just as much as personal relationships. And he didn't use a single sports simile! I kept my eyes carefully downcast when I went up to take communion, and tried to think about God rather than Aubrey when he pressed the wafer into my hand.

As we were folding up our kneelers, I saw one of the couples who had spoken to Aubrey while he and I were in line at the movies. They gave me a smile and wave, and huddled to talk to the man and woman with whom I'd been sharing a pew. After that, I was beamed on even more radiantly, and the movie couple introduced me to the pew couple, who asked me about twenty questions as rapidly as they could so they'd have the whole scoop on the pastor's honey.

I felt like I was flying under false colors – we'd only had one date. I began to wish I hadn't come, but Aubrey'd asked me, and I had enjoyed the service. It seemed now I had to pay for it, since there was no quick exit. The crowd had bottlenecked around the church door, shaking hands and exchanging small talk with Aubrey.

'What a good sermon,' I told him warmly, when it was finally my turn. My hand was taken in both of his for a moment, pressed and released. A smooth gesture, in one quick turn showing me I was special, yet not presuming too much.

'Thanks, and thanks for coming,' he said. 'If you're going to be home this afternoon, I'll give you a call.'

'If I'm not there, just leave a message on my machine and I'll call you back. I may have to go over to the house.'

He understood I meant Jane's house, and nodded, turning to the old lady behind me in line with a happy 'Hi, Laura! How's the arthritis?'

Leaving the church parking lot, I felt a distinct letdown. I guess I had hoped Aubrey would ask me to Sunday lunch, a big social event in Lawrenceton. My mother always had me over to lunch when she was home, and I wondered, not for the first time, if she'd still want me to come over when she and John Queensland got back from their honeymoon. John belonged to the country club. He might want to take Mother out there.

I was so dismal by the time I unlocked my back door that I was actually glad to see the message light blinking on the answering machine.

'Hi, Roe. It's Sally Allison. Long time no see, kiddo! Listen, what's this I hear about you inheriting a fortune? Come have lunch with me today if this catches you in time, or give me a call when you can, we'll set up a time.'

I opened the phone book to the A's, looked up Sally's number, and punched the right buttons.

'Hello!'

'Sally, I just got your message.'

'Great! You free for lunch since your mom is still out of town?'

Sally knew *everything*.

'Well, yes, I am. What do you have in mind?'

'Oh, come on over here. Out of sheer boredom, I have cooked a roast and baked potatoes and made a salad. I want to share it with someone.'

Sally was a woman on her own, like me. But she was divorced, and a good fifteen years older.

'Be there in twenty minutes, I need to change. My feet are killing me.'

'Well, wear whatever you see when you open your closet. I have on my oldest shorts.'

'Okay, bye.'

I shucked off the blue and white dress and those painful sandals. I pulled on olive drab shorts and a jungle print blouse and my huaraches and pounded back down the stairs. I made it to Sally's in the twenty minutes.

Sally is a newspaper reporter, the veteran of an early runaway marriage that left her with a son to raise and a reputation to make. She was a good reporter, and she'd hoped (a little over a year ago) that reporting the multiple murders in Lawrenceton would net her a better job offer from Atlanta; but it hadn't happened. Sally was insatiably curious and knew everyone in town, and everyone knew that, to get the straight story on anything, Sally was the person to see. We'd had our ups and downs as friends, the ups having been when we were both members of Real Murders, the downs having mostly been at the same time Sally was trying to make a national, or at least regional, name for herself. She'd sacrificed a lot in that bid for a life in the bigger picture, and, when the bid hadn't been taken up, she'd had a hard time. But now Sally was mending her fences locally, and was as plugged in to the Lawrenceton power system as she ever had been. If her stories being picked up by the wire services hadn't gotten her out of the town, it had certainly added to her power in it.

I had always seen Sally very well dressed, in expensive suits and shoes that lasted her a very long time. When I reached her house, I saw Sally was a woman who put her money on her back, as the saying goes. She had a little place not quite as nice as Jane's, in a neighborhood where the lawns weren't kept as well. Her car, which hadn't been washed in weeks, sat in dusty splendor uncovered by carport or garage. Getting in it would be like climbing in an oven. But the house itself was cool enough, no central air but several window air conditioners sending out an icy stream that almost froze the sweat on my forehead.

Sally's hair was as perfect as ever. It looked like it could be taken off and put on without one bronze curl being dislodged. But instead of her usual classic suits, Sally was wearing a pair of cutoffs and an old work shirt.

'Girl, it's hot!' she exclaimed as she let me in. 'I'm glad I don't have to work today.'

'It's a good day to stay inside,' I agreed, looking around me curiously. I'd never been in Sally's house before. It was obvious she didn't give a damn about decor. The couch and armchairs were covered by throws that looked very unfortunate, and the cheap coffee table had rings on top. My resident manager's eye told me that the whole place needed painting. But the bookcase was wonderfully stuffed with Sally's favorite Organized Crime books, and the smell coming from the kitchen was delicious. My mouth watered.

Of course I was going to have to pay for my dinner with information, but it just might be worth it.

'Boy, that smells good! When's it going to be on the table?'

'I'm making the gravy now. Come on back and talk to me while I stir. Want a beer? I've got some ice cold.'

'Sure, I'll take one. It's the "ice cold" that does it.'

'Here, drink some ice water first for your thirst. Then sip the beer for your pleasure.'

I gulped down the glass of ice water and twisted the cap off the beer. Sally had put out one of those round plastic grippers without my even having to ask. I closed my eyes to appreciate the beer going down my throat. I don't drink beer any other time of the year, but summer in the South is what beer was made for. Very cold beer. 'Ooo,' I murmured blissfully.

'I know. If I didn't watch out, I could drink a whole sixpack while I cooked.'

'Can I set the table or anything?'

'No, I already got everything done, I think. Soon as this gravy is ready – whoa, let me look at the biscuits – yep, they're nice and brown – we'll be ready to eat. Did I get the butter out?'

I scanned the table, which at least was a few feet from the stove. Sally must have been burning up over there.

'It's here,' I reassured her.

'Okay, here we go. Roast, biscuits, baked potatoes, a salad, and for dessert' – Sally took off a cake cover with a flourish – 'red velvet cake!'

'Sally, you're inspired. I haven't had red velvet cake in ten years.'

'My mama's recipe.'

'Those are always the best. You're so smart.' A good southern compliment that could mean almost anything, but this time I meant it quite sincerely. I am not a person who often cooks whole meals for herself. I know single people are supposed to cook full meals, lay the table, and act like they had company, really – but how many single people actually do it? Like Sally, when I cook a big meal, I want someone else to appreciate it and enjoy it.

'So, what's this about you and the man of the cloth?'

Closing in for the kill already. 'Sally, you need to wait till I've eaten something,' I said. Was the roast worth it?

'What?'

'Oh Sally, it's really nothing. I've had one date with Aubrey Scott, we went to the movies. We had a nice time, and he asked me to come to the church today, which I did.'

'Did you now? How was the sermon?'

'Real good. He's got brains, no doubt about it.'

'You like him?'

'Yes, I like him, but that's it. What about you, Sally, are you dating anyone in particular?'

Sally was always so busy asking other people questions, she hardly ever got asked any herself. She looked quite pleased.

'Well, since you ask, I am.'

'Do tell.'

'This is gonna sound funny, but I'm dating Paul Allison.'

'Your husband's brother?'

'Yes, that Paul Allison,' she said, shaking her head in amazement at her own folly.

'You take my breath away.' Paul Allison was a policeman, a detective about ten years older than Arthur – not much liked by Arthur or Lynn, if I remembered correctly. Paul was a loner, a man never married who did not join in the police force camaraderie with much gusto. He had thinning brown hair, broad shoulders, sharp blue eyes, and a suggestion of a gut. I had seen him at many parties I'd attended while I dated Arthur, but I'd never seen him with Sally.

'How long has this been going on?' I asked.

'About five months. We were at Arthur and Lynn's wedding, I tried to catch you then, but you left the church before I could. I didn't see you at the reception?'

'I had the worst headache, I thought I was starting the flu. I just went on home.'

'Oh, it was just another wedding reception. Jack Burns had too much to drink and wanted to arrest one of the waiters he remembered having brought in before on drug charges.'

I was even more glad I'd missed it now.

'How's Perry?' I asked reluctantly, after a pause. I was sorry to bring poor, sick Perry up, but courtesy demanded it.

'Thanks for asking,' she said. 'So many people don't even want to, because he's mentally sick instead of having cancer or something. But I do want people to ask, and I go see him every week. I don't want people to forget he's alive. Really, Roe, people act like Perry's dead because he's mentally ill.'

'I'm sorry, Sally.'

'Well, I do appreciate your asking. He's better, but he's not ready to get out yet. Maybe in two more months. Paul's been going with me to see Perry the past three or four times.'

'He must really love you, Sally,' I said from my heart.

'You know,' she said, and her face brightened, 'I really think he does! Bring your plate over, I think everything's ready.'

We served ourselves from the stove, which was fine with me. Back at the table, we buttered our biscuits and said our little prayer, and dug in like we were starving.

'I guess,' I began after I had told Sally how good everything was, 'that you want to hear about Jane's house.'

'Am I as transparent as all that? Well, I did hear something, you know how gossip gets around, and I thought you would rather me ask you and get it straight than let all this talk around town get out of hand.'

'You know, you're right. I would rather you get it right and get it out on the gossip circuits. I wonder who's started the talk?'

'Uh, well . . .'

'Parnell and Leah Engle,' I guessed suddenly.

'Right the first time.'

'Okay, Sally. I am going to give you a gossip exclusive. There's no way this could be a story in the paper, but you see everyone in town, and you can give them the straight scoop from the horse's mouth.'

'I am all ears,' Sally said with a perfectly straight face.

So I told her an amended and edited account. Leaving out the cash amount, of course.

'Her savings, too?' Sally said enviously. 'Oh, you lucky duck. And it's a lot?'

Glee rolled over me suddenly as it did every now and then

when I forgot the skull and remembered the money. I nodded with a canary-full grin.

Sally closed her eyes in contemplation of the joy of having a lot of money all of a sudden.

'That's great,' she said dreamily. 'I feel good just knowing someone that's *happened* to. Like winning the lottery.'

'Yeah, except Jane had to die for me to get it.'

'My God, girl, she was old as the hills anyway.'

'Oh, Sally, Jane wasn't so old as people go nowadays. She was in her seventies.'

'That is plenty old. I won't last so long.'

'I hope you do,' I said mildly. 'I want you to make me some more biscuits sometimes.'

We talked some more about Paul Allison, which seemed to make Sally quite happy. Then I asked her about Macon Turner, her boss.

'I understand he's seeing my new maybe-neighbor, Carey Osland,' I said casually.

'They are hot and heavy and have been,' Sally said, with a wise nod. 'That Carey is really appealing to the opposite sex. She has had quite a dating – and marriage – history.'

I understood Sally exactly. 'Really?'

'Oh, yes. First she was married to Bubba Sewell, back when he was nothing, just a little lawyer right out of school. Then that fell through, and she married Mike Osland, and by golly one night he goes out to get diapers and never comes home. Everyone felt so sorry for her when her husband left, and, having been in something of the same position, I did feel for her. But at the same time, I think he might have had some reason to take off.'

My attention sharpened. A number of instant scenarios ran through my head. Carey's husband kills Carey's lover, then flees. The lover could have been Mark Kaplan, the Rideouts' vanished tenant, or some unknown. Or maybe Mike Osland could be the skull, reduced to that state by Carey's lover or Carey.

'But she has a little girl at home,' I said in the interest of fairness.

'Wonder what she tells that little girl when she has overnight company?' Sally helped herself to more roast.

I disliked this turn of the conversation. 'Well, she was very nice to me when she came over to welcome me to the neighborhood,' I stated, flatly enough to end that line of conversation. Sally shot me a look and asked if I wanted more roast.

'No thanks,' I said, giving a sigh of repletion. 'That was so good.'

'Macon really has been more agreeable at the office since he began dating Carey,' Sally said abruptly. 'He started seeing her after his son went away, and it just helped him deal with it a lot. Maybe Carey having somebody leave her, she was able to help Macon out.'

'What son?' I didn't remember Mother mentioning any son during the time she'd dated Macon.

'He has a boy in his late teens or early twenties by now, I guess. Macon moved here after he got divorced, and the boy moved here with him, maybe seven years ago now. After a few months, the boy – his name was Edward, I think – anyway, he decided he was just going to take some savings his mother had given him and take off. He told Macon he was going to India or some such place, to contemplate or buy drugs or something. Some crazy thing. Of course, Macon was real depressed, but he couldn't stop him. The boy wrote for a while, or called, once a month . . . but then he stopped. And Macon hasn't seen hide nor hair of that child since then.'

'That's terrible,' I said, horrified. 'Wonder what happened to the boy?'

Sally shook her head pessimistically. 'No telling what could happen to him wandering by himself in a country where he didn't even speak the language.'

Poor Macon. 'Did he go over there?'

'He talked about it for a while, but when he wrote the State Department they advised him against it. He didn't even know where Edward had been when he disappeared . . . Edward could have wandered anywhere after he wrote the last letter Macon got.

I remember someone from the embassy there went to the last place Edward wrote from and, according to what they told Macon, it was sort of a dive with lots of Europeans coming and going, and no one there remembered Edward, or at least that's what they were saying.'

'That's awful, Sally.'

'Sure is. I think Perry being in the mental hospital is better than that, I really do. At least I know where he is!'

Incontrovertible truth.

I stared into my beer bottle. Now I'd heard of one more missing person. Was a part of Edward Turner's last remains in my mother's pink blanket bag? Since Macon told everyone he'd heard from the boy since Edward had left, Macon would have to be the guilty one. That sounded like the end of a soap opera. 'Tune in tomorrow for the next installment,' I murmured.

'It is like a soap,' Sally agreed. 'But tragic.'

I began my going-away noises. The food had been great, the company at least interesting and sometimes actually fun. Sally and I parted this time fairly pleased with each other.

After I left Sally's I remembered I had to check on Madeleine. I stopped at a grocery and got some cat food and another bag of cat litter. Then I realized this looked like permanency, rather than a two-week stay while the Engles vacationed in South Carolina.

I seemed to have a pet.

I was actually looking forward to seeing the animal.

I unlocked the kitchen door at Jane's with my free hand, the other one being occupied in holding the bags from the grocery. 'Madeleine?' I called. No golden purring dictator came to meet me. 'Madeleine?' I said less certainly.

Could she have gotten out? The backyard door was locked, the windows still shut. I looked in the guest bedroom, since the break-in had occurred there, but the new window was still intact.

'Kitty?' I said forlornly. And then it seemed to me I heard a noise. Dreading I don't know what, I inched into Jane's bedroom. I heard the strange mew again. Had someone hurt the cat? I began shaking, I was so sure I would find a horror. I'd left the door to Jane's closet ajar, and I could tell the sound was coming from there. I pulled the door open wide, with my breath sucked in and my teeth clenched tight.

Madeleine, apparently intact, was curled up on Jane's old bathrobe, which had fallen to the bottom of the closet when I was packing clothes. She was lying on her side, her muscles rippling as she strained.

Madeleine was having kittens.

'Oh *hell,*' I said. 'Oh – hell hell hell.' I slumped on the bed despondently. Madeleine spared me a golden glare and went back to work. 'Why me, Lord?' I asked self-pityingly. Though I had to concede it looked like Madeleine would be saying the same thing if she could. Actually, this was rather interesting. Would Madeleine mind if I watched? Apparently not, because she didn't hiss or claw at me when I sat on the floor just outside the closet and kept her company.

Of course Parnell Engle had been fully aware of Madeleine's impending motherhood, hence his merriment when I'd told him Madeleine could stay with me.

I pondered that for a few seconds, trying to decide if Parnell and I were even now. Maybe so, for Madeleine had had three kittens already, and there seemed to be more on the way.

I kept telling myself this was the miracle of birth. It sure was messy. Madeleine had my complete sympathy. She gave a final heave, and out popped another tiny, slimy kitten. I hoped two things: that this was the last kitten and that Madeleine didn't run into any difficulties, because I was the last person in the world who could offer her any help. After a few minutes, I began to think both my hopes had been fulfilled. Madeleine cleaned the little things, and all four lay there, occasionally making tiny movements, eyes shut, about as defenseless as anything could be.

Madeleine looked at me with the weary superiority of someone who has bravely undergone a major milestone. I wondered if she were thirsty; I got her water bowl and put it near her, and her food bowl, too. She got up after a moment and took a drink but didn't seem too interested in her food. She settled back down with her babies and looked perfectly all right, so I left her and went to sit in the living room. I stared at the bookshelves and wondered what in hell I would do with four kittens. On a shelf separate from those holding all the fictional and nonfictional murders, I saw several books about cats. Maybe that was what I should dip into next.

Right above the cat shelf was Jane's collection of books about Madeleine Smith, the Scottish poisoner, Jane's favorite. All of us former members of Real Murders had a favorite or two. My mother's new husband was a Lizzie Borden expert. I tended to favor Jack the Ripper, though I had by no means attained the status of Ripperologist.

But Jane Engle had always been a Madeleine Smith buff. Madeleine had been released after her trial after receiving the Scottish verdict 'Not Proven,' wonderfully accurate. She had almost certainly poisoned her perfidious former lover, a clerk, so she could marry into her own respectable upper-middle-class milieu without the clerk's revealing their physical intimacy. Poison was a curiously secret kind of revenge; the hapless L'Angelier had deceived himself that he was dealing with an average girl of the time, though the ardency of her physical expressions of love should have proved to him that Madeleine had a deep vein of passion. That passion extended to keeping her name clean and her reputation intact. L'Angelier threatened to send Madeleine's explicit love letters to her father. Madeleine pretended to effect a reconciliation, then slipped arsenic into L'Angelier's cup of chocolate.

For lack of anything better to do, I pulled out one of the Smith books and began to flip through it. It fell open right away. There was a yellow Post-it note stuck to the top of the page.

It said, in Jane's handwriting, *I didn't do it.*

Chapter Seven

I didn't do it.

The first thing I felt was overwhelming relief. Jane, who had left me so much, had not left me holding the bag, so to speak, on a murder she herself had committed.

She *had* left me in the position of concealing the murder someone else had committed, a murder Jane also had concealed, for reasons I could not fathom.

I had believed the only question I had to answer was Whose skull? Now I had also to find out who put the hole in that skull.

Was my situation really any better? No, I decided after some consideration. My conscience weighed perhaps an ounce less. The question of going to the police took on a different slant now that I would not be accusing Jane of murder by taking in the skull. But she'd had something to do with it. Oh, what a mess!

Not for the first (or the last) time, I wished I could have five minutes' conversation with Jane Engle, my benefactress and my burden. I tried to think of the money, to cheer myself up; I reminded myself that the will was a little closer to probate now, I'd be able to actually spend some without consulting Bubba Sewell beforehand.

And, to tell you the truth, I still felt excellent about that money. I had read so many mysteries in which the private detective had sent back his retainer check because the payer was immoral or the job he was hired to do turned out to be against his code of honor. Jane wanted me to have that money to have fun with, and she wanted me to remember her. Well, here I was remembering her every single day, by golly, and I certainly intended to have fun. In the meantime, I had a problem to solve.

It seemed to me that Bubba knew something about this. Could

I retain him as my lawyer and ask him what to do? Wouldn't attorney-client privilege cover my admission I'd located and rehidden the skull? Or would Bubba, as an officer of the court, be obliged to disclose my little lapse? I'd read a lot of mysteries that had probably contained this information, but now they all ran together in my head. The laws probably varied from state to state, too.

I could tell Aubrey, surely? Would he be obligated to tell the police? Would he have any practical advice to offer? I was pretty confident I knew what his moral advice would be; the skull should go into the police station now, today, pronto. I was concealing the death of someone who had been dead and missing for over three years, at a minimum. Someone, somewhere, needed to know this person had died. What if this was Macon Turner's son? Macon had been wanting to know the whereabouts of his son for a long time, had been searching for him; if there was even a faint chance his son's letters to him had been forged, it was inhumane to keep this knowledge from Macon.

Unless Macon had caused the hole in the skull.

Carey Osland had believed all these years her husband had walked out on her. She should know he had been prevented from returning home with those diapers.

Unless Carey herself had prevented him.

Marcia and Torrance Rideout needed to know their tenant had not voluntarily skipped out on his rent.

Unless they themselves had canceled his lease.

I jumped to my feet and went into the kitchen to fix myself – something. Anything. Of course, all that was there was canned stuff and unopened packages. I ended up with a jar of peanut butter and a spoon. I stuck the spoon in the jar and stood at the counter licking the peanut butter off.

Murderers needed to be exposed, truth needed to see the light of day. Et cetera. Then I had another thought: whoever had broken into this house, searching for the skull, had been the murderer.

I shivered. Not nice to think.

And even now, that little thought trickled onward, that murderer was wondering if I'd found the skull yet, what I'd do with it.

'This is bad,' I muttered. 'Really, really bad.'

That was constructive thinking.

Start at ground zero.

Okay. Jane had seen a murder, or maybe someone burying a body. For her to get the skull, she had to know the body was there, right? Jane literally knew where the bodies were buried. I actually caught myself smiling at my little joke.

Why would she not tell the police immediately?

No answer.

Why would she take the skull?

No answer.

Why would anyone pick Jane's demise as the time to look for the skull, when she'd obviously had it for years?

Possible answer: the murderer did not know for sure that Jane was the person who had the skull.

I imagined someone who had committed a terrible crime in the throes of who knew what passion or pressure. After hiding the body somewhere, suddenly this murderer finds that the skull is gone, the skull with its telltale hole, the skull with its identifiable teeth. Someone has taken the trouble to dig it up and take it away and the killer doesn't know who.

How horrible. I could almost pity the murderer. What fear, what terror, what dreadful uncertainty.

I shook myself. I should be feeling sorry for The Skull, as I thought of it.

Where could Jane have seen a murder?

Her own backyard. She had had to know where the body was buried exactly; she had had to have leisure to dig without interruption or discovery, presumably; she could not have carted a skull any distance. My reasoning of a few days before was still valid, whether or not Jane was the murderer. The murder had happened on this street, in one of these houses, somewhere where Jane could see it.

So I went out in the backyard and looked.

I found myself staring at the two cement benches flanking the birdbath. Jane had been fond of sitting there in the evenings, I recalled her saying. Sometimes the birds had perched on the bath while she sat there, she could sit so still, she had told me proudly. I did wonder if Madeleine had been outside with Jane enjoying this, and dismissed the thought as unworthy. Jane had been many things – I seemed to be finding more and more things she'd been every day – but she hadn't been an out-and-out sadist.

I sat on one of the cement benches with my back to Carey Osland's house. I could see almost all the Rideouts' sun deck clearly, of course: no Marcia in red there today. I could see their old garden plot and some clear lawn. The very rear of their yard was obscured by the bushes in my own yard. Beyond the Rideouts' I could discern one little section of Macon Turner's, which had lots of large bushes and rather high grass. I would have to come out here at night, I thought, to find if I could see through the windows of any of these houses.

It was hot, and I was full of roast beef and peanut butter. I slid into a trance, mentally moving people around their backyards, in various murderous postures.

'What you doing?' asked a voice behind me curiously.

I gasped and jumped.

A little girl stood behind me. She was maybe seven or eight or even a little older, and she was wearing shorts and a pink T-shirt. She had chin-length, wavy, dark hair and big dark eyes and glasses.

'I'm sitting,' I said tensely. 'What are you doing?'

'My mom sent me over to ask you if you could come drink some coffee with her.'

'Who's your mom?'

Now that was funny, someone not knowing who her mom was.

'Carey Osland.' She giggled. 'In that house right there,' she pointed, obviously believing she was dealing with a mentally deficient person.

The Osland backyard was almost bare of bushes or any

concealment at all. There was a swing set and a sandbox; I could see the street to the other side of the house easily.

This was the child who had needed diapers the night her father left the house and never returned.

'Yes, I'll come,' I said. 'What's your name?'

'Linda. Well, come on.'

So I followed Linda Osland over to her mother's house, wondering what Carey had to say.

Carey, I decided after a while, had just been being hospitable.

She'd gone the afternoon before to pick up Linda from camp, had spent Sunday morning washing Linda's shorts and shirts, which had been indescribably filthy, had listened to all Linda's camp stories, and now was ready for some adult companionship. Macon, she told me, was out playing golf at the country club. She said it like she had a right to know his whereabouts at all times and like other people should realize that. So, if their relationship had had its clandestine moments, it was moving out into the open. I noticed that she didn't say anything about their getting married, and didn't hint that was in the future.

Maybe they were happy just like they were.

It would be a great thing, not to want to get married. I sighed, I hoped imperceptibly, and asked Carey about Jane.

'I feel myself wanting to get to know her better now,' I said, with a what-can-you-do? shrug.

'Well, Jane was a different kettle of fish,' Carey said, with a lift of her dark brows.

'She was an old meanie,' Linda said suddenly. She'd been sitting at the table cutting out paper doll clothes.

'Linda,' her mother admonished, without any real scolding in her voice.

'Well, remember, Mama, how mad she got at Burger King!'

I tried to look politely baffled.

Carey's pretty, round face looked a little peeved for just a second. 'More coffee?' she asked.

'Yes, thanks,' I said, to gain more time before I had to go.

Carey poured and showed no sign of explaining Linda's little remark.

'Jane was a difficult neighbor?' I asked tentatively.

'Oh.' Carey sighed with pursed lips. 'I wish Linda hadn't brought that up. Honey, you got to learn to forget unpleasant things and old fights, it doesn't pay to remember stuff like that.'

Linda nodded obediently and went back to her scissors.

'Burger King was our dog; Linda named him of course,' Carey explained reluctantly. 'We didn't keep him on a leash, I know we should have, and of course our backyard isn't fenced in . . .'

I nodded encouragingly.

'Naturally, he eventually got run over. I'm ashamed of us even having an outside dog without having a fence,' Carey confessed, shaking her head at her own negligence. 'But Linda did want a pet, and she's allergic to cats.'

'I sneeze and my eyes get red,' Linda explained.

'Yes, honey. Of course, we had the dog when Jane had just gotten her cat, and of course Burger King chased Madeleine every time Jane let her out, which wasn't too often, but every now and then . . .' Carey lost her thread.

'The dog treed the cat?' I suggested helpfully.

'Oh yes, and barked and barked,' Carey said ruefully. 'It was a mess. And Jane got so mad about it.'

'She said she would call the pound,' Linda chimed in. 'Because there's a leash law and we were breaking it.'

'Well, honey, she was right,' Carey said. 'We were.'

'She didn't have to be so mean about it,' Linda insisted.

'She was a little shirty,' Carey said confidentially to me. 'I mean, I know I was at fault, but she really went off the deep end.'

'Oh dear,' I murmured.

'I'm surprised Linda remembers any of this because it was a long time ago. Years, I guess.'

'So did Jane end up calling the animal control people?'

'No, no. Poor Burger got hit by a car over on Faith, right here to the side of the house, very soon after that. So now we have Waldo here' – and the tip of her slipper poked the dachshund affectionately – 'and we walk him three or four times a day. It's not much of a life for him, but it's the best we can do.'

Waldo snored contentedly.

'Speaking of Madeleine, she came home,' I told Carey.

'She did! I thought Parnell and Leah picked her up from the vet's where she'd been boarded while Jane was sick?'

'Well, they did, but Madeleine wanted to be at her own house. As it turns out, she was expecting.'

Linda and Carey both exclaimed over that, and I regretted telling them after a moment, because of course Linda wanted to see the little kitties and her mother did not want the child to cough and weep all afternoon.

'I'm sorry, Carey,' I said as I took my leave.

'Don't worry about it,' Carey insisted, though I was sure she wished I had kept my mouth shut. 'It's just one of those things Linda has to learn to live with. I sure hope someday I can afford to fence the backyard; I'll get her a Scottie puppy, I swear I will. A friend of mine raises them, and those are the cutest puppies in the world. Like little walking shoe brushes.'

I considered the cute factor of walking shoe brushes as I went through Carey's backyard to my own. Carey's yard was so open to view it was hard to imagine where a body could have been buried on her property, but I couldn't exclude Carey either; her yard might not have been so bare a few years before.

I could be rid of all this by getting in my car and driving to the police station, I reminded myself. And for a moment I was powerfully tempted.

And I'll tell you what stopped me: not loyalty to Jane, not keeping faith with the dead; nothing so noble. It was my fear of Sergeant Jack Burns, the terrifying head of the detectives. The sergeant, I had observed in my previous contacts with him, burned for truth the way other men burn for a promotion or a night with Michelle Pfeiffer.

He wouldn't be happy with me.

He would want to nail me to the wall.

I would keep the skull a secret a little longer.

Maybe somehow I could wriggle out of this with a clear conscience. That didn't seem possible at this moment, but then it hadn't seemed possible someone would die and leave me a fortune, either.

I went in to check on Madeleine. She was nursing her kittens and looking smug and tired at the same time. I refilled her water bowl. I started to move her litter box into the room with her, but then I reconsidered. Best to leave it in the place she was used to going.

'Just think,' I told the cat, 'a week ago, I had no idea that soon I'd have a cat, four kittens, a house, five hundred and fifty thousand dollars, and a skull. I didn't know what I was missing.'

The doorbell rang.

I jumped maybe a mile. Thanks to Jane's cryptic note, I now knew I had something to fear.

'Be back in a minute, Madeleine,' I said, to reassure myself rather than the cat.

This time, instead of opening the door, I looked through Jane's spyhole. When I saw lots of black, I knew my caller was Aubrey. I was smiling as I opened the door.

'Come in.'

'I just thought I'd drop by and see the new house,' he said hesitantly. 'Is that okay?'

'Sure. I just found out today I have kittens. Come see them.'

And I led Aubrey into the bedroom, telling him Madeleine's saga as we went.

The proximity of the bed startled him a little, but the kittens entranced him.

'Want one?' I asked. 'It occurs to me I'll have to find homes for all of them in a few weeks. I'll have to call a vet and find out when they can be separated from her. And when I can have her neutered.'

'You're not going to take her back to Jane's cousin?' Aubrey asked, looking a little amused.

'No,' I said without even thinking about it. 'I'll see how I like living with a pet. She seems pretty attached to this house.'

'Maybe I will take one,' Aubrey said thoughtfully. 'My little house can get lonely. Having a cat to come home to might be pretty nice. I do get asked out a lot. That's where I've been since church, as a matter of fact; a family in the church asked me to their home for lunch.'

'I bet it wasn't as good as my lunch.' I told him about Sally's roast beef, and he said he'd had turkey, and we ended up sitting by the kittens talking about food for a while. He didn't cook for himself much, either.

And the doorbell rang.

We had been getting along so cozily, I had to resist an impulse to say something very nasty.

I left him in the bedroom staring at the kittens, all asleep and tiny, while I scrambled into the living room and opened the door.

Marcia Rideout, wide awake and gorgeous in white cotton shorts and a bright red camp shirt, smiled back at me. She certainly wasn't drunk now; she was alert and cheerful.

'Good to see you again,' she said with a smile.

I marveled again at her perfect grooming. Her lipstick was almost professionally applied, her eye shadow subtle but noticeable, her hair evenly golden and smoothly combed into a page boy. Her legs were hairless and beautifully brown. Even her white tennis shoes were spotless.

'Hi, Marcia,' I said quickly, having become aware I was staring at her like a guppy.

'I'll just take a minute of your time,' she promised. She handed me a little envelope. 'Torrance and I just want to give a little party on our sun deck this Wednesday to welcome you into the neighborhood.'

'Oh, but I—' I began to protest.

'No no, now. We wanted to have a little cookout anyway, but your inheriting the house just makes a good excuse. And we have new neighbors across the street, too, they're going to come. We'll all get to know each other. I know this is short notice, but Torrance has to travel this Friday and won't be back until late on Saturday.' Marcia seemed like a different person from the indolent drunk I'd met a few days before. The prospect of entertaining seemed to bring her to life.

How could I refuse? The idea of being honored at the same party with Lynn and Arthur was less than thrilling, but refusal would be unthinkable, too.

'Do bring a date if you want, or just come on your own,' Marcia said.

'You really won't mind if I bring someone?'

'Please do! One more won't make a bit of difference. Got anyone in mind?' Marcia asked, her brows arched coyly.

'Yes,' I said with a smile, and said no more. I was just hoping with all my might that Aubrey would not choose this moment to emerge from the bedroom. I could picture Marcia's eyebrows flying clean off her face.

'Oh,' Marcia said, obviously a little taken aback by my marked lack of explanation. 'Yes, that'll be fine. Just come as you are, we won't be fancy, that's not Torrance and me!'

Marcia seemed very fancy indeed to me.

'Can I bring anything?'

'Just yourself,' Marcia responded, as I'd expected. I realized that the party preparations would keep her excited and happy for the next three days.

'I'll see you then,' she called as she bounced down the steps and started back over to her house.

I took the little invitation with me when I went back to Aubrey.

'Could you go to this with me?' I asked, handing it to him. I thought if he turned me down I was going to be horribly embarrassed, but I had no one else to ask, and if I was going to a party with Arthur and Lynn present, I was damn sure going to have a date.

He pulled the invitation out and read it. It had a chef on the front wearing a barbecue apron and holding a long fork. 'Something good is on the grill!' exclaimed the print. When you opened it, it said, '. . . and you can share it with us on *Wednesday, 7:00* at *Marcia and Torrance's* house. See you then!'

'A little on the hearty side,' I said, as neutrally as I could. I didn't want to seem uncharitable.

'I'm sure I can, but let me check.' Aubrey pulled a little black notebook out of his pocket. 'The liturgical calendar,' he explained. 'I think every Episcopalian priest carries one of these.' He flipped through the pages, then beamed up at me. 'Sure, I can go.' I blew out a sigh of sheer relief. Aubrey produced a little pencil in disgraceful shape and wrote in the time and address, and, to my amusement, 'Pick up Aurora.' Would he forget me otherwise?

Stuffing the book back into his pocket, he got to his feet and told me he'd better be going. 'I have youth group in an hour,' he said, checking his watch.

'What do you do with them?' I asked as I walked him to the door.

'Try to make them feel okay about not being Baptists and having a big recreation center to go to, mostly. We go in with the Lutherans and the Presbyterians, taking turns to have the young people on Sunday evening. And it's my church's turn.'

At least it was too early in our relationship for me to feel at all obliged to take part in that.

Aubrey opened the door to leave, then seemed to remember something he'd forgotten. He bent over to give me a kiss, his arm loosely around my shoulders. There was no doubt this time about the jolt I felt clear down to the soles of my feet. When he straightened up, he looked a little energized himself.

'Well!' he said breathlessly. 'I'll give you a call this week, and I look forward to Wednesday night.'

'Me, too,' I said with a smile, and saw past his shoulder the curtains in the house across the way stir.

Ha! I thought maturely, as I shut the door behind Aubrey.

Chapter Eight

Monday turned out to be a much busier day than I'd expected. When I went in to work to put in what I thought would be four hours, I found that one of the other librarians had caught a summer cold ('The worst kind,' all the other librarians said wisely, shaking their heads. I thought any cold was the worst kind). The head of the library, Sam Clerrick, asked if I'd put in eight hours instead, and after a little hesitation I agreed. I felt very gracious, because now I had it within my financial power (well, almost within my financial power) to quit my job completely. There's nothing like patting yourself on the back to give you energy; I worked happily all morning, reading to a circle of preschoolers and answering questions.

I did feel justified in taking a few extra minutes on my coffee break to call the phone company and ask them if the number I had at the town house could also be the number for Jane's house, at least for a while. Even if that wasn't possible, I wanted Jane's phone hooked back up. To my pleasure, it was possible to get my number to ring at Jane's, and I was assured it would be operational within the next couple of days.

As I was hanging up, Lillian Schmidt lumbered in. Lillian is one of those disagreeable people who yet have some redeeming qualities, so that you can't write them off entirely – but you sure wish you could. Furthermore, I worked with Lillian, so it was in my interest to keep peace with her. Lillian was narrow-minded and gossipy, but fair; she was a devoted wife and mother, but talked about her husband and daughter until you wanted them to be swallowed up in an earthquake; she knew her job and did it competently, but with so much groaning and complaining about minute details that you wanted to smack her. Reacting to Lillian, I sounded like a wild-eyed Communist, an incurable Polyanna, and a free-sex advocate.

'It's so hot outside, I feel like I need another shower,' she said by way of greeting. Her forehead was beaded with perspiration. She pulled a tissue from the box on the coffee table and dabbed at her face.

'I hear you had a windfall,' she continued, tossing the tissue into the trash and missing. With a deep sigh, Lillian laboriously bent over to retrieve it. But her eyes flicked up to take in my reaction.

'Yes,' I said with a bright smile.

Lillian waited for me to elaborate. She eyed me wryly when I didn't say anything. 'I didn't know you and Jane Engle were such good friends.'

I considered several possible responses, smiling all the while. 'We were friends.'

Lillian shook her head slowly. 'I was a friend of Jane's, too, but she didn't leave me any house.'

What could I say to that? I shrugged. If Jane and Lillian had had any special personal relationship, I certainly couldn't recall it.

'Did you know,' Lillian continued, switching to another track, 'that Bubba Sewell is going to run for state representative in the fall?'

'Is he really.' It wasn't a question.

Lillian saw that she'd made an impression. 'Yes, his secretary is my sister-in-law, so she told me even before the announcement, which is tomorrow. I knew you'd be interested since I saw you talking to him at Jane's funeral. He's trying to get his house in order, so to speak, so he doesn't want even a whiff of anything funny that might be dug up during the campaign. He's going to be running against Carl Underwood, and Carl's had that seat for three terms.'

Lillian had gotten to give me information I hadn't possessed, and that had made her happy. After a couple more complaints about the school system's insensitivity to her daughter's allergies, she stumped off to actually do some work.

I remained seated on the hard chair in the tiny coffee-break room, thinking hard about Bubba Sewell. No wonder he hadn't wanted to know what was fishy in Jane's house! No wonder he had catered to her so extensively. It was good word of mouth for him, that he would go to such lengths for his elderly client, especially since he wasn't gaining anything from her will – except a fat fee for handling it.

If I told Bubba Sewell about the skull he'd hate me for the rest of his life. And he was Carey Osland's first husband; maybe somehow he was involved in the disappearance of Carey's second husband?

As I washed my mug in the little sink and set it in the drainer, I dismissed any urge I'd ever felt to confide in the lawyer. He was running for office; he was ambitious; he couldn't be trusted. A pretty grim summation for someone who might be my elected representative in the statehouse. I sighed, and started for the check-in desk to shelve the returned books.

On my lunch hour, I ran over to the house on Honor to let the cat out and check on the kittens. I picked up a hamburger and drink at a drive-through.

When I turned off Faith I saw a city work crew cleaning the honeysuckle and poison ivy from around the DEAD END sign at the end of the street. It would take them hours. Vines and weeds had taken over the little area and had obviously been thriving for years, twining around the sign itself and then attaching to the rear fence of the house backing onto the end of our street. The city truck was parked right in the middle of the road down by Macon Turner's house.

For the first time since I'd inherited Jane's house, I saw the newspaper editor himself, perhaps also returning to his home for lunch. Macon's thinning, brownish-gray hair was long and combed across the top of his head to give his scalp some coverage. He had an intelligent face, thin lipped and sharp, and wore suits that always seemed to need to go to the cleaners; in fact, Macon always gave the impression that he did not know how to take care of himself. His hair always needed trimming, his clothes needed ironing, he usually seemed tired, and he was always one step behind his schedule. He called to me now as he pulled letters out of his mailbox, giving me a smile that held a heavy dose of charm. Macon was the only man my mother had ever dated that I personally found attractive.

I waited, standing in the driveway with my little paper bag of lunch in one hand and my house keys in the other, while Macon walked over. His tie was crooked, and he was carrying his suit coat, a lightweight khaki, almost dragging the ground. I wondered if Carey Osland, whose house was not exactly a model of neatness, realized what she was taking on.

'Good to see you, Roe! How's your mother and her new husband?' Macon called before he was quite close enough. The cleanup crew, two young black men being watched by an older one, turned their heads to cast us a glance.

It was one of those moments that you always remember for no apparent reason. It was dreadfully hot, the sun brilliant in a cloudless sky. The three workmen had huge, dark stains on their shirts, and one of the younger men had a red bandanna over his head. The ancient city dump truck was painted dark orange. Condensation from the cup containing my soft drink was making a wet blotch on the paper bag; I worried that the bag would break. I was feeling glad to see Macon, but also impatient to get inside the cool house and eat lunch and check on Madeleine's brood. I felt a trickle of sweat start up under my green-and-white-striped dress, felt it roll its ticklish way down under my belt to my hips. I looped my purse strap over my shoulder so I could have a free hand to hold up my hair in the vain hope of catching a breeze across my neck; I hadn't had time to braid my hair that morning. I looked down at a crack in the driveway and wondered how to get it repaired. Weeds were growing through in unattractive abundance.

I was just thinking that I was glad Mother had married John Queensland, whom I found worthy but often boring, rather than Macon, whose face was made disturbingly attractive by his intelligence, when one of the workmen let out a yell. It hung in the thick, hot air; all three men froze. Macon's head turned in midstride, and he paused as his foot hit the ground. All movement seemed to become deliberate. I was acutely aware of turning my head slightly, the better to see what the man with the red bandanna was lifting off the ground. The contrast of his black hand against the white bone was riveting.

'God almighty! It's a dead man!' bellowed the other worker, and the slow motion speeded up into a sequence too swift for me to replay afterward.

I decided that day that the dead person could not be Macon Turner's son; or, at least if it was, Edward had not been killed by Macon. Macon's face never showed the slightest hint that this find might have a personal slant. He was excited and interested and almost broke his door down to get in to call the police.

Lynn came out of her house when the police car appeared. She looked pale and miserable. Her belly preceded her like a tugboat pulling her along.

'What's the fuss?' she asked, nodding toward the workmen, who were reliving their find complete with quotes and gestures while the patrolman peered down into the thick weeds and vines choking the base of the sign.

'A skeleton, I think.' I said cautiously. Though I was sure it was not a *complete* skeleton.

Lynn looked unmoved. 'I bet it turns out to be a Great Dane or some other big dog. Maybe even some cow bones or deer bones left over from some home butchering.'

'Could be,' I said. I looked up at Lynn, whose hand was absently massaging her bulging belly. 'How are you doing?'

'I feel like . . .' She paused to think. 'I feel like if I bent over, the baby's so low I could shake hands with it.'

'Oo,' I said. I squinched up my face trying to imagine it.

'You've never been pregnant,' Lynn said, a member of a club I'd never belonged to. 'It's not as easy as you might think, considering women have done it for millions of years.' Right now, Lynn was a lot more interested in her own body than in the body at the end of the road.

'So you're not working now?' I asked, keeping one eye cocked at the patrolman, who was now using his radio. The workmen had calmed down and moved into the shade of a tree in Macon's front yard. Macon disappeared into his house, popping back out with a camera and notepad.

'No. My doctor told me I had to take off work and keep my feet up for as long each day as I can. Since we got most of the boxes unpacked and the nursery is ready, I just do house things about two hours each day, and the rest of the time,' she told me gloomily, 'I just wait.'

This was so – un-Lynn.

'Are you excited?' I asked hesitantly.

'I'm too uncomfortable to be excited. Besides, Arthur is excited enough for both of us.'

I found that hard to picture.

'You don't mind anymore, do you?' Lynn asked suddenly.

'No.'

'You dating anyone else?'

'Sort of. But I just stopped minding.'

Luckily Lynn stopped there, because I simply would not say anything more about it.

'Do you think you'll keep the house?'

'I have no idea.' I almost asked Lynn if it would bother her if I did, then I realized I didn't want to know the answer.

'Are you going to that party?' Lynn asked after a moment.

'Yes.'

'We will too, I guess, though I'm not much in partying shape. That Marcia Rideout looked at me like she'd never seen a pregnant woman when she came over to meet me and leave the invitation. She made me feel like the Goodyear blimp and an unmade bed all at once.'

I could see how that would be, given Marcia's aggressively good grooming.

'I better go check on the kittens,' I told Lynn. The situation down at the end of the street was static. The patrolman leaned against his car, waiting for someone else to show up, apparently. Macon was standing at the end of the pavement looking down at the bones. The workmen were smoking and drinking RC Colas.

'Oh, you have kittens? Can I see?' For the first time, Lynn looked animated.

'Sure,' I said with some surprise. Then I realized Lynn was in the mood to see baby anything.

The kittens were more active today. They tumbled over one another, their eyes still not open, and Madeleine surveyed them with queenly pride. One was coal black, the others marmalade and white like their mother. Soon their energy ran out and they began to nurse, dropping off into sleep directly after. Lynn had carefully lowered herself to the floor and watched silently, her face unreadable. I went into the kitchen to replenish Madeleine's water and food, and I changed the litter box while I was at it. After I washed my hands and had a gulp of my drink and most of my hamburger, I went back to the bedroom to find Lynn still staring.

'Did you watch them being born?' she asked.

'Yep.'

'Did it look like she hurt?'

'It looked like it was work,' I said carefully.

She sighed heavily. 'Well, I expect that,' she said, trying to sound philosophical.

'Have you gone to Lamaze?'

'Oh, yeah. We do our breathing exercises every night,' she said unenthusiastically.

'You don't think they're going to work?'

'I have no idea. You know what's really scary?'

'What?'

'No one will tell you.'

'Like who?'

'*Anyone*. It's the damnedest thing. I really want to know what I'm up against. So I ask my best friend, she's had two. She says, "Oh, when you see what you get it's worth it." That's no answer, right? So I ask someone else who didn't use any anesthesia. She says, "Oh, you'll forget all about it when you see the baby." That's not an answer either. And my mom was knocked out, old-style, when she had me. So she can't tell me, and she probably wouldn't. It's some kind of mom conspiracy.'

I thought it over. 'Well, I sure can't answer any questions, but I'd tell you the truth if I could.'

'I expect,' Lynn said, 'that I'll be telling you, and pretty soon.'

When I left the house to return to the library, I saw two police cars parked in Macon Turner's driveway, and the city truck was gone. The rest of the skeleton having been found was a great relief to me. Now the police would be working on finding out who it was. Perhaps the remaining bones would be enough? If they could find out from the bones, I mentally promised The Skull I would give it a decent burial.

I was guiltily aware I was not taking any morally firm position.

That evening the doorbell rang just as I had eased off my shoes and rolled my panty hose down. I hastily yanked them off, pushed them under my chair, and stuck my bare feet into my shoes. I was a hot, wrinkled mess with a headache and a bad conscience.

Sergeant Jack Burns filled my doorway from side to side. His clothes were always heavy on polyester, and he had long Elvis sideburns, but nothing could detract from the air of menace that emanated from him in a steady stream. He was so used to projecting it that I think he might have been surprised if you had told him about it.

'May I come in?' he asked gently.

'Oh, of course,' I said, backing to one side.

'I come to ask you about the bones found today on Honor Street,' he said formally.

'Please come have a seat.'

'Thank you, I will, I been on my old feet all day,' he said in a courtly way. He let himself down on my couch, and I sat opposite him in my favorite chair.

'You just come in from work?'

'Yes, yes I did.'

'But you were at Jane Engle's house on Honor Street today when the road crew found the skeleton.'

'Yes, I had come there on my lunch hour to feed the cat.'

He stared and waited. He was better at this than I was.

'Jane's cat. Uh – she ran away from Parnell and Leah Engle and came back home; she had kittens in the closet. In Jane's bedroom.'

'You know, you sure turn up a lot for a law-abiding citizen, Miss Teagarden. We hardly seem to have any homicides in Lawrenceton without you showing up. Seems mighty strange.'

'I would hardly call having inherited a house on the same street "mighty strange," Sergeant Burns,' I said bravely.

'Well, now you think about it,' he suggested in a reasonable voice. 'Last year when we had those deaths, there you were. When we caught them that did it, there you were.'

About to get killed myself, I said, but only in my head, because you didn't interrupt Sergeant Jack Burns.

'Then Miss Engle dies, and here you are on the street with a skeleton in the weeds, a street with a suspicious number of reported break-ins, including one in this house you just inherited.'

'A suspicious number of break-ins? Are you saying other people on Honor besides me have reported their house being entered?'

'That's what I'm saying, Miss Teagarden.'

'And nothing taken?'

'Nothing the owner would admit to missing. Maybe the thief took some pornographic books or some other thing the home-owner would be embarrassed to report.'

'There certainly wasn't anything like that in Jane's house, I'm sure,' I said indignantly. Just an old skull with some holes in it. 'It may be that something was missing, I wouldn't know. I only saw the house after the burglary. Ah – who else reported their houses had been broken into?'

Jack Burns actually looked surprised before he looked suspicious.

'Everyone, now. Except that old couple in the end house on the other side of the street. Now, do you know anything about the bones found today?'

'Oh, no. I just happened along when they were discovered. You know, I've only been in the house a few times, and I've never stayed there. I only visited Jane, over the past couple of years. Before she went into the hospital.'

'I think,' Jack Burns said heavily and unfairly, 'this is one mystery the police department can handle, Miss Teagarden. You keep your little bitty nose out of it.'

'Oh,' I said furiously, 'I will, Sergeant.' And as I rose to show him out, my heel caught on the balled-up panty hose under my chair and dragged them out for Jack Burns's viewing.

He gave them a look of scorn, as if they'd been sleazy sexual aids, and departed with his awful majesty intact. If he had laughed, he would've been human.

Chapter Nine

I'd only had half a cup of coffee the next morning when the phone rang. I'd gotten up late after an uneasy sleep. I'd dreamed the skull was under my bed and Jack Burns was sitting in a chair by the bed interrogating me while I was in my nightgown. I was sure somehow he would read my mind and bend over to look under the bed; and if he did that I was doomed. I woke up just as he was lifting the bedspread.

After I'd poured my coffee, made my toast, and retrieved my Lawrenceton *Sentinel* from the front doorstep, I settled at the kitchen table for my morning read. I'd gotten the page one lead story (SEWELL CHALLENGES INCUMBENT) skimmed and was just searching for the comics when I was interrupted.

I picked up the phone, convinced the call was bad news, so I was pleasantly surprised to here Amina's mom on the other end. As it turned out, my original premise was correct.

'Good morning, Aurora! It's Joe Nell Day.'

'Hi, Miss Joe Nell. How you doing?' Amina bravely called my mother 'Miss Aida.'

'Just fine, thanks, honey. Listen, Amina called me last night to tell me they've moved the wedding day up.'

I felt a chill of sheer dismay. Here we go again, I thought gloomily. But this was Amina's mother. I stretched my mouth into a smile so my voice would match. 'Well, Miss Joe Nell, they're both old enough to know what they're doing,' I said heartily.

'I sure hope so,' she said from the heart. 'I'd sure hate Amina to go through another divorce.'

'No, not going to happen,' I said, offering reassurance I didn't feel. 'This is going to be the one.'

'We'll pray about it,' Miss Joe Nell said earnestly. 'Amina's daddy is fit to be tied. We haven't even met this young man yet.'

'You liked her first husband,' I said. Amina would always marry someone nice. It was staying that way that was the problem. What was this guy's name? Hugh Price. 'She had so many positive things to tell me about Hugh.' He was positively good-looking, he was positively rich, he was positively good in bed. I hoped he wasn't positively shallow. I hoped Amina really loved him. I wasn't too concerned about him loving Amina; I took that as an easy accomplishment since I loved her.

'Well, they're both veterans of the divorce wars, so they should know what they want and don't want. Anyway, why I called you, Aurora, moving up the wedding day means you need to come in and get fitted for your bridesmaid's dress.'

'Am I the only one?' I hoped desperately I could wear something personally becoming rather than something that was supposed to look good on five or six different females of varying builds and complexions.

'Yes,' said Miss Joe Nell with open relief. 'Amina wants you to come down and pick what you want as long as it will look good with her dress, which is a mint green.'

Not white. I was kind of surprised. Since Amina had decided to send out invitations and have a larger wedding because her first one was so hole-in-the-wall, I'd felt she'd do the whole kit and caboodle. I was relieved to hear she was moderating her impulse.

'Sure, I can come in this morning,' I said obligingly. 'I don't have to work today.'

'Oh, that's just great! I'll see you then.'

This was when your mother owning a dress shop was really convenient. There was sure to be something at Great Day that would suit me. If not, Miss Joe Nell would find something.

When I went upstairs to get dressed, on impulse I turned into the back bedroom, the guest room. The only guest who'd ever slept in it had been my little half-brother Phillip when he used to come spend an occasional weekend with me. Now he was all the way in California; our father and his mother had wanted to get him as far away from me and Lawrenceton as possible, so he wouldn't have to remember what had happened to him here. While he was staying with me.

I fought off drearily familiar feelings of guilt and pain, and flung open the closet door. In this closet I kept the things I wasn't wearing currently, heavy winter coats, my few cocktail and evening dresses . . . and my bridesmaid dresses. There were four of them: a lavender ruffled horror from Sally Saxby's wedding, Linda Erhardt's floral chiffon, a red velvet with white 'fur' trim from my college roommate's Christmas 'nuptials,' and a somewhat better pink sheath from Franny Vargas's spring marriage. The lavender had made me look as if I'd been bushwhacked by a Barbie doll, the floral chiffon was not bad but in blonds' colors, the red velvet had made me look like Dolly Parton in the chest but otherwise we'd all looked like Santa's helpers, and the pink sheath I'd had cut to knee length and had actually worn to some parties over the years.

I'd worn jeans to Amina's first, runaway wedding.

That had been the most useful bridesmaid's outfit of all.

Now that I had worked myself into an absolutely great mood, what with thinking of Phillip and reviewing my history as a bridesmaid, I decided I'd better get myself in gear and go do things.

What did I need to do besides go by Great Day?

I had to go check on Madeleine and the kittens. I had to go by Mother's office; she'd asked me to on the message left on my machine, and I hadn't done it yet. I felt an urge to go check on the skull, but I decided I could be pretty sure it hadn't gone anywhere.

'Stupid,' I muttered at my mirror as I braided my hair. I slapped on a little makeup and pulled on my oldest jeans and a sleeveless T-shirt. I might have to go by Mother's office, but I wasn't going to look like a junior executive. All her salespeople were sure I would go to work for Mother someday, completely disrupting their food chain. Actually, showing houses seemed like an attractive way to pass the time, and now that I had my own money – almost – I really might think about looking into it seriously.

But of course I didn't have to work for Mother. I gave the

mirror a wicked grin, picturing the furor for a happy second, before I lapsed back to reality. Wrapping the band around the end of the braid to secure it, I admitted to myself that of course I would work for Mother if I did decide to take the plunge and switch jobs. But I'd miss the library, I told myself as I checked my purse to make sure I had everything. No I wouldn't, I realized suddenly. I'd miss the books. Not the job or the people.

The prospect of possibly resigning kept me entertained until I got to Great Day.

Amina's father was a bookkeeper, and of course he did the books for his wife's business. He was there when I came in, the bell over the door tinkling to announce my arrival. Miss Joe Nell was using some kind of hand-held steamer to get the wrinkles out of a newly arrived dress. She was a very attractive, fair woman in her middle forties. She'd been young when she had Amina, her only daughter. Amina's younger brother was still in graduate school. Miss Joe Nell was very religious, and, when my mother and father had gotten divorced when I was a teenager, one of my many fears was that Miss Joe Nell would disapprove of the divorce so much she wouldn't let me stay with Amina anymore. But Miss Joe Nell was a loving woman and sympathetic, too; my worry had been banished quickly.

Now she put down the steamer and gave me a hug.

'I just hope Amina's doing the right thing,' she whispered.

'Well, I'm sure she is,' I said with a confidence I was far from feeling. 'I'm sure he's a good man.'

'Oh, it's not him I worry about so much,' Miss Joe Nell said, to my surprise. 'It's Amina.'

'We just hope she's really ready to settle this time,' rumbled Mr Day. He sang bass in the church choir, had for twenty years, and would until he could sing no more.

'I hope so, too,' I admitted. And we all three looked at one another rather dolefully for a long second.

'Now, what kind of dress does Amina want me to try on?' I asked briskly.

Miss Joe Nell shook herself visibly and led me over to the

formal dresses. 'Let's see,' she said. 'Her dress, like I said, is mint green, with some white beading. I have it here, she tried on several things when she was home for your mother's wedding. I thought she was just sort of dreaming and planning, but I bet she had a little idea back then that they would move the date up.'

The dress was beautiful. Amina would look like an American dream in it.

'So we can coordinate my dress easily,' I said in an optimistic tone.

'Well, I looked at what we have in your size, and I found a few things that would look lovely with this shade of green. Even if you pick a solid in a different color, your bouquet could have green ribbons that would sort of tie it together . . .'

And we were off and running, deep in wedding talk.

I was glad I'd braided my hair that morning, because by the time I'd finished hauling dresses off and on it would have been a crow's nest otherwise. As it was, loose hairs crackling with electricity were floating around my face by the time I was done. One of the dresses became me and would coordinate, and, though I doubted I would ever have occasion to wear it again, I bought it. Mrs Day tried to tell me she would pay for it, but I knew my bridesmaid's duty. Finally she let me have it at cost, and we both were satisfied. Amina's dress had long, see-through sleeves and solid cuffs, a simple neckline, beaded bodice, and a full skirt, plain enough to set off the bridal bouquet but fancy enough to be festive. My dress had short sleeves but the same neckline, and it was peach with a mint green cummerbund. I could get some heels dyed to match – in fact, I thought the heels I'd had dyed to match Linda Erhardt's bridesmaid's dress might do. I promised Miss Joe Nell I'd bring them by the store to check, since my dress had to remain at Great Day to have its hem raised.

And it had only taken an hour and a half, I discovered when I got back in my car. I remembered when I'd gone dress hunting with Sally Saxby and her mother, and four other bridesmaids. The expedition had consumed a whole very long day. It had taken me awhile to feel as fond of Sally as I had before we went dress hunting in Atlanta.

Of course, now Sally had been Mrs Hunter for ten years and had a son almost as tall as me, and a daughter who took piano lessons.

No, I would *not* be depressed. The dress had been found, that was a good thing. I was going by the office, that was another good thing. Then I would go see the cats at the new house, as I was trying to think of it. Then I would treat myself to lunch somewhere good.

When I turned into the rear parking lot of my mother's office, I noticed no one dared to park in her space though she was actually out of the country. I pulled into it neatly, making a mental note to tell Mother this little fact. Mother, thinking 'Teagarden Homes' was too long to fit on a Sold sign, had instead named her business Select Realty. Of course this was a blatant attempt to appeal to the 'up' side of the market, and it seemed to have worked. Mother was a go get 'em realtor who never let business call her if she could get out there and beat the bushes for it first. She wanted every realtor she hired to be just as aggressive, and she didn't care what the applicant looked like as long as the right attitude came across. An injudicious rival had compared Select realtors to a school of sharks, in my hearing. Marching up the sidewalk to the old home Mother had bought and renovated beautifully, I found myself wondering if my mother would consider me a suitable employee.

Everyone who worked at Select Realty dressed to the nines, so I was fairly conspicuous, and I realized my choice of jeans and T-shirt had been a mistake. I had wanted to look as unlike a realtor as I could, and I had succeeded in looking like an outdated hippie.

Patty Cloud, at the front desk, was wearing a suit that cost as much as a week's salary from the library. And this was the *receptionist*.

'Aurora, how good to see you!' she said with a practiced smile. Patty was at least four years younger than me, but the suit and the artificial ease made her seem as much older.

Eileen Norris passed through the reception area to drop some papers labeled with a Post-it note on Patty's desk, and stopped in her tracks when she recognized me.

'My God, child, you look like something the cat dragged in!' Eileen bellowed. She was a suspiciously dark-haired woman about forty-five, with expensive clothes from the very best big women's store. Her makeup was heavy but well done, her perfume was intrusive but attractive, and she was one of the most overwhelming women I'd ever met. Eileen was something of a town character in Lawrenceton, and she could talk you into buying a house quicker then you could take an aspirin.

I wasn't exactly pleased with her greeting, but I'd made an error in judgment, and Eileen was not one to let that go by.

'I'm just dropping in to deliver a message. Mother is extending her honeymoon a little.'

'I'm so glad she is,' Eileen boomed. 'That woman hadn't taken a vacation in a coon's age. I bet she's having a real good time.'

'No doubt about it.'

'And you're checking up on the children while their mama's away?'

There was also no doubt Eileen wasn't happy with the idea of the boss's daughter 'checking up.'

'Just wanted to see that the building was still standing,' I said lightly. 'But I do have a realty question to ask.'

Mackie Knight, a young black realtor Mother had just taken on, came in just then with clients, a pair of newlyweds I recognized since their picture had been in the paper the same day Mother and John's had been. The couple looked a little dazed, and were arguing in a weary way between a house on Macree and a house on Littleton. Safely ahead of them, Mackie rolled his eyes at us as they passed through.

'He's working out good,' Eileen said absently. 'The younger couples don't mind having a black realtor, and the black clients love it. Now, you said you had a realty question?'

'Yes, I do. What are houses in the area right around the junior high selling for?'

Patty and Eileen snapped to attention. This was Business.

'How many bedrooms?'

'Ah – two.'

'Square footage?'

'Maybe fourteen hundred.'

'A house on Honor in that area just sold,' Eileen said promptly. 'Just a minute and I'll look that up.'

She marched back to her desk, her high heels making little thumps on the carpet. I followed her through the unobtrusively attractive gray and blue halls to her office, second in size only to Mother's. It had probably been the second best bedroom. Mother had what had been the master bedroom, and the kitchen had the copying machine and a little snack area. The other rooms were much smaller and occupied by Mother's lesser minions. Eileen's desk was aggressively busy, papers everywhere, but they were in separate stacks, and she doubtless was capable of juggling many balls at a time.

'Honor, Honor,' she muttered. She must have been looking up the price of the little house Arthur and Lynn had bought. Her ringed fingers flipped expertly through a stack of listings. 'Here we go,' she murmured. 'Fifty-three,' she said more loudly. 'Are you interested in buying or selling?' I could tell Eileen was no longer concerned with my blue jeans and messy braid.

'Maybe selling. I inherited the house right across the street from that house you're looking at now.' I nodded at the listing sheet.

'Really,' Eileen said, staring. 'You? Inherited?'

'Yes.'

'And you may want to sell the house instead of living in it?'

'Yes.'

'Is the house paid for by the previous owner? The owner doesn't owe any money on it, I mean?'

'No, it's paid for.' I thought I remembered Bubba Sewell telling me that. Yes, I did. Jane had been paying on the house until her mother died, when she'd had the cash to complete buying it in one whack.

'You have a completely free house and you don't want it? I

would've thought a two bedroom was just the right size for you. Not that I wouldn't love to list it for you,' Eileen said, recalled to her senses.

A frail, pretty woman in her late thirties stuck her head in. 'Eileen, I'm off to show the Youngman house, if you've got the key handy,' she said with a teasing smile.

'Idella! I can't believe I did it again!' Eileen hit her forehead with the heel of her hand, but very lightly so as not to smear her makeup.

'I'm sorry, I didn't know you had company,' the woman continued.

'Idella, this is Aurora Teagarden, Aida's daughter,' Eileen said, rummaging through her purse. 'Aurora, you may not know Idella Yates yet? She came in with us earlier this year.'

While Idella and I exchanged nice-to-meet-you's, Eileen kept up with her search. Finally she unearthed a key with a large label attached. 'Idella, I'm sorry,' Eileen boomed. 'I don't know why I don't remember to put the keys back on the keyboard. That seems to be one thing I cannot remember. We're supposed to put them back on the main keyboard, that Patty watches, every time we use a key to show a house,' Eileen explained to me. 'But for some reason, I just cannot get it through my head.'

'Don't worry about it,' Idella said sweetly, and with a nod to me she left to go show the house. She did glance at her watch rather pointedly as she left, letting Eileen know that, if she was late to meet her client, Eileen was the one to blame.

Eileen sat staring after Idella with a curiously uneasy look on her face. Eileen's face was only used to positive emotions, emerging full-blown. Something like 'uneasy' sat very oddly on her strong features.

'There's something funny about that woman,' Eileen said abruptly and dismissively. Her face fell back into more familiar lines. 'Now, about that house – do you know things like how old the roof is, whether it's on city water, how old the house itself is? Though I think all the houses in that area were built about nineteen fifty-five or so. Maybe some in the early sixties.'

'If I make up my mind definitely, I'll get all that information,' I promised, wondering how on earth I'd find out about the roof. I might have to go through every one of Jane's receipts, unless perhaps one of her neighbors might remember the roofing crew. Roofing crews usually made their presence felt. A vagrant thought crossed my mind. What if one of the houses was older than it appeared, or had been built on the site of a much older home? Maybe there was a basement or a tunnel under one of the houses where the body had been until it had been tossed into the weeds at the end of the street?

Admittedly this was a pretty stupid idea, and when I asked Eileen about it she dismissed it as it deserved. 'Oh, no,' she said briskly, beginning to shake her head before I even finished my sentence. 'What a strange notion, Roe. That area is much too low for basements, and there wasn't anything there before the junior high was built. It was timberland.'

Eileen insisted on walking me out of the office. I decided it was because I was a potential client, rather than because I was Aurora Teagarden. Eileen was not a toady.

'Now, when is your mother coming back?' she asked.

'Oh, soon, sometime this week. She wasn't definite. She just didn't want to call in to the office; maybe she was scared if she talked to one of you she'd just get to talking about work. She was just using me as a messenger to you all.' All of the other offices that I passed were busy or showed signs of work in progress. Phones were ringing, papers were being copied, briefcases were being packed with paperwork.

For the first time in my life, I wondered how much money my mother had. Now that I didn't need it anymore, I was finally curious. Money was something we never talked about. She had enough for her, and did her kind of thing – expensive clothes, a very luxurious car (she said it impressed clients), and some good jewelry. She didn't play any sport; for exercise she had installed a treadmill in one of the bedrooms of her house. But she sold a lot of real estate, and I assumed she got a percentage from the sales of the realtors she employed. I was very fuzzy on how that worked, because I'd just never thought it was my business. In a moment I was not too proud of, I wondered if she'd made a new will now that John and she had married. I frowned at myself in the rearview mirror as I sat at a stoplight.

Of course, John already had plenty of money of his own, and he had two sons . . .

I shook my head impatiently, trying to shake those bad thoughts loose. I tried to excuse myself by reasoning that it was really no wonder that I was will-and death-conscious lately, or for that matter that I was more than usually interested in money matters. But I wasn't happy with myself, so I was quicker to be displeased when I pulled into the driveway of the house on Honor to find Bubba Sewell waiting for me.

It was as if I'd conjured him up by thinking about him.

'Hello,' I said cautiously as I got out of the car. He got out of his and strode over to me.

'I took a chance on finding you here. I called the library and found out you were off today.'

'Yes, I don't work every day,' I said unnecessarily. 'I came to check on the kittens.'

'Kittens.' His heavy eyebrows flew up behind his glasses.

'Madeleine came back. She had kittens in the closet in Jane's room.'

'Have Parnell and Leah been over here?' he asked. 'Have they given you much trouble?'

'I think Parnell feels we're even now that I have four kittens to find homes for,' I said.

Bubba laughed, but he didn't sound like he meant it.

'Listen,' he began, 'the county bar association dinner-dance is next weekend and I wondered if you would go with me?'

I was so surprised I almost gaped at him. Not only was he reportedly dating my beautiful friend Lizanne, but also I could have sworn that Bubba Sewell was not the least bit interested in me as a woman. And though my dating schedule was certainly not heavy, I had learned long ago that it was better to be home alone with a good book and a bag of potato chips than it was to be out on a date with someone who left you cold.

'I'm sorry, Bubba,' I said. I was not accustomed enough to turning down dates to be good at it. 'I'm just very busy right now. But thank you for asking me.'

He looked away, embarrassed. 'Okay. Maybe some other time.'

I smiled as noncommittally as I could.

'Is everything going – all right?' he asked suddenly.

How much did he know?

'You read about the bones found around the dead end sign?' It had been below the report about Bubba's run for representative: CITY WORKERS FIND BONES. It had been a very short story; I expected a much fuller account in the next morning's paper. Maybe, I suddenly thought, now that the law had the bones, there would be more information on the sex and age of the skeleton included in the next story. The few paragraphs this morning had stated that the bones were going to a pathologist for examination. I swam out of my thoughts to find Bubba Sewell eyeing me with some apprehension.

'The bones?' he prompted. 'A skeleton?'

'Well, there wasn't a skull,' I murmured.

'Was that in the paper?' he asked sharply. I'd made a mistake; as a matter of fact, the skeleton's skull-lessness had not been mentioned in the story.

'Gosh, Bubba,' I said coolly. 'I just don't know.'

We stared at each other for a minute.

'Gotta be going,' I said finally. 'The cats are waiting.'

'Oh, sure.' He tucked his mouth in and then relaxed it. 'Well . . . if you really need me, you know where I am. By the way, had you heard I'm running for office?'

'Yes. I'd heard that, sure had.' And we looked at each other for a second more. Then I marched up the sidewalk and unlocked the front door. Madeleine slithered out instantly and headed for the soft dirt around the bushes. Her litter box was only a backup system: she preferred to go out-of-doors. Bubba Sewell was gone by the time I locked the front door behind me.

Chapter Ten

I rattled around restlessly in the 'new' house for a few hours. It was mine, all mine, but somehow I didn't feel too cheerful about that anymore. Actually, I preferred my town house, a soulless rental. It had more room, I was used to it, I liked having an upstairs I didn't have to clean if company was coming. Could I stand living across the street from Arthur and Lynn? Next door to the unpredictable Marcia Rideout? Jane's books were already cramming the bookcases. Where would I put mine? But if I sold this house and bought a bigger one, probably the yard would be bigger, and I hadn't ever taken care of one . . . If Torrance hadn't mowed the yard for me, I wouldn't know how to cope. Maybe the yard crew that did the lawn at the town houses?

I maundered on in my head, opening the kitchen cabinets and shutting them, trying to decide which pots and pans were duplicates of mine so I could take them to the local Baptist church, which kept a room of household goods for families who got burned out or suffered some equal disaster. I finally chose some in a lackadaisical way and carried them out to the car loose; I was out of boxes. I was treading water emotionally, unable to settle on any one task or course of action.

I wanted to quit my job.

I was scared to. Jane's money seemed too good to be true. Somehow, I feared it might be taken away from me.

I wanted to throw the skull in the lake. I was also scared of whoever had reduced the skull to its present state.

I wanted to sell Jane's house because I didn't particularly care for it. I wanted to live in it because it was safely mine.

I wanted Aubrey Scott to adore me; surely a minister would have a specially beautiful wedding? I did not want to marry

Aubrey Scott because being a minister's wife took a lot more internal fortitude than I had. A proper minister's wife would have marched out of the house with that skull and gone straight to the police station without a second thought. But Aubrey seemed too serious a man to date without the prospect of the relationship evolving in that direction.

I did run the pots and pans to the Baptist church, where I was thanked so earnestly that it was soothing, and made me think better of my poor character.

On the way back to the new house, I stopped at Jane's bank on impulse. I had the key with me, surely? Yes, here it was in my purse. I went in hesitantly, suddenly thinking that the bank might present difficulties about letting me see the safe deposit box. But it wasn't too difficult. I had to explain to three people, but then one of them remembered Bubba Sewell coming by, and that made everything all right. Accompanied by a woman in a sober business suit, I got Jane's safe deposit box. Something about those vaults where they're kept makes me feel that there's going to be a dreadful secret inside. All those locked boxes, the heavy door, the attendant! I went into the little room that held only a table and a single chair, shut the door. Then I opened the box, telling myself firmly that nothing dreadful could be in a box so small. Nothing dreadful, but a good deal that was beautiful. When I saw the contents of the long metal box, I let my breath out in a single sigh. Who would ever have imagined that Jane would want these things?

There was a pin shaped like a bow, made out of garnets with the center knot done in diamonds. There were garnet and diamond earrings to match. There was a slim gold chain with a single emerald on it, and a pearl necklace and bracelet. There were a few rings, none of them spectacular or probably extremely valuable, but all of them expensive and very pretty. I felt I had opened the treasure chest in the pirate's cave. And these were mine now! I could not attach any sentiment to them, because I'd never seen Jane wear them – perhaps the pearls, yes; she'd worn the pearls to a wedding we'd both attended. Nothing else rang any bells. I tried on the rings. They were only a little loose. Jane and I both had small fingers. I was trying to imagine what I could wear the bow pin and earrings to; they'd look great on a winter white suit, I decided. But as I held the pieces and touched them, I knew that despite Bubba Sewell's saying there was nothing else in the safe deposit box, I was disappointed that there was no letter from Jane.

After I'd driven back to the house, despite an hour spent watching Madeleine and her kittens, I still could not ground myself. I ended up throwing myself on the couch and turning on CNN, while reading some of my favorite passages from Jane's copy of Donald Rumbelow's book on Jack the Ripper. She had marked her place with a slip of paper, and for a moment my heart pounded, thinking Jane had left me another message, something more explicit than *I didn't do it*. But it was only an old grocery list: eggs, nutmeg, tomatoes, butter . . .

I sat up on the couch. Just because this piece of paper had been a false alarm didn't mean there weren't any other notes! Jane would put them where she would think I'd find them. She had known no one but me would go through her books. The first one had been in a book about Madeleine Smith, Jane's main field of study. I riffled through Jane's other books about the Smith case. I shook them.

Nothing.

Then maybe she'd hidden something in one of the books about the case that most intrigued me – well, which one would that be? Either Jack the Ripper or the murder of Julia Wallace. I was already reading Jane's only Ripper book. I flipped through it but found no other notes. Jane also had only one book on Julia Wallace, and there again I found no message. Theodore Durrant, Thompson-Bywater, Sam Sheppard, Reginald Christie, Crippen . . . I shook Jane's entire true-crime library with no results.

I went through her fictional crime, heavy on women writers: Margery Allingham, Mary Roberts Rinehart, Agatha Christie . . . the older school of mysteries. And Jane had an unexpected shelf of sword-and-sorcery science fiction, too. I didn't bother with those, at least initially; Jane would not have expected me to look there.

But in the end I went through those as well. After two hours, I had shaken, riffled, and otherwise disturbed every volume on the shelves, only a trace of common sense preventing me from flinging them on the floor as I finished. I'd even read all the envelopes in the letter rack on the kitchen wall, the kind you buy at a handcraft fair; all the letters seemed to be from charities or old friends, and I stuffed them irritably back in the rack to go through at a later date.

Jane had left me no other message. I had the money, the house, the cat (plus kittens), the skull, and the note that said *I didn't do it*.

A peremptory knock on the front door made me jump. I'd been sitting on the floor so lost in the doldrums I hadn't heard anyone approach. I scrambled up and looked through the peephole, then flung the door open. The woman outside was as well-groomed as Marcia Rideout, as cool as a cucumber; she was not sweating in the heat. She was five inches taller than me. She looked like Lauren Bacall.

'Mother!' I said happily, and gave her a brief hug. She undoubtedly loved me, but she didn't like her clothes wrinkled.

'Aurora,' she murmured, and gave my hair a stroke.

'When did you get back? Come in!'

'I got in really late last night,' she explained, coming into the room and staring around her. 'I tried to call you this morning after we got up, but you weren't home. You weren't at the library. So after a while, I decided I'd phone in to the office, and Eileen told me about the house. Who is this woman who left you the house?'

'How's John?'

'No, don't put me off. You know I'll tell you all about the trip later.'

'Jane Engle. John knows – John knew her, too. She was in Real Murders with us.'

'At least that's disbanded now,' Mother said with some relief. It would have been hard for Mother to send John off to a monthly meeting of a club she considered only just on the good side of obscenity.

'Yes. Well, Jane and I were friends through the club, and she never married, so when she died, she left me – her estate.'

'Her estate,' my mother repeated. Her voice was beginning to get a decided edge. 'And just what, if you don't mind my asking, does that estate consist of?'

I could tell her or I could stonewall her. If I didn't tell her, she'd just pull strings until she found out, and she had a bunch of strings to pull.

'This Jane Engle was the daughter of Mrs John Elgar Engle,' I said.

'The Mrs Engle who lived in that gorgeous mansion on Ridgemont? The one that sold for eight hundred and fifty thousand because it needed renovation?'

Trust Mother to know her real estate.

'Yes, Jane was the daughter of that Mrs Engle.'

'There was a son, wasn't there?'

'Yes, but he died.'

'That was only ten or fifteen years ago. She couldn't have spent all that money, living here.' Mother had sized up the house instantly.

'I think this house was almost paid for when old Mrs Engle died,' I said.

'So you got this house,' Mother said, 'and . . . ? '

'And five hundred and fifty thousand dollars,' I said baldly. 'Thereabouts. And some jewelry.'

Mother's mouth dropped open. It was the first time in my life I think I'd ever astonished my mother. She's not a moneygrubbing person, but she has a great respect for cash and property, and it is the way she measures her own success as a professional. She sat down rather abruptly on the couch and automatically crossed her elegant legs in their designer sportswear. She will go so far as to wear slacks on vacation, to pool parties, and on days she doesn't work; she would rather be mugged than wear shorts.

'And of course I now have the cat and her kittens,' I continued maliciously.

'The cat,' Mother repeated in a dazed way.

Just then the feline in question made her appearance, followed by a chorus of forlorn mews from the kittens in Jane's closet.

Mother uncrossed her legs and leaned forward to look at Madeleine as if she had never seen a cat before. Madeleine walked right up to Mother's feet, stared up at her for a moment, then leaped onto the couch in one flowing motion and curled up on Mother's lap. Mother was so horrified she didn't move.

'This,' she said, 'is a cat you inherited?'

I explained about Parnell Engle, and Madeleine's odyssey to have her kittens in 'her' house.

Mother neither touched Madeleine nor heaved her legs to remove her.

'What breed is she?' Mother asked stiffly.

'She's a mutt cat,' I said, surprised. Then I realized Mother was evaluating the cat. Or valuing her. 'Want me to move her?'

'Please,' my mother said, still in that stiff voice.

Finally I understood. My mother was scared of the cat. In fact, she was terrified. But, being Mother, she would never admit it. That was why we'd never had cats when I was growing up. All her arguments about animal hair on everything, having to empty a litter tray, were just so much smoke screen.

'Are you scared of dogs, too?' I asked, fascinated. I carefully scooped Madeleine off Mother's lap, and scratched her behind the ears as I held her. She obviously preferred Mother's lap, but put up with me a few seconds, then indicated she wanted down. She padded into the kitchen to use her litter box, followed by Mother's horrified gaze. I pushed my glasses up on my nose so I could have a clear view of this unprecedented sight.

'Yes,' Mother admitted. Then she took her eyes off Madeleine and saw my face. Her guard snapped up immediately. 'I've just never cared for pets. For God's sake, go get yourself some contact lenses so you'll stop fiddling with those glasses,' she said very firmly. 'So. Now you have a lot of money?'

'Yes,' I admitted, still enthralled by my new knowledge of my mother.

'What are you going to do?'

'I don't know. I haven't made any plans yet. Of course, the

estate has to go through probate, but that shouldn't take too long, Bubba Sewell says.'

'He's the lawyer who's handling the estate?'

'Yes, he's the executor.'

'He's sharp.'

'Yes, I know.'

'He's ambitious.'

'He's running for office.'

'Then he'll do everything right. Running for office has become just like running under a microscope.'

'He asked me out, but I turned him down.'

'Good idea,' my mother said, to my surprise. 'It's never wise to have a social relationship mixed up with money transactions or financial arrangements.'

I wondered what she would say about a social relationship mixed up with religion.

'So you had a good time?' I asked.

'Yes, we did. But John came down with something like the flu, so we had to come home. He's over the worst, and I expect he'll be out and about tomorrow.'

'He didn't want to stay there until he got over it?' I couldn't imagine traveling with the flu.

'I suggested it, but he said when he was sick, he didn't want to be in a resort where everyone else was having fun, he wanted to be home in his own bed. He was quite stubborn about it. But, up until that time, we really had a great honeymoon.' Mother's face looked almost soft as she said that, and it was borne in on me for the first time that my mother was in love, maybe not in as gooey a way as Amina, but she was definitely feeling the big rush.

It occurred to me that John had come back to Lawrenceton and gotten in Mother's bed, not his own. 'Has John sold his house yet?' I asked.

'One of his sons wanted it,' Mother said in as noncommittal a voice as she could manage. 'Avery, the one that's expecting the baby. It's a big old house, as you know.'

'How did John David feel about that? Not that it's any of my business.' John David was John's second son.

'I wouldn't have presumed to advise John about his family business,' Mother began answering indirectly, 'because John and I signed a prenuptial agreement about our financial affairs.'

This was news to me, and I felt a distinct wave of relief. I'd never considered it before, but all the complications that could arise when both parties had grown children suddenly occurred to me. I'd only thought of what Mother might leave when she died, this very day. I should have known, as property conscious as she was, she would have taken care of everything.

'So I didn't advise him,' Mother was continuing, 'but he thought out loud when he was trying to figure out what was fair to do.'

'You're the obvious person for input when it comes to real estate questions.'

'Well, he did ask me the value of the house on the current market.'

'And?'

'I had it appraised, and I think – now I don't know, but I think – he gave John David the cash value of the house, and deeded over the house to Avery.'

'So John David didn't want the house at all?'

'No, his work requires that he transfer every few years, and it didn't make sense for him to own a house in Lawrenceton.'

'That worked out well.'

'Now I'm going to tell you what I did about my house.'

'Oh, Mom!' I protested.

'No,' she said firmly. 'You need to know this.'

'Okay,' I said reluctantly.

'I think a man needs to know he has a home that's his,' she said. 'And since John gave up his house, I have left him mine for his lifetime. So if I die before John, he gets to stay in the house until he dies. I thought that was only right. But, after John passes away, it's yours to do with as you will, of course.'

This was just my season for having things willed to me.

Suddenly I realized that Mother would leave me her business and her money, as well as the house; with Jane's money, and her little house, too, I need never work another day in my life.

What a startling prospect.

'Whatever you do is fine with me,' I said hastily, aware that Mother was looking at me in a funny way. 'I don't want to talk about it.'

'We'll have to sometime,' Mother warned.

What was with her today? Had getting remarried somehow awakened or reinforced her feelings of her own mortality? Was it signing the prenuptial agreement with all these arrangements for what would happen after her death? She was just back from her honeymoon. She should be feeling pretty frisky.

'Why are you talking about all this now?' I asked bluntly.

She considered this. 'I don't know,' she said in a puzzled way. 'I certainly didn't come here expecting to talk about it. I was going to tell you about the hotel and the beach and the tour we took, but somehow I got sidetracked. Maybe when we talked about what Jane Engle left you, I started thinking about what I was going to leave you. Though, of course, now you won't need it as badly. It does seem strange to me that Jane left all her money and property to someone who isn't even a member of the family, someone who wasn't even that close a friend.'

'It seems strange to me, too, Mom,' I admitted. I didn't want to tell my mother that Jane had left everything to me because she saw me starting out like her, single and bookish, and maybe Jane had seen something else in me that struck a chord with her; we were both fascinated by death between the pages of a book. 'And it's going to seem strange to a lot of other people.'

She thought about that for a little. She waited delicately to see if I would enlighten her about Jane's motives.

'I'm glad for you,' Mother said after a minute, seeing I wasn't going to offer any more information about my relationship with Jane. 'And I don't expect we have to worry about what people say.'

'Thanks.'

'I'd better get back to my sick husband,' Mother said fondly.

How strange it was to hear that. I smiled at her without thinking about it. 'I'm glad for you, too,' I told her honestly.

'I know that.' She gathered her purse and keys, and I rose to walk her to her car.

She was discussing a dinner party an old friend was planning to give for her and John, and I was wondering if I should ask to bring Aubrey, when Marcia Rideout came out of her front door. She was wearing another matched and beautifully ironed shorts set, and her hair was a little blonder, it seemed to me.

'Is that your momma I see with you?' she called when she was halfway down her drive. 'Do you just have a minute?'

We both waited with polite, expectant smiles.

'Aida, you may not remember me,' Marcia said, with her head tilted coyly to one side, 'but you and I were on the Fallfest committee together a couple of years ago.'

'Oh, of course,' Mother said, professional warmth in her voice. 'The festival turned out very well that year, didn't it?'

'Yes, but it was sure a lot of work, more than I ever bargained for! Listen, we're all just so thrilled Roe is moving on our street. I don't know if she told you yet or not, I understand you've been away on your honeymoon, but Torrance and I are giving Aurora and our other new neighbors' – and Marcia nodded her smooth head at the little yellow-shuttered house across the street – 'a little get-together tomorrow night. We would just love it if you and your new husband could come.'

Nothing nonpluses Mother. 'We'd love to, but I'm afraid John came back from the Bahamas with just a touch of flu,' she explained. 'I tell you what, I may just drop in by myself for a few minutes, just to meet Aurora's new neighbors. If my husband is feeling better, maybe he'll come, too. Can I leave it that indefinite?'

'Oh, of course, that poor man, the flu in this pretty weather! And on his honeymoon! Bless his heart!'

'Who are the other new people on the street?' Mother inquired, to stem Marcia's pity.

'A police detective and his brand-new wife, who is also a police detective! And she's going to have a baby just any time now. Isn't that exciting? I don't think I'd ever met a real detective until they moved in, and now we have two of them on the street. We should all be real safe now! We've had a lot of break-ins on this street the past few years – but I'm sure your daughter is as safe as can be, now,' Marcia tacked on hastily.

'Would that detective be Arthur Smith?' Mother asked. I heard the permafrost under her words. I could feel my face begin to tighten. I had never known how much Mother knew or guessed about my relationship with Arthur, but I had a feeling she'd gotten a pretty accurate picture. I turned my face away a little under pretext of pushing up my glasses.

'Yes. He's such a solemn young man, and handsome, too. Of course, not as handsome as the man Roe is dating.' Marcia actually winked.

'You don't think so?' my mother said agreeably. I bit my upper lip.

'Oh, no. That minister is so tall and dark. You can tell from my marrying Torrance, I like tall, dark men. And that mustache! It may not be nice to say this about a man in the ministry, but it's just plain sexy.'

My mother had been totting up this description. 'Well, I'll sure try to come, thanks so much for inviting me,' she said in a perfectly polite but unmistakably conclusive way.

'I'll just go back to cleaning the house,' Marcia said brightly, and, after a chorus of good-byes, off she trotted.

'Dating Father Scott?' Mother asked when she was sure Marcia was out of earshot. 'And you're over that lousy policeman?'

'Yes to both.'

Mother looked quite unsettled for a minute. 'You turned down a date with Bubba Sewell, you're over that Arthur Smith, and you're dating a minister,' she said wonderingly. 'There's hope for your love life after all.'

As I waved to her as she drove down the street, it was a positive satisfaction for me to think of the skull in her blanket bag.

Chapter Eleven

In a burst of morning energy, I was singing in the shower when the telephone rang. Blessing answering machines, I barely paused in my rendition of 'The Star-Spangled Banner.' The shower is probably the only place our national anthem should be sung, especially by people with a limited vocal range, a category that definitely includes me. As I rinsed the shampoo out of my hair, I did a medley of my favorite ads. For my finale, as I toweled I warbled 'Three Little Ducks.'

There is something to be said for living by oneself when one wants to sing unheard.

It would be hard to say why I was in such a festive mood. I had to go in to work for five hours, then come back to the town house to prepare for the party. I was pleased at the prospect of seeing Aubrey, but not goo-goo eyed. I was more or less getting used to being rich by now (though the word still gave me a thrill up my spine), and I was on standby regarding action on the skull. I squinted into my makeup mirror as I put on a little eye shadow.

'I'm going to quit my job,' I told my reflection, smiling.

The *pleasure* of being able to say that! To decide, just like that! Money was wonderful.

I remembered the phone message and pressed the play button, beaming at my reflection in the mirror like an idiot, my drying hair beginning to fly around my head in a dark, wavy nimbus.

'Roe?' began the voice, faint and uncertain. 'This is Robin Crusoe, calling from Italy. I called in and got your message from Phil . . . the guy subletting my apartment. Are you all right? He said Arthur married someone else. Can I come see you when I get back from Europe? If that's not a good idea, send a note to my old address. Well, write me either way, and I'll get it when I get back.

That should be in a few weeks, probably late next month. Or earlier. I'm running out of money. Good-bye.'

I had frozen when I first heard the voice begin. Now I sat breathing shallowly for a few seconds, my brush in my hand, my teeth biting my lower lip gently. My heart was beating fast, I'll admit. Robin had been my tenant and my friend and almost my lover. I really wanted to see him again. Now I would have the pleasure of composing a note that would say very delicately that I *definitely* wanted him to come calling when he got back. I didn't want him to get the impression I was sitting in Lawrenceton with my tongue hanging out while I panted, but I did want him to come, if he was of the same mind in a few weeks. And if I was. I could take my time composing that note.

I brushed my hair, which began to crackle and fly around even more wildly. I gathered it all together and put a band on it about halfway down its length, not as stodgy as a 'real' ponytail. And I tied a frivolous bow around the band. However, I did wear one of my old 'librarian' outfits that so disgusted Amina: a solid navy skirt of neutral length with a navy-and-white-striped blouse, plain support hose, and unattractive but very comfortable shoes. I cleaned my glasses, pushed them up on my nose, nodded at my reflection in the full-length mirror, and went downstairs.

If I'd known how to cha-cha, I think I would have done it going up the ramp from the employees' parking lot into the library.

'Aren't we happy today?' Lillian said sourly, sipping from her cup of coffee at the worktable in the book-mending room.

'Yes, ma'am, we are,' I said, depositing my purse in my little locker and snapping the padlock shut. My only claim to fame in my history as a librarian in Lawrenceton was that I had never once lost my padlock key. I kept it on a safety pin and pinned it to my skirt or my slip or my blouse. Today I pinned it to my collar and marched off to Mr Clerrick's office, humming a military tune. Or what I imagined was a military tune.

I tapped on the half-open door and stuck my head in. Mr Clerrick was already at work on a heap of papers, a steaming cup of coffee at his elbow and a smoldering cigarette in the ashtray.

'Good morning, Roe,' he said, looking up from his desk. Sam Clerrick was married with four daughters, and, since he worked in a library, that meant he was surrounded by women from the moment he got up to the moment he went to bed. You would think he would have learned how to treat them. But his greatest and most conspicuous failure was in people management. No one would ever accuse Sam Clerrick of coddling anyone, or of favoritism; he didn't care for any of us, had no idea what our home lives were like, and made no allowances for any individual's personality or work preferences. No one would ever like him; he would never be accused of being unfair.

I had always been a little nervous around someone who played his emotional cards as close to his chest as Sam Clerrick. Suddenly leaving did not seem so simple.

'I'm going to quit my job,' I said quietly, while I still had some nerve. As he stared, that little bit of nerve began to trickle away. 'I'm on part-time anyway, I don't feel like you really need me anymore.'

He kept peering at me over his half-glasses. 'Are you giving me notice, or quitting, no more work as of today?' he asked finally.

'I don't know,' I said foolishly. After I considered a moment, I said, 'Since you have at least three substitute librarians on your call list, and I know at least two of them would love to go regular part-time, I'm quitting, no more work as of five hours from now.'

'Is there something wrong that we can talk about?'

I came all the way into the room. 'Working here is okay,' I told him. 'I just don't have to anymore, financially, and I feel like a change.'

'You don't need the money,' he said in amazement.

He was probably the only person working at the library, or perhaps the only person in Lawrenceton, who didn't know by now about the money.

'I inherited.'

'My goodness, your mother didn't die, I hope?' He actually put his pencil down, so great was his concern.

'No, no relative.'

'Oh – good. Well. I'm sorry to see you go, even though you were certainly our most notorious employee for a while last year. Well, it's been longer than that now, I suppose.'

'Did you think about firing me then?'

'Actually, I was holding off until you killed Lillian.'

I stared at him blankly until I accepted the amazing fact that Sam Clerrick had made a joke. I began laughing, and he began laughing, and suddenly he looked like a human being.

'It's been a pleasure,' I said, meaning it for the first time, and turned and left his office.

'Your insurance will last for thirty days,' he called after me, running a little truer to form.

As luck would have it, that morning at the library business was excruciatingly slow. I didn't want to tell anyone I'd quit until I was actually leaving, so I hid among the books all morning, reading the shelves, dusting, and piddling along. I didn't get a lunch break, since I was just working five hours; I was supposed to bring it with me or get one of the librarians going out to bring back something from a fast-food place, and eat it very quickly. But that would mean eating in the break room, and there was sure to be someone else in there, and having a conversation without revealing my intention would be seen as fraudulent, in a way. So I dodged from here to there, making myself scarce, and by two o'clock I was very hungry. Then I had to go through the ritual of saying good-bye, I enjoyed working with you, I'll be in often to get books so we'll be seeing each other.

It made me sadder than I thought it would. Even saying good-bye to Lillian was not the unmitigated pleasure I had expected. I would miss having her around because she made me feel so virtuous and smart by contrast, I realized with shame. (*I* didn't moan and groan about every little change in work routine, *I* didn't bore people to tears with detailed accounts of boring events, *I* knew who Benvenuto Cellini was.) And I remembered Lillian finally standing by me when things had been so bad during the murders months before.

'Maybe you can hunt for a husband full-time now,' Lillian said in parting, and my shame vanished completely. Then I read in Lillian's face the knowledge that the only thing she had that I could possibly want was a husband.

'We'll see,' I told her, and held my hands behind my back so I wouldn't choke her.

I retrieved my purse and turned in my locker key, and I walked out the back door for the last time.

I went straight to the grocery store. I wanted something for lunch, I wanted something to put in the refrigerator at the house on Honor for snacks while I was there. I zoomed through the grocery store tossing boxes and produce bags in my cart with abandon. I celebrated quitting my job by getting one of the really expensive microwave meals, the kind with a neat reusable plate. This was getting fancy for me, for lunch anyway. Maybe now I would have time to cook. Did I want to learn to cook in any more detail? I could make spaghetti, and I could make pecan pie. Did I need to know anything else? I debated it as I stood in front of the microwave at the town house.

I could decide at my leisure. I was now a woman of leisure.

I liked the sound of it.

The woman of leisure decided to celebrate by buying a new outfit to wear to the Rideouts' party. I would not go to Great Day, I decided; I'd share the wealth and go to Marcus Hatfield instead. Usually Marcus Hatfield made me nervous; though it was a mere satellite of the big Atlanta store, the selection was just too great, the saleswomen too aggressively groomed. Maybe my contact with Marcia was inuring me to immaculate grooming; I felt I could face even the cosmetics-counter woman without flinching.

I pulled my skirt straight and stiffened my spine before I entered. I can buy anything in this store, I reminded myself. I marched through the doors in my hopeless librarian's outfit. I was almost immediately confronted by a curvy vision in bright flowers, perfect nails, and subtle makeup.

'Hey, neighbor,' exclaimed the vision. It was Carey Osland in her working getup. I could see why she preferred loafers and housedresses. She looked marvelous, almost edible, but definitely not comfortable. 'I'm glad to see you,' Carey was saying warmly while I was decoding her identity.

'Good to see you, too,' I managed.

'Can I help you today?'

'I need something new to wear tonight.'

'To the sun-deck party.'

'Yes. It's so nice of the Rideouts to be giving it.'

'Marcia loves to entertain. There's nothing she likes better than to have a bunch of people over.'

'She said she didn't like it when her husband had to be away overnight.'

'No. I expect you noticed she drinks a little then. She's been like that as long as I've known her, I guess . . . though I don't know her very well. She knows a lot of people around town, but she never seems to be close friends with anyone. Were you thinking of a sports outfit or did you want a sundress, something like that?'

'What?'

'For the party.'

'Oh, sorry, I was off in the clouds somewhere. Um . . . what are you going to wear?'

'Oh, I'm too fat to wear a sundress,' Carey said cheerfully. 'But you'd look real pretty in one; and, so it wouldn't be too dressy, you could wear flat sandals and go real plain on your jewelry.'

I looked dubiously at the dress Carey had pulled out. Mrs Day would never have suggested it for me. But, then, Mrs Day didn't carry too much like this at her shop. It was white and orange, very pretty but very casual, and there wasn't a back to it.

'I couldn't wear a bra with that,' I pointed out.

'Oh, no,' Carey agreed calmly.

'I would jiggle,' I said doubtfully.

'Go try it on,' Carey said with a wink. 'If you don't like it, we have all kinds of cute shorts sets and lightweight pants, and any of them would be just fine, but just put this dress on.'

I had never had to almost completely undress to try on clothes before. I pulled on the dress and bounced up and down on the balls of my feet, my eyes on the dressing-room mirror. I was trying to gauge the amount of jiggle. I am chesty for such a small person, and there was enough jiggle to give me pause.

'How is it?' Carey called from outside my cubicle.

'Oh . . . I don't know,' I said doubtfully. I bounced again. 'After all, I'm going with a minister.'

'He's human,' Carey observed. 'God made bosoms, too.'

'True.' I turned around and observed my back. It looked very bare. 'I can't carry this off, Carey,' I told her.

'Let me see.'

I reluctantly opened the door of the cubicle.

'Wow,' said Carey. 'You really look *good*,' she said with squinted eyes. 'Very sexy,' she added in a conspiratorial whisper.

'I just feel too conspicuous. My back feels cold.'

'He'd love it.'

'I don't know about that.'

I looked in a bigger mirror at the end of the row of dressing rooms. I considered. No, I decided finally. I could not go out in that dress with someone I hadn't slept with.

'I'm not going to wear it tonight, so I still need to find something else for that,' I told Carey. 'But I think I'll buy it anyway.'

Carey became the complete saleswoman. The orange-and-white dress was whisked away to be put on a hanger, and she brought several more things for me to try on. Carey seemed to be determined that I wanted to present a sexy, sophisticated image, and I became sorry I hadn't gone to Great Day. Finally we found a cotton knit shorts and shirt that represented a compromise. The shirt was scoop-necked and white with red polka dots, and the red shorts were cut very full, like a little skirt, with a long tie belt that matched the shirt. I certainly had a lot of exposed skin, but at least it wasn't on my back. Carey talked me into red sandals and red bracelet and earrings to match before I called a halt to my shopping.

When I carried my purchases back to the town house, I called Aubrey at his church. 'Who's calling?' the church secretary asked, when I wanted to be connected to Aubrey.

'Roe Teagarden.'

'Oh!' she said breathlessly. 'Sure, Roe, I'll tell him. He's such a nice man, we just love him here at St. John.'

I stared at the phone for a second before I realized I was being given a boost in my assumed effort to win the heart of their priest. The congregation of St. John's must think it was time their leader married again, and I must be respectable enough at first glance to qualify as a suitable mate.

'Roe?'

'Hi, Aubrey,' I said, shaking myself out of my thoughts. 'Listen, would you meet me tonight at the house on Honor instead of picking me up here at the town house? I want to feed the cat before the party.'

'Sure. Are we supposed to bring anything? A bottle of wine?'

'She didn't want me to bring anything to eat, but if you want to bring a bottle of wine, I imagine they'd be glad.' A nice thought on Aubrey's part.

'This is casual, right?'

'It's going to be on their sun deck, so I'm sure it is.'

'Good. I'll see you at your new house at seven, then.'

'That's just fine.'

'I look forward to it,' he said quietly.

'Me, too.'

I got there early, and pulled my car all the way inside the carport so there'd be room for Aubrey's. After tending to Madeleine's needs, I thought of the clothes still in Jane's drawers. I'd cleaned out the closet, but not the chest of drawers. I pulled one open idly to see what I had to contend with. It turned out to be Jane's sleepwear drawer. Jane had had an unexpected taste in nightgowns. These certainly weren't what I'd call little-old-lady gowns, though they weren't naughty or anything like that. I pulled out the prettiest, a rose pink nylon, and decided I might actually keep it. Then I thought, Maybe I'll just spend the night here. Somehow the idea struck me as fun. The sheets on the bed were clean, changed by the maid hired to straighten everything out after Jane had gone into the hospital. Here was a gown. I'd just put a little food in the refrigerator. The air conditioner was running. There was a toothbrush in a sealed container in the bathroom, and an unopened tube of toothpaste. I would see what waking up in my new house was like.

The doorbell rang, announcing Aubrey's arrival. I answered it feeling a little self-conscious because of the scoop neckline. Sure enough, Aubrey's eyes went instantly to my cleavage. 'You should have seen the one I didn't wear,' I said defensively.

'Was I that obvious?' he said, a little embarrassed.

'Carey Osland says God made bosoms, too,' I told him, and then closed my eyes and wished the ground would swallow me up.

'Carey Osland says truly,' he said fervently. 'You look great.'

Aubrey had a knack for taking the embarrassment out of situations.

'You look nice yourself,' I told him. He was wearing what would be a safe outfit at ninety percent of Lawrenceton's social occasions: a navy knit shirt and khaki slacks, with loafers.

'Well, now that we've admired each other, isn't it time to go?'

I glanced at my watch. 'Right on the dot.'

He offered his arm like the usher at a wedding, and I laughed and took it. 'I'm going to be a bridesmaid again,' I told him. 'And you know what they say about women who are bridesmaids so often.' Then I felt furious with myself all over again, for even introducing the subject of weddings.

'They say, "What a beautiful bridesmaid",' Aubrey offered tactfully.

'That's right,' I said, relieved. If I couldn't do better than this, I'd have to keep my mouth shut all evening.

From my first glimpse of Marcia it was apparent to me that she lived to entertain. The food even had little mesh tents over it to keep flies off, a practical touch in Lawrenceton in the summer. The cloths covering the tables erected on the sun deck for the occasion were starched and bright. Marcia was her usual well-turned-out self, as starched and bright as the tablecloths in blue cotton shorts and blouse. She had dangly earrings and painted nails, top and bottom. She exclaimed over the wine and asked if we wanted a glass now. We refused politely and she went in to put it in the refrigerator, while Torrance, looking exceptionally tan in his white shorts and striped shirt, took our drink orders. We both took gin and tonics with lots of ice, and went to sit on the built-in bench that ran all the way around the huge deck. My feet could barely touch the deck. Aubrey sat very close when he sat next to me.

Carey and Macon came in right on our heels, and I introduced them to Aubrey. Macon had met him before at a ministerial council meeting Macon had covered for the paper, and they immediately plunged into an earnest conversation about what the council hoped to accomplish in the next few months. Carey eyed my outfit and winked at me, and we talked over the men about how good Marcia and the party food looked. Then the couple who lived in the house across from Carey, the McMans, came up to be introduced, and they assumed that Aubrey and I owned Jane's house together, that we were cohabiting. As we were straightening that out, Lynn and Arthur came in. Lynn was elephantine and obviously very uncomfortable in a maternity shorts outfit. Arthur was looking a little worried and doubtful. When I saw him I felt – nothing.

When Arthur and Lynn worked their way around to us, he seemed to have shaken off whatever had been troubling him. Lynn looked a little more cheerful, too. 'I wasn't feeling too well earlier,' she confided as Arthur and Aubrey tried to find something to talk about. 'But it seems to have stopped for the moment.'

'Not good – how?'

'Like gas pains,' she said, her mouth a wry twist at this confession. 'Honestly, I've never been so miserable in my life. Everything I eat gives me heartburn, and my back is killing me.'

'And you're due very soon?'

'Not for a couple more weeks.'

'When's your next doctor's appointment?'

'In your last month, you go every week,' Lynn said

knowledgeably. 'I'm due to go back in tomorrow. Maybe he'll tell me something.'

I decided I might as well admit wholesale ignorance. Lynn certainly needed something to feel superior about. She had looked sourly on my red and white shorts outfit. 'So what could he tell you?' I asked.

'Oh. Well, for example, he could tell me I've started dilating – you know, getting bigger to have the baby. Or he could tell me I'm effacing.'

I nodded hastily, so Lynn wouldn't explain what that meant.

'Or how much the baby has dropped, if its head is really far down.'

I was sorry I'd asked. But Lynn was looking in better spirits, and she went on to tell Aubrey how they'd decorated the nursery, segueing neatly from that domestic subject to a discussion of the break-ins on the street, which were being generally discussed. The McMans complained about the police inaction on the crimes, unaware that they were about to become very embarrassed.

'You're going to have to understand,' Arthur said, his pale blue eyes open wide, which meant he was very irritated, 'that if nothing is stolen and no fingerprints are found, and no one sees anything, the burglar is going to be almost impossible to find unless an informant turns in something.'

The McMans, small and mousy and shy, turned identical shades of mortification when they realized that the new couple next door were both police detectives. After an embarrassing bumble of apologies and retractions, Carey talked about her break-in – which had occurred when she and her daughter were at Carey's folks' house for Thanksgiving two years ago – and Marcia related her experience, which had 'scared her to death.'

'I came back from shopping, and of course it was when Torrance was out of town; nothing happens but when Torrance is out of town' – and she gave him a knife of a glance – 'and I saw the back window of the kitchen was broken out, oh you should have seen me make tracks over to Jane's house.'

'When was that?' I asked. 'Around the time Carey's house was broken into?'

'You know, it was. It was maybe a month later. I remember it was cold and we had to get the glass fixed in a hurry.'

'When was your house broken into?' I asked Macon, who was holding Carey's hand and enjoying it.

'After the Laverys,' he said, after a moment's thought. 'They're the people who owned the house you bought,' he said to Arthur. 'They got transferred five months ago, so I know they're relieved not to have to make two house payments. My break-in, and the Laverys', was like the others . . . back window, house searched and messed up, but nothing apparently taken.'

'When was that?' I persisted. Arthur shot me a sharp look, but Lynn seemed more interested in her stomach, which she was massaging slowly.

'Oh, sometime about a year and a half ago, maybe longer.'

'So Jane's house was the only one that hadn't been broken into until very recently?'

Carey, Macon, the McMans, and Marcia and Torrance exchanged glances.

'I think that's right,' Macon said. 'Come to think of it. And it's been quite awhile since the last one, I know I hadn't thought about it in ages until Carey told me about Jane's house.'

'So everyone's been broken into – everyone on the street?' Was that what Jack Burns had told me?

'Well,' Marcia said, as she poured dressing on the salad and tossed it, 'everyone but the Inces, whose house is on the two lots across from Macon and us. They're very, very old and they never go out anymore. Their daughter-in-law does everything for them, shopping and taking them to doctor appointments and so on. They haven't been bothered, or I'm sure Margie – that's the daughter-in-law – would've come over and told me about it. Every now and then she comes over and has a cup of coffee after she's been to see them.'

'I wonder what it means?' I asked no one in particular.

An uncomfortable silence fell.

'Come on, you all, the food's all ready and waiting!' Marcia said cheerfully.

Everyone rose with alacrity except Lynn. I heard Arthur murmur, 'You want me to bring you something, hon?'

'Just a little bit,' she said wearily. 'I'm just not very hungry.'

It didn't seem to me that Lynn would have any room left for food, the baby was taking up so much.

Torrance went through the house to answer the front doorbell. The rest of us shuffled through the line, oohing and ahhing appropriately at the gorgeous food. It was presented in a beautiful way, all the dishes decorated and arranged as if far more important people than we were coming to taste it. Unless Marcia had had help, this table represented hours of work. But the food itself was comfortingly homely.

'Barbecued ribs!' exclaimed Aubrey happily. 'Oh boy. Roe, you're just going to have to put up with me. I make a mess when I eat them.'

'There's not a neat way to eat ribs,' I observed. 'And Marcia has put out extra large napkins, I see.'

'I'd better take two.'

Just then I heard a familiar voice rising above the general chatter. I turned to peer around Aubrey, my mouth falling a little open in a foolish way.

'Mother!' I said, in blank surprise.

It was indeed Mother, in elegant cream slacks and midnight blue blouse, impressive but casual gold necklace and earrings, and her new husband in tow.

'I'm so sorry we were late,' she was apologizing in her Lauren Bacall gracious woman mode, the one that always made people accept her apology. 'John wasn't sure until the last minute whether he felt like coming or not. But I did so want to meet Aurora's new neighbors, and it was so kind of you to invite us . . .'

The Rideouts gushed back, there was a round of introductions, and suddenly the party seemed livelier and more sophisticated.

Despite his tired eyes, John looked well after their honeymoon, and I told him so. For a few minutes, John seemed a little puzzled as to what exactly Aubrey was doing at the party, but when it sunk in that his minister was my date, John took a deep breath and rose to the occasion, discussing church affairs very briefly with Aubrey, just enough to make them comfortable with each other without boring the non-Episcopalians. Mother and John joined in the food line behind us, Mother sparing a cold glance for Arthur, who was sitting beside his wife and eating while giving her a solicitous look or laying his hand on her shoulder every few seconds.

'She's about to pop. I thought they just got married a few months ago,' Mother hissed in my ear.

'Mom, hush,' I hissed back.

'I need to talk to you, young lady,' Mother responded in a low voice so packed with meaning that I began to wonder what I could have done that she'd heard of. I was almost as nervous as I'd been at six when she used that voice with me.

We sat back down at the picnic tables set with their bright tablecloths and napkins, and Marcia rolled around a cart with drinks and ice on it. She was glowing at all the compliments. Torrance was beaming, too, proud of his wife. I wondered, looking at Lynn and Arthur, why the Rideouts hadn't had children. I wondered if Carey Osland and Macon would try to have another one if they married. Carey was probably forty-two, but women were having them later and later, it seemed. Macon must have been at least six to ten years older than Carey – of course, he had a son who was at least a young adult . . . the missing son.

'While I was in the Bahamas,' John said quietly into my ear, 'I tried to get a minute to see if the house of Sir Harry Oakes was still standing.'

I had to think for a minute. The Oakes case . . . okay, I remembered.

'Alfred de Marigny, acquitted, right?'

'Yes,' said John happily. It was always nice to talk to someone who shared your hobby.

'Is this a historical site in the Bahamas?' Aubrey asked from my right.

'Well, in a way,' I told him. 'The Oakes house was the site of a famous murder.' I swung back around to John. 'The feathers were the strangest feature of that case, I thought.'

'Oh, I think there's an easy explanation,' John said dismissively. 'I think a fan blew the feathers from a pillow that had been broken open.'

'After the fire?'

'Yes, had to have been,' John said, wagging his head from side to side. 'The feathers looked white in the picture, and otherwise they would've been blackened.'

'Feathers?' Aubrey inquired.

'See,' I explained patiently, 'the body – Sir Harry Oakes – was found partially burned, on a bed, with feathers stuck all over it. The body, I mean, not the bed. Alfred de Marigny, his son-in-law, was charged. But he was acquitted, mostly because of the deplorable investigation by the local police.'

Aubrey looked a little – what? I couldn't identify it.

John and I went on happily hashing over the murder of Sir Harry, my mother to John's left carrying on a sporadic conversation with the mousy McMans across from her.

I turned halfway back to Aubrey to make sure he was appreciating a point I was making about the bloody handprint on the screen in the bedroom and noticed he had dropped his ribs on his plate and was looking under the weather.

'What's the matter?' I asked, concerned.

'Would you mind not talking about this particular topic while I eat my ribs, which looked so good until a few minutes ago?' Aubrey was trying to sound jocular, but I could tell he was seriously unhappy with me.

Of course I was at fault. That had the unfortunate result of making me exasperated with Aubrey, as well as myself. I took a few seconds to work myself into a truly penitent frame of mind.

'I'm sorry, Aubrey,' I said quietly. I stole a peek at John out of the corner of my eye. He was looking abashed, and my mother had her eyes closed and was silently shaking her head as if her children had tried her beyond her belief, and in public at that. But she quickly rallied and smoothly introduced that neutral and lively subject, the rivalry of the phone companies in the area.

I was so gloomy over my breach of taste that I didn't even chip in my discovery that my phone company could make my phone ring at two houses at the same time. Arthur said he was glad that he had been able to keep his old phone number. I wondered how Lynn felt about giving up her own, but she didn't look as if she gave a damn one way or another. Right after Arthur finished eating and they had thanked Marcia and Torrance in a polite murmur for the party, the good food, and the fellowship, they quietly left to go home.

'That young lady looks uncomfortable,' Torrance commented in a lull in the telephone wars. Of course, that led to a discussion of Arthur and Lynn and their police careers, and since I was also a newcomer on the street the discussion moved logically to my career, which I was obliged to tell them – including my mother – had come to an end.

I thought if my mother's face held its mildly interested smile any longer, it would crack.

Aubrey had finished his supper finally and joined in the conversation, but in a subdued way. I thought we were going to have to talk sometime soon about my interest in murder cases and the fact that he found them nauseating. I was trying not to think about how much fun it had been to talk to John about the fascinating Oakes case . . . and it had occurred while the duke and duchess of Windsor were governing the islands! I'd have to catch my new stepfather alone sometime and we could really hash it over.

I was recalled to the here and now by my mother's voice in my ear. 'Come to the bathroom for a moment!'

I excused myself and went in the house with her. I'd never been in the Rideouts' before, and I could only gather an impression of spotless maintenance and bright colors before I was whisked into the hall bathroom. It seemed like a teenager sort of thing to do, going into the bathroom together, and just as I opened my mouth to ask my mother if she had a date to the prom, she turned to me after locking the door and said—

'What, young woman, is a skull doing in my blanket bag?'

For what felt like the tenth time in one day I was left with my mouth hanging open. Then I rallied. 'What on earth were you doing getting a blanket out in this weather?'

'Getting a blanket for my husband while he was having chills with the flu,' she told me through clenched teeth. 'Don't you dare try to sidetrack me!'

'I found it,' I said.

'Great. So you found a human skull, and you decided to put it in a blanket bag in your mother's house while she was out of town. That makes perfect sense. A very rational procedure.'

I was going to have to level with her. But locked in Marcia Rideout's bathroom was not the situation.

'Mom, I swear that tomorrow I'll come to your house and tell you all about it.'

'I'm sure any time would be okay with you because you have no job to go to,' my mother said very politely. 'However, I have to earn my living, and I am going to work. I will expect you to be at my house tomorrow night at seven o'clock, when I had better hear a good explanation for what you have done. And while I'm saying drastic things, I might as well tell you something else, though since you have been an adult I have tried not to give you any advice on your affairs of the heart – or whatever. Do *not* sleep with my husband's minister. It would be very embarrassing for John.'

'For John? It would be embarrassing for *John*?' Get a hold, I told myself. I took a deep breath, looked in the gleaming mirror, and pushed my glasses up on my nose. 'Mother, I can't tell you how glad I am that you have restrained yourself, all these years, from commenting on my social life, other than telling me you wished I had more of one.'

We looked at each other in the mirror with stormy eyes. Then I tried smiling at her. She tried smiling at me. The smiles were tiny, but they held.

'All right,' she said finally, in a more moderate voice. 'We'll see you tomorrow night.'

'It's a date,' I agreed.

When we came back to the sun deck, the party talk had swung around to the bones found at the end of the street. Carey was saying the police had been to ask her if there was anything she remembered that might help to identify the bones as her husband's. 'I told them,' she was saying, 'that that rascal had run off and left me, not been killed. For weeks after he didn't come back, I thought he might walk back through that door with those diapers. You know,' she told Aubrey parenthetically, 'he left to get diapers for the baby and never came back.' Aubrey nodded, perhaps to indicate understanding or perhaps because he'd already heard this bit of Lawrenceton folklore. 'When the police found the car at the Amtrak station,' Carey continued, 'I knew he'd just run off. He's been dead to me ever since, but I definitely don't believe those bones are his.' Macon put his arm around her. The mousy McMans were enthralled at this real-life drama. My mother stared at me in sudden consternation. I pretended I didn't see it.

'So I told them he'd broken his leg once, the year before we got married, if that would tell them anything, and they thanked me and said they'd let me know. But after the first day he was gone, when I was so distraught; well, after the police told me they'd found his car, I didn't worry about him anymore. I just felt mad.'

Carey had gotten upset, and was trying very hard not to let a tear roll down her cheeks. Marcia Rideout was staring at her, hoping her party was not going to be ruined by a guest weeping openly.

Torrance said soothingly, 'Now, Carey, it's not Mike, it's some old tramp. That's sad, but it's nothing for us to worry about.' He stood, holding his drink, his sturdy body and calm voice somehow immensely reassuring.

Everyone seemed to relax a little. But then Marcia said, 'But where's the skull? On this evening's television news they said there wasn't a skull.' Her hand was shaking as she put the lid on a casserole. 'Why wasn't the head there?'

It was a tense moment. I couldn't help clenching my drink tighter and looking down at the deck. My mother's eyes were on me; I could feel her glare.

'It sounds macabre,' Aubrey said gently, 'but perhaps a dog or some other animal carried off the skull. There's no reason it couldn't have been with the rest of the body for some time.'

'That's true,' Macon said after a moment's consideration.

The tension eased again. After a little more talk, my mother and John rose to leave. No one is immune to my mother's graciousness; Marcia and Torrance were beaming by the time she made her progress out the front door, John right behind her basking in the glow. The McMans soon said they had to pay off their babysitter and take her home, since it was a school night. Carey Osland, too, said she had to relieve her sitter. 'Though my daughter is beginning to think she can stay by herself,' she told us proudly. 'But for now she definitely needs someone there, even when I'm just two houses away.'

'She's an independent girl,' Macon said with a smile. He seemed quite taken with Carey's daughter. 'I'd only been around boys before, and girls are so different to raise. I hope I can do a better job helping Carey than I did raising my son.'

Since the Rideouts were childless, and so was I, and so was Aubrey, we had no response that would have made sense.

I thanked Marcia for the party, and complimented her and Torrance on the decorations and food.

'Well, I did barbecue the ribs,' Torrance admitted, running his hand over his already bristly chin, 'but all the rest of the fixing is Marcia's work.'

I told Marcia she should be a caterer, and she flushed with pleasure. She looked just like a department store mannequin with a little pink painted on the cheeks for realism, so pretty and so perfect.

'Every hair is in place,' I told Aubrey wonderingly as we walked over to his car parked in my driveway. 'She wouldn't ever let her hair do this,' and I sunk my hands into my own flyaway mop.

'That's what I want to do,' Aubrey said promptly, and, stopping and facing me, he ran his hands through my hair. 'It's beautiful,' he said in an unministerly voice.

Woo-woo. The kiss that followed was long and thorough enough to remind me of exactly how long it had been since I had biblically known anyone. I could tell Aubrey felt the same.

We mutually disengaged. 'I shouldn't have done that,' Aubrey said. 'It makes me . . .'

'Me, too,' I agreed, and he laughed, and the mood was broken. I was very glad I hadn't worn the orange-and-white dress. Then his hands would have been on my bare back . . . I started to chatter to distract myself. We leaned against his car, talking about the party, my new stepfather's flu, my quitting my job, his retreat for priests he'd be attending that Friday and Saturday at a nearby state park.

'Shall I follow you home?' he asked, as he slid into his car.

'I might spend the night here,' I said. I bent in and gave him a light kiss on the lips and a smile, and then he left.

I walked to the kitchen door and went in. The moon through the open kitchen curtains gave me plenty of light, so I went to the bedroom in darkness. The contrast of quiet and dark with the talk, talk, talk I'd done that day made me sleepier than a pill would have. I switched on the bathroom light briefly to brush my teeth and shuck my clothes. Then I pulled the rose pink nightgown over my head, switched off the bathroom light, and made my way to the bed in darkness. To the quiet hum of the air-conditioning and the occasional tiny mew from the kittens in the closet, I fell fast asleep.

Chapter Twelve

I woke up. I knew where I was instantly – in Jane's house. I swung my legs over the side of the bed automatically, preparing to trek to the bathroom. But I realized in a slow, middle-of-the-night way that I didn't need to go.

The cats were quiet.

So why was I awake?

Then I heard movement somewhere else in the house, and saw a beam of light flash through the hall. Someone was in the house with me. I bit the insides of my mouth together to keep from screaming.

Jane's clock radio on the bedside table had a glowing face that illuminated the outline of the bedside phone. With fingers that were almost useless, I lifted the receiver, taking such care, such care . . . no noise. Thank God it was a push-button. From instinct I dialed the number I knew so well, the number that would bring help even faster than 911.

'Hello?' said a voice in my ear, groggy with sleep.

'Arthur,' I breathed. 'Wake up.'

'Who is this?'

'It's Roe. I'm across the street in Jane's house. There is someone in the house.'

'I'll be there in a minute. Stay quiet. Hide.'

I hung up the phone so gently, so delicately, trying to control my hands, oh Lord, let me not make a sound.

I knew what had given me away: it was my downward glance when the skull was mentioned, at the party. Someone had been watching for just such a reaction.

I slid my glasses on while I was thinking. I had two options on hiding: under the bed or in the closet with the cats. The intruder was in the guest bedroom, just a short hall length away. I could see the flashlight beam bobbing here and there; searching, searching again, for the damn *skull*! The best place to hide would be the big dirty-clothes closet in the bathroom; I was small enough to double up in there, since it was almost square to match the linen closet on top of it. If I hid in the bedroom closet, the intruder might hear the cat noises and investigate. But I couldn't risk slipping into the bathroom now, with the light flashing in the hallway unpredictably.

In response to my thoughts, it seemed, the light bobbed out of the guest bedroom, into the little hall, through the big archway into the living room. When it was well within the living room, I slid off the bed onto my feet with the tiniest of thumps . . .

. . . and landed right on Madeleine's tail. The cat yowled, I screamed, a startled exclamation came from the living room. I heard thumping footsteps and, when a blob was in the doorway, pausing, maybe fumbling for a light switch, I leaped. I hit someone right in the chest, wrapped my right arm around a beefy neck, and with my left hand grabbed a handful of short hair and pulled as hard as I could. Something from a self-defense course I'd taken popped into my mind and I began shrieking at the top of my lungs.

Something hit me a terrible blow on the back, but I tightened my grip on the short hair and my stranglehold on the neck. 'Stop,' wheezed a heavy voice, 'stop, stop!' And blows began raining on my back and legs. I was being shaken loose by all the staggering and my own weight, and I had to stop screaming to catch my breath. But I sucked it in and had opened my mouth to shriek again when the lights came on.

My attacker whirled to face the person who'd turned on the light, and in that whirl I was slung off onto the floor, landing not quite on my feet and staggering into the bedpost to collect a few more bruises.

Lynn Liggett Smith stood leaning against the wall in the hall, breathing heavily, the gun in her hand pointing at Torrance Rideout, who had only a flashlight dangling from his hand. If the flashlight had been a knife, I'd have been bleeding from a dozen wounds; as it was, I felt like Lee's Army had marched over me. I held on to the bedpost and panted. Where was Arthur?

Torrance took in Lynn's weak stance and huge belly and turned back to me.

'You have to tell me,' he said desperately, as if she wasn't even there, 'you have to tell me where the skull is.'

'Put your hands against the wall,' Lynn said steadily but weakly. 'I'm a police officer and I will shoot.'

'You're nine months pregnant and about to fall down,' Torrance said over his shoulder. He turned to me again. '*Where is the skull?*' His broad, open face was crossed with seams I'd never noticed before, and there was blood trickling down from his scalp onto his white shirt. I seemed to have removed a square inch of hair.

Lynn fired into the ceiling.

'Put your hands against the wall, you bastard,' she said coldly.

And he did.

He hadn't realized that if Lynn really shot at him she stood an excellent chance of hitting me. Before he got the idea, I moved to the other side of the bed. But then I couldn't see Lynn. This bedroom was too tight. I didn't like Torrance being between me and the door.

'Roe,' Lynn said from the hall, slowly. 'Pat him down and see if he's got a gun. Or knife.' She sounded like she was in pain.

I hated getting so close to Torrance. Did he respect the gun enough? Had he picked up on the strain in Lynn's voice? I wished, for a moment, that she had gone on and shot him.

My only ideas about patting a suspect down came from television. I had a shrinking distaste for touching Torrance's body, but I pursed my lips and ran my hands over him.

'Just change in his pocket,' I said hoarsely. My screaming had hurt more than Torrance's ears.

'Okay,' said Lynn slowly. 'Here are the cuffs.'

When I looked right in her face, I was shocked. Her eyes were wide and frightened, she was biting her lower lip. The gun was steady in her hand, but it was taking all her will to keep it so. The carpet looked dark around her feet, which were wearing slippers that were dark and light pink. I looked more closely. The darkness on her slippers was wetness. She had fluid trickling down her legs. There was a funny smell in the air. Lynn's water had broken.

Where was Arthur?

I closed my eyes for a second in sheer consternation. When I opened them, Lynn and I were staring at each other in panic. Then Lynn hardened her glare and said, 'Take the cuffs, Roe.'

I reached through the narrow doorway and took them. Arthur had shown me how to use his one day, so I did know how to close them on Torrance's wrists.

'Hold out your hands behind you,' I said as viciously as I could. Lynn and I were going to lose control any minute. I'd gotten one cuff on when Torrance erupted. He swung the arm with the cuff on it around, and the flying loose cuff caught me on the side of the head. But he mustn't get the gun! I gripped whatever of him I could grab, blinded by pain, and hobbled him enough to land us both on the floor, rolling around in the limited space, me hanging on for my own dear life, him desperately trying to be rid of me.

'Torrance, stop!' shrieked yet another voice, and we were still, him on top of me panting and me underneath barely breathing at all. Past his shoulder I could see Marcia, her hair still smooth, her blue shorts and shirt obviously hastily pulled on.

'Honey, it doesn't make any difference anymore, we have to stop,' she said gently. He got off me to swing around and look at her heavily. Then Lynn moaned, a terrible sound.

Torrance seemed mesmerized by his wife. I crawled past him and past her, actually brushing her leg as I went by. They both ignored me in the eeriest way.

Lynn had slid down the wall. She was making a valiant attempt to hold the gun up but couldn't manage anymore. When she saw me, her eyes made an appeal and her hand fell to the floor and released the gun. I took it and swung around, fully intending to somehow shoot both the Rideouts, our recent hosts. But they were still wrapped up in each other, and I could have riddled them both for all they paid attention to me. With the affronted feeling of being a child whose anger adults won't take seriously, I turned back to Lynn.

Her eyes were closed, and her breathing was funny. Then I realized she was breathing in a pattern.

'You're having the baby,' I said sadly.

She nodded, still with her eyes closed, and kept her breathing going.

'You called some backup, right?'

She nodded again.

'Arthur must have been out on a call; that was you on the phone,' I observed, and I went into the bathroom right at my back to wash my hands and get some towels.

'I don't know nothin' 'bout birthin' no babies,' I told my reflection, pushed my glasses up on my nose, had the fleeting thought that it was nothing short of amazing they hadn't been cracked, and went to squat by Lynn's side. I gingerly pulled up her nightgown and lay towels on the floor beneath her drawn-up knees.

'Where is the skull?' Torrance asked me. His voice sounded defeated.

'At my mom's house in a closet,' I said briefly, my attention absorbed by Lynn.

'So Jane had it all the time,' he said, in a wooden voice from which all the wonder was leached. 'That old woman had it all the time. She was furious after the tree thing, you know. I couldn't believe it, all those years we were good neighbors, then there was this trouble about the damn tree. Next thing I know, there was a hole in the yard and the head was gone. But I never connected the two things. I even left Jane's house for last because I thought she was least likely to have it.'

'Oh, Torrance,' Marcia said pitifully. 'I wish you had told me. Was it you who broke into all the houses?'

'Looking for the head,' he said. 'I knew someone around here had to have it, but it never occurred to me it could be Jane. It had to be someone who could have seen me burying him, but not

Jane, not that sweet little old lady. I just knew that if she'd seen me burying him, she'd have called the police. And I had to wait,' Torrance meandered on, 'so long between each house, because after each break-in, people would be so cautious for a long time . . .'

'You even pretended to break into our house,' marveled his wife.

Gingerly I stole a peek under the nightgown. I was instantly sorry.

'Lynn,' I told her hesitantly, 'I see what I think is the baby's head, I guess.'

Lynn nodded emphatically. Her eyes flew open, and she focused on a point on the wall opposite. Her breathing became ragged for a few moments. 'Get yourself together!' I said earnestly. Lynn was the only person who knew what was happening. Lynn seemed to take that as advice offered from compassion, and squeezed my hand till I thought of screaming again.

Suddenly she caught her breath, and her whole body tensed.

I peeked again.

'Oh dear,' I breathed. This was really quite a lot worse than watching Madeleine the cat. I followed my own advice and pulled myself together, despite my desire to run screaming out of this house and never come back. I let go of Lynn's hand and moved between her legs. There was barely room. It was lucky I was a small person.

Lynn strained again.

'Okay, Lynn,' I said bracingly. 'It's coming. I'll catch it.'

Lynn seemed to rest for a moment.

'Whose skull?' I asked Torrance. Marcia had sunk to the floor, and they were sitting knee to knee holding hands.

'Oh,' he said as if he'd lost interest. 'The skull is Mark. Mark Kaplan. The boy who rented our apartment.'

Lynn gathered herself and pushed again. Her eyes were glazed, and I was scared to death. I hesitantly put my hands where they might do some good.

'Lynn, I see more of the head,' I told her.

Amazingly, Lynn smiled. And she gathered herself. And pushed.

'I've got the head, Lynn,' I told her in a shaky voice. I was trying to sound confident, but I failed. Would the baby's neck break if I let its head flop? Oh dear Jesus, I needed help, I was so inadequate.

Lynn did it again.

'That's the shoulders,' I whispered, holding this tiny, bloody, vulnerable thing. 'One more push should do it,' I said bracingly, having no idea at all what I was talking about. But it seemed to hearten Lynn, and she started pulling herself together again. I wished that she could take a break, so I could, but I had told her the truth out of sheer ignorance. Lynn pushed like she was in the Olympics of baby extrusion, and the slippery thing shot out of her like a hurtling football, or so it seemed to me. And I caught it.

'What?' asked Lynn weakly.

It took me a second of sheer stupidity to understand her. I should be doing something! I should make it cry! Wasn't that important?

'Hold it upside down and whack it on its back,' Marcia said. 'That's what they do on TV.'

Full of terror, I did so. The baby let out a wail. So it was breathing, it was alive! So far so good. Though still hooked up to Lynn, this child was okay for now. Should I do something to the umbilical cord? What? And I heard sirens coming, thank the Lord.

'What?' Lynn asked more urgently.

'Girl!' I said jerkily. 'A girl!' I held the little thing as I had seen babies held in pictures and made plans to burn the rose pink nightgown.

'Well,' said Lynn with a tiny smile, as pounding began on the front door, 'damn if I'm going to name it after you.'

It took some time to sort out the situation in Jane's little house, which seemed more crowded than ever with all the policemen in Lawrenceton.

Some of the policemen, seeing Arthur's former flame kneeling before his new wife, both bloody, assumed I was the person to arrest. They could hardly put cuffs on me or search me though, since I was holding the baby, who was still attached to Lynn. And when they all realized I was holding a newborn baby and not some piece I'd ripped from Lynn's insides, they went nuts. No one seemed to remember that there'd been a break-in, that consequently the burglar might be on the scene.

Arthur had been out on a robbery call, but when he arrived he was so scared he was ready to kill someone. He waved his gun around vaguely, and when he spotted Lynn and the blood, he began bellowing, 'Ambulance! Ambulance!' Jack Burns himself pushed right by the Rideouts to use the phone in the bedroom.

Arthur was by me in a flash, babbling. 'The baby!' he said. He didn't know what to do with his gun.

'Put the gun away and take this baby,' I said rather sharply. 'It's still attached to Lynn, and I don't know what to do about that.'

'Lynn, how are you?' Arthur said in a daze.

'Honey, put a towel over your suit and take your daughter,' Lynn said weakly.

'My – oh.' He holstered his gun and reached down and took a towel off the stack I'd brought out. I wondered if Jane could ever have imagined her monogrammed white cotton towels being used for such a purpose. I handed the baby over with alacrity, and stood up, trembling from a cocktail of fear, pain, and shock. I was more than glad to vacate my position between Lynn's legs.

One of the ambulance attendants ran up to me then and said, 'You the maternity? Or have you been injured?'

I pointed a shaky finger at Lynn. I didn't blame him for thinking I'd been seriously hurt; I was covered with smears of blood, some of it Lynn's, some of it Torrance's, a little of it mine.

'Are you all right?'

I looked to the source of the voice and found I was standing next to Torrance. This was so strange.

'I'll be okay,' I said wearily.

'I'm sorry. I was never cut out to be a criminal.'

I thought of the inept break-ins, Torrance not even taking anything to make them look like legitimate burglaries. I nodded.

'Why did you do it?' I asked him.

Suddenly his face hardened and tightened all over. 'I just did,' he said.

'So when Jane dug up the skull, you dug up the rest of the body and put the bones by the dead end sign?'

'I knew no one would clean up that brush for years,' he said. 'And I was right. I was too scared to carry the bones in my trunk, even for a little while. I waited till the next night when Macon went over to Carey's, and I carried the bones in a plastic bag through his backyard and up the far side of his house; then it was just a few feet to the brush . . . no one saw me *that* time. I was so sure whoever had taken the skull would call the police. I waited. Then I realized whoever had the skull just wanted . . . to have it. For me to squirm. I had almost forgotten that trouble about the tree. Jane was so ladylike. I never believed . . .'

'And he never told me about it,' said Marcia, to his left. 'He never let me worry, too.' She looked at him fondly.

'So, what did you do it for?' I asked Torrance. 'Did he make a pass at Marcia?'

'Well . . .' said Torrance hesitantly.

'Oh, honey,' Marcia said, reproving. She leaned over to me, smiling a little at a man's silly gesture. 'He didn't do it,' she told me. 'I did it.'

'You killed Mark Kaplan and buried him out in the yard?'

'Oh, Torrance buried him when I told him what I'd done.'

'Oh,' I said inadequately, swallowed by her wide blue eyes. 'You killed him because—?'

'He came over while Torrance was gone.' She shook her head sadly as she told me. 'And I had thought he was such a nice person. But he *wasn't*. He was very dirty.'

I nodded, just to be responding somehow.

'Mike Osland, too,' Marcia ran on, still shaking her head at the perfidy of men.

I felt suddenly very, very cold. Torrance closed his eyes in profound weariness.

'Mike,' I murmured interrogatively.

'He's under the sun deck, that's why Torrance built it, I think,' Marcia said earnestly. 'Jane didn't know about him.'

'She's confessing,' said an incredulous, hoarse voice.

I turned from Marcia's mesmerizing eyes to see that Jack Burns was sitting on his haunches in front of me.

'Did she just confess to a murder?' he asked me.

'Two,' I said.

'Two murders,' he repeated. He took his turn at head shaking I would have to find someone at whom I could shake *my* head incredulously. 'She just confessed two murders to you. How do you do it?'

Faced by his round, hot eyes, I became aware that I was in a torn and disheveled and rather skimpy-at-the-top nightgown that had become quite soiled in the course of the night. I was definitely reminded that I was not Jack Burns's favorite person. I wondered how much Lynn would remember of what she'd overheard while she was having the baby – was it possible she would remember my telling Torrance that I knew the whereabouts of the skull?

Lynn was being carried out on a stretcher now. I presumed that the afterbirth had been delivered and disposed of. I hoped I wouldn't find it on the bathroom floor or something.

'This man,' I told Jack Burns, as I pointed to Torrance, 'broke into my house tonight.'

'Are you hurt?' asked Sergeant Burns, with reluctant professional solicitude.

I turned to look in Torrance Rideout's eyes. 'No,' I said clearly. 'Not at all. And I have no idea why he broke in here or what he was looking for.'

Torrance's eyes showed a slow recognition. And, to my amazement, he winked at me when Jack Burns turned away to call his cohorts over.

After an eternity, every single person was gone from Jane's house but me, its owner. What do you do after a night you've had a burglary, been battered, delivered a baby, and nearly been mown down by the entire detective force of Lawrenceton, Georgia? Also, I continued enumerating as I hauled the remains of the nightgown over my head, heard a confession of double murder and had your scarcely covered bosom ogled by the same detectives who had been about to mow you down minutes earlier?

Well. I was going to take a hot, hot bath to soak my bruises and strains. I was going to calm a nearly berserk Madeleine, who was crouching in a corner of the bedroom closet hoping she was concealed underneath a blanket I'd thrown in there. Madeleine, as it happened, did not react well to home invasion. Then, possibly, I could put my tired carcass back between the cool sheets and sleep a little.

There'd be hell to pay in the morning.

My mother would call.

But I only slept four hours. When I woke it was eight o'clock, and I lay in bed and thought for a moment.

Then I was up and brushing my teeth, pulling back on my shorts set from the night before. I managed to get a brush through my hair, which had been damp from the tub when I'd fallen asleep the night before. I let Madeleine out and back in – she seemed calm again – and then it was time to get to Wal-Mart.

I walked in as the doors were unlocked and found what I was looking for after a talk with a salesperson.

I stopped in at the town house and got out my box of gift wrap.

At Mother's house both cars were gone. I'd finally gotten a break. I used my key one last time; I never would again now that John lived here, too. I sped up the stairs and got the old blanket bag out of the closet and left the gift-wrapped blanket bag on the kitchen table on my way out. I left my key by it.

Quickly out to my car then, and speeding back to the house on Honor.

Another stroke of luck; no police cars at the Rideouts' yet.

I went out the back kitchen door and looked around as carefully as Torrance Rideout must have the night he buried Mark Kaplan, the night he buried Mike Osland. But this was daylight, far more dangerous. I'd counted cars as I pulled into my own driveway:

Lynn's car was at the house across the street, Arthur's was gone. That figured; he was at the hospital with his wife and his baby.

I did falter then. But I reached up and slapped myself on the cheek. This was no time to get weepy.

The elderly Inces were not a consideration. I peered over to Carey Osland's house. Her car was home. She must have been told of the confession by Marcia Rideout that Mike Osland was in the Rideouts' backyard. I could only hope that Carey didn't decide to come look personally.

As I started across my backyard, I had to smother an impulse to crouch and run, or slither on my belly. The pink blanket bag seemed so conspicuous. But I just couldn't bring myself to open it and carry the bare skull in my hands. Besides, I'd already rubbed my prints off. I got to the sun deck with no one shouting, 'Hey! What are you doing?' and took a few deep breaths. Now hurry, I told myself, and unzipped the bag, grabbed the thing inside by hooking a finger through the jaw, and, trying not to look at it, I rolled it as far as I could under the deck. I was tempted to climb the steps to the deck, look between the boards, and see if the skull showed from on top. But instead I turned and walked quickly back to my own yard, praying that no one had noticed my strange behavior. I was still clutching the zip bag. Once inside, I glanced in the bag to check that no traces were left of the skull's presence, and folded one of Jane's blankets, zipped it inside, and shoved the bag to the back of the shelf in one of the guest bedroom closets. Then I sat at the little table in the kitchen, and out the window toward the Rideouts' I saw men starting to take apart the sun deck.

I had just made it.

I shook all over. I put my head in my hands and cried.

After a while, that seemed to dry up, and I felt limp and tired. I made a pot of coffee and sat at the table and drank it while I watched the men demolish the deck and find the skull. After the hubbub that caused was over and after the skull had been placed carefully in a special bag of some kind (which actually made me smile a little), the men began digging. It was hot, and they all sweated, and I saw Sergeant Burns glance over to my house as though he'd like to come ask me a few questions, but I'd answered them all the night before. All I was ever going to answer.

Then one of the men gave a shout, and the others gathered round, and I decided maybe I wouldn't watch anymore. At noon the phone rang, and it was my mother, thanking me crisply for the lovely new blanket storage bag and reminding me that we were going to eat dinner together and have a long talk.

'Sure, Mom,' I said, and sighed. I was sore and stiff; maybe she would cut it short. 'Mom, tomorrow I'm going to come in and list this house.'

Well, that was business. That was different. Or maybe not. 'I'll list it myself,' she promised meaningfully, and hung up.

The phone was on the wall by the letter rack and the calendar, a sensible and convenient arrangement. I stood staring blankly at the letter rack for a few seconds, finally taking down a charity appeal, pulling out the begging letter, looking it over, throwing it away. I took out another letter, which should have been a bill from the bug-spray people by the envelope . . . why didn't Bubba Sewell have it? He should have all the bills. But the stamp had been canceled months before.

Suddenly I knew what this was, knew even as I shook the paper out of the slit that it was not going to be a bill from Orkin.

Of course: 'The Purloined Letter.' Jane liked *classics*.

'On a Wednesday night in the summer, four years ago,' the letter began abruptly,

> I, Jane Engle, was sitting in my backyard. It was very late because I had insomnia, and I often sit in the garden in the dark when I have insomnia. It was about midnight, when I saw Mark Kaplan, the Rideouts' boarder, go to Marcia's back door and knock. I could see him clearly in the floodlight the Rideouts have at their back door. Marcia always leaves it on all night when Torrance is out of town. Marcia came to the door, and Mark Kaplan, right away, attacked her. I believe he had been drinking, that he had a bottle in his hand, but I am

not sure. Before I could go to her help, she somehow knocked him down, and I saw her grab something from her kitchen counter and hit Mark Kaplan on the back of the head with it. I am not sure what she picked up, but I think it was a hammer. Then I became aware another car had pulled up into the Rideouts' carport, and I realized that Torrance had come home.

I went inside, thinking that soon I would hear police cars and I would have to talk to the police about what I'd seen. So I changed into my regular clothes – I'd had my nightgown on – and sat in the kitchen and waited in the dark for something to happen.

Instead of police cars, sirens, and whatnot, I saw Torrance come out in a few minutes with a tablecloth. Clearly something body size was wrapped in it, and I was sure it was Mark Kaplan. Torrance proceeded over to their old garden plot, and began to dig. I stayed awake the rest of the night, watching him. I didn't call the police, though I gave it some thought. I knew what testifying in court would do to Marcia Rideout, who has never been any too stable. Also, Mark Kaplan did attack her, and I knew it.

So I said nothing.

But a little over a year and a half later, I got into a dispute with Torrance over my tree, from which he arrogantly trimmed some branches. Every time I looked out my kitchen window, the tree looked worse. So I did something I'm not proud of. I waited till the Rideouts were both out of town, and I went over in the night and dug where I'd seen Torrance dig many months before. It took me three nights, since I am an old woman, but I reached the skull. I removed it and brought it home with me. And I left the hole open, to be sure Torrance knew someone had the head, someone knew.

I am truly not proud of this. Now I am too sick to put the skull back, and I am too afraid of Torrance to just give it to him. And I have been thinking of Mike Osland; he disappeared before Mark Kaplan was killed, and I remember seeing him look at Marcia at parties. I think now that Marcia, just a little eccentric on the surface, is actually quite disturbed, and I think Torrance knows this; and yet he goes on with his life as though by denying she needs special care, she will get better.

I am too close to my own death to worry about this anymore. If my lawyer finds this, he must do as he thinks best; I don't care what people say about me when I am gone. If Roe finds this, she must do as pleases her. The skull is in the window seat.

Jane Engle

I looked down at the paper in my hands, then refolded it. Without really considering it, I began shredding the letter, first in halves, then quarters, then thirds, until finally I had a little pile of confetti on the counter. I gathered it all up and dropped it down the sink, running the water and starting the disposal. After it had rumbled for a moment, I turned off the water and carefully checked all the other letters in the rack. They were exactly what they seemed.

I looked at Jane's calendar, still turned to two months before. I took it down and flipped it to the right page and hung it back up. It was perfectly blank. The strangest thing about not having a job was that it made the whole week so shapeless. I wasn't even taking a day off from anything. Suddenly emptiness spread out in front of me like a slippery ramp. Surely there was something I had to do?

Sure there was. I shook my head in horror. I'd almost forgotten that today was the day I was supposed to pick up my altered bridesmaid's dress.

Miss Joe Nell would have had a fit if I'd forgotten.

And then I knew what I'd do tomorrow.

I'd start looking for my own house.

I detoured by the cemetery on my way to Great Day. I walked up the little hill to Jane's headstone, already in place. If Bubba Sewell could get things done that fast, perhaps he was worth voting for. Feeling stupid and sentimental, I stared at the headstone for a few seconds. This had been a dumb idea. Finally, I said, 'Okay, I'm going to enjoy it.'

I hadn't needed to come out to the cemetery to do this. I could've talked to Jane from anywhere. A trickle of sweat tickled my spine. 'Thanks a lot,' I said, hoping I didn't sound sarcastic. 'But don't do me any more favors,' I told the stone, and began laughing.

I got back in my car and went to pick up the bridesmaid's dress.

Three Bedrooms, One Corpse

My thanks to
Atlanta-area Realtor/broker Joanne Kearney,
who provided me with much helpful information.
If I have misused it, the fault is mine.

Chapter One

My career as a real estate salesperson was short and unofficial, but not uneventful. It started in the lobby of Eastern National Bank at nine thirty on a weekday morning with my mother glancing at her tiny, expensive gold watch.

'I can't make it,' she said with controlled savagery. A person who couldn't manage her appointments was inefficient in my mother's estimation, and to find herself coming up short in that respect was almost intolerable. Of course, her dilemma was not her fault.

'It's those Thompsons,' she said furiously, 'always late! They should have been here forty-five minutes ago! Late for their own house closing!' She stared down at her tiny elegant watch as if she could change its reading by the force of her will. Her slim crossed legs were jiggling with impatience, one navy-pump-shod foot swinging back and forth. When she got up, there might be a hole in the bank's ersatz oriental carpeting.

I sat beside her in the chair I would vacate for Mrs Thompson, when and if she showed up. A couple standing up Aida Brattle Teagarden Queensland for their own house closing was simply amazing; the Thompsons were gutsy, or so rich they wore an impervious armor of self-assurance.

'What are you going to be late for?' I was eyeing her crossed legs enviously. My own legs will never be long enough to be elegant. Actually, my feet couldn't even touch the floor. I waved at two people I knew in the time in took my mother to answer. Lawrenceton was like that. I'd lived in this small Georgia town all my life, and figured I'd be here forever; sooner or later, I'd join my great-grandparents in Shady Rest Cemetery. Most days that gave me a warm, fluid feeling; just part of that ole southern river of life.

Some days it made me crazy.

'The Bartells. He's come in from Illinois as plant manager of Pan-Am Agra, they're looking for a "really nice home," and we have an appointment to see the Anderton house. Actually, they've been here, or he's been here, I didn't get the details – he's been here for three months living in a motel while he gets things lined up at Pan-Am Agra, and now he has the leisure to house-hunt. And he asked around for the best Realtor in town. And he called me, last night. He apologized beautifully for disturbing me at home, but I don't think he was really a bit sorry. I know the Greenhouses were thinking they would get him, since Donnie's cousin is his secretary. And I'm going to be *late*.'

'Oh,' I said, now understanding the depths of Mother's chagrin. She had a star listing and a star client, and being late for introducing one to the other was a professional disaster.

Getting the Anderton house listing had been a real coup in this smallish town with no multiple-listing service. If Mother could sell it quickly, it would be a feather in her cap (as if her cap needed any more adornment) and of course a hefty fee. The Anderton house might truthfully be called the Anderton mansion. Mandy Anderton, now married and living in L.A., had been a childhood acquaintance of mine, and I'd been to a few parties at her house. I remembered trying to keep my mouth closed so I wouldn't look so impressed.

'Listen,' said Mother with sudden resolution, 'you're going to meet the Bartells for me.'

'What?'

She scanned me with business eyes, rather than mother eyes. 'That's a nice dress; that rust color is good on you. Your hair looks okay today, and the new glasses are very nice. And I love your jacket. You take this fact sheet and run along over there – please, Aurora?' The coaxing tone sat oddly on my mother, who looked like Lauren Bacall and acted like the very successful Realtor/broker she is.

'Just show them around?' I asked, taking the fact sheet hesitantly and sliding forward to the edge of the blue leather chair. My gorgeous brand-new rust-and-brown suede pumps finally met the floor. I was dressed so discreetly because today was the third day I'd followed Mother around, supposedly learning the business while studying for my Realtor's license at night. Actually, I'd spent the time daydreaming. I would much rather have been looking for my own house. But Mother had pointed out cleverly that if I was in the office, I'd get first chance at almost any house that came up for sale.

Meeting the Bartells might be more interesting than observing Mother and the banker going through the apparently endless paperwork-and-signature minuet that concludes a house sale.

'Just till I get there,' my mother said. 'You're not a licensed Realtor, so you can't be *showing* them the house. You're just there to open the door and be pleasant until I get there. Please explain the situation to them, just enough to let them know it's not my fault I'm late. Here's the key. Greenhouse Realty showed the house yesterday, but one of them must have given it to Patty early this morning; it was on the key board when I checked.'

'Okay,' I said agreeably. *Not* showing a rich couple a beautiful house was bound to be much more entertaining than sitting in a bank lobby.

I stuffed my paperback into my purse, put the Anderton key on my key ring, and kept a safe grip on the fact sheet.

'Thanks,' Mother said suddenly.

'Sure.'

'You really are pretty,' she said unexpectedly. 'And all the new clothes you bought are so much better than your old wardrobe.'

'Well . . . thanks.'

'Since Mary Elizabeth Mastrantonio was in that movie, your hair seems to strike people as fashionable rather than unmanageable. And,' she went on in an unprecedented burst of candor, 'I've always envied you your boobs.'

I grinned at her. 'We don't look like mother and daughter, do we?'

'You look like my mother, not me. She was an amazing woman.'

My mother had stunned me twice in one morning. Talking about the past was something she just didn't do. She lived in the here and now.

'Are you feeling okay?' I asked nervously.

'Yes, fine. I just noticed a little more gray this morning.'

'We'll talk later. I'd better get going.'

'Goodness, yes! Get over there!' Mother had looked at her watch again.

Luckily I'd met Mother at the bank instead of going with her from the office, so I had my own car. I got to the Anderton mansion in plenty of time to park to one side so my practical little car wouldn't mar the view from the curb. Two months ago, when old Mr Anderton had died, Mandy Anderton Morley (his sole heir) had flown in from Los Angeles for the funeral, put the house on the market the next day, and flown back out to her rich husband after clearing her father's clothes out of the master bedroom and emptying all the drawers into boxes that she had shipped to her home. All the furniture was still in place, and Mandy had indicated to my mother she would negotiate with the buyers if they wanted some or all of the furnishings. Mandy had never been a sentimental person.

So when I unlocked the double front doors and reached in to turn on the lights in the cold, stale two-storey foyer, the house looked eerily as it had when I was a child. I left the front doors open to let in some fresh air and stood just inside, looking up at the chandelier that had so awed me when I was eleven. I was sure the carpet had been replaced since then, but it seemed the same creamy color that had made me terribly conscious of any dust on my shoes. A huge brilliant silk-flower arrangement glowed on the marble table opposite the front doors. After you circled the marble table, you arrived at a wide staircase that led up to a broad landing, with double doors across from the top of the staircase echoing the double front doors below. I ran to turn the heat up so the house wouldn't be so chilly while I was not-showing it, and returned to shut the front doors. I flipped on the switch that lit the chandelier.

I had enough money to buy this house.

The realization gave me a tingle of delight. My spine straightened.

Of course I'd be broke soon after the purchase – taxes, electricity, etc. – but I actually had the asking price.

My friend – well, really, my friendly acquaintance – Jane Engle, an elderly woman with no children, had left me all her money and belongings. Tired of my job at the Lawrenceton Library, I'd quit; tired of living in a row of townhouses I managed for my mother, I'd decided to buy my own house. Jane's house, which I now owned, just wasn't what I wanted. For one thing, there wasn't room for our combined libraries of true and fictional crime. For another, my old flame Detective Arthur Smith, with his new wife, Lynn, and their baby, Lorna, lived right across the street.

So I was looking for my own new home, a place just mine, with no memories and no nerve-racking neighbors.

I had to laugh as I pictured myself eating tuna fish and Cheez-Its in the Anderton dining room.

I heard a car crunch up the semicircular gravel drive. The Bartells were arriving in a spotless white Mercedes. I stepped out onto the large front porch, if you can call a stone-and-pillars edifice a porch, and greeted them with a smile. The wind was chilly, and I pulled my wonderful new fuzzy brown jacket around me. I felt the wind pick up my hair and toss it around my face. I was at the top of the front steps looking down at the Bartells as he helped his wife from the car. Then he looked up at me.

Our eyes met. After a startled moment I blinked and collected myself.

'I'm Aurora Teagarden,' I said, and waited for the inevitable. Sure enough, sleek, dark Mrs Bartell sniggered before she could stop herself. 'My mother is delayed, which she very much regrets, and she asked me to meet you here so you could begin looking. There's so much to see in this house.'

There, I'd done my mother proud.

Mr Bartell was about five-ten, forty-fiveish, prematurely white-headed, with a tough, interesting face, and was wearing a suit even I could tell was a major investment. His eyes, which I was trying hard to avoid, were the lightest brown I'd ever seen. 'I'm Martin Bartell, Miss Teagarden,' he said in an unaccented Voice of Command, 'and this is my sister, Barbara Lampton.'

'Barby,' said Barbara Lampton with a girlish smile. Ms Lampton was maybe forty, broad in the beam but camouflaging it very skill-fully, and not altogether happy at being in Lawrenceton, Georgia, pop. 15,000.

I raised my eyebrows only very slightly (after all, my mother wanted to sell this house). A Barby was laughing at an Aurora? And she wasn't Mrs Bartell, after all. But was she really his sister?

'Nice to meet you,' I said neutrally. 'Now, I'm not really showing you this house, I'm not a licensed Realtor, but I do have the fact sheet here in case you have any questions, and I am familiar with the layout and history of the house.'

So saying, I turned and led the way before Martin Bartell could ask why this was any different from showing the house.

'Barby' commented on the marble-topped table and the silk flowers, and I explained about the furniture.

To the right of the foyer, through a doorway, was a very sizable formal living room and a small formal dining room, and to the left the same space was divided into two large rooms, a 'family room' and a room that could be used for just about anything. Martin Bartell examined everything very carefully and asked several questions I was quite unable to answer, and a few I was.

I was careful always to be looking down at the fact sheet when he turned to ask me something.

'You could use this back room for your gym equipment,' Barby remarked.

So that was where the athletic movement and the muscles came from.

They wandered farther back and looked through the kitchen

with its informal dining nook, then into the formal dining room, which lay between the kitchen and the living room.

Was his sister going to live with him? What would he do in a house this large? He would need a maid, for sure. I tried to think of whom I could call who might know of a reliable person. I tried *not* to picture myself in one of those 'French maid' outfits sold in the back of those strange confession magazines. (A junior-high girl left one in the library one time.)

All the time we were walking and looking, I kept in front of him, behind him, anywhere but facing him.

Instead of taking the kitchen stairs, I maneuvered Martin Bartell and Barby back to the main staircase. I had always loved that broad staircase. I glanced at my watch. Where was Mother? The upstairs was really the climax of the house, or at least I'd always thought so, and she should be the one to show it. Mr Bartell seemed content with me so far, but having me instead of Mother was like having hamburger when you'd been promised steak.

Though I had a very strong feeling Martin Bartell didn't think so.

This was turning out to be a complicated morning.

This man was at least fifteen years older than I, belonged to a world I hadn't the faintest inkling of, and was silently bringing to my attention the fact that for some time now I had been dating a minister who didn't believe in premarital sex. And before Father Aubrey Scott, I hadn't dated anyone at all for months.

Well, I couldn't keep them standing in the foyer while I reviewed my sex life (lack of). I mentally cracked a whip at my hormones and told myself I was probably imagining these waves of interest that washed over me.

'Up these stairs is one of the nicest rooms in the house,' I said determinedly. 'The master bedroom.' I looked at Mr Bartell's chin instead of his eyes. I started up, and they followed obligingly. He was right behind me as I mounted the stairs. I took a few deep breaths and tried to compose myself. Really, this was *too stupid*.

'There are only three bedrooms in this house,' I explained, 'but all of them are marvelous, really almost suites. Each has a dressing room, a walk-in closet, and a private bathroom.'

'Oh, that sounds wonderful,' said Barby.

Maybe they really *were* brother and sister?

'The master bedroom, which is behind these double doors at the head of the stairs, has two walk-in closets. The blue bedroom is the door on the right end of the landing, and the rose bedroom is the one on the left. The extra door to the left is to a small room the Andertons used as a homework and TV room for the children. It would be a good office, or sewing room, or . . .' I trailed off. The room was useful, okay? And it would be much more suitable for Martin Bartell's exercise equipment than a downstairs, public, room. 'The extra door to the right leads to the stairs that come up from the kitchen.'

All the bedroom doors were closed, which seemed a little odd.

On the other hand, the situation gave me a great dramatic moment. I turned both knobs simultaneously, swept open the master bedroom doors, and instantly moved to one side to give Mother's clients an unobstructed view while I glanced back to get their reaction.

'Oh, my *God*!' said Barby.

It wasn't what I'd expected.

Martin Bartell looked very grim.

Slowly and reluctantly, I turned to see what they were staring at.

The woman in the middle of the huge bed was sitting propped up against the headboard, with the white silk sheets pulled up to her waist. Her bare breasts shocked the eyes first; then her face, dark and swollen. The teased and disheveled black hair had been smoothed back to some semblance of normality. Her wrists, positioned at her sides, had some leather thongs around them.

'That's Tonia Lee Greenhouse,' remarked my mother from behind her clients. 'Aurora, please go make sure Tonia Lee is dead.'

That's my mother. Always say 'please', even when you're asking someone to check the vital signs of an obvious corpse. I had touched a dead person before, but it was not an experience I wanted to repeat. However, I had taken a step forward before a strong hand closed around my wrist.

'I'll do it,' Martin Bartell said unexpectedly. 'I've seen dead people before. Barby, go downstairs and sit in that big front room.'

Without a word, Barby did as she was told. The Voice of Command even worked on a sister. Mr Bartell, his shoulders stiff, strode across the wide expanse of peach carpet and leaned across the huge bed to put his fingers to the neck of the very deceased Tonia Lee Greenhouse.

'As you can tell, she's definitely dead and has been for a while,' Mr Bartell said matter-of-factly enough. His nose wrinkled, and I knew he was getting a much stronger whiff than I of the very unpleasant smell emanating from the bed. 'Are the phones hooked up?'

'I'll see,' said Mother briefly. 'I'll try the one downstairs.' She spoke as if she'd decided that on a whim, but when I turned to look at her, her face was completely white. She turned with great dignity, and as she went down the stairs, she began to shake visibly – as though an earthquake only she could feel was rocking the staircase.

My feet had grown roots into the thick carpet. Though I wished myself somewhere else, I seemed to lack the energy to take me there.

'Who was this woman?' asked Mr Bartell, still bending over the bed but with his hands behind him. He was scrutinizing her neck with some detachment.

'Tonia Lee Greenhouse, half of Greenhouse Realty,' I said. It was a little surprising to hear my own voice. 'She showed this house yesterday. She had to get the key from my mother's office, but it was back there this morning.'

'That's very remarkable,' Mr Bartell said unemphatically.

And it surely was.

I stood there rooted, thinking how atypically everyone was behaving. I would have put money on Barby Lampton screaming hysterically, and she hadn't squeaked after her first exclamation.

Martin Bartell hadn't gotten angry with us for showing him a house with a corpse in it. My mother hadn't ordered me to go downstairs to call the police, she'd done it herself. And instead of finding a solitary corner and brooding, I was standing stock-still watching a middle-aged businessman examine a naked corpse. I wished passionately I could cover up Tonia Lee's bosom. I stared at Tonia Lee's clothes, folded on the end of the bed. The red dress and black slip were folded so neatly, so oddly, in tiny perfect triangles. I brooded over this for some moments. I would have sworn Tonia Lee would be a tosser rather than a folder. And any dress subjected to that treatment would be a solid mass of wrinkles when it was shaken out.

'This lady was married?'

I nodded.

'Wonder if her husband reported her missing last night?' Mr Bartell asked, as if the answer would be interesting, no more. He straightened up and walked back over to me, his hands in his pockets as though he were passing the time until an appointment.

My brain was not moving so very quickly. I finally realized he was doing his best not to touch anything in the room.

'I'm sure we shouldn't cover her up,' I said wistfully. For once, I was wishing I hadn't read so much true and fictional crime, so I wouldn't know I was not supposed to adjust the corpse.

Martin Bartell's light brown eyes looked at me very thoroughly. They had a golden touch, like a tiger's.

'Miss Teagarden.'

'Mr Bartell . . . ?'

His hand emerged from his pocket and moved up. I tensed as though I were about to be jolted by electricity. I lost the technique of staring at his chin and looked right at him. He was going to touch my cheek.

'Is the body in here?' asked Detective Lynn Liggett Smith from perhaps three feet away.

Downstairs, at least thirty minutes later, I had recovered my composure. I no longer felt as if I was in heat and would rip

Martin Bartell's clothes off any minute. I no longer felt that he, out of all the people in the world, had the power to look underneath all the layers of my personality and see the basic woman, who had been lonely (in one particular way) for a very long time.

In the 'family room,' with my mother and Barby Lampton to provide protective chaperonage, I was able to collect all my little foibles and peculiarities back together and stack them between myself and Martin Bartell.

My mother felt obligated to hold polite conversation with her clients. She had introduced herself formally, gotten over her surprise on finding out that Mr Bartell's companion was his sister, not his wife, and had established the fact that Martin Bartell had received good impressions of Lawrenceton in the weeks he'd spent here. 'It's been a pleasant change of pace after the Chicago area,' he said, and sounded sincere. 'Barby and I grew up on a farm in a very rural area of Ohio.'

Barby didn't seem to enjoy being reminded.

He explained a little about his reorganization of the local Pan-Am Agra plant to my mother, a born manager, and I kept my eyes scrupulously to myself.

We waited for the police for a long time, it seemed. I heard familiar voices calling up and down the stairs. I'd dated Lynn Liggett's husband, Arthur Smith (before they married, of course), and during our 'courtship' I'd become acquainted with every detective and most of the uniforms on Lawrenceton's small force. Detective Henske's cracker drawl, Lynn's crisp alto, Paul Allison's reedy voice . . . and then came the sound I dreaded.

Detective Sergeant Jack Burns.

I turned in my chair to group myself protectively with the other three. What were they talking about now? Martin Bartell had said he'd been at work every day of the three months he'd spent in Lawrenceton, and had invited Mother to tell him about the town. He couldn't have asked anyone more informed, except perhaps the Chamber of Commerce executive, a lonely man who worked touchingly hard to persuade the rest of the world to believe in Lawrenceton's intangible advantages.

I listened once more to the familiar litany.

'Four banks,' Mother enumerated, 'a country club, all the major automobile dealerships, though I'm afraid you'll have to get the Mercedes repaired in Atlanta.'

I heard Jack Burns shouting down the stairs. He wanted the fingerprint man to 'get his ass in gear'.

'Lawrenceton is practically a suburb of Atlanta now,' Barby Lampton said, earning her a hard look from my mother. Most Lawrencetonians were not too pleased about the ever-nearing annexation of Lawrenceton into the greater Atlanta area.

'And the school system is excellent,' my mother continued with a little twitch of her shoulders. 'Though I don't know if that's an area of interest—?'

'No, my son just graduated from college,' Martin Bartell murmured. 'And Barby's girl is a freshman at Kent State.'

'Aurora is my only child,' Mother said naturally enough. 'She's worked at the library here for what – six years, Roe?'

I nodded.

'A librarian,' he said thoughtfully.

Why was it librarians had such a prim image? With all the information available in books right there at their fingertips, librarians could be the best-informed people around. About anything.

'Now she's thinking about going into real estate, and looking for her own home at the same time.'

'You think you'd like selling homes?' Barby said politely.

'I'm beginning to think maybe it's not for me,' I admitted, and my mother looked chagrined.

'Honey, I know this morning has been a horrible experience – poor Tonia Lee – but you know this is not something that happens often. But I *am* beginning to think I'll have to establish some kind of system to check on my female Realtors when they are out showing a house to a client we don't know. Aurora, maybe Aubrey wouldn't like you selling real estate? My daughter has been dating our Episcopalian priest for several months,' she explained to her clients with an almost-convincing casualness.

'Episcopalians have a reputation for being generally liberal,' Martin Bartell remarked out of the blue.

'I know, but Aubrey is an exception if that really is true,' Mother said, and my heart sank. 'He is a wonderful man – I've come to know him since I married my present husband, who is a cradle Episcopalian – but Aubrey is very conservative.'

I felt my cheeks turn red in the cold room. I ran a nervous hand under the hair at my neck, loosening the strands that had gotten tucked in my jacket collar, and tilted my head back a little to shake it straight.

Thinking about Tonia Lee Greenhouse was preferable to feeling like a parakeet that is extremely excited at the prospect of being eaten by the cat.

I thought about the loathsome way Tonia had been positioned, a parody of seductiveness. I thought about the leather thongs on Tonia's wrists. Had she been tied to the ornate wooden headboard? Old Mr and Mrs Anderton must be turning in their graves. I thought about Tonia Lee in life – tall, thin, with teased dark hair and bright makeup, a woman who was rumored to be often unfaithful to her husband, Donnie. I wondered if Donnie had just gotten tired of Tonia Lee's ways, if he'd followed her to her appointment and taken care of her after the client had left. I wondered if Tonia had been overcome by passion for her client and had bedded him here in the invitingly luxurious master bedroom, or if she'd had an assignation with someone she'd been seeing for a while. Maybe the house-showing had been a fictitious cover to let her romp in one of the prettiest houses in Lawrenceton.

'Mackie brought her the key yesterday,' I said suddenly.

'What?' asked my mother with reproof in her voice. I had no idea what they'd been talking about.

'Yesterday about five o'clock, while I was waiting for you in the reception room, Tonia Lee called your office and asked for the key. She said she'd been held up – if anyone was getting off work, she'd be really obliged if they could drop it off here; she'd meet them. I handed the phone to Mackie Knight. He was leaving just then, and he said he'd do it.'

'We'll have to tell the police. Maybe Mackie was the last one to see her alive – or maybe he saw the man she was going to show the house to!'

Then Jack Burns was in the doorway, and I sighed.

Detective Sergeant Jack Burns was a frightening man, and he really couldn't stand me. If he could ever arrest me for anything, he'd just love to do it. Luckily for me, I'm very law-abiding, and since I had come to know Jack Burns, I'd made sure I got my car inspected right on the dot, that I parallel-parked perfectly, and that I didn't even jaywalk.

'If it isn't Miss Teagarden,' he said with a terrifying affability. 'I declare, young woman, you get prettier every time I see you. And I always do seem to see you when I come to a murder scene, don't I?'

'Hello, Jack,' said my mother with a distinct edge to her voice.

'Mrs Teagarden – no, Mrs Queensland now, isn't it? I haven't seen you since your wedding; congratulations. And these must be our new residents? Hope you don't feel like running back north after today. Lawrenceton used to be such a quiet town, but the city is reaching out to us here, and I guess in a few years we'll have a crime rate like Atlanta's.'

Mother introduced her clients.

'Guess you won't want this house after today,' Jack Burns said genially. 'Ole Tonia Lee looked pretty bad. I'm sure sorry you all ran into this, you being new and all.'

'This could have happened anywhere,' Martin said. 'I'm beginning to think being a real estate agent is a hazardous occupation, like being a convenience-store clerk.'

'It certainly does seem so,' Jack Burns agreed. He was wearing a hideous suit, but I'll give him this much credit – I don't think he cared a damn about what he wore or what people thought about it.

'Now, Mr Bartell, I believe you touched the deceased?' he continued.

'Yes, I walked over to make sure she was dead.'

'Did you touch anything on the bed?'

'No.'

'On the table by the bed?'

'Nothing in the bedroom,' Martin said very definitely, 'but the woman's neck.'

'You notice it was bruised?'

'Yes.'

'You know she was strangled?'

'It looked like it to me.'

'You have much experience with this kind of thing?'

'I was in Vietnam. I've had more experience with wounds. But I have seen one case of strangulation before, and this looked similar.'

'What about you, Mrs Lampton? You go in the room?'

'No,' Barby said quietly. 'I stayed on the landing outside. When Miss Teagarden opened the doors, of course I saw the poor woman right away. Then my brother told me to go downstairs. He knows I don't have a strong stomach, so of course it was better for me to go.'

'And you, Mrs – Queensland?'

'I came up the stairs just after Aurora opened the bedroom doors. I actually saw her swing them open from downstairs after I started up.' Mother explained about the Thompsons and her delegation of me to open the house for the Bartells. 'Excuse me, Mr Bartell and Mrs Lampton.'

'You're his sister,' Jack Burns said, as if trying to get that point quite clear. He swung his baleful gaze on poor Barby Lampton.

'Yes, I am,' she said angrily, stung by the doubt in his voice. 'I just got divorced, my only child's in college, I sold my own home as part of the divorce settlement, and my brother invited me to help him house-hunt down here out of sheer kindness.'

'Of course, I see,' said Jack Burns with disbelief written on every crease in his heavy cheeks.

Martin Bartell's hair might be white, but his eyebrows were still dark. Now they were drawn together ominously.

'When was the last time you saw Mrs Greenhouse, Roe?' Jack Burns had switched his questioning abruptly to me.

'I haven't seen Tonia Lee to speak to in weeks, and then it was only a casual conversation at the beauty parlor.' Tonia Lee had been having a dye job and a cut, and I'd been having one of my rare trims. She had tried the whole time to find out how much money Jane Engle had left me.

'Mr Bartell, had you contacted Mrs Greenhouse about looking at any homes?' Jack Burns shot the question at the Pan-Am Agra manager as though he would enjoy beating the answer out of him. What a charmer.

I could see Martin taking a deep breath. 'Mrs Queensland here is the only Realtor I have contacted in Lawrenceton,' he said firmly. 'And now, if you'll excuse me, Sergeant, my sister has had enough for this morning, and so have I. I have to get back to work.'

Without waiting for an answer, he got up and put his arm around his sister, who had risen even faster.

'Of course,' Burns said smoothly. 'I'm so sorry I've been holding you all up! You just go on, now. But please, folks, keep everything you saw at the scene of the murder to yourselves. That would help us out a whole bunch.'

'I think we'll be going, too,' my mother said coldly. 'You know where we'll be if you need us again.'

Jack Burns just nodded, ran a beefy hand over his thinning no-color hair, and stood with narrowed eyes watching us leave. 'Mrs Queensland!' he called when Mother was almost out the door. 'What about keys to this house?'

'Oh, yes, I forgot . . .' And Mother turned back to tell him about Mackie Knight and the key, and I walked out into the fresh chill of the day, away from the thing in the bedroom upstairs and the fear of Jack Burns.

And right into Martin Bartell.

Over his shoulder I saw Barby was in the front seat of the Mercedes and buckled up already. She was dabbing at her eyes with a tissue. She'd waited until she was outside to shed a few tears; I admired her control. I felt a sympathetic tear trickle down my own face. One way or another, the morning had been a dreadful strain.

I was looking at a silk tie in a shade of golden olive, with a white stripe and a thin sort of red one.

He wiped the tear from my face with his handkerchief, carefully not touching me with his fingers.

'Am I imagining this?' he asked very quietly.

I shook my head, still not meeting his eyes.

'We have to talk later.'

I couldn't speak, for once in my life. I was terrified of seeing him again; and I would rather have shaved my head than not see him again.

'How old *are* you? You're so tiny.'

'I'm thirty,' I said, and finally looked up at him.

He said after a moment, 'I'll call you.'

I nodded, and walked quickly over to my car and got in. I had to sit for a moment so I could stop shivering. Somehow I had his handkerchief clutched in my hand. Oh, that was just great! Maybe he had an old high school letter jacket I could wear? I was mad at my hormones, upset about the awful death of Tonia Lee Greenhouse, and horrified at my own perfidy toward Aubrey Scott.

There was knock on my window that made me jump.

My mother was bending, gesturing for me to roll the window down. 'I've never met Jack Burns in his professional capacity before,' she was saying furiously, 'and I pray I never do again. You told me he was like that, Aurora, but I couldn't quite credit it! Why, when I sold him and his wife that house, he was just so polite and nice!'

'Mom, I'm going to go to my place.'

'Why, sure, Aurora. Are you okay? And poor Donnie Greenhouse . . . I wonder if they've called him yet.'

'Mother, what you have to worry about, right now, is how that key got back on your key board. Someone at Select Realty put it there. The police are going to be all over your office asking questions just as quick as quick can be.'

'You definitely have a mind for crime,' Mother said disapprovingly, but she was thinking fast. 'It's that club you were in, I expect.'

'No. I was in Real Murders because I think that way, I don't think that way because I was in the club,' I said mildly. But she wasn't listening.

'Before I go back,' said Mother suddenly, 'I was thinking I should ask Martin Bartell and his sister – I can't believe a woman that age is answering to "Barby"—' This from a woman with a name like Aida. 'I should get them over to the house for dinner tomorrow night. Why don't you and Aubrey come?'

'Oh,' I said limply, horrified at the prospect. How was I going to excuse myself – 'Mom, this guy I just met, well, if we see each other again, we just may have at it on the floor'?

My mother, usually so sharp, did not pick up on my turmoil. Of course, she had a few more things on her mind.

'I know you have to ask Aubrey first, so just give me a call. I really think I should make some gesture to try to make up to them—'

'For showing them a house with a dead Realtor in it?'

'Exactly.'

Suddenly my mother realized that the Anderton house was going to be impossible to move, at least for a while, and she closed her eyes. I could see it in her face, I could read her mind.

'It'll sell sooner or later,' I said. 'It was too big for Mr Bartell anyway.'

'True,' she said faintly. 'The house on Ivy Avenue would be more appropriate. But if the sister is going to live with him, the separate bedroom suites would have been great.'

'See you later,' I said, starting my car.

'I'll call you,' she told me.

And I had no doubt she would.

Chapter Two

An hour after I'd gotten home I began to feel like myself again. I'd huddled wrapped in an afghan, with Madeleine the cat purring in my lap (an effective tranquilizer), while I watched CNN to feed my mind on impersonal things for a while. I was in my favorite brown suede-y chair with a diet drink beside me, comfortable and nearly calm. Of course, Madeleine was getting cat hairs all over the afghan and my lovely new dress; I'd had to resist the impulse to change into blue jeans when I got home. I still felt my new clothes were costumes I was wearing, costumes I should doff when I was really being myself.

I'd had Madeleine neutered after I'd given away the last kitten, and the scar still showed through her shorter tummy hair. She had quickly adjusted to the switch from Jane's house to the town-house, though she was still angry at not being let outside.

'A litter box will just have to do until I find a house with a yard,' I told her, and she glared at me balefully.

I'd calmed down enough to think. I pushed the OFF button on the remote control.

I was horrified at what had happened to Tonia Lee, and I was trying very hard not to picture her as I'd last seen her. It was far more typical of Tonia Lee to remember her as she'd been at the beauty shop during our last conversation – her hair emerging glossy dark from the beautician's curling iron, her long oval nails perfectly polished by the manicurist, her brain trying to frame an impolite query politely, her dissatisfied face momentarily intent on extracting information from me. I was sorry she'd had such a dreadful end, but I'd never liked the little I knew of Tonia Lee Greenhouse.

Over and above being tangentially connected to her nasty

death, I had a personal situation on my hands, no doubt about it. What had happened – and what was going to happen – between me and Martin Bartell?

I should call Amina, my best friend. Though she lived in Houston now, it would be worth the long-distance daytime call. I peered at the calendar across the room by the telephone in the kitchen area. Today was Thursday. The wedding had been five weeks ago . . . Yes, they should have gotten back from the cruise and the resort at least two weeks ago, and Amina wouldn't go back to work until Monday.

But if I called Amina, that would be validating my feeling.

So what was this feeling? Love at first sight? This didn't seem to be centered around my heart, but somewhere considerably lower.

And amazingly, he felt it, too.

That was what was so shocking – that it was mutual. After a lifetime of considering and dissecting, I was seriously in danger of being swept away by something I couldn't control.

Oh – sure I could! I slapped myself lightly on one cheek. All I had to do was *never see Martin Bartell again.*

That would be the honorable thing. I was dating Aubrey Scott, a fine man and a handsome one, and I should count myself lucky.

Which introduced a drearily familiar train of thought.

Where was my relationship with Aubrey going? We'd been dating for several months now, and I was sure his congregation (including my mother and her husband) expected great things. Of course, someone had told Aubrey about my involvement in the Real Murders deaths – due to my membership in a club devoted to discussing old murder cases, my half-brother Phillip and I had almost gotten killed – and we'd talked about it a little. But on the whole, other people seemed to consider our relationship suitable and unsurprising.

We found each other attractive, we were both Christians (though I was certainly not a very good one), neither of us drank more than the occasional glass of wine, and we both liked reading and popcorn and going to the movies. He enjoyed kissing me; I liked being kissed by him. We were fond of each other and respected each other.

But I would be a terrible minister's wife, inwardly if not outwardly. He must know that by now. And he wouldn't be right for me even if he was a – well, a librarian.

But I hated to do anything fast and drastic. Aubrey deserved better than that. My het-up feelings for Martin Bartell might disappear as suddenly as they'd appeared. And at least half of me fervently hoped those feelings would vanish. There was something degrading about this.

Also something terribly exciting, the other half admitted.

The phone rang just as I was about to go through my whole thought cycle again.

'Roe, are you all right?' Aubrey was so concerned it hurt me.

'Yes, Aubrey, I'm fine. I guess my mother called you.'

'She did, yes. She was very upset about poor Mrs Greenhouse, and worried about you.'

Maybe that wasn't exactly what Mother had been feeling, but Aubrey put the nicest interpretation on everything. Though he was certainly not naive.

'I'm all right,' I said wearily. 'It was just a tough morning.'

'I hope the police can catch whoever did this, and do it fast,' Aubrey said, 'if there's someone out there preying on lone women. Are you sure you want to go into this real estate business?'

'No, actually I'm not sure,' I said. 'But not because of Tonia Lee Greenhouse. My mother has to carry a calculator all the time, Aubrey.'

'Oh?' he said cautiously.

'She has to know all about the current interest rate, and she has to be able to figure out what someone's house payment will be if he can sell his house for X amount so he can put that down on the next house, which costs twenty thousand dollars more than the house he has . . .'

'You didn't realize that was involved in house-selling?' Aubrey was trying hard to sound neutral.

'Yes, I did,' I said, trying equally hard not to snap. 'But I was thinking more of the house-showing part of it. I like going into people's houses and just looking.' And that was the long and short of it.

'But you don't like the nuts and bolts part,' Aubrey prompted, probably trying to figure out if I was nosy, childish, or just plain weird.

'So maybe it's not for me,' I concluded, leaving him to judge.

'You have time to think about it. I know you want to do *something* – right?' My being completely at liberty, except for the nominal duty of listening to any complaints that might arise from the townhouse tenants in Mother's complex, made Aubrey very uneasy. Single women worked full-time, and for somebody other than their mothers.

'Sure.' He was not the only one who found the concept of a woman of leisure unsettling.

'Did your mother mention her plan for tomorrow night to you?'

Oh, *damn*. 'The dinner at her house?'

'Right. Did you want to go? I guess we could tell her we had already made other plans.' But Aubrey sounded wistful. He loved the food Mother's caterer served. 'Caterer' was a fancy term for Lucinda Esther, a majestic black woman who made a good living 'cooking for people who are too lazy', as she put it. Lucinda also got extra mileage out of being a 'character', a factor of which she was fully aware.

Oh, this was going to be awful. And yet, maybe it would clear the air in some way.

'Yes, let's go.'

'Okay, honey. I'll pick you up about six thirty.'

'I'll see you then,' I said absently.

'Bye.'

I said good-bye and hung up. My hand stayed on the receiver.

Honey? Aubrey had never called me an endearment before. It sounded to me as if something was happening with Aubrey . . . or maybe he was just feeling sentimental because I'd had a very bad experience that morning?

Suddenly I saw Tonia Lee Greenhouse as she had been in that huge bed. I saw the elegant matching night tables flanking the bed. I could see the strange color of Tonia Lee's body against the white sheets, the red of the dress folded so peculiarly at the foot of the bed. I wondered where Tonia Lee's shoes were – under the bed?

And speaking of missing things – here a thought hovered on the edge of my mind so insistently that my eyes went out of focus as I tried to pin it down. Missing things. Or something at least not included in my mental picture of the bed and surrounding floor. The night tables . . .

There it was. The night tables. My mental camera zoomed in on their surfaces. I picked up the phone and punched in seven familiar numbers.

'Select Realty,' said Patty Cloud's On-the-Ball voice.

'Patty, this is Roe. Let me speak to my mother if she's handy, please.'

'Sure, Roe,' said Patty in her Warm Personal voice. 'She's on another line – wait, she's off. Here you go.'

'Aida Queensland,' said my mother. Her new name still gave me a jolt.

'When you first listed the Anderton house,' I said without preamble, 'think about going in the bedroom with Mandy.'

'Okay, I'm there,' she said after a moment.

'Look at the night tables.'

A few seconds of silence.

'Oh,' she said slowly. 'Oh, I see what you mean. Yes, I have to call Detective Liggett right away. The vases are missing.'

'She should check the formal dining room, too. There was a crystal bowl with crystal fruit in there that cost a fortune.'

'I'll call her right away.'

We hung up at the same moment.

It had been years since I was at the Anderton house, but I still remembered how impressed I'd been that instead of tissues or bed lamps, Mandy's parents had Chinese vases on their bedside tables. In her charming way, Mandy had bragged about how much those vases had cost. But she had never liked them. So when I realized they were gone, I didn't for an instant think she'd had them packed up and shipped to Los Angeles. She would have left them to coax a buyer. Anyone who would have enough money to consider buying her parents' house would not want to steal vases, right?

I dumped an indignant Madeleine from my lap and moved around the room restlessly. I was standing at the window staring out at my patio, thinking I'd have to bring in my outdoor chairs and table and store them down in the basement during the coming weekend, when the phone rang. I reached out to the kitchen wall extension.

'It's me again,' said my mother. 'We're having a meeting this afternoon for everyone on the staff, two o'clock. You're going to need to come, too.'

'Did the police question Mackie?'

'They took him to the police station.'

'Oh, no.'

'It turns out Detective Liggett – I mean Detective *Smith* – was already here when I was on the phone with you. I'm sure this all happened as a result of what I told Jack Burns, about Mackie taking Tonia Lee the key. I was only thinking of Mackie having possibly seen who was at the house with Tonia Lee. It didn't occur to me until too late that they might pick up Mackie as a suspect.'

'Do you think it's because he's—?'

'Oh, I'd hate to think that. I hope our police force is not like that. But you know, being black may work in his favor, actually. Tonia Lee would never have gone to bed with Mackie. She didn't like blacks at all.'

'They might just say he raped her.'

There was a long pause while Mother digested this. 'You know, somehow it didn't . . . well, I can't say why. And I only looked for a second. But it didn't look like a rape, did it?'

I paused in turn. Tonia completely undressed, the sheets pulled back as if two people had actually gotten in the bed together . . . Mother was right, it looked like a seduction scene, not a hasty rape, even though the leather thongs might indicate force. My first thought had been consensual kinky sex. But maybe Mother and I were both factoring in Tonia Lee's known reputation for infidelity. When I suggested this to Mother, she agreed.

'Anyway, I'm sure Mackie is not involved,' she said staunchly. 'I like him a lot, he's a hard worker, and for the year he's been here, he's been totally honest and aboveboard. Besides . . . he is too smart to put the key back.'

After we'd hung up, I wondered about that. Why had the Anderton house key been put back on the hook so mysteriously? That key had enabled us to enter and find the body.

I thought a number of interesting questions depended on the answer to that riddle.

The office meeting ought to be stimulating.

I ate an apple and a leftover chicken breast while flipping through Jane Engle's copy of *The Murderers' Who's Who*. I read the entries for some of my favorite cases and wondered if an updated edition would include our local murderous duo whose dreadful but brief career had made national headlines; or perhaps our only other claim to fame might rate an entry, the disappearance of an entire family from a house outside of Lawrenceton. That had been – what? – five or six years ago.

My familiarity with old murder cases was my mother's despair. Now, since the disbandment of the Real Murders club, I had no one to share it with. I sighed over spilt milk.

After putting my dishes in the dishwasher, I glumly mounted the stairs to get ready for the meeting. For one thing, I had to brush all the cat hairs off my skirt.

Mother's office building, with its soothing gray and blue carpeting and walls, peaceful prints, and comfortable chairs, exuded calm and profitable efficiency. That was Mother's essence, and she and the office designer had captured it when they renovated the building. Mother had insisted on a conference room, for staff meetings. Every Monday every Realtor working for Mother had to attend this meeting. She'd planned to expand, and the room was still more than large enough for the whole staff.

I saw with interest that one of John Queensland's daughters-in-law had been brought in to answer the phones and take messages while Mother held the meeting. I knew my stepfather's sons and their wives only slightly, and as I nodded to Melinda Queensland, I tried to figure out what my relationship to her was. Stepsister-in-law? It looked to me as if I was going to be a stepaunt in a few months, but Melinda had had several miscarriages and I wasn't going to ask.

Melinda was sitting at Patty Cloud's desk, which of course was not only orderly but also decorated with a tidy plant and a picture in an expensive frame. Patty's desk faced the front door, and her underling, Debbie Lincoln, had a desk at right angles to it, in effect forming the start of the corridor down to the conference room and Idella's and Mackie's offices. In the square created by two walls and the desks, firmly screwed to the wall behind Patty, was the key board, a large peg-board striped with labeled hooks. The more popular letters of the alphabet claimed two or even three hooks. A person of even the feeblest intelligence could figure out the system in seconds, and every other agency in town had something similar.

I snapped out of my study of the key board to find that Melinda was waiting for me to acknowledge her, and her smile was growing strained as I stared at the wall behind her. I gave her a brisk nod and started down the hall to the conference room. I was in time to sit at Mother's left, a chair left vacant deliberately for me, I presumed. All the Realtors expected me to inherit this business from Mother, and saw my presence in the office this week as the first step in my becoming second-in-command.

This was far from true. I had quit my job at the library on a whim, and I already regretted it more than I ever would have believed possible. (Of course, even regretting it mildly was more than I ever would have believed possible.)

Idella Yates, a frail-looking fair woman in her mid-thirties, divorced with two children, slid into the chair at the end of the table and put a briefcase on the table in front of her as if building a barrier between herself and the room. Her short straight hair was the color of dead winter grass. Eileen Norris bustled in, carrying a large stack of papers and looking abstracted. Eileen was Mother's second-in-command, the first Realtor Mother had hired after she'd gone out on her own. Eileen was big, brassy, loud, and cheerful on the surface; underneath, she was a barracuda. Patty Cloud, the receptionist/secretary, groomed to a tee, had perched her bottom dead in the center of the chair next to Idella's. Patty, who was maybe all of twenty-four, baffled and irritated me far more than she should have. Patty worked hard at being perfect, and she had damned near succeeded. She was always helpful on the phone, always turned out high-quality work, never forgot anything, and never, never came to work in anything frumpy or out of style or even wrinkled. She was already studying for her Realtor's license. She would probably pass at the top of her group.

Patty's underling, Debbie Lincoln, was a rather dim and cowed girl right out of high school. She was a full-figured black with hair expensively corn-rowed and decorated with beads. Debbie was quiet, punctual, and could type very well. Other than that, I knew little about her. At the moment she was sitting quietly by Patty with her eyes on her hands, not chatting back and forth like the others.

Eileen finally got settled, and we all looked at Mother expectantly. Just as she opened her mouth, the conference room door opened and in came Mackie Knight.

His dark round face looked strained and upset, and he responded to our various exclamations with a wave of his hand. He collapsed into a chair by Eileen with obvious relief, automatically adjusting his tie and running a hand over his very short hair.

'Mackie, I thought I was going to have to send a lawyer down to the station to get you out!'

'Thanks, Mrs Queensland. You were going to be my one phone

call,' he said. 'But they seem to believe, at least for the moment, that I didn't do it.'

'What did happen yesterday?' Eileen asked.

We all leaned forward to listen.

'Well,' Mackie began wearily, telling a story he'd obviously told several times already, 'the phone rang here five minutes after Patty went home for the day, and I was standing out in the reception room talking to Roe, so I answered it.'

Patty looked chagrined that she hadn't worked late the day before.

'It was Mrs Greenhouse, and she said she had an appointment to meet a client to show him the Anderton house. She had forgotten to come by earlier to get the key – if anyone happened to be leaving our office soon, could they bring it by? She was worried she'd miss her client if she left to come to our office.'

'She didn't name the client?' Mother asked.

'No name,' Mackie said firmly. 'She did say "he", I'm almost positive.'

Idella Yates, beside me, shuddered and clutched her arms as if she were feeling a chill. I think we all did; Tonia Lee, making arrangements to meet her own death.

'Anyway, this is the part the police have the most trouble with,' Mackie continued. 'What I did, instead of driving up and leaving the key and going on home . . . I went home first, put on my jogging clothes, and went out for my run. I stuck the key in the pocket of my shorts and stopped on my run to hand it to Mrs Greenhouse. That only made maybe seven to ten minutes' difference in the time I actually got there, and it suited me better. To tell you the honest truth, I wasn't so excited about doing her work for her. No one here would be that sloppy. When I got there, she was at the house by herself. If anyone else was there, I didn't see him. Hers was the only car. It was parked in the back, outside the kitchen, so that was the door I went to.'

'Why does that seem funny to the police?' Mother asked. 'It doesn't seem odd to me.'

'They seem to think that I ran instead of driving my car so no one would identify my car as being in the driveway, later. They said a woman living across the street from the Anderton house, she was waiting for her daughter to get home from spending a week out of town. So she was sitting in her front room, looking out the window, and reading a book, for the best part of two hours . . . the daughter had had a flat on the interstate, turns out. This woman might have missed a person on foot, but not a car.'

'What about the back door?' Eileen asked.

'The people who live behind the Andertons were watching TV in their den with the curtains open, since they knew no one was in the Anderton house. They told the police that they saw Tonia Lee's car pull up when it was still daylight, but fading fast. One woman got out. They sat watching TV and eating in their den while they watched, and no other car ever pulled up. They figured someone else had come to the front door. They did see Tonia Lee's car pull out after dark, way after dark, but of course they couldn't see who was in it. They were pretty interested, someone being in the house for that long; they thought someone might really be thinking of buying.'

We all mulled that over for a minute.

'I wonder why the police told you so much?' Patty asked.

Mackie shook his head. 'I guess they thought they would pressure me into confessing or something. If I'd been guilty, it might have worked.'

'You run every night, you've always told us that, and I've often seen you. That's not suspicious at all,' my mother said staunchly. We all murmured agreement, even Patty Cloud, who was none too fond of having to do work for a black man, I'd observed. Though having Debbie working for *her* didn't seem to be a problem.

'Lots of people run or ride bikes in the evening,' Idella said suddenly. 'Donnie Greenhouse does . . . Franklin Farrell does.'

Franklin Farrell was another local Realtor.

'I bet it was Donnie,' Eileen said bluntly. 'He just couldn't stand Tonia Lee screwing around anymore.'

'Eileen,' Mother said warningly.

'It's true, and we all know it,' Eileen said.

'I'm sure she just made an appointment with someone who used a false name, and the man killed her,' Idella said in so low a voice we had to strain to hear her. 'It could happen to any of us.'

We were all silent for a moment, staring at her.

'Except Mackie, of course,' Eileen said briskly, and we all broke into laughter.

'Naw, I just get framed for it,' Mackie said after the last chuckle had died away. And we were all sober again.

Patty Cloud said suddenly, 'I think it was the House Hunter.'

'Oh,' my mother said doubtingly. 'Come on, Patty.'

'The House Hunter,' said Eileen consideringly. 'It's possible.'

'Who's that?' I asked. I was apparently the only one not in the know.

'The House Hunter,' Idella said softly, 'is what all the Realtors in town call Jimmy Hunter, the owner of the hardware store. On Main, you know?'

'Susu's husband?' I asked. There were several women named Sally in Lawrenceton, so most of them went by distinguishing nicknames. 'I was in their wedding,' I said, as if that made it impossible for Jimmy Hunter to be peculiar.

'We all know him,' Mother said dryly. 'And we christened him the House Hunter because he just loves to look at houses. Without Sally with him. He's always going to buy her a house for her birthday, or some such thing. And he's got the money to actually do it, that's the only reason we put up with him.'

'He's not really in the market?'

'Oh, hell no,' Eileen boomed. 'They're going to stay in that old house they inherited from Susu's folks till hell freezes over. He's just some mild kind of pervert. He just likes to look at houses.'

'With women,' Idella added.

'Yes, when we sent him out with Mackie, he didn't call us back for months,' Mother said.

'He won't make appointments with Franklin, either,' Idella added. 'Just that Terry Sternholtz that works with him.' Eileen laughed at that, and we all looked at her curiously.

'Maybe he called Greenhouse Realty instead,' Mackie said quietly.

'And since the Greenhouses are hard up, Donnie sent Tonia Lee out with him, just on the off chance he might really buy something.' This was Eileen's contribution.

'Let me get this straight. He doesn't make passes?' I asked.

'No.' Mother shook her head emphatically. 'If he did, none of us would show him a doghouse. He just likes to look through other people's homes, and he likes to have a woman who isn't his wife with him. Who knows what's going through his head?'

'How long has Jimmy been doing this?' I was fascinated with this bizarre behavior on the part of my friend's husband. 'Does Susu know?'

'I don't have any idea. How would any of us tell her? On the other hand, it does seem strange that gossip hasn't informed her that her husband is house-hunting. But as far as I know, she's never said anything. You were close to Susu in high school, weren't you, Roe?'

I nodded. 'But we don't see each other much nowadays.' I forbore from adding that that was because Susu was always ferrying her children somewhere or involved in some PTA activity. I was having trouble picturing thick-featured Jimmy Hunter, still broad-shouldered and husky as he'd been in his football days but now definitely on the heavyweight side, wandering dreamily through houses he didn't want to buy.

'If it's not the House Hunter,' Patty suggested, 'maybe Tonia Lee's murder has something to do with the thefts.'

This caused an even greater reaction than Patty's first suggestion. But this reaction was different. Dead silence. Everyone looked upset. Beside me, Idella rubbed her hands together, and her pale blue eyes brimmed with tears.

'Okay,' I said finally, 'fill me in on *this*. The real estate business in this town just seems to be full of secrets, these days.'

Mother sighed. 'It's a serious problem, not something like the House Hunter, whom we more or less treat as a joke.' She paused, considering how to proceed.

'Things have been stolen from the houses for sale for the past two years,' Eileen said bluntly.

Even Debbie Lincoln was roused by this. She slid her eyes sideways at Eileen.

'In houses just listed by a particular Realtor? In houses that have just been shown by one Realtor every time?' I asked impatiently.

'That's just the trouble,' Mother said. 'It's not like – say, the refrigerator vanished every time Tonia Lee showed a house. That would make it clear and easy.'

'It's small things,' Mackie said. 'Valuable things. But not so small a client could slip them into a pocket while we were showing the home. And even though the property might be listed with one realtor, of course we let any other Realtor show it – that's the way you have to be in a town this size. We all have to cooperate. We all leave a card when we show a house, whether the owner's home or not . . . you know the procedure. If only we'd gotten the multiple-listing system, we could use lockboxes. None of this would have happened.'

What he meant was, none of the police station routine would have happened to *him*, because he wouldn't have had to take a key to the Anderton house. Tonia Lee would be just as dead, presumably. Mother was in favor of paying for one of the multiple-listing services most of the Atlanta area towns used, but the smaller Realtors in town – particularly the Greenhouses – had balked.

'And it was never the same people, never, any more than coincidence could explain,' Mother was saying. 'I don't think the houses had been shown by the same person – or to the same person – before the items were missed, any time.'

'You all borrow keys back and forth,' I said.

The Realtors nodded.

'So anyone could have them copied and use them at his or her leisure.'

Again, glum nods all around.

'So why haven't I read about this in the paper?'

Distinctly guilty looks.

'We all got together,' Eileen said. 'Us, Select Realty; Donnie and Tonia Lee, Greenhouse Realty; Franklin Farrell and Terry Sternholtz, Today's Homes; even the agency that deals mostly in farms, Russell & Dietrich, because we had shown some of the farmhouses.'

'City people who want to say they own property in the country,' Mother told me, raising her eyebrows in derision.

'And what happened at the meeting?' I asked everyone at the table.

No one seemed in any big hurry to answer.

'Nothing was settled,' Idella murmured.

Eileen snorted. 'That's putting it mildly.'

'Lots of mutual accusations and a general clearinghouse of old grievances,' Mother said. 'But finally, to keep this out of the papers, we agreed to reimburse the homeowner for anything missing while the house was listed.'

'That's pretty broad.'

'Well, there couldn't be any signs of a break-in.'

'And there never were?'

'Oh, token ones, and the police came in at first. That Detective Smith,' said Mother distastefully. She was unshakable in her conviction that Arthur Smith had done me wrong and that Lynn Liggett had somehow stolen him from my arms, despite the fact that Arthur and I had broken up before he began dating Lynn. Maybe a week before, it's true. And I'd only broken up with Arthur maybe twenty seconds before he was going to break up with me, so I could salvage some dignity. But what the hell . . . it was all over.

'And what did he find?'

'He found,' said Mother carefully, 'that in his expert opinion, the break-ins were staged to cover up the fact that the thief had entered with a key. And later on, the thief didn't even pretend to break in.'

'But there was no one to accuse – any of us could have been guilty or innocent,' Mackie said. 'As usual, they checked me out first.' He wasn't disguising his bitterness.

'No one was showing any sudden affluence. No one was taking lots of trips to Atlanta to dispose of the stolen items, at least as far as he could tell. Of course, we all go to Atlanta often,' Eileen said. 'And I gather the Lawrenceton police force is not large enough to follow all the Lawrenceton Realtors wherever they go.'

Would Arthur tell me any more? I wondered. Had he, for example, staked out a house that might be robbed? Had he had any suspicions that he couldn't prove?

'As far as we know, the investigation is ongoing,' Mother said with apparent disbelief. 'The whole thing is still up in the air and has been for a long time, too long. We're all sick to death of watching our every move for fear it'll be misinterpreted. At least the talk about this isn't so widespread that people are afraid to list their houses, but it may come to that.'

'That would really hurt business,' Eileen said, and there was a reverent silence.

'So who,' I asked, moving on to the vital question, 'put the key back on the board?'

Chapter Three

That question had to be asked and answered sooner rather than later, and I stuck my neck out to ask it because I was very interested in the answer.

But you would have thought I was a policeman with a rubber hose, one who was furthermore holding their kids as hostages.

'We have to find out,' my mother said. 'Someone in this office got that key and put it back on the key board. No one here knew I was going to show the Anderton house this morning. I didn't know it myself until last night, when Mr Bartell called me at home. So it was likely the body wouldn't be found for a long time – how often do we show the Anderton house? Maybe one client in ten can afford a house like that.'

For the first time Debbie Lincoln opened her mouth. 'Someone,' she offered softly, 'could have come in when Patty and me were both gone from the reception area.'

Patty shot her a look. 'We're never supposed to both be gone from the reception area. But there was a period of maybe five minutes this morning when both Debbie and I were not there,' she admitted. 'While Debbie was in the back copying the sheet for the Blanding house, I had to visit the ladies' room.'

'I walked through while no one was there,' Eileen said immediately. 'And I didn't see anyone coming in from outside.'

'So that narrows the time someone could have come in by a few more seconds,' I observed.

Mother said, 'It would have to be someone who knew our system and could find the right hook for the Anderton key very quickly.'

'Every Realtor in town knows where our key board is, and that we label every hook alphabetically,' Mackie said.

'So you're saying whoever returned the key is another Realtor, or one of you,' I pointed out. 'Though I think anyone coming into the office could figure out the key board in seconds. But it does make more sense for a Realtor to have returned it, to have realized *not* having the key on the board would have alerted us much sooner than the key being there. It's just bad luck for whoever killed Tonia Lee that Martin Bartell wanted to see some big houses this morning, and that he called Mother at home last night after the office was closed.'

Again I was aware of my lack of popularity as the people around the table realized they'd just been boxed in.

'All right,' said Patty defensively and illogically, 'where is Tonia Lee's car? Why wasn't it at the Anderton house this morning?'

That was another interesting question. And one I hadn't thought of . . . nor had anyone else in the room.

'It's parked behind Greenhouse Realty,' said a new voice from the door. 'And wiped clean of fingerprints.'

My old buddy Lynn Liggett Smith, making another of her silent entrances.

'Your daughter-in-law told me to come on back,' she told my mother, who had a particularly nasty gleam in her eye. I didn't think Melinda would be asked to answer the phones anymore.

Lynn was a tall, slim woman with short brown hair very attractively styled. She wore little or no makeup, always pumps or flats, and plain solid-color suits with bright blouses. Lynn was brave and smart, and sometimes I regretted that because of Arthur we would never be good friends. Lynn was also the only detective specifically designated 'homicide' at the Lawrenceton police department; she'd served on the Atlanta police force before taking what she thought would be a lower-stress job. She hadn't counted on Detective Sergeant Jack Burns.

'When did you find her car?' Mother was scrambling to regain her composure.

'This afternoon. Mr Greenhouse knew it was there this morning, but he didn't think that was important, because he thought Mrs Greenhouse had driven off in someone else's car. He just plain didn't know where Mrs Greenhouse was, and when she didn't come home last night, he thought she was just spending the night with someone else. I gather it's common knowledge she was prone to do that sort of thing.' Lynn had made a little pun, and she gave me the ghost of a smile.

'But today Mr Knight has told us that Mrs Greenhouse's car was in the driveway of the Anderton house last night, so she got there under her own steam. Someone, presumably the murderer, drove that car to Greenhouse Realty and left it there out of sight of the street.' Lynn cocked, her head and scanned our faces.

The absence of the car would have been noticed by Donnie Greenhouse, just as the absence of the key would have been noticed at our office, sooner or later.

But the murderer had had bad luck, no doubt about it.

'So,' Lynn continued, 'who put the key back?'

'My daughter brought that up, too,' Mother said smoothly. 'We have decided that at one point this morning, early, someone could have entered the reception area without being seen.'

'How long a time would this one point have lasted?'

'Five minutes. Or less,' Patty Cloud said reluctantly.

'No one wants to 'fess up, I guess,' Lynn said hopefully.

Silence.

'Well, I'll need to talk to each of you separately,' she said. 'If you all have finished your meeting, perhaps I could just stay in here? I'll start with you, Mrs Tea – No, Mrs Queensland. That okay?'

'Of course,' Mother said. 'Back to your work, the rest of you. But don't leave until the detective has a chance to talk to you. Rearrange your appointments.'

Beside me Idella Yates sighed. She picked up her briefcase and pushed back her chair. I turned to make some remark and suddenly realized Idella had been crying silently, something I have never mastered. I caught her eye as she dabbed at her cheeks with a handkerchief.

'Stupid,' she said bitterly. Feeling rather puzzled, I watched her leave the room. If Idella and Tonia Lee had been friends, it would have surprised me considerably. And Idella's reaction seemed a little extreme otherwise.

I made my own exit wondering where I would wait for my turn with Lynn. My mother's office, I decided, and started down the hall.

A young woman was standing in the reception area. I vaguely recognized her as I went through on my way to the left-hand corridor that led to Mother's office.

'Miss Teagarden?' she said hesitantly. I turned and smiled with equal uncertainty.

'I believe I met you at the church last week,' she said, holding out a slim hand. I jogged my memory.

'Oh, of course,' I said, none too soon. 'Mrs Kaye.'

'Emily,' she said, smiling.

'Aurora,' I told her, and to her credit, her smile barely faltered.

'Do you work here?' she asked. 'At Select Realty?'

'Not really,' I confessed. 'It's my mother's agency, and I'm trying to find out a little more about how the business works.' That was close enough to the truth.

Emily Kaye was at least five inches taller than I, no great feat. She was slim and small-breasted and dressed in a perfect suburban sweater and skirt and low-heeled shoes . . . and her purse matched, too. Her jewelry was small, unobtrusive, but real. Her hair was golden brown and tossed back from her face in a smooth, well-cut mane.

'Did you like the church?' I asked.

'Oh, yes, and Father Scott is so nice,' she said earnestly.

Huh?

'He is so good with children,' she went on. 'My little girl, Elizabeth, just loves him. He promised he'd take her to the park soon.'

He *what*?

All my senses went on full alert.

'You're so lucky,' she said.

My stare must have made her a bit nervous.

'To be dating him,' she added hastily.

So she'd been doing some research. I was thinking a number of things, so many that it would have taken a long time to have completed each thought.

Aubrey loved children? Aubrey had already visited his new parishioner and invited her little girl to the park?

'You play the organ, don't you?' I said thoughtfully.

'Oh, yes. Well, not very well.' She was lying through her teeth, I just knew it. 'I did play for the church in Macon.' Suspicion confirmed.

'You're – excuse me, you're a widow?'

'Yes,' she said briskly, to get quickly over a painful subject. 'Ken died last year in a car wreck, and it was hard to live in Macon after that. I don't have any family there, we were there just because of his job . . . but I do have an aunt, Cile Vernon, here in Lawrenceton, and she heard there was a teacher's job available at the kindergarten here, and I was lucky enough to get it. So now I'm house-hunting for a little place for Elizabeth and me.'

'Well, you came to the right Realtor,' I said, trying to brighten up the conversation and not give way to my deep suspicions. I had a feeling that if I looked over Emily Kaye's shoulder, I would see the writing on the wall for my relationship with Father Aubrey Scott.

'Yes, Mrs Yates is so nice. I'm really looking seriously at a little house on Honor right by the junior high school. It's just a couple of blocks from the kindergarten, and there's a preschool for my little girl nearby, too. Of course, I'd really like to quit work and stay home with Elizabeth,' she said wistfully.

That writing got darker and darker. *Sure* she would.

And to top it all off, that was my house, the house I'd inherited from Jane Engle, she was thinking of buying.

She'd be right across the street from Lynn and Arthur and their baby.

Aubrey would drop me and fall in love with this organ-playing widow with the cute little girl.

No, I was being paranoid.

No, I was being realistic.

'Mrs Kaye,' Idella's sweet voice said, just in the nick of time. 'I'm so sorry, we have to rearrange our appointment to see the house again.'

'Oh, and I had my aunt keep Elizabeth just so I could see it by myself!' Emily Kaye said, regret and accusation mingling in her voice.

I was battling a tide of rage and self-pity that had torn through me with the force of a monsoon. And I would rather have died than for Emily Kaye to notice that anything was wrong with me.

'Why don't you just go ask Detective Smith if you could run over for a half hour and show the house to Mrs Kaye?' I suggested to Idella, who was looking distressed at her client's disappointment. My voice rang a little hollow in my ears, and I felt my expression probably didn't match my concerned words, but I was doing the best I could.

'I'll do that,' Idella said with unaccustomed decision. 'Excuse me just a second.'

'Oh, thanks,' Emily told me with a warm sincerity that made me want to throw up. 'I hated to ask Aunt Cile to keep Elizabeth this morning. I don't want her to think I moved here just to have a free babysitter!'

'Think nothing of it,' I answered with equal sincerity. I wanted to get out of that room so badly my feet were itching. Any minute I was going to slap the tar out of Emily Kaye.

And why? I asked myself as I gave her a final, civil nod and glided off down the hall to Mother's office. Because, I answered myself angrily, Emily Kaye was going to get married, she would marry Aubrey, and even if I didn't want to marry him, I would once again be *left*. I knew I was being childish, I knew there was nothing logical about my feeling, and still I couldn't help it. This was not my finest hour.

It was time for one of my pep talks.

It is better not to be married than to be married unhappily.

Women do not need to be married to have rich, fulfilled lives.

I didn't want to marry Aubrey anyway, and I probably wouldn't have accepted if Arthur Smith had asked me. (Well, yes I would, but it would've been a mistake.)

All relationships fail until you find the right one. It's inevitable.

The failure of a relationship to lead to marriage does not mean you are unworthy or unattractive.

Having told myself all this, I recited the list again.

By the time Mother returned to her office, I'd completed the circuit three times. Mother was not in the best of humor, either. She was fuming about the disruption of the office, about being questioned again by the police, about the nerve of Tonia Lee, turning up dead in a Select Realty listing. Of course, she didn't use those words, but that was the gist of her diatribe.

'Oh, listen to me!' she said suddenly. 'I can't believe I'm going on like this, and a woman I know is probably lying on a table somewhere waiting to be autopsied.' She shook her head at her own lack of empathy. 'We'll just have to put up with all this. I wasn't crazy about Tonia Lee, God knows, but no one should have to go through what she must have.'

'You did tell Lynn about the thefts?'

'Yes. I let her draw her own conclusions. I'd already told her about the vases missing from the Anderton house. So I went on and told her about the pilfering that's been going on. Of course, it's more than pilfering. Someone in our little group of Realtors is seriously dishonest.'

'Mom, have you happened to think that Tonia Lee found out who stole the stuff from the houses? That maybe that was why she got killed?'

'Yes. Of course. I hope the thefts had nothing to do with the murder.'

'That would mean that a Realtor is the killer.'

'Yes. Let's just drop the subject. We don't know anything. It was probably one of Tonia Lee's conquests that did her in.'

'Probably. Well, I'm going to go home as soon as Lynn talks to me.'

'You don't have a feel for the business, do you?' Mother said reluctantly.

'I don't think so,' I said with equal regret.

She reached across her desk and patted my hand, surprising me for the second time today. We are not touchers.

'Excuse me,' Debbie Lincoln said from the doorway. 'That woman wants you, Miss Teagarden.'

'Thanks,' I said. I retrieved my purse from the floor and fluttered my fingers at my mother. 'See you tomorrow night, Mom, if not sooner.'

'Okay, Aurora.'

That night, after I'd taken my shower and wrapped myself up in a warm robe, something that had been picking at the edges of my mind finally surfaced.

I looked up a number in the little Lawrenceton phone book and dialed.

'Hello?'

'Gerald, this is Roe Teagarden.'

'My goodness, girl. I haven't seen you in a year, I guess.'

'How are you doing, Gerald?'

'Oh, pretty well. You know, don't you, that I've remarried?'

'That's what I heard. Congratulations.'

'Mamie's cousin Marietta came to help me clean out her stuff after Mamie – died, and we just hit it off.'

'I'm so glad, Gerald.'

'Is there anything I can do for you, Roe?'

'Listen, I heard a name today and I'm trying to pin a case to it. Think you can help me?'

'I'll sure give it a shot. It's been a long time since I've read any true crime. Mamie getting killed kind of made my interest in crime fade . . .'

'Of course. I'm being so stupid calling you . . .'

'But lately I've thought about taking it up again. So what's your question?'

'You were always our walking encyclopedia in Real Murders, Gerald. So here's the question. Emily Kaye?'

'Emily Kaye . . . hmmmm. A victim, not a killer, I remember that right off the bat.'

'Okay. American?'

'Nope. Nope. English . . . early this century, 1920s, I think.'

I kept a respectful silence while Gerald rummaged through his mental attic of old murder cases. Since Gerald was an insurance salesman, his interest in wrongful death had always seemed rather natural.

'I got it!' he said triumphantly. 'Patrick Mahon! Married man who killed and cut up his mistress, Emily Kaye. There were pieces of her all over the holiday cottage he'd rented; he'd tried several methods to dispose of the body. He'd bought a knife and saw before he'd gone down to the cottage, so the jury didn't believe his excuse that she'd died accidentally. Let me flip open this book, Roe. Okay . . . his wife, who'd thought he was fooling around, found a ticket to retrieve a bag from the train station . . . and in the bag was a woman's bloodstained clothing. She told the police, I believe. So they backtracked Mahon and found the body parts. That what you needed to know?'

'Yes, thank you, Gerald. I appreciate your help.'

'No trouble at all.'

The early Emily Kaye was certainly a far cry from the present-day Emily. I couldn't imagine the Emily I knew going to a cottage for an illicit vacation with a married man.

So a little niggling point had been settled. I knew where I'd heard the name.

But there was no one I could share this fascinating bit of information with, no one who would appreciate it. For the second time in one day, I regretted the disbanding of Real Murders. Call us ghouls, call us just plain peculiar, we had had a good time with our admittedly offbeat hobby.

What had happened to the members of our little club? Of the twelve, one would go on trial soon for multiple murder, another had committed suicide, one had been murdered, one had been widowed, one had died of natural causes, one had been arrested for drug trafficking (Gifford's unusual lifestyle had finally attracted the wrong attention), one was in a mental institution . . . on the other hand, LeMaster was still busy and prosperous with his dry-cleaning business, presumably, though I hadn't seen him since Jane Engle's funeral. John Queensland had married my mother. Gerald had remarried. Arthur Smith had gotten married. And I . . .

It seemed LeMaster Cane and I were the only ones who were basically unchanged in life condition in the eighteen months or so since Real Murders had had its last meeting.

Chapter Four

Friday morning I woke with that blank feeling I'd had lately. Nothing specific to do, nowhere particular to go. No one expected me anywhere.

Even though library funding cuts had meant I'd only been part-time, my work hours had shaped my week. I had an increasingly strong feeling I wouldn't be throwing my lot in with Mother's at Select Realty, so I wouldn't be studying for my real estate license.

Lying in bed drowsily was not such a pleasure if it wasn't illicit, even with Madeleine's heavy warm body curled up against my leg. Before, I'd used this time to map out my day. Now the time lay like a wasteland before me. I didn't want to think about the dinner party tonight, didn't want to feel again the alternating apprehension and attraction Martin Bartell aroused in me.

So I scolded myself out of bed, down the stairs, and popped an exercise video into the VCR after switching on the coffeepot. I stretched and bent and hopped around obediently, grudging every necessary minute of it. Madeleine watched this new part of my morning routine with appalled fascination. Now that I was thirty, calories were no longer burning themselves off quite so easily. Three times a week my mother, clad in gorgeous exercise clothes, went to the newly opened Athletic Club and did aerobics. Mackie Knight, Franklin Farrell, and Donnie Greenhouse, plus a host of other Lawrencetonians, ran or biked every evening. I'd seen Franklin's cohort, Terry Sternholtz, out 'power walking' with Eileen. My mother's new husband was a golfer. Almost everyone I knew did *something* to keep her muscles in working order and her body in the proper shape. So I'd succumbed to the necessity myself, but with little grace and less enthusiasm.

At least I felt I'd earned my coffee and toast, and my shower was a real pleasure afterward. While I was drying my hair, I decided that today I'd start looking at houses seriously. I needed a project, and finding a house I really liked would do. Jane's books and the few things from her house I'd wanted to keep were stacked in odd places around the townhouse, and I was beginning to feel claustrophobic. Mother had hinted heavily that Jane's dining room set would be welcome in her third bedroom for a short time only.

Of course, I'd have to go through Select Realty, and I didn't think I ought to have Mother showing me around. Eileen, Idella, or Mackie? Mackie could use the vote of confidence, I reflected, standing bent at the waist with my hair hanging down so I could dry the bottom layer. But though I didn't have anything against Mackie, I never had been too crazy about him, either. I didn't think it was because he was black or because he was male. I just wasn't that comfortable with him. On the other hand, Eileen was smart and sometimes funny, but too bossy. Idella was sweet and could leave you alone when you needed to think, but she was no fun at all.

After a moment's consideration, I chose Eileen. I phoned the office.

Patty said she wasn't in.

I looked up Eileen's home number and punched it with an impatient finger.

'Hello?'

'May I speak to Eileen, please?'

'May I tell her who's calling?'

'Roe Teagarden.' Who the hell was this? Eileen's personal home secretary? On the other hand, it wasn't exactly my business.

Eileen finally came on the line.

'Hi, Eileen. I've decided to start moving on finding a house of my own. Can you show me some, pretty soon?'

'Sure! What are you looking for?'

Oh. Well, four walls and a roof . . . I began speaking as I thought. 'I want at least three bedrooms, because I need a room for a library. I want a kitchen with some counter space.' The townhouse was definitely deficient in that department. 'I want a large master bedroom with a very large closet.' For all my new clothes. 'I want at least two bathrooms.' Why not? One could always be kept pretty for company. 'And not lots of traffic.' For Madeleine, who was weaving around my ankles, rumbling her rough purr.

'What price range do you have in mind?'

I was still talking to an investment banker about what I would have to live on if I didn't use any of Jane's capital. But I could buy the house outright and then invest the rest, or I could put the money from the sale of Jane's house down on the new place . . . I let all this swirl around in my head, and then an answer popped to the top of my brain, like the answer popping up to the window of a fortune-telling ball.

'Okay,' Eileen said. 'Seventy-five to ninety-five gives us some room. There are quite a few for sale in that range since Golfwhite closed its factory here.' Golfwhite – which, logically enough, manufactured golf balls and other golfing accessories – had closed its Lawrenceton factory and moved all its people who were willing to move to the larger factory in Florida.

'I don't really need anything awfully big or important-looking,' I told Eileen, assailed by sudden doubts.

'Don't worry, Roe. If you don't like it, you don't have to buy it,' she said dryly. 'Let's get a start tomorrow afternoon. I'll see what I can get lined up in that time.'

After I'd dressed in my lime green blouse and navy blue pants and sweater, I had nothing better to do than drop in on my old friend Susu Saxby Hunter. The house she'd inherited from her parents was in the oldest part of Lawrenceton. The house had been built in the last quarter of the previous century, and had charming high ceilings and huge windows, negligible closets, and wide halls, a feature I was especially fond of for some reason. Wide halls are a great location for bookshelves, and Susu was wasting a whole lot of prime space, in my opinion. Of course, she had other things to worry about, I found out that morning. In a house the age of hers, the heating and cooling bills were extortionate, drafts were inescapable, curtains had to be custom-made because nothing was of standard size, and all the electric wiring had had to be replaced recently. To say nothing of the antiquated toilets and tubs that Susu had just replaced.

'But you love this house, don't you?' I said, sitting across from Susu at her 'country pine' kitchen table. Susu's kitchen was so heavily 'country', including a pie safe in the corner (lovingly refinished and containing no pies whatsoever), that you expected a goose to walk in with a blue bow around its neck.

'Yes,' she confessed, putting out her third cigarette. 'My great-grandparents built it when they were first married, and then my parents inherited and they redid it, and now I'm redoing it. I guess I always will be. It's lucky Jimmy's in the hardware business! The only thing it would be better if he did is if he were a licensed electrician. Or had a fabric store. Want some more coffee?'

'Sure,' I said, reflecting I'd have to view the renovated bathrooms quite soon at this rate. 'How's Jimmy doing?'

Susu didn't look quite as happy as she had when discussing the house. 'Roe, since we've been friends a long time, I'll tell you . . . I'm not sure how Jimmy's doing. He goes to work, and he works hard. He's really built the business up. And he goes to Rotary, and he goes to church, and he coaches Little Jim's baseball team in the summer. And he goes to Bethany's piano recitals. But sometimes I have the funniest feeling . . .' Her voice trailed off uncertainly, and she stared down at her smoldering cigarette.

'What, Susu?' I asked quietly, suddenly feeling a return of my high school affection for this bright, blond, plump, scared woman.

'His heart's not in it,' she said simply, and then gave a little laugh. 'I know that sounds stupid . . .'

Actually, she sounded quite perceptive, something I'd never suspected.

'Maybe he's just having sort of an early midlife crisis?' I suggested gently.

'Of course, you're probably right,' Susu said, obviously embarrassed by her own frankness. 'Come see how I decorated

Bethany's room! She'll be a teenager before I know it. Roe, I expect her to tell me any day that she's started her *periods*!'

'Oh, no!'

And we oohed and aahed our way up the stairs to Bethany's pretty-as-a-picture room, still decorated with childish things like favorite dolls – but the dolls were sharing space with posters of sullen young men in leather. Then we viewed Little Jim's room, with its duck-laden wallpaper and masculine plaids. It seems to be the view of those who design 'male' decorations that the male DNA includes a gene that requires duck-killing.

Then we moved on to Sally and Jim's room, resplendent with chintz and framed needlework, an antique cedar chest, and ruffled pillows on the beds. A picture from their wedding hung by Sally's dressing table, one of the whole carefully arranged wedding party.

'There you are, Roe, second from the end! Wasn't that a wonderful day?' Susu's pink fingernail landed on my very young face. That face, with its stiff smile, brought that day back to me all too vividly. I had known exactly how unbecoming the dreadful lavender ruffled bridesmaid's dress had been, and my unruly hair was topped with a picture hat trailing a matching lavender ribbon. My best friend, Amina, also a bridesmaid, had fared much better in that get-up because of her height and longer neck, and her smile was unreserved. Susu herself, radiant in fully deserved white, was gorgeous, and I told her so now. 'That was the wedding of the year,' I said, smiling a little. 'You were the first of us to be married. We were so envious.'

The memory of that envy, the thrill of being the first, momentarily warmed Susu's face. 'Jimmy was so handsome,' she said quietly.

Yes, he had been.

'Honey, I'm here for lunch,' bellowed a voice from downstairs. Susu's plump face aged again. 'You won't believe who's here, Jimmy!' she called gaily.

And down the stairs we tripped, stuck in a time warp between that picture-book wedding and the reality of two children and a house.

Jimmy Hunter quickly brought me back to the present. It had been a long time since I'd seen him close up, and he'd aged and coarsened. The basic goodwill that had always lain behind his character seemed to be gone now, replaced by something like confusion, laced with a dose of wondering resentment. How could Jimmy Hunter's life not be idyllic? he seemed to be wondering. What could possibly be missing? I'd always thought of him as an uncomplicated jock. I saw I would have to revise this assessment of Jimmy just as I'd had to correct my reading of his wife.

'You look great, Roe,' Jimmy said heartily.

'Thanks, Jimmy. How's the hardware business?'

'Well, it keeps us in hamburger, with steak on the weekends once in a while,' he said casually. 'How's the realty market in Lawrenceton?'

Of course everyone in town had heard by now I'd left the library, and heard and speculated about my legacy from Jane Engle.

'Kind of upset, right now.'

'You mean about Tonia Lee? That gal just didn't know when to quit, did she?'

'Oh, Jimmy,' Susu protested.

'Now, sugar, you know as well as I do that Tonia Lee would cheat on her husband any time it came in her head to do it. She just did it once too often, with the wrong man at the wrong time.'

As right as he might be, he said this in a very unpleasant way, a way that made me want to defend Tonia Lee Greenhouse. Jimmy was the kind of man who would say a woman deserved to get raped if she wore a low-cut blouse and tight skirt.

'She was unwise,' I said levelly, 'but she didn't deserve to be murdered. No one deserves to be killed for making some mistakes.'

'You're right,' said Jimmy, backing down instantly, though obviously not changing his opinion at all. 'Well, I can see you ladies have a lot to talk about, so I'll just take myself outside to work in the toolshed. Call me when lunch is ready, Susu.'

'Okay,' she responded warmly. When he was out the back door and down the steps, her face seemed to fold in.

'Oh, Roe, he's always going out to that toolshed! He's redone it as a workshop, and he spends hours out there piddling with this or that. He's a good husband as far as providing goes, and he loves the kids, but I just don't feel like he really lives here half the time.'

Caught unawares, I couldn't think of what to say. I patted her shoulder awkwardly, uncomfortable as usual when touching people.

'You know what he does?' Susu asked as she rummaged in the refrigerator and emerged with some leftover dishes. 'He goes and looks at houses! When we have this lovely home that I don't want to give up, ever! He just makes these appointments and looks at houses!' She popped the dishes in the microwave and punched in a time setting. 'I don't know how he explains to the Realtors that I'm never with him – I'm sure they expect his wife to come along if he's really house-hunting. I've had people whose homes were for sale ask me how Jimmy liked their house, and I didn't know anything about it!' Susu grabbed a tissue from a crochet-covered tissue box and blotted her eyes with ferocious intensity. 'It's so humiliating.'

'Oh, Susu,' I said with considerable distress, 'I have no idea why Jimmy would do that.' The microwave beeped, and Susu began pulling things out and then got two plates from the cupboard.

'I'll bet you've heard about it, though, haven't you?' She could tell my answer by my face. 'Everyone has. Even Bethany came home from school asking me if it was true her daddy was peculiar.'

'Maybe this house is just so much yours,' I said hesitantly. I knew it was stupid to open my mouth, but I did it anyway.

'Of course it's mine,' Susu said grimly. 'It's been my family's and it's in my name and I love it and it's going to stay that way.'

There seemed little more to say. Susu had drawn a line, and her husband was stepping over it, his fanciful house-hunting an odd symptom of a deep dissatisfaction.

Or at least that was the way I saw it. (I am as bad at practicing amateur psychology as anyone I know.)

I tried to get up and leave, having turned down repeated invitations to eat with them, but Susu determinedly kept me talking, though lunch was seemingly ready. She wanted us to talk about all the other bridesmaids. These reminiscences seemed to feed her something she needed. Naturally, all of them but me were married; some had been married more than once. Or twice.

'I heard you've been dating Aubrey Scott,' Susu said encouragingly.

'We've been going out for a few months.'

'What's it like to date a minister? Does he want to kiss and everything?'

'He wants to kiss; I don't know about "everything". He's got hormones, same as anyone else.' I had to smile at her.

'Oooh, oooh,' said Susu, shaking her head in mock horror. 'Roe, you may not have gotten married, but you've dated more interesting people than any of us ever dated.'

'Like who?'

'That policeman, for one. And that writer. And now a priest. Don't the Episcopalians call 'em priests like Catholics do? And remember, even when you were in high school, you dated . . .'

Now, I knew Susu intended this list to cheer me up, but it had exactly the opposite effect. Like looking at my closetful of bridesmaid dresses. So as soon as I could, I started the parting process. As I was getting into my car, I said as casually as I could, 'Did Little Jim have a football game Wednesday evening? I thought I saw your van parked at the Youth Club field.'

'What time?'

'Oh, I guess it was about five thirty.'

'Let me think. No, no, Wednesday afternoon is Bethany's Girl Scout meeting, and Little Jim has Tae Kwon Do at the same time, so Jimmy has to take him to that while I go with Bethany to Scouts. Jimmy has Wednesday afternoons off anyway – that's the afternoon the store is closed, because it's open on Saturdays. I think the older league had a game scheduled for Wednesday. There are lots of vans like ours.'

'Little Jim's Tae Kwon Do is in that building in the shopping center on Fourth Street?'

'Yes, right by that carpet and linoleum place.'

'Does Jimmy get to stay and watch Little Jim's class?'

'No, the teacher won't let parents stay except for special occasions. He says it distracts the boys, especially the littler ones. But the lessons are just half an hour or forty-five minutes. So Jimmy takes a book and reads in the car, or runs an errand. And it's right before supper, too, at five o'clock, so on Wednesdays I have to have leftovers or run home from Scouts and get something out of the freezer to microwave.'

Susu didn't seem to think it was strange I was interested in her family's schedule, something she enjoyed detailing anyway. Like any specialist, she wanted to air her knowledge.

As I finally took my leave and drove away, I was thinking that if Jimmy Hunter had killed Tonia Lee, he'd done it on a tight time budget. Susu hadn't actually said her husband had eaten with the family on Wednesday night, but she hadn't mentioned it was different from any other Wednesday, either. So I had to decide this was inconclusive. But the odds were a little more in favor of Jimmy Hunter's being innocent. It looked as if Patty Cloud's favorite suspect had been sitting outside the Tae Kwon Do studio with a newspaper or a book, or sitting at the country pine table eating supper, at the time Tonia Lee Greenhouse had been killed.

Chapter Five

There was a blinking light on my answering machine.

The first message was from my mother. 'If you haven't taken anything by Donnie Greenhouse's, you need to do that. I took by a chicken casserole this morning, Franklin Farrell said he was going to take a fruit salad of some kind, and Mark Russell from Russell and Dietrich says his wife is making a broccoli casserole. But no one's made a dessert. I know her mother's church will take a lot of stuff, but if you could make a pie, that would mean that the Realtors had provided a full meal. Okay?'

'Make pie,' I wrote on my notepad. (Despite the fact that I was not a Realtor, and I supposed Eileen or Idella knew how to make a pie – probably Mackie, too, for that matter.)

'This is Martin Bartell,' began the second message. 'I'll see you tonight at your mother's.'

I swear the sound of his voice made something vibrate in me. I had it bad, no doubt about it. It was a helpless feeling, kind of like developing rabies, I figured. Though they had shots now for that, didn't they? I wished I could take a shot and be over this thing with Martin Bartell. Aubrey was sexy, too, and a lot safer; perhaps, despite my doubts, our relationship was viable. With an effort, I dismissed Martin from my thoughts and began to rummage through the freezer to see if I had enough pecans for pecan pie.

Not enough pecans. Not enough coconut for German chocolate pie. (Yes, pie. I never make the cake.) Not any cream cheese for cheesecake. I turned my search to the cabinets. Ha! There was a can of pumpkin that must have come out of Jane's cupboard. I would make a pumpkin pie. I took off my navy blue sweater and put on my old red apron. After tying back my hair, which tends to fly into batter or get caught in dough, I set to work. After I cleaned up and ate my lunch – granola and yogurt and fruit – the pie was ready to go to Donnie Greenhouse's.

Tonia Lee and Donnie's modest home was surrounded by cars. I recognized Franklin Farrell's Lincoln parked right in front, and several more cars looked familiar, though I am not much of a one for remembering cars. Franklin Farrell's was the only powder blue Lincoln in Lawrenceton, and had been the subject of much comment since he'd bought it.

Donnie Greenhouse was right inside the door. He looked white and stunned and yet somehow – exalted. He took my hand, the one that wasn't balancing the pie, and pressed it with both of his.

'You are so kind to come, Roe,' he said with doleful pleasure. 'Please sign the guest book.'

Donnie had been handsome when Tonia Lee had married him seventeen years before. I remembered when they'd eloped; it had been the talk of the town, the high-school-graduation-night elopement that had been 'so romantic' to Tonia Lee's foolish mother and 'goddamned stupid' to Donnie's more realistic father, the high school football coach. Tonia Lee seemed to have worn Donnie thin. He'd been a husky football player when they'd married; now he was bony and looked undernourished in every way. Tonia Lee's horrible death had given Donnie a stature he'd lacked for a long time, but it was not an attractive sight. I was glad to get my hand back, murmur the correct words of condolence, and escape to put the pie in the kitchen, which was already full of more homemade food than Donnie had eaten in the past six months, I'd have been willing to bet.

The cramped little kitchen, which had probably been ideal for Tonia Lee, a minimalist cook, was full of Tonia's mom's church buddies, who seemed to be mostly large ladies in polyester dresses. I looked in vain for Mrs Purdy herself and asked a couple of the ladies, who suggested I try the bathroom.

This seemed a bit odd, but I made my way through the crowd to the hall bathroom. Sure enough, the door was open and Helen Purdy was seated on the (closed) toilet, dissolved in tears, with a couple of ladies comforting her.

'Mrs Purdy?' I said tentatively.

'Oh, come in, Roe,' said the stouter of the two attendants, whom I now recognized as Lillian Schmidt, my former co-worker at the library. 'Helen has cried so hard she's gotten herself pretty sick, so just in case, we came in here.'

Oh, great. I made my face stick to its sympathetic lines and nervously approached Helen Purdy.

'You saw her,' Helen said pitifully, her plain face soggy with grief. 'How did she look, Aurora?'

A vision of Tonia Lee's obscenely bare bosom flashed through my head. 'She looked very' – I paused for inspiration – 'peaceful.' The bulging eyes of the dead woman, staring blankly out from her posed body, looked at me again. 'At rest,' I said, and nodded emphatically to Helen Purdy.

'I hope she went to Jesus,' wailed Helen, and began crying again.

'I hope so, too,' I whispered from my heart, ignoring the wave of doubt that washed unbidden through my mind.

'She never could find peace on earth, maybe she can find it in heaven.'

Then Helen just seemed to faint, and I backed hastily out of the little bathroom so Lillian and her companion could work over her.

I saw one of the local doctor's nurses in the family room and told her quietly that Helen had collapsed. She hurried to the bathroom, and feeling that I'd done the best I could, I looked around for someone to talk to. I couldn't leave yet – I hadn't been there quite long enough, my inner social clock told me.

I spied Franklin Farrell's head of thick gray hair over the heads crowding the room, and 'excuse me'd' over to him. Franklin, a spectacularly tan and handsome man, had been selling real estate since coming to Lawrenceton thirty or more years before.

'Roe Teagarden,' Franklin said as I reached his side, giving every appearance of great pleasure. 'I'm glad to see you, even though I'm sorry it's here, on such a sad occasion.'

'I'm sorry it's here, too,' I said grimly. I told him about Helen.

He shook his handsome head. 'She has always been wrapped up

in Tonia Lee,' he said. 'Tonia Lee was Helen's only child, you know.'

'And Donnie's only wife.'

He looked taken aback. 'Well, yes, but as we all know . . .' Here he realized that bringing up Tonia Lee's infidelities would hardly be proper.

'I know.'

'I brought a fruit salad with Jezebel sauce,' he said, to change the subject. Franklin was one of the few single men in town who didn't mind confessing that he cooked for himself and did it well. His home was also definitely decorated, and beautifully so. Despite his flair for interior design, and his penchant for cooking something other than barbecue, no one had ever accused Franklin of being effeminate. Too many well-known cars had been parked overnight in the vicinity of his house.

'I brought a pumpkin pie.'

'Terry's bringing marinated mushrooms.'

I tried not to gape. It was hard to picture Donnie and Helen Purdy appreciating marinated mushrooms.

'Terry doesn't always have a solid sense of occasion,' Franklin said, enjoying my expression.

Franklin and Terry Sternholtz were certainly the odd pair of the Lawrenceton realty community. Franklin was sophisticated, smooth, a charmer. Everything about him was planned, immaculate, controlled, genial. And here Terry came, covered dish in her hand, her chin-length red hair permed and tossed into fashionable disarray. Terry Sternholtz said just about anything that entered her head, and since she was well-read, an amazing number of things did. She nodded at her boss, grinned at me, and mouthed 'Let me get this to the kitchen' before being swallowed by the crowd. Terry had freckles and an open, all-American face.

In sharp contrast, I found myself staring at a picture of Tonia Lee that hung over the fireplace. It had been taken at one of those instant-glamour photography places that dot suburban malls. Tonia was elaborately made-up, her hair sexily tousled and softer than her normal teased style. She had a black feather boa trailing across her neck, and her dark eyes were smoldering. It was quite a production, and to have hung it over her fireplace where she could view it constantly meant Tonia Lee had been very pleased with it.

'She was quite a woman,' Franklin said, following my gaze. 'Couldn't sell real estate worth a damn, but she was determined her personal life was going to be memorable.'

That was a strange but appropriate epitaph for the misguided and horribly dead Tonia Lee Greenhouse, née Purdy.

'You go out running every evening right after work, don't you?' I asked him.

'Yes, almost always, unless it's raining or below freezing,' Franklin said agreeably. 'Why?'

'So you must have been out Wednesday evening.'

'I guess so. Yes, it hasn't rained this week, so I must have run.'

'Did you see Mackie Knight?'

He thought. 'So often I see the same people who exercise at the same time I do, and I'm not sure if I did see Mackie that evening or not. I don't always, because I vary my route. There are two I like, and I pretty much alternate them. Mackie seems to pick his at random. I remember it was Wednesday when I saw Terry and Eileen; they walk together most evenings. But I remember only because Terry congratulated me again on a sale I'd made that day. I saw Donnie, riding his bike, that new ten-speed . . . I'm sorry, Roe, I just can't remember about Mackie specifically. How come?'

I told him about Mackie's questioning by the police.

'I can't believe they're so sure another car wasn't there!' Franklin looked very skeptical. 'Someone must have shut their eyes for a minute or two, either the woman across the street or the couple behind the Anderton house. And it seems pretty strange to me that both doors were watched that very night.'

I shrugged. But I thought of what the killer had had to do – move Tonia Lee's car to the rear of Greenhouse Realty, then get home on foot. If the killer's car had been at the house, too, he'd either have had to go all the way back to the Anderton house from Greenhouse Realty to move his own car, or return from taking his own car home to get Tonia Lee's. It seemed almost certain someone would have noticed the other car.

I was thinking of the killer as 'he' because of Tonia Lee's nudity.

Terry Sternholtz returned while I was still thinking it through.

'You look awful grim, Roe,' she said.

'Considering the occasion . . .'

'Sure, sure. It's terrible what happened to Tonia Lee. All us females are going to have to be more careful – right, Eileen?' Eileen had just appeared at Terry's elbow, looking especially impressive in a black-and-white suit and huge black earrings.

'I'm glad we took that self-defense course,' Eileen said.

'When was this?' I asked.

'Oh, a year ago, I guess. We drove into Atlanta to take it. And we practice the moves the woman taught us. But I guess, if Tonia let herself be tied up like that, she wouldn't have had a chance anyway.' Terry shook her head.

Franklin looked startled. He must not have heard that titillating fact. Even worse, Donnie Greenhouse was standing very close, with his back to us, talking to a woman whose hair and glasses were exactly the same gray-blue. But Donnie didn't turn around, so apparently he hadn't heard Terry. She, too, had spotted Donnie and was making a horrified face at us to show she realized her gaffe. Eileen gave her the reproving look you give a close friend, the one that says, 'You blockhead, you did it again, but I love you anyway.'

Eileen and Terry were apparently closer than I'd realized. Now that I considered it, I believed it was Terry who'd answered the phone at Eileen's when I'd called this morning. Eileen was at least ten or more years older than Terry, but they had a lot in common, it seemed. They worked for competing real estate firms, but they were the only single female real estate dealers in Lawrenceton. Well, there was Idella, but she hadn't been divorced very long.

I'd always assumed (along with everyone else in Lawrenceton) that Terry and Franklin were lovers, at least occasionally, because with Franklin's reputation it was impossible to believe he could share an office with a woman and not try to seduce her, and it was assumed in Lawrenceton (especially by the male population) that almost all of his seduction attempts were successful. But the way Franklin and Terry were standing, the way they spoke to each other, didn't add up to an intimate relationship. If I'd had to pick a pair of lovers out of our little group, it would have been Eileen and Terry.

This was an idea I had to adjust to. I had no problem with it. I just had to adjust.

Donnie Greenhouse joined our little circle, and my attention was claimed by his doleful face and his strangely exultant eyes. Somewhere behind those pale compressed lips lurked a grin of triumph. I realized I would rather mash the pumpkin pie in his face than have him eat it, and stomped the thought down into my 'Examine Later' compartment. That compartment was filling up rapidly today. Donnie put his hand on Franklin's shoulder.

'Thanks so much for coming,' the new widower said. 'It's great to know our – my – fellow professionals are showing such support.'

Embarrassed, we all mumbled appropriate things.

'Tonia Lee would have been so pleased to see you all here. Mrs Queensland was here this morning, and Mark Russell and Jamie Dietrich were here, and I see Idella coming in the door . . . this has meant so much to me and Tonia Lee's mom. She's had to lie down in the guest bedroom.'

'Do you have any idea yet when the funeral will be?' Eileen asked.

'Not for sure . . . probably next week sometime. I should be able to get Tonia Lee's – remains back from the autopsy by then. Now, Terry – you be sure and come to the funeral.'

Terry looked considerably surprised. 'Of course I will, Donnie.'

We were all shuffling around trying to figure out what to say when Donnie suddenly burst out, 'I know you all will back me up with the police and tell them I couldn't have hurt Tonia Lee! That woman detective seems to think I could have killed Tonia, but let me tell you' – suddenly he was breathing very fast and other people were turning to look at us – 'if I'd been going to do it, I'd have done it long before this!'

Now *that* I could believe.

The room hushed, and everyone tried to find somewhere else to look. As if moved by one impulse, we all gazed at the ridiculous glamour photograph blown up to such huge proportions above the fireplace. Tonia Lee's false smoldering eyes stared back at us. Her widower broke out in sobs.

This was undoubtedly a scene that would be forever enshrined in Lawrenceton folklore, but telling about it in a year would be a lot more fun than being here at the actual moment it occurred. We all looked at the front door longingly, and as soon as decently possible, the crowd began to flow out, washing the little cluster of Realtors with it. Donnie had pulled himself together enough to shake the hands of those leaving.

I noticed quite a number of them managed to wipe their hands against their clothes, unobtrusively.

I know I did.

An hour of reading the newest Joan Hess restored me. I may have dozed off a little, because when I looked at the clock, I found it was past time to get ready for Mother's dinner party. I dashed up the stairs, took a very brief shower to freshen up, and stood in front of my open closet, faced with a sartorial dilemma. I had to look nice for Aubrey without having it seem as if I was looking my best for Martin Bartell. Well, that was treading a very fine line indeed. What would I have worn if I'd never met Martin? If I were just going to a dinner to greet a new person in town?

I'd wear my royal blue dress and matching pumps, with my pearl earrings. Too dressy? Maybe I should wear nice pants and a pretty blouse? I called my mother to find out what she was wearing. A dress, she told me definitely. But the royal blue suddenly looked boring – high-necked and vaguely military with its two rows of buttons up the front. Then I caught myself thinking of Martin, and I resolutely pulled the blue dress over my head. My hair crackled as I brushed it back and secured the top part over to one side with a fancy barrette. I popped in the pearl earrings, dabbed on a very little scent, and worked on my makeup until the doorbell rang. Before I went down to let Aubrey in, I examined myself in the full-length mirror I'd inherited from Jane. For the thousandth time, I regretted my inability to wear contact lenses, which I'd finally gotten around to trying the previous month. A corner of my mouth turned down. There I was, short, chesty, with round dark brown eyes and so much wavy hair. And round tortoiseshell glasses, and short plain nails with messy cuticles.

It came to me that in my life anything was still possible, but that time might be coming to a close.

Aubrey was clerical that evening – all in black, with his reverse collar. And he looked wonderful that way. He'd seen my dress before, but he still complimented me.

'That's your color,' he said, kissing me on the forehead. 'You ready? You know how I am about dinners at your mother's. Did she hire Mrs Esther?'

'Yes, Aubrey,' I answered with a mocking air of long-suffering. 'Let me get my coat, and we'll go tend to your appetite.'

'It's really cold,' he warned me.

I kept my coats in a downstairs closet. I looked at them for a second before pulling out the new black one. It was beautifully cut, with a high collar. I handed it to Aubrey, who liked to do things like help me on with my coat, even though in my thirty years I'd had plenty of experience. I slid my arms in while he held it, and then he tenderly gathered my hair and pulled it out of the coat and spread it on my shoulders. That was the part he enjoyed. He bent to kiss my ear, and I gave him a sidelong smile.

'Have you seen your new parishioner lately?' I asked.

'Emily, with the little girl?'

There was, something a little different in his voice. I knew it.

'Yes. She was in the office yesterday. She's thinking about buying the house I inherited from Jane.'

I'd discovered Aubrey was interested in me the very day I found out Jane had left me her home and her money and a secret, one I'd never told Aubrey . . . or anyone else. Aubrey had always felt a little uncomfortable about Jane's legacy, since his sensitive cleric's antennae told him people had talked mightily about that strange bequest.

'It's a pretty little house. That would be a good place to raise a child.'

Aubrey had that child on the brain. He hadn't had any with his wife, who had died of cancer.

'I didn't know you were fond of children, Aubrey,' I said very carefully.

'Roe, there's never a good time to talk about this, so I'll talk to you about it now.'

I swung around to face him. My hand had actually been on the doorknob. I know I must have looked alarmed.

'I can't have children.'

He could see from my expression that I was struggling for a response.

'When my wife began to get sick, before we found out what was wrong, we'd been trying, and I went in for tests before her. I found out I was sterile . . . and we found out she had cancer.'

I closed my eyes and leaned against the door for a second. Then I stepped over to Aubrey and put my arms around him and leaned my head against his chest. 'Oh, honey,' I said softly, 'I'm so sorry.' I stroked his back with one hand.

'Does it make a difference to you?' he asked me softly.

I didn't raise my head. 'I don't know,' I said sadly. 'But I think it makes a difference to you.' I turned up my face then, and he kissed me. Despite Aubrey's principles, we came very close to falling over the edge then and there, at the end of our relationship. There was more emotion in back of our touching than there ever had been before.

'We'd better go,' I said.

'Yes,' he said regretfully.

We were silent all the way to my mother's house on Plantation Drive. We were both a little sad, I think.

Chapter Six

Martin's Mercedes was already parked in front of my mother's house. I took a deep breath and exhaled it into the nippy air as I swung my legs out of the front seat of Aubrey's car. He extended his hand and helped me out, and we went up the long flight of steps to the front door still holding hands. The glass storm door showed us the fireplace, lit and welcoming, and my mother's new husband, John Queensland, standing in front of it with a glass of wine. He saw us coming and held the door for us.

'Come in, come in, it's cold out tonight! I think winter is just about really here,' John said genially. I realized that he now felt at home in the house, he was the host. I, therefore, must be a guest.

This evening was beginning on several jarring notes.

My mother swept in from the kitchen. She could sweep even in quite narrow dresses; you'd think lots of material would be required for that gesture, but not with Aida Teagarden Queensland.

'Aubrey! Aurora! Come get warm and have a glass of wine with our guests,' Mother said, giving me a peck on the cheek and patting Aubrey's shoulder.

He was sitting on the couch, his back to me. I had a little time to get myself steeled. I held Aubrey's hand tighter. We went around the corner of the couch to enter the little 'conversation group' before the fire.

'Have you gotten over your shock of yesterday?' asked Barby Lampton. She was wearing an unbecoming dress in dark green and mustard.

'Yes,' I said briefly. 'And you?'

Aubrey was sliding my coat off. He smoothed my hair gently before he handed the coat to John to hang up. My eyes finally met

Martin Bartell's. His face was quite expressionless. His eyes were hot.

'I guess so,' Barby said with a little laugh. 'Nothing like that has ever happened to me before, but a woman I met at the local library this morning was telling me *you've* had an exciting life.'

'Were you taking out a library card?' I asked after a moment.

'Oh, no,' Barby said, letting out a little shriek of laughter. 'I wanted to look at the *New York Times*, at the sale ads. I was thinking about flying up to New York before I go home.'

Her marriage must have left her pretty affluent.

'You're going back so soon?' John asked hastily. Aubrey and I sat on one of the love seats flanking the couch, and Aubrey took my hand again.

'I'm sorry. I must not be cut out for rural living,' Barby said rather smugly. 'This is such a sweet little town, all the people are so – talkative.' And her eyes cut toward me. 'But I miss Chicago more than I thought I would. I'll have to go back and start apartment-hunting. I think Martin was hoping I'd keep house for him, but I don't think I'm quite ready for that.' She smirked at us significantly.

'I understand you got hurt quite badly a couple of years ago?' Barby went on, oblivious to the fact that my mother's back got very straight and even John looked rather grim. Martin's eyes were going from one face to another curiously.

'Not seriously,' I said finally. 'My collarbone was broken, and two ribs.'

Aubrey was looking studiously at his wineglass. My brush with death had always seemed a little lurid to him.

'Oh, my God! I know that hurt!'

'Yes. It hurt.'

'How did it happen?'

My side began to ache, as it always did when I thought about that horrible night. I heard myself screaming and felt the pain all over again.

'It's old news,' I said.

Barby opened her mouth again.

'I hear you have a wonderful cook, Aida,' Martin said clearly and smoothly.

Barby looked at him in surprise, Mother in gratitude.

'Yes,' she agreed instantly, 'but Mrs Esther is not my cook, really. She's a local caterer. If she knows you well, she'll come into your home and cook for you. If she doesn't know you well, she'll prepare it all and leave it in your kitchen with instructions. Fortunately for me, she knows me well. She picks her own menu, and the next day everyone gets to talk about what Mrs Esther felt like cooking for Mrs Queensland, or Mr Bartell, or whomever. We've all tried to figure out how she selects her dishes, but no one can pick out a pattern.'

Mrs Esther's cooking and character had provided more conversational fodder for parties than any other topic in Lawrenceton. Martin segued smoothly from Mrs Esther to catering disasters at parties he'd attended, Aubrey ran that into bizarre weddings at which he'd officiated, and we were all laughing by the time Mrs Esther appeared in the doorway in a spotless white uniform to announce that it was time to come to the table. She was a tall, heavy black woman with hair always arranged in braids crowning her head, and thick gold hoops in her ears. Mrs Esther – no one ever called her Lucinda – was a serious woman. If she had a sense of humor, she kept it a secret from her clients. Mr Esther was a secret, too. Young Esthers were always on the honor roll printed in the newspaper, and they were apparently as closemouthed as their mother.

We all went into Mother's dining room with a sense of anticipation. Sometimes Mrs Esther cooked French, sometimes traditional Southern, once or twice even German or Creole. Most often it was just American food well prepared and served. Tonight we had baked ham, sweet potato casserole, green beans with small new potatoes, homemade rolls, Waldorf salad, and Hummingbird Cake for dessert. Mother had placed herself and John on the ends, of course, and Aubrey and I faced Barby and Martin, respectively.

I looked at Martin when I thought he was unfolding his napkin.

He instantly looked up, and we stared at each other, his hand frozen in the act of shaking out the napkin.

Oh, dear, this was just awful. I would have given anything to be miles and miles away, but there was no excuse I could make to leave just then. I looked away, addressed some remark at random to Aubrey, and resolutely kept my eyes turned down for at least sixty seconds afterward.

Mrs Esther did not serve, though she did remain to clean up afterward. So we were all busy passing dishes and butter for a few minutes. Then Mother asked Aubrey to say grace, and he did with sincerity. I poked at the food on my plate, unable for a few minutes to enjoy it. I stole a quick glance across the table. He was freshly shaved; I bet he'd needed to, he was probably a hairy man. His hair must have been black before it turned white early, his eyebrows were still so dark and striking. His chin was rounded, and his lips curved generously. I wanted Martin Bartell so much it made me sick. It was a dangerous feeling. I had always been wary of dangerous feelings.

I turned to Aubrey, who had chosen this evening of all evenings to tell me about his sterility. To tell me how lovely Emily Kaye's little girl was. To warn me that he wanted children and couldn't have them with me, but that Emily already had a child who could be his in all but name. I had always theoretically wanted a baby of my own, but – I thought now – if I loved Aubrey enough, I would have forgone my own children. If he had loved me enough.

This was not going to happen. Aubrey was not going to hold me fast to his anchor while the danger of Martin Bartell passed by. He was going to cast me adrift, I thought melodramatically. I took a bite of my roll. Martin looked at me, and I smiled. It was better than smoldering at him. He smiled back, and I realized this was the first time I'd seen him look happy. My mother eyed us, and I took another bite of roll.

An hour later we were all protesting how full we were and that the cake had been the clincher. Chairs were pushed back, everyone stood up, my mother swept into the kitchen to compliment Mrs Esther, Barby excused herself, and I walked back into the living room. Martin fell in beside me. Behind us Aubrey and John discussed golf.

'Tomorrow night,' Martin said quietly. 'Let's eat dinner in Atlanta tomorrow night.'

'Just us?' I didn't mean to sound stupid, but I didn't want to be surprised when he turned up with his sister.

'Yes, just us. I'll pick you up at seven.' His fingers brushed mine.

After thirty or forty more minutes of polite conversation, the little dinner party broke up.

Aubrey and I went to his car after Martin and Barby had pulled away, and we exclaimed over how cold it was and how soon Thanksgiving seemed, all of a sudden. Talking about the food lasted us until my place, where he courteously got out to walk me to the door. This was where our dates usually ended; Aubrey wasn't taking chances on being swept away by passion. Tonight he kissed me on the cheek instead of the lips. I felt a surge of grief.

'Good night, Aubrey,' I said in a small voice. 'Good-bye.'

'Good-bye, sweetheart,' he said with some sadness. He kissed me again and was gone.

I dragged myself up the stairs to the bedroom and undressed, moving slowly with an exhaustion so deep it was like a drug. Once I'd washed my face and pulled on my nightgown, I crawled into bed and was out when my head hit the pillow.

I woke up slowly the next day. It was sunny and cold. The tree on the front lawn of the townhouse row flicked its bare branches at my window. I was house-hunting this afternoon and had a date for the evening: that made it a very crowded day indeed, by my recent (non-working) standards. I pulled on an old pair of jeans and a shirt, some thick socks and sneakers, and made myself a big breakfast: biscuits, sausage, eggs.

Then I had three hours before Eileen picked me up. Rather than wander around restlessly thinking about Martin, I began to clean. Starting with the downstairs, I picked up, scrubbed, dusted, vacuumed. Once the downstairs was done to my satisfaction, I moved to the upstairs. The guest bedroom was full of boxes of things from Jane's I'd decided to keep, and another bedstead was leaning up against the wall; so cleaning wouldn't be of much use. But in my bedroom I really went to town. My sheets got changed, the bed was perfectly made, the bathroom shone with cleanliness, the towels were fresh, and all my makeup was put away in the drawer where it belonged instead of cluttering the top of my vanity table. I even refolded everything in my chest of drawers.

Then I decided to pick out my clothes for the evening, in case I had a lot of houses to look at today and got home late. What did you wear to a presumably fancy restaurant with a worldly older man you had the hots for?

I'd recently discovered a women's clothing place in the city that stocked things just for petites. My purchases there were among my best and most becoming, because my friend Amina's mom's shop, Great Day, just didn't carry that many petites. Now that I had money, I could buy things even when I didn't need them at the moment. I had one dress I'd been saving for something fancy, if only I had the guts to wear it. It was teal and it shone; it was a little above the knee and had a low neckline and was cut exactly along my body. I took it out of the closet and eyed it nervously. It wasn't what I thought of as indecent, but it certainly complemented my figure.

Now came the indecent part. On the same day, I'd bought an amazing black lace bra and a matching garter belt. This was being seriously naughty for me, and I had been very embarrassed at the cash register. With a sense of casting all caution to the winds, I laid out these garments on the bed, along with some sheer black hose and high-heeled black pumps, and hoped I wouldn't disgrace myself by falling over in them. I wasn't at all sure I had enough confidence to wear this ensemble, but the time was now, if ever. I would aim for this, and if my confidence seeped away during the day and I wore more ordinary undergarments, no one would know I'd chickened out but myself.

It was now almost time for Eileen to come, and I walked through the whole townhouse checking it for details. Everything was clean, orderly, and inviting. I only hoped I wouldn't run into Martin today, since I looked my worst right now.

The doorbell rang at one o'clock on the dot, and when I opened it with my purse in hand and coat halfway on, I was relieved to see Eileen wasn't wearing one of her 'Realtor' outfits, but a pair of nice slacks and a blouse, with a bright fuchsia jacket and sneakers.

'Hi, Roe! Ready to start looking?'

'Sure, Eileen. Is the wind blowing?'

'You bet, and colder than a witch's tit.'

At least it wasn't raining or snowing. But by the look of the leaden sky and the way the trees were tossing, it felt as if it would be raining before long.

'You seemed unsure about what you really wanted,' Eileen began when we were buckled up, 'so I just called around and found out what I could show you today, in your size and price range. We have five houses to see.'

'Oh, that's good.'

'Yes, better than I expected at such short notice. The first one's on Rosemary. Here's the sheet on it . . . it has three bedrooms, two baths, a large kitchen and family room, a formal living room, small yard, and is all electric . . .'

The house on Rosemary needed new carpet and a new roof. That was not insurmountable. What struck it off my list was the narrow lot. My neighbors could look right in my bedroom window and shake hands with me, if they should be so inclined. I'd had too many years of townhouse living for that. If I was going to own a house, I wanted privacy.

The next house had four bedrooms, which I liked, and a poky kitchen with no storage room, which I didn't.

The third house, a two-story in a rather run-down part of Lawrenceton, was most attractive. It needed some renovation, but I could pay for that. I loved the master bedroom, and I loved the breakfast area overlooking the backyard. But the house next door had been divided into apartments, and I didn't like the thought of all the in-and-out traffic – there again, I'd had enough.

The fourth house was a possible. It was a smaller house in a very nice area of town, which meant it cost the same as a larger home elsewhere. But it was only ten years old, was in excellent shape, and had a beautifully landscaped, low-maintenance yard and lots of closets. Also a Jacuzzi in the master bath, which I eyed with interest. It was over my price limit, but not too drastically.

By the time we pulled up in front of the fifth house, Eileen and I had learned a lot about each other. Eileen was intelligent, conscientious, made a note to find out the answer to each and every small query I had, tried to stay out of my way as I considered each property, and was in general a really great Realtor. She at least pretended to consider that not knowing exactly what you wanted was normal.

I was trying to overlook things that I could do something about if I were really interested in the house, and concentrate instead on things that would absolutely knock the house out of the running. These things could be pretty nebulous, though, and then I felt obliged to come up with a concrete reason to give Eileen.

The fifth house was the killer. There was nothing wrong with it. It was a three-bedroom with a pleasant yard, a small but adequate kitchen, and the usual number of closets. It was certainly big enough for one person. If toys were any evidence, it was not quite big enough for a couple with several children. It was very similar to its neighbors . . . the exterior was one of three or four standardly used in this subdivision. I was sure anyone on the street would have no trouble finding her way to any particular room or closet in any house.

'I hate this house,' I said.

Eileen tapped her fingernails absently on the imitation wooden-block Formica of the kitchen counter. 'What is it you dislike so much, so I won't waste our time showing you anything else with that feature?' A reasonable question.

'It's too much like all the other houses on the street. And everyone else on this street seems to have little children. I wouldn't feel a part of the neighborhood.'

Eileen was resigning herself to the fact that I wasn't going to be the easiest sell she'd ever had.

'This is just the first day,' she said philosophically. 'We'll see more. And it's not like you have a time limit.'

I nodded, and Eileen dropped me back at my place, thinking out loud the whole time about what she could line up to show me in the coming week. I listened with half my attention, the other half wrapped up in my date tonight. I was trying to keep my mental screen absolutely blank, trying not to imagine any scenes from the evening, trying not even to conjecture on its outcome.

Of course, I still had time to kill when I got home, and with the house clean and my clothes selected, nothing to kill it with. So I turned on the television, and when that failed, I tried to concentrate on an old Catherine Aird, counting on her never-failing blend of humor and detection to get me through a couple of hours. After ten minutes of concentrated effort, Aird worked, as she always did. I even forgot to look at my watch for minutes at a time.

Then I remembered I hadn't done my exercise video that morning. Madeleine came to watch with her usual amazement, and I worked up quite a sweat and felt very virtuous.

Finally it really was time for a shower.

I hadn't scrubbed myself this much since my senior prom. Every atom of my skin and inch of my hair was absolutely clean, every extra hair was shaved from my legs, and when I emerged I slapped everything on myself I could think of, even cuticle cream on my messy cuticles. I plucked my eyebrows. I put on my makeup with the care and deliberation of a high-fashion model, and dried my hair to the last strand, brushing it afterward at least fifty times. I even cleaned my glasses.

I wiggled into my incredible underwear without looking in the mirror, at least not until I pulled the black slip over my head. Then, very carefully, the teal dress, which I zipped up with some difficulty. I switched purses, put on my high-heeled pumps, and surveyed myself in Jane's mirror.

I looked as good as I possibly could, and if it wasn't good enough . . . so be it.

I went downstairs to wait.

Chapter Seven

The doorbell rang exactly on the dot.

Martin was wearing a gorgeous gray suit. After a moment I stepped back to let him in, and he looked around.

Suddenly we realized we weren't observing the amenities, and both of us burst into speech at once. I blurted 'How've you been doing?' as he said 'Nice apartment.' We both shuddered to a halt and smiled at each other in embarrassment.

'I reserved a table at a restaurant the board of directors took me to after they'd decided to hire me for the job here,' Martin said. 'It's French, and I thought it was very good. Do you like French food?'

I wouldn't understand the menu. 'That'll be fine,' I said. 'You'll have to order for me. I haven't tried to speak French since high school.'

'We'll have to rely on the waiter,' Martin said. 'I speak Spanish and some Vietnamese, but only a little French.'

We had one thing in common.

I got my black coat from the coat closet. I slid it on myself, not being ready for him to touch me. I lifted my hair out of the collar and let it hang down my back, acutely conscious that he watched my every move. I thought if we made it out the door it would be amazing, so I kept my distance; and when he opened the door for me to pass through, I did so as quickly as I could. Then he opened the patio gate and the door of his car. I hadn't felt so frail in years.

His car was wonderful – real leather and an impressive dashboard. It even smelled expensive. I had never ridden in anything so luxurious. I was feeling more pampered by the moment.

We swept imperially through Lawrenceton, attracting (I hoped) lots of attention, and hit the short interstate stretch to Atlanta.

Our small talk was extremely small. The air in the car was crackling with tension.

'You've always lived here?'

'Yes. I did go away to college, and I did some graduate work. But then I came back here, and I've been here ever since. Where have you lived?'

'Well. I grew up in rural Ohio, as I mentioned last night,' he said.

I could not picture him being rural at any point in his life, and I said so.

'I've spent my lifetime eradicating it,' he said with some humor. 'I was in the Marines for a while, in Vietnam, the tail end, and then when I came back, after a while I began to work for Pan-Am Agra. I finished college through night school, and Pan-Am Agra needed Spanish speakers so much that I became fluent. It paid off, and I began working my way up . . . this car was the first thing I got that said I had arrived, and I take good care of it.'

Presumably the big house in Lawrenceton would be another acquisition affirming that he was climbing the ladder successfully.

'You're – thirty?' he said suddenly.

'Yes.'

'I'm forty-five. You don't mind?'

'How could I?'

Our eyes moved simultaneously to a lighted motel sign looming over the interstate.

The exit was a mile away.

I thought I was about to give way to an impulse – finally.

'Ah – Aurora—'

'Roe.'

'I don't want you to think I don't want to spend money on you. I don't want you to think I don't want to be seen with you. But tonight . . .'

'Pull off.'

'What?'

'Pull off.'

Off the interstate we rolled at what seemed to me incredible speed, and suddenly we were parked in front of the bright office of the motel. I couldn't remember the name of it, where we were, anything.

Martin left the car abruptly, and I watched him register. He carefully did not turn to look back at me during the interminable process.

Then he slid back into the car with a key in hand.

I turned to him and said through clenched teeth, 'I hope it's on the ground floor.'

It was.

It rained during the night. The lightning flashed through the windows, and I heard the cold spray hit the pavement outside. He had been sleeping; he woke up a little when I shivered at the thunder. 'Safe,' he said, gathering me to him. 'Safe.' He kissed my hair and fell back into sleep.

I wondered if I was. In a practical way I was safe, yes; we were not stupid people; we took precautions. But in my heart I had no feeling, none at all, of safety.

The morning was not the kind that ordinarily made me cheerful. It was colder, grayer, and puddles of muddy water dotted the parking lot of the motel. But I felt good enough to overcome even the faint sleaziness of putting back on the same clothes I'd worn. We ate breakfast in the motel coffee shop, and both of us were very hungry.

'I don't know what we've started,' Martin said suddenly, as he was about to get up to pay our bill, 'but I want you to know I have never felt so wrung out in my life.'

'Relaxed,' I corrected smilingly. 'I'm relaxed.'

'Then,' he said with raised eyebrows, 'you didn't work hard enough.'

We smiled at each other. 'A matter of opinion,' I said, quite shocked at myself.

'We'll just have to try again until we're both satisfied,' Martin murmured.

'What a fate,' I said.

'Tonight?' he asked.

'Tomorrow night. Give me a chance to recoup.'

'See, you do know some French words,' he replied, and we smiled at each other again. He glanced at his watch as we drove back. 'I'm usually working at the plant alone on Sunday, but today we're having a special meeting at twelve thirty, followed by an executives' lunch. It's a kickoff for our next production phase.'

'What will they say if you're a few minutes late?' I asked him softly when he kissed me good-bye at my townhouse door.

'They won't say anything,' he told me. 'I'm the top dog.'

For the first time in a long time, I was going to skip church. I staggered up the stairs and stripped off all my clothes, pulled a nightgown over my head, and after turning off the bell of the phone, crawled in bed to rest. I began to think, and with an effort turned off the trickle of thought like a hand tightening a faucet. I was sore, exhausted, and intoxicated, and soon I was also asleep.

My mother called at eleven, as soon as she got home from church. The Episcopalians in Lawrenceton had a nine thirty service, because Aubrey went to another, smaller church forty miles away to hold another service directly after the Lawrenceton one. I was drowsing in bed, trying to think of what to do with the remainder of the day, persuading myself not to call Martin. I felt so calm and limp that I thought I might slide out of bed and ooze across the carpet to the closet. I barely heard the downstairs phone ringing.

'Hello, Aurora,' Mother said briskly. 'We missed you at church. What have you been doing today?'

I smiled blissfully at the ceiling and said, 'Nothing in particular.'

'I called to find out about the annual Realtors' banquet,' she said. 'Would you and Aubrey like to come? It's for families, too, you know, and you might enjoy it, since you know everyone.' Mother tried to get me there every year, and the last year I'd broken down and gone. The annual Realtors' banquet was one of those strange events no one can possibly like but everyone must attend. It was a local custom that had begun fifteen years before when a Realtor (who has since left town) decided it would be a good thing if all the town professionals and their guests met once a year and drank a lot of cocktails and ate a heavy meal, and afterward sat in a stupor listening to a speaker.

'Isn't the timing a little bad this year?' I was thinking of Tonia Lee.

'Well, yes, but we've made the reservations and selected the menu and everyone's kept that night free for months. So we might as well go through with it. Shall I put you and Aubrey down? This is the final tally of guests. I'll be glad when Franklin's in charge of this next year.' Each agency in Lawrenceton took the task in turn.

'He'll leave most of the arrangements to Terry Sternholtz, the same way you left them to Patty,' I said.

'At least it won't be our agency that looks inefficient if anything goes wrong.'

'Nothing's going to go wrong. You know how efficient Patty is.'

'Lord, yes.' My mother sighed. 'I sense you're putting me off, Aurora.'

'Yes, actually I am. I just wanted to sort of tell you something . . .'

' "Sort of"?'

'I'm trying to glide into this.'

'Glide. Quickly.'

'I'm not dating Aubrey anymore.'

An intake of breath from Mother's end.

'I'm really just . . . I think . . . I'm seeing Martin. Bartell.'

Long silence. Finally Mother said, 'Were there any bad feelings, Aurora? Do John and I need to skip church for the next couple of weeks? Aubrey was a little somber today, maybe, but not so much that I thought anything about it until I talked to you.'

'No bad feelings.'

'All right. I'll have to hear the whole story from you sometime.'

'Sure. Yes, well, Martin and I will come, I think . . . maybe.' I had a sudden attack of insecurity. 'It's next Saturday night, right?'

'Right. And Tonia Lee will be buried Tuesday. Donnie called today. The church service is at' – Mother checked her notes – 'Flaming Sword of God Bible Church,' she finished in an arid voice.

'Golly. That's out on the highway, isn't it?'

'Yes, right by Pine Needle Trailer Park.' Mother's voice could have dried out the Sahara.

'What time?'

'Ten o'clock.'

'Okay. I'll be there.'

'Aurora. You're okay? About this change in beaus?'

'Yes. So is Aubrey. So is Martin.'

'All right, then. See you Tuesday morning, if not before. I think Eileen mentioned she had some more properties to show you this afternoon; she should be calling you soon.'

'Okay. See you.'

I took a quick shower, pulled on a green-, rust-, and brown-striped sweater, the matching rust-colored pants, and my brown boots. A glance outside had shown that the day had not brightened, but remained resolutely cold, windy, and wet.

Downstairs I found my answering-machine light was blinking. I'd been too tired to glance that way this morning.

'Roe, this is Eileen, calling on Saturday evening. I have two houses to show you Sunday afternoon if it's convenient for you, in the afternoon. Give me a call.'

A moment of silence between messages.

'Roe, are you asleep?' My face flushed when I heard Martin's voice. He'd probably called while I was in the shower. 'I'm calling from work, sweetheart. I can hardly wait until tomorrow night. I can't make it to Atlanta that night since I have a meeting early Tuesday morning, but we can at least go to the Carriage House.' That being Lawrenceton's best restaurant. 'I want to see you again,' he said simply. 'You made me very happy.'

I was pretty damn happy myself.

I called Eileen back to make an appointment for two o'clock, then decided to treat myself to lunch somewhere. On impulse, I punched the number of my reporter friend, Sally Allison, and we arranged to meet at the local Beef 'N More.

Thirty minutes later we were settled opposite each other, after waiting in line through the Sunday church crowd. Sally was working on a hamburger and a salad, and I had virtuously opted for the salad bar only, though I could certainly get enough calories from what was spread up and down its length.

Sally was older than I by more than twelve years, but we're good friends. She was a Sally who wouldn't tolerate a nickname. Sally had bronze hair, never out of place, and she bought expensive clothes and ran them into the ground. She was wearing a black suit I'd seen on her countless times, and it still looked good. For once, she had some news to impart before she started digging for more.

'Paul's working today. He and I got married last weekend,' she said casually, and the cellophane package of crackers I was trying to open exploded. I hastily began to gather up the crumbs.

'You married your first husband's brother?'

'You know we've been dating for a long time.'

'Well, yes, but I didn't know it was going to result in a marriage!'

'He's great.'

We chatted away. I was dying to know what the first Mr Allison thought of this new situation, but was aware I really must not ask.

The third time Sally was explaining to me how wonderful Paul was (she knew I'd heard while dating Arthur Smith that Paul had never been popular with his fellow detectives), I was sufficiently bored and skeptical to look around me. To my surprise, I spied Donnie Greenhouse eating lunch with Idella. They were sitting in one of the few places in the steak house where you could talk without being overheard. Donnie was leaning over the table, talking earnestly and quickly to Idella, whose delicate coloring was showing unbecoming blotches of stress. Idella was shaking her head from side to side.

What an odd couple! It was a little strange to see Donnie out in public, even though I dismissed that reaction on my part as uncharitable. But with Idella?

'They certainly look put out with each other,' Sally said. She'd followed my gaze. 'I don't think this is a widower on the rebound, do you?'

There sure wasn't anything loverlike in their posture or in the way they were looking at each other. Suddenly Idella sprang up, grabbed her purse, and headed for the women's room. Donnie scowled after her. I thought Idella was crying.

Sally and I exchanged glances.

'I guess I better go check,' I said. 'There's a fine line between showing concern and butting in, and this situation is right on it.'

The two-stall salmon-and-tan women's room was empty except for Idella. She was indeed crying, shut in one of the booths.

'Idella,' I said gently. 'It's Roe. I'm holding the door shut so no one else can come in.' And I braced my back against the door.

'Thanks,' she sobbed. 'I'll straighten up in a minute.'

And sure enough, she pulled herself together and emerged from the booth, though not until I'd had time to decipher the last batch of graffiti through a layer of tan paint. Showing some wear and tear, Idella ran some cold water on a paper towel and held it over her eyes.

'It's going to ruin my makeup,' she said, 'but at least my eyes won't be so puffy.'

It was oddly difficult to talk to her with her eyes covered like that, in this bleak room with the smell of industrial disinfectant clogging my nostrils.

'Idella, are you all right?'

'Oh . . . yes, I'll be okay.' She didn't sound as though she were certain. 'Donnie just has some crazy idea in his head, and he won't let it go, and he's hounding me about it.'

I waited expectantly. I was so curious I finally prodded her. 'He surely doesn't think you had anything to do with Tonia Lee's death?'

'He thinks I know who did do it,' Idella said wearily. 'That's just ridiculous, of course.' She stared bleakly into the mirror; she looked even more haggard under the harsh light, her dead-grass hair a limp mess around her pale face. 'He says he saw my car pulling out of the Greenhouse Realty parking lot the night Tonia Lee was killed.'

'How could he possibly think that?'

But Idella was through confiding, and when someone pushed behind me hard enough to make the door move a little, she seized the chance to go back to her table. 'Thanks,' she said quickly. 'I'll see you later.'

I moved away from the door to let her out, and she shouldered her way past the door-pusher, who turned out to be Terry Sternholtz.

She gave us a very peculiar look; she knew I'd been holding the door shut. I wondered if she'd been out there long.

'Idella seemed upset,' Terry said casually as she pulled open one of the stalls. She looked very bright today, her bouncing red hair contrasting cheerfully with a kelly green suit.

'Some upset she had,' I said dismissively, and went back to my table. Sally was waiting, and raised her eyebrows expectantly as I slid into my chair.

'I don't know,' I said to answer Sally's unspoken query. 'She wouldn't really say.' I didn't want to repeat the conversation. It seemed evident Idella was in trouble of some kind, and she had always been so nice to me I didn't want to compound it by starting a rumor. Sally looked at me sideways, to show me she knew I was evading her. 'I don't know why you think I tell everyone everything I know,' she said with more than a little pique in her voice. It looked as if we'd have our own little quarrel.

Just then the group of Pan-Am Agra executives came in for their campaign kick-off lunch, among them Martin. It was just like seeing the boy who'd given you your first kiss the night before. As if I'd had on a homing signal, Martin immediately turned and scanned the crowd, finding me quickly. He excused himself from his companions and left the line to come over. My face felt hot. Sally's back was to him, and she was saying 'You look like you just swallowed a fish, Roe,' when he came up, bent over, and gave me a kiss that was just short enough not to be vulgar. Then we beamed at each other.

'This is my friend Sally Allison, Martin,' I said abruptly, suddenly aware of Sally's interested face.

'Hello,' he said politely, and shook Sally's proferred hand.

'Aren't you the new plant manager of Pan-Am Agra?' she asked. 'I think Jack Forrest did a business-page article on you.'

'I saw it. It was well written,' Martin said. 'More than I can say for some of the stories written about me. What time tomorrow night, Roe?'

'Seven?' I said at random.

'I'll be there at seven.' He kissed me again very quickly, nodded to Sally, and rejoined his group, who were watching with great attention.

'You certainly got branded in public,' Sally said dryly.

'Huh?' I had my face turned down to my plate.

' "Property of Martin Bartell. Do Not Touch".'

'Sally, I don't want to look like we're talking about him,' I hissed. I looked at her sternly. 'Just talk about something else for a while.'

'Okay,' she said agreeably. 'Is he going to ask you to the prom?'

'Sally!'

'Oh, all right. Donnie left in a snit as soon as Idella emerged from the women's room and hot-footed it out the door. Donnie looked right sullen. What did she tell you?'

'That Donnie thought . . . oh, Sally!'

'Just curious, just curious! Since when are you and Martin Bartell an item?'

'Very recently.' Like last night.

'Well, isn't life on the up-and-up for us? I get married, and you get a sweetie.'

I rolled my eyes. Thinking of Martin as a 'sweetie' was like thinking of a Great Dane as a precious bundle of fur.

'He was in Vietnam, wasn't he?' Sally asked.

'Yes.'

'I think he brought home some medals. He wouldn't talk about it to Jack, but one of the other Pan-Am Agra execs told Jack that Bartell came out of the war with a bit of glory.'

'When was the story in the paper?' I hadn't seen it.

'Soon after he arrived, at least six weeks ago.'

'Can you send me a copy, Sally?'

'Sure. I'll track it down when I go to the office tomorrow.'

We computed tips and gathered our purses. My shoulder blades itched, and I looked behind me. Martin, surrounded by his employees, was sitting at one of the larger round tables, watching me, smiling a little.

He looked hungry.

I floated out to my car.

Chapter Eight

I had agreed to meet Eileen at the office, and it was close enough to the time for me to head that way. There were several cars parked outside; Sunday was often a busy day at Select Realty.

The first person I saw was Idella, who said 'Hi, Roe!' as brightly as if I hadn't seen her boo-hooing in the women's room at a restaurant not forty-five minutes before.

'Hello, Idella,' I said obligingly.

'I just got an offer on your house on Honor. Mrs Kaye is offering three thousand less than your asking price, plus she wants the microwave and the appliances to stay.'

We went to Idella's little office, decorated exclusively with pictures of her two children, together and separate, the boy about ten and very heavyset, the girl perhaps seven and thin, with lank blond hair. I sat in one of her client chairs and considered for a moment.

'Tell her – her offer needs to be up by a thousand, and she can have everything but the washer and dryer.' Mine came with the townhouse, and I'd need a set when I moved.

'What about the freezer in the carport toolshed?' Idella asked. 'It's not spelled out here whether she is including that under appliances or not.'

'I don't really care that much about the freezer. If she wants it, she can have it.'

'Okay. I'll take your counteroffer over to her aunt's house right now.'

Idella was obviously determined not to refer to the scene at Beef 'N More. Of course, I wanted to know what it was about, but in all decency I would have to wait until she felt like confiding in me.

'I'm really pleased about this offer,' I told her, and she smiled.

'It was an easy sell, the right person at the right time,' she said dismissively. 'She needs a small decent house in good shape, you have a small decent house in good shape; the dead-end street location and the price are right.'

The phone rang while Idella gathered papers. She picked up with one hand while her other kept busy. 'Idella Yates speaking,' she said pleasantly. The first words of her caller changed Idella's demeanor dramatically. Her free hand stilled, she sat up straighter, the smile vanished from her face. 'I'll have to talk later,' she said swiftly. 'Yes, I have to see you . . . well . . .' She closed her eyes in thought. 'Okay,' she said finally. She hung up and sat very still for a moment. The cheer, the bustle, had seeped right out of her. I didn't know whether to say anything or not, so I settled for looking concerned, as I certainly was.

Idella decided to stonewall. 'I think I've got everything here,' she said in a dreadful simulation of her previous cheerful efficiency.

'If you need help, you know you can count on me and my mother,' I told her, and left her office for Eileen's.

Just as Eileen got up to go, she received an unexpected call from an out-of-town client who'd decided to make an offer on a house he'd seen the week before. The house was listed with Today's Homes, but the client had been referred to Eileen personally, so she had shown it along with a lot of Select Realty listings. It took Eileen some time to hammer out the client's offer, assure the client that she'd call Today's Homes that very second, then hang up and immediately lift the phone to dial. I had fished my book out of my purse several minutes before and was reading contentedly.

'Franklin? Eileen. Listen, that Mr and Mrs McCann I showed the Nordstrom house to last week, they just called . . . Yep, they want to make an offer . . . I know, I know, but here it is . . .' As Eileen relayed the offer to Franklin, I became immersed in my book. I was almost through with the Catherine Aird.

Finally Eileen was ready to set out. I told her the good news about the probable sale of my own house as we got into her car.

'Does Idella seem okay to you?' I asked cautiously.

'Lately, no.'

'I think something's wrong.'

'What? Anything we can do something about?'

'Well – no.'

'If we don't know, and she doesn't ask for help, seems like we aren't wanted,' Eileen said, giving me a straight look.

I nodded glumly.

At the first house, the owners were on their way out as we pulled up to the curb. Eileen had cleared the showing with them first, of course, and she went up to talk to them while I surveyed the yard, which badly needed raking.

'How are the two of you?' Eileen said in her booming voice. 'Ben, you ready to go out with me yet?'

'The minute Leda lets me off the rope,' the man answered with equally heavy good humor. 'You better get out your dancing shoes.'

'Haven't you found Mr Right yet, Eileen?' the woman asked.

'No, honey, I still haven't found anyone who's man enough for me!'

They chuckled their way through some more faintly bawdy dialogue, and then the couple pulled off in their car while Eileen unlocked the front door.

'What?' Eileen said sharply.

I hadn't known anything was showing on my face.

'Why do you do that, Eileen?' I asked as neutrally as I could. 'Is that really you?'

'No, of course not,' she said crisply. 'But how many houses am I going to sell in this small town if Terry and I go out in public holding hands, Roe? How would we make a living here? It's a bit easier for Terry in some ways . . . Franklin actually wanted someone working for him who was immune to his charm. He didn't want to fall into bedding an employee. But still, if everyone knew . . . and the people who do know have to be able to pretend not to.'

I could see her point, though it was depressing.

'So here is the Mays' house,' Eileen said, resuming her Realtor's mantle with a warning rattle. 'We have – three bedrooms, two baths, a family room, a small formal living room . . . mmmm . . . a walk-in closet off the master bedroom . . .'

And we strolled through the Mays' house, which was dark and gloomy, even in the kitchen. I could tell within two minutes I would never buy this house, but this seemed to be a day for pretense. I was pretending I might, Eileen was pretending the preceding conversation hadn't taken place. Idella had been pretending she wasn't upset by the phone call in her office.

My lack of sleep began to catch up with me by the hall bathroom, which I viewed dutifully, opening the linen closet and yawning into it, noting the hideous towels the Mays had wisely put away.

'Are you with me today, Roe?'

'What? Oh, I'm sorry, I didn't sleep too well last night.'

'Do you even want to go see this other house?'

'Yes, I promise I'll pay attention. I just don't like this one, Eileen.'

'Just say so. There's no point in our spending time in a house you don't want.'

I nodded obediently.

We were short on conversation and long on silence as we drove to our next destination. Lost in daydreams, I barely noticed when Eileen began to leave town.

Just a mile east out of Lawrenceton, we came to a house almost in the middle of a field. It had a long gravel driveway. It was a two-storey brick house, and the brick had been painted white to set off the green shutters and a green front door. There was a screened-in porch. The second storey was smaller than the first. There was a separate, wide two-car garage to the left rear, with a covered walk from a door in the side of the garage to the house.

There was a second storey to the garage, with a flight of stairs also covered, leading up to it.

The sun was beginning to set over the fields. It was much later than I'd thought.

'Eileen,' I said in amazement, 'isn't this—'

'The Julius house,' she finished.

'It's for sale?'

'Has been for years.'

'And you're showing it to me?'

She smiled. 'You might like it.'

I took a deep breath and got out of the car. The fields around the house were bare for the winter, and the yard was bleached and dead. The huge evergreen bushes that lined the property were still deep green, and the holly around the foundation needed trimming.

'The heirs have kept it going all this time,' I said in amazement.

'Just one heir. Mrs Julius's mother. She wanted to turn the electricity off, of course, but the house would just have rotted. There's been surprisingly little vandalism, for the reputation it has.'

'Well. Let's go in.'

This was turning out to be an unexpectedly interesting day. Eileen led the way, keys in hand, up the four front steps with their wrought-iron railing painted black, badly needing a touch-up now. We went in the screen door and crossed the porch to the front door.

'How old is it, Eileen?'

'Forty years,' she said. 'At least. But before the Juliuses disappeared, they had the whole house rewired . . . they had a new roof put on . . . a new furnace installed. That was . . . let me check the sheet . . . yes, six years ago.'

'And they had the extra storey put on the garage?'

'Yes, it was a mother-in-law apartment. Mrs Julius's mother lived there. But of course you remember.'

The disappearance of the Julius family had been the sensation of the decade in Lawrenceton. Though they had some family in town, few other people had had a chance to get to know them, so almost everyone had been able to enjoy the unmitigated thrill of the mystery and drama of their vanishing. T. C. and Hope Julius, both in their early forties, and Charity Julius, fifteen, had been gone when Mrs Julius's mother came over for breakfast, as was her invariable habit, one Saturday morning. After calling for a while, the older woman had searched through the house. After she'd waited uneasily for an hour, and finally checked to see that their vehicles were still there, she'd called the police. Who of course had at first been skeptical.

But as the day progressed, and the family car and pickup truck remained parked in the garage, and no member of the Julius family called or returned, the police became as uneasy as Mrs Julius's mother. The family hadn't gone bike riding, or hiking, hadn't accepted an invitation from another family.

They never came back, and no one ever found them.

Eileen pushed open the front door, and I stepped in.

I don't know what I'd expected, but there was nothing eerie about the house. The cold sunshine poured through the windows, and instead of sensing ghostly presences of the unfound Julius family, I felt peace.

'There's one bedroom downstairs,' Eileen read, 'and two upstairs, plus a room up there used for an office or a sewing room . . . of course, that could be a bedroom, too. And there's an attic, with a boarded floor. Very small. Access through a trapdoor in the upstairs hall.'

We were in the family room, a large room with many windows. The pale carpet smelled mildewy. The double doors into the dining room were glass-paned. The dining room had a wood floor and a built-in hutch and a big window with a view of the side yard and the garage. After that came the kitchen, which had an eat-in area and many, many cabinets. Lots of counter space. The linoleum was a sort of burnished orange, and the wallpaper was cream with a tiny pattern of the same color. The kitchen curtains were cream with a ruffle of the burnished orange. There was a walk-in pantry that had apparently been converted into a washer-dryer closet.

I loved it.

The downstairs bathroom needed work. New tile, recaulking, a new mirror.

The downstairs bedroom would make a great library.

The stairs were steep but not terrifying. The banister seemed quite solid.

The largest bedroom upstairs was very nice. I didn't like the wallpaper too much, but that was easily changed. Again, the upstairs bath, which opened into the hall, needed some work. The other bedroom needed painting. The small room, usable as a storeroom or sewing room, also needed painting.

I could do that. Or better yet, I could have it done.

'You look pretty happy,' Eileen observed.

I had forgotten anyone else was there.

'You are actually considering buying this house,' she said slowly.

'It's a wonderful house,' I said in a daze.

'A little isolated.'

'Quiet.'

'A little desolate.'

'Peaceful.'

'Hmmm. Well, as far as price goes, it's a bargain . . . and of course, there's the little apartment over the garage that you can rent to whomever . . . that'll help with the isolation, too.'

'Let's see the apartment.'

So down the stairs and out the kitchen door we trooped. The flight of stairs up to the little second floor seemed sturdy enough; of course, this addition was only six years old. I followed Eileen up, and she unlocked the glass-paned door.

It was really one large open area, the only sealed-off part being a bathroom at one end. The bathroom had a shower, no tub. The kitchen was just enough for one person to heat up a few things from time to time; the mother had gone over to the house for most of her meals. Some nice open shelves had been built in, and there were two closets. There was a window air conditioner, but no hint of how it had been heated.

'A kerosene space heater is my guess,' Eileen said. 'There shouldn't be any problem in an area this size.'

Perhaps I could rent this to a student at Lawrenceton's little Bible college or to a single schoolteacher. Someone quiet and respectable.

'I really like this,' I told Eileen unnecessarily.

'I can tell.'

'But I need to think about it, of course.'

'Of course.'

'I can afford it, and the repairs, and pay for it outright. But it is stuck out of town, and I need to decide if that would make me nervous. On the other hand, I can practically see Mother's house from here. And if you could find out who owns this field, I'd appreciate it. I wouldn't want to buy out here and then discover someone was putting up a discount mall. Or a chicken farm.'

Eileen scribbled a note to herself.

I told myself silently that if any of these variables didn't work out, I would hire an architect and have a house very similar to this one built from scratch.

'And I'll keep looking, too,' I told Eileen. 'I just don't want to see anything cramped.'

'Okay, you're the boss,' Eileen said agreeably. It had grown dark enough for her to switch on the car lights as she turned around on the apron to the side of the garage to negotiate the long driveway.

We went back to town in silence, Eileen obviously trying not to give me some good advice, I in deep thought. *I really liked that house.*

'Wait a minute,' Eileen said, her voice sharp.

I snapped out of my reverie.

'Look, that's Idella's car. But she's not showing the Westley house today. My God, look at the time! I'm showing it in an hour to a couple who work different shifts all week. I'm going to need that key.'

Eileen was seriously miffed. If I'd been just any client, she would have waited until she got me back to the office and then returned to or called the listing, but since I was part of the Realtor family, she felt free to vent in front of me. Eileen pulled into the driveway and swung out of her car with practiced ease. I got out, too. Maybe Idella would know if Emily Kaye had already responded to my counteroffer.

There was no client car parked by Idella's.

'The Westleys moved last week,' Eileen said, and opened the front door without knocking. 'Idella!' she hooted. 'I'm going to need this key in an hour, woman!'

Nothing. All within was dark. We went in slowly.

For once, Eileen seemed disconcerted.

Eileen called again, but with less expectation that she would be answered. The blinds and curtains were all open, letting in some light from the streetlamp one lot away. Eileen tried to flip on a light, but the electricity had been turned off.

The house was very cold, and I pulled my coat tighter around me.

'We should leave and call the police,' I said finally.

'What if she's hurt?'

'Oh, Eileen! You know . . .' I couldn't finish the sentence. 'All right,' I said, bowing to the inevitable. 'Do you have a flashlight in your car?'

'Yes, I do. I don't know where my head is!' Eileen exclaimed, thoroughly angry with herself. She fetched the flashlight and swept its broad beam around the family room. Nothing but dust on the carpet. I followed her and her flashlight into the kitchen . . . nothing there. So, back past the front door and down the hall to the bedrooms. Nothing in the first one to the left. Nothing in the bathroom. By now, tears were running down Eileen's face and I could actually hear her teeth chattering.

Nothing in the second bedroom.

Nothing in the hall linen closet.

Idella was in the last bedroom. The flashlight caught her pale hair, and the beam reluctantly went back to her and stayed.

She was crumpled in a corner like a discarded bedspread. Tonia Lee had been arranged, but Idella had just been dumped. No living person could have been lying that way.

I made myself step forward and touch Idella's wrist. It was faintly warm. There was no pulse. I held my hand in front of her nostrils. No breath. I touched the base of her thin neck. Nothing.

You never know about people. I heard a slithery sound, and the flashlight beam played wildly over the walls as tough Eileen Norris slid to the floor in a dead faint.

Of course, there wasn't a phone in the Westley house. I had the sudden feeling I was on an island in the middle of a populous stream. I hated to leave Eileen alone in the dark and silence with Idella's corpse, but I had to get help. There was a car at the house to the right of the Westleys', the helpful flashlight revealed, and I knocked on the screen door.

A toddler answered, in a red-checked shirt and overalls. I couldn't tell if it was a little boy or a little girl. 'Could I speak to your mommy?' I said. The child nodded and left, and after a moment a young woman with a towel around her hair came to the door.

'I'm sorry, I've told Jeffrey not to answer the door, but if I don't hear the doorbell in time, he zooms to it,' she said, making it clear she thought that very clever of Jeffrey. 'Can I help you?'

'I'm Aurora Teagarden,' I began, and her face twitched before the polite lines reasserted themselves. 'I need you to call the police for me. There's been a – an accident next door at the Westley house.'

'You're really serious,' she said doubtfully. 'No one should be in that house, it's for sale.'

'I promise you I am serious. Please call the police.'

'All right, I will. Are you okay, yourself?' she asked, terrified I would ask to be let into her home.

'I'm fine. I'll go back over there now if you'll call.' I had the distinct feeling that she would much rather have gone back to washing her hair and forgotten that I'd knocked.

'I'll call right now,' she promised with sudden resolution.

So I went back over to the cold black house next door. Eileen was stirring around but still out of it. I gripped the flashlight defensively as I crouched next to her on the nasty brown carpet, and stared dully at a dead beetle while I waited for the police.

At least Jack Burns didn't show up. I would rather have been in a locked room with a pit bull than have faced Sergeant Burns at that moment. He had regarded me with baleful mistrust ever since we'd come across each other during the Real Murders investigation. He seemed to think I was the Calamity Jane of Lawrenceton, that death followed me like a bad smell. If I'd been Jonah, he'd have thrown me to the whale without a qualm.

Lynn Liggett Smith seemed to take my presence as a matter of course. That was almost as disturbing.

Eileen came out of her faint, we were allowed to tell the little we knew, and then I drove a shaken Eileen back to the office. My mother had already been called by the police, so she had waited there. Eileen went to Mother's office in a wobbly parody of her usual brisk trot. There were lights on down the hall. I slid into the client chair in Mackie Knight's office. With considerable astonishment, Mackie put down the paperwork he was doing.

'What's happening, Roe?'

'Have you been here all afternoon, Mackie? Till now?' I saw by the clock on the office wall that it was already seven.

'No. I just came back after spending all afternoon at church and eating supper at home with my folks. Just as my mom put her lemon meringue pie in front of me, I remembered that I didn't have all the papers ready for the Feiffer closing tomorrow morning.' There was lemon meringue smeared on a Styrofoam plate and a used plastic fork on a corner of his desk.

'Was anyone else at your folks'?'

'Yeah, my minister. What's this about?'

'Idella was just killed.'

'Oh, no.' Mackie looked sick. 'Where?'

'At the empty Westley house.'

'How?'

'I don't know.' I hadn't seen a weapon, but Idella's coat had been covering her throat. The poor light hadn't been reliable, but I'd thought her face had had the same funny tone as Tonia Lee's. 'Maybe strangled.'

'The poor woman. Who's told her kids?'

'I guess the police. Or maybe whoever she left the kids with while she worked.'

'And I couldn't have done it!' Mackie said, the penny finally dropping. 'I've been with someone every blessed minute, except driving time from my folks' back here.'

'Maybe this wasn't planned as well as Tonia Lee's murder.'

'You think Tonia Lee was killed at the time she was killed and the place she was killed because there would be a lot of available suspects.'

'Sure, don't you?'

'I hadn't thought about it that way,' he said slowly, 'but it makes good sense. Poor Idella.' Mackie shook his head in disbelief. 'She sure had been acting funny lately, almost apologetic, every time I talked to her.'

'She knew you didn't kill Tonia Lee, Mackie. I think she knew who did, or suspected.'

We both sat and thought for a while, and then my mother came to the door and asked gently if she could speak to me for a moment.

'Mackie,' she said as I got up to leave his office, 'you went to church after Idella left the office? Or before?'

'Before. She was still in her office when I walked out the door. I said good-bye to her.'

'Oh, thank God. You're in the clear, then.'

'Yes, I think I am.' Mackie was having a hard time with conflicting emotions.

Lynn was waiting in Mother's office.

'I hear you had an interesting conversation with Idella at Beef 'N More,' she said.

I thought Lynn was bluffing, but I'd intended telling her what

Idella had said anyway, vague though it was. The only person who could have told Lynn that I'd talked to Idella at lunch was Sally Allison, and Sally didn't know what Idella had said to me. No, I wasn't being fair to Sally . . . there was Terry Sternholtz.

I told Lynn all about Idella's and my little bathroom tête-à-tête. We went over and over it while my mother listened or worked quietly. I wondered why I was sitting here instead of going down to the police station. I told Lynn, frontward and backward and upside down, every little nuance of Idella's apparent fight with Donnie Greenhouse, her flight to the women's room, my half-hearted attempt to help her, her few comments to me, and her departure from the restaurant. My next glimpse of her at the office, my brief conversation with her here, the exchange with an unknown person she'd had over the telephone, and her statement that she was going to go to Emily Kaye with my counteroffer. Then how I'd found her at the empty house.

By the time Lynn was satisfied she'd gotten everything out of me she could get, I was heartily sorry I'd spoken to Idella at the restaurant. Sometimes good impulses backfire.

'Go talk to Donnie Greenhouse,' I said irritably. 'He was the one who upset her, not me.'

'Oh, we will,' Lynn assured me. 'In fact, someone's talking to him right now.'

But Donnie Greenhouse, who'd let Tonia Lee stomp on him for so long, would not yield an inch to the police. He called my mother while I was still in her office and told her triumphantly he hadn't given Paul Allison the time of day.

'He told Paul that no matter what Roe Teagarden said Idella told her, he and Idella had discussed nothing more than business and Tonia Lee's funeral.' My mother's famous eyebrows were arched at their most skeptical.

'He might as well wear a sign that says "Please Kill Me. I Know Too Much",' I said.

'Donnie doesn't have enough sense to come in out of the rain,' but I didn't think he was this dumb,' Mother said. 'And why he's doing it, instead of telling the police all he knows, I cannot fathom.'

'He wants to avenge Tonia Lee himself?'

'God knows why. Everyone knows she made his life hell on wheels.'

'Maybe he always loved her.' Mother and I pondered that separately.

'I personally don't think a rational person with a sense of self-preservation could continue to love under such a stream of abuse as that,' my mother said.

I wondered if she was right. 'So Donnie's not rational and has no sense of self-preservation,' I said. 'And what about Idella? Evidently the call she got in her office was from someone she suspected might be the killer. And yet she apparently agreed to meet this person in an empty house. Doesn't that sound like she loved whoever it was?'

'I just don't love that way,' said Mother finally. 'I loved your father until he was unfaithful.' This was the first time she'd ever said one word to me about her marriage with my father. 'I loved him, in my opinion, very deeply. But when he hurt me so much, and things weren't going well otherwise, it just killed the love. How can you keep on loving when someone lies to you?' She really could not understand it.

I didn't know, with my limited experience, if my mother just had an extraordinarily strong sense of self-preservation, or if the world was full of irrational people.

'It seems from what I've read, and observed,' I said hesitantly, 'that lots of people aren't that way. They keep on loving, no matter what the hurt or cost.'

'No self-respect. That's what I believe,' my mother said crisply. She stared out her window for a moment, at the bare branches of the oak tree outside, which made a bleak abstract pattern against the gray sky. 'Poor Idella,' she said, and a tear oozed down her cheek. 'She was worth ten Tonia Lees, and she had children. She'd done so much for herself since her husband left her. I'd gotten pretty fond of her without ever getting really close to her.' Mother looked back at me. Our eyes met. 'She must have been so frightened.' Then she shook herself. 'I'll have Eileen call Emily Kaye to find out if Idella'd actually gotten over there with your counteroffer, honey. The police should let us have the papers in her car, soon. We can get on with the house sale, with Eileen or me taking Idella's part. I'll let you know.'

I hadn't been worried about it at all. 'Thanks,' I said, trying to look relieved. 'I think I'll go home now.' But I turned at her office door to say, 'You know, I'll bet money that Donnie doesn't really know anything at all. If he does get killed, it'll be over absolutely nothing.'

I was really glad I hadn't agreed to meet Martin tonight. I needed a little time to get over this horror. Driving home, I felt the impulse to call him nonetheless. But I shook my head. No telling what he was doing. Still trying to inspire Pan-Am Agra executives, eating supper with a client, working in his motel room on important papers. I hated him to find out how lonely I was, so soon.

I kept thinking about Idella, her children, her death from love.

Chapter Nine

The next morning my best friend, Amina Day – now Amina Day Price – called me. I'd just pulled on my blue jeans, and I lay across the bed on my stomach to grab the phone.

'Hi, it's me!'

'Amina,' I said happily, feeling my mouth break into a smile, 'how are you?'

'Honey, I'm pregnant!'

'Ohmigod!'

'Yes! Really, really. The ring in the tube turned the right color this morning, and I lost my breakfast, too. So I'm home lying down.'

'Amina, I can't believe it. What does Hugh say?'

'He's just thrilled. He's ready to go out now and buy a car seat and a crib. I told him he better wait a while, my mother always told me it was bad luck to start getting ready too soon.'

'Have you seen a doctor?'

'No, I have an appointment for next week with the obstetrician all the wives of Hugh's partners go to.'

Hugh is an up-and-coming lawyer in Houston.

'I'm so glad for you,' I told her honestly.

We talked for a while. Or, rather, I listened while Amina talked to me about the baby and what she wanted and didn't want for this exceptional infant.

'So what's new with you?' she asked finally.

'Well . . . I'm seeing someone.'

'Not the minister?'

'No, not anymore. This man – Martin – he's the new plant manager at Pan-Am Agra.'

'Wo-wo. How old is he?'

'Older.'

'Rich?'

'Well-to-do.'

'Of course, that doesn't make any difference anymore, since you inherited all that loot.'

'No, but it's nice anyway. He likes having money.'

'Tell me all!'

'Well, his name is Martin Bartell, he's forty-five, he has white hair but his eyebrows are black . . .'

'Sexy!'

'Yes, very . . . he's tough, strong, intelligent, and . . . ruthless. You wouldn't want to try to bullshit him.'

'These are not Boy Scout attributes.'

'You know, you're right,' I said thoughtfully. 'He's definitely not a Boy Scout type. More of a street fighter.'

'I hope he's not too tough for you.'

'No matter what he is,' I confessed, 'this is the worst I've ever had it. I'm scared to death. I couldn't stay away from him if he were on fire.'

'Oh, wow. You do have it bad. I hope he's worthy of this. This sounds like a "love at first sight" thing.'

'Yes, the first time I've ever experienced it. And, I hope, the last. It's awful.'

'I've never had it like that,' Amina said. 'So what else is happening?' It wasn't like Amina to change the subject. Could she be a bit envious?

But I filled her in on Tonia Lee's murder and the resultant confusion. Then I told her about Susu Hunter's husband and his strange secret persona as the House Hunter.

'Oh, I'm like that to a lesser extent,' Amina said instantly. 'It's not so weird.'

'You just like to look at houses?'

'Sure, don't you? I get a tingle at the base of my spine when I walk into a house that's not mine, that I can look at all I want. It's like stepping into someone else's life for a while. You can open the closets, and find out what they pay for electricity, and how many clothes they have, and how clean their furniture is . . . I have had the best time since Hugh and I started looking for a house. I wish I could look at houses all the time. In fact, I thought about becoming a Realtor instead of a legal secretary until I realized I'd have to get out in all kinds of weather and deal with jerks who didn't know what they wanted . . . you know.'

'That's interesting, Amina,' I said, and meant it.

'Of course, now we're looking at *bigger* houses,' she added, and we were back on her favorite topic of the moment.

By the time we hung up, I'd agreed to be the baby's godmother and Amina had urged me to hurry and marry Martin if we were going to anyway, so she could be a matron of honor before her stomach got too big.

I just laughed and said good-bye. It made me nervous to think of marriage and Martin in the same sentence, as if it were a jinx. I finished dressing, trying not to feel sorry for myself, only glad for Amina and Hugh.

I found myself wondering if Jimmy Hunter had been Idella's lover. It would make perfect sense, given his house-hunting aberration, for him to pick a Realtor as a lover. But how would that tie in with the things missing from houses listed with local Realtors? Surely Jimmy hadn't been lifting them while he toured the houses? He just couldn't have, not without a Realtor noticing. And it wasn't always Idella who'd shown him around. Hadn't someone at the meeting at Select Realty said the Greenhouses had always made sure Tonia Lee escorted him? Had something in Tonia Lee's sharp nature punctured the balloon of Jimmy's fantasy life as a house hunter, something so upsetting he'd killed her for it?

Jimmy Hunter drove a blue Ford Escort, and so had Idella. Maybe it had been Jimmy's car Donnie Greenhouse had seen Wednesday night. Come to think of it, what had Donnie been doing out himself? It must have been after the presumed time of Tonia Lee's death, which must have taken place before the neighbors to the rear of the Anderton place had noticed her car had gone. About the time of Tonia Lee's death, Jimmy had been parked outside the Tae Kwon Doe studio waiting for his son.

I shook my head at myself while I peered in the mirror applying my makeup. I was just getting confused. I wasn't going to speculate about depressing things anymore. I was going shopping to buy a dress to wear tonight. I was going to find out if Emily Kaye had accepted my counteroffer on the house on Honor. It would be nice and tidy to have that little chapter of my life closed, Jane's house settled and all my things ready to put into a home I owned. And I thought of the Julius house again: the sun through the windows, the warm kitchen, the porch.

'You'd like it,' I told Madeleine, who was squinting at me doubtfully in the one pool of sunshine in my bedroom. She rolled on her back to invite me to tickle her stomach, and I obliged. We went downstairs together to change her water and fill her food bowl.

I called Mother's office before I set out for my petite dress shop in Atlanta. Eileen said that the police had given her the contract for my house, signed by Emily Kaye. It had been in Idella's car. The changes I had stipulated had been penciled in, and Emily herself had called that morning after she heard the news of Idella's death, to confirm that she had agreed to the price and to my wanting the washer and dryer. So on my way out of town, I stopped by the office and signed the contract, too. And Jane's house was on its way to becoming Emily Kaye's house, having never really been my house at all.

I was willing to drive all the way into the city instead of going to Great Day, Amina's mom's store, because I wanted something that Amina called a 'Later, Baby' dress. Amina had always been a dating specialist, one who picked her clothes with as much care as she picked her makeup. Your clothes always said something to your date, she claimed, and she had had such a long and varied and successful dating career that I figured she knew what she was talking about.

'It has to be modest enough to where you could see your mom

while you were in it without turning red,' she had advised. 'But it has to kind of growl to your date, "Later, baby!" '

It was a slow day at the petite shop, Short 'n Sweet (hey, I didn't name it), and the saleswoman who'd helped me before was glad to see me. I was too embarrassed to spell out what I wanted, but I tracked it down eventually. It was a sweater dress, soft and beige and shapeless but clingy, with a big cowl collar – and you wore it almost off the shoulders. I had to buy a strapless bra to go under it, and then big gold earrings, and then some shoes, so I made the saleswoman's afternoon a happy one. Quite a switch for someone who had worn her college and high school clothes for ten years.

I ate lunch in the city and visited my favorite bookstore, so I came home to Lawrenceton fairly laden down with good things.

I tuned in to the local radio station as I left the interstate. It was time for the news. 'Police are questioning a suspect in the murder of a Lawrenceton Realtor,' said the newswoman chattily. 'Today a prominent local businessman was taken in for questioning regarding the death of Tonia Lee Greenhouse, who was found strangled in an empty home last week. Though police would not comment, an unnamed source says police will also question James Hunter in connection with the death of Idella Yates, whose body was found yesterday.'

I sucked in my breath. Jimmy Hunter. Poor Susu! Poor kids! I wondered what new evidence Lynn had uncovered that had led to Jimmy's being taken to the police station. I thought perhaps the police had found some of the stolen things in Jimmy's possession. Or maybe . . . but it was no use speculating.

Martin was ten minutes early.

He took in the dress appreciatively.

'I just have to brush my hair,' I said, my hands extended to hold him off.

'Let me,' he suggested, and I could feel a blush that began at my toes.

'We'll never get there if I do,' I said with a smile, and scampered up the stairs before he could grab me.

'One kiss,' he said as I came back down minutes later. He and Madeleine had been regarding one another warily.

'One,' I said strictly.

It was very sweet at first, but then it began to steam up.

'My glasses are fogging,' I murmured.

He laughed. 'Okay, we'll go.'

But it wasn't until a few minutes later that we got into his car. It didn't take long to get to the Carriage House, which had actually formerly been what its name implied. It was the only fancy restaurant in Lawrenceton, and had very good food and service. It was small, dark, and expensive, with a large added-on room at the back where local groups held dinners. We were shown a comer table and sat side by side on the L-shaped banquette.

Being so close to Martin was seriously interfering with my paying attention to anything else, but I was determined to get through a normal-date evening with him. We talked about what wine to order, and I selected my food; and he talked to the waiter, and the wine arrived.

'Jimmy Hunter's being questioned about the death of the woman whose body we found,' I told him.

'I heard someone was. Do you know the man?'

So I told Martin about Jimmy and Susu, and Jimmy's little quirk.

'He likes to look at houses with female Realtors? That's pretty – kinky.'

'But he's never done anything to anybody,' I pointed out fairly. 'And frankly, I hope the police have got something more on him than that, as I assume they must, because I find it very hard to believe that Jimmy did it.' I hadn't known I felt that way until it came out of my mouth. 'And they haven't charged him in Tonia Lee's murder, or Idella's, and surely the same person killed them both.'

But Martin hadn't heard about my finding Idella's body, and I had to tell him now, his light brown eyes fixed on my face.

'I wish you had called me when you were upset,' he said. I had an uneasy feeling that he might be a little angry with me.

'I thought about you. Of course. It's just that – really – for all our emotions for each other, we really don't know each other that well. And you're the plant manager, you have all kinds of duties and responsibilities that I don't know anything about, Martin. Even on Sunday night, I just felt very hesitant about interrupting you.'

I had been able to picture all too clearly his exasperated face as he turned away from some important papers to answer a call from his one-night flame.

'Listen,' he said intently. 'Don't. We haven't learned a lot about each other, but this is not just a bed thing. I hope. On my part, anyway, and I think for you, too.'

I didn't know, yet.

He touched my hair. 'If you need me, I'll come. That's all there is to it. We have time to get to know each other. But if anything bothers you or upsets you, you call me.'

'Okay,' I said finally, with misgivings.

Our salads arrived and we began eating, very conscious of each other.

'Martin, you'll have to tell me about your company,' I said. 'I have only the vaguest idea of what Pan-Am Agra does.'

'We arrange for the exchange of good used farm machinery for the produce from some of the South American countries,' he explained. 'Also, we manufacture some agricultural goods and food using raw materials from North and South America, which is what we do at the plant here. And we own land in South America where we're trying to use North American farming methods to produce better yields. Those are the main things Pan-Am Agra does, though there are a few other things, too.'

'What kind of products does Pan-Am Agra make?'

'Some fruit blends, some products containing coffee, some fertilizer.'

'Do you have to travel to South America much?'

'When I was at company headquarters in Chicago, I had to go

often, at least once every month. Now I won't fly down as much. But I will have to visit the other plants.'

'Is the government very much involved in what you do?'

'As a regulatory agency, yes, too much so. They're forever thinking we're smuggling drugs in or weapons out, knowingly or unknowingly, and our shipments are almost always searched.'

I thought of searching fertilizer, or the raw materials thereof, and wrinkled my nose.

'Exactly,' Martin said.

'So what is a pirate like you doing in an agricultural company?'

'Is that the way you see me? A pirate?' He laughed. 'What is a quiet, slightly shy, introverted librarian doing dating a pirate like me? Your life has changed a lot lately, if what you tell me and what other people tell me is true.'

I noticed he hadn't answered my question.

'My life has changed a lot,' I said thoughtfully. 'I'm changing with it, I guess.' Funny, I'd never thought of myself changing, just my circumstances. 'I guess it started – oh, almost two years ago,' I told him, 'when Mamie Wright was killed the night it was my turn to address Real Murders.'

The salads left, and the main course came while I was telling Martin about Real Murders and what had happened that spring.

'You're certainly not going to think I'm quiet after hearing all that,' I said ruefully. 'You had better tell me about your growing up, Martin.'

'I don't like to think about it much,' he said after a moment. 'My father died in a farm accident when I was six . . . a tractor overturned. My mother remarried when I was ten. He was a hard man. Still is. He didn't put up with any nonsense, and he had a broad definition of nonsense. I didn't mind him at first. But I couldn't stand him after a few years.'

'What about your mom?'

'She was great,' he said instantly, with the warmest smile I'd seen. 'You could tell her just about anything. She cooked all the time, did things you just see mothers in old sitcoms doing now. She wore aprons, and she went to church, and she came to every game I played – baseball, basketball, football. She did the same for Barbara.'

'You said you grew up in a small town, too?'

'Yes. A few miles outside the town, actually. So I wasn't sorry to get the chance at this job here, I wanted to see what it would be like to be back in a small town again, though Lawrenceton is really on the edge of Atlanta.'

'Your mother isn't alive anymore?'

'No, Mom died when I was in high school. She had a brain aneurysm, and it happened very – very suddenly. My stepfather is still alive, still on the farm, but I haven't seen him since I came home from the war. Barbara goes back to town every now and then, just to show off how far beyond that little place she is now, I think . . . she doesn't see him, either.'

'There was a rift?'

'He won't sell the farm.'

I didn't think that answered my question.

'Mother left the farm to him for his lifetime, and left us a little cash. Of course, she didn't have much. But we're supposed to get a third of the proceeds if he ever sells it, or if he dies before selling it, we get the land. We wanted him to sell when she died so we could move into town. But he wouldn't sell, out of some damn stubbornness. Now the situation for small farms is even worse, as I'm sure you're aware.' I nodded soberly. 'So the farm's falling down, the barn has a hole in the roof, he hasn't made money in years, and the whole thing is rotting. He could sell anytime to our nearest neighbor, but out of sheer meanness he won't.' Martin stabbed his steak with his fork.

We ate for a minute in silence. I thought over what he'd said.

'Um – how many times have you been married?' I asked apprehensively.

'Once.'

'Divorced?'

'Yes. We had been married for ten years . . . we had a son, Barrett. He's twenty-three now . . . he wants to be an actor.'

'A chancy profession.' I thought of my mystery-writer friend,

Robin Crusoe, now in California writing a television movie script based on his latest book, and wondered how he was making out.

'That's what I told him. Funny thing – he already knew it!' Martin said wryly. 'But he wanted so much to try, I gave him the money to get started. If he doesn't make it, he at least needs to know he gave it his best shot.'

'You sound as though you didn't get the encouragement you needed at some point.'

He looked surprised for a moment. 'I guess that's right. Though it's hard to say what I really wanted to do. I don't know that I ever formulated it. Something big,' and his hands made a circle in the air. We laughed. 'It had to be something I could leave my hometown for.'

'I've never wanted to leave my hometown,' I said.

'Would you?'

'I've never had a reason to. I don't know.' I tried to remember what it had been like when I went to college: not knowing anyone, not knowing where anything was, the first two weeks of uncertainty.

The waiter came up at that moment to see if we needed anything. 'Will you be wanting any dessert tonight?'

Martin turned questioningly to me. I shook my head.

'No,' he told the waiter. 'We'll have ours later.' He smiled at me, and I felt a quiver that went down to my shoes.

Martin paid the bill, and I realized I hadn't said a word about it being my turn. Something about Martin discouraged such offers. We would have to talk about that.

But not right away.

We were quite ready for dessert when we got to my place.

Chapter Ten

'Martin,' I said later in the night, 'can you go with me to the Realtors' banquet Saturday night?'

'Sure,' he said sleepily. He wound a strand of my hair around his finger. 'Do you ever wear it up?' he asked.

'Oh, sometimes.' I rolled over so it hung around his face like a curtain.

'Could you wear it up Saturday night?'

'I guess so,' I said warily.

'I love your ears,' he said, and demonstrated that he did.

'In *that* case,' I said, 'I will.'

A thud on the foot of the bed made Martin jump.

'It's Madeleine,' I said hastily.

I could feel him relax all over. 'I have to get used to the cat?'

'Yes, I'm afraid so. She's old,' I said consolingly. 'Well, actually, middle-aged.'

'Like me, huh?'

'Oh, yes, you practically have one foot in the grave,' I said.

'Ooo – do that again.'

So I did.

'I have to go out of town late this afternoon,' Martin said over toast early the next morning. He had stowed some extra clothes and shaving gear in his car, so he was ready for work.

'Where to?' I tried not to feel dismayed. This relationship was so new and perilous and fragile, and I was so constantly afraid Martin did not feel what I felt, so often aware of the differences in our ages, experiences, goals.

'Back to Chicago, to report on the plant reorganization to the higher-ups. I've been cutting out a lot of deadwood, finding out the weak points in the plant management. That's what I was brought in to do.'

'Not a popular job.'

'No. I've made some people mad,' he said matter-of-factly. 'But it's going to make the plant more efficient in the long run.'

'How long will you be gone?'

'Just Wednesday and Thursday. I'll fly back in Friday morning. But why don't we have lunch today? Meet me out at the Athletic Club at twelve thirty, and we'll go from there, if that suits your plans.'

'Okay. But please let me take you to lunch this time, my treat.'

The look on his face had to be seen to be believed. I burst into giggles.

'You know, that's the first time a woman ever offered to take me out,' he said finally. 'Other men have told me it's happened to them. But never to me. A first.' He tried very hard not to glance around at my apartment, so much humbler than any place he'd be used to living in since he'd climbed the business ladder.

'We don't have to go to McDonald's,' I said gently.

'Sweetheart, you don't have a job—'

'Martin, I'm rich.' Gosh, that word still gave me a thrill. 'Maybe not what you would think of as rich, but still I have plenty of money.'

'Inherited?' he asked.

'Uh-huh. From a little old lady who just wanted me to have it.'

'No relation?'

'None.'

'You're just a lucky woman,' Martin said, and proceeded to demonstrate just how lucky I was.

'You'll mess up your suit,' I said after a moment.

'Damn the suit.'

'You told me you have an appointment at eight thirty.'

He released me reluctantly.

'See you later,' he said.

I gave him a light kiss on the cheek. 'Twelve thirty,' I said.

*

I had an unpleasant task to face that morning. I had decided I should go see Susu. All the people who wrote in to 'Ann Landers' and 'Dear Abby' complained that they felt neglected when someone in the family had serious legal problems or went to jail, that people tried to act as if it hadn't happened or stayed away entirely. While Jimmy hadn't exactly been arrested, I didn't want to be a fair-weather friend to Susu, though time and circumstance had certainly created a gulf between us. So I pulled on a bright sweater and black pants, and red boots to go with the sweater. Cheerful, casual – as if it were an everyday catastrophe that had befallen the Hunter family.

It took me a second to recognize Susu when she came to the door. Her veneer was stripped away, and so much of Susu depended on that veneer. Her shoulders sagged, her eyes were red-rimmed, her clothes were – it seemed – deliberately shabby and old. She looked as if she'd reached back in her closet for the things she was saving to pull on when she painted the carport. There were dirty dishes piled up in the sink. Susu was not only genuinely a woman in the midst of a crisis, she was also acting out the part.

'Where are the kids?' I asked cautiously.

'I sent them to my sister in Atlanta.' As if she'd put them in a box and taken them down to the post office.

'You're here all by yourself?'

'Not a soul has come by except our minister.'

'What's the story on Jimmy?'

'He's down at our lawyer's office right now. They kept him all day yesterday. I think they may arrest him today.'

'Susu, you think he did it!'

'What else can I think?'

'Well, *I* don't think he did it.'

'You don't?' She sounded amazed.

'Susu! Of course not!'

'His fingerprints were in the Anderton house.'

'So? Hasn't it occurred to you there are several ways they could have gotten there without him having been the one to kill Tonia Lee?'

'Like how, Roe? Just tell me how!'

'Maybe some other Realtor showed him over the house. Maybe Tonia Lee did show him the house, and then he left and her date showed up and killed her!'

'Jimmy must have been having an affair with her, Roe. Then she threatened to tell me or the kids and he killed her. He must have just lost his temper.'

'I could kick you in the rear, Susu Hunter. You are making up things you can't possibly know. You get yourself into that shower upstairs and get your nice clothes on and put on your makeup and go down to your lawyer's office and you *ask him yourself*.'

I was probably doing exactly the wrong thing. Susu would get down there and Jimmy would say, 'Yeah, I did it. And I had been having an affair with her, too.'

Saint Aurora, I told myself sardonically.

But Susu was actually doing it. She went up the stairs at a pace a little brisker than her previous shamble. She was patting her hair absently, doing some damage-control evaluation.

I washed the dishes. I left them in the drainer to irritate Susu into putting them away.

She came down in thirty minutes, looking more like herself.

'When is he supposed to have done her in?' I asked.

'Well, Wednesday night.'

'But he took your son to karate practice, or something, that evening, didn't he? And he was at work until then, right? After practice, he came right home to supper?'

'Yes.'

So much for it having been Jimmy's car Donnie had seen.

'So when did he find time to go over to the Anderton house, screw Tonia Lee, and kill her?' I asked.

'That's true,' she said slowly. 'I guess I was just so quick to believe he did it because he's been acting so funny lately.'

'He may be going through a hard time, Susu. He may even

need therapy or something. But I really don't think Jimmy ever killed anyone.'

'I'd better get down there. Thanks for coming by, Roe. I just kind of gave up.'

'Sure,' I said, not feeling noble at all.

'Of course, if he did do it, 'I'll never want to see you again,' she said with a tiny smile.

'I know.'

She'd never been as dumb as she liked to seem.

I was getting back into my car when suddenly I realized that this was the morning of Tonia's funeral. *Another* unpleasant task. I looked at my watch. I had thirty minutes. I raced back to the townhouse, dashed up the stairs, tore off my clothes and pulled on my winter black dress, loose and long with a drop waist. No time to bother with a slip; no time to pull on panty hose. I rummaged through the closet and got my black boots. The dress needed a necklace or scarf or something, but there simply wasn't time, and my earrings would just have to do. I yanked on my coat and ran to the car.

The Flaming Sword of God Bible Church was a rectangular cement-block building painted white, with a parking lot of ruts and dust. A cold wind whistled straight through my clothes as I got out of my car. I pulled my coat tighter around me with one hand and held my hair out of my face with the other. I gusted into the little church along with the chilly wind. The parking area had been crowded, and the church was jammed to capacity. I'd seen a television news truck outside, parked in the rear along with the hearse, and the camera crew was in the church. I was willing to bet Donnie was responsible for that. There was no place to sit; every pew was jam-packed with solid Lawrencetonians in their winter coats. I hovered at the back, trying to spot a dark corner. My mother's basilisk glare found me anyway. Of course, she'd arrived on time, and was seated decorously in the middle of the church, along with the other members of the staff of Select Realty.

They were all there except Debbie Lincoln, who presumably was manning the phone at the office.

For a moment I looked for Idella, before I remembered.

The coffin was sitting at the front of the church. I was thankful it was closed. It was covered with a pall of red carnations, and the sharp scent of the flowers carried through the chilly air. There was no organ, but a pianist was playing something subdued and doleful, maybe 'Nearer, My God, to Thee'. The minister entered from a door by the altar. He was a plain young acne-scarred man, with eyebrows and lashes so light they were almost invisible. He clutched a Bible, and he had on a cheap dark suit, white shirt, and black tie. There was a shifting on all the hard pews. I recognized Mrs Purdy down at the front, wearing navy blue and pearls. Beside her, Donnie's white face stood out over a suit of unrelieved black.

'Let us bow our heads in prayer,' the minister intoned. His voice was unexpectedly rich. I did so, uneasily aware that a member of the camera crew was eyeing me with speculation. I began to edge away as unobtrusively as possible. I was afraid I had been recognized. The cameras had caught me before, when the Real Murders deaths had taken place. Surely no one would approach me until the service was over. The cameraman had poked the reporter, a very young woman I recognized faintly from the very few times she'd been on the air. He was whispering in her ear, and she was staring in my direction. My name had not been in the newspaper accounts of Tonia Lee's death, thank God, at least as far as I knew.

I had a hard time concentrating on the sermon, which from the snatches I caught seemed to be a combination of 'She is at peace now, whatever her life and last moments were like' and 'We must forgive the erring human who has strayed so far from God . . . Vengeance is mine, saith the Lord'. The congregation seemed to meet this last idea with some resistance at first, but by the time the minister ended, heads were nodding in agreement. I hadn't caught the man's name, but this preacher seemed to be a man of some persuasion.

The whole thing seemed to go by quickly, what with one thing and another. The pallbearers assembled and began to carry out the coffin, with some head-nods and murmurs among them to coordinate the lifting. Everyone rose, and the piano began to mourn again. For the last time, Tonia Lee left a house of the living. The camera crew became busy filming this, and I managed to work my way down the line of pews until I was even with the one where the Select Realty crowd was situated. After allowing enough time for the coffin to be loaded into the hearse, which I'd heard pulling around to the front door, the minister gave a closing prayer, doleful and fervent, and the congregation began to file out to their cars. All I had to do was whisper to Mother that the cameraman had recognized me, and the Select Realty staff closed around me. I managed to get to Mother's car thus camouflaged, and squeezed in with Mother, Eileen, Patty, and Mackie, who had stood out in the Flaming Sword of God Bible Church like a chocolate drop on a wedding cake.

I hadn't planned on going to the cemetery, but it seemed as though I had to.

None of us talked much on the ride to Shady Rest. I was thinking of how soon we'd be doing this again, whenever Idella was buried. Eileen was still washed out and subdued from our experience Sunday. Mackie was always quiet in a social setting, at least in one involving whites. For all I knew, he sang solo in the choir at the African Methodist Episcopal church.

Mother was grim about the news crew. Patty was upset by the funeral itself. 'I've never been to one before,' she explained, and I wondered if she'd only come to this one because my mother had assumed she would.

I looked around the crowd at the gravesite. Under the green tent, in the front row of folding chairs, sat Mrs Purdy and Donnie and a thin-lipped woman I recognized as Donnie's older sister. Tonia Lee's aunt and cousins sat behind them.

The chilly wind whipped among the mourners, making the tent awning flap and the red pall ripple. It brought tears to eyes that otherwise wouldn't have shed any. Franklin Farrell, his gray hair for once ruffled, was standing at the back of the crowd, looking a little bored. Sally Allison was there in a neat dark gray suit, her tan eyes flickering over the assemblage. Lillian, my former co-worker, had ended up with her face to the wind and was blinking furiously and shivering. Lynn Liggett Smith, muffled in a heavy brown coat, was scanning the crowd with sharp eyes.

At least the graveside service was short. It helped that Donnie had decided to play the dignified widower rather than opting for histrionics. He contented himself with throwing a single red rose on the coffin. Mrs Purdy burst into sobs at this romantic gesture, and had to be consoled with patting and hugging during the remainder of the service. I thought perhaps she was the only person there who genuinely regretted the ending of Tonia Lee's life.

On our subdued ride back to the church, where Mother dropped me off by my car, I found myself wondering how Susu and Jimmy were getting along.

I looked at my watch. It was almost time to meet Martin. I looked dreadful. Standing still in the cold had drained all color from my face, and my hair had been whipped around until it looked like a long dust mop. In the rearview mirror, I looked at least five years over my age. I pulled some lipstick out of my purse and put it on. I did have a brush, so I tried to tame my hair. I was marginally more presentable when I got through.

The Athletic Club was a fairly new enterprise in Lawrenceton. Built only a couple of years before, it offered memberships to businesses and individuals. It featured weight rooms, exercise classes, and racquet-ball courts, plus a sauna and whirlpool. My mother took aerobics classes there. I explained to the dismayingly fit woman at the front desk – she was wearing orange-and-pink-striped spandex and had her hair in a ponytail – that I was meeting Martin Bartell, and she told me he was still playing racquetball on the second court. 'You can watch if you climb those stairs,' she said helpfully, pointing to the easily visible stairs five feet to her left.

Sure enough, one side of the second-floor hall was faced with Plexiglas that overlooked the racquetball courts. The other side had ordinary doors in an ordinary wall, and from behind one of them I could hear shouted instructions ('Okay! Now BEND!') to an exercise class, backed by the deep-bass beat of rock music. The first racquetball court was empty, but in the second court the only sounds were the rebound of bodies and the ball from the walls, and the grunts of impact. Martin was playing killer racquetball with a man about ten years younger than he, and Martin was playing with a single-minded will and determination that gave me pause. In the five or six minutes they played, I learned a lot about Martin. He was ruthless, as I'd sensed. He was a man who could push the edge of fair play, staying just on the good side. He was a little frightening.

Was it possible this man, this pirate, was content to be an executive of an agricultural company? There was a barely contained ferocity about Martin that was exciting and disturbing. I'd already known he was a competent, forceful, and decisive man, a man who made his mind up quickly and kept it made. Now he seemed more complicated.

The game was over at last, and Martin had apparently defeated the younger man, who was shaking his head ruefully. They were both pouring with sweat. I heard someone mounting the stairs heavily, then sensed a presence to my left. Someone else was standing there looking down at the racquetball court. When I glanced sideways, I saw a blond man in his forties, burly and dressed in a suit that was rather too tight. He was staring at Martin with a look that alarmed me.

When I looked back down, Martin had spotted me and was signaling that he'd be with me in ten minutes. I nodded and tried to smile. He looked puzzled, and then his eyes moved to the man next to me. Martin's grimace of recognition was irritated, no more. He gave the man a curt nod. But then his face became angry, and when I looked back at the blond man, I found out why. The man, now only three feet away, was looking at me – and not with the hate-filled glare he'd aimed at Martin but with a spiteful speculation.

I was all too aware that the hall was empty. I'd never had anyone look at me like this, and it was horrible. I was considering if the situation warranted screaming – surely the only way the exercise class would ever hear me – when I heard more footsteps thudding up the stairs. Martin, covered with sweat, said easily, 'Sam, did you want to talk to me?' He had his racket in his hand, and though his voice was relaxed, he wasn't.

'This your little squeeze, Bartell?' asked the blond man in the sort of voice you use to say insulting things.

Little squeeze?

The man hadn't decided what to do yet; I could tell by the set of his shoulders. If only I could step past him to Martin, we could simply leave. I hoped. But the burly man, who carried maybe twenty extra pounds around the middle, blocked my way. Deliberately. Now Martin's racquetball partner appeared behind Martin, and I vaguely recognized him as one of the Pan-Am Agra executives who'd been with Martin at the steak house Monday. He looked excited and interested; this was like the gunfight at the O.K. Corral.

We were all frozen for a minute.

This was absurd.

'Excuse me,' I said suddenly, clearly, and very loudly. They all jumped. The blond man halfway turned to look at me, and I just stepped right on by him, close enough to tell he'd been drinking – in the middle of the day, too! noted my puritan streak.

'Martin, we have to go to lunch, I'm starving,' I told him, and held his elbow firmly. Because I continued walking, he had to turn and the younger man had to go down the stairs ahead of me. I didn't look at Martin, and I didn't look back over my shoulder.

'I'll wait out here for you to shower,' I said at the bottom of the stairs. The blond man had not followed. I waited for Martin and his racquetball opponent to go through the doors marked MEN'S LOCKERS AND SHOWERS before I seated myself in the safe proximity of the incredible spandex girl at the reception desk.

After a moment the blond man stomped down the stairs and, giving me another long look, left.

'Do you know who that was?' I asked the receptionist. She looked up from her book – Danielle Steel, I noted – to say, 'He's not an individual member, but he used to come here on the Pan-Am Agra membership. I think his name is Sam Ulrich. They took him off the list last week, though.'

'So why didn't you tell him he couldn't come in?'

'He went too fast.' She shrugged. 'Besides, one of the guys in the men's locker room would see he wasn't on the list and tell him to leave if he went in to change.'

Security was really tight at the Athletic Club.

I stared blankly at an out-of-date magazine until Martin emerged, dressed for once in casual clothes.

When he held out his hand, I took it and rose, conscious of the receptionist's gaze. She was really making those orange-and-pink stripes ripple for Martin's benefit. But he was not in the mood.

Martin said over his shoulder to her as we left, 'I'm going to have to call the manager today. You should have informed me Sam Ulrich was in the club, and I would have escorted him out.' I caught one glimpse of her dismayed and beginning-to-be-angry face as the door swung shut.

'Are you all right?' he asked. He put his arms around me. I was kind of glad to lean against him for a moment.

'Yes. It shook me up, though,' I admitted. 'Who was that man?'

'A very recent ex-employee. Part of the deadwood I was hired to cut out of the company. He took it pretty bad.'

'Yes, I could tell,' I said dryly.

'I'm sorry you had to be there. If you see him again, call me instantly, okay?'

'Do you think he'd hurt me to get at you?' I asked Martin.

'Only if he's a more complete idiot than I think he is.'

Not too good an answer, really. But how could Martin tell what the man would do?

'Are you really worried about Sam?' he asked. 'Because, if so, I can cancel my trip and stay here.'

'I thought for a minute. 'No, not so much worried about him, though that did shake me up. It's just been a down morning, Martin. I went to see Susu Hunter, and that was depressing. Then I went to Tonia Lee's funeral.'

'You told me when it was and I forgot. I was so involved in getting everything assembled for my trip.'

'I didn't expect you to come. It was pretty bleak, and very cold.'

'Where are we going to lunch?' he asked. 'You need something to warm you up.'

I was recalled to my hostess duties. 'Michelle's, have you been there? They have a buffet lunch with lots of vegetables.'

'In my three months here living in the motel, I think I've visited every restaurant in Lawrenceton at least ten times.'

'I didn't think about that, Martin. I'll have to cook for you soon.'

'Can you cook?'

'I have a limited repertoire,' I admitted, 'but the food is edible.'

'I like to cook once in a while,' he said.

We talked about cooking until we got to Michelle's, where we collected our plates and went through the line. I saw Martin was careful in his selections and realized he was weight- and health-conscious as well as an exercise enthusiast. We sat on the same side of the booth, and even in that prosaic setting, his nearness was disturbing.

It had been a harrowing morning, and now Martin was leaving town. Ridiculously, I felt like bursting into tears. I had to get over this. This intensity was terrifying me. I sat with my fork poised in my hand, staring straight ahead, willing myself not to cry.

'Do you want me to ignore this?' Martin murmured.

I nodded vehemently.

So he kept on quietly eating.

At last, I gathered myself together and put some cauliflower in my mouth, making myself chew and swallow.

I was going to have to keep busy while Martin was gone.

After a while I said conversationally, 'So you're leaving this afternoon?'

'About five o'clock. I'll have a meeting first thing tomorrow morning, and it may go on all day. Then I meet with another group Thursday. So I'll stay over that night and catch the first flight out Friday morning. Will you cook for me Friday night?'

'Yes,' I said, and smiled.

'And Saturday night is the Realtors' thing?'

'Yes, the annual banquet. We've booked the Carriage House, so at least the food will be good. There'll be a speaker, and cocktails. Usual stuff.'

'You handled that situation at the Athletic Club with great . . . aplomb,' he said suddenly. 'I don't think I've ever said that word out loud. But it's the only one that fits.'

'Um. I figured I could rescue myself this time.'

'Let me do it next time. My turn, okay?'

'Okay,' I said, and laughed.

He took me back to the Athletic Club to pick up my car, and we parted there in the parking lot. He gave me the phone number of his hotel and made me promise to call if I saw Sam Ulrich again. Then we kissed, and he was gone.

Chapter Eleven

Madeleine had a checkup at the vet's office scheduled the next morning. I got out the stout metal cage Jane had bequeathed me and opened the little door. I put one of Madeleine's toys inside. I set the cage, door open, on the kitchen table. I put on gardening gloves.

I had profited by experience.

Madeleine knew the instant the cage came out. She could find places to hide you'd swear a fat old cat could never squeeze into. I'd quietly gone upstairs first and closed all the doors while Madeleine was in plain view on the couch, and even closed off the front downstairs living room and the downstairs bathroom. But still, Madeleine had disappeared.

I groaned and started searching.

This time she'd wedged herself under the television stand.

'Come on, old girl,' I coaxed, knowing I was wasting my breath.

The battle raged for nearly twenty minutes. Madeleine and I cursed at each other, and very nearly spat at each other. But after that twenty minutes, Madeleine was in the cage, staring out with the haunted expression of a political prisoner being filmed by Amnesty International.

I dabbed some antibiotic ointment on the worst scratches and pulled on my coat. I was bracing myself for the ordeal to come.

Madeleine wailed all the way to Dr Jamerson's office. Nonstop.

Sometimes I loathed that cat.

'Oh, good, Madeleine's right on time,' said Dr Jamerson's nice receptionist with a distinct lack of enthusiasm. I returned a grim nod.

'Let's see. What does Madeleine need today?'

She knew damn good and well.

'All her shots.'

'Charlie'll get his gloves,' she said, heaving a resigned sigh. 'He'll be with you in just a minute.'

Charlie helped Dr Jamerson with the really difficult animals. He was a huge cheerful young man, working at the vet's office until he had enough saved to go to college full-time instead of part-time.

'Is she here yet?' I heard Charlie ask the receptionist apprehensively. A moment later Charlie stuck his head out into the waiting room.

'Right on time, as always, Miss Teagarden! And how is your kitty today?'

Madeleine yowled. The Labrador on the other side of the room began to whine and pressed his nose against his owner's leg. Charlie winced.

'Better bring her back,' he said with false assurance. 'Doctor's waiting.'

I struggled with the heavy carrier, knowing I'd have to heft it myself, since Madeleine had found out last time that her paw could fit through the mesh door nicely, even with her claws fully extended. Dr Jamerson had all Madeleine's shots laid out ready, plus a generous supply of cotton balls and antiseptic. His jaw was set, and he gave me a grim smile.

'Bring her on, Miss Teagarden. We got through her neutering before, we'll get through her shots now, Thank God she's a healthy cat.'

That thought certainly gave me pause. If Madeleine was like this when she felt *good* – 'Oh, dear,' I said.

I pulled my gloves back on. 'Are you ready?'

'Let's do it,' Dr Jamerson said to Charlie and me, and we all nodded simultaneously. I unlatched the cage door and pulled it open.

Fifteen minutes later I emerged from the vet's office, lugging the cage with the cat screaming triumphantly inside. She'd had her shots. And we'd pretty much had ours, too.

'He didn't bleed very much, Mother,' I said reassuringly when she called to see how Dr Jamerson was doing.

'I sold him a house. He's such a nice man,' she sighed. 'I wish you'd take that cat to Dr Caitlin. He went through Today's Homes.'

'He wouldn't see her,' I said.

'Oh.'

'What time Saturday night?' I asked. 'The banquet.'

'What did you do with your invitation?'

'It got lost or something.'

'You need a bulletin board and some thumbtacks.'

'Yes, I know. What time do we need to be there?'

'Drinks at seven, dinner at seven thirty.'

'Okay.'

'I'm going to be showing him some more houses, you know.'

'Oh – no, we didn't talk about it.'

'Nothing as grand as the Anderton place, but all in the one to two hundred thousand range. He must be planning on doing a lot of entertaining.'

'He's the head man here. I guess so.'

'Still, a single man . . . why does he want that much room?'

'I don't know.' Because he came from a poor farm in America's heartland? I had no idea.

'Well, I hope you know what you're doing.'

'I do too,' I said softly.

'Oh, Roe, have you got it bad?' My mother was suddenly distressed.

'Yes,' I said, and closed my eyes.

'Oh, dear.'

'I'll see you Saturday night,' I said hastily. 'Bye, Mother.'

'Bye, baby.' My mother was worried.

I'd rented a movie to watch that night, and I was curled up in front of the television wrapped in a quilt and eating crackers and peanut butter when Martin called. He just wanted to see if I was okay, he told me, after the incident with Sam Ulrich the morning before. He was lonely in his hotel room, he told me.

After I hung up, I thought about his exercise equipment and his running and his racquetball, and I closed the peanut butter jar.

And before I went to bed, I thought about Sam Ulrich – and Idella and Tonia Lee – and I double-checked all my doors and windows.

I'd just pulled on my jeans and a sweater the next morning when the phone rang.

'Roe,' said the warm voice on the other end, 'how are you this morning?'

'Oh, hi, Franklin.' Mild curiosity stirred within me. 'I'm all right.'

'Not too shaken up by your dreadful experience?'

'You mean finding Idella. It was just horrible, Franklin, but I haven't dwelt on it.' I'd been dwelling on something else. I felt myself smiling, and was ashamed.

'That's good. Life goes on,' he said offhandedly. 'I called to see if by chance you would go with me to the Realtor's banquet?'

Well, well. The legendary Franklin Farrell was asking little old me for a date. He'd probably gone out with every other woman in Lawrenceton.

'Franklin, how nice of you to ask. I'm flattered. But I already have plans for that night.'

'Oh, that's too bad. Well, another time then.'

'Thanks for calling.'

If anyone had been there to see me, I would have raised my eyebrows in amazement. Franklin Farrell without a date, and the banquet so close? Something must have happened to his original plans. Did this mean someone had canceled on Franklin? That would indeed be news.

I drummed my fingers on the kitchen counter.

The next thing I knew, I was asking Patty to connect me with Eileen.

'How are you doing, honey?' Eileen asked, but without her usual boom.

'I'm just fine. You?'

'Still upset, Roe. I just can't stop seeing Idella, thrown down like a sack of garbage.'

'It had to have been quick, Eileen. Maybe she didn't know anything about it.'

The paper had quoted Lynn as saying it was believed Idella'd been strangled like Tonia Lee, though that wouldn't be a certainty until the autopsy. I did hope it had been quick, but I had a conviction that Idella had known exactly who was killing her and that she was being killed. I tried so hard not to imagine that that I bit my lip.

'I hope not,' Eileen was sighing. 'Listen, Roe, not to change the subject, but I have to get on with my work, I guess. I took yesterday off. Do you want to do any more house-hunting today?'

'I don't think so, Eileen. I've kind of lost my taste for it, for a little while at least. I liked the Julius house so much better than anything I've seen, but I have to ponder long and hard about whether I could live out of town without getting the willies every night.'

'I can understand that, believe me. Just give me a call when you make up your mind.'

'Listen, Eileen. Do you know if Idella had been dating anyone special?'

'If she was, she didn't tell me who. But she had been very "up" lately, dressing more carefully, cheerful, eyes shiny, etcetera. Idella wasn't one to talk about her personal life. I worked with her for a month without her mentioning her children!'

'She *was* closemouthed,' I said, impressed. 'I just wondered if she hadn't been dating Franklin Farrell.'

'I would be extremely surprised,' Eileen said instantly. 'You know what a reputation he has as a ladies' man. Idella was very shy.'

She'd have been a real challenge to a Franklin Farrell.

'You heard they questioned Jimmy Hunter?' Eileen told me suddenly.

'Yes, but I don't believe he's guilty.'

'It's got to be someone,' Eileen said practically. 'Though I hear his alibi for the time Idella was killed is pretty strong.'

'So there are two stranglers in Lawrenceton, attacking real estate saleswoman?'

'You've heard about copycat killers. Maybe this is one.'

'What about the thefts?'

'I'm not the police,' Eileen said irritably. 'I'm just hoping all this is over and I can go back to my job without being scared every time I have an appointment to meet someone at an empty house.'

'Sure,' I said, instantly contrite. 'I'm a friend of Susu's, or at least I used to be in high school.'

'We're not going to come out of this with everyone happy.'

'Of course not. Listen, when do you walk every evening?'

'Terry and I usually walk at five in the winter, seven in the summer. Did you want to join us?'

'Oh, how nice of you! No, I'd just slow you down. I thought I might give it a try, but I'd better go by myself at first.'

'Then be careful.'

'Okay. See you Saturday night.'

'Bye.'

I actually found myself a tiny bit regretful I wasn't going to see Franklin in action. Amina had told me a date with Franklin was like being in a warm, soothing bubble bath. You felt cherished and delicate and pamperable. And of course you wanted that to go on and on, so the date extended very easily into bed. Once or twice, or perhaps even for a month. And then Franklin stopped calling and you had to come back to the real world.

If Martin hadn't happened, I would certainly have accepted, just to sample the experience. I would have stopped short of bed, I told myself firmly.

I put out fresh food and water for Madeleine, who was still hiding somewhere in the townhouse, sulking about the great indignity done her at the vet's.

And the phone rang again.

This time it was Sally Allison.

'The police searched the Hunters' house and came up with zilch,' she said without preamble.

'Oh, thank God. Maybe he's not such a suspect anymore?'

'Could be. The afternoon Idella Yates was killed, he was in the hardware store without a break, in full view of at least three people at any given moment. And he says he did look at the Anderton house with Tonia Lee, but on a different day. That's how his fingerprints got on the night table.'

'Is it okay for you to be telling me this?'

'If you don't tell anyone else. Otherwise, Paul will have my guts for garters.'

'I understand.'

'I know you're a friend of Susu's, so I just wanted you to know.'

'Thanks, Sally. Listen, did you ever date Franklin Farrell?'

'No,' she said, and laughed. 'I didn't want to be a cliché. He tries to date you when he thinks you're especially lonely, or rebounding from a relationship, or if you're a little stupid. I understand he really wines and dines you before the Big Move, but when he called me, I was too scared I'd join the ranks to accept.'

'Just wondered.'

'Oh, did you get that newspaper article I sent you?'

'Oh, shoot. I forgot to check my mail yesterday. I'll bet it's out there. I'll go see.'

'Okay. If you don't get it, call me.'

I reached in my mailbox eagerly and came out with a handful. Yes, here was the article Sally had sent me as she'd promised. There was Martin's picture. I sighed absurdly. Martin, I read, had a background in agriculture (I assumed that was his being raised on a farm); a distinguished service record, including two purple hearts (that explained the scars I hadn't yet asked him about); and a long work history with Pan-Am Agra . . . a brief chronicle of his steady rise through the ranks followed . . . then a noncommital statement of Martin's, about his plans for the plant.

There wasn't anything much to it, really, but for some reason it was very exciting to read about my – well, whatever – in the paper. So I read it over. And over.

'Isn't that strange,' I said out loud.

Martin had mentioned casually to me that he had gotten out of the Army in 1971. This article stated that he'd begun work at Pan-Am Agra in 1973.

What had Martin been doing for those two years? I wondered.

Chapter Twelve

Little tasks consumed the rest of my day. I had to stop by the dry cleaner's and go to the grocery store with a list of ingredients for the supper I was going to cook Martin the next night. I did my laundry and a little ironing. I sent Amina and her husband a 'congratulations' card and a copy of Dr Spock's famous book on baby care.

And I went by the library to check out some books. Every time I went into my former place of employment, I felt a pang of regret. There were so many things I missed about working there: seeing all the new books first (and free), having a chance to see and learn about so many people in the town I wouldn't run across otherwise, the companionship among the librarians, just being in the presence of so many books.

What I didn't miss was the companionship of Lillian Schmidt. So of course it was Lillian who was at the checkout desk today. I politely asked after Tonia Lee's mother and got a blow-by-blow account of Mrs Purdy's collapse after the funeral and her continued depression, Mrs Purdy's relief on hearing there had been an arrest, Mrs Purdy's horror and disbelief on hearing who was being questioned, Mrs Purdy's confusion on hearing that there was no concrete proof against Jimmy Hunter.

'Oh, that's great!' I said involuntarily.

Lillian was affronted. Her oversized bosom heaved under its striped polyester covering. 'I just think it's one of those technicalities,' she said. 'I bet they'll be sorry when some other woman gets killed in her bed.'

I forbore remarking that the bed Tonia Lee had been killed in was not exactly her own. 'If someone else does die, it won't be because Jimmy Hunter wasn't arrested,' I said firmly if confusingly, and picked up my books.

By the time I got home and unloaded my car, it was a little after four, and becoming dark and colder. This was getting close to the time of day Tonia Lee had been killed. With no other car having been seen in the driveway, the police had thought Mackie might be involved, since he ran every evening at this time. I thought the theory was sound, even though they'd had the wrong person. This evening, I'd walk myself. Just to see what could be seen.

Twenty minutes later I was shaking my head and muttering to myself. The streets were practically teeming with walkers and joggers. I had had no idea that the residential areas of Lawrenceton were so busy at an hour I normally associated with winding down and preparing supper. Every other block, it seemed, I passed another walker, or a runner, or a biker. Sometimes two. Everyone in town was out in the streets! Arms swinging energetically, Walkmans (Walkmen?) fixed on ears, expensive athletic shoes pounding the pavement . . . it was amazing.

I was heading toward the Anderton house, of course, walking at as swift a clip as I could manage. I passed Mackie, running in a sweatshirt and gym shorts, pouring sweat in the chilly air; he gave me the quick nod that was apparently all that was expected of runners. Next I saw Franklin Farrell, keeping trim for all those ladies, running at a more moderate pace, his long legs muscular and lean. No wonder he seemed so much younger than I knew he must be. True to his nature, he managed an intimate smile even through his careful breathing. Eileen and Terry marched by together, weights on their ankles and wrists, arms swinging in unison, not talking, and keeping a pace I knew would have me panting in minutes.

This was much more interesting than my exercise video. All these people, including half the real estate community, all out and about at the time the murderer must have arrived at the Anderton house. Even Mark Russell, the farm broker, strode by, in an expensive walking outfit from the Sports Kitter shop. And perfect Patty Cloud, bless my soul, in an even more expensive pale pink silky-looking running suit, her hair drawn up and back into a perky ponytail with matching pink bow. Patty even jogged correctly.

And here came Jimmy Hunter on a very fancy bike.

'Jimmy!' I said happily. He pulled to a stop and shook my hand.

'Susu told me you came by yesterday when everyone else was staying away,' he said gruffly. 'Thanks.'

'Are you okay?' I asked inadequately. He'd been through such an ordeal.

'I will be,' he said, shaking his head slightly as though a fly were circling it. 'It's going to be hard getting over this feeling that everyone was against me, that everyone believed I'd done it, right off the bat.'

'Susu okay?'

'She's tired, but she's regrouping. We have a lot to talk about. I think we'll leave the kids with their aunt and uncle for a while.'

'I hope everything—' I floundered. 'I'm really glad you're home,' I finally said.

'Thanks again, Roe,' he said, and wheeled away.

Seconds later I was in front of the Anderton house, its Select Realty sign still stuck forlornly in the yard, doomed to be frosted and snowed upon all winter and covered with the quick grass of spring and the weeds of summer, I was sure.

I didn't think the Anderton house, or the little ranch-style where we'd found Idella, would sell anytime soon.

After all, these deaths hardly seemed to be the work of a random killer, striking where he could find a woman alone.

I wondered if anyone had seen a car at the house where Idella'd been found.

A client arriving by foot would have been unusual, even unnerving, especially to Idella, who'd already been made nervous by Tonia Lee's death, who'd already heard that the police suspected someone of arriving at the Anderton house on foot . . . surely she'd have run screaming from the house instantly?

Yes, if it had been a random client who called to set up an appointment.

But not if it had been someone she knew, someone who said, maybe, 'My run (or my bike ride) takes me by there, so I'll see you at the Westley house', or something of the sort. And what more impersonal place to kill than someone else's empty house? You could just leave the body where it fell. The killer hadn't had a chance to divert suspicion, hadn't had the opportunity to move Idella's car somewhere else; since it had been dusk, not dark, when Idella had been murdered, her car couldn't have been moved without the driver being seen. Idella had had to be silenced quickly or she would have told what she knew . . . and Donnie Greenhouse thought she knew who'd killed his wife.

There he was now, as if my thinking of him had conjured him up, alternately walking and jogging, dressed in ancient dark blue sweats. He was dangerously hard to see in the gathering dark. I could just make out the features of his face.

'Roe Teagarden,' he said by way of greeting. 'What are you doing out tonight?'

'Walking, like everyone else in Lawrenceton.'

He laughed without humor. 'Decided to join the crowd, huh? I come here every evening,' he said with an abrupt change in tone. 'I come stand here while I'm out running. I think about Tonia Lee, about what she was like.'

This was weird.

A car went by, its headlights underlining the suddenly increasing darkness. I had a rather long walk home. I began to shift my feet uneasily.

'She was quite a woman, Roe. But you knew her. She was one of a kind.'

That was the absolute truth. I was able to nod emphatically.

'Everyone wanted her, and not just men, either; but she was my wife,' he told me proudly. His words had the feeling of a mantra he'd chanted over and over.

My scalp began to crawl.

'She'll never cheat with anyone else again,' Donnie said with some satisfaction.

'Um, Donnie? Do you think it's really that good for you to keep on coming over here?'

He turned to me, but I couldn't see his face well enough to discern his expression.

'Maybe not, Roe. You think I should resist the temptation?' His voice was mocking.

'Yes,' I said firmly. 'I think so. Donnie, why didn't you tell the police what you and Idella talked about that day at the restaurant?'

'So that's how they knew. Idella talked to you in the women's room.'

'She told me you were saying you saw her car come out of your office parking lot.'

'Yeah. I was out looking for Tonia Lee. So I cruised by the office. Sometimes she would take people there if she couldn't find anywhere else.'

'Was Idella driving?'

'I couldn't tell. But it was her car. It had that MY CHILD IS AN HONOR STUDENT AT LCS bumper sticker.'

'You can't believe that Idella killed Tonia Lee.'

'No, Roe, I've never believed that. But I think she gave a ride home to whomever left Tonia Lee's car at the office. And I think I know who that was.'

'You should tell the police, Donnie.'

'No, Roe, this is mine. My vengeance. I may take my time about it. But Tonia Lee would have wanted me to avenge her.'

I drew in a deep, cautious breath. The conversation could only go downhill from here. 'It's really dark, Donnie. I'd better go.'

'Yes, don't get caught alone with someone you don't know very well.'

I took a tiny step backward.

'And don't go into houses with strangers,' he added, and ran away, the measured thud of his Reeboks fading into the distance.

I headed in the opposite direction. I would have gone that way even if it hadn't been the way home.

*

I walked back to the townhouse more quickly than I'd set forth. It was too dark to be out by now, and my brown coat rendered me invisible to cars. I hadn't prepared very well for my walk, and I was unnerved by my encounter with Donnie. I pulled my keys out when I neared the back of my townhouse – I'd automatically walked into the parking lot instead of going to my closer but seldom-used front door. The lighting back here was good, but I glanced around carefully as I approached my patio gate.

I caught a little movement, from the corner of my eye, back by the dumpster in the far corner of the lot.

There weren't any strange cars parked under the porte cochere. All the vehicles belonged to residents. I stared into the dark corner where the Dumpster squatted. Nothing moved.

'Is anyone there?' I called, and my voice was disgracefully squeaky.

Nothing happened.

After a long moment I very reluctantly turned my back, and moving quicker than I had on my walk, I raced through my patio and turned the key in the back door, closing and shutting it behind me with even greater rapidity.

The phone was ringing.

If the caller had been Martin, I probably would have told him how scared I was. But it was my mother, wanting to know the news about the police questioning of Jimmy Hunter. I talked with her long enough to calm down, carefully not mentioning why I was so breathless. I hadn't really seen anything, and if I possibly *had* seen just a tiny movement, what I'd glimpsed was a cat prowling around the Dumpster in search of mice or scraps. There was, it was true, a murderer at large in Lawrenceton, but there was no reason on earth to believe he or she was after me. I knew nothing, had seen nothing, and was not even in real estate.

But the feeling of being observed would not leave, and I wandered restlessly around the ground floor of the townhouse, making sure everything was locked and all the curtains and shades were drawn tight.

Finally, after telling myself several times in a rallying way that I was being ridiculous, I went upstairs to change. Even in the cold, I'd sweated during my walk. Normally, I would have taken a shower, but this night, I could not bring myself to step in the tub and close the shower curtain. So I pulled on my ancient heavy bathrobe, a thick saddle blanket of a robe in green-and-blue plaid, the most comforting garment I have ever known.

It didn't work its magic. I found myself scared to turn on the television for fear the noise would block out the sounds of an intruder. But nothing happened, all evening. I was caught up in some kind of siege mentality; I got a box of Cheez-Its and a diet Coke and holed up in my favorite chair, with a book I'd read many times, one of William Marshall's Yellowthread Street series. But even his endearingly bizarre plotting could not relax me.

I wondered if men had evenings like this.

The time passed, somehow. I turned on my patio and front door lights, intending to leave them burning all night. I switched off the interior lights. I went from window to window, sitting in the dark and looking out. I never saw anything else; about one o'clock, I heard a car start up somewhere close and drive away. Though that could have signaled any number of things, perhaps none of them concerning me, I was able to sleep in fits and starts after that.

Chapter Thirteen

It was raining Friday evening when Martin came to supper. He had barely shed his raincoat when he gathered me up in his arms.

'Martin,' I whispered, finally.

'Humm?'

'The water for the spaghetti is boiling over.'

'What?'

'Let me go put in the spaghetti so we can eat. After all, you need to build up your strength.'

Which earned me a narrow-eyed look.

I can never manage to get all the elements of a meal ready simultaneously, but we did eventually eat our salad and garlic bread and spaghetti with meat sauce. Martin seemed to enjoy them, to my relief. While we ate, he told me about his trip, which seemed to have consisted mainly of small enclosed spaces alternating with large enclosed spaces: airplane, airport, meeting room, dining room, hotel room, airport, airplane.

When he asked me what I'd been doing, I almost told him I'd sat up last night afraid of the bogey man. But I didn't want Martin to think of me as a shaking, trembly kind of woman. Instead, I told him about my walk, about the people I'd seen.

'And they all had a chance to kill Tonia Lee,' I said. 'Any one of them could have walked up to the house in the dusk. Tonia Lee wouldn't have been too surprised to see any one of them, at least initially.'

'But it had to have been a man,' suggested Martin. 'Don't you think?'

'We don't know if she'd actually had sex,' I pointed out. 'She was positioned to look like it, but we don't have the postmortem report. Or she could have had sex, and then been killed by someone other than her sex partner.' Martin seemed to take this conversation quite matter-of-factly.

'That would assume a lot of traffic in and out of the Anderton house.'

'Doesn't seem too likely, does it? But it could be. After all, the presence of a woman wouldn't scare Tonia Lee at all. And Donnie Greenhouse said several very strange things last night.' I told Martin about Donnie's remark that not only men had wanted Tonia Lee, and about his sighting of Idella's car. But I didn't say anything about Eileen and Terry; just because they were the only lesbians I knew about in Lawrenceton didn't mean they were the only ones in town.

Aubrey would have been nauseated by this time.

'So what's your assumption?' Martin asked.

'I think . . . I think Tonia Lee learned who was stealing those things from the houses for sale. I think she was having an affair with whoever it was, or he – or she – seduced her when she asked him to come to the Anderton house to talk about the thefts. Maybe he asked her to meet him under the guise of having a romp in the hay there, when he meant to finish her all along. So they romp or they don't, but either way he fixes it to look as if they had. I'm sure he planned it beforehand. He arrives by foot or bicycle, he kills Tonia Lee, he positions her sexually to make us think it's just one of her paramours who got exasperated, he moves her car, he goes home, he somehow gets the key back to our key board. He thinks that that way no one will look for Tonia Lee for days, days during which all alibis will be blurred or forgotten or unverifiable. Maybe he returns the key in the few minutes Patty and Debbie are both out of the front room at the office.'

Martin had been listening quietly, thinking along with me. Now he held up his hand.

'No,' he said. 'I think Idella must have put back the key.'

'Oh, my God, yes. Idella,' I said slowly. 'That's why he killed her. She knew who had had the key. She got it from whoever was at Greenhouse Realty.'

That made so much sense. Idella, crying at the staff meeting right after Tonia's body was discovered. Idella, red-eyed and upset during the days after the killing.

'It must have been someone she was incredibly loyal to,' I murmured. 'Why wouldn't she tell? It would have saved her life.'

'She couldn't believe it, she wouldn't believe this person did it,' Martin said practically. 'She was in love.'

We stared at each other for a minute.

'Yes,' I said quietly. 'That must have been it. She must have been in love.'

I thought of Idella after Martin fell asleep that night. Deluded in the most cruel way, Idella had died at the hands of someone she loved, someone of whom she could believe no evil, no matter how compelling the evidence. In a way, I thought drowsily, Idella had been like me . . . she'd been alone for a while, coping with her life on her own. Maybe that had made her all too ready to trust, to depend. It had cost her everything. I prayed for her, for her children, and finally for Martin and me.

I must have coasted off into sleep, because the next thing I was aware of was waking. I woke up just a little, though; just enough to realize I'd been asleep, just enough to realize something unusual had roused me.

I could hear someone moving very quietly downstairs. Martin must be getting a drink and doesn't want to disturb me – so sweet, I thought drowsily, and turned over on my stomach, pillowing my face on my bent arms. My elbow touched something solid.

Martin.

My eyes opened wide in the darkness.

I froze, listening.

The slight sound from downstairs was repeated. I automatically reached out to the night table for my glasses and put them on.

I could see the darkness much more clearly.

I slid out of bed as silently as I could, my slithery black nightgown actually of some practical use, and crept to the head of the stairs. Maybe it was Madeleine? Had I fed her before we came up to bed?

But Madeleine was in her usual night place, curled on the little cushioned chair by the window, and she was sitting up, her head turned to the doorway. I could see the profile of her ears against the faint light of the streetlamp a block north on Parson Road, coming in through the blinds.

I glided back to the bed, very careful not to stumble over scattered clothes and shoes.

'Martin,' I whispered. I leaned over my side of the bed and touched his arm. 'Martin, there's trouble. Wake up.'

'What?' he answered instantly, quietly.

'Someone downstairs.'

'Get behind the chair,' he said almost inaudibly, but very urgently.

I heard him get out of bed, heard him – just barely heard him – feeling in his overnight bag.

I was ready to disobey and take my part in grabbing the intruder – after all, this was my house – when I saw in that little bit of glow from the streetlight that Martin was holding a gun.

Well, it did seem time to get behind something. Actually, the chair felt barely adequate all of a sudden. I left Madeleine right where she was. Not only would she very probably have yowled if I'd grabbed her, but I trusted her survival instincts far more than mine.

I strained as hard as I could to hear but detected only some tiny suggestions of movement – maybe Martin going to the head of the stairs. Despite the dreadful hammering of my heart, I said a few earnest prayers. My legs were shaking from fear and the cramped crouching position I'd assumed.

I willed myself to be still. It worked only a little, but I could hear some sounds coming up the stairs. This intruder was no skilled stalker.

I found I was more frightened of what Martin might do than I was of the intruder. Only slightly, though.

I heard the someone enter the room. I covered my face with my hands.

And the lights came on.

'Stop right there,' Martin said in a deadly voice. 'I have a gun pointed at your back.'

I peeked around the chair. Sam Ulrich was standing inside the room with his back to Martin, who was pressed against the wall by the light switch. Ulrich had a length of rope in one hand, some wide masking tape in the other. His face was livid with shock and excitement. Mounting my stairs must have been pretty heart-pounding for him, too.

'Turn around,' Martin said. Ulrich did. 'Sit on the end of the bed,' Martin said next. The burly ex-Pan-Am Agra executive inched back and sat down. Slowly I got up from my place behind the chair, finding out that during those few moments I'd spent there, my muscles had become strained and sore from the tension. My legs were shaking, and I decided sitting in the chair would be a good idea. My robe was draped over the back of it, and I pulled it on. Madeleine had vanished, doubtless irritated at having her night's sleep so rudely interrupted.

'Are you all right, Roe?' Martin asked.

'Okay,' I said shakily.

We stared at our captive. I had a thought. 'Martin, where did you park when you came tonight? Are you in your car?'

'No,' he said slowly. 'No, I parked out back in one of the parking slots, but I'm in a company car. I don't like to leave my car parked at the airport.'

'So he didn't know you were here,' I observed.

Martin absorbed that quickly. From looking perplexed and angry, his expression went to murderous.

'What were you going to do with the rope and the tape, Sam?' he asked very quietly.

I felt all the blood drain from my face. I hadn't followed through on my own idea until Martin asked that critical question.

'You son of a bitch, I was going to hurt you like you hurt me,' Sam Ulrich said savagely.

'I didn't rape your wife.'

'I wasn't going to rape her,' he said, as if I weren't there. 'I was going to scare her and leave her tied up so you'd know what it was like to see your family helpless.'

'Your logic escapes me,' Martin said, and his voice was like a brand-new razor blade.

I knew this was a quarrel between the two men, but after all, it was I who would have been tied up.

'Didn't you feel it might be a little cowardly,' I said clearly, 'to creep up in the dark and tie up a woman who wasn't even your real enemy?'

It seemed Sam Ulrich had never put it to himself quite that way. He turned even redder in a slow, ugly way.

'I'd like to kill you,' Martin said very quietly. I didn't doubt his sincerity, and I could tell from the hunch of his shoulders that Ulrich didn't, either. Martin, even in pajama bottoms, had more authority than Sam Ulrich would have had in a suit. 'But since it's Roe's house you broke into, and her you were going to harm, maybe she should decide what should happen to you.'

I knew that Martin would kill this man if I asked him to.

I thought of calling the police. I thought of cops I knew from having dated Arthur, perhaps even Arthur himself, up here in my bedroom looking at me in my black nightie. I thought of their eyes as they found out Martin and I had been asleep together when I heard someone downstairs. I thought of the report taken from the police blotter that appeared daily in the Lawrenceton *Sentinel*. Then I thought of letting this dreadful coward go scot-free. But my flesh crawled when I pictured myself alone here with this frustrated man and his rope and his tape.

And I'll tell you what I just plain liked about Martin. He let me think. He didn't say one word, or look impatient, or even make a face.

'Do you have a wife?' I asked Sam Ulrich.

'Yes,' he mumbled.

'Children?'

'Two.'

'What are their names?'

He looked more and more humiliated. 'Jannie and Lisa,' he said reluctantly.

'Jannie and Lisa wouldn't like to see their father's name in the paper for attacking an unarmed woman in her home.'

I thought that between anger and humiliation he might cry.

I got a pen and a notepad from my bedside drawer.

'Write,' I said.

He took the pen and paper.

'Date it.'

He wrote the date.

'I am dictating this now. Start writing,' I told him. 'I, Sam Ulrich, broke into the townhouse of Aurora Teagarden tonight . . .' His hand finally moved. When it stopped, I continued. 'I had with me some rope and masking tape.' Done. 'She was asleep in bed with all the lights out, and I did not know anyone was in the townhouse with her.' His fingers moved even slower. 'I was only prevented by her house guest from doing her harm. If I do not abide by the conditions she sets forth, she will send this letter to the police, with a copy to my wife.' And as he finished writing, I told him to sign it.

He waited to hear my conditions.

'What I want to see is your house up for sale tomorrow, and for God's sake don't list it with Select Realty. And I want you out of here, moved, family and all, within the week. I never want you to come back here, and I never want to see you again. You may not get a job like you're used to, but anything, I think, would be better than being in jail for what you wanted to do to me.'

Martin's face was blank.

Ulrich was so upset his features were distorted. I wondered if between rage, and relief, and shock, he would have a heart attack on the way home, and I found myself not much caring if he did.

'Martin, could you please walk Mr Ulrich to his car?'

'Sure, honey,' Martin agreed, with a dangerous kind of smoothness. 'Come on, Ulrich. You're lucky I asked the lady. I would have put you in the hospital if it had been up to me.'

Or the morgue, I thought.

Sam Ulrich rose slowly. He took a step forward and then stopped. He was afraid to go closer to Martin. He was not such a fool as he looked. Martin moved back, and Ulrich preceded him down the stairs.

I heard the back door open and close, and wondered if I'd left it unlocked when we'd gone upstairs for the night. I didn't think so. Not a very good lock. I'd get a better one.

Being left alone for a few minutes was a great relief, and I burst into tears and tried very hard not to picture myself at the mercy of the man now being marched to his car.

I was rinsing my face at the sink, the cold water making me shudder, when Martin returned. I saw his reflection in the mirror beside mine.

'You've been crying,' he said very gently, putting his gun on my vanity table, where it lay looking as out of place as a rattlesnake. I turned and put my arms around him. His bare chest was cold from the outside air, and I rubbed my cheek against him.

'He's driving home,' he said, answering a question I was scared to ask.

'Martin,' I said, 'if you hadn't been here . . .'

'You would have called 911, because I wouldn't have been between you and the phone,' he said practically. 'They would have been here in two minutes, maximum, and you would have been fine.'

'So this doesn't count as a rescue?' I asked shakily.

'We're even on this one. You kept me from doing something stupid to him. I would hate to have to spend the night down at the police station because of Sam Ulrich. You saved his family, too.'

'Martin. Let's just get in bed and pile all the blankets on, and you can hold me.'

I was trembling from head to toe. I realized, as I lay with my eyes wide open in the dark, that I had had to wait to find that Sam Ulrich had left in his own car – alive – before I could let myself have the luxury of relaxing, believing the incident was over.

Martin was awake, too, listening. I didn't think Ulrich was stupid enough to come back; he should be in his own bed counting his blessings.

I began to count my own.

At least Martin didn't try to get to the plant early on Saturday, but he felt he should go in, especially since he'd been out of town. 'I think my weekend hours will decrease now things are beginning to shape up at this plant,' he told me over our morning coffee, 'especially now that I have a reason to stay away.'

I tried to smile back, but my attempt must have been a miserable failure.

'Roe,' he said seriously, 'it's me that got you into the trouble last night, and for that I am so sorry. He wouldn't have come here if it wasn't for me. I hope you don't hate me for that.'

'No,' I said, surprised. 'No, never think it. I'm just tired, and it was very upsetting. And you know – you do have to tell me why you brought a gun when you came to spend the night with me.'

'I've had a hard life,' Martin said after a moment. 'I have a job that requires me to do difficult things to other people, people like Ulrich.'

I closed my eyes briefly. This was all probably true, as far as it went. 'All right,' I said.

'Do you think you'll feel like going to that banquet tonight?'

I'd forgotten all about it. Of course, I wasn't wild about going, but on the other hand, when I pictured my mother asking me why we hadn't come, I just couldn't come up with a believable excuse.

'I guess so,' I said unenthusiastically. 'I'd rather drag myself there than think about last night.'

'Don't forget to wear your hair up,' Martin reminded me later as he gathered all his things to stow in his company car. 'What time should I come by?'

'I think cocktails start at six thirty.'

'Six thirty it is. Dressy?'

'Yes. Everyone can bring two other couples as guests, so there's usually a decent crowd, and there's a speaker.'

I was leaning on the door frame, and Martin was halfway to his car when he dropped the things he was carrying and came back. He held my hand.

'You aren't off me because of last night?' He looked at me steadily as he asked.

I shook my head slowly, trying to analyze what I did feel, why things seemed so grim. 'I just realized I'd taken on more than I'd anticipated,' I said, giving him the condensed version.

He looked at me quizzically. I was so tired that my judgment was impaired, and I went on. 'You're a dangerous man, Martin,' I said.

'Not to you,' he told me. 'Not to you.'

Especially to me, I thought, as I watched him drive away.

I had completely forgotten to make an appointment to get my hair put up. Of course, all the hairdressers who were open on Saturday were fully booked. But with some wheedling and bribing, I got my mother's regular woman to stay open late to work with my mane. I would be done barely in time for the dinner.

That suited me just fine. I climbed wearily up my stairs and went back to bed. It was becoming a habit.

When I woke again at two o'clock, the gray day didn't look any more inviting, but I felt much better. I decided to cram the night before into a mental closet for the time being, to take some pleasure in going to a social function in Lawrenceton with Martin for the first time. I was human enough to relish the anticipation of eyebrows lifted, of envious women. I was convinced any woman with hormones would want Martin.

I even turned on my exercise tape and got at least halfway through it before getting fed up with the dictatorial instructress. Madeleine watched me, as usual, her eyes round and disbelieving. She followed me upstairs for my shower, watched me put on my makeup and dry my hair. I changed my sheets, too, and ran a carpet sweeper over the bedroom hurriedly.

I would be running so short on time I decided to put on everything but the actual dress before I left for my hair appointment. So I looked through my closets. I'd wear the dress I'd worn the year before. Martin hadn't seen it, even if everyone else had, and I'd only worn it that once. It was green, and after simple long sleeves and a scoop neck, the bodice descended to a point in front, and the short skirt flounced out in gathers all around. I'd have to wear black heels . . . I needed some of those shiny lamé-looking shoes that were so popular now, but I didn't have the energy or time to go shopping. Black would have to do. I had a little black evening purse, too. So I put on the right bra and slip and hose, and a dress that buttoned down the front over them.

I hurried out to my car and started across town to my mother's hairdresser. I'd looked up an address before leaving home, and I took a little detour. There was the Ulrich house, a three-bedroom ranch style in one of Lawrenceton's prettier middle-class neighborhoods.

And there was a FOR SALE sign in the yard.

Chapter Fourteen

'How do you want it done?' Benita asked briskly. It was clearly the end of a long day for her. Her own red hair was wild and dark at the roots, and the beige-and-blue uniform all the operators at Clip Casa wore was rumpled and – well, hairy.

'Could you do it like this?' I'd spent my waiting time leafing through professional magazines.

'Yes,' Benita said briefly after a thorough look at the enigmatically smiling model, and set to work.

It was one of those hairdos with the braid miraculously inside-out. French braiding, I thought it was called. I'd never understood how that was done, and now it was about to be accomplished on my very own head. In the picture the model's hair wasn't pulled back tightly but puffed around her face. The length of hair at the base of the neck was also braided, and the model had a ribbon around the end. I had no fancy bows, but Benita had some for sale, including a gold lamé one I thought would be pretty. I didn't know if Martin would like the hairstyle, but it struck me as very fashionable. Plus, it didn't seem possible that my hair could come loose, as all too often happened when I put it up myself.

'Roe,' drawled a voice close by, and I recognized the apparition under the dryer as my beautiful friend Lizanne Buckley.

'I haven't seen you in a coon's age!' I said happily. 'How are you doing?'

'Just fine,' said Lizanne in her slow sweet way. 'And you?'

'Pretty good. What have you been doing?'

'Oh, I'm still down at the power company,' she said contentedly. 'And I'm still dating our local representative.'

Lawyer J. T. (Bubba) Sewell, whom I'd met in a professional capacity, would be home from the Capitol for the weekend, and he and Lizanne were also going to the Realtors' banquet, she told me. In fact, Bubba was the speaker.

'Are you two engaged?' I asked. 'That's what someone told me, but I wanted to hear it straight from the horse's mouth.'

Lizanne smiled. She had a habit of that. She was stunningly beautiful, and no slave to the bone-thin convention of female figures. She was just right. 'Oh, I expect we are,' she said.

'Someone's finally going to walk you down the aisle,' I marveled. Men had tried for years to marry Lizanne and she would have none of it, the world being the unfair place it is.

'Oh, I don't think we'll get married in a church,' Lizanne demurred. 'I haven't been in one since Mamma and Daddy died, and I don't expect to go. I believe Bubba sees that as my only drawback, a politician's wife not going to church.'

There was no possible response, and Lizanne didn't expect any. I felt like someone who was walking over a familiar sunny beach, only to discover that it had changed into quicksand.

'I hear you've been dating that new man at Pan-Am Agra,' Lizanne said after a few minutes. Lizanne heard everything.

'Yes.'

'He coming with you tonight?'

I nodded until a sharp exclamation from Benita reminded me to hold still.

'I'll be glad to meet him; I've heard a lot about him.'

I didn't know if I wanted to hear or not. 'Oh?' I said finally.

'He's got everyone out there shivering in their shoes. There's evidently been a lot of slack and some thieving, and he was sent in to be the man to get everything straight. He's firing and moving around people and looking into everything.'

Lizanne reached back and turned off her dryer, lifting the hood to reveal a head covered with large rollers. She patted them to make sure her hair was dry, took one down experimentally, nodded. 'Janie, I'm done,' she called to the beige-and-blue-uniformed beautician drinking a cup of coffee in the back of the shop. The phone rang, and Janie answered it. It was for Benita, one of her children with a household emergency, and with an exclamation of impatience, she ran to take the call. I noticed the whole time she talked, she worked on her hair with a comb she picked up from the counter; if Benita was standing, she was working on hair.

'I have a friend at the police station,' Lizanne said casually, standing by my chair and looking into my mirror. 'Jack Burns – your good buddy, Roe – has decided that since no one has been killing Realtors until now, the murderer must be someone new to town. Some of the detectives don't agree, but since they questioned Jimmy Hunter and let him go, all kinds of people have been pressuring the chief of police to find someone else. Jimmy Hunter's parents have got lots of friends in this town, and the arrest of someone else would take the suspicion off Jimmy for good. So I hear the police are going to make an arrest soon in the murders of those two women. They're probably going to be taking someone in for questioning tomorrow.'

My eyes met Lizanne's in the mirror. She was giving me a message. But I had to decipher it.

'My goodness, Lizanne Buckley!' exclaimed Benita, coming back at that inopportune moment. 'Who told you that?'

'Little bird,' Lizanne said laconically, and wandered off to her beautician's station, where she began to remove her own rollers, tossing them in one of the wheeled bins. Janie drained her cup and unhurriedly began helping Lizanne, whose easygoing attitude seemed to rub off on people. I remembered Bubba Sewell's slow good-ole-boy manner and his sharp brain and decided (in a remote corner of my own brain) that he and Lizanne would make a most interesting couple.

But mostly I was trying to figure out what Lizanne had meant.

We'd been talking about Martin. Then she'd talked about the arrest. Surely she didn't mean the police suspected Martin?

She had been letting me know Martin was going to be arrested. At the least, taken in and questioned.

I stared at the mirror as two spots of color rose to stain my cheeks. I was gripping the padded arms of the swivel chair with undue force.

'Honey, are you cold?' Benita asked. 'I can sure turn up the heat.'

'Oh. No, I'm fine, thanks.'

Ridiculous. This was ridiculous.

The police had been wrong once. They were wrong again. Of course they were wrong again, I told myself fiercely. The thefts. They'd begun long before Martin had moved here.

But the murders, of course, had begun after.

I remembered my mother wondering what on earth Martin was doing looking at such a large house. Logically, a bachelor would be looking at a smaller place, not a virtual mansion like the Anderton house. The police might think he'd made an appointment to see the Anderton house because he wanted his handiwork found. Martin had been in town some weeks before I met him, long enough to meet Tonia Lee and Idella. Tonia Lee, who would go to bed with almost anyone, would undoubtedly have licked her chops when she met Martin. Idella, wispy, palely pretty, and lonely, would have been thrilled to meet someone who could pay such close and flattering attention to her.

Of course, that was what the *police* might think.

I shut my eyes.

'Are you okay, sweetie?' Benita was asking with concern.

'I'm fine,' I lied automatically. 'Are we about finished?'

'Just about. Do you like it?'

'It's different,' I said, startled enough to peek out from under my personal black cloud. 'Gosh, I don't look like me.'

'I know,' said Benita proudly. 'You look very sleek and sophisticated. Just beautiful.'

'Gee,' I said slowly. 'I do.'

'All you need to do is go home and put on your dress and some lipstick, and you'll be ready to step out.'

I did need lipstick. And I needed some spine, too, I decided grimly. I wasn't going to let these black thoughts overwhelm me. I *knew* Martin, on some level, knew him thoroughly.

I thought.

I paid Benita handsomely, and went home to slide into my

green flouncy dress and put on some lipstick. I'm going to go and have a good time, I told myself. I'm going with a handsome, sexy man who considers me absolutely necessary. He might have wanted to kill nasty Sam Ulrich last night, but he wouldn't have killed Tonia Lee and Idella. Absolutely not.

At least my inner turmoil wasn't showing on the outside. When I looked in my bathroom mirror to put on my bronzy lipstick, I looked just as good as I had in the beauty shop.

I almost wished I'd polished my nails, but that would have been absolutely out of character; and with my hair put up, I hardly knew myself, as it was.

Instead of bustling around thinking of something to do, I sat on the ottoman in front of my favorite chair, my current book lying neglected on the table beside it. I decided to pop the dress on at the last second. It hung on the bathroom door, looking festive and fancy, mocking me. I stared into space and thought about Martin gone, Martin in jail, Martin on trial.

He was as necessary to me as he said I was to him.

When the doorbell rang, it actually surprised me. I pulled off my robe, pulled the dress over my head, and zipped it up in record time. I slid my feet into my high-heeled pumps and pulled myself together to answer the door, wondering vaguely why everything looked so funny.

Martin took in a deep breath when I opened the door. He looked down at me with some unreadable emotion.

'Do I look all right?' I asked, suddenly anxious.

'Oh, yes,' he said. 'Oh, yes.'

'Do you like the hair?' I asked nervously when he still stared.

'Yes . . . very much.' He finally stepped in so I could close the door against the cold. He was wearing a black overcoat, and his white hair was strikingly attractive.

Once again I had the unsettling feeling that he was grown up and I wasn't.

'Where are your glasses?'

'Oh,' I exclaimed, 'that's why everything looked so funny.' In some relief, I found them on the little table beside my chair and popped them on. 'I tried contact lenses,' I told him defensively, 'but I'm one of those people who can't wear them. They just drove me crazy.'

'I'm glad you wear glasses.'

'Why?'

'So no one else can see you with them off,' he said, and bent to give me a kiss on the cheek. His finger traced the line of my neck. I shivered. My fears abated now that I was with him. When I was close to him, I felt that Martin would not *let* himself be arrested.

'Come look in the bathroom mirror,' he suggested.

'What?'

'Just for a minute; come with me.'

'Is my hair coming down?' My hands flew up.

'No, no,' Martin said, and smiled.

So into the bathroom we went, and I looked at myself in the mirror, Martin's face rising neatly above mine in the reflection. He pulled off his gloves, and his hand went into a pocket.

Suddenly I realized I should be absolutely terrified.

But if he wanted to kill me, he would. I took a deep breath, looking steadily at his eyes in the mirror, and from his pocket he pulled a little gray velvet box and set it on the counter. Gently and expertly he removed my earrings, plain gold balls, and opening the velvet box, he extracted gorgeous amethyst-and-diamond earrings and with no fumbling at all fixed them in my ears.

'Oh, Martin,' I said, stunned. I felt as if I'd put on my brakes at the edge of a precipice.

'Sweetheart, do you like them?' he said finally.

'Oh, yes,' I said, trying hard not to cry. 'Yes, Martin. They're beautiful.' My hands were shaking, and I clenched my fists so he wouldn't notice.

'Didn't you tell me November was your birthday?'

'Yes, it is.'

'And here it is November. I didn't know which day, but I wanted to get you a present. I know topaz is your birthstone, but none I saw seemed warm enough to me. These look like you. If you didn't know it, you look beautiful tonight.'

The stones glittered. The amethysts were rectangular and edged with small diamonds.

'I'm overwhelmed. Martin, I don't know what to say.' I'd never spoken truer words.

'Tell me you love me.'

I looked into the mirror.

'I love you.'

'That's all I wanted to hear.'

'Martin.'

His hand touched my cheek.

'Do you—?'

'Yes,' he said into my ear, kissing my neck. 'Oh, yes. I love you.'

After a while he said, 'Do we have to go?'

'Unless we want my mother coming here to find out what happened to me, yes.'

Actually, I needed a space to think, to calm down. If we stayed here, I certainly wouldn't get it.

Talk about warring emotions. Someone loved me. I loved him back. He might be questioned tomorrow for murder. He'd given me the most romantic gift, the kind women wait a lifetime for. And I'd thought for a moment that he was going to strangle me.

Martin fetched my coat from the closet while I reexamined my earrings in the mirror. 'Can you stop looking long enough to put on your coat?' he asked, laughing.

'I guess so,' I said reluctantly. The moment of terror was oozing out and filling up with delight. 'Martin, what's that clipped to your coat pocket?'

'Oh, a beeper. We've been having trouble with a particular man on the night shift. His supervisor is watching him tonight, and if he catches him stealing, he's going to beep me so I can go have it out with the guy.'

In my now almost complete wave of euphoria, I did a Scarlett O'Hara and decided to think about the bad stuff later. Maybe I couldn't put it off until tomorrow, but I could savor this minute, surely.

Martin and I were a little late, among the last to arrive. We picked glasses of white wine off the tray a waiter carried by. I spotted Lizanne and Bubba Sewell immediately. Lizanne did not hint in her greeting to me that she had given me a warning that afternoon. Maybe her liquid dark eyes rested on me a little sadly, but that was all. Bubba started one of those conversations with Martin designed to link them in the male network: he connected what he was working on as a representative with what Martin was trying to achieve at Pan-Am Agra, he told Martin that he could call him any time he wanted to 'talk things over', he illustrated his intelligence and grasp of Pan-Am Agra's interests, and he implied that Martin was the best thing that had happened to the company since sliced bread.

Martin responded cautiously but with interest.

Lizanne told me how pretty my hair looked, and admired my earrings.

'Martin gave them to me,' I said proudly.

She looked worried for a minute, then properly complimented me and drew Bubba's attention to them.

'Did you show them your ring?' he responded after a token remark.

Lizanne, with her lovely slow smile, held out her hand on which glittered a notable diamond. 'My engagement ring,' she said calmly.

'Oh,' I said. 'Oh, Lizanne, it's beautiful.' I sighed, suddenly realized I was doing so, and tried to make it silent. 'When's the wedding?'

'In the spring,' Lizanne said offhandedly. 'We've got to sit down with a calendar and pick a date. It depends on the legislature, and of course I have to give notice at my job.'

'You're quitting work?' I didn't mean to sound startled, but I was. What on earth would Lizanne do all day?

'Oh, yes. We're going to be living in my house for a while, until Bubba's career plans are finalized, but there's a lot I need to do to it . . . and I'm bored with my job anyway.'

I hadn't known boredom was a concept Lizanne understood. Also, Lizanne heard every bit of news in her job, since the power company was a place everyone had to go sooner or later, and she had the most amazing capacity to attract confidences. I would have supposed Bubba would want Lizanne right where she was.

'Congratulations, Lizanne,' I said quietly as Bubba drew Martin off to meet another Lawrenceton mover and shaker.

She bent down to kiss me on the cheek. 'Thanks, honey,' she murmured. Then she whispered, 'They're going to take your friend in tomorrow for questioning. For sure. I'm not going to tell you how I know.'

That was why she was so popular. She never told how she knew. And she certainly hadn't told her fiancé; otherwise, he wouldn't be sucking up to Martin. He'd be avoiding him as though Martin were a leper.

'Thanks, Lizanne,' I said in almost as low a voice. Suddenly curious, I asked, 'Why are you telling me?'

'You helped me the day my parents were killed.'

I nodded, and pressed her hand. I had never been sure Lizanne had been aware of my presence or my identity on that horrible day. She and I gave each other a look and drifted apart, and I strolled over to my mother, my wineglass clutched in a death grip.

'Where'd you get the earrings?' she asked instantly. 'They're gorgeous.'

'Martin gave them to me tonight,' I said numbly, turning my head from side to side so she could get the full effect, all the time wondering what I could do to prevent tomorrow from happening.

'He did?' Mother raised her perfect brows. 'But you've only known each other such a short time!'

I shrugged.

'Oh, you have got it bad,' she said darkly. 'But at least he does, too. They're very nice, dear.'

'What are you admiring, Mrs Queensland?' Patty Cloud, in her favorite pink, this time a rose shade, appeared at my mother's shoulder, trailing a delicate cloud of expensive perfume and a staggeringly handsome date, some man from Atlanta she'd met at a Sierra Club meeting, she managed to let me know. I talked to them for a few minutes of stultifying conversation about white-water canoeing before Martin rescued me.

'How'd you get along with Bubba Sewell?' I murmured as we went to our places around the table.

'He's on the rise,' Martin said thoughtfully. 'I won't be surprised if he makes U.S. Senate some day.'

'Really?' I tried not to sound skeptical.

'He's doing everything right. A lawyer, but not a criminal lawyer. Comes from a local family with a clean record, worked himself through law school, practiced for a while before running, going to marry a beautiful wife who can't possibly offend anyone. She's planning to quit work and stay at home, producing the right picture, and I bet they have a baby before they've been married two years. It'll look good on the campaign poster, a family picture.'

I tried to think about this, to care about Bubba's career, all the while turning nonsensical schemes over in my mind. I should tell Martin. Then he could brace himself. Or run. (I staved that thought off.) I should *not* tell Martin, so he would show unfeigned surprise when the police came to Pan-Am Agra. I pictured Martin being taken from his office, his humiliation; at least the people who worked for him would see it as humiliation. I checked the rein on my imagination; surely the police could not arrest him without warning, on the little or no evidence they had. But still . . .

Of all the people I knew, the one best qualified to fend for himself was Martin. Why was I worrying?

I yanked myself out of this anxious silent yammering to introduce Martin to Franklin Farrell and his date, who were seated across from us. Franklin must have been calling his reserve list, the day he'd called me; maybe this woman had been next, in alphabetical order. She was in her late forties, remarkably well groomed and dressed. Physically she was a good match for the immaculate Franklin. She glittered in a hard way, and her practiced conversation aroused my instant distrust. Her name I didn't catch, but she was full of glib comments that gave no clue to her character. She was playing up to Franklin in a rather desperate way, and I could tell they hadn't been out together before. He was being courteously cool.

The meal was served, and I talked to Mackie on my left, and Martin on my right, and Franklin and Miss Glitter across the way, though what I said I couldn't have told you afterward.

Even through the worry, I could tell Martin and I were attracting a certain amount of attention. The tables had been arranged in a large U. Martin and I were seated on the outside of one arm of the U, and as Franklin bent to retrieve his lady friend's napkin, I realized someone across from us at the far side of the U's other arm was staring. With some amazement, I recognized my former flame Arthur Smith sitting with his wife, homicide detective Lynn Liggett Smith. Who on earth had invited them? Arthur was looking at me with all too apparent concern, his fair brows drawn together and his fingers drumming on the table. Lynn was eating and listening to Eileen Norris, who had come in with Terry, announcing to the room at large that the single ladies had just decided to come together.

I raised my eyebrows very slightly, and Arthur looked down, flushing red.

I knew then that Lizanne was right. Martin was under suspicion. Perhaps I hadn't been quite sure Lizanne had gotten the true word before, but I knew it now.

'Are you all right?' Martin asked me.

'I'm all right. I need to—' I started to say 'talk to you later,' but what an irritating thing that is to do to someone. 'I'm fine,' I said clearly. 'Do you like this salad?'

'Too much vinegar in the dressing,' he said critically, but his sharp look told me he knew something was in the wind.

Somehow I did the right things through the meal, but when Bubba got up to make his address about new legislation for the real estate industry, I was able to tune out completely. In fact, it was hard to keep my eyes aimed in the right direction. I gnawed at my problem, poked at my fear, which was like a monster with many faces; I was afraid of Martin's getting arrested, afraid of losing him, afraid of what it would do to his job and self-esteem to be questioned at the police station; and maybe afraid he was guilty.

My eyes traveled across the faces around the Carriage House's elaborate wine-and-cream banquet room. All these faces, almost all familiar. One of these people was most probably the person the police really wanted, if I could just make them see it.

The murderer was a Realtor, or connected with realty in some way – someone who'd known how to get the key replaced.

The murderer had been able to arrive at the Anderton house without a car and had been part of the scenery while doing so – someone who ordinarily walked or jogged or biked in the evening.

The murderer had to be someone Idella Yates trusted, someone she'd been willing to risk a lot for, since it seemed pretty certain Idella had replaced the key.

I looked at Mackie's dark neck as he turned his face politely to the speaker. His date beyond him was picking at her nails, though she, too, was keeping a courteous face turned in the right direction. Across the room, Eileen was dabbing her lips with her napkin. Beside her, Terry, in a dark blue dress with big fake diamond buttons, was listening to Bubba with a skeptical lift to one corner of her mouth. Mark Russell and his wife were sitting with the practiced posture of those who listen to many speakers; his partner, Jamie Dietrich, a lanky man with a huge Adam's apple, stifled a yawn. Patty was all attention, though her date was doing something surreptitious under the tablecloth that brought a tiny secret smile to her face. Even young Debbie Lincoln, more beads woven into her hair than I would have thought possible, was turned to Bubba and trying to pay attention, though her date was openly, elaborately bored. Conspicuously alone, Donnie Greenhouse had deliberately left an empty chair beside him to remind people that he was a brand-new widower. Somehow I'd known he wouldn't miss an opportunity to star in a public drama, even if he had to point it out himself.

Close to Lizanne, my mother inclined her head regally to one side, her resemblance to Lauren Bacall especially pronounced. John was resting his arm on the back of her chair. John looked ready to go home. Across the table from Martin, Miss Glitter appeared riveted. Franklin was listening with slightly drawn mouth, his long, thin hands arranging and rearranging his cloth napkin.

He pleated it, unpleated it. I returned my eyes to Mackie's neck, prepared to plunge back into my fears and my dreadful burden of love. Then my attention shot back to Franklin. He pleated, unpleated. Then he folded the napkin into neat triangles, triangles that got smaller and smaller but never less neat. His long white fingers smoothed the napkin out. Then he pleated it. Then again, the triangles. Meticulously neat triangles. Where had I—?

His eyes began to turn toward me, and I instantly looked forward, my heart thumping.

Through no great feat of ratiocination, I, Aurora Teagarden, had solved a mystery.

Franklin Farrell was the murderer.

He was folding and refolding his napkin in the same curious way Tonia Lee's clothing had been treated. It was as unmistakable as a fingerprint.

Franklin Farrell.

Chapter Fifteen

I couldn't jump up and scream and point to him. I had to force myself back down in my seat. I gripped my hands together, willing them to be still.

Charming, handsome Franklin, who'd had so many conquests they must have become boring and routine by now. Franklin, with a house we all entered only once a year for his annual party, a house that could be full of things stolen from homes he was showing.

Franklin could have had Tonia Lee just by crooking his finger, and his legendary charm could have persuaded lonely and shy Idella to do something she must have known was incredibly suspicious. How had he persuaded her to return the key to the key board, or to give him a ride from Greenhouse Realty to his house? He must have told her that he had arrived at the Anderton house to find Tonia Lee already dead – though what explanation he could have given her for going to the Anderton house at all I couldn't imagine.

Maybe he'd told Idella that putting back the key would lessen the chances of his being suspected of something he hadn't done, but Idella couldn't stand up to the heavy secret she carried, the guilt she felt. I remembered her crying in the bathroom of Beef 'N More, the day of her death. And Franklin, of course, could tell Idella was cracking. Even if she couldn't face the fact that Franklin was almost certainly the murderer, she would feel terribly conscious that she had lied to the police. And to her employer.

'Roe? Roe? Are you all right?'

'What?' I jumped.

Martin was leaning toward me, his incredible light brown eyes full of concern. His innocent light brown eyes, I thought with a swelling heart.

'Um, as a matter of fact, Martin, I don't feel too well.' People were getting up, chatting. Time to go.

'Let's get you home, then.'

Martin retrieved our coats while I sat at the table, afraid to look up for fear I'd meet Franklin's eyes. He and his date were still sitting across from me.

'Let's leave, honey,' she was saying.

'Want to stop at The Pub for a drink?' he asked, his voice warm and inviting as a crackling fire on a freezing night.

'Sure. Then we'll see after that,' she said teasingly.

There wouldn't be much to see, I thought. It was already a case of my-place-or-yours. And, my mind raced, I was willing to bet it would be hers. Franklin probably still had the vases from the Anderton place in his house. Somewhere. He'd be afraid to sell them in Atlanta, surely, with the case still so fresh. On the other hand, I argued with myself, keeping the vases in his house would be so dangerous! His car would be an even riskier place, though . . .

I slipped into my coat without even thinking about Martin, who was holding it for me.

How could I get the police to search Franklin's house?

Martin's arm was around me. 'Are you going to make it to the car?' he asked, concerned.

'Martin, I'm thinking,' I told him. He looked at me oddly.

'Honey, I'm going to get the car. I'm worried about you. I'll bring it around as quickly as I can.'

I nodded absently, and was only vaguely aware when he left.

'It was so nice to meet you,' a voice at my elbow said with routine courtesy.

I looked up at Miss Glitter. 'Enjoyed it,' I said automatically. I tried not to look at Franklin, standing at her elbow. Terry Sternholtz and Eileen came up, Terry looking very pretty in the dark blue, her curly red locks tamed into a striking hairdo. It felt strange to realize that Terry had dressed up as much for her date with Eileen as I had for my date with Martin.

'I'll be late Monday,' Terry told her boss. 'I have an early appointment with the Stanfords.'

'I'll be in Atlanta all day,' Franklin said casually. 'I'll see you Tuesday.'

But as Eileen, Franklin, and his date walked away, I gripped Terry's arm. I must not have been gentle; she looked surprised as she asked me what I wanted.

'Terry. Do you remember saying, when we were at the Greenhouses', that a self-defense course wouldn't have helped Tonia Lee? Because she had been tied up?'

Terry groped in her memory. 'Sure,' she said finally. 'I remember. So?'

'Do you by any chance remember who told you Tonia Lee had been tied?'

'Oh. Yeah, it was Franklin, next morning at the office. I get sick at grisly stuff like that, but Franklin gets into it.'

'Thanks, Terry. I was just curious.' Terry looked at me doubtfully, but then Eileen called her impatiently from the door, and she left, giving me a suspicious glance.

Donnie Greenhouse's stupidity had maybe saved his life. He'd heard Terry make the comment about Tonia Lee's being tied and realized its significance long before I did – well, maybe he wasn't so dumb after all. He'd probably been plotting some elaborate revenge against Terry, never thinking to ask her where she'd gotten that damning piece of information. All the time, it had been secondhand.

I stood lost in thought until I realized Arthur had taken my hand. His wife was across the room talking to my mother.

I was eager to tell Arthur what I'd seen; okay, napkin-folding can't be used as evidence, but at least I'd get a message to Lynn surreptitiously, an indicator that the police should look Franklin's way very quickly.

But Arthur had his own agenda, and in a particularly

maddening gesture I remembered vividly from our relationship, he raised his hand when I started to talk.

'Roe, that guy is bad news,' he said, fixing me with his flat blue eyes. His voice was low and steady and absolutely sincere. 'Because of the good times we had together, I'm warning you. Get away from him, and stay away. This isn't sour grapes on my part. We've done a background check on him, and he's not—'

'Arthur,' I said with great force, to stop whatever he was going to say. I was thrown completely off-track. 'I appreciate your concern. But I am telling you that I am in love. Now, you listen to this—'

'If you won't shuck him, I can't make you.'

'You are so right—'

'But you have to know that that man is dangerous.'

'Who's dangerous?' asked Martin with a ferocious cheerfulness.

'Mr Bartell,' Arthur said, hostility in his voice. 'I'm Arthur Smith, a detective on the local force.'

Martin and Arthur shook hands, but looked as if they would just as soon have arm-wrestled.

If they'd had fur around their necks, it would have been standing on end.

'Glad I met you,' Martin said enigmatically. 'Roe, I brought the car around.'

'Thanks, honey,' I said, and Martin slid an arm around me and we turned to go to the car.

'Tell Lynn I need to speak to her,' I told Arthur over my shoulder.

'What's happening, Roe?' Martin said after we'd left the Carriage House parking lot. 'Are you really feeling sick?'

'No. But something happened tonight, and we have to talk about it.' Who else was more qualified to handle dangerous situations than Martin? He was dangerous himself. Maybe he would have an idea.

'Does it concern that policeman? Is he someone you've gone out with?'

'He's married and has a baby,' I said firmly. 'I went out with him a long time ago.'

'Was he warning you about me?'

'Yes, but that's not what I want—'

'He said I was dangerous. Do you believe that?'

'Oh, yes. But—'

And suddenly we were in the middle of our first argument, which I couldn't quite figure out. Somehow he was angry because Arthur had enough feelings for me to want to warn me off Martin, and I gathered it wasn't the warning but the feelings that upset Martin. And then also, he felt that Lizanne's engagement ring had overshadowed the beautiful earrings he'd given me, and he was mortified. And I was trying to tell Martin I loved the earrings and wouldn't have taken an engagement ring if he'd given it to me, which was completely untrue and a very stupid thing to say. If we had fallen in love like teenagers, we were quarreling like teenagers, and if we had been a little younger, I'd have given him back his letter jacket. And his class ring.

And then, just as we pulled into my parking lot, his beeper went off.

Martin said something truly terrible.

'I have to go.' He was suddenly calm.

'I have to tell you something,' I told him urgently, 'about Franklin Farrell. *Before* tomorrow!'

'I can't believe I said all those things.'

'Please come back.' I was almost crying. I'd been through too many emotions in one day, and they were seeking their natural vent.

'As soon as I handle the situation at the plant, I'll come back.'

'Wait a second,' I said as I slid out of the car. I ran to unlock my back door and ran back to the car. 'Here's my key.' I put it in his hand and closed his fingers around it. 'I have another I'll use. Come on in when you get back.'

We looked at each other searchingly. 'I've never given anyone a key to my own house before,' I said, slamming the car door and running into the town-house.

Madeleine was standing curiously in the cold draft from the door I'd left open, and she rubbed against my legs as I stood in the kitchen area wondering what on earth I was going to do.

I wandered up the stairs, pulling off my finery with little regard for my hair. I left my earrings in, and sat at my dressing table admiring them absently while I tried to figure out what to do.

What if I called the police station and said there was a kidnapped woman in Franklin's house? Wouldn't they be obliged to break in to see?

Maybe not. I could hardly call Arthur to find out.

Report a fire?

Well, the firemen wouldn't recognize the vases, as indeed most of the policemen wouldn't. Of course, we didn't have photographs of them, and my mother had only a general memory of their shape and position on the night tables.

Tomorrow Martin would be taken in for questioning if I couldn't draw attention to Franklin *now*. Day after tomorrow, Franklin would take the vases to Atlanta and sell them or drop them in the river on the way, if he hadn't done it already.

He'd be out of his house tonight, with Miss Glitter.

I stood there in the bathroom with my fists balled, trying to steel myself against the decision I was about to make.

Okay. I'd have to do it.

Thinking harsh thoughts about how incredibly stupid I was, I pulled on heavy socks and blue jeans and a T-shirt and a sweatshirt. I zipped up my black boots and found an old jacket with deep pockets. I found a knit scarf that had a hood for the head and then two long ends that tossed around the neck, which I pinned so I wouldn't have to keep fooling with them. Everything I had on was black or dark brown or navy blue. I looked like someone who'd dressed with only a tiny amount of light in the closet, just enough to pick out dark colors, but not the right dark colors. Amina would have a fit, I thought wryly.

I did keep on my beautiful earrings.

Downstairs I trudged, terrified and determined, to stuff my

pockets with screwdrivers and anything that looked as if it might be helpful in breaking into Franklin Farrell's house.

I added a heavy, fist-sized rock to my collection of potential burglary tools. I'd brought it home as a souvenir of a trip to Hot Springs, and it was dark with a protrusion of clear crystal. Then I remembered a crowbar in a box of Jane Engle's tools I'd had stored in my extra bedroom.

I dumped everything into the car. It was eleven o'clock, my dashboard informed me. I am a law-abiding person, I told myself grimly. I don't litter. I don't even jaywalk. I never park in handicapped spaces. I pay my taxes on time. I only lie when it's polite. Lord have mercy on me for what I'm about to do.

That thought, from my saner self, sent me right back inside. I took a piece of paper and a pencil and wrote, 'Martin: Franklin Farrell is the man who killed Tonia Lee Greenhouse. I am going to go break into his house and get back the vases he took from the Anderton place. Eleven o'clock. Roe.' Somehow writing this note made me think I was being much more prudent, a totally unjustified feeling. But I locked the door to the townhouse before I shut it, thus burning my bridges behind me, since I'd forgotten to get my extra key and Martin now had mine.

I left my car two blocks south and one block east of Franklin Farrell's house, which was inconveniently located (for me) on a main thoroughfare, where no parking was possible. Franklin had an older home on a street that was now almost all commercial, but he had painted it an eye-catching combination of dove gray and yellow, and tricked it up with expensive antiques and gadgets until it was now one of the town's notable homes. Entrance to it was very restricted, though. Franklin entertained women there sometimes, it was generally understood, but had only one social gathering a year in his home. It was carefully planned, lavish, and invitations were much prized. Otherwise, Franklin entertained clients and other business associates at restaurants. He never asked uninvited guests in, no matter how attractive they were, a quirk of his that was much discussed and secretly envied by those who were too cowardly to do likewise.

All this I knew about Franklin. All this, and now much more.

I probably wasn't particularly silent as I stole across his backyard and up to his back door. But in that cold, who had their windows open to hear? I was shivering as I tried the back door knob, just for the hell of it. Of course, the door was locked. Franklin's car wasn't there, so I assumed he and Miss Glitter were having a good time. I hoped it was real good, and that he'd stay the night. I had no plan to conceal the break-in, because I thought I'd be damned lucky to get in at all, much less try to be clever about it. So after an attempt or two with the screwdrivers, I just smashed a pane in the kitchen door window with my souvenir rock, which I popped back into my pocket. I reached in carefully and unlocked the door. It should have opened then, but it didn't. Though my coat and sweatshirt gave my arm some protection, I became worried that the glass remaining in the frame would cut me as I prodded around inside, trying to discover what was still holding the door.

Finally I risked using my flashlight. With my face pressed against an upper pane and flashing the light up and down the inside of the door, I discovered at long last that Franklin had put a sliding bolt at the top of the door. The moment I saw it, I switched the flashlight off.

I was too short to reach the sliding bolt.

I took a few deep breaths and poked through with the longest screwdriver. I stood on tiptoes. I closed my eyes to concentrate. The tip of the screwdriver finally touched the knob of the bolt. With every bit of stretch I could summon, I pushed the bolt back.

I had to crouch down and shake for a minute when the door finally yielded. I took a deep breath, stood, and entered.

This is dumb, this is dumb, my more intelligent side was insisting as I stepped inside. *Get out.*

But I didn't listen. I examined the kitchen as carefully as I could by flashlight. Then, through the dining room, the hutch full of an impressive array of gleaming silver. Then into the living room, color-coordinated to a depressing degree in creamy shades, with cranberry wallpaper. The fireplace across the room was flanked on either side by windows, and matching sofas faced each other in front of them. My flashlight flicked over the furniture, the gleaming hardwood floor, and the marble fireplace. And came back to the fireplace.

The vases were on the mantle. I caught my breath at the sheer gall of it. Placed as carefully as if they were legitimate, they looked lovely on either end, with a dried-flower arrangement in between. If they'd been stashed in a closet, they'd have seemed much more suspicious. I walked up the alley formed by the two sofas to examine them more closely. These were the right ones. I remembered the pictures of rivers and valleys that had so entranced me as a child.

Hah! I could feel myself smiling in the dark, though the insistent pulse in my brain kept telling me, This is dumb, this is dumb.

And it was, too, because just then Franklin turned on the light.

'I didn't hear you pull up,' I said lamely after I swung around to face him.

'That's obvious,' he said. 'I saw a light dancing around in my living room from two blocks away, so I left my car parked on the street.' If he'd seen me through the open curtains, someone else could, too, I thought hopefully. Franklin reached out one arm casually and pressed a button. Behind me I heard the curtains electronically swish shut.

Of all the damned gadgets.

We stood looking at each other. I was wondering what happened next. Maybe he was, too.

'Why on earth did you do this?' he said almost wearily. The handsome face drooped on its elegant bones. He tossed his overcoat over the back of the sofa as though he were about to sit in his favorite chair and open the newspaper. Instead, he pulled a long, thin scarf from his overcoat pocket.

'Oh, you just carry one with you now? Just in case you run across someone who needs killing?' The words popped out before my brain could censor them.

'Tonia Lee was a piece of trash, Roe,' he said coldly. 'But she was clever enough to spot some things in my house that she shouldn't have. She was willing enough to keep quiet for some – exotic – rolls in the hay. Unusual places. Being tied up. Tonia Lee liked that kind of thing. But I got tired of obliging.' I pictured him sitting at the foot of the bed while Tonia Lee was tied to it, talking to her while methodically folding her clothes, Tonia Lee knowing all the while that she was going to die. 'A piece of trash,' he repeated.

He wasn't slotting her in a social class or giving a character assessment. He was dismissing her as nonhuman, inconsequential. On a par, perhaps, with a mole that was making ridges in his lawn. It made me sick.

'What about Idella?' I asked involuntarily.

'She was so easy to get to bed after I'd finally convinced her to just go out with me. I was glad I'd gone to the trouble of overcoming her scruples at dating a man with my reputation with women, because when I needed her to put back that key, it wasn't hard at all to persuade her. I told her it would ruin my business if I had to tell the police I'd been in the house with Tonia Lee's body. I told her I'd had an anonymous call that I should hurry over to the Anderton house, that the caller said it was Idella who was hurt there. How could Idella refuse to help me after that?' He raised his eyebrows mockingly. 'Obviously, someone wanted to frame me for Tonia Lee's death, someone who knew I'd go rushing to help Idella. It was after she had time to think that she became difficult. She sensed – some implausibility. She was scared of being single, scared of being alone; but she became even more scared of me,' said the man who was quite happy with being alone because he was so fond of himself.

'And me?'

'You're a little different,' he conceded. 'But now you know about me, and no one else does. No one else even suspects. Why did you have to do this?'

'Why'd you have to come home? I thought you were all set for the night.'

'Oh, Dorothy?' He actually thought for a moment. 'You know,' he said almost musingly, 'I just couldn't be bothered.'

He stepped toward me. I glanced at the front door, since Franklin was between me and the back door. The front door was locked and had a similar bolt at the top. I would take seconds reaching it, and more seconds stretching up to the bolt. There was no way. The doorway to my left was shut, but it might be a coat closet, for all I knew. And probably was, because right by it was an ornately carved openwork umbrella stand, appropriately holding a fancy umbrella with a long ferrule.

'I had to do this,' I began, moving slowly to my left around the end of the sofa, compelling him with all my will to watch my face and not my feet, 'because tomorrow the police were going to get Martin.'

'Martin – oh, the new boyfriend. The reason you wouldn't go out with me.' His voice held a mild interest as he came closer. 'Why are you edging left, Roe?'

I pulled the umbrella from the stand. 'Because I hope to hurt you some before you hurt me.' I gripped it determinedly with both hands, pointing the sharp ferrule in his direction.

He laughed. He really did. Wrapping the scarf around both hands in a practiced move, he held out the taut length so I could admire the shine of the blue silk. 'This is Terry's scarf. I think I'll leave it on you so maybe they'll think Terry killed you because Eileen had the hots for you. What a hoot.'

Ha ha. 'Martin will kill you for this,' I said with absolute assurance.

'Your latest honey? I think not.'

And before this could go any further, I charged at him with all my strength and yelled as loud as I could, which was pretty damn loud.

I was short and he was tall, and I was bent over in my charge.

I caught him just in the pit of his stomach. Actually, a *little* lower.

He shrieked, his arms flew up linked by the scarf, and he began to double over. I reeled back from the impact, staggered, went down on my face.

He fell right on top of me.

I fought to get him off, though the air had been mostly knocked out of me. I bucked and pushed and heaved, but he was too heavy. He was growling now, a horrible animal sound, and the glimpse I caught of his face was terrifying, if I could have been any more frightened than I was. He had apparently never been hurt before, because he went berserk with rage. He'd let go of one end of the scarf. He was tearing at any part of me he could get hold of, and I heard a rip and then some clinking, rolling sounds as one of my pockets was absolutely torn off my coat, its contents spilling out.

He grabbed my mass of braided hair and banged my face against the hardwood floor. For a moment of blinding pain my brain went dark, and I heard a cracking sound I couldn't understand. Then he lifted himself on his knees to get a good swing at my head, and I seized the second to turn over. Now I had one free arm, but he came down on the other one. When I tried to bite him, his suit coat prevented me. He grabbed my hair again and banged the back of my head against the wooden floor. I had another moment of darkness, and then with the little energy I had left I grabbed his ear with my one free hand and pulled and pulled, though he tossed and twisted to shake me off. My other arm, trapped between our bodies, hurt dreadfully, though I had no time to think about that.

I realized I was losing consciousness, the weight of him pushing the air out faster than the struggle was letting me take it in. I dug my fingernails into his ear to mark him, since I was losing, and had the satisfaction of feeling wetness under my fingers. But it almost made me lose my grip on his ear. He'd remembered the scarf now, wrapped it around his free hand, and then put it around my neck. I had the wooly scarf pinned there, though, and the collar of my coat, too. But I began to feel myself blanking in and out, like a flickering picture on a black-and-white television. My hand finally lost its grip and slipped to the floor. My fingers landed on a rough lump. My souvenir rock. I forced my fingers to curl around it, and with my last strength I swung the rock and made direct contact with the side of Franklin's head. The sound was dull and nauseating.

The weight on top of me went limp. There were some oddly peaceful moments, because of the silence, the stillness; most of all the cessation of fear. Then I became aware of hearing noise again. Was someone talking to me?

'Let go,' said a fuzzy voice, urgently.

Of what? I wondered if I was barely clinging to my life. Should I let go of it? I wanted it.

'Let go of the rock.'

It was a voice I could trust. I let go, moaning at the sudden pain in my cramped fingers.

I heard sounds, sort of – dragging sounds, and something bumped down the length of my body. Franklin Farrell's head, as someone dragged him off me. I tried to focus, but achieved only a blur.

'I can't see,' I whispered.

'It's me, it's Martin, Roe. Lie still.'

Now that I could do.

'I'm going to call the hospital.' Footsteps retreated and came back. At some point. Everything was fuzzy and blurry and vague.

'Did I hurt him bad?' I mumbled through thick lips. They also hurt. I was finding that a lot of things hurt as my adrenaline ebbed.

I heard a choked sound.

'I called the ambulance for *you*.'

'Why can't I see, Martin?'

'He broke your glasses. They cut your face. Maybe your nose is broken. Maybe your arm, too.'

'Oh. My eyes okay?'

'They may be once the swelling goes down.'

'Did – I – kill him?' I was having some difficulty enunciating.

'Don't know. Don't care.'

'Tough guy,' I mumbled.

'Tough woman,' I thought he said. I would have snorted derisively if my face hadn't hurt so badly.

'Hurts, Mar'in,' I commented, trying not to whine.

'Go to sleep,' he advised.

It was surprisingly easy to do.

Chapter Sixteen

Rubber soles against tile. Trays banging against a metal cart. A voice over a public-address system.

Hospital sounds. I turned my head.

'You're making a habit of this, Aurora,' my mother said sternly. 'I don't want to get one more call from the hospital in the middle of the night telling me my daughter's been brought in beaten up.'

'I promise I won't do it again,' I mumbled painfully.

'For a librarian, you are . . .' And her voice faded out. But when I was all there again, it was still going on. 'John and I are not as young as we were, and we need our sleep, so if you could just get beaten up in the daytime . . .' She was stomping around verbally, because ladies couldn't just stomp around.

'Mother. Am I hurt bad?'

'You're going to feel terrible for a while, but no, no permanent damage has been done. You may have some scarring around the eyes from the cuts your glasses caused, but it's probably going to fade. By the way, I called Dr Sheppard this morning to get a new pair made up. They had a record of what frames you ordered the last time, so they'll be just like your other glasses. He promised he'd have them later today. To continue – the muscles and ligaments in your left arm are strained badly, but the bones aren't broken. Your nose, however, is. Your lips are cut and swollen. Your whole face is black and blue. You look like hell on wheels. You have an engagement ring on your left hand.'

'. . . What?'

'He came in and put it on this morning – he got it right after the jeweler's opened, he said.'

I couldn't lift my arm to look. It was taped or bound somehow.

'You're not supposed to use that arm for a while,' Mother said sharply. 'Wait a minute. I'm going to push the button to raise the head of the bed.'

I opened my eyes cautiously and saw blurry pale blue walls and my mother's arm. It really was daytime. Then as the angle of the bed moved, I was able to see down without shifting my head, which felt as if it might fall off if I did so. My pale left hand was sticking out of a sling, and on it, sure enough, glittered a diamond bigger than Lizanne's.

Of course he would get one bigger than Lizanne's.

'Where is he?' I mumbled through my swollen lips.

'He had to stay at the police station this morning, to talk about the man his foreman caught stealing last night, and about – Franklin.' My mother's voice said the name reluctantly.

'There's some doubt about Franklin's bail hearing,' she went on more cheerfully, 'because you hit him hard enough to put him in this hospital – right down the hall, with a policeman in there with him and his arm handcuffed to a bedrail.'

Franklin's arm, not the policeman's, I assumed.

'You hit him with a rock, I believe,' my mother said remotely.

'Vases,' I said urgently.

'Yes, they know those are the vases from the Anderton house. The senior Andertons had some pictures taken of their more valuable doodads and stored the pictures in their lockbox, and Mandy just now got around to opening the things she had shipped from Lawrenceton to Los Angeles. When the police here called her about the vases being missing, she mailed the pictures, and they arrived yesterday. There's proof. They'll nail that bastard.'

I'd never heard my mother say that particular word.

But I wondered if they could find proof to stick the murders to him. Besides what he'd said to me. I would have to appear in court. Again.

I heard a light knock, and my mother called, 'Come in.'

'Oh,' she said rather stiffly. 'All finished at the police station?'

Martin.

He murmured something to her.

'I'll just leave for a minute to get a cup of coffee, since you're here,' she said with assumed offhandedness.

The door swished again, and I heard him approach the bed. I wiggled the fingers of my left hand, and he laughed.

'Do you like it?' he asked quietly.

He came into my field of blurry vision then. I had a good right hand, and though any movement was not without its cost, I reached out and placed it on his chest. Then I patted my left hand with my right.

'You're cocky,' I mumbled.

This was so romantic.

'I didn't want to take any chances. For all I knew, the doctor might be a former flame who took this chance to rekindle the relationship.'

I giggled, which was quite uncomfortable.

'Roe,' he said more seriously, 'why did you do it? Why did you place yourself in danger like that?'

I was amazed he didn't know. Somehow, I'd assumed the police would tell him. Of course they wouldn't. I beckoned him to bend over with my good hand, so I wouldn't have to talk as loud.

'They were going to question you.'

'You—' He walked away from the bed, stared out the window for a minute, stalked back. 'You did that because you thought I might be arrested?'

I nodded. 'I had it from some reliable sources. I realized at the banquet that Franklin was the killer. No proof.'

'You crazy woman! He could have killed you. If I hadn't been able to settle the problem at the plant in record time, get back and read your note, find out where the hell Franklin Farrell lived . . . at least I still had the map of Lawrenceton in my glove compartment that the Chamber of Commerce gave me when I moved here. You could still be lying there with him on top of you.'

I wondered hazily what would have happened. Would he have regained consciousness before I'd managed to crawl out from under him and get to a telephone? I was glad I hadn't had to find out.

Martin was still running on. 'Did it strike you that I might be able to find the damn vases? Did you think of telling me? I would have broken into his house.'

And possibly been arrested, and lost his job . . .

'It never occurred to me,' I enunciated with some difficulty, 'to ask you.'

There was a harder, brisker knock at the door. Martin went to open it.

'It's the police,' he told me more gently. 'They need a statement about last night.'

'If you can stay,' I managed to say.

So Martin sat beside me, or stood beside me, or walked around the bed, while I mumbled my story to Lynn Liggett and Paul Allison, whom I remembered to congratulate on his marriage to Sally. He seemed a little surprised and uncomfortable. Lynn treated me like a mental case she'd given up all hope on. I edited Franklin's remarks about Terry and Eileen; no point in dragging their relationship into the limelight because of a chance whim on the part of Franklin Farrell.

Finally the two detectives seemed satisfied, if disgusted, with me, and after telling me ominously she would be talking to me again, Lynn strode out of the room. Paul Allison followed after giving me a hard look and shaking his head.

Martin did his circuit of the room again. I waited for him to calm down.

Another knock, this time perfunctory.

'Here's your pain medication. Need some?' asked a plump nurse with curly silver hair. I was delighted to see her, and the two pills I swallowed had an almost instant effect. Martin had to stomp around some more after she left, while I got drowsier and more comfortable. Everyone seemed quite angry with me today.

Finally he came to rest by the bed. My eyes met his. 'We are going to have to do a lot of talking when you can talk a little better,' he said.

We needed a change of topic.

'Talk about the wedding,' I said clearly, and coasted off to sleep.

The Julius House

My thanks to
the Reverend Gary Nowlin,
attorney Mike Epley,
Arkansas state park ranger Jim Gann,
chemist Glenn McCelland,
Dennis of the Georgia State forensic Department,
and Dr Aung Than
for their help with various parts of this book.
Mistakes are my own, not theirs.

Chapter One

The Julius family vanished six years before I married Martin Bartell.

They disappeared so abruptly that some people in Lawrenceton phoned the *National Enquirer* to tell a reporter that the Juliuses had been abducted by aliens.

I had been home from college for several years and was working in the Lawrenceton Public Library when – whatever it was – happened to T.C., Hope, and Charity Julius. And I was as full of speculation as anyone else.

But as time went by with no trace of the Julius family, I forgot to wonder about them, except for an occasional frisson of creepiness when the name 'Julius' came into a conversation.

Then Martin gave me their house as a wedding present.

To say I was surprised to get a house is an understatement: 'stunned' is more accurate. We did want to buy a house, and we had been looking at fancier homes firmly anchored in the newer suburbs of Lawrenceton, an old southern town that itself is actually in the regrettable process of becoming a commuter suburb of Atlanta. Most of the houses we'd been considering were large, with several big rooms suitable for entertainment; too big for a couple with no children, in my opinion. But Martin had this streak that yearned for the outer signs of financial health. He drove a Mercedes, for example, and he wanted our house to be a house where a Mercedes would look at home.

We'd looked at the Julius house because I'd made a point of telling my friend and Realtor Eileen Norris to put it on the list. I'd seen it when I was searching for a house for myself alone.

But Martin hadn't loved the Julius house instantly, as I had. In fact, I could tell he found my affection for the house strange. His arched dark eyebrows rose, the pale brown eyes regarded me questioningly.

'It's a little isolated,' he said.

'Just a mile out of town. I can almost see my mother's house from here.'

'It's smaller than the house on Cherry Lane.'

'I could take care of it myself.'

'You don't want a maid?'

'Why would I?' I don't have anything else to do, I added privately. (And that was not Martin's fault, but my own. I'd quit my job at the Lawrenceton library before I'd even met him, and as time went on, I regretted it more and more.)

'There's that apartment over the garage. Would you want to rent it out?'

'I guess so.'

'And the garage being separate from the house . . .'

'There's a covered walkway.'

Eileen tactfully poked around elsewhere while Martin and I conducted this little dialogue.

'You do wonder what happened to them,' Eileen said later, as she locked the door behind her and dropped the labeled key into her purse.

And Martin looked at me with a sudden illumination in his eyes.

So that's why, when we exchanged wedding gifts, I was stunned at his handing me the deed to the Julius house.

And he was equally bowled over by my gift. I'd been amazingly clever.

I'd given him real estate, too.

Choosing Martin's present had been terrifying. The plain fact was we didn't know each other that well, and we were very different. What could I give him? Had he ever expressed a want?

I sat in my brown suede-y chair in the 'family' room of the town house I'd lived in for years now and cast my thoughts around frantically trying to think of the perfect gift. I had no idea what his previous wife had given him, but I was determined this present would be more meaningful. Madeleine the cat spilled over from my lap to the cushion, her heavy warm mass moving slightly with her purring. Madeleine seemed to know when I began thinking she was more trouble than she was worth, and she would make some demonstration of an affection I was sure was false. Madeleine had been Jane Engle's cat, and my spinster friend Jane had died and left me a fortune, so I suppose Madeleine reminded me of good things – friendship and money.

Thinking of Jane led me to think of the fact that I'd wrapped up the sale of her house, so now I had even more money. I began thinking of real estate in general – and suddenly, I knew what Martin wanted.

Sophisticated corporation man Martin was from rural Ohio, oddly enough. The only obvious tie-in this had with his present life was that he now worked for Pan-Am Agra, manufacturing farming products in conjunction with some of the more agricultural Latin American countries, principally Guatemala and Brazil. Martin's father had died early in Martin's life, and his mother had remarried. Martin and his sister Barby had never gotten along with husband number two, Joseph Flocken, particularly after the death of Martin's mother. Martin had told me bitterly that the farm was falling to ruin because the stepfather was too consumed with arthritis to work it, yet he wouldn't sell, to spite Martin and his sister.

By golly, I'd buy the farm for him.

The tricky part had been thinking of a good reason to be absent from town for a few days. I'd finally told Martin I was going to visit my best friend Amina, now living in Houston and into the second trimester of her pregnancy. I phoned Amina and asked her if she and Hugh would mind letting their answering machine screen their calls for a few days. I'd call her every night and if Martin had called me, I could call him back from Ohio. Amina thought my idea was very romantic, and reminded me she'd be driving over to Lawrenceton soon, with her husband, Hugh, for the festivities preceding the wedding and the wedding itself. 'I can hardly wait to meet Martin,' she said happily.

'Don't turn on your charm for him, now,' I said cheerfully, and suddenly became aware I meant it. I felt quite savage when I thought about Martin being charmed by another woman.

'How charming can I be?' Amina shrieked. 'I'm poking out to China, honey!'

I figured Amina probably had a slight convex curve to her tummy.

We closed with our usual chatter, but my jealous reaction gave me thinking material for that flight to Pittsburgh (the nearest airport), and on the drive west in the rental car to the town nearest Martin's family's farm. This town, Corinth, a little smaller than Lawrenceton, boasted a Holiday Inn where I'd reserved a room, not being sure what else I'd find.

You have to understand, for me this was an exotic adventure. Though I told myself repeatedly that other people traveled by themselves to unfamiliar places all the time, I was highly nervous. I'd studied the map repeatedly during the plane trip, I'd sat in the airport parking lot anxiously checking over the Ford Taurus I'd rented, I'd marveled over the fact that no one in the world knew exactly where I was.

My first impression of Corinth, Ohio, was of how familiar it seemed. True, the land configuration was slightly different, and the people dressed a little differently, and maybe the prevailing architecture was more heavily red brick, more often two-storey . . . but this was a small farming center grouped around a downtown with inadequate parking space, and there were plenty of John Deere tractors in the big sales lot right outside town.

I checked in to the Holiday Inn and called a Realtor. There were only three listed; Corinth was modest about its saleability. The company that advertised specializing in farms ('agricultural acreage') was Bishop Realty. I hesitated, my hand actually on the receiver. I was about to do some lying, and I wasn't used to it.

'Bishop Realty, Mrs Mary Anne Bishop speaking,' said a brisk voice.

'This is Aurora Teagarden,' I said clearly, and waited for the snicker. It was more like a snort. 'I want to look at some farms in the area, specifically ones that are not in the best shape. I want somewhere pretty isolated.'

Mary Anne Bishop digested this in thoughtful silence.

'What size property did you want to see?' she asked finally.

'Not too big,' I said vaguely, since I hadn't wriggled that information out of Martin.

'I could line some things up for you to see tomorrow morning,' Mrs Bishop said. She sounded rather cautious about it. 'If you could tell me – are you actually planning to farm the land? If I knew what you intended to do with it, maybe I could select properties to show you . . . that would suit you better.' She was trying awfully hard not to sound nosy.

I closed my eyes and drew a breath, glad she couldn't see me.

'I represent a small but growing religious community,' I said. 'We want a property that we can repair ourselves, and modify to suit our needs. We'll be doing some farming, but mostly we want the extra land for privacy.'

'Well,' Mrs Bishop said, 'you're not Moonies, are you? Or those Druvidians?'

Druids? Branch Davidians?

'Gosh, no,' I said firmly. 'We're Christian pacifists. We don't believe in drinking or smoking. We don't dress funny, or ask for donations on street corners, or preach in the stores, or anything!'

With an effort, Mrs Bishop joined in my light laughter. The Realtor gave me clear directions to her office, recommended a couple of restaurants for supper ('If you're allowed to do that'), and said that she'd see me in the morning.

I located the soft drink machine, bought a Coke, and watched the news while sipping a bourbon-and-Coke made from the second half of my airline bottle. I was glad Mrs Bishop wasn't there to see the conduct of this purported member of a religious cult.

After a while, feeling strangely anonymous in this little town where no one knew me, I drove around, staring through the fading light at the town Martin had known so well growing up. I went past the ugly brick high school where he had played football. Through a light drizzle in the gray spring evening, I peered at the houses where Martin must have had friends, acquaintances, girls he'd dated, boys he'd gone drinking with. Some of them, perhaps most of them, were surely still here in this town . . . maybe men he'd gone to Vietnam with. Perhaps they mentioned it as seldom as he did.

I felt as if I were eavesdropping on Martin's life.

I had a book in my purse, as usual (tonight it was the paperback of Liza Cody's *Stalker*), and I read as I ate supper at the diner Mrs Bishop had recommended. The menu was slightly alien – none of the southern diner standbys. But the chili was good, and it was with reluctance I left half of everything on my plate. Now that I was over thirty, gravity and calories seemed to be having a little more effect than they used to. When you're four feet, eleven inches, a few extra calories end up looking like a lot.

No one bothered me, and the waitress was pleasant, so I had a nice time. I took the light rain as a sign I should not walk or run tonight, though I'd virtuously brought my sweats and running shoes. As a palliative to my conscience, I did some stretches and calisthenics when I got back to my room. The exercise did relieve some of the cramped feeling the plane and the long car ride had caused. I checked in with Amina, who told me Martin had indeed left a message on her machine not thirty minutes ago.

I smiled fatuously, since no one was there to see me, and called him. The minute I heard his voice, I missed him with a dreadful ache. I pictured his meticulously groomed thick white hair, the black arched brows and pale brown eyes, the heavily muscled arms and chest. He was at work, he'd told Amina's machine, so I could imagine him at his huge desk, covered with piles of paper that were nonetheless neatly stacked and separate. He would be wearing a spotless white shirt, but he would have taken his tie off when the last employee left. His suit jacket would be hanging on a padded hanger on a hook in his very own bathroom.

I loved him painfully.

I couldn't remember ever having told Martin lies before, and I kept having to remind myself of where I was supposed to be.

'Is Amina talking a lot about the baby?' he asked.

'Oh, yes. She's scheduled to take Lamaze in a couple of months, and Hugh's gung-ho about coaching her.' I hesitated a moment. 'Did you take Lamaze when Barrett was born?'

'I don't remember taking the course, but I was there when he was born, so I guess Cindy and I did,' he said doubtfully.

Cindy. Wife number one, and mother of Martin's only child, Barrett, who was now trying to become a successful actor in Los Angeles.

Martin was saying, 'Roe, is Amina being pregnant giving you ideas?'

I couldn't tell how he felt from his voice. He'd spoken so much about Barrett lately I'd felt it wasn't a good time to talk about another child.

'How do you feel about that?' I asked.

'I don't know. I'm pretty old to be changing diapers. It's daunting to think of starting all over again.'

'We can talk about it when I get home.'

We talked about a few other things Martin wanted to do when I got home. By a pleasant coincidence, I wanted to do them, too.

After I hung up, I picked up the little Corinth phone book. Before I could reconsider, I flipped to the *B*'s.

Bartell, C. H., 1202 Archibald Street.

Now, this may sound fishy, but up until that moment I hadn't thought of Martin's former wife being in Corinth.

I discovered I was burning with the urge to see Cindy Bartell. A particularly ridiculous jealousy had flared in my heart; I wanted to *see her*.

Wise or not, I decided to lay eyes on Cindy Bartell while I was here. I took off my glasses and relaxed on the slablike motel bed, with an uneasy feeling that I was being seriously stupid, and wracked my brain to try to remember what Cindy did for a living. Surely Martin had mentioned it at some point or other? He was not one to discuss his past much, though he seemed fascinated with the placidity of mine . . .

I almost fell asleep fully dressed, and when I forced myself to get up and wash my face and put on my nightgown, I had dredged up the fact that Cindy Bartell was, or had been, a florist.

The little telephone book informed me that there was a listing for a Cindy's Flowers.

I fell asleep as if I'd been sandbagged, still not having decided if my good taste and good sense would keep me away from Cindy's shop.

The next morning I showered briskly, put my mass of long, wavy hair up in a bun that I hoped would make me look religious, went light on the makeup, and cleaned my glasses carefully. I wore a suit, a khaki-colored one with a bronze silk blouse, and modest brown pumps. I wanted to look ultrarespectable, so Mrs Bishop would be reassured, yet I wanted the religious cult front to be objectionable enough to tempt Joseph Flocken to sell the farm to spite his stepchildren. Unfortunately, I didn't know the location of the farm, since Flocken didn't have a phone listing. I was simply hoping I'd spot it during my driving around with the real estate agent.

I scanned myself in the motel mirror, thought I would pass whatever test Mrs Bishop chose to give, and went off to have a little breakfast before I met her.

Her directions proved excellent, which boded well for her efficiency.

Bishop Realty was in an old house right off Main Street. As I entered the reception area, a door to the right opened, and a tall, husky blond woman emerged. She was wearing a cheap navy blue suit and a white blouse.

'The Lord be with you,' I said promptly.

'Miss Teagarden?' she said cautiously, after a glance at my ring finger. Naturally, I'd left my huge engagement ring in a zippered pouch in my purse. It hardly fit my new image.

'I do have a few places to show you this morning,' Mary Anne Bishop said, still obviously feeling her way with me. 'I hope you like one of them. We look forward to having your group settle in our area. It is a church, I understand?' She waved me into her office and we sat down.

'We're a small pacifist religious group,' I said with equal caution, wondering about tax exemptions and other hitches connected with claiming to be an actual church. 'We like privacy, and we're not rich,' I continued. 'That's why we want a farm a fair way out of town, one that we can fix up.'

'And you want at least – what – sixty acres?' asked Mrs Bishop.

'Oh, at least. Or more. It would depend,' I said vaguely. I had no idea how big the Bartell/Flocken farm was.

'Excuse me for asking, but I was wondering why your group was interested in this part of Ohio. You seem southern, and there is so much farming land available down there . . .'

'God told us to come here,' I said.

'Oh,' Mrs Bishop said blankly. She shrugged her broad shoulders and assumed her Selling Smile. 'Well, let's go find that place that's just right for you. We'll go in my Bronco, since we're looking at farms.'

So for a whole morning I drove around in rural Ohio with Mary Anne Bishop, looking at fields and fences and run-down farmhouses, thinking about how cold and isolated some of these farms would be in winter, how the land would look covered with snow. It made me shiver to imagine it.

None of these farms was Martin's.

How on earth could I get her to show me the right place? Evidently Flocken hadn't listed it with anyone, was just sitting on it to keep Martin and Barby out. I began to hate Joseph Flocken, sight unseen.

We returned to town for lunch, after which Mary Anne excused herself to recheck the afternoon's appointments. I sat alone in the waiting room and fretted about seeing the right property. Even after that, maybe he wouldn't sell to me. I got up to look in the mirror on the wall above a tiny decorative table, a little closer to Mary Anne's office. My hair, which leads its own life, was escaping from the bun in a tightly waving chestnut nimbus. I began repair work.

If I listened really hard, I found, I could make out Mary Anne's words.

'So I'll bring her out this afternoon, Inez, if you're ready. No, she doesn't wear funny clothes or anything like that. She's tiny, and young, and she's wearing a suit that cost a mint . . .'

Damn! I should have gone and picked out something at WalMart.

'. . . but she's very polite and not at all weird. A real southern accent, you-all!'

I winced.

'No, I don't think the pastor would mind,' Mary Anne said persuasively. 'This group evidently doesn't drink, smoke, or believe in having guns. They can only have one wife. It sounds pretty respectable, and if they're off in the country by themselves . . . well, I know, but she has the money, it seems . . . okay, see you in a little while.'

Mary Anne strode out of her office with a bright face and a sheaf of papers on the various places we'd see this afternoon. My heart sank down to join my spirits.

It was a long afternoon. I learned more about agriculture in mideastern Ohio than I ever wanted to know. I met many nice people who really wanted to sell their farms, and felt sorry for most of them, victims of our economic times. But I couldn't afford *all* those farms.

By four o'clock I'd toured everything Mary Anne Bishop had lined up. There were three more places to see the next morning. I was pretending to consider seriously two of the properties we'd looked at, but found sufficient fault with them to make her eager for tomorrow. We were pretty sick of each other by the time I got in my rental car, which had been parked at her office all day. I'd tried a couple of times to steer her conversation toward the years

Martin had been growing up here, but she'd never mentioned the Bartells, though she and her husband were both natives of the town.

I missed Martin dreadfully.

I was almost through with my paperback, so when I saw a bookstore on my way back to the motel, I pulled into its parking lot with happy anticipation. Any place books are massed together makes me feel at home. It was a small, pleasant shop in a little strip with a dry cleaner's and a hair salon. A bell over the door tinkled as I went in, and a gray-haired woman on a stool behind the cash register looked up from her own paperback as I paused just inside the door, savoring the feeling of being surrounded by words.

'Do you want anything in particular?' she asked politely. Her glasses matched her hair, and she was wearing, unfortunately, fuchsia. But her smile was wonderful and her voice was rich.

'Just looking. Where are your mysteries?'

'Right wall toward the rear,' she said, and went back to her book.

I had a happy fifteen or twenty minutes. I found a new James Lee Burke and an Adam Hall I hadn't read. The true crime section was disappointing, but I was willing to forgive that. Not everyone was a buff, like me.

The woman rang up my books with the same cheerful live-and-let-live air. Without thinking at all, I asked her where Cindy's Flowers might be.

'Around the corner and one block down,' she said succinctly, and reopened her book.

I started my rental car and hesitated for maybe thirty seconds before going to Cindy's Flowers instead of the Holiday Inn.

It looked like a prosperous place on the outside, with a very pretty Easter-decorated front window. I powdered my nose and inexplicably took the pins out of my hair and brushed it out before I left the car. The front of the store held displays of both silk flowers and live plants, and some samples of special arrangements for weddings and funerals. There was a huge refrigerator case, a small counter for paying. The large work area in the back was almost totally open to view. Two women were working there. One, an artificial blond in her fifties, was putting white lilies on a styrofoam cross. The other, who had very short dark hair and was about ten years younger, seemed to be making a 'congratulations on the male baby' bouquet in a blue straw basket shaped like a bassinet. Being a florist was a rites-of-passage occupation, like being a caterer – or a minister.

The women glanced at each other to see who was going to help me, and the dark-haired woman said, 'You finish, Ruth, you're almost done.' She came forward to help me silently and quickly in her practical Nikes, ready to listen but obviously in a hurry.

'What can I do for you?' she asked.

She had large dark eyes and a pixie haircut. Her face and her whole body were lean. She was beautifully made up and wore bifocals. Her nails were long and oval and covered with clear polish.

'Um. I'm just here for a couple of days, and I suddenly realized my mother's birthday is tomorrow. I'd like to send her some flowers.'

'From the sunny South,' she commented, as she picked up a pad and pen. 'What did you have in mind?'

I wasn't used to being so identifiable. Every time I opened my mouth, people knew one thing about me for sure: I wasn't from around here.

'Mixed spring flowers, something around forty dollars,' I said at random.

She wrote that down. 'Where are you from?' she asked suddenly, without looking up.

'Georgia.'

Her pen stopped for a second.

'Where do you want these sent?'

Uh-oh. I'd walked right into this. If I'd had the brains God gave a goat, I'd have sent the flowers to Amina, but since I'd said they were for my mother, I felt stupidly obliged to send them to my mother. I had sustained a deception all day, and perhaps I was just tired of deceiving.

'Twelve-fourteen Plantation Drive, Lawrenceton, Georgia.'

She kept writing steadily, and I shed an inaudible sigh of relief.

'It's an hour later in Georgia, so I don't know if I can get anything there today,' Cindy Bartell pointed out. 'I'll call first thing in the morning, and I'll do my best to find someone who can deliver them tomorrow. Will that do?'

She looked up, her eyes questioning.

'That'll be fine,' I said weakly.

'You have a local number?'

'The Holiday Inn.' She was past being pretty; she was striking. She was a good six inches taller than I.

'How'd you want to pay?'

'What?'

'Cash? Credit card? Check?'

'Cash,' I said firmly, because that way I wouldn't have to give her my name. I thought I was being crafty.

I'd been watching the blond woman work on the funeral cross; I always like to watch other people do something well. When I looked back at Cindy Bartell, I caught her staring at me. She glanced down at my left hand, but of course my engagement ring was still zipped in my purse. 'Do you have relatives here, Miss?'

'No,' I said with a bland smile. And I handed over my money.

I am not totally without resources.

As I picked up supper from a fast food restaurant and took it to the Holiday Inn, I wondered why I'd done such a stupid thing. I couldn't come up with a very satisfactory answer. I hadn't given Martin's past life much thought, and I'd been overwhelmed with sudden curiosity. Surely prospective wife number two always wonders about wife number one?

I watched the news as I ate, my book propped up in front of me to occupy my eyes during the ads. It was a relief to be myself after pretending to be someone else all day. While I enjoyed imagining this or that in my head from time to time, sustained deception was another matter.

The knock at my door scared me out of my wits.

No one knew where I was except Amina, and she was in Houston.

I pitched the remains of my supper in the trash on my way to the door. I'd put the chain on. Now I opened the door a crack.

Cindy Bartell was standing there looking tense and miserable.

'Hi,' I said tentatively.

'Can I come in?'

I had some bad thoughts: 'Rejected Wife Murders Bride-to-Be in Motel Room.'

She interpreted my hesitation correctly. 'Whoever you are, I don't mean you any harm,' she said earnestly, as embarrassed by the melodrama as I was.

I opened the door and stood aside.

'Are you . . .' She stood in the middle of the floor and twisted her keys around and around. 'Are you Martin's new fiancée?'

'Yes,' I said, after a moment's thought.

'Then I'm not making a fool of myself.' She looked relieved.

I thought that remained to be seen. There was an awkward pause. Now we *really* didn't know what to say.

'As you know,' she began, 'or I think you know?' She paused to raise her eyebrows interrogatively. I nodded. 'So you know I'm, I was, Martin's wife.'

'Yes.'

'Martin doesn't know you're here.'

'No. I'm here to buy his wedding present.' I indicated she should have one of the two uncomfortable chairs on either side of the round table. She sat on the edge of it, doing the thing with the key ring again.

'He told Barrett he was getting married again, and Barrett called me,' she explained. 'Barrett said his dad told him you were very small,' she added wryly, 'and he wasn't kidding.'

'For Martin's wedding present,' I said steadily, 'I want to buy him the farm he grew up on. Can you tell me where it is? I haven't told the Realtor I want to see this one particular farm because of course she'll know I want it for some reason, and Joseph Flocken won't sell to me if he knows I'm going to give it to Martin.'

'You're right, he won't. I'll tell you what you need to know. But then I'm going to give you some advice. You're a lot younger than me.' She sighed.

'It's a good idea, getting the farm for him,' she began. 'He always hated someone else having it, someone else letting it fall into ruin. But Joseph always had it in for Martin, in particular, though he wasn't too fond of Barby. I'm not either, for that matter. One of the disadvantages of being married to Martin is that Barby becomes your sister-in-law . . . I'm sorry, I promised myself I wasn't going to be bitchy. Barby had a hard time as a teenager. The reason the blood's so bad between the kids and Flocken – Martin'll never tell you this, Barby told me – is that she got pregnant when she was sixteen, and when Mr Flocken found out, he stood up in front of the whole church – not a mainstream church, one of these little off-sects, or off sex, ha! – and told everyone in the church about it, with Barby sitting right there, and asked their advice. So she got sent to one of those homes and missed a year of school and had her baby, and gave it up for adoption. And nothing ever happened to the kid who was the *dad*, of course, he just went around town telling everyone what a slut she was, and what a stud he was. So Martin beat him up and blacked Mr Flocken's eye.'

What a dreadful story. I tried to imagine being publicly denounced in that fashion, and cringed at the thought.

'Okay, the farm is south of town on Route 8, and you can't see the house from the road, but there's a mailbox with "Flocken" on it by the gate.'

I copied the directions onto the little pad the motel left in the drawer below the telephone. 'Thanks,' I told her. And I braced myself for the advice.

'Martin has a lot of good qualities,' she said unexpectedly.

She was giving the good news before the bad.

'But you don't know everything about him,' she went on slowly.

I had long suspected that.

'I don't want to know unless he tells me,' I said.

That stopped her dead. And I couldn't quite believe that had come out of my mouth. 'Don't tell me,' I said. 'He has to.'

'He never will,' she said with calm certainty. Then her mouth twisted. 'I'm not trying to be bitchy, and I wish you luck – I think. He never was bad to me. He just never told me everything.'

I watched her while she stared into a corner of the room, gathering her strength around her, regretting already her display of emotion. Then she just got up and left.

It took everything I had not to get up and run after her.

The next morning I met Mary Anne Bishop at her office. I was in a brisk frame of mind. I asked her which farms we were to see today, looked at the spec sheets, and asked that we see the one on Route 8 first. Looking a little puzzled, she agreed, and off we went. I looked carefully at each mailbox as we passed, and spotted one labeled 'Flocken' just before the farm we'd come to see, which we toured quickly. I paved the way by telling Mary Anne that the area felt right, but the farmhouse was too small. On our way back to town, I asked her about the road that led from the mailbox over a low hill. Presumably, the farmhouse was not too far from that. 'I liked not having the house visible from the road,' I commented. 'Who owns that property?'

'Oh, that's the Bartell farm,' she said instantly. 'The man who owns it now is called Jacob – no, Joseph – Flocken, and he's got a reputation for being cranky.' But she pulled to the side of the road and tapped her teeth with a pencil thoughtfully.

'We could just drop in and see,' Mary Anne said finally. 'I've heard he wants to move, so even though he hasn't listed the farm, we can check.'

The farmhouse was large and dilapidated. It had been white. Now the paint was peeling and the shutters were falling off. It was two-storey, undistinguished, blocky. The barn to the right side and back a hundred yards or so was in much worse shape. It had housed no animals for some time, apparently. A rusted tractor sat lopsidedly in a field of weeds and mud.

A tall, spare man came out of the screeching screen door. He didn't have his teeth in, and he was leaning heavily on a cane. But he was shaven and his overalls were clean.

'Good morning, Mr Flocken!' Mary Anne said. 'This lady is in the market for a farm, and she wanted to know if she could take a look at yours.'

Joseph Flocken didn't speak for a long moment. He looked at me suspiciously.

I looked straight back at him, trying hard to keep my face guileless.

'I represent the Workers for the Lord,' I said, making it up on the spot. 'We want to buy a farm in this area that needs work, a secluded farm that we can renovate. When the work is done, we'll use the dormitories we build as shelter for our members.'

'Why this farm?' he said, speaking for the first time.

Mary Anne looked at me. Why indeed?

'Not only does it meet the criteria my church lays down for me,' I said staunchly, praying for forgiveness, 'but God guided me here.'

Out of the corner of my eye, I could see Mary Anne looking over the mess of mud and weeds dubiously. Perhaps she was thinking God apparently had it in for me.

'Well, then, look around,' Joseph Flocken said abruptly. 'Then come on in and look at the house.'

There wasn't much to look at outside, so we murmured together about acreage and rights-of-way and wells, and then went inside.

Martin's childhood home.

I gave Flocken some credit for trying to keep the kitchen, the downstairs bathroom, and his bedroom clean. Beyond that he had not troubled, and observing the pain it caused him to move, I could not blame him. I tried to imagine Martin as a child running out this kitchen door to play, climbing up the stairs to the second floor to go to bed, but I just could not do it. Despite the immeasurable difference loving parents would have made, I could not see this place as anything but lonely and bleak. So great was my wish to be away that I negotiated for the farm in an abstract way. Flocken obviously relished details of how the church members would have to work their butts off to build their own shelter, so I managed several references to the strict work habits my church required and encouraged. He nodded his gray head in agreement. This man did not want anyone to have a free ride, or even a pleasant one.

He and Mary Anne began to discuss the selling price, and suddenly I realized I had won. All it took was someone asking, someone he was convinced Barby and Martin would not want the farm to go to.

I wanted to *leave*.

I leaned forward and looked into his mean old eyes.

'I'll give you this much and no more,' I said, and told him the sum.

Mary Anne said, 'That's a fair price.'

He said, 'It's worth more.'

'No, it's not,' I snapped.

He looked taken aback. 'You're a tough little thing,' he said finally. 'All right, then. I don't think I can take another winter here, and my sister in Cleveland has a spare bedroom she says I can have.'

And just like that, it was accomplished.

I shook his hand with reluctance; but it had to be done.

Chapter Two

The purchase went swiftly since there was no loan to approve. I'd thought I'd have to do a lot by mail, or perhaps make a return trip, but it wasn't necessary, to my relief. The essential work had been accomplished after three days were up. By the time I drove my rental car back to the airport in Pittsburgh, I'd paid two more visits to the bookshop, eaten in every restaurant in town, and rigorously avoided Cindy's Flowers. If I could have announced who I really was to someone, I might have passed the time with people who knew the man I loved, but I had to stay in character when I wasn't in my motel room. The chances seemed distant that someone would find out the real reason I wanted the farm, someone who liked Joseph Flocken enough to tell him. But I couldn't risk it. So I was virtuous, and ran in the morning, tried not to eat too much out of sheer boredom, cruised all the local shopping, and was heartily sick of Corinth, Ohio, by the time I left.

I swore I'd never wear my hair in a bun again.

I wanted Martin to meet me at the airport, so passionately I could taste it, but of course he'd want to know why he was meeting a flight from Pennsylvania, and I didn't want to give him his wedding present in the airport.

When I got off the plane in Atlanta I felt more relaxed than I had in a week. Carrying my luggage as though it were featherlight, I located my old car in the longer-term parking, paid the exorbitant amount it took to get it out, and drove off to Lawrenceton reveling in the familiarity of home, home, home.

When I passed the Pan-Am Agra plant on my way in to town, I had to stop.

I had only been in the plant a couple of times before, and felt very much out of place. At least Martin's secretary knew who I was.

'I'm glad you're back,' Mrs Sands said warmly, her grandmotherly voice at odds with the luridly dyed black hair and lavender suit. 'Maybe now he'll be happier.'

'Something wrong?'

'Oh, he got some mail from South America that made him angry, and he was on the phone all day that day, but he's back to normal now, just about. Go on in.'

But I knocked, because he was at work; so he was looking up when I came in.

He dropped his pen, rolled back in his chair, and came around the desk in a second.

After a few minutes, I said, 'We should either lock the door or postpone this until tonight.'

Martin glanced at his watch. 'I guess it'll have to be tonight,' he said with an effort. 'I should have an appointment sitting out in the reception area by now. Mrs Sands is probably wondering what to do. However – I don't mind keeping him waiting . . .'

'No,' I said, trying not to giggle. 'I have to confess, it makes me feel a little self-conscious knowing Mrs Sands is sitting out there. Tonight, then?'

'We'll go out to eat,' he said. 'I know you won't feel like cooking, and I won't get through here until seven, so I won't have time.'

Martin's cooking is limited to grilling steaks, but he never minds doing it.

'See you then,' I whispered, giving him one last kiss.

He tried to pull me back, but I wiggled away and grinned over my shoulder at him as I left the room.

'Bye, Mrs Sands,' I said in what I hoped was a collected voice. It probably would have been more effective if I hadn't suddenly realized my blouse wasn't tucked into my skirt any longer. I scooted across the room quickly, catching just a glimpse of the dark-complected man waiting to see Martin; a man with a heavy, piratical mustache, thick black hair, and ropelike arm muscles. He looked more like a nightclub bouncer than a job applicant.

I called my mother from the town house to tell her I was home, and learned what had happened in town in the few days I was gone.

'Thanks for the flowers, Aurora. I don't know what the occasion was, but they were lovely.'

I started. I'd forgotten all about sending the flowers from Ohio. I mumbled something deprecating.

'Have you seen Martin yet?' Mother was asking. She sounded as if the question were loaded. I could see her at her desk at Select Realty, thin and elegant and self-possessed, remarkably like Lauren Bacall.

'Yes. I stopped by the plant. But he didn't have much time. We're going out tonight.' If I'd had antennae, they would have been pointing in Mother's direction. Something was afoot. 'How's John?' I asked.

'He's just fine,' she said fondly. 'He's been planting a garden.'

'In the backyard?'

'Yes, something wrong with that?'

'No, no,' I said hastily. If I'd ever doubted my mother adored her recently acquired second spouse, I knew differently now. I could not imagine in a million years my mother allowing someone to dig up her carefully groomed backyard to plant tomatoes.

I hung up shaking my head, decided to put off retrieving Madeleine from the vet until the next day, and carried my bag upstairs to unpack, happily, in my own bedroom.

I scrubbed my out-of-state trip away in my own shower. I dried my hair. I took a nap. After I woke up, I went down to my basement to pop a load of clothes into the washer. The neighbor who'd been collecting my mail brought it over. I thanked her and she left. I stood by the kitchen counter leafing through the assorted junk. Suddenly, I let all the pleas from new resort areas and all the sweepstakes offers slip through my fingers to land in a heap on the beige formica.

Perhaps because I was tired, or shaken out of my usual routine . . . I don't know why. Suddenly I was asking myself, Why am I marrying Martin? There were gaps in his history. He was more than he seemed. There were moments when I found him a man of frightening capabilities. He could be tough and ruthless and hard.

But not with me.

I was getting maudlin, silly. I shrugged physically and mentally, shaking off the dramatic notions I'd entertained. I sounded like the heroine of one of those romance novels, the gals who think with their vaginas. I tried to imagine Martin and me posing for one of those covers, me with my bodice artfully slipping, him with his 'poet shirt' strategically ripped. Then to complete the picture I added my favorite glasses in their bright red frames, and the half-glasses Martin wore when he read. I laughed. By the time I had put on makeup and chosen a dress, one Martin had bought me and made me promise to wear with no one but him, I felt better.

Actually, he'd said, 'Never wear that unless you're with me, because you look so good I'd be afraid someone would try to lure you away.'

Maybe *that* was the reason I was marrying Martin.

He arrived at seven on the dot. I had the deed tucked in my purse. I was determined we wouldn't give in to our hormones, but would actually make it to the restaurant, because I'd had this movie in my head of us swapping wedding presents in a restaurant, and I couldn't get rid of it. I think we were supposed to wait until the rehearsal dinner, but I knew I couldn't keep a secret from him until then, even a short three weeks.

We went to the Carriage House, because it was the fanciest place in Lawrenceton, and our reunion was a fancy occasion.

We ordered drinks, and then our food.

'It's early to do this, Roe,' Martin said and reached across the table to take my hand, 'but I've got your gift, and I want to give it to you tonight.'

'I have your gift, too,' I said. We laughed a little. We were both nervous about this exchange. I supposed he'd gotten me a diamond bracelet, or a new car – something costly and wonderful – but I never expected a real *surprise*. He reached in his coat and pulled out a legal envelope.

He'd changed his will? Gee, how romantic. I disengaged my hand and took the envelope, trying to make my face blank so he wouldn't read disappointment. I slid a sheaf of stiff paper out, unfolded it, and began reading, trying to force comprehension. Suddenly it came.

I now owned the Julius house.

I felt tears in my eyes. I hated that; my nose turns red, my eyes get bloodshot, it messes up my eye makeup. But whether I wanted to or not, my eyes began to leak down my face.

'You know how much this means to me,' I said very quietly. 'Thank you, Martin.' I picked up my huge cloth napkin and gently patted my face. Then I fished my own legal envelope out of my purse and shoved it across the table. He opened it with much the same apprehensive look I must have had. He scanned the first page and looked away, over the heads of the other diners, blinking.

'How'd you do it?' he asked finally.

I told him, and he laughed in a choky way when I talked about my representation of myself as a religious cultist. But he kept looking away, and I knew he would not look at me for fear of crying.

'Let's go,' he said suddenly, and groping for his wallet, threw some money on the table.

We got out the door, adroitly dodging the young woman with the reservations book, who clearly wanted to ask us what was wrong. I put my arm around Martin's waist, and his arm snaked around me, and I went across the gravel parking lot pretty briskly for a short woman wearing heels. Of course Martin wouldn't forgo opening my door for me, though I had often reminded him I had functioning arms, and by the time he had gotten in his side, he was really breathless from trying to tamp the emotion back down inside. I turned around in the seat to face him and slid my arms around him. Sometimes I am very glad I am small. His arms went around me ferociously.

He was crying.

My husband-to-be handed me the keys to our house the next morning.

'Go see it. Make some plans,' he said, knowing that was exactly what I wanted to do. I was pleased to be going by myself, and he knew that, too.

I showered and pulled on blue jeans and a short-sleeved tee, slapped on some makeup, stuck in some earrings, tied my sneakers, and drove a mile north of town.

The Julius house lay across open fields from Lawrenceton, the fields usually planted in cotton. As I'd pointed out to Martin, you could see my mother's subdivision from the house – if you went to the very back of the yard, out of the screen of trees the original owner had planted around the whole property, which was about an acre.

A family named Zinsner had built the house originally, about sixty years ago. When the second Mrs Zinsner had been widowed, she'd sold the house for a song to the Julius family. ('No Realtor,' my mother had sniffed.)

The Julius family had lived in the house for a few months six years ago. They had renovated it. T. C. Julius had added an apartment over the garage for Mrs Julius's mother. They had enrolled their daughter in the local high school.

Then they had vanished.

No one had seen the Juliuses since the windy fall day when Mrs Julius's mother had come over to the house to cook breakfast for the rest of the family, only to find them all gone.

The wind was blowing today, too, sweeping quietly across the newly planted fields, a spring wind with a bite to it. The trustee for the estate, a Mrs Totino, Martin had told me, had had the yard mowed from time to time and kept the house in decent shape to discourage vandals and gossip. It had been rented out occasionally.

Today the yard was full of weeds, tall weeds, but this early in the spring, they were mostly tolerable ones like clover. The clover was blooming, yards and yards of it, bright green with bobbing white flowers. It looked cold and sweet, as though lying on it would be like lying on a chilly, fragrant bed.

The long driveway was in terrible shape, deeply rutted, the gravel almost all gone. Martin had already arranged to have more gravel hauled in.

The huge yard was full of trees and bushes, all tall and full. An enormous clump of forsythia by the road was bursting into yellow blooms. The house was brick, painted white. The front door and the door to the screened-in porch were green, as were the shutters on the downstairs windows and the awning on the second-floor triple window overlooking the front yard.

I went up the concrete steps to the screen door opening onto the front porch that extended the width of the house. The wrought-iron railing by the steps needed painting; I made a note on my little pad. I crossed the porch and turned my key in the front door for the first time.

I threw down my purse on the smelly carpet and wandered happily through the house, my pad and pencil at the ready. And I found a lot to note.

The carpet needed replacing; the walls needed new paint. Martin had told me to pick what I liked, as long as avocado green, gold, and raspberry pink weren't included. The fireplace in the front room should be flanked by bookshelves, I decided dreamily. The dining room that lay between the front room and the kitchen had a built-in hutch to hold our silver and placemats and tablecloths, the gifts that were already accumulating in my living and dining rooms at the town house.

There were plenty of cabinets in the kitchen, and the cream and golden-orange scheme was just right. I'd have to reline the shelves; I made another note. The Juliuses had begun renovating the downstairs bathroom, but I didn't like the wallpaper, and the tub needed replacing. I made another note. Would we want to use the downstairs bedroom, or turn it into a smaller, less formal family room? Perhaps an office – did Martin bring work home?

I went up the stairs to look at the size of the two upstairs bedrooms. The largest one looked out over the front of the house; it was the one with a row of three windows with an awning to keep out the afternoon sun. I was drawn to them immediately. I looked out over the ridge of the porch roof, which was separate; the porch must have been an afterthought. The impression from the front yard was of looking at a large piece of typing paper folded lengthwise – that was the roof of the house – echoed by a smaller piece of notepaper folded the same way lower down, the porch roof. However, this roof didn't intrude on the view, which swept across the fields to a series of distant hills. No other houses in sight. The fireplace downstairs in the large front room was echoed in the fireplace up here.

I loved it.

This would be our bedroom.

Closet space was a definite problem. The double closet was just not adequate. I went across the landing to the little room with no apparent use. Perhaps it had been a sewing room originally? Could we build an extra closet in here? Yes, it was possible. There was a blank wall that would make a larger closet than the one we had in the bedroom. And there was room enough for Martin's exercise equipment. The other upstairs bedroom could be the guest bedroom.

Books – where would I put my books? I had so many, with my library combined with Jane's . . . I took time for fond thoughts of Jane, with her silver chignon and her little house, her Sears dresses and modest ways; rich Jane, who'd left me all that money. I sent waves of affection and gratitude toward her, wherever she was, and hoped she was in the heaven I believed in.

I went slowly down the stairs, looking below me as I went. The stairs ended about six feet inside the front door and divided the large front room from the wide hall that gave access to the bathroom and downstairs bedroom, and another way to get to the kitchen, rather than going through the dining room.

What a nice wide hall. Wouldn't it look great repapered and lined with bookshelves?

I laughed out loud. It seemed there could hardly be anything more entertaining than to have a house to redo and enough money to redo it.

This was the happiest morning of my life, spent all alone, in the Julius house.

Chapter Three

I picked up Madeleine from the vet's, where I'd boarded her while I was gone. The entire staff could hardly wait until she left; Madeleine hated everyone who worked there and let them know it. Growls issued from her carrier all the way to the town house, but I ignored her. I was riding on a happy wave and no fat marmalade cat could make me crash.

I met Martin for lunch at Beef 'N More, and once we'd said hello to half a dozen people, we were free to talk about the house. Really, Martin listened to me talk. I set my notepad by my plate and had to keep pushing up my glasses as I referred to it.

'You're happy,' he said, dabbing his mouth with his napkin.

'More than I've ever been.'

'I got you the right thing.'

'Absolutely.'

'Would you mind if I left you with the whole responsibility of seeing to the changes we need to make in the house?'

'Is this a nice way of saying, "Since you're not working, could this be your job?" '

Martin looked disconcerted for a second. 'I guess it is,' he admitted. 'I want our house to look nice, of course, and be comfortable for us; I mean, I care what it looks like! But I have some business trips coming up—'

I made a little sound of dismay. 'Trips?'

'I'm sorry, honey. This was totally unexpected. I promise in three weeks I won't budge.' Three weeks from now was the wedding. 'But there are a lot of things I have to tie up before I take off for the wedding and our honeymoon.'

To tell the truth, the prospect of having free rein on the house renovation was very attractive. I felt he was dangling that as recompense for the business trips, but okay. I bit.

'What have we got in the next three weeks that I need to be on hand for?' he said, getting his pocket calendar out.

I whipped out my own and went over the schedule: a supper party, a shower for me. 'Then,' I went on, 'we have a barbecue in our honor at Amina's parents' lake house, a week from Saturday. It's informal. Amina and her husband will be driving in from Houston for that.'

Amina would be my only attendant. The fit of her dress and the chance of her getting nauseated during the ceremony added yet another note of suspense to an already nerve-wracking rite.

'Southern weddings,' my beloved said darkly.

'It would be a lot worse if we weren't so old and established,' I told him. 'If I were twenty-two instead of thirty-one and you were twenty-four instead of forty-five, we'd have at least double this schedule.'

Martin was aghast.

'I'm not joking,' I assured him.

'And then, at the reception, you just have cake and punch,' he said, shaking his head.

'I know it's hard to understand, but that's the way we do things in Lawrenceton,' I said firmly. 'I know when Barby got married she had a supper buffet and a band, but believe me, we're stretching it by having champagne.'

He took my hand and once again I felt that oozy, melty feeling that was disgustingly like a forties song.

'I heard from Barby,' he said, and I kept my face smiling happily with some effort. My future sister-in-law wasn't my favorite part of the wedding package.

'She's flying in two days before the wedding, and she accepted your mother's offer of her guest bedroom. I'll call your mother and thank her,' Martin said, making a note. 'And Barrett called.'

Martin's son called Martin about once a month, to recount his ups and downs on the road to an acting career in California.

'Is Barrett still going to be your best man?'

'He can't make it.'

I stiffened, dropping all pretense at smiling.

'He has a part in a movie filming then,' Martin said expressionlessly. 'He's waited a long time for this part; he has lines and is on screen for several scenes . . . the hero's best friend.'

We looked at each other.

'I'm sorry,' I said finally.

Martin looked over the heads of the other diners. I was glad we were in one of the little alcoves that make Beef 'N More at least a tolerable place to eat.

'There's something I want to talk to you about,' he said after a moment. The subject of Barrett was clearly closed.

I shifted my face around to 'Expectant.'

'The garage apartment,' he said.

I raised my eyebrows even higher.

'I have a friend who just came into town from Florida. He lost his job. He and his wife are very capable people. I wondered – if you didn't mind – if they could have the garage apartment.'

'Of course,' I said. I'd never met a friend of Martin's, an old friend. He had made a few connections locally, mostly at the Athletic Club, upper-management men like himself. 'You knew him from—?'

'Vietnam,' he said.

'So what's his name?'

'Shelby. Shelby Youngblood. I thought . . . with all the renovation . . . it might be nice to have someone else on the spot out at the house. Shelby will probably work out at Pan-Am Agra in shipping and receiving, but Angel, his wife, could be there when he's not.'

'Okay,' I said, feeling I'd missed something important.

'When I found out Barrett couldn't come,' Martin said, almost as an afterthought, 'I called your stepfather, and he's agreed to be my best man.'

I smiled with genuine pleasure. In many ways, it was easier to marry an older man who was used to fending for himself. 'That was a good idea,' I said, knowing John must have been pleased to be asked.

We parted in the parking lot. He took off back to work, and I was going to my favorite paint/carpet/wallpaper store, Total House, to start the Julius place on its road to becoming our house. But halfway there, I pulled over to the curb and sat staring ahead, my window open for the cool fresh air.

Martin, in his 'mysterious' mode, had put one over on me.

Who the hell was this Shelby Youngblood? What kind of woman was his wife? What sort of job in Florida had he lost, and how did he know where to find Martin? I drummed my fingers on the steering wheel, wondering.

Probably this was the *downside* of marrying an older man who was used to fending for himself. He also was not used to having to explain himself. And yet Martin deserved to keep his past life a secret, I thought confusedly; I was hardly telling *him* all . . . No! I had told him everything that might make a difference to our life together. I wasn't wanting to know the names of his sexual partners in the past years, which of course he should keep to himself. But I had a right, didn't I, a right to know – what? What was really frightening me?

But we hadn't known each other that long, I told myself. We had plenty of time for Martin to tell me whatever heavy and grim passages from his past he wanted me to know.

I was *going to marry Martin*. I started my car and pulled back into the modest stream of traffic that was Lawrenceton's lunch-hour rush.

Because really, trickled on a tiny cold relentless voice in the very back of my mind, really, if you asked him and he told you, you might learn something that would force you to cancel the wedding.

The prospect of being without him was so appalling, I just couldn't risk it.

At the second stoplight, I swept this all neatly under my mental carpet as prewedding jitters and took a right turn to Total House.

There I made a few salesmen very, very happy.

*

I met Martin at the Episcopal church, St James, that night for our fourth premarital counseling session with Father Aubrey Scott. The two men were standing out in the churchyard talking when I arrived – Martin shorter, more muscular than Aubrey, more intense. It felt odd walking over to them under their scrutiny; Aubrey had been my escort for several months and we had been rather fond (though never more than that) of each other. If they were asked to describe me, I suddenly thought, they would describe totally different people. I stowed that thought away to chew at later.

Martin had met me when I was dating Aubrey, and consequently always felt extra possessive when Aubrey was around, I'd noticed. Now, he slid his arm around me as I joined them, while keeping their desultory conversation going.

'—the Julius house?' Aubrey was saying in some surprise.

I looked up, way up, at his mildly handsome face with its carefully groomed dark mustache.

'Her wedding present,' Martin said simply.

'Quite a gift,' Aubrey said. 'But, Roe, won't it bother you?'

'What?' I asked, deliberately obtuse.

'The missing family. I've been in Lawrenceton long enough to hear the story, several times. Though I'm sure it's gotten embroidered over the years. Can there really have been hot food still on the table when the mother came over from the garage apartment?'

'I don't know, I hadn't heard that particular twist,' I said.

'And it won't make you nervous?' Aubrey persisted.

'It's a wonderful house,' I said. 'It makes me happy just to walk in the door.'

'Emily would be too nervous to stay an hour.'

Aubrey always had to drag Emily Kaye into the conversation. I figured the sexual dynamics went something like this: Aubrey and I had parted when Martin and Emily appeared on our horizons. Emily had the child Aubrey wanted and couldn't have (he was sterile) and Martin had so much electricity for me I felt the air crackled when we were together. But Aubrey had dated me first, and perhaps a little resented my recovering from his gentle 'good-bye' speech so thoroughly and quickly. So Emily Kaye, his all-but-in-name fiancée, was sure to be mentioned whenever I saw him.

It's stuff like that that made me so glad to be almost married. After so many years of dating and not-dating, I was heartily sick of all these little undercurrents and maneuverings. I was ready to be devastatingly straightforward. There is no telling what my reputation for eccentricity would have become if Martin hadn't chanced to want to see a house my mother, the real estate queen of Lawrenceton, was too busy to show him. She'd sent me in her stead and we had met for the first time on the front steps.

The phone rang in Aubrey's office, and he excused himself to answer it. I seized the opportunity to turn Martin's face toward mine and give him a very thorough kiss. That was certainly one of the biggest differences in my relationship with Martin; the sex was frequent, uninhibited, and absolutely wonderful. My sexual experience was not extensive, though I'd had what I thought was good sex before, but I had found a whole new dimension to the subject with Martin Bartell.

He said, 'If it's the suit, I'll wear it every day.'

'I was just thinking about the first time I saw you.'

'Can we go back and stand on the steps of that house again?'

'No, Mother sold it last week.'

'Well—' Martin bent to resume where we'd left off, but Aubrey came out of his office then. The churchyard was getting dark, and he called to us to come in. We went in hand and hand, and while we talked in his office, the darkness outside became complete.

'I had supper tonight with Shelby Youngblood,' Martin said. He was leaning against his car, I against mine, side by side in the church parking lot. The security lights overhead made his face colorless and cast deep shadows under his eyes.

Martin was going to spend the night at his apartment since he was leaving early in the morning to catch a plane to the Pan-Am Agra plant in Arkansas.

'I should meet him,' I murmured.

'That's what I wanted to set up. Can he come out to the new house tomorrow morning? That's where you'll be?'

I nodded. 'Martin, what's this man like?'

'Shelby? He's . . . trustworthy.'

That wasn't exactly what I'd expected to hear. A strange capsule biography.

'I guess I wanted a little more than that,' I said. 'Does he drink, smoke, gamble? Where does he come from? What did he do before he came here?'

'He doesn't talk much about himself,' Martin said after a pause. 'I guess you'll have to find out what he's like from his actions.'

I'd made Martin angry. Perhaps he felt I was questioning his judgment.

'You know what I call the way you look now?' I asked.

Martin raised his eyebrows in polite query. He really was angry.

'Your "Intruder Alert" face.'

He looked surprised, then irritated, and finally he began laughing.

'Am I that bad?' he asked. 'I know I have a problem talking about some things. No one ever called me on it before.'

I waited a little while.

'I don't talk about Vietnam easily, because it was dirty and scary,' he said finally. 'And there are some people I don't talk about, because they're connected with that time . . . I guess Shelby's one of them. He's from Tennessee, from Memphis. We were in the same platoon. We were good friends. After the war, we hung around together for a while. We kept in touch. Maybe once every three months I'd get a phone call or letter, for at least four years or so. Then I didn't hear from Shelby for a long, long time. I thought something must have happened to him.'

Martin turned to look at the floodlit church, the lights shining full on his face for a minute, making him look – old.

'I got a letter from him about a year ago, and we resumed the connection. He had married Angel.'

Martin stopped abruptly and I realized I had gotten all I was going to get.

It was a start.

I was at the Julius house by seven the next morning. I looked at each room, slowly and carefully, revising my room-by-room list of the changes that needed to be made. At eight fifteen the carpenters came, followed me around, took notes, and left. At nine the paint, wallpaper, and carpet people came, measured, and left. At nine forty-five the plumber showed up, trailing a miserable-looking assistant with a cigarette stuck in his mouth.

'Please don't smoke in here,' I said as pleasantly as possible.

The lanky red-haired boy, who couldn't have been more than eighteen, threw me a sullen look and retreated to the front yard, where I was willing to bet he'd leave his cigarette butt in the grass. After years at the library, I could fairly accurately predict which teenagers were going to behave and which were going to be problems. This one was a problem. I looked at my plumber.

'I know, I know,' John Henry said. 'I don't think he'll last long. It's a pain riding in the truck with him. But his mama is my wife's best friend.'

We sighed simultaneously.

John Henry and I discussed the bathrooms, worked out a schedule (as soon as possible), and then he crawled under the house to check out the plumbing. 'I'm a little scared to explore too much here,' he confessed with a broad grin. 'Who knows but what they're all under the house?'

'Oh, the Juliuses.' I smiled back. 'Well, I bet the police checked that out pretty thoroughly at the time.'

'Sure. Still, I bet you wonder if they'll show up here somewhere. It'd give me the creeps, Roe.'

'It doesn't bother me,' I said dismissively, and turned to the open front door to see a stranger standing there. He was looking back over his shoulder at the red-haired boy smoking on the lawn. When he turned to me, I recognized the dark man who'd been sitting in Martin's waiting room the day I'd returned from Ohio.

This was Shelby Youngblood. He looked at me in that moment, and we had a good rude stare at each other.

He was about five foot ten, swarthy-skinned, with muscles that were truly impressive, even to one used to Martin's muscular build. His hair was a dusty black, shaggy, only a few threads of gray, and his mustache was the kind that framed his mouth. His eyes were blue, and he wore old jeans and a faded T-shirt. His hands looked broad and hard.

'Miss Teagarden?' he asked, in a pleasant voice. 'I'm Shelby Youngblood.' I'd expected him to growl.

'I'm glad to meet a friend of Martin's,' I said honestly. 'Please call me Roe.'

We shook hands. His were very hard, ridged and scarred.

'Come see the garage apartment,' I suggested.

I got my keys and led the way, out the kitchen, under the roofed walkway, over to the garage with the covered stairs running up the side closest to the house. I unlocked the door at the top, and we went in. Since the garage was not only more than wide enough for two cars, but had a deep storage room running all its width along the back, the apartment was larger than one expected from outside. It was a very good size for one person – it was basically one large open room. I hoped two people would be comfortable there. The bathroom was small but adequate, and more modern than the ones in the house, since it was the Juliuses who had turned what had been a glorified hayloft into an apartment for Mrs Julius's mother. The tiny kitchen was not meant for producing a full Thanksgiving feast, but would be bearable for someone who was not an enthusiastic cook.

I looked at Shelby Youngblood inquiringly.

'Is this okay?' I asked, when he didn't say anything.

'It's fine,' he said with some surprise, as if he hadn't realized I was waiting for his verdict.

'This carpet is mildewed, I think the carpet pad is, too,' I said, wrinkling my nose. I hadn't noticed this the other time I'd looked at the apartment. 'I'll replace it. Is there any color you particularly like? Anything that might match your furniture . . . ?'

'Right now, we don't have any,' he said calmly.

He seemed amused.

All right! What was so damn funny about not having furniture, about my wanting to know if their furniture was any color I should be mindful of when I ordered carpet! Didn't most people in their forties have furniture? It wasn't as if I'd asked about his racial origin or asked him to describe a shrimp fork. I could feel myself turning red.

'Angel and I haven't been in one place long enough to accumulate much,' he said, and I nodded curtly.

'Then I'll rent it furnished,' I said, and turned and walked out.

I stomped down the stairs breathing heavily.

I spied John Henry's wife's best friend's son going into my house with a cigarette in his mouth.

'Excuse me!' I called.

He stopped and turned.

This kid had an attitude, no doubt about it. He looked at me as if I'd crawled out from under a rock to question his God-given right to smoke in my house.

'Please put out the cigarette before you go in,' I said as evenly as I could manage, coming to a stop in the front yard a few feet away from the boy as he stood on my front steps.

He rolled his eyes and sneered. It was one of those teenage grimaces that make you amazed that so many of them survive to adulthood. Of course teenagers had acted like this in the library, and I had handled it then, but a few months away had resensitized me.

Already angry, I was now inwardly berserk. What this translated to on the outside was that I had my hands clenched in fists by my side, my jaw felt soldered together, and all I needed to complete my Shirley Temple imitation was to stick my lip out.

The boy dropped the cigarette on my wooden porch and ground it out with his foot. He took another step inside.

'Pick it up,' suggested a quiet voice from behind me.

'Huh?' The boy's mouth was open in amazement at this novel idea.

'Pick it up and put it in your pocket,' the quiet voice said, as if it were implanting a posthypnotic suggestion.

With a fearful stare over my shoulder, the boy reached down, picked up his cigarette butt, dropped it in his pocket, and scuttled into the house.

'Now,' I said, pivoting on my heel, 'I could have handled that by myself.'

'I made you mad in the first place,' Shelby said.

I tried to think that out, but couldn't while he was standing there looking at me.

'We should start again,' he said.

'Yes.'

'Hi, I'm Shelby Youngblood, a friend of Martin's.'

'Hi. I'm Roe Teagarden, Martin's fiancée.'

We didn't shake hands again, but regarded each other warily.

'I hope you don't mind Martin suggesting we live here,' Shelby said.

That wasn't easy for him. He wasn't used to being beholden to anyone.

I blew out a long breath silently, gradually cooling down. I decided on simple positive sentences. 'I am very glad for you to be in the apartment. I know that you plan to help out while the renovation is going on. I'm anxious to get it done as soon as possible. We'll get married in three weeks, and be back from our honeymoon two weeks after that, so I hope to have most of it done by then.'

'If I start work at Pan-Am Agra before then, Angel will be more than able to supervise whatever work is left to be done,' Shelby said. 'And by the way, she likes light orange – I think she calls it peach – and green.'

I could feel the tension ease out of my face.

'Will you go back to – Florida, right? – to get her, or . . .'

'Yeah. I'll fly back tomorrow, and we'll wrap things up there and start driving up here in maybe three or four days.'

'Okay. That'll work out great.' By the time the Youngbloods were in place, I should be more and more wrapped up in wedding plans, and it really would be a help to have them actually on the spot.

For the first time I saw how Shelby Youngblood had gotten out to the house. He was driving Martin's car.

'He really does trust you,' I said.

'Yeah.'

We gave each other another long look.

'Catch you later,' Shelby said casually, and strode off, starting up Martin's car and driving off in it.

It felt very strange to see someone else in Martin's car.

I ran into town to tell the carpet and paint people they had a new job, and one that took priority. By great good fortune, they had a peach-colored carpet in stock. Since the white walls in the apartment were still in very good shape, I asked the painter to do the baseboards and door and window frames in green. I was lucky enough to find white curtains with a little peach-colored figure at WalMart (I was in too much of a hurry to have some made), and as for furniture . . . gee, this was getting expensive. I looked in the for-sale ads of the *Lawrenceton Sentinel* and called some of the numbers listed. By late afternoon, I'd found a very nice used bedroom suite and a couch and two armchairs in a neutral beige, and had run back to WalMart and bought queen-size sheets and a bedspread (green). The living-room set was in good shape but needed cleaning. I made a note to buy a spray cleaner, and then rushed back to the town house to get ready for the wedding shower.

As I sank into the warm water of the bathtub, I realized that I hadn't eaten lunch and didn't have time to eat supper. I was astonished. Meals were not something I skipped without noticing. Well, I certainly hadn't missed the calories, but I wouldn't be able to keep up this pace unless I took better care of myself. I consciously relaxed everything from my toes on up, practicing slow regular breathing. I was going to enjoy tonight. I'd waited all these years for a bridal shower in my honor; by golly, this was my night.

Luckily, I'd decided in advance what to wear. I pulled the purple with white polka dots from the closet, put in the amethyst earrings Martin had bought me, slid my feet into one of my few pairs of high heels. After surveying my reflection, I added a small gold bracelet. I brushed my hair carefully and then put on a braided headband to keep the mass out of my face (and my drink, and my food).

Food. I hoped Eileen and Sally had a tableful. Maybe those sausage and biscuit balls?

My mouth watered while I swapped purses, and when my mother rang the doorbell, I was feeling ravenous.

My mother, Aida Brattle Teagarden Queensland, looked aristocratic and slim and cool as ever in a gorgeous royal blue suit. She is a woman dauntingly difficult to criticize. Her clothes and behavior are always appropriate for the occasion. She always thinks before she speaks. Her extensive and successful business dealings are always ethically aboveboard, and her employees have excellent health benefits and a profit-sharing program.

But she is definitely not a woman you would run up and hug without a fair warning and a good reason, and she is not sentimental, and she never forgets anyone who does not deal fairly with her.

Mother gave me a careful, cheerful kiss on the cheek. She was finally marrying me off, enjoying all the mother-of-the-bride things that she'd been denied. And she knew I was happy. And she approved of Martin, though I sensed reservations. Martin was closer to her age than to mine, and that worried her a bit. (She had asked me if I'd seen his company's insurance policy, for example.) And, being my mother and extremely property oriented, she wanted to know how much money Martin had in the bank, what his salary was, how much of that he saved, and what his pension program was. Since it was impossible for her to ask Martin these things pointblank, it had been amusing to hear her try to maneuver the conversation delicately around to what she wanted to know.

'I'm willing to give her a full, typed financial statement,' Martin had told me after we'd eaten supper with Mother and John one night.

'That would be too direct,' I told him. 'I don't know why she's in such a lather, anyway.' (Though actually, my mother in a lather was pretty unimaginable.) 'I have plenty of money of my own, safely invested, well protected.'

'She's just watching out for you,' Martin said fondly.

I had dark thoughts about why everyone seemed to feel I needed 'watching out for,' but considering my mother had a right to if anyone did, I kept quiet.

Now as Mother swept me into her superior car (she'd picked me up because she considered my old Chevette to be too plebeian for The Bride) she checked me over as though I were going on my first date, gave a quick little nod of approval, and asked me if I'd heard from my father lately.

'Not since he called me after he talked to Betty Jo about coming,' I answered. Betty Jo was my father's second wife, down to earth, plain, and homey as all get out. When he'd fled my mother, Father had certainly run in the opposite direction. He and Betty Jo lived in California now, with their child, my brother Phillip, age nine. I hadn't seen my father or Phillip or Betty Jo in nearly three years.

'He said they were?'

'If he could take his vacation time then. He was going to ask.'

'And you haven't heard back,' my mother murmured, almost to herself.

I didn't say anything.

'I'll call him tomorrow,' she said decisively. 'He has to let us know.'

'I'd like Phillip to be ring-bearer if they're coming,' I said suddenly.

It was lucky we were in Mother's big Lincoln, because it was full of thoughts unsaid. Phillip had had a traumatic experience the last time he spent the weekend with me. They'd moved to California in a (to me) mistaken attempt to help Phillip recover, and he'd been seeing a counselor for a year afterward. According to my father's rare letters, Phillip was fine now.

Then, as we parked at Eileen's house, I caught a glimpse through the picture window of a table covered in white with white and silver wedding bells hanging from the light fixture, and Eileen carrying in a big tray of something sure to be edible, and Sally Allison, her co-hostess, stirring a huge silver bowl of punch. On a table nearby presents wrapped in white and silver and pastels were heaped. Sally and Eileen were dressed to the teeth.

As I slid out of the car it hit me smack in the psyche.

This was for *me*.

I was getting *married*.

I put one hand out to the roof of the car and the other touched my chest as if I were pledging my allegiance.

I knew a moment of delight, followed by a groundswell of panic.

'Just hit you, huh?' Mother asked.

I nodded, unable to say a word.

We stood in the dark, looking through that window, for a couple of minutes. It was oddly companionable.

'Which way is it going to be?' Mother finally asked.

It was the first time she'd spoken to me as if I were absolutely grown up.

'Let's go in,' I said, and started up the sidewalk to the front door.

Chapter Four

Mother and I stood nervously in the foyer waiting to say hello to the first arrivals before being put wherever we were supposed to sit during the present opening. Though Mother was nervous, she looked as composed and cool as she always did, as though she couldn't sweat. But one eyelid twitched from time to time.

One of Mother's friends came in first, and then Amina's mom, Miss Joe Nell, one of my favorite people. And then the guests came too fast for me to talk much to each one; it was like a 'This Is Your Life' theme party. The pile of presents rose higher and higher, and the room got fuller and fuller, and older women who had been my mother's friends for years mixed with women my own age whom I'd known all my life – Susu Hunter, Lizanne Buckley Sewell, Linda Erhardt, and several others – and women who had to be asked because of some connection to my life, like Patty Cloud, my mother's office manager, and Melinda, wife of my mother's husband's son, and a couple of women I'd asked just to say 'Ha!' such as Lynn Liggett Smith (wife of my former flame Arthur Smith) and Emily Kaye (love of my former flame the Reverend Aubrey Scott).

After the usual twenty minutes or so of chatter, during which I answered the same questions six or seven times, Sally made a little speech about my upcoming marriage, including a joke about how long we'd all waited for that day – thanks, Sally – and then the present opening began. I had registered my color preferences in towels and bathroom items with the local stores, and of course I got lots of those, and toothbrush holders and wastebaskets and even a monogrammed towel rack, which left me practically speechless. I could hardly wait to show it to Martin, and picturing his face started a fit of the giggles I had trouble suppressing. I passed each present around the circle of women so it could be admired and its giver complimented on her choice.

It was the lingerie, of course, that provoked the most oohs and ahhs. I got a leopard print teddy from Susu, which engendered quite a few risqué comments, and some silk pajamas from my mother in a champagne color, and from the shower hostesses a truly gorgeous negligee set in black lace. Showing that to Martin was going to be fun, too.

Sally and Eileen had popped in and out during the present opening, vanishing to the kitchen after commenting on a gift or two, and now they both appeared and took their place at the loaded dining-room table, Sally pouring punch into delicate glass cups and Eileen cutting and serving the cake on her best china at the opposite end. As the honoree, I was expected to go first, one of the other nice things about being a bride. We all made the ritual comments about how good everything looked, and about how we'd just eaten supper so we weren't sure we could jam in another bite, and then we loaded down our plates and stuffed ourselves.

Of course it was all good, but it could have been sawdust and I would still have enjoyed it. Some women reminisced about their showers and weddings, some asked Sally and Eileen for recipes, others talked about ordinary Lawrenceton happenings, others asked me about the wedding plans, and a few of the older ladies quizzed me about Martin and who 'his people' were.

As some of the guests were returning their empty plates to the sideboard, a very old lady came to sit in the chair beside me that my mother had temporarily vacated. She had wrinkles like cobwebs gridding her face, her eyes were the color of bleached denim, and her thinning hair was snowy. She was wearing one of those flowered dresses that were the staple of Lawrenceton fashion. This particular example was sky blue with pink flowers, and the lady who wore it was the same thickness all the way up and down. This was Mrs Lyndower Dawson, christened Eunice, but since childhood called Neecy.

'How are you, Miss Neecy?' I asked.

'I get long pretty good, Aurora. As long as the Lord lets me, I want to get around on my own,' Neecy told me solemnly.

In Lawrenceton, we were a little worried about the Lord letting Miss Neecy get around, since she was still driving and tended to take the middle of the road and ignore little things like stop signs.

'Now, tell me something, Aurora,' Neecy said slowly, and I realized we were getting to the crux, here. 'I hear that that young man of yours has bought you the so-called Julius house.'

'That's right,' I said agreeably, tickled at Martin being my 'young man' and curious about what she was going to tell me.

'They call it the Julius house, but of course it isn't really.'

'Oh?'

'Of course not; those people just lived there a few months. It's really the Zinsner house, they originally built it and lived in it for oh, sixty or sixty-five years before Sarah May sold it to those Juliuses.'

'Is that right?' Actually, I'd known that, but I didn't want to dam Miss Neecy in midflow.

'Oh, yes, honey, the Zinsners were an old Lawrenceton family. They got here before my family, even. And the branch that built that house was the last of the family. They built out there when town was two and a half miles away on a poor dirt road, rather than a mile away on a paved one.'

I nodded encouragingly.

'I remember when they were building that house, John L. and Sarah May were fighting like cats and dogs about how to do it. John L. wanted things one way, Sarah May wanted 'em another. Sarah May wanted a gazebo in the backyard, and John L. told her she'd have to build one with her own hands if she wanted it. Sarah May was one smart woman, but that she couldn't do. But she had her own way about the porch. After the house was all but finished, she told John L. she had to have a front porch, a big one. Now John L. had already had the roof completed, and he didn't want to tear it up again, so that's why the roof of the porch is separate. John L. just put in guttering between the two parts. Then Sarah wanted a two-car garage instead of a one-car, and though they only had one car, John L. added another stall for another car. And then she wanted an extra closet, but John L. and her had a fight and he boarded it up to spite her!' Neecy shook her head as she remembered the battling Zinsners.

'They're both gone now?' I asked gently.

'Gosh, no, someone as mean as Sarah May takes a long time to kill,' Neecy said cheerfully. 'She's over in Peachtree Leisure Apartments, a nice name for that old folks' home on Pike Street, where the old fire station used to be. I go to visit my friends out there from time to time, and I see Sarah May right often, though some days she doesn't know me. And that woman is out there, too, come to think of it.'

'What woman do you mean, Miss Neecy?'

'That Julius woman's mother. Got an Italian name. Totino. Melba Totino.'

I hadn't known the family who'd built the house still had living members, and I hadn't known The Mother-in-law (as she was invariably referred to in local legend) was still living, much less still living in Lawrenceton.

'There, you didn't know all that, did you?' said Neecy in a pleased way. 'Not too many of us around to remember things the way they were.'

'Thanks for telling me,' I said sincerely.

'Oh, we old people aren't much good for anything except remembering,' Neecy said with a deprecatory wave of her hand.

Of course, I protested as I was supposed to, and she ended up happy, which she was supposed to. I thanked her profusely for her gift of scented 'guest' soap shaped like seashells, and that pleased her, too.

She got up to go and thought of one more thing to say. 'That man you're marrying, Aurora, is it true he's from Chicago, Illinois?'

'Well, he moved here from Chicago. Actually, he grew up in Ohio.'

Neecy Dawson shook her head slowly from side to side. She patted me absently on the shoulder and began steering her way over to my mother. I saw her engage my mother in serious conversation.

Later, when we were loading the presents into the trunk of Mother's car, I asked her what Neecy had been saying. Mother laughed.

'Well, if you really want to know – she asked me if it was really true that you were marrying a Yankee. I said, "Well, Miss Neecy, he *is* from Ohio." And she said, "Poor Aida. I know you're worried. But there *are* some nice ones. Aurora will be all right, honey".'

Chapter Five

Now that I'd taken on renovating the Julius house – I just couldn't think of it as the Zinsner house – the time before the wedding flew by. I got the apartment above the garage finished first. The carpet was laid within three days after the painter finished the trim. I cleaned the furniture I'd bought, positioned it invitingly, relined the kitchen shelves, cleaned the stove, and made the bed. I'd gotten a set of china for four at WalMart, and some wedding gift pots and pans I didn't need went into the kitchen cabinets. I put towels in the bathroom, hung a shower curtain, and arranged some of the seashell soap in a soap dish. It looked pretty and inviting and clean, and I hoped I'd done Martin's friends proud.

The work on the big house went slower. Some of the workmen I wanted were busy, and the carpet took longer to come than it was supposed to, and I had a hard time picking out paint and wallpaper. I was frantic to have it finished; my town house and Mother's guest bedroom were overflowing with the wedding gifts and furniture I'd kept from Jane Engle's house. Martin's furniture was still in storage at a warehouse closer in to Atlanta, and I made a trip there to see what he had. In between making decisions, fretting over delays, and spending hours worrying, I had to get dressed appropriately and punctually for the remaining parties in our honor.

Now, these are all very pleasant problems to have, I know. But I did begin to get tired, and frayed, and desperate. Martin seemed unprecedentedly grim, too, though his bad mood didn't seem to have anything to do with the wedding.

So I was really glad to greet the Youngbloods when they arrived from Florida. I was at the Julius house when they drove in at noon one day about a week and a half before the wedding.

Angel Youngblood emerged from the dusty old Camaro first. Her legs swung out and out and out, and then the rest of her followed. I gaped. Angel was easily as tall as her husband. Muscular and sleek as a cheetah, she had pale blond hair gathered up in a ponytail. She was wearing the loose sheeting pants that weightlifters wear when they train, and a gray tank top. She had a broad, thin-lipped mouth, a straight nose, and brilliant blue eyes in a narrow face. She wore no makeup. She looked around her carefully, her eyes gliding right over me and then coming back to note me. We looked at each other curiously.

'I'm Aurora,' I said finally, shaking her hand, which was an experience for both of us. 'You must be Angel?'

'Yes,' she said. 'It's been a long drive. It's good to get out of the car.'

She stretched, an impressive process that showed muscles I didn't even know women had.

Her husband came to stand beside her. He looked even swarthier, his face more pock-marked, against her smooth sleekness.

'Shelby, nice to see you again,' I said.

'Aurora,' he nodded.

The carpet layers, who were carrying in the pad, stopped to stare at Angel. Shelby looked at them. They hastily headed into the house.

It wasn't that she was pretty. She wasn't. And her chest was almost flat. She was just very obviously strong and fit and golden tan, and her hair was such a pretty color. It was really just like seeing a wild animal walk into the yard – beautiful and scary at the same time.

'Please come see the garage apartment,' I said a little shyly. 'I hope you like it.' I turned to precede them up the steps. Suddenly I reconsidered. 'No,' I said, turning. 'Here are the keys.'

It was theirs, they should see it alone, without me there to make them feel that they had to admire it. I left to start overseeing the carpet layers.

About an hour later they came to the house, looking about them carefully, like cats examining a new environment.

While Shelby went upstairs at my invitation to finish the tour, Angel put a broad hand on my shoulder to get my attention. I looked up at her.

'It's the nicest place we've lived in years,' she said unexpectedly. 'Shelby told me what it was like before. Thank you for everything.'

'You're welcome. If you want to change anything, now is the time, with all these home repair people coming in and out.'

She looked at me blankly, as if changing her environment was an alien concept. 'Where do you want us to park?'

'Since Martin and I don't have both cars here, just park in the garage. I don't know what we'll work out later after the wedding, but we'll think of something.'

'Okay. We've carried our suitcases up, and we're ready to start work.'

'Work' sounded more formal than the casual 'helping you out' relationship Martin had suggested. But I certainly did need help.

'Let me tell you what I want to do here in the house, and how far I've gotten on each item,' I began. To my surprise, she pulled a small ruled pad out of her pocket, and uncapped a pen clipped to it. Shelby was suddenly beside her, listening just as attentively as if I were updating them on a missile launch. Feeling nervous and awkward, I started explaining, room by room, the plans I'd made, and showed them the paint, wallpaper, and carpet samples for each room that I'd sorted into a divided accordion folder. In the section I'd accorded each room was also a list of necessary repairs or changes, and taped to the front was a list of things I had yet to do before we left on our honeymoon. This list included such things as 'Start paper delivery. Order new return-address stickers. New library card. Box books in town house. New stove will be delivered Monday A.M., be there . . .' and it went on and on.

'I think we can take care of this,' Shelby said after a thorough briefing.

'You do?' I know I sounded idiotic, but I was stunned. It had never occurred to me they'd take the whole thing off my hands.

'Of course we can't sign things for you,' Angel said. 'And you'll want to come see for yourself, at least once a day. I know I would. But I think we can make sure all this happens on time, and I see you've got a list of all the phone numbers we might need, taped here to the folder.'

I am capable of organization.

'You'd do that?' I was still having trouble grasping the idea that relief was standing right before me.

'Of course,' Angel said again, surprised in turn. 'That's what we're here for.'

'When will Shelby start work at Pan-Am Agra?'

'Oh, not until you all are back,' Shelby said. 'Martin wanted us to be sure everything kept on going while you were gone, and that's what Angel and I intend to do.'

'Oh . . . that's wonderful. Thank you,' I said from the bottom of my heart.

They both looked uncomfortable and glanced at each other.

'It's our job,' Angel said, with a little shrug. A little shrug on Angel was a pretty large gesture.

I had to relax them before I left. 'Now,' I said briskly, 'the carpenter building the bookshelves here in the hall is supposed to come this afternoon, but he'll get his wife to call with some excuse, about 12:30. So tell him that if he doesn't come in to finish the job, we'll hire someone else tomorrow.'

'Okay,' Shelby nodded. 'And who will we call tomorrow? Or am I bluffing?'

'Bluffing. He'll come in today, but he just needs prodding. He likes to go fishing.'

'So do I,' Shelby said. 'I feel for him. Well, go on if you have something else you need to be doing. We'll handle things here.'

'Thank you,' I said again, and I meant it just as much.

That evening we had scheduled another session with Aubrey. I got to St James early, but Aubrey was already there, sitting on the steps of the church. He was watching the sun go down, a little ritual he liked to observe every now and then. I plopped down by him, glad to sit and let my brain rest for a little bit.

After our hellos, we slumped together companionably for a few minutes, thinking our separate thoughts, watching the splendor unfold to the west. Aubrey had a wonderful quality of restfulness, the inner relaxation of a man who is square with the world and its maker.

'Martin's not early, for once,' Aubrey observed, after a while.

'No . . . guess he had a meeting.'

'I think he usually comes early because he doesn't want to leave you alone with me.'

'You think so?'

'Could be,' Aubrey said neutrally.

'He knows I love him,' I said.

'He knows other people love you.'

I mulled that over.

'You're implying that he's extremely jealous?'

'Could be.'

'Do you like Martin?'

'I admire him. He has many fine qualities, Roe. I don't think you'd pick a man who didn't. He's intelligent, strong, a leader. And he obviously loves you. But you're going to have to stand up to him on everything, every point, not let him get the upper hand. Once he has that, he won't be able to stop.'

'This is a surprise, Aubrey.' I watched an ant toiling across the gray concrete of the sidewalk.

'I care about you. Of course, I care about everyone in this congregation, but you're a special person to me, and you know it. In these counseling sessions, I've seen how much Martin loves you and how much you love him, and I've seen that both of you believe in God and are trying to lead the good life. But Martin feels he is a law to himself, that he and God are each autonomous.'

We were sitting with our knees almost in our faces because the steps were so shallow. I leaned my head down on my knees, felt their hard caps and the movement of my muscles underneath, the amazing way my body worked. I was trying not to feel scared.

'You'll perform the wedding?'

'Yes. And I'm not saying anything to you I won't say to Martin. I just wanted to talk to you because I felt I was being prevented from doing it. And because I'll always be fond of you.'

'Are you going to marry Emily?' I was being impertinent, but the evening and the quiet of the neighborhood around the church encouraged intimacy.

'We're thinking about it. She hasn't been a widow very long, and her little girl is still trying to understand her daddy's absence.' Emily's husband had been killed in a wreck the year before, and she'd moved to Lawrenceton because she had an aunt living here.

Emily Kaye was dull as dishwater, but of course I wasn't going to say that to Aubrey. At least my intended was exciting.

And here he came in his Mercedes. Martin was groomed to a T even after a long day at work, his striped shirt still crisp, his suit unwrinkled. My heart gave its familiar lurch at the sight of him, and I sighed involuntarily.

'You're really in love,' Aubrey said very quietly, as if to reassure himself.

'Yes.'

I smiled at Martin as he got out of the car and came toward us, and he didn't look jealous or even uneasy at Aubrey and me sitting tête-à-tête. But he pulled me up by my hands and gave me a kiss that lasted too long and was almost ferocious.

'I'll go unlock the office,' Aubrey murmured, and rose from the steps.

'Your friends got in today,' I told Martin.

'Shelby called me. What did you think of Angel?'

'I've never met anyone like her, or like Shelby, for that matter.'

'What do you mean?' We began walking down the south sidewalk to the parish hall where Aubrey's office was, the dusk gathering around us. I could see the desk lamp shining through Aubrey's uncurtained window.

'Well,' I said slowly and carefully, 'they seem used to having very little, to needing very little.' I was uncertain how to phrase my next thought. 'They're very quick to understand your wishes and act on them, and they don't reveal anything about themselves, about what they want. Oh, gosh, that makes them sound like a maid and a butler, and they're anything but that. But do you see what I mean?'

He didn't answer for a moment, and I was afraid I'd offended him.

'They're very independent, and very capable of making quick judgment calls, Angel even faster than Shelby maybe,' Martin said finally. 'But I understand you. Shelby has never been one to talk about himself, and I was sure he'd marry someone who talked nonstop, but he married Angel. She'll tell you more about herself than Shelby will, but she isn't any chatterer.'

'They're going to be great help with getting the house finished,' I said carefully, when it became apparent Martin wasn't going to volunteer any more – like, who were these people? Where had they come from, and what had they been doing there? Why were they willing to be in Lawrenceton, doing what they were doing here? 'It's a relief knowing they're there.'

'Great, honey. I wanted you to get some quiet time before the wedding. That house was running you ragged.'

Ragged? I felt the urge to pop in the nearest women's room and stare into the mirror, suddenly terrified I'd see crow's feet and gray hair. Normally I am not morbidly self-conscious about my appearance, but the fittings for the wedding dress and the fuss over clothes in general for the past couple of months had made me very aware of how I looked.

'They took notes,' I told Martin absently. 'I think they'll do a great job.'

'I want you to be happy,' he said.

'I am,' I told him, surprised. 'I've never been happier in my life.'

Then we were at the door to Aubrey's office, and we joined hands and went in. Our last session before the wedding, and Aubrey wasn't going to make it easy. He asked hard questions and expected honest answers. We had gone over what we expected from each other financially, emotionally, and in the matter of religion. And we had talked again about having children, with both of us unable to decide. Maybe indecision wasn't good, but it was better than holding opposing views. Right?

The counseling sessions had opened vistas of complexities I'd never imagined, the little and big adjustments and decisions of sharing life with another adult human being. It was the 'working' aspect of marriage I'd somehow missed when my friends talked about their married lives. Martin, who was more experienced by reason of his previous marriage, had mentioned Cindy in the course of the sessions more than I'd ever heard him mention her before. Especially since I'd met Cindy, I listened carefully. And this evening, Aubrey asked Martin The Big Question.

'Martin, we've concentrated, naturally, on your relationship with Roe, since you're going to be married. But I wondered if you wanted to share your feelings about why your previous marriage didn't work out. Have we covered anything in these evenings together that rang any bells?'

Martin looked thoughtful. His pale brown eyes focused on the wall above Aubrey's dark head, his hands loosened the knot of his tie. 'Yes,' he said quietly, after a few seconds. 'There were some things we never talked about, important things. Some things I liked to keep to myself. I don't like to think about the woman I love worrying about them.'

My eyes widened. My mouth opened. Aubrey shook his head, very slightly. I subsided, but rebelliously. I would worry if I damn well chose to; I deserved the choice.

'But,' Martin continued, 'that wasn't the way the marriage could survive. Cindy ended up not trusting me about anything. She got sadder and more distant. At the time, I felt that if she had enough faith in me, everything would be okay, and I was resentful that she didn't have that faith.'

'But now?' Aubrey prompted.

'I wasn't being fair to her,' Martin said flatly. 'On the other hand, she began to do things that were calculated to gain my attention . . . flirt with other men, get involved with causes she had very little true feeling for . . .'

'And you didn't communicate these feelings to each other?'

'It was like we couldn't. We'd been talking so long about things like Barrett's grades, what time we had to be at the PTA meeting, whether we should install a sprinkler system, that we couldn't talk about important things very effectively. Our minds would wander.'

'And now, in your marriage to Aurora?'

'I'll try.' He glanced toward me finally, apologetically. 'Roe, I'll try to talk to you about the most important things. But it won't be easy.'

As we were leaving, Aubrey said, 'I almost forgot, Roe. I was visiting a few members of the congregation who live in Peachtree Leisure Apartments yesterday. We were in that big common room in the middle, and an older lady came up to me and asked if I was the minister who was going to conduct the ceremony for your wedding.'

'Who was she?'

'A Mrs Totino. You know her? She said she'd read the engagement notice in the paper. She wanted to meet you.'

'Totino,' I repeated, trying to attach a face to the name. 'Oh, I know! The Julius mother-in-law! I heard at the shower that she was still alive and living here, and I'd completely forgotten it.'

'I never met her when I bought the house. Bubba Sewell ran back and forth with all the papers,' Martin said.

'Is she in good health, Aubrey?' I asked.

'She seemed pretty frail. But she was full of vinegar and certainly all there mentally. The old gentleman I was visiting says she's the terror of the staff.'

I pictured a salt-and-peppery little old lady who would say amusingly tart things the staff would quote to their families over supper.

'I'll go see her after the wedding,' I said.

Chapter Six

Lately I'd been feeling as if I were in one of those movies where calendar pages fly off the wall to indicate the passage of time. Events and preparations made the time blur. Only a few things stood out clearly when I thought about it later.

The night we were riding home from the barbecue Amina's parents held for us, out at their lake house, Martin finally told me where we were going on our honeymoon. He had asked what I wanted, and I had told him to surprise me. I had half-expected the Caymans, or perhaps a Caribbean cruise.

'I wanted you to have a choice, so I've made initial preparations for two things,' he began, as the Mercedes purred down the dreadful blacktop that led to the state highway back into town. I leaned back against the seat, full of anticipation and barbecued pork.

'We can either go to Washington for two weeks, and do the Smithsonian right.'

I breathed out a sigh of delight.

'Or we can go to England.'

I was stunned. 'Oh, Martin. But is there really something – I mean, both of those are things you would enjoy too?'

'Sure. I've been to the Washington area many times, but I've never had time to see the Smithsonian. And if you pick England, we can go on a walking tour of famous murder sites in London, if you'll come with me to get some suits made on Savile Row, or as close to Savile Row as I can manage.'

'How can I pick?' I chewed on my bottom lip in happy agony. 'Oh . . . England! I just can't wait! Martin, what a great idea!'

He was smiling one of his rare broad smiles. 'I picked the right things, then.'

'Yes! I thought for sure we'd be going to some island to lie on gritty sand and get all salty!'

He laughed out loud. 'Maybe we can do that sometime, too. But I wanted you to have a really good time, and a beach honeymoon just didn't sound like you.'

Once again, Martin had surprised me with his perception. If we'd sat down and consulted on it, I would never have thought of suggesting England (going farther than the Caribbean had never crossed my mind), and if I had, I would have dismissed the idea as something that wouldn't have appealed to Martin.

We had an absolutely wonderful time after we got to the town house.

Another moment I remembered afterward was Amina's introduction to Martin. I was very excited about her meeting him and attributed her unusual silence thereafter to the bouts of nausea she was still experiencing. Amina, who had always been happily unconscious of her good health, was having a hard time adjusting to the new limits and discomforts her pregnancy was imposing on her. Her hair was hanging limply instead of bouncing and glowing, her skin was spotty, her ankles were swelling if she sat still for more than a short time, and she seemed to alternate nausea with heartburn. But every time she thought about the baby actually arriving, she was happy as a clam at high tide.

So at first I thought it was just feeling demoralized about her appearance that made Amina uncharacteristically silent. Finally, unwisely, I asked her directly what she thought about Martin.

'I know I'm not my normal self right now, but I'm not crazy, either,' Amina began. I got that ominous feeling, the one you get when you know you're about to get very angry and it's your own fault. We were standing out in the front yard of the Julius house, which was beginning to look as my imagination had pictured it when I had first seen it. John Henry's legs, in their plumbers' overalls, were protruding from the crawl space under the house, a young black man was trimming the foundation bushes, and the Youngbloods were doing a strange Asian thing on the broad driveway in front of the garage. It was some kind of martial ballet alternating sudden kicks and screams with hissing breathing and slow graceful movements. Amina watched them for a moment and shook her head in disbelief. 'Honey,' she said, looking directly into my eyes, *'who are those people?'*

'I told you, Amina,' I said, 'Shelby is an old army buddy of Martin's, and he lost his job in Florida—'

'Cut the crap.'

I gaped at my best friend.

'What job? Where, exactly? Doing what? And what does she do? Does she look like Hannah Housewife to you?'

'Well, maybe they're not exactly like the people we know . . .'

'Damn straight! Hugh said they looked more like people the criminal-law side of his firm would defend!'

Bringing in Hugh, her husband, was a mistake, Amina realized instantly. 'Okay, okay,' she said, holding up her hands, 'truce. But listen, honey, those people seem very strange to me. Martin wanting them to live out here with you all – I don't know, it just looks . . . funny.'

'Be a little more specific, Amina,' I said very stiffly. 'Funny? How?'

Amina shifted from foot to uncomfortable foot. 'Could we sit down?' she asked plaintively. I recognized a delaying tactic, but she really was tired. I pushed a folding lawn chair in her direction. I pulled over one for myself. Martin and I had been sitting out on the lawn the evening before, looking at the house and talking about our plans.

'I shouldn't have started this,' Amina muttered to herself and tried to arrange her altering body in the light aluminum-frame chair. 'I'm just worried about you,' she said directly. 'If Martin was a regular guy in a regular job who came home every night, I'd like him fine. And I do like him as he is, because he obviously thinks you're the greatest thing since sliced bread. But he's gone so much, he works so hard, such long hours. Why does he have to be out of town so much? Plant managers are supposed to stay at the plant, right? And these Youngbloods.' She shook her head.

'Amina, stop.'

'Your mom's worried, too.' She was crying.

The Youngbloods had finished their strange ritual and were doing some kind of exercise in which they faced each other, squatted, and whacked each other's arms.

My mother, I reflected, had been smart enough not to say anything.

To tell the truth, this conversation shook me.

I handed Amina a Kleenex from my shoulder bag.

'I'm just scared that – it almost looks like you'll be their prisoner.'

'Amina, I think you need to go lie down,' I said, after a little silence.

'Don't patronize me! I may be pregnant but I'm not stupid.'

'Then you'll believe me when I say that I don't want to hear any more of this.'

We each stared off angrily in opposite directions, composing ourselves, trying to be friends again.

It took a few days.

The ceremony itself was brief and beautiful. Lawrencetonians filled up my side of the church and half the rows on Martin's. Being older, and having moved so many times, Martin had not invited many people, and those who came were business associates from Pan-Am Agra, a few old friends from Ohio, and his sister Barbara. I had some sympathy for Barby since I'd learned more of her history while I was in Corinth, but still I knew she would never become my favorite person or my confidante. (She brought her daughter, a sophomore at Kent State, a pretty, dark, plump, young woman named Regina. Regina was not blessed with many brains and asked far too often why her cousin Barrett hadn't come to see his dad get married.)

So St James Episcopal Church was full, Emily Kaye played the organ beautifully, my mother walked down the aisle with the dignity that was her trademark, Martin appeared from Aubrey's study with John at his side – Martin looked absolutely delicious in his tux – and Amina went down the aisle in her full-skirted dress that fairly well concealed her pregnancy. Then it was my turn.

My father and his wife had finally decided to come, pretty much at the last minute; you can imagine how their lack of enthusiasm made me feel. And then they'd left my brother Phillip with some friends in California.

My crushing disappointment had permanently altered the way I felt about my father.

I am no apple-cart upsetter. I am no flouter of tradition. And I am not a person who likes last-minute changes in plans. But when my father had arrived, I had told him I wanted to walk down the aisle by myself. My mother drew in a sharp breath, opened her mouth to say something, then looked at me and shut it. And I didn't explain my decision to Father, or wait for his reaction, or tell him not to get his feelings hurt. And Betty Jo had no say at all. So Father and Betty Jo had walked in before Mother.

That's why I came down the aisle by myself when Emily began playing the music I'd waited so many years to hear. I'd had my hair put up, I was wearing the earrings Martin had given me the night before we'd gotten engaged, I was wearing full bride regalia. I felt like the Homecoming Queen, Miss America, a Pulitzer Prize winner, and a Tony Award nominee, all rolled into one.

And we got married.

Chapter Seven

We pulled into our very own gravel driveway, groggy from the trip, glad to be home. I knew Martin had started thinking about the plant again, and I had been visualizing my own – our own – bed, and my washing machine, and staying in my nightgown until I was good and ready to get dressed. And my own coffee! Our honeymoon, which had been as sweet as honeymoons are supposed to be, had been wonderful, but I was really ready to be back in Lawrenceton. It was hard to believe we had to get through the rest of the day before going to bed. Martin had slept some on the airplane coming across the ocean, and I had too, but it wasn't especially restful sleep.

The house looked wonderful. The new carpet, paint, and the bookshelves were in. God bless the Youngbloods; they'd arranged the furniture I'd thought would be lined up against the walls. I'd left diagrams of how I wanted the bedrooms to be situated, but I hadn't been able to visualize the living room. It actually looked very nice, though I was sure I'd want to change a couple of things. Madeleine had already chosen a chair and mastered the pet door in the kitchen. Judging by her girth, the Youngbloods had been feeding her too well. She seemed faintly pleased to see me, and as always, totally ignored Martin.

In that distracted way people have when they come home from a trip and can't settle, we wandered separately around the house. Martin went to the large box of mail on the coffee table and began to sort through it – his pile, my pile – while I roamed through the dining room, noting all the wrapped presents on the table, to check out the kitchen. I'd moved most of my kitchen things here myself and gotten them in place before the wedding, and Martin's household goods had been retrieved from storage before the wedding, too, but there was a box or two yet to unpack; the essential things that I'd kept at my apartment until the day of the wedding. I'd have cleaned out the apartment and moved in with Mother if the furniture left me by Jane Engle hadn't already been taking up the third bedroom, and the second one had been promised to Barby Lampton for the week of the wedding.

I knew, catching sight of the back of Martin's head as I began to open the belated wedding presents stacked on the dining-room table, that I was going to experience an after-wedding slump, as we began the day-to-day part of our life together, so I was glad there was some work left to do on the house. I stared blearily at yet another set of wine glasses, and checked the box to see if they were from the Lawrenceton gift shop; they were. I could take them back tomorrow and trade them in on something we really needed, though what that might be, I didn't know, since it seemed to me we had enough things to last us our lifetimes.

The next package contained purple and silver placemats of such stunning hideousness that I had to call Martin to see them. We puzzled over the enclosed card together, and I finally deciphered the crabbed handwriting.

'Martin! These are from Mrs Totino!'

'Mrs who?'

'The mother-in-law! The one who found out they were all missing! Why has she sent us a present?'

'Probably glad to have the house off her hands after all these years.'

'The money. I guess she's glad to have the money. The house did belong to her?' A sudden thought occurred to me. 'Has the family been officially declared dead?'

'Not yet. Later this year, in a few months, in fact. The check to buy the house went into the estate. It was a strange house closing. Bubba Sewell represented the estate. Mrs Totino, evidently, was appointed the conservator for the estate after a year. I don't think there are any other relatives.'

I lifted one of the suitcases to take it upstairs. 'I am headed for our own shower in our own bathroom with our own soap.'

'And a nap in our bed?' he asked.

'Yep. Right after I call Mother and tell her we're back.'

'Can I join you?'

'The phone call? The shower? The nap?'

'Maybe we can delay the phone call and work something in between the shower and the nap?'

'Could be,' I said musingly. 'But you'd better catch me quick, or the nap will claim me first.'

'I don't know if I can move fast enough,' Martin admitted, tucking the card back in the box with the placemats and walking through the living room to join me at the stairs, 'but I can try.'

He was fast enough. We inaugurated our new house in a very satisfactory manner.

After a day to rest, Martin went happily to work, and I settled into the rest of my life. The downstairs bathroom hadn't been completed, and I had to harass a few people over that, but the upstairs had been finished and it was beautiful. Our bedroom was French blue, gray, and white; I'd used Martin's bedroom furniture in the guest room, and his bedspread had been maroon and navy, so I had worked those colors in there. The anonymous little room now housed Martin's exercise equipment and the clothes that couldn't fit in our closet. The wood of the stairs had been refinished and polished and the carpet that ran throughout the top floor ran down the stairs, too, a light blue.

When I'd had the carpet ripped up downstairs, I'd found the floors were all hardwood, and had had them refinished. There was a large oriental rug in the living room, another in the dining room, and a runner going down the hall. We'd turned the downstairs bedroom into an informal 'family' sitting room. Martin's desk was in one corner, the television was in there, as well as a couple of comfortable chairs grouped with tables and lamps.

Jane Engle's mother's antique dining-room table and chairs now graced our dining room, and our living room was composed of things from Jane's, mine, and Martin's households, an eclectic mix but one that pleased the eye, I thought.

And the built-in bookcases lining the hall looked wonderful. Any space not taken up by books was filled with knick-knacks we'd gotten as wedding presents, a china bird here, a vase there. Two of Jane's bookcases – they were lawyer bookcases with wonderful glass doors – were in the family room, and the rest of the bookcases were in a storage lockup with some of Martin's things, awaiting our final decision.

I wondered what had happened to the Julius family's belongings.

I was sitting at the butcher-block table in the kitchen, drinking my coffee and trying to suppress the desire for another piece of toast, when I saw Shelby Youngblood coming down the stairs to the apartment. He walked around the far side of the garage and I heard a car start. They must have decided that was the most discreet place to park. He backed out, used the concrete turnaround apron, and left (I presumed) for work. His car crunched as it hit the gravel; sooner or later we would have to have the rest of the driveway paved. I thought about Angel Youngblood in her peach and green apartment, and I remembered what Amina had blurted out before the wedding. Amina's concern had stuck to me like a cockleburr, irritating and hard to dislodge.

I found myself wondering what Angel would do with herself all day. It wasn't really any of my business; but I am curious about the people around me. They're what I use to keep myself entertained.

I put the breakfast dishes in the dishwasher, wiped the counters, and went upstairs to get dressed. After wearing all my new 'honeymoon' clothes, it was nice to get back into my oldest blue jeans and my mystery bookstore T-shirt. I did put on some makeup, so as not to give Martin too complete a shock when he came home today. I had picked out my red-framed glasses to wear and was brushing my hair and planning my day when I heard a double rap on the kitchen door.

Angel was wearing one of those spandex exercise outfits that practically outline your arteries and veins. This bra-and-shorts combination was in a striking black and pink flame design. She had a warmup jacket on over the bra. Her legs were long columns of muscle ending in heavy pink socks and black running shoes.

'Welcome back,' she said briefly.

'Come in.'

'Just for a minute.'

'Thanks for arranging all the furniture.'

She shrugged and managed a smile. It suddenly dawned on me that Angel was shy.

'I just dropped by before my run to tell you that later, when you're ready, I can come help you move the living-room stuff into the position you want. We just kind of put it to where it looked like a real room, but I figured you would want to rearrange when you got home.' Angel had to look down and down at me, but she didn't seem either to mind or to feel it gave her an edge.

'Angel, what are you exactly?'

'Huh?'

'Are you my employee? Martin's employee, like Shelby? If so, what's your job description? I feel like I'm missing something.'

I hoped I wasn't being rude, but it made me feel uneasy, her doing me all these favors, since she wasn't a personal friend. If she was getting paid for it, that was another matter.

That proved to be the case.

'Martin pays Shelby and me,' she answered after looking at me consideringly for a moment. 'Of course, Shelby gets a paycheck from the plant, but we get some money besides. For helping you all out here. Because this house is a little far from town, out of earshot . . . and Martin's gone a lot, Shelby tells me.'

'Sit down, please.' We faced each other over the table. 'What does helping me out include?'

'Ah . . . well. Working in the yard, this is a lot of yard to keep trimmed and mowed and planted. And if you need heavy things done in the house. And to house-sit when you go somewhere and Martin's gone, too . . . like that.'

We regarded each other intently. This was very interesting. What on earth had this woman's life been like?

'Thanks, Angel,' I said finally, and she shifted a little in her chair. 'Have a good run.' She rose without haste, nodded, and drifted to the kitchen door, which opened onto the backyard.

'I'll be thinking about the living room while you run, and maybe later after you shower and everything, you could come over.'

'Sure,' she said, sounding relieved. 'Should be about an hour, maybe a little longer.'

'Fine.' And I closed the door behind her, leaned against it, and wondered what she hadn't told me.

At the end of a morning spent moving heavy objects, I knew a little more about Angel. She and Shelby had been married for seven years. They had worked together on their previous job. What that job was, was vague. I am southern enough to have trouble asking direct questions; I'd used up my quota for the day that morning in the kitchen. And Angel, whether deliberately or not, did not respond to anything but flat-out bald-faced directness. I still had no clear fix on her character.

Martin had a lunch meeting that day, and Mother was taking some clients out, so I sat down at the kitchen table and worked out a meal plan for the week, which was one of the things I'd heard good housewives did, and shopped at the grocery accordingly. I'd cooked for Martin before, of course, and he'd grilled meat for us many times, but this would be the first meal I cooked for him as his wife in our new home, and I thought it should be fancy, but not so fancy that he got inflated ideas about what our daily cuisine would be and also not so difficult that I ruined it. We'd gotten at least five cookbooks as wedding presents, and I mildly looked forward to our eating our way through them.

I sat in our little family room and watched the news, reading through our backlog of magazines during the ads. Then I wrote some more thank-you's, managing to acknowledge over half the gifts that had arrived in our absence. When I walked to the end of the drive to put the notes in the mailbox, I noticed for the first time that the Youngbloods had put up their own mailbox. That made sense, since we had the same address; it was a problem I hadn't thought of before, and here it was already solved. I ambled back up the drive, looking idly through the load of bills and occupant notices and free samples I'd found in the box. As we'd decided in our premarital counseling, I would be responsible for paying the month-to-month bills from our joint account, into which Martin and I each deposited a predetermined amount from our separate incomes. So I pulled out our brand-new joint checkbook, paid the bills, and signed the checks 'Aurora Teagarden.'

Okay, okay. I'd kept my name, that absurd and ridiculous name that had been my bane my whole life. When it got right down to it, I just couldn't become anyone else. Martin had had a hard time about that, but I had a gut feeling I was right. When I feel like that, I am fairly immovable. And I can't tell you how much better it made me feel. I had my own money, I had my own friends and family, I had my own name. I was one lucky woman, I told myself as I sliced strawberries.

Martin opened the front door and yelled gleefully, 'Hi, honey! I'm home!'

I started laughing.

I was actually able to turn from the sink and say, 'Hello, dear. How did your day go?' just like a sitcom mom.

I was one lucky, uneasy woman.

Chapter Eight

The next morning, on a whim, I went to Peachtree Leisure Apartments, a sort of independent old folks' home, as Neecy Dawson had so cheerfully pointed out. I'd been there before to visit various people, but not in a long time. There'd been a few changes. Before, there'd been a directory in the large lobby, and you could just walk in and take the elevator to the floor you needed. Now, there was a very large black man with a narrow mustache seated at a desk, and the directory was gone. There was a television camera pointed from one corner that embraced almost the whole lobby area.

'They was getting robbed,' the man explained when I asked about the change. 'People was coming in here, reading a name and apartment number, and just wandering through the building till they found who they wanted. They'd sell them magazines the old people didn't need, if they thought the old person was senile enough, or they'd just rob them if the old folks were feeble. So now I am here. And at night, from five until eleven, there's another man. Now, who did you come to see?'

Somewhat shaken at this picture he painted of wolves roaming the halls in Peachtree Leisure Apartments, I told him I'd come to see Mrs Melba Totino.

'She expecting you, Miss?'

'Mrs No, Ms' What was I going to call myself? He was eyeing me warily. 'No, Mrs Totino isn't expecting me. I just came to thank her for the wedding present.'

'She *gave* you something?' The brown eyes widened in a burlesque of surprise. 'You *must* be a friend.'

'I take it this is unusual?'

But after his little joke, he wasn't going to say anything else.

'I'll call her, if you just wait a minute,' he said.

He picked up the phone, dialed, and told Melba Totino about my presence in the lobby. She would see me.

'Go on up,' he said. 'She don't get too many visitors.'

The elevator smelled like a doctor's office, like rubbing alcohol and disinfectant and cold steel. The guard had told me there was a physician's assistant actually in residence; and of course a doctor on call. There was a cafeteria in the building for those who 'enrolled' for that service, and groceries could be delivered from one of the local stores. Everything was very clean, and the lobby had been dotted with old people who at least looked alert and comfortable, if not exactly happy. I supposed, if you couldn't live entirely on your own, this would be a good place to live.

Mrs Totino's apartment was on the third floor. I could tell by the spacing of the doors that some apartments were larger than others. Hers was one of the small ones. I knocked, and the door swung open almost before I could remove my hand.

I could look her straight in the eyes, so she wasn't more than five feet tall. Her eyes were dark brown, sunk in wrinkles that were themselves blotched with age spots. She had a large nose and a small mouth. Her wispy white hair was escaping from a small bun on the back of her head. She wore no glasses, which surprised me. Her ludicrously cheerful yellow and orange striped dress was covered with a gray sweater and the air that rushed out smelled strongly of air freshener, talcum powder, and cooking.

'Yes?' Her voice was deep and pleasant, not shaky as I'd expected.

'I'm Aurora Teagarden, Mrs Totino.'

'That's what Duncan said. Now, what kind of name is Duncan for a black man? I ask you.' And she backed into her apartment to indicate I should enter. 'I asked him that, too,' she said with great amusement at her own daring. 'I said, "I never knew no black man called Duncan before." He said, "What you think I should be called, Miz Totino? LeRoy?" That Duncan! I laughed and laughed.'

Who-wee, what a knee-slapper. I bet Duncan had thought so, too.

'Have a seat, have a seat.'

I looked around me nervously. There were seats to be had, but everything was so busy I wasn't sure if they were occupied or not. The sofa and matching chair were violently flowered in orange and brown and cream. The table between the chair and the sofa contained a *TV Guide*, the ugliest lamp in the universe, a red-and-white glass dish containing hard candy, a pair of reading glasses, a box of Kleenex, and a stunningly sentimental figurine of a little girl with big eyes petting a cuddly puppy with the legend across the base, 'My Best Friend.' I finally decided one of the couch cushions was empty and lowered myself gingerly down.

'This apartment building is very nice,' I offered.

'Oh, yes, the new security makes all the difference in the world! Can I get you a cup of coffee? I'm afraid I only have instant decaffeinated.'

Then why have coffee at all? 'No, thank you.'

'Or a – Coke? I think I have a Coke stuck in the refrigerator.'

'Okay, thanks.'

She walked bent over, and haltingly. In the jammed tiny room there were two doorways, one at the rear left leading into the kitchen and one at the right into the bedroom. I heard the sounds of fumbling and muttering in the kitchen and took the chance to look around me.

The walls were covered with doodads of every description. Gold-tone butterflies in a group of three, one rather pretty painting of a bowl of flowers, two awful prints of cherubic children being sweet with cute animals, a straw basket holding dried flowers that looked extremely dusty, a plaque with The Serenity Prayer . . . I began to feel dazed at the multitude of things that presented themselves for inspection. I thought of all the room in our house and felt a stir of guilt.

Then the television caught my attention. All this time it had been on, but I had not paid any attention to the picture. I realized now that the scene I was seeing was the apartment building lobby.

An old man with a walker moved slowly across the screen as I watched. Good Lord. I wondered if many of the residents chose to watch life in their lobby.

Mrs Totino tottered back into the room with a glass of Coke and ice clutched in her shaking hand. The ice was tinkling against the glass with a quick tempo that was distinctly nerve-wracking.

'Did you like the placemats?' Mrs Totino asked suddenly and loudly.

We negotiated the transfer of the Coke from her hand to mine.

'I've never seen any like them,' I said sincerely.

'Now, I know you won't be offended when I tell you that they were wedding presents for T.C. and Hope. They'd been packed away in a drawer for these many years, and I thought, why not let someone else enjoy them? And they've never been used – it's not like I gave you a *used* gift!'

'Recycled,' I suggested.

'Right, right. Everything's this recycling now! I recycled them.'

I had hoped to see a picture of the Julius family, but in all this clutter, there were only two photographs, in a double frame balanced precariously on the television set. Both photographs were very old. One showed a stern small woman with dark hair and eyes standing stiffly beside a somewhat taller man with lighter hair and a thin-lipped shy face. They were wearing clothes dating from somewhere around the twenties, I thought. In the other picture, two girls who strongly resembled each other, one about ten and the other perhaps twelve, hugged each other and smiled fixedly at the camera.

'Me and my sister, her name's Alicia Manigault, isn't that a pretty name?' Mrs Totino said fondly. 'I've always hated my name, Melba. And the other picture is the only one ever taken of my parents.'

'Your sister is still . . . does she live close?'

'New Orleans,' Mrs Totino said. 'She has a little house in Metairie, that's right by New Orleans.' She sighed heavily. 'New Orleans is a beautiful place; I envy her. She never wants to come see me. I go there every now and then. Just to see the city.'

I wondered why she didn't just move. 'You have relatives here now, Mrs Totino?'

'No, not since . . . not since the tragedy. Of course you know about that.'

I nodded, feeling definitely self-conscious.

'Yet you bought the house, or your husband bought it for you, I understand from Mr Sewell.'

'Yes, ma'am.'

'You aren't scared? Other people backed down from buying it at the last minute.'

'It's a beautiful house.'

'Not haunted, is it? I don't believe in that stuff,' said Mrs Totino robustly. I looked surreptitiously for a place to deposit my glass. The Coke was flatter than a penny on a railroad track.

'I don't either.'

'When that lawyer with the stupid name called to say someone really wanted to buy it, and he said it was a couple about to be married, I thought, I'll just send them a little something . . . after all these years, the house will be lived in again. What kind of shape was it in?'

So I told her about that, and she asked me questions, and I answered her, and all the while she never talked about what I was most interested in. Granted, the disappearance of her daughter, her granddaughter, and her son-in-law had to have been dreadful, but you would think she would mention it. Aside from that stiff reference to 'the tragedy' she didn't bring it up. Of course she was most interested in changes we had made to the apartment over the garage, the one built for her, the one she'd inhabited such a short time. Then she moved to the house, conversationally. Had we repainted? Yes, I told her. Had we reroofed? No, I told her, the real estate agent had ascertained that Mr Julius had had a new roof put on when he bought the house.

'He came here to be near relatives?' I asked carefully.

'His relatives,' she said with a sniff. 'His aunt Essie never had any children, so when he retired from the Army, he and Charity moved here to be close to her. He'd saved for years to start his own business, doing additions onto houses, carpentry work, stuff he'd always wanted to do. He could have gone anywhere he wanted, but he picked here,' she said gloomily.

'And asked you to live with them?'

'Yes,' she admitted. 'Want some more Coke? There's half a can left in the kitchen. No? Yes, they had figured out how they could add an apartment on the garage. Didn't want me in the house with 'em. So I moved from New Orleans – I'd been sharing a place with my sister – and came up here. Left her down there.' She shook her head. 'Then this all happened.'

'So,' I said, about to ask something very nosy but unable to stop myself, 'why did you stay?'

'Why?' she repeated blankly.

'After they disappeared. Why did you stay?'

'Oh,' she said with comprehension. 'I get you. I stayed here in case they turned up.'

'Don't you think that's kind of eerie, Martin?' I asked that night, as he put away the leftovers and I washed the dishes.

'Eerie? Sentimental, maybe. They're obviously not going to turn up alive, after all these years.'

I recalled the saccharine pictures in the apartment, the figurine. All very sentimental. 'Maybe so,' I conceded reluctantly.

'Did you see that Angel and I had rearranged the living room?' I asked after a moment. I squeezed out my sponge and pulled the plug. The sink water drained out with a big gurgle, like a dragon drinking water.

'It looks good. I think the gallery table Jane left you needs some work, though. One of the legs is loose.'

'I think maybe you'd better tell me about the Youngbloods, Martin.'

'I told you, Shelby needed a job . . .'

I gathered my courage. 'No, Martin, tell me really.'

He was hanging up the dishtowel on a rack mounted beside the sink. He got it exactly straight.

'I wondered when you were going to ask,' he said finally.

'I wondered when you were going to tell.'

He turned to face me and leaned against the counter. I leaned against the one at right angles to him. I crossed my arms across my chest. His sleeves were rolled up and his tie was loosened. He crossed his arms across his chest, too. I wondered what a body-language expert would make of this.

'Are the Youngbloods my jailers? Are they here to keep an eye on me?' I thought I'd lead off with the most obvious question.

Martin swallowed. My heart was pounding as if I'd been running.

'I knew Shelby in Vietnam,' he began. 'He helped me get through it.'

I nodded, just to show I was registering this information.

'After the war . . . after our part of the war . . . I'd met some intelligence people in Vietnam. I spoke some Spanish already, and so did Shelby. We had some Hispanic guys in our unit and we spoke Spanish with them, got a lot better. It was something to do.'

Martin's knuckles were white as he gripped his crossed arms.

'So, after we left Nam, we left the Army but we signed on with another company that was really the government.'

'You were asked?'

'Yes.' His eyes met mine for the first time, the pale brown eyes edged with black lashes and brows that were Martin's most immediately striking feature. 'We were asked. And in our – working with us, was Jimmy Dell Dunn, a swamp boy from Florida who'd grown up next to some exiled Cubans. His Spanish was even better than ours.' Martin half smiled and shook his head at some fleeting memory of a time and place I couldn't even imagine.

'What we did was,' he resumed, 'sell guns. Really, we were giving them away. But it was supposed to seem like we were an independent company selling them. What can I say, Roe? I thought, at least at the beginning, that I was doing something good for my country. I never made any personal profit. But it's become harder and harder to know who the good guys are.' He was looking out the window into the night. I wondered if the

Youngbloods could look outside the side window of their apartment and down into our kitchen. I could not move to draw the curtain.

And Martin had his own private view of darkness.

Guns. Guns were better than drugs. Right? Of course with all Martin's trips to South America, I had been worried Martin's pirate side had led him into the dangerous and lucrative drug trade, though Martin had often expressed profound contempt for those who used drugs and those who sold them. Guns were better.

'And we delivered them, in some very remote places, to right-wing groups. Some of these people were okay, some were crazy. They were all very tough. A few were just – bandits.'

I pulled my glasses off and rubbed my eyes with my hand. I had a headache. I put them back on and pushed them up on my nose with a finger. I stared past Martin's arm. I needed to get some Bon Ami and really scrub that sink.

'And one day – it was about midmorning, we were up in the Chama Mountains . . . we were making a delivery to one of the better guys. Out of nowhere, we were ambushed by another group who'd heard somehow about the delivery. I got the scar on my shoulder, Shelby got a worse wound in the leg. And Jimmy Dell got his head blown off.'

I took in my breath quickly. I was married to man who had witnessed this barbarity, this horror, had been part of it. I began to shiver. I wanted this story over.

'Shelby and I got out of there, just barely. We had to leave Jimmy Dell, and he was our pilot. Shelby knew enough about the copter to get us out, though he was bleeding like a stuck pig. And then it took us a while to heal. We heard the group we were supposed to take the guns to were all dead before we got there. When we came back to the States, Shelby went to see Jimmy Dell's family in Florida. Jimmy Dell had been the oldest kid by far, and there were five more after him. The youngest one was Angel. She was too young then, Shelby thought, and Mr Dunn surely thought so, too. So Shelby wandered for a while.'

And Martin had gone to stay on that isolated farm in Ohio with a man he hated, just to have a familiar place to recover. And while he was there, he hooked back up with Cindy. And they married. And he never told her this. Or not all of it. Ridiculously, I could not stop shivering.

'After a few years Shelby went back to Florida. Angel had gotten interested in martial arts in high school after something happened to her, and she got Shelby interested, too. They got married, and they began working as a team of bodyguards.'

Gee, I wondered whom you would work for in southern Florida.

'But they didn't want to work for that kind.' My face must have spoken for me. 'So later, mostly they worked at the smaller movie studios up and down the East Coast, guarding people who were there temporarily. Some of the people were pretty famous.' Martin attempted a smile. 'And they did some stunts in karate movies, too. Their last job was for a woman who told Shelby she owed a lot of money to the wrong people.

'She didn't owe it, Roe.' Martin looked directly at me. 'She'd stolen it, and they found her. They let the Youngbloods live, but they gave them a beating they'd remember. Angel was in the hospital, still, when Shelby came up here to find me. In their line of work, you can't get insurance, and they were broke, and they needed to leave the area for a while. I'd been worried about you being out here by yourself when I was out of town, and the apartment being empty . . . you're shaking.'

He came over to me in two steps, waited a moment to see if I would hit him if he touched me, then put his arms around me. I felt his heavy muscles encircle me, and I had the stray thought that the workouts I had attributed to a desire to stay fit and look good were actually aimed toward keeping him ready for self-defense. I lay my head against his thick chest and let some of the shaking be absorbed by him.

'So,' he said to the top of my hair, almost in a whisper, 'what's going to happen now?'

'I'm going to get some Bon Ami and scrub the sink.'

Martin held me away from him. He was angry. 'I'll go in the family room and work until you feel like talking.'

He left the kitchen through the hall door, his shoes making little noises on the hardwood as he crossed the hall.

I got the Bon Ami and a sponge with a rough scrubbing side, and set to work. I thought of a conversation I'd had with my mother. We'd been talking about love, and she'd said that women who stay with men who damage them have some deep need to be damaged; they can't possibly love the damager, that can't be the reason they stay. A woman with a strong sense of self-preservation will leave the bad relationship to save herself; the self-preservation will kill the love, so the individual will leave and be saved from further harm. My mother had cited herself: When my father had begun to be unfaithful, she had left, and she no longer loved him.

I loved Martin so much it made me catch my breath, sometimes. He had not told me the whole truth. I was going to stay. I had no idea what he was thinking, sitting there in our new room in our new house.

I rinsed the Bon Ami out of the sink. It was gleaming. It had probably never been so clean in its entire existence.

I seemed unable to string a coherent chain of thought together. I was relieved beyond measure that it hadn't been drugs. I would have had to leave. Guns were bad. Could I live with guns? I could live with the guns. And why on earth had Martin fallen in love with me, anyway? It was like a mating between a Martian and a Venusian. I doubled over and put my head on my arms on the counter and began to cry.

Martin heard and came in. He hated it when I cried. He turned me around and held me, and this time I pressed against him, hard, as though I were trying to crawl inside his skin. After a few moments, this had the inevitable effect, even under the emotional circumstances. Martin moved restlessly, and I kept my arms wrapped around him and raised my face to his.

Chapter Nine

Martin left for work the next morning still eyeing me warily but apparently relieved that I was quietly working on whatever reaction his revelations had raised.

I watched him walk to the garage. I had the window open to let in the cool morning air, so I heard him tell Madeleine in no uncertain terms to get off the hood of his Mercedes. Martin was so fond of his car that he would not leave it parked at the airport when he had to catch a plane, but instead invariably took one of the company cars, so the cat was living dangerously. Madeleine sauntered insolently out of the garage as Martin backed out, reversed on the concrete apron, and took off down the gravel. I went out with the bag of cat food and filled her bowl. She rewarded me with a perfunctory purr. I sat on the steps in my bathrobe and watched her eat every bit of kibble.

I went through the rest of my little morning rituals in the same numb way. I'd been faced with something so bizarre it was just going to take me a little time to assimilate it. I thought of the men some of my classmates had married: a hardware store owner, an insurance salesman, a farmer, a lawyer. My dating a police officer had been thought very exotic by my friends. Police officers were too close to the wormy side of life, the side we didn't see because we didn't turn rocks over.

For whatever reason.

From our beautiful triple bedroom windows that looked out over our front yard, and across the road, to rolling fields, I spied Angel Youngblood going out for her morning run. This time she was wearing solid gold. She did her stretches, in itself an impressive sight, and then she began to run. I watched her lope down the driveway and out onto the road, long legs pumping in rhythm, blond ponytail bouncing. Angel was energetic. Soon she would be bored.

I had an idea.

I was watching for her when she came back, and when I figured she'd had time to shower and dress, I called her. I'd found their number written on the pad by the telephone on Martin's desk when I'd gone to make an errand list the day before.

'Angel,' I said after she answered. 'If you wouldn't mind coming over after you've run whatever errands you need to run, I have a project.'

That morning I grasped the true beauty of the concept of having an employee. Angel and I didn't know each other, were bound by no ties of friendship or kin or community, but she was bound to help me achieve my goal.

And since Angel was an employee, she had to help me without protest. She had come over in blue jeans and a T-shirt and sneakers, looking like a healthy farm girl who tossed bales of hay up to the loft with her bare hands. I had braided my hair to keep it out of the way. I had assembled a retractable metal tape measure, a pad and pencil, and a copy of the most comprehensive newspaper article dealing with the Julius family's disappearance. I'd had that stuck away in a file for years, since I'd thought of doing a presentation on it for the Real Murders Club.

I intended, of course, to find the Julius family.

I handed the article to Angel and waited till she read it.

> Police continue their search for the T. C. Julius family, reported missing yesterday morning by Mrs Julius's mother, Melba Totino.
>
> Mrs Totino called the police after walking across to the family home from her adjacent garage apartment Saturday morning and finding no one at home. After some hours of waiting, and the discovery that the family car and truck were still in the garage, Mrs Totino reported the disappearance.
>
> Missing are T. C. Julius, a retired army sergeant who had hoped to open a business locally; his wife, Hope; and their

> daughter Charity, 15. Julius is described as 5–11, 185 pounds, 46, with graying . . . brown hair and blue eyes. Hope Julius has dark brown hair, blue eyes, is 5–4 and 100 pounds. She is 42 years old, and is suffering from cancer. Charity Julius, who had just begun attending the Lawrenceton High School, has blue eyes and shoulder-length brown hair. She is approximately 5–4 and 120 pounds.
>
> The Juliuses had moved to Lawrenceton four months ago to be close to Mr Julius's only surviving relative, his aunt, Essie Nyland. Mrs Nyland is described by friends as being distraught at the disappearance. 'She'd been so happy at T.C. moving here, since she's in poor health,' said one neighbor, Mrs Lyndower Dawson. 'I'm afraid this will finish her.'
>
> The day before the disappearance appeared to be a normal one, Mrs Totino told local authorities. She reported spending most of the day in her own apartment and joining the family for meals, as usual. She said Harley Dimmoch, a friend of Charity Julius's from their previous hometown of Columbia, S.C., visited the family. He left before dark, having spent the day helping Mr Julius around the house.
>
> In the late afternoon, local contractor Parnell Engle arrived to pour the concrete for a new patio T. C. Julius had planned at the rear of the house. He saw and spoke to Hope and Charity Julius, who both seemed normal at that time.
>
> Detective Jack Burns describes his department as 'pursuing all leads with the utmost vigor.'
>
> 'It doesn't look as though they left voluntarily, since the family vehicles are still in the garage,' he commented. 'On the other hand, there are no signs of violence and all their possessions are still here.'
>
> . . . He urged any resident who has knowledge of the Julius family to call the police station immediately.

There were pictures with the article: a shot of the house and a studio portrait of the family. T. C. Julius was a sturdy man with an aggressive smile and a square face. His wife, Hope, looked thin, frail, and ill, shrunken to the same size and frame as their teenage daughter. Charity Julius had shoulder-length hair that turned under neatly and an oval face like her mother's. She wasn't a pretty girl, but she was attractive, and she held herself like a girl who's used to being a force to reckon with.

'That's this house,' Angel commented, studying the picture. She checked the date at the top of the article. 'Over six years ago.'

'Where do you think they are?' I asked.

'I think they're dead,' she answered without hesitation. 'He just moved here. He was going to open a new business. No mention of trouble in the marriage. No mention of the daughter getting into trouble with the law. He'd just built the apartment for the mother-in-law, so he must have been able to tolerate her. No apparent reason for him to do a flit, especially taking the wife and daughter with him.'

'I think they're still here. The car was still here.'

'But the killer could have taken them away in his or her own car,' Angel objected reasonably. 'What if the Dimmoch boy took them away and dumped them on the way home?'

'Then why haven't the bodies turned up?'

'Not found yet. They haven't found Hoffa, have they?'

I would not be daunted. 'I just think with the car here, with the bodies not having been found elsewhere, that the chances are good they're here somewhere.'

'So, what do you want us to do?'

'I want us to measure every wall and floor and anything else we can think of.'

'You don't think the police did all that?'

'I don't know what they did, and I'm not sure I can find out. But I'll try. This is just step one.'

'Step one. Huh.' She thought about it for a second and shrugged. 'Where do we start?'

'The apartment, I'm afraid.'

'But the mother-in-law, Totino, says she was in the apartment all day. Or at least most of the day,' Angel amended, checking the story again.

'So we start with the least likely and eliminate that,' I said.

Angel looked at me consideringly. 'Okay,' she said, and we gathered our paraphernalia and started to work.

We were halted after an hour and a half by the arrival of Susu Hunter, who had been my friend my whole life. She hollered from the front porch.

'Roe! I know you're here somewhere!'

Angel and I extracted ourselves from the tool shed at the back of the garage, dusty and warm and fairly covered with cobwebs. The toolshed was an area I had overlooked during my house renovation. You could tell Mr Julius had intended to use it often: There was pegboard lining the walls with hooks still protruding, and a workbench with a powerful fluorescent light overhead had been added. He had also altered the doors, apparently: They were extra-wide doors that swung back completely. Now it held some boxes of tools Martin had apparently not opened since he had been transferred to Chicago and lived in an apartment instead of a house. The boxes were keeping company with a lawnmower whose pedigree I could not figure out; perhaps it had been Jane Engle's. Assorted rakes, hoes, shovels, a sledgehammer, and an ax filled out our tool repertoire. Everything was grimy.

So, as I say, when Angel and I emerged, we weren't at our best.

'Look at you, Roe!' Susu said in some amazement. 'What on earth have you been doing?'

'Rearranging the garage,' I said, not untruthfully. We had done a certain amount of straightening since we were in there already. 'Susu, this is Angel Youngblood, a new arrival to Lawrenceton.'

Susu said warmly, 'We're so glad to have you here! I hope you like our little town. And if you don't have a church home yet, we'd just love to have you at Calgary Baptist.'

I wished I had a camera tucked in my pocket. Angel's face was a picture. But underneath the gritty life she'd led in the past few years, Angel Dunn Youngblood was a true daughter of the South. She rallied.

'Thank you. We like it here very much so far. And thanks so much for inviting us to your church, but right now Shelby and I are very interested in Buddhism.'

I turned to Susu in anticipatory pleasure.

'How fascinating!' she exclaimed, without missing a beat. 'If you ever have a free Wednesday noon, first Wednesday in the month, we'd love to have you come speak at the Welcome to Town Luncheon.'

'Oh. Thanks so much. Excuse me now, I'm expecting Shelby to come home to eat in half an hour or so.' And Angel retired gratefully, bounding up the stairs to their apartment. I was relieved to see a little smile – a nonmalevolent smile – on her thin lips as she shut the door behind her.

'What an interesting woman,' Susu said with careful lack of emphasis.

'She really is,' I said sincerely.

'How on earth did she come to be living in your garage apartment?'

We began to stroll toward the house. Susu looked pretty, and a few pounds heavier than she'd been the year before. She'd just had her hair done in a defiant blond, and she was wearing sky blue polka-dotted slacks with a white shirt.

'Oh, her husband is a friend of Martin's.'

'Is he any bigger than her?'

'A little.'

'No children, I guess?'

'No . . .'

'Because I hate to think what size baby they'd have.'

I laughed, and we began to talk about Susu's 'babies,' Little Jim and Bethany. Bethany was heavily involved in tap dancing, and Little Jim, the younger by a couple of years, was up to his brown belt in Tae Kwon Do.

'And Jimmy?' I asked casually. 'How's he doing?'

'We're going to family therapy,' Susu said in the voice of one determined not to be ashamed. 'And though it's early to tell, Roe, I really think it's going to do us some good. We just went along for too long ignoring how we were really feeling, just scraping the surface to keep everything looking good for the people around us. We should have been more concerned about how things really were with us.'

What an amazing speech for Susu Saxby Hunter to have made. I gave her a squeeze around the shoulders. 'Good for you,' I said inadequately and warmly. 'I know if you both try, it'll work.'

Susu gave me a shaky smile and then said briskly, 'Come on! Show me this dream house of yours!'

Susu's dream house was the one her parents had left her, the one her grandparents had built. No house would ever measure up to it in her sight, and she was fond of dismissing our friends' new homes in new subdivisions as 'houses, not homes!' But she pronounced this house a real home.

'Does it ever give you the creeps?' she asked with the bluntness of old friends.

'No,' I said, not surprised she'd asked. Old friends or not, quite a lot of people had asked me that one way or another. 'This is a peaceful house. Whatever happened.'

'I'll bet sometimes you just wonder where they are.'

'You're right, Susu. I do. I wonder that all the time.'

Susu gave a theatrical shudder. 'I'm glad it's yours and not mine,' she said. 'Can I smoke?'

'No, not inside. Let's sit out on the porch. I have one ashtray to go out there on the porch furniture.'

There was now a swing attached to the roof of the porch, and some pretty outside chairs arranged in a circle including the swing. There were two or three small tables available, and I found an ashtray for Susu to use.

While we sat and talked of this and that, Shelby Youngblood pulled into the driveway and waved as he emerged from his car. We waved back and he ran up the stairs to his apartment, to his Angel.

'Wow, he is big,' Susu commented. 'Not a looker, is he?'

'I think he is,' I said, surprising myself.

'And you're the woman married to Hunk of the Year.'

'Shelby is attractive,' I said firmly. 'I may be married, but I'm not blind.'

'All those acne scars!'

'Just make him look lived-in.'

'Does Martin come home for lunch?'

'So far, no. But he's still catching up from the time we spent away.'

'Jimmy had Rotary today. Let's go in the kitchen and scrounge around for lunch.'

We ate ham sandwiches and grapes and potato chips, and talked about my honeymoon and the latest meeting of the Ladies' Prayer Luncheon. My old friend Neecy Dawson had objected to the guest speaker's theology in loud, persistent terms, casting the ladies into a turmoil, and causing not a few of them to express the opinion it was time Neecy met God face-to-face.

'She was a friend of Essie Nyland's, wasn't she?' I asked casually.

'Neecy? Yep. Essie was a good friend of my grandmother's, too, outlived her by twenty years, I guess. Miss Essie died . . . what? Six years ago now, must be. Neecy's still going strong. She still knows everyone in this town, what they've done, and when they did it.'

It struck me that I could have a profitable conversation with Miss Neecy. She'd told me of the arguments between the Zinsners when they built this house. It was that conversation that had given me the idea that there might be several hidey-holes the bodies of the Julius family could be in. That was the reason for the ground-zero search Angel and I were conducting.

'You remember when the Julius family vanished?' I asked. I picked up Susu's empty plate and my own and carried them over to the sink, admiring my new stoneware as I did every time I looked at it. Earth tones in a southwestern pattern . . . why on earth I, a native Georgian, felt compelled to have southwestern dishes I do not know.

'Yes,' Susu said. 'I'd just had Little Jimmy. You were working at the library, I think you'd only been there a year, right?'

'Right. Over six years ago, now.' We shook our heads simultaneously at Time's inexorable march.

Susu looked at her watch and gave a little shriek. 'Woops! Roe! I was supposed to pick up old Mrs Newsman at the beauty parlor ten minutes ago! I'm sorry, I've got to run! I invited myself and then I stick you with the dishes,' she wailed, and yanked her car keys out of her purse on her way out the front door.

I stuck the dishes unceremoniously in the dishwasher, started our supper pork chops marinating in honey and soy sauce and garlic, and sat down to make one of those lists that were supposed to make me much more efficient.

1. Finish measuring the house.
2. Talk to Miss Neecy about Essie Nyland, also the Zinsners – where was the boarded-up closet?
3. Possible to find the boyfriend, Harley Dimmoch?
4. See if Parnell Engle will tell me about the day he poured the concrete.
5. Ask Lynn or Arthur if I could see the file on the Julius disappearance, or if he would just tell me about it in detail.
6. See if I could worm anything out of Mrs Totino's lawyer, Bubba Sewell (who was incidentally my lawyer and the husband of my friend, the former Lizanne Buckley).

I was pleased. This looked as if it would keep me busy for quite a while. Right now, busy-ness was what I wanted. Maybe while I worked on the problem of the Juliuses, the problem of my husband's secret life would sort of solve itself.

Right.

Chapter Ten

'Sally,' I said quietly into the telephone on Martin's desk. 'I want to have lunch with you at my place or your place soon, okay? I need to ask you some questions. You covered the Julius disappearance, didn't you? Do you still have a file on it somewhere, of your notes you took at the time?' Sally, cohostess at my bridal shower, had worked at the *Lawrenceton Sentinel* for at least fifteen years.

'I don't keep my notes on fiftieth wedding anniversaries or who won the watermelon-seed-spitting contest, but I do keep my notes on major crimes.'

She sounded a little testy.

'Okay, okay!' I said hastily. 'I'm sorry. I don't know how reporters do things!'

'Yes, I have the file right here,' she said in a mollified tone. 'And I can certainly understand why you're interested. My better half – well, my other half – is attending a seminar in Augusta on interrogation techniques, so I'm footloose and fancy free for two days. What suits you?'

'What about here, tomorrow, for lunch at noon?' I asked. I knew Sally, like all of Lawrenceton, wanted to see the house.

I hung up as Martin came down the stairs, sweating and relaxed after his session with the Soloflex. He played racquetball at the Athletic Club too, but sometimes the hours didn't suit him. He liked having the exercise equipment at home.

'I'm sweaty,' he warned me. I didn't care since I could use a shower myself after my work in the garage that morning. Angel and I had finished our measurements later in the afternoon, and there was a four-inch question mark running down the middle of the garage, but I figured that was just where Mrs Zinsner had demanded Mr Zinsner make it a two-car garage. I didn't think four inches was enough space to hide three bodies, and Angel agreed.

I hugged Martin, sliding my hands around his waist and up his back.

'Roe,' he said hesitantly.

'Um?'

'Are you mad?'

'Yes. But I'm working on it.'

'Working on it.'

'Yeah. I suppose you didn't tell me all that before we got married in case I wouldn't marry you if I knew it. Is that right? Or did you just hope I wouldn't ever ask? Or did you just think I was desperate or stupid enough not to notice that there were a few holes in your story?'

'Well . . .'

'I'll give you a clue, Martin. There's only one correct answer to that.'

'I was afraid you wouldn't marry me if you knew.'

'And that was the correct answer.'

'Good.'

'So now I have to decide how I feel about you wanting me to enter into marriage, a very serious thing, not knowing all the facts about your life. Am I flattered that you were so anxious to keep me that you wouldn't risk it? Sure.' I traced his spine with my fingernail and felt him shiver. 'Am I angry that you treated me like some fifties little woman, the less I knew the better? You bet.' I dug the fingernail in. He gasped. 'Martin, you have to be honest with me. My self-respect – I can't stand being lied to, no matter how much I love you.'

The next day, the day I was going to have Sally Allison over to lunch, Martin and I had also been invited to dinner at the home of one of Pan-Am Agra's division chiefs. This man, Bill Anderson, was a new employee, hired by Martin's boss and sent to Lawrenceton to evaluate and expand the plant's safety program. So I woke with a certain sense of anticipation. Martin was shaving as I groped past him into the bathroom for a quick stop on my way downstairs to the coffeepot. We were beginning to find our routine.

He liked to be at his desk when the other Pan-Am Agra executives arrived. And Martin always looked spic and span. His clothes were all expensive and he liked his shirts taken to the laundry to be starched, which frankly suited me. I didn't mind in the least dropping them by or picking them up. I hated ironing worse than anything in the world, and Martin, who could do a competent job of it, didn't have the time or inclination unless there was an emergency.

Luckily, we both liked noncommunication until coffee had been consumed. He would come downstairs and make his own breakfast and pour his own coffee. By that time I would have finished the front section of the paper, which I had fetched from the end of the driveway. He would read that, then I would hand him the inside sections. Martin was not much interested in team sports, I had noted silently. One-on-one sports, now that was something he checked the scores on.

When Martin had finished the paper and his breakfast, we had a brief conversation about appointments for the day. He went upstairs to brush his teeth. I poured another cup of coffee and worked the crossword puzzle in the newspaper.

He came downstairs, gathered his briefcase, checked with me to make sure we didn't need to talk about anything else, told me he was going to be out of his office most of the afternoon, and kissed me good-bye. He was gone by seven thirty, or earlier.

I felt we had made a success of mornings, anyway. So far.

This morning Angel reported about eight thirty.

'Shelby says,' she began without preamble, 'that we need to find out if an aerial search was made, particularly of the fields around the house.'

'Hmmmm,' I said, and made a note on my list. 'I'll remember to ask that at lunch. A local reporter is a friend of mine, and she's coming over for lunch.'

'You sure have a social life.'

'Oh?'

'You're always having people over, or you go out, or people call you, seems like.'

'I grew up here. I expect if you were still in the town you were born in, it would be the same.'

'Maybe,' said Angel doubtfully. 'I've never had that many friends. When I grew up, we lived way out in the swamps. I had my brothers and sisters. What about you?'

'I have a half-brother, but he's in California. He's a lot younger than me.'

'Well, except for some Cubans, it was just us out there. We pretty much kept to ourselves. When I was a teenager, I began to date . . . but even then, I was usually glad to get home. I wasn't much good at small talk, and if you didn't talk and drink, they wanted to do the other thing, and I didn't.'

We smiled at each other for the first time.

Then Angel clammed up, and I realized she would only speak about herself in rationed drips, and I had had my allotment for the day.

We went out into the bright spring air to measure the outside of the house. Then we measured each inside room and drew a detailed map of our house.

'I guess sometime having this will come in handy,' I sighed, a comparison of figures having shown that the walls were only walls and not secret compartments with grisly contents. So much for a hidden closet.

'Oh, I'm sure,' Angel said drily. 'The next time someone wants to know how to get to the bathroom, all you have to do is tell him to go forty-one inches from the newel post, due east, then north two feet.'

I stared at her blankly for a second and then suddenly began to laugh.

Maybe our strange association was going to be more fun than either of us had anticipated.

Angel looked down at the plans.

'There was something in the attic,' she said.

'What! What?'

'Nothing, most likely. But you know the chimney comes up from the living room, runs up one end of your bedroom where you have a fireplace, goes through the attic and out the roof.'

'Right.'

'It seemed to me that in the attic there was too much chimney.'

'They might be sealed up in there,' I said breathlessly.

'They might not. But we can see.'

'Who can we call to knock it down?'

'Shoot, I can do it. But you got to think, here, Roe. What if there's nothing there? What if you're just knocking down a perfectly good chimney for the hell of it?'

'It's my chimney.' I crossed my arms on my chest and looked up at her.

'So it is,' she said. 'Then let's go. You go up there and look, and I'll go to the garage and get a sledgehammer and one or two other things we might need.'

I let down the attic steps and climbed up. In the heat of the little attic, with sunlight coming in through the circular vent at the back of the house, I calmed down. The attic was floored, with the old original floorboards, wide and heavy. They creaked a little as I crossed to look at the chimney. Sure enough, the bricks looked a little different from the bricks downstairs, though I couldn't say they looked newer. And the chimney was wider.

I remained skeptical. I felt sure the police would have noticed fresh brickwork.

Angel came up the stairs in a moment, the sledgehammer in her hand.

She eyed the bricks. She slid on a pair of clear plastic safety goggles. I stared at her.

'Brick fragments,' she said practically. 'You should stand well back, since you don't have safety glasses.'

I retreated as far as I could, back into an area where I could barely stand, and on Angel's further advice I turned my back to the action. I heard the thunk as the hammer hit the bricks, and then more and more thunks, until gradually that sound became accompanied by the noises of cracking and falling.

Then Angel was still, and I turned.

She was looking at something in the heap of dislodged bricks and mortar chips.

'Oh, shit,' she breathed.

I felt my skin crawl.

I scuttled over to Angel and stood by her looking down as she was doing.

In the rubble was a small figure wrapped in blankets blackened by smoke and soot.

My hand went up over my mouth.

We stood for the longest moments of my life, staring down at that little bundle.

Then I knelt and with shaking hands began to unwrap the blanket. A tiny white face looked up at me.

I screamed bloody murder.

I think Angel did, too, though she afterward denied it hotly.

'It's a doll,' she said, kneeling beside me and gripping my shoulders. 'It's a doll, Roe. It's china.' She shook me, and I believe she thought she was being gentle.

Later on, after we'd both showered and Angel had called a mason to come repair the chimney, we speculated on how the compartment had gotten sealed up, how the doll had been left inside. I figured that the story of Sarah May Zinsner's desire for a closet and her husband's sealing one up out of sheer cussedness had its basis in whatever had happened by the chimney. We ended up deciding that she'd ordered an extra frame of brickwork for shelving, to store – who knew what? Maybe she'd intended the shelving for the use of the maid who may have been living in the attic. But that final change had been the straw that had metaphorically broken John L. Zinsner's back. He'd had the shelves bricked up, and while the mason was working, perhaps one of the daughters of the house had set her wrapped-up 'baby' temporarily (she thought) on the shelves. Now I had it, all these years later, and it had scared the hell out of Angel and me.

Somehow, when my mother called while I was slicing strawberries for lunch, I didn't tell her about my morning's adventure. She would be horrified that I was looking for the Julius family; also, I didn't care to relate how deeply upset I'd been when I'd seen that tiny white face.

For once, she didn't sense that I was less than happy. That was remarkable, since we spoke on the phone or in person almost every day. She was all the family I had, since my father had moved with my half-brother to California. That was something I had in common, I realized, with the Julius family. They had been nearly as untangled from the southern cobweb of family connections as I was.

'I had a closing this morning,' Mother said. She was as proud of each sale as though it were her first, which I found sort of endearing. When I was in my early teens, when she'd begun to work but before she was independent and very successful, I'd felt each house she sold should be celebrated by a party. Mother seemed just as driven now as she had been after she'd separated from my father and become a needy wage earner; my father had never been too good about sending child support payments.

'Which one?' I asked, to show polite interest.

'The Anderton house,' she said. 'Remember, I told you I had it sold last week. I was scared until the last minute that they were going to back out. Some idiot told them about Tonia Lee Greenhouse.' Tonia Lee, a local Realtor, had been murdered in the master bedroom. 'But it went through.'

'That'll make Mandy happy. By the way,' the similar names had reminded me, 'we're going to dinner at Bill Anderson's tonight. You sold them a house, didn't you? What's his wife like?'

'Nice enough, not too bright, if I remember correctly. They're renting, with an option to buy.'

After we said our good-byes, and I returned to my task at the sink, hurrying because the attic escapade had made me late, I tried to imagine what my mother would do in my present predicament – but it was like trying to picture the pope tap dancing.

Sally arrived punctually, in a very expensive outfit that she intended to wear to rags. Sally had been forty-two for a number of years. She was an attractive woman with short permed bronzey hair. She was neither slim nor fat, neither short nor tall.

During the past two or three years, Sally had been close to breaking into the big time with a larger paper, but it just hadn't happened. She had settled for being the mentor and terror of the young cub reporters who regularly came and went at the *Sentinel* as they learned their trade.

For the first time, Sally gave me a ritual hug. It was a recognition of the big things I'd undergone since last we met, the fact that I was now a respectable married woman, and not only married, but married to a real prize, an attractive plant manager who presumably had an excellent income. This really can all be conveyed in a hug.

'You look great, Roe,' Sally pronounced.

I don't know why people seem impelled to tell brides that. Is regular sex supposed to make you prettier? A number of acquaintances had told me how great I looked since we'd come back from the honeymoon. Maybe only married sex made you look better.

'Thanks, Sally. Come on in and see the house.'

'I haven't been in here in years. Not since it happened. Oh, who would have known there were hardwood floors! It looks wonderful!' Sally followed me around, exclaiming appropriately at each point of interest.

As I put lunch on the table, she told me all about her son Perry and the wonderful girl he'd met in his therapy group, and about her husband Paul and the shakiness of their new marriage.

'Surely you can work it out, Sally! You had such high hopes when you married him, and it's only been a few months!'

'Fourteen,' she said precisely, spearing a strawberry with her fork.

'Oh. Well. Would marriage counseling help, do you think? Aubrey Scott is really good.'

'Maybe,' she said. 'We'll talk about it when Paul gets back from Augusta.'

'So, can you tell me all about the disappearance?' I asked gently, when she'd poked at her dill pickle for a few seconds of recovery.

'Do you have the stories from the *Sentinel*?'

'Yes, the main one. I really want to know what you didn't put in the paper, or what stuck out in your mind. Were you out here then?'

'Along with a slew of other reporters. Though I did get an exclusive for one day. The disappearance was really hot for a while, until a week had passed with no news. But being the local reporter paid off.'

Sally laid down her fork and opened her briefcase. She extracted a few pages of computer printout from a file folder.

'Those are your notes?' I'd expected a spiral notebook with scribbles.

'Yes,' Sally said with a hint of surprise. 'Of course I put them on a disk when I get back to the office. Let me see . . . this will be a reconstruction.' She glanced over the pages, organizing herself, and nodded.

'When the police got here,' she began . . .

There's an old woman standing out in the driveway. She's small, and gray, and alternately distraught and grumpy. Her name, she says, is Melba Totino, and she is the mother of Mrs Julius, Hope Julius. They're all gone, she says: Hope, and her husband, T.C., and their girl, Charity. They vanished in the night. She herself had risen at her usual hour and gone over to the house to prepare breakfast, as she always did. She had expected all of them to be there, even Charity, who had been home sick the day before. Charity is a sophomore at Lawrenceton High, newly enrolled. She'd had a hard six weeks getting used to being in a new school, missing her boyfriend, but finally she'd adjusted. She'd had a low fever the past couple of days. But Charity, sick or not, now wasn't in the house.

Melba Totino goes in by the front door, since the back door of the kitchen faced outward over a new expanse of concrete, poured the day before to make a patio. She is unsure whether or not it's okay to walk on the concrete yet, so she goes to the front. The door's unlocked. No lights on inside. No stirring, no movement.

Mrs Totino steps inside hesitantly, calling. She doesn't want to stroll in without warning. But no one answers her call. She creeps through the house, now anxious, looking about for signs of the untoward. The house is clean and peaceful. The cuckoo clock in the living room makes its brainless noise, and the old lady jumps.

Where is her daughter? Where is Hope? With approaching panic, the old lady finally screams up the stairs, but no one answers. Telling herself she is being ridiculous, and she'll give them a real talking to when they come home, Melba Totino sits at the kitchen table, waiting for someone to come. She doesn't dare to touch a thing. The dishes are all put away. There is no coffee perking, nothing baking in the oven. After half an hour, she walks back out the front door and looks in the garage. She hadn't bothered on her way over – why would she?

And now, as far as she can see, everything is the same. She doesn't drive, she doesn't know anything about cars, but this car is her daughter's family car, the truck is her son-in-law's pickup, with 'Julius Home Carpentry' proudly painted on the side, phone number right below. No one is in either vehicle.

She goes from the entrance to the garage past the stairs leading up to her apartment, across the covered walkway over to the house, into the big backyard. She is glad she has her sweater on, there's a nip in the air for sure. There's a turkey buzzard circling in the sky. The yard itself is empty. She looks up to the second story of the house, hoping to see movement at Charity's window, but there is nothing.

Bewildered, trying to keep her terror a secret from herself, the old woman walks slowly back to the front of the house, still trying to keep pristine that new concrete that the owners of the house will never see again. Finally, after some interminable hours, she calls the police.

'Parnell Engle drove by that morning in his pickup truck,' Sally explained, 'and since he'd poured the concrete the day before, naturally he glanced at the place as he went by. After he saw all the police cars there, he just happened to stop by the paper to check on his classified ad, and just happened to wander into the newsroom and let me know what he'd seen.'

'Naturally,' I agreed.

'Of course, this was a couple of years before he "found the Lord".' Sally said. 'Lucky for me, because I was able to talk to the old lady before any other reporters even knew something had happened. By the next day she wasn't talking to anyone. Wonder where she is now?'

'In Peachtree Leisure Apartments,' I said smugly. 'She gave me a wedding present.' It was not often I got to impart news to Sally.

'It's odd she chose to stay here, with no family. I gather she and her sister had been living in New Orleans. Wonder why she didn't go back?'

'She told me she was waiting for the Juliuses to turn up.'

Sally shuddered, and took a sip of her iced tea. 'That's creepy in more ways than one. You know, Hope Julius would be dead by now, even if she was alive.'

I raised my eyebrows, and after a second, Sally realized what she'd said. She shook her head in self-exasperation.

'What I mean is, Hope Julius had cancer,' Sally explained. 'She had ovarian cancer, I think, very advanced. Though there was apparently little hope, she was undergoing radiation treatment in Atlanta. All her hair had fallen out . . . I remember seeing one wig and one empty stand in her room when the police let me walk through the house . . . Mrs Totino said it was okay. One wig, a curly one that she wore almost every day, was gone. The one that was left was fancier, like she'd had her hair put up. She wore that one to church and parties.'

'Oooo,' I said. 'That's *awful.*' A woman's false hair, sitting there in her room when the woman was gone.

'It really was,' Sally agreed. She turned over a page of her notes.

'Why was the wig there, I wonder? That makes it look bad for Mrs Julius.'

'Yes, it does. She wouldn't leave without her extra wig, would she? And the wig made the whole scene eerier . . . like Martians had beamed them up right after they'd made their beds that morning, but before they'd gone down to breakfast.'

'They'd made their beds,' I repeated.

'Yes, unless something happened during the night, before they went to bed but after Mrs Totino had gone to sleep up in her apartment.'

'And what time was that, do you remember?'

'Yes, I have it here . . . nine thirty, she said. She was extra tired from all the activity of the day . . . the Dimmoch boy coming to visit Charity and help T.C., Parnell coming to pour the patio.'

It was hard picturing that as exhausting since someone else had done all the work. I said as much to Sally.

'Yes, but you see, since her daughter was so ill she'd been doing most of the cooking, the evening meals anyway, and lots of the laundry, I gathered.'

'Maybe that was why T.C. was agreeable to building her the apartment? Because Hope was so sick?'

'That's what I presumed. I never met him. The few people who did meet him, like Parnell Engle, liked him, and liked Hope, too. The picture I get is of a rigid kind of man, very honest and above-board, very meticulous in his dealings, punctual, orderly; of course, some of that might be from being in the service for so long. As far as I can tell, Hope was not a strong person, emotionally or physically, and I'm sure her illness had sapped her.'

'And Charity?'

'Charity was a typical teenager, according to the local kids who knew her for a few weeks. She talked all the time about her boyfriend she'd had to leave behind when she moved here, but most of the girls I interviewed seemed to feel that was a ploy to make her look important. Though since the Dimmoch boy cared enough to drive over, I guess they were wrong. Her grades, if I am remembering correctly, weren't that good, implying either that she wasn't bright or that she was more interested in other things; don't know which. She was an attractive girl, they all said that in one way or another, even though she didn't seem so pretty in a photo. I managed to talk to a couple of kids who knew her when she lived in Columbia, and they all spoke of her as being a strong girl, one with a lot of adult qualities, especially after her mother got sick.'

I offered Sally another glass of tea. She looked down at her wrist.

'No, thanks. I've got to be at a City Council meeting in ten minutes.'

Sally left me with a lot to think about as I put the dishes in the dishwasher. And I realized I'd forgotten to ask her about the aerial search.

After I saw Angel leave on some errand of her own that afternoon, I did something peculiar.

I retraced Mrs Totino's movements of the morning of the disappearance – no, the morning the disappearance was reported – as she had told them to Sally. I walked in the front door, looked around, went to the kitchen, went out the front door again, looked in the garage, went between the garage and the house to the backyard. I looked around it, and up at the window of our guest bedroom, the room that had been Charity's. Then I went in the front door yet another time.

I was certainly glad we lived out in the country so no one would see this bizarre exercise, which netted me exactly nothing but chills up and down my spine.

I called Lynn Liggett Smith that afternoon. Conversations between Lynn and me were always egg-walking exercises. On the one hand, she'd married Arthur Smith, the policeman whom I'd dated and been very fond of for months before he up and married Lynn – who was pregnant. I didn't care so much about that anymore, but Lynn felt a certain delicacy. On the other hand, we would have liked each other if it hadn't been for that, I'd always thought.

'How's Lorna?' I asked. I pictured Lynn at her desk at the Lawrenceton police station, tall, slim Lynn who'd lost all her baby-weight very fast and resumed her tailored suits and bright blouses with ease. I'd seen Lynn at the wedding, but of course she and Arthur hadn't brought the baby. Since I'd seen Lorna being born, I was always interested in her progress. 'Is she walking yet?' I had a very shaky idea of baby chronology.

'She's been walking for months now,' Lynn said. 'And she's talking. She knows at least forty words!'

'Eating real food?'

'Oh, yes! You ought to see Arthur feeding her yogurt.'

I thought I would pass that up.

'So what can I help you with today, Roe?'

'I wondered,' I said, 'if you would mind very much looking in the file on the Julius disappearance, and telling me exactly how the police searched.'

Long silence.

'That's all you want to know?' Lynn asked cautiously.

'Yes, I think so.'

'I can't think of a good reason why not.'

The phone clunked as it hit Lynn's desk, and I heard other detectives talking in the background as the click of Lynn's pumps receded.

With the phone clamped awkwardly between my shoulder and ear, I wiped the kitchen counter. I tried to decide what I'd wear to dinner that night. Should we take a bottle of wine with us? What if the Andersons were teetotalers? Lots of people in this area were.

'Roe?'

I jumped. The telephone was speaking to me.

'Every inch of the house was searched, and the garage apartment, too. No bloodstains. No signs of foul play. Gas in both vehicles, both vehicles running normally . . . so they hadn't been disabled. Beds stripped and mattresses tested . . . yard gone over inch by inch. The fields visually surveyed. According to the file, Jack Burns requested an aerial search but the city didn't have enough money left in the budget to pay for one.'

'Golly. Since there wasn't enough money, one wasn't done?'

'You got it.'

'That's wrong.'

'That's fiscal responsibility.'

'I just never thought about police department budgets not permitting things like that.'

Lynn laughed sardonically, and did a good job of it, too. 'Budgets don't permit lots of things we'd like to do. Our budget doesn't even permit us to do some of the things we need, much less the things we'd like.'

'Oh,' I said inadequately, still at a loss.

'But short of that, the investigation was very thorough. And the search was meticulous. There was a complete search of the house, an exhaustive search of the yard and the field around the house, and a lab examination of the two vehicles, all of which turned up absolutely nothing. Bus stations, airlines, train stations, all queried for anyone answering the description of any or all members of the family. That took some time, since they were all more or less average looking, though Hope was visibly ill. But no leads.'

'Eerie.' I jumped at the sound of the pet door as Madeleine entered. She walked over to her food bowl and deposited something in it, something furry and dead.

'Jack still talks about that case, when he's had a beer or two. Which is more often—' Lynn stopped, reconsidered, and changed the subject. 'So how's your husband?'

'He's fine,' I said, a little surprised. Arthur had strong views about Martin, and he had shared them with Lynn, I could tell.

'He is a little older than you?'

'Fifteen years. Well, fourteen plus.'

I could feel my brows contracting over my nose. I took off my glasses – the tortoiseshell pair today – and rubbed the little spot where tension always gathered. Madeleine was waiting for me to come over and compliment her.

'I want to talk to you sometime soon,' Lynn said, with an air of suddenly made decision.

Arthur and Lynn, through some law-enforcement channel, had heard something about Martin's former activities, I thought. All I needed at this point was someone else lecturing me. Or telling me something I didn't know about my own husband, pitying me.

'I'll give you a call when I'm free,' I said.

Chapter Eleven

A spring dinner at an employee's house; our first social engagement as a couple since our wedding. I finally chose a short-sleeved bright cotton dress and pumps. Martin brushed my hair for me, something he enjoyed doing. I was ready to get it cut. Its waviness and resultant bushiness made it a pain if it got too long, but Martin really liked it below my shoulders. I would tolerate the extra trouble until another Georgia summer. Since the dress was blue and red, I wore my red glasses, and I felt they added a cheerful touch. For some reason, my husband found them amusing.

Martin wore a suit, but when we got to the Andersons', only a few houses down Plantation Drive from my mother's, we found Bill Anderson shedding his tie.

'It's already heating up for summer,' he said. 'Let's get rid of these things. The ladies won't mind, will you, Roe? Bettina?'

Bettina Anderson, a copper-haired, heavy woman in her mid-forties, murmured, 'Of course not!' at exactly the same moment I did.

Our host took Martin down the hall to deposit his coat. They were gone a little longer than such an errand warranted. While they were gone, I asked Bettina if there was anything I could help her with, and since she didn't know me, she had to say there was nothing.

I was glad we hadn't brought the wine when we were offered nothing to drink stronger than iced tea.

Bill and Martin reappeared, Martin wearing a scowl that he made an effort to smooth out. Bettina vanished into the kitchen within a few minutes and was obviously flustered, but I noticed that when the doorbell rang again, it was Bettina who answered it.

I wondered how long the Andersons had been married. They didn't actually talk to each other very much.

To my pleasure, the other dinner guests were Bubba Sewell and his wife, my friend Lizanne Sewell, née Buckley. Bubba is an up-and-coming lawyer and legislator, and Lizanne is beautiful and full-bodied, with a voice as slow and warm as butter melting on corn. They had married a few months before we had, and the supper they'd given us had been the best party we'd had as an engaged couple.

I gave Lizanne a half-hug, rather than a full frontal hug, befitting our friendship and the length of time we hadn't seen each other.

Bettina turned down Lizanne's offer of help as well; so she was certainly determined to keep us 'company.' We chattered away while our hostess slaved out of sight in the kitchen and dining room. Lizanne inquired about the honeymoon, but without envy: She never wanted to leave the United States, she said. 'You don't know where you are in those other countries,' she said darkly. 'Anything can happen.'

I could see Bill Anderson had overheard this and was about to take issue, an incredulous look on his face. (I was beginning not to like Bill, and unless I was mistaken, Martin didn't like him either. I wondered if this was something we would have to do often, dine with people with whom we had nothing in common.)

'Are you enjoying not having to go to work every morning?' I asked Lizanne instantly, to spare her discomfort. (Lizanne probably wouldn't care one bit what Bill Anderson or anyone else thought about her opinions, but her husband would.)

'Oh . . . it's all right,' Lizanne said thoughtfully. 'There's a lot to do on the house, yet. I'm on some good-works committees . . . that was Bubba's idea.' She seemed slightly amused at Bubba's efforts to get her into his own up-and-coming pattern.

We were called to the dining room at that moment, and since I had my own agenda, I was pleased to see I was seated between Martin and Bubba at the round table.

After the flurry of passing and serving and complimenting an anxious Bettina on the chicken and rice and broccoli and salad, I quietly asked our state representative if he had been the lawyer in charge of the Julius estate since their disappearance. It was heartless of me, since the conversation had turned to regional football.

'Yes,' he said, dabbing his mustache carefully with his napkin. 'I handled the house purchase, when Mrs Zinsner sold the house to T. C. Julius. So after they vanished, Mrs Totino asked me to continue as the lawyer in the case.'

'What's the law about disappearances, Bubba?'

'According to Georgia law, missing people can be declared dead after seven years,' Bubba told me. 'But Mrs Totino was able to show she was the sole remaining relative of the family, and since she had very little without their support – she'd been living with a sister in New Orleans, scraping by with Social Security – we went to court and got her appointed conservator of the estate, so I could arrange for her to have enough money to live on. After a year, we got a letter of administration, so she could sell the property whenever she could find a buyer. Of course, this is all a matter of public record,' he concluded cautiously.

'So in a few months, the Juliuses will be declared dead.'

'Yes, then the remainder of their estate will be Mrs Totino's.'

'The house sale money.'

'Oh, no. Not just the house sale money. He'd been saving for a while, to start his own business when he retired from the Army.' And Bubba indicated by the set of his mouth that this was the end of the conversation about the Julius family's financial resources.

'Did you like him?' I asked, after we'd eaten quietly for a minute.

'He was a tough man,' Bubba said thoughtfully. 'Very much . . . "everything goes as I say in my family". But he wasn't mean.'

'Did you meet the others?'

'Oh, yes. I met Mrs Julius when they bought the house. Very sick, very glad to be within driving distance of all the hospitals in Atlanta. A quiet woman. The daughter was just a teenager; not giggly. That's all I remember about her.'

Then our host asked Bubba what was coming up in the legislature that we needed to know about, and my conversation with him about the Julius family was over.

On the way home, I related all this to Martin, who listened abstractedly. That wasn't like Martin, who was willing to be interested in the Julius disappearance if I was.

'I have to fly to Guatemala next week,' he told me.

'Oh, Martin! I thought you weren't going to have to travel as much now that you're not based in Chicago.'

'I thought so, too, Roe.'

He was so curt that I glanced over with some surprise. Martin was visibly worried.

'How long will you be gone?'

'Oh, I don't know. As long as it takes . . . maybe three days.'

'Could . . . maybe I could go, too?'

'Wait till we get home; I can't pay attention to this conversation while I'm driving.'

I bit my lip in mortification. When we got home, I stalked straight into the house.

He was just getting out of the car to open my door, and I caught him off guard. He didn't catch up to me until I was halfway down the sidewalk to the kitchen side door.

Then he put his hand on my shoulder and began, 'Roe, what I meant . . .'

I shook his hand off. 'Don't you talk to me,' I said, keeping my voice low because of the Youngbloods. Here we lived a mile out of town, and I still couldn't scream at my husband in my own yard. 'Don't you say *one word*.'

I stomped up the stairs, shut the door to our bedroom, and sat on the bed.

What was the matter with me? I'd never had open quarrels with anyone in my life, and here I was brawling with my husband, and I'd been within an ace of hitting him, something I'd also never done. This was so *trashy*.

I had to do some thinking, and now. Our relationship had always been more emotional than any I'd ever had, more volatile.

But these bright, hot feelings had always served to leap the chasms between us, I realized, sitting on the end of our new bedspread in our new house with my new wedding ring on my finger. I took off my shoes and sat on the floor. Somehow I could think better.

'He's still not telling me the truth,' I said out loud, and knew that was it.

I could hear him faintly, stomping about downstairs. Fixing himself a drink, I decided. I felt only stunned wonder – how had I ended up sitting on the floor in my bedroom, angry and grieved, in love with a man who lived a life in secret? I remembered Cindy Bartell saying, 'He won't cheat on you. But he won't ever tell you everything, either.'

I had a moment of sheer rage and self-pity, during which I asked myself all those senseless questions. What had I done to deserve this? Now that I'd finally, finally gotten married, why wasn't it all roses? If he loved me, why didn't he treat me perfectly?

I lay back on the floor, looking up at the ceiling. More importantly, what was I going to do during the next hour?

A creaking announced Martin's progress up the stairs and across the landing.

'I won't knock at my own bedroom door,' he said, from outside.

I stared at the ceiling even harder.

The door opened slowly. Perhaps he was afraid I'd throw something at him? An intriguing mental image. Maybe Cindy had thrown things.

He appeared at my feet, two icy glasses of what appeared to be 7-and-7 in his hands. I saw the wet stain on his off-white shirt, where he'd tucked the extra glass between arm and chest while he'd used his other hand to open the door.

'What are you doing, Roe?'

'Thinking.'

'Are you going to talk to me?'

'Are *you* going to talk to *me*?'

He sat on the stool in front of my vanity table. He leaned over to hand me a drink. I held it centered under my breasts with both hands gripping the heavy glass.

'I still . . .' he began. He stopped, looked around as if a reprieve would come, took a drink. I looked up at him from the floor, waiting.

'I still sell guns.'

I felt as if the ceiling had fallen on my head.

'Do you want to know any more about it than that?'

'No,' I said. 'Not now.'

'I don't think Bill Anderson is who he says he is,' Martin said.

I cut my gaze over to him without turning my head.

'I think he's government.'

I looked back at my glass. 'I thought you were government.'

His mouth went down at one corner.

'I thought I was, too. I suspect something's changed that I don't know about. That's why I need to go to Guatemala. Something's come unglued.'

I struggled with so many questions I couldn't decide what to ask first. Did I really want to know the answers to any of them?

'Are you really a man with a regular job with a real company?' I asked, hating the way my voice faltered.

He looked sad. 'I'm everything I ever told you I was. Just – other things, too.'

'Then why couldn't you be satisfied?' I said bitterly and futilely.

I sat up, tears coursing down my cheeks without my knowing they had started, not sobbing, just – watering my dress. I took a drink from my glass; yes, it was 7-and-7.

When I could bear to, I looked at him.

'Will you stay?' he asked.

We looked at each other for a long moment.

'Yes,' I said. 'For a while.'

I never finished that drink, yet the next morning I felt I had a hangover. I had to take my mind off my life. I dressed briskly, putting on powdered blush more heavily than usual because I looked like hell warmed over, and went to Parnell Engle's cement business.

It was a small operation north of Lawrenceton. There were heaps of different kinds of gravel and sand dotting the fenced-in area, and a couple of large cement trucks were rumbling around doing whatever they had to do. The office was barren and utilitarian to a degree I hadn't seen in years. There was a cracked leather couch, a few black file cabinets, and a desk in the outer office. That desk was commanded by a squat woman in stretch pants and an incongruous gauzy blouse that was intended to camouflage the rolls of fat. She had good-humored eyes peering out of a round face, and she was dealing with someone over the phone in a very firm way.

'If we told you it would be there by noon, it will be there by noon. Mr Engle don't promise nothing he can't do. Now the rain, we cain't control the rain . . . No, they cain't come sooner, all our trucks are tied up till then . . . I know the weather said rain, but like I told you . . . All right then, we'll see you *at noon.*' And she hung up with a certain force. There was an old Underwood typewriter on the desk, and not a computer in sight.

'Is Mr Engle in?' I asked.

'Parnell!' she yelled toward the door behind her. 'Someone here to see you.'

Parnell appeared in the door in a moment dressed in blue jeans, work boots, and a khaki shirt, his hand full of papers.

'Oh,' he said unenthusiastically. 'Roe Teagarden. You enjoying all that money my cousin left you?'

'Yes,' I said baldly.

After a moment of Dodge-City staring at each other, Parnell cracked a smile. 'Well, at least the Lord has shined on you,' he said. 'I hear you got married last month. God meant for woman to be a companion to man.'

'Amen,' I said sadly.

'You need to talk to me?'

'Yes, if you have a minute.'

'That's about all I do have, but come on in.' He made a nearly gracious sweep with his handful of papers, and I went across the creaking wooden floor to Parnell's sanctum. I felt a surge of fondness for Parnell; his office was exactly what I expected. It was as dilapidated as the outer room, and there was a large reproduction of the Last Supper on the wall, and plaques with Bible verses were stuck here and there, along with a huge map of the country and a calendar that featured scenery rather than women.

'You know I bought the Julius house,' I said directly. Parnell neither expected nor appreciated small talk. 'I want to know about the day you poured the patio there.'

'I went over and over it at the time,' he remarked. 'And I don't know why you want to know, but I suppose it's none of my business. It's been a long time since I thought of that day.'

He leaned back in his chair, wove his fingers together across his lean stomach. He pursed his thin lips for a moment, then began. 'I was still working most of the jobs I got myself. I've prospered in the last few years, praise the Lord. But when T.C. called, I was glad to come. He'd made the form himself, it was all ready, he told me. I knew he was trying to set up his own carpentry business, handyman work, that kind of thing, so I knew he'd have done a competent job. So I went out there with the truck and the black man working for me then, Washington Prescott, he's dead now, had an aneurysm. We got there. The form looked fine, just like I expected. There was some rubble down in it, like people throw in sometimes, extra bricks, things you want to get rid of; but nothing like a body or anything that could have held a body. Stones, old bricks, seems like I remember a couple of pieces of cloth, rag. The girl Charity came out and said hi. I'd met the family before at church so I knew her. She said her dad had gone on an errand and called to say he wouldn't make it back in time, I should just go on and pour and send him a bill.'

'You never saw him?'

'Just said that, didn't I?'

'Did you see other members of the family?'

'I'm about to tell you. You're the one wanting to know all about it.'

'Sorry.'

'Charity's boyfriend, Harley, came out to help if I needed him. And the mother-in-law, don't remember her name, came out of the garage apartment and watched us for a spell. While we were pouring, Washington was in the form getting everything to flow right, and then we were both finishing it. I could see in the kitchen window. Hope was in there wearing an apron, fixing supper, looked like. She waved at me but didn't come out to speak. I thought, She must be in a hurry. They must be going out later.'

'She was usually friendly?'

'Hope? Oh, yes, she was a friendly woman, meek. That cancer was really draining her, but that day she looked better and moved easier than she had in the month or two I'd known her.'

He'd seen every member of the Julius family but T.C.

'Was the light in the kitchen on?' I asked.

'No, I don't think so. There was still plenty of light. I got there at four, and it was late October; it wasn't real bright, come to think of it. But it was Hope I saw.'

'And there's no way that after you left, bodies could have been put in the concrete.'

'I went out late the next day after I'd talked to the police. That concrete was exactly like me and Washington left it, and no one had touched it.'

Parnell said this with a finality that was absolutely believable. He leaned up in his chair to a squeal of springs, and said, 'Now, I think that's it, Roe.'

He got up to walk me to the door, so I slung my purse over my shoulder and obediently preceded him. I thought of one last question.

'Parnell, why did you think Mrs Julius was going out later?'

'Well,' he said, and then stopped dead. 'Now why did I?' he wondered, scratching the side of his nose with the papers he'd picked up again. His narrow face went blank as he rummaged through his memory. 'Because of the wig,' he said, pleased at his ability to recall. 'Hope was wearing her Sunday wig.'

Next I went to the church.

I couldn't think of anywhere else to go. It was unlocked. I could see across the right angle formed by the church and the parish hall, where the office was. Aubrey was seated at his desk. But I went in the church. It was warm and dusty. I sat at the back, let down a kneeler, and slid down on it.

I was hoping to bring order to chaos.

I'd promised Martin to stay with him, when we married. I loved him.

But he was – a Bad Guy. Or, at the very least, a Not-So-Good Guy.

I winced as I formulated the thought, but I couldn't deny its truth.

If someone came to me – say, Aubrey – and told me, 'I know a man who sells arms illegally to desperate people in Latin America,' what would I assume?

I would assume that this man was bad, because no matter what else was good in his life, it would not balance that piece of – evil.

This man who was doing that evil act was my husband, the man who had made alternate honeymoon plans so he'd be sure I was happy, the man who thought he was extremely lucky to marry me, the man who'd fought a horrible war in Vietnam, a man who loved and supported an ungrateful son.

I was convinced Martin was doing what he was doing not because he was intrinsically evil but because he was addicted to danger, adventure, and maybe because he thought he was serving his country. But what he was doing would poison our life together, no matter how much good that life contained. He was my sweetheart, he was my lover, he was an agricultural company executive, he was a veteran, he was an athlete, but I could not forget what else he did.

I cried for a while. I heard the door of the church open quietly. I felt someone standing in the narthex behind me: Aubrey. He must have noticed my car. But I didn't turn around because I didn't want him to see my face. After a while I felt his hand brush my hair in a caress and rest lightly on my shoulder. He gave me a pat, and I heard the door squeak shut behind him.

Peachtree Leisure Apartments. A different security guard, also black, less formidable and less good-natured. This man's name was Roosevelt, which I was sure pleased Mrs Totino. She was less pleased with me, however; her voice, which I could hear crackling over the lobby phone, was not enthusiastic. Perhaps she was regretting the purple and silver placemats.

'You been crying,' she said sharply, standing back from her door with none too gracious an air. Why the sudden coolness? I remembered she had a reputation for being disagreeable. Maybe she'd just reverted to character.

'I wanted to ask you something,' I said. 'I'm sorry I didn't call before I came.' Actually, that had been a stroke of luck, I now considered.

She wasn't going to ask me to sit.

'What?' she said rudely.

'The day the concrete was poured for the patio . . .'

She nodded curtly, her thin bent figure outlined in the sun coming through the one window in the cramped and crowded living room.

'Can you think of any reason why your daughter would be wearing her Sunday wig?'

'Go!' she shrieked at me suddenly. 'Go! Go! Go! You bought the house! That's an end of it! You can't leave it alone, can you? We'll never know! You know what one old fool here told me? Told me they'd got eaten by Martians! I've listened to it for years. I just can't stand it!'

Utterly taken aback and deeply embarrassed at having provoked such a ruckus – doors were opening up and down the hall – I stepped back and gave her the room she needed to slam the door in my face.

*

To cap off a perfect twenty-four hours, Martin telephoned from work to say his superior at the main office in Chicago had called an urgent meeting of all plant managers for as soon as everyone could get there. He'd come home to pack and I hadn't been there, and no one had known where I was.

Whom had he asked? I wondered.

'So I'll have to fly straight from Chicago to Guatemala,' he said.

I made a little noise of protest. I couldn't reach any decision about my life with Martin, but I knew I would miss him and I hated for him to leave the country before we could resolve our problems.

'Roe,' he said in a more private, less brisk, voice. 'I'm going to quit.'

Unfortunately, I started crying again.

'Promise,' I sobbed, like a nine-year-old.

'I promise,' he said. 'This last trip is it. I'll start disentangling myself while I'm down there. There are people I have to talk to, arrangements I have to make. But it's over for me.'

'Thank God,' I said.

I thought I'd wept more in my four-week marriage to Martin than I had in the previous four years.

Chapter Twelve

The next day, I called Harley Dimmoch's parents to find out where their son was now. The name was not exactly common, and Columbia, South Carolina, is not that big. There were three Dimmochs; the second listing was the right one.

I told Harley Dimmoch's mother that I had just bought the house the Julius family had lived in. 'I'm interested in the history of the house. I was hoping he could tell me about the day before they disappeared.'

'He doesn't like to talk about it. He was really sweet on the girl, you know.'

'Charity.'

'Yes. I hadn't thought of that in a year or two, Harley is so different now.'

'Does he live in Columbia with you?'

'No, he lives close to the Gulf Coast now, working in a lumber yard. He's got a girlfriend now, oh for several years he's been seeing this young woman. He comes home to visit about once a year, to let us have a look at him.'

'And you say he doesn't talk about Charity's disappearance?'

'No, he's real touchy about it. His dad and me, we always thought he felt kind of guilty. Like if he'd stayed instead of coming on home that night, he could have stopped whatever happened.'

'So he came home the day—'

'He came home very late the night before Mrs Totino found they were gone. Oh, the police came over here and talked to him forever, we were afraid he'd lose his temper, which he's a little prone to do, and say something that would make them think he'd done it . . .'

I liked this woman. She was loquacious.

'But he just seemed stunned, like. He hardly knew what he was doing. He told us a thousand times, "Mama, Daddy, I helped Mr Julius with the roof and I watched that man pour the concrete for the patio and I ate supper, and I left".'

'He never mentioned they were quarreling with each other, or strangers came to the door, or anything odd?' I was trolling, now.

'No, everything was just as usual, he kept on telling us that like we doubted him. And the police went over and over that old car of his, like to drove us crazy. He was just nuts about Charity. He has never been the same since that time.'

'Oh, really?'

'Yes, he just couldn't settle down after that. He is older than – well, Charity was fifteen or sixteen, and Harley was eighteen when it happened. It's hard to believe my baby is twenty-four now, almost twenty-five! We had hoped he'd stay with us, maybe think about going to a junior college, or something like that. He had just gotten laid off at his first job when he went over to see Charity that time. But after it happened, he just wanted to take off on his own, didn't want to stay around here. And the shock of it. It's like he don't want more surprises, ever in his life again. He don't like phone calls if he's not expecting us to call. We call him on Sunday, or not at all. We don't drive down to see him on the spur of the moment, so to speak, we tell him way in advance.'

I made an indeterminate sound that was meant to be encouraging.

'So I'd better not give you his number, Miss. Because he wouldn't appreciate a phone call from out of the blue. But if you'll give me your number, I'll pass it on to him the next time we speak.'

I gave her my name and phone number, thanked her sincerely, and hung up.

I related this conversation to Angel as we sat on the front porch with lemonade two days later. The house was measured all over and we'd knocked on walls for hollow places. We'd scanned the yard. Neecy Dawson, whom I wanted to ask about the sealed-up closet, had gone to Natchez to tour antebellum homes with a busload of other ladies. Bettina Anderson had left a message on my answering machine. I'd seen my mother and John off to a real estate brokers' convention in Tucson, and the weather was swiftly getting hotter. There was never enough spring in Georgia.

Martin had called to say he'd arrived in Chicago, and Emily Kaye had called to ask me to join St James's Altar Guild. Both calls had made me anxious, though on different levels. Martin had sounded worried but determined; it was the worried part that frightened me. Would it be easy to extricate himself from this business? Emily, in her very nicest way, had quite refused to take no for an answer and had sweetly demanded I attend the Altar Guild meeting today to find out more about it.

'So what have you learned?' Angel was asking in her flat Florida voice.

'I have learned,' I began slowly, 'that Mrs Julius was wearing her Sunday wig on a weekday night. I have learned that Mrs Totino doesn't want to talk about the disappearance anymore. I have learned that there were no bodies under the concrete, and none could have been put there afterward. I have learned that Harley Dimmoch was a changed person after Charity Julius disappeared, but that at the time the police were satisfied with his story, because Mrs Totino saw the Juliuses after he left – presumably.'

'So Mrs Totino's word is all you have that they were alive?'

'Yes,' I conceded. 'But after all, she's the mother of the woman who's missing. She was part of the family. Her daughter had cancer.'

'Maybe you should talk to the sister. Mrs Totino's sister. The one in Metairie.'

'I don't know what she could tell me. According to Mrs Totino, the sister's never been up here. Mrs Totino is so in love with New Orleans she goes down there every now and then, she says, though somehow it sounded like the sister wasn't exactly happy to have her.'

'Wonder why?'

'Well, she can certainly pitch a fit when she wants to, and

evidently from what the security guard said the first day I visited, she has a reputation for being unpleasant.'

'If she's such a bitch, how come the Juliuses wanted her around?'

'To help in the house, while Mrs Julius was having her cancer treatments, I guess.'

'But wouldn't that have made everything worse? I mean, you've got a sick woman, and a teenage girl mad because she had to move away from her boyfriend, and a husband trying to start his own business in a new town. Wouldn't a woman like that be more trouble than she was worth? They could've hired a maid cheaper than building onto the garage.'

Put like that, it *was* mysterious. I would mull it over when I had the time. Right now I had to meet with the members of the Altar Guild, presumably to talk about altar topics, whatever that might include.

'I've got to go,' I said reluctantly. I moved to pick up the glasses.

'I'll get them,' Angel said. 'I'll just put them in the kitchen and lock the back door on my way out.'

So we went inside together, since I needed my purse and keys. I was wearing what I hoped was a suitable tailored khaki skirt and a striped blouse with a bright yellow barrette to hold back my hair, and my soberest pair of glasses, the ones with the tortoiseshell rims. My purse was right inside, at the front door, so I was going down the front porch steps before Angel had even reached the kitchen. It was warm, but not that breathless glaring heat you get in a full-blown Georgia summer. I scuffled through the grass, thinking that buying a riding mower at Sears might be a good idea; the yard was so big.

Madeleine suddenly ran from the garage, crossed the yard with speed surprising in such a fat cat, and disappeared under the bushes around the front porch. What on earth had spooked her? I looked into the shadowy interior, walking slowly now, anxious without formulating exactly why.

The tool-room door was open a crack. Surely Angel and I had shut it the day we'd been in there measuring and straightening.

Angel came out of the side kitchen door and was halfway across the sidewalk between the house and the garage.

I took another step and it seemed to me the crack widened some.

'Angel,' I called, panic sparking along my nerves and surely showing in my voice.

She had a reaction that even at the time struck me as extraordinary.

Instead of saying 'What?' or 'Got a problem?' she broke into a dead run and moved so fast that she was in front of me one split second after the tool-room door had burst open. The man erupting from it was heading straight for us, and he had our ax in his hands.

'Run!' Angel said fiercely. 'Run, Roe!'

That seemed extremely disloyal to me, but also intensely desirable. I couldn't abandon Angel, I decided nobly, idiotically, since the man was swinging the ax and yelling and coming straight for us. Angel ducked under his arm, attempted to grab the ax handle, lost her footing on the loose gravel, and went down. My purse was all I had, and I swung it on its long shoulder strap and had the shock of seeing the ax sever the straps and my purse hit the ground. However, that took up one swing and he had to haul back for another try, and that gave Angel time to lunge from her prone position and grab his ankles, so his next step toward me brought him down as the ax whistled harmlessly past me. He hit the driveway with a thud but kept a grip on the ax, and he was trying to maneuver to use it on Angel when I stomped on his hand.

With a howl he let go of the ax, and I stooped and grabbed the handle and slung it as far away as I could sling. I instinctively wanted the ax out of the equation, since sharp cutting edges make me very nervous. But he used his hands after that, spinning, grabbing Angel's ponytail and hitting her face against the gravel. She did not allow the pain to deflect her, but with an expression of absolute determination reached for a spot on his arm and pressed in with her strong fingers. He screamed and let go, and aimed a kick at Angel's head. Swift as a snake she rolled, and the kick landed on her shoulder instead, but I saw her mouth open in pain. She was slowed down enough for him to jump to his feet. I'd been circling futilely, trying to see a vulnerable spot, but they were so fast it was bewildering. When he jumped up, I insanely tried to block him, but he straightarmed me, and my feet in their leather-soled suburban low-heeled pumps flew right out from under me, and with a *whump!* I landed flat on my back with all my wind knocked out. I was quite unable to move as I heard heavy running steps crunch down the driveway.

Angel's face, scraped and bleeding, appeared over me. 'All right?' she asked urgently.

I managed to waggle my head a little, still waiting for the intake of breath that would make me whole.

She ran after the intruder, her footfalls lighter and swifter. But I heard a car start up, and I knew Angel would be back soon.

She was, but in no mood to sit around and rehash our experience.

'Into the house, now!' she said harshly, scooping me off the ground with one movement. I drew in some air finally. The relief was immense. Angel's arm was under mine and I was being dragged/marched into the house. Angel had my damaged purse in her other hand, extracting the keys as we went, and she cast my purse down while she twisted the key in the lock. She more or less pitched me into the living room while she locked the door and shot the deadbolt behind us. While I sat there still trying to figure out what had happened, Angel ran to the kitchen, with blood from the abrasions on her face dropping down to spot the floor.

I heard her voice, quick and calm. She was on the phone calling the police.

I struggled to my feet and wobbled into the kitchen.

Angel was hanging up the phone. She turned to the side kitchen door and shot the deadbolt on it; then the back kitchen door received the same treatment. She went around the kitchen yanking the curtains shut.

Then she turned to me and I realized she was furious. There was nothing slow and deliberate about Angel anymore.

'When I tell you to run, you run,' she said in a low, barely controlled voice. 'You don't hang around to save my ass. You were in the way out there. I told you to *run*.'

'Angel,' I said, realization dawning. 'You're my *bodyguard*.'

We stood staring at one another. Both of us had a lot to think about.

'Why didn't you run?' she asked.

'I couldn't leave you out there.' I reached behind me for a towel and handed it to her. 'You're dripping all over,' I said.

She took it absently and began patting at her face. She glanced down at the towel and seemed surprised at the red blotches on it.

'You have to go to the doctor.'

'No,' she said. 'We'll take care of it. We're not going anywhere until Shelby checks the road between here and town. That's what he's doing now.'

'That's who you called.'

She nodded. She went to look out the curtains.

'You didn't call the police.' I said this cautiously, feeling I was saying something quite naive.

I was right. Angel raised one eyebrow and shook her head.

I didn't even have to ask why. Angel thought this attack was related to Martin's illegal activities. Angel and Shelby, of course, had known all along, I realized in an ever-widening ripple of revelation; Martin had brought them here to protect me before we were even married, had bought me the Julius house because of the garage apartment for the Youngbloods to stay in, had foreseen the possibility that something like this might happen.

I got the first-aid kit from the bathroom, feeling as if I were already half-dead. I was shocked by the attack, humiliated by all I now knew. I should be grateful; I would undoubtedly be dead by now if it weren't for Angel Youngblood. But I felt cold and stony; I hated them all, Angel and Shelby and Martin. I thumped the first-aid kit down on the counter in the kitchen; I picked up the phone. Angel made a face of protest, but before she could speak I turned on her a face so dreadful that she went back to staring out a gap in the curtains.

'Emily,' I said, when I heard the voice on the other end of the line, 'I won't be able to come to Altar Guild this afternoon, I'm so sorry.' Appropriate, but rather huffy, noises from Emily.

'Well, I fell on my way to the garage – yes, I know that's an old-lady thing to do – the gravel was slippery and my shoes are leather-soled – no, I'm fine really, I'm just bruised. I'll be there next time, for sure! Give the ladies my regrets.'

I hung up the phone. I stood there, my hand on it, staring off down the black hole I'd fallen into. I got a white washrag out from under the sink, moistened it, wrung it out.

'Sit down,' I told Angel.

She abandoned her post but insisted we drag a chair over to the window. She kept watch while I cleaned her face. I knew it hurt; I didn't care. Once her abrasions and cuts were clean, I dabbed antibiotic ointment all over them. She was a sight.

Shelby's car crunched down the drive. He pulled into the Youngbloods' accustomed parking spot on the far side of the garage, so he was hidden from view. Angel had appropriated a knife from my kitchen drawer; she stood watching for her husband intently, the knife gripped in her right hand.

'Unlock the kitchen door,' she told me.

I did it.

'Stand back from it.'

I rolled my eyes and went back to lean against the counter. I could see through Angel's little gap. Finally Shelby crossed it, walking warily, eyes going everywhere at once. In his hands was a shotgun.

My mouth fell open.

A number of things had hit me that day, literally and metaphorically. But the most telling thing, the moment of truth, was seeing that shotgun in Shelby Youngblood's hands.

Someone had tried to kill *me*. That man had been trying to get *me*. Angel had just been an obstacle in his eyes; he'd had no idea of her function or capability. His focus had been on killing me. I thought of that ax coming down on my head. Suddenly my knees were wobbly.

Shelby came in the kitchen door with a rush. Angel was on hand to lock it after him the instant he was in.

'You okay?' he asked her.

She nodded. 'Mad,' she said. 'I'm mad as hell. I couldn't get him. My feet went out from under me. She got the ax away from him, not me.' Angel obviously did not need or expect any fuss about her damaged face; Shelby's dark eyes had assessed her injuries quickly and dismissed them. Angel was a professional, it was borne in on me more strongly every minute. If I was dealing with my own humiliation, so was she; she had failed in her job.

'Roe got the ax?' Shelby said incredulously.

'It's in the middle of the front yard. She threw it.'

'Roe did.' Shelby still couldn't quite absorb it.

'He got very close,' Angel said angrily. 'If I hadn't already been out of the house, he'd of got her.'

I had to sit down quite suddenly.

I pulled one of the breakfast-table chairs out. The legs made a scraping noise.

'So I guess you didn't spot him on your way through town.'

'No blue Chevy Nova.'

'Tags were covered with mud,' Angel said sullenly. I could tell she'd already told Shelby this on the phone and he'd been on the lookout on the way here.

No one could say my married life was placid. No rut for the Bartells!

I giggled.

They glanced at me uneasily, then went back to their consultation.

'It's quiet out there now. We'd better get moving,' Shelby said.

'I'll call him,' Angel said. She was obviously bent on confessing her failure to someone. After a beat I realized she meant she was going to call Martin, and I just snapped.

'Excuse me,' I said viciously. 'If anyone is going to call my husband, I am.'

They both looked startled at my speaking, and dismayed by what they were hearing.

'You should pack, and talk to Martin tonight,' Shelby said gently. But the gentleness was costing him, I could tell. Good.

'I will talk to my husband whenever I damn well please.'

They were considerably taken aback. Though I hadn't known the true nature of the Youngbloods, they were finding out a thing or two about me.

They had Martin's telephone numbers where he was staying. They knew where he was and why he was out of town. They knew all about our lives.

They were my bodyguards. I had a little shock whenever the word entered my mind.

Well, Shelby with his acne-scarred face and unruly black hair was nothing like Kevin Costner.

'I will go use the phone in the other room,' I told them. I stalked across the hall to sit at Martin's desk and call him in Chicago.

The secretary who took the call was quite sure that Martin's meeting ('He's in conference with the president,' she said severely) was more important than my call, but I said, 'I really have to insist. This is his wife, and there is an emergency.'

After a pause of nearly five minutes, Martin was on the phone, and at the sound of his voice I almost broke down.

'What is it?' he asked tensely. 'Are you all right?'

'I'm all right.' My voice was shaky. I sat for a moment gathering myself. 'Angel is a little hurt,' I said with shameful satisfaction.

'Angel? You're all right and *Angel's* hurt? What happened? Is Shelby there?'

'Yes, Martin, Shelby is here and you can talk to him in a minute so you guys can *handle* everything.' By golly, I was still mad at everyone. 'A man was hiding in the garage, and if he'd had the sense to wait till I was in there, he would've had me. But I noticed something was wrong and he charged out and Angel was able to get there in time, and I got the ax away. But he ran and got in a car and left.' Now my voice was shaking again. I certainly wished I could pick an emotion and stick with it. Fear, anger, humiliation, shock. A cocktail of feelings.

'Baby. Are you really all right? Hurt anywhere?'

'Not physically, Martin,' I said with great restraint.

'Does Angel need to be in the hospital?'

'No, I took care of it with the first-aid kit.'

'That's good. Very good. Okay, honey. Here's what I need you to do. I need you to do whatever Shelby and Angel tell you to do. They're there to keep you safe. I'll catch a flight home tomorrow morning. I'll go to Guatemala once I make sure you're going to be all right.'

'Okay,' I said tersely. There really wasn't any point in saying anything else.

'Now, I need to talk to Angel and Shelby. I'm – thank God you're okay. I'm so sorry.'

I looked across the hall. They were standing close to the kitchen doorway. Shelby had his arms around Angel. A weak moment.

'Phone,' I said. 'Angel.'

Looking as if she'd rather face wrestling an alligator, Angel Youngblood, my protector, came to talk to Martin.

I went upstairs and lay on my bed.

Chapter Thirteen

It was a long night.

Angel slept in the office/family room downstairs on the couch. Shelby was out patrolling the grounds. I lay awake in our bedroom. Sometimes I read. Sometimes I slept. Sometimes I brooded. In a million years, I could never have imagined myself in the situation in which I found myself now.

I was glad my mother was out of town. I couldn't envision successfully concealing from her all the misery and fear I felt.

Before we'd all gone to our assigned spots for the night, Shelby had questioned us about the appearance of the man. It had all happened quickly, and he'd been in movement the whole time, but I found that if I shut my eyes and replayed him exploding from the tool-room door I could get a fair picture.

'He had on a short-sleeved khaki work shirt,' I said first. Angel nodded agreement.

'And safety shoes,' Angel contributed, rubbing her shoulder.

'What are safety shoes?' I asked.

'Steel toes,' she told me, looking faintly amazed.

'Oh. And he had on dark brown work pants.'

'So now we've got his wardrobe. What did he look like?' asked Shelby with very obvious patience.

I had a good mind to stomp up to my room and slam the door, but I was aware that Shelby, of course, was just doing his job and my acting childish would not help the situation. I was sorely tempted, though.

'He had dark curly hair,' Angel said.

'He was Angel's height,' I contributed. 'He was young. Not more than thirty, I doubt that old.'

'He does heavy work for a living,' Angel said. 'Based on his musculature.'

'Clean-shaven. Blue eyes, I'm pretty sure. Heavy jaw.'

'He never said anything in any language?' Shelby asked us.

'No.'

'No.'

And that was the sum total of our knowledge of the man in the garage.

The next morning was clear again, definitely hotter. The Youngbloods switched; Shelby went up to their apartment to sleep, and Angel was detailed to stay with me. We ate breakfast and did the dishes in silence, and when we were facing each other dressed in blue jeans and T-shirts, we fidgeted. Angel hadn't gotten her run in. I had finished my last library book, and I was not a daytime television watcher. After one round of the news on CNN, I switched the set off.

Normally, at this time, I would be getting ready to start my round of errands, or at least figuring out what that round should consist of – cleaners, grocery, bank, library – making phone calls, or writing letters. But today I couldn't; they didn't want me to go into town.

'Can we go outside?' I asked Angel finally.

She considered.

'Yes, in the front yard,' she said at last. 'There are too many trees and bushes that block the view in the backyard.'

That was one of the things I liked about it so much.

'In the front yard I can see what's coming,' Angel said. 'Last night, Shelby took out that clump of bushes out by the road that hid the car.'

'He what?'

Taken aback, Angel repeated, 'He cut down that clump of yellow bells.'

'The forsythia is gone,' I said unbelievingly. During the night, Shelby had cut down my bushes, a huge beautiful growth of three forsythias that had been happily expanding and blooming for twenty years, I estimated.

'They were down by the road, and they hid things from the house,' Angel explained further, puzzled at the degree of my dismay.

'Okay,' I said finally. 'Okay. Let's go.'

'What are we going to do?'

I was punch drunk with lack of sleep and shock.

'Got a Frisbee, Angel?'

'Sure,' she said, as though I'd asked her whether she had a nose.

'Well. Let's play Frisbee.'

So after a preliminary reconnaissance, we came out into the fresh day. I ignored the shotgun Angel carried out; she put it on the chair on the porch, where she could reach it quickly. Then she got her Frisbee and cocked her wrist to spin it to me, an anticipatory grin stretching her thin lips. I prepared myself for some running.

Ten minutes later I was panting, and even Superwoman was breathing a little heavily. Angel had gotten surprised all over again. I was no mean Frisbee player. But my aerobic exercise videotape hadn't prepared me for this, and I felt the first trickle of sweat for the summer season gliding down my back and then between my hips. On the whole, I was having a good time. I dashed inside for a drink of water.

Angel must have felt mildly challenged. She had backed out toward the road a little, and as I was coming down the front steps, she flicked her wrist and the red disk took off. A sudden breeze gusting over the open field across the road picked up the Frisbee and wafted it even higher. With a thunk, the Frisbee grazed the top of the first roof peak (the roof of the porch) and rolled into the space under my bedroom windows.

'Aw, shit,' Angel said. 'Listen, I'll be back in a second. Let me go blot my face, the sweat's getting into my scrapes and making them sting.'

'Sure,' I said. 'I'll be getting the ladder.'

It felt creepy going into the garage and opening the door to the tool shed in the back. I knew the Youngbloods had checked it out and searched everything on the property before it got dark the night before, but in my brief hours of sleep, I'd had nightmares about a dark figure running toward me with an upraised ax.

I maneuvered the long ladder out of the tool shed and shouldered it to get it to the front of the house. Angel descended the apartment steps with a tender look on her face; the sight of Shelby sleeping certainly still rang her bells.

I pushed back the hooks that held the extension down parallel with the base of the ladder, and with Angel's help ran it up to the roof. Since the house was built up on a high foundation, the climb was no short one.

'Do you mind,' Angel said almost shyly, 'I know I threw it up there, but if there's one thing I can't handle, it's heights . . . now if it bothers you, I'll go on and do it, or Shelby can get up there when he gets up . . .'

I gaped at her, before I remembered my manners and nodded matter-of-factly. 'No problem,' I said briskly.

She seemed to relax all over. 'I'll brace the ladder,' she said with equal briskness.

So up I started. I am not automatically afraid of heights; I am fairly phobia-free. But it was quite a climb, and since I was showing off for Angel, I found I needed to keep my eyes looking up and my progress steady. Stopping, I had a strong feeling, would not be good.

Actually – come to think of it – I had never been on a roof before. The porch roof was steep. Really steep. Nervously, I transferred from the ladder to the shingles, already warm from the spring sun. I'd never been right next to shingles before; I had a good look at their pebbly grayness while I was bracing myself to reach the peak. I stretched and grasped it, and pushed with the sides of my feet, glad I was wearing sturdy rubber-soled hi-tech sneakers. The Frisbee should be on the downslope of this roof, where it joined the roof of the house; I remembered Miss Neecy telling me about the feuding couple who'd built the house, Sarah May Zinsner's last-minute insistence on a porch.

'I hear a car coming, Roe,' Angel said quietly down below.

I froze. 'What should I do?'

'Get over that roofline.'

So I scrambled up and over in no time at all. A little incentive was all I needed. In the valley between the two roofs, formed like a forty-five-degree angle with the wall under my bedroom windows being the straight line and the upward slope of the porch roof being the angle line, lay the bright red Frisbee and an old gray tarp so exactly matching the shingles that I had to land on it to notice it.

I peeked over the roofline to see what Angel was doing. The shotgun was in her hands now, and she was against the inside wall of the garage, the far side where Martin's Mercedes was parked. The car was visible as it came closer, thanks to Shelby's butchery of my forsythia, and it was a white car that was a little familiar. It turned in the driveway, and Angel raised the shotgun. The white car crunched slowly up the drive and pulled to a halt on the gravel a few feet behind my car, on the near side of the garage. The driver's door opened. Martin stepped out.

I was smiling without even realizing it for a second.

Angel came out of the garage with the shotgun lowered, and though I couldn't hear what they said, she pointed at the roof.

'Up here!' I called. Martin turned and went to the front of the house, looking up with a quizzical expression. He wasn't wearing a suit for once, and he needed a shave.

'How are you, Roe?' he asked.

I still loved him.

'I'm all right, Martin. Be down in a minute. Here's the Frisbee.' I sailed it over the peak down to them. Martin's arm shot out and he caught it neatly.

'There's something else up here,' I called. 'There's a gray plastic tarp.'

Angel's expression changed to alarm. 'Don't touch it!' she and Martin yelled simultaneously.

'It's been here for ages,' I reassured them. 'There're pine needles and bird poop and dirt all over it.'

The two faces upturned to me relaxed somewhat.

'What do you think it is, builder's material?' Martin asked.

'Well, I'm going to find out.' I maneuvered a turn in the little valley in which I found myself. A gutter had been installed in this valley, to carry off rainwater, and the covered bundle had been shoved just clear of it under my bedroom window. In fact it was so closely packed into this one straight stretch of roof that I knew why I hadn't ever noticed it: It was so close under my window that I would have had to stick out my head and shoulders and look down to see it.

The tarp was stiff and crackly with age and exposure. It was weighted down with bricks. When I shoved one off the tarp and raised one corner, the whole thing moved, and I was treated to a comprehensive view of what lay beneath.

It took me a moment to understand what I was seeing. I tried to believe that someone had been up on the roof eating ribs and had thrown the discarded bones in a heap after he was through. Maybe lots of people; there were so many . . . I saw the ribs first, you see. They weren't pretty and white: they were yellowish and had little bits of dried dark stuff on them. But there were other bones, tiny and large, one whole hand with a few strings of tendon still holding it together . . . The skulls had rolled a little, but I counted them automatically.

'Roe?' Martin called from below. 'What's happening up there? Are you okay?'

The breeze was gusting again. For the first time in over six years, it wafted under the gray plastic. The hair on one of the skulls lifted.

I wanted *off this roof.*

I flung myself upward, swung my legs over the peak, and began backing down in record time.

'Roe,' called Martin again, definitely alarmed.

My feet hit the first rung. It seemed like long minutes before my hands could grasp the metal and then my feet flew down once I was totally supported by the ladder.

Martin and Angel were both asking me questions at once. I

leaned against the metal, my feet finally on the ground, a safe distance from the horror on the roof.

'They're there,' I managed to say at last. 'They've been there all along.'

Martin still looked blank, but Angel, who had helped me look, got the point immediately.

'The Julius family,' she told Martin. 'They're on the roof.'

We had to tell the police about this. Angel stored away the shotgun and made the phone call. Then I saw her bounding up her apartment steps, presumably to wake Shelby.

We were sitting on the porch in one of the chairs. I was folded up on Martin's lap.

'Martin,' I whispered. 'She still had on her wig. But there was just a skull underneath it.'

Everyone came. It was like a lawn party for law enforcement personnel in Spalding County.

Our house was just within the city limits, so the chief of police came first. Padgett Lanier was sharp-nosed, tall, with thinning blond hair and nearly invisible eyelashes and eyebrows. He had a paunch, and a mouth that was too small for his face. He had been chief of police of Lawrenceton for twenty years. I'd met him at various parties while I was dating Arthur Smith.

I was sitting in a separate chair by then, but still on the porch, hoping to keep everyone out of our home. Martin had pulled his chair over by mine and was holding my hand. Shelby and Angel were sitting on the porch itself, blocking the front door, watching the activity with impassive faces.

'Mrs Bartell?' Lanier asked from the front lawn.

'Ms Teagarden,' I said.

'You the one that found them?'

'Yes. They're up on the roof. Under the plastic.'

'The picture man should be here in a minute,' he said. It sounded as though he were talking about Mr Rogers; Padgett Lanier was one of those people who think because I'm small, I'm childlike. 'I'd better let him go up first. Did you touch anything while you were up there, honey? How'd you happen to go up on the roof? Wait, here comes Jack; you might as well tell both of us at once.'

Detective Sergeant Jack Burns came next, and I heaved a sigh when I saw him emerge from his car. He hated my guts. On the other hand, he treated me like an adult. Burns was wearing one of his hideous suits, which he apparently bought at garage sales held on dark nights. He stood looking at the ladder with a face even grimmer than usual. He did not relish making the climb. His no-color hair was scantier than when I'd last seen him, and the flesh of his face was sagging.

Lynn Liggett Smith was right behind him, looking as slim, tall, and competent as ever, and she had the 'picture man' with her. Several other cars pulled in after Lynn's, and it began to seem that whoever was off duty or had decided they weren't needed at the moment had driven out to the Julius place to see what was happening. It was the place to be if you were a cop.

Martin murmured, 'Is there no other crime in this town that needs investigating? Surely somebody is running a stop sign somewhere.'

'Most of them, probably, were here six years ago,' I said.

After a thoughtful moment, he nodded.

Padgett Lanier conferred with Jack Burns, and the picture man was dispatched up the ladder first. Lynn went up after him to help carry his equipment. Fortunately, she was wearing slacks. She looked through the rungs at me on her way up. She shook her head slightly, as if I'd gotten up to another naughty trick.

The yard fell silent. All the policemen – and aside from Lynn, they were all male – looked up at the roof above our heads. I could hear the scrape of the photographer's shoes as he scrambled up the roof; the pause as he reached the top, saw the tarp. He said something to Lynn; I heard her reply, 'Here,' as she handed him his camera from her place on the ladder. I could only see her feet from my chair. Presumably he took a few pictures. I heard him say, 'Lift the tarp for me, Detective,' and then Lynn's progress across the roof. I swear I heard the rattle of the stiff, cracking plastic as Lynn raised it.

'They're stacked on top of each other, Martin,' I murmured. 'I guess it's all three of them.'

'Mostly bones, Roe?' Martin asked. His face was calm, and I knew he was being matter-of-fact because he knew I needed it. And because he had seen death far more often than I.

'Yes . . . mostly. The wig is on her skull. I told you that. I don't understand about the wig.'

'Probably a synthetic.'

'No, no. It's the wrong wig.'

His eyes were questioning and he leaned closer, but at that moment Lynn came down the ladder, turned to her superiors, and nodded curtly.

'Three of them,' she said. 'Three skulls, anyway.'

A collective sigh seemed to go up from the people on my front lawn.

'Jerry's going to pass the tarp down,' she said. 'Then he'll take more pictures.' She went to her car and got a large plastic garbage bag. She beckoned to a patrolman. He sprang to help, and they spread the mouth of the garbage bag wide. There were a series of scraping sounds as the photographer/policeman removed the tarp.

'Need someone up here to pass it down!' he called.

Jack Burns shambled forward to the foot of the ladder and began to climb heavily. He had pulled on plastic gloves.

They made an effort to pass the tarp down folded, so nothing would spill from its surface, but it was cracking with age and a few pieces had to be retrieved from the bushes around the porch. Finally it was sealed in the garbage bag and placed in Lynn's car.

'Get whoever's on dispatch to call Morrilton Funeral Home to come out here. Tell them what to expect,' she told the patrolman who'd helped hold the bag. He nodded and went to his patrol car radio.

Some of the men approached Lynn with a request, and after a moment's thought, she nodded. They converged at the foot of the ladder. One by one the men climbed up. We would hear the scrape of heavy official shoes, a silence as he peeked over the porch roof, then he would come down. The process would be repeated. While that was going on, Lynn and her two superiors congregated on the porch. Shelby got up and arranged three chairs facing ours. Angel took Martin's chair. He and Shelby stood on the side of the porch, where Angel and I could see them. This did not suit Jack Burns, I could tell, but he could hardly tell our husbands to leave when Angel and I were innocent bystanders to another family's tragedy.

'Could we move inside?' he asked, with as much geniality as he could muster.

Angel had actually shifted in her seat preparatory to rising when I said, 'I'd really rather not.' She shot me a startled look and tried to settle back as though she'd never moved. I saw from the corner of my eye that Martin had blinked in surprise, and Shelby turned to one side to hide a grin.

Lynn, Lanier, and Jack Burns all looked surprised, too.

I didn't want my house invaded.

'Well, it is a right nice day out here,' Lanier said smoothly.

'How did you come to go up on the roof, Roe?' Lynn asked.

'Angel and I were playing Frisbee.'

Lanier looked from Angel to me, comparing our sizes, and put his hand over his mouth to shield his smile.

'Angel threw the Frisbee, there was a gust of wind, and it ended up going up on the roof. I got the ladder, climbed up, got the Frisbee, and found – them.'

'You were there, Mrs Youngblood?' Lynn asked politely.

'I was holding the ladder. I'm scared of heights.'

'What happened to your face, young lady?' Jack Burns asked, in tones of tender solicitousness.

'I fell on the gravel driveway, and I couldn't catch myself in time,' Angel said. Her hands, resting on the arms of the chair, were perfectly relaxed.

'And you, Mr Bartell?' Lynn asked suddenly, swinging around in her seat to look at Martin. 'Where were you when your wife went up on the roof? And Mr Youngblood?'

'I was driving in from the airport. I got here while my wife was up on the roof,' Martin responded. 'I've been away on a business trip.'

'I was asleep,' Shelby said.

'You're not working today?'

'I felt sick this morning, and didn't go in. As a matter of fact, I started feeling real bad yesterday afternoon, all of a sudden. I came home from work then and haven't been back since.'

Shelby had neatly covered his sudden departure from work yesterday afternoon after Angel had called him. A 'just in case' move, I thought.

That was really all Lynn could ask us, given the circumstances. Perhaps it was even one or two questions more than she should have asked us, come to think about it.

'I'm taking my wife inside now, she's had a shock,' Martin said. The police cars were vanishing one by one, but local people were beginning to drive by; someone had been listening to a scanner. A hearse from Morrilton Funeral Home pulled into our driveway, and abruptly I could hardly wait to be inside the house.

There was no reason for me to stay, so Lynn nodded. Shelby and Angel came in with us. Martin pulled the drape cord in the living room and blocked out the cruising cars and the police and the funeral-home men. But nothing could block out the sounds from the roof.

Chapter Fourteen

I wanted the Youngbloods to go to their apartment. I wanted to forget about the mad ax-man and the bones on the roof. I wanted to watch an old movie on the TV, curled up on the couch with a big bowl of popcorn and maybe a beer. I wanted Martin upstairs after the movie was over. Or even earlier.

But his agenda was different, I realized with a sigh.

He gathered us around the table in the kitchen.

'Now, what happened yesterday?' he asked.

I told him again, and then Angel began her part, her battered face more testimony than her words.

I slumped back in my chair sullenly. A night short on sleep and two days of violent emotions were taking their toll. I was very tired and very sick of crises. I wanted this all to go away, just for a little while, so I could make one of my slow adjustments. But of course I was thinking again of the man who had run at me, and now that I was too tired to be scared, I thought more of his face. While Martin was saying something about security to the Youngbloods, something about the bushes, I realized that there had been something faintly familiar about the man. I associated him with construction, building . . .

The phone rang. I went to the counter to answer it. Sally Allison wanted to know all about the skeletons on the roof; she was not in her 'friend' mode, but in her 'reporter' mode. I told her.

'You know,' she said, 'the police will call in the forensic anthropologist on this one. Did you know Georgia is the only state with a forensic anthropologist on the payroll? He's never been called to a case in Spalding County before! He'll be here tomorrow.'

'Wouldn't it be funny,' I said, 'if it wasn't the Juliuses?'

Dead silence. Then Sally laughed uncertainly. 'Who else could it be, Roe?' she asked, as carefully as though she were speaking to a lunatic.

I thought, If I were rested I could figure this out, something important. 'Never mind,' I said. 'See you later, Sally.' I hung up, and the phone rang again. I dealt with that call. Then another. Finally, I switched off the sound and turned on the answering machine.

I sat down at the table with the others, who had been conferring in low voices all this time.

'Roe,' Martin began, and I knew he was about to tell me what to do.

'Martin,' I interrupted. 'I think Angel and I will take a few days off and fly to New Orleans.'

They all gaped at me. It was very gratifying.

'I know you need to go to Guatemala, and I expect Shelby needs to be getting back to work before the other people at the plant start to ask questions, so the best thing, with the phone ringing off the wall and all, would be for me – and Angel, since you think I need a bodyguard – to just go somewhere. And I think we might go to New Orleans. It's been years since I was there.'

Martin looked suspicious. But he said, 'That sounds good, Roe. Angel, how does that sound to you?'

'Suits me,' Angel said cautiously. 'I can pack and be ready to go in thirty minutes.'

'That would give me a chance to look into having some security installed here,' Shelby said.

'I don't want to find an armed fortress when I come back,' I told him.

He did not even look at Martin; give him credit for that. 'I won't do anything until I talk to you both,' he said.

I nodded and stood up in a very pronounced way. The Youngbloods rose instantly and left for their apartment. Martin went to the living room and looked through the crack in the drapes.

'They're leaving,' he said, not turning around. 'All the police. The hearse has gone.'

I waited.

He finally faced me. 'Roe, I don't know what to tell you now. Nothing has turned out as we planned. I wanted a good life for us, I wanted to provide for you and take care of you, and I never wanted any harm or upset to come to you. I thought I could keep the gun thing separate. I thought I would go to work at the plant and come home and you would tell me about whatever you were interested in and I would enjoy it and we would make love every night.'

Maybe I had sort of planned on all that, too.

'Well, Martin. It looks like we're not going to have that, exactly.' I walked over and put my arms around him, lay my head against his chest. He squeezed me so hard I thought I would squeak. 'We'll have something different, though. If you can disentangle yourself from this arms thing . . .' we have a chance, I finished silently. 'But,' I resumed, 'we can still go for part of your expectations.'

'Hmmmm?'

'We can make love every night.'

'Let's go upstairs.'

'Good idea.'

Readers, he carried me.

New Orleans. In New Orleans, Angel's battered face attracted little attention. Angel followed me grimly through the gorgeous new Aquarium of the Americas at the foot of Canal Street. Angel sulkily refused iced coffee and *beignets* at the Cafe du Monde. Angel accepted the rooms and the service at the Hyatt Regency with calm disdain. When a tattooed man on Bourbon Street grabbed my arm and made a suggestion so bizarre and indecent that my jaw dropped open, Angel stepped up from behind me, pressed his arm in a particular spot right above his elbow, and glanced back with grim satisfaction while he rubbed his useless arm and cursed.

'Why are we really here?' she asked after I'd bought my mother some antique earrings at a little shop in the French Quarter.

'Let's go on the walking tour of the cemetery,' I suggested. We met the tour guide at a little cafe close to the police station. The cafe was loaded with charm and fancy versions of coffee. The guide was also loaded with charm, if an offbeat brand, and I found myself as curious about his sex life as I was about the tour, which was very interesting – though I can't say Angel seemed too impressed. After we'd received the lecture about staying with the group since there'd been some muggings in the cemetery, I saw from Angel's restive gaze and alert stance that she was aching for someone to try to attack us.

'Why are we really here?' she asked, as we ate in a Cajun restaurant across from the convention center.

'Let's go to the zoo tomorrow,' I suggested.

When we got back to the Hyatt, I found Martin had left a voice message on my room telephone. 'I'm here, I'm trying hard, and it looks possible but difficult,' he said. 'I miss you more than I can say.' I had a sudden blur of tears in my eyes and sat on the side of my bed gripping a Kleenex.

It wasn't the message I'd hoped for. Dawdling in New Orleans, having a good time, wasn't going to work. I was going to have to try Plan B.

I should have called Sally Allison. It would have helped a lot. But frankly, it never occurred to me.

'Tomorrow, Angel,' I said, 'we're going to work.'

'About damn time.'

Chapter Fifteen

Angel was driving. She was very comfortable and competent behind the wheel. She'd opened up enough to tell me she'd taken several driving courses especially for bodyguards. We were going out to Metairie, a giant suburb of New Orleans, where Melba Totino had lived with her sister before she'd moved to Lawrenceton.

There was a phone listing for Mrs Totino's sister, Alicia Manigault, in the Metairie phone book.

Mrs Totino had gotten all misty when she spoke of her former home, but I couldn't see much about Metairie to love, from the interstate, anyway. There were hundreds of small houses jammed into tiny lots, charmless and styleless, leavened by an occasional motel or restaurant or strip shopping center. Surely there were prettier parts of Metairie somewhere?

The heat had begun in earnest here, and I shuddered when I thought of what it must be like in July or August. We had the air-conditioning on in the rental car, and I still felt sticky when we got out on the short, narrow street where Alicia Manigault lived. Scrubby, stunted palms were planted here and there in tiny yards. All the houses were very small and one story, and though some of them were spic and span, others were in need of repair and paint. I would hate living in a place like this more than anything I could imagine. I felt very there-but-for-the-grace-of-God.

The squat flat-roofed house at the phone book address was moderately well cared for. The grass was mowed, but there were no ornamental touches to the yard, beyond some straggly foundation bushes. The house, formerly barn red, was peeling, and the side facing the afternoon sun was noticeably lighter than the rest of the house.

Angel unfolded herself from the dark green rental car and

surveyed the street expressionlessly. 'What do you want to do?' she asked.

'Ring the doorbell.'

The whole property was enclosed in a low chain-link fence. The gate creaked.

There didn't seem to be a doorbell, so I knocked instead. My heart was beating uncomfortably.

A young woman answered.

I had never seen her before. She was very fat, very fair, wearing a pink dollar-store 'Plus-Size' muumuu.

'What you want?' she asked. She didn't look unfriendly, just busy.

'Is Mrs Manigault here?' I asked.

'Alicia? No, she's not here.'

'She doesn't live here?'

'Well, it's her house,' the young woman said, her small blue eyes blinking in a puzzled way behind blue-framed glasses.

'And you rent it from her,' Angel said.

'My husband and me, yeah, we do. What you want with Alicia?' A strange sound behind her made the young woman turn her head.

'Listen, come on in,' she said. 'I got a sick dog in here.'

We followed, her into the tiniest living room I had ever seen. It was jammed with vinyl furniture covered with crocheted afghans in a variety of patterns. The only thing they had in common was a stunningly dreadful combination of colors. Angel and I gaped.

'I know,' the woman said, with a little laugh, 'everyone just cain't believe it. I sell them at craft shows on the weekend, but the ones in here are my favorites. I just couldn't sell them. My husband always says, "You'd think we got cold here!" '

She bent over a basket in the corner by a doorway into, I thought, the kitchen. When she straightened, she had in her arms a tiny black dog with brown on its muzzle – a Toy Manchester, I thought.

'Kickapoo,' she said proudly. 'That's his name.'

Angel made a snorting noise and I realized she was trying not to laugh. I was too concerned by the obvious illness of the dog. It was limp and listless in her arms.

'What's the matter?' I asked, not at all sure I really wanted to know.

'He got hurt,' she said. 'A bad man kicked our little doggy two days ago, didn't he, Kickapoo?'

'Oh, that's terrible!'

'Kickapoo couldn't hurt anyone, you can see that,' said the woman, dreadful indignation printed deep in folds of fat. 'I don't know what was the matter with him.' I assumed she was referring to the kicker. 'He was in a bad mood that day, but he never has done nothing like that.'

'Not your husband?' I inquired incredulously.

'Oh, no! Carl loves our little doggy,' she said, 'doesn't he, Kickapoo?'

The dog didn't nod.

'No, this was a friend of Alicia's, the man she has collect the rent and tend to things for her. 'Course, we mow the lawn and take care of the little repairs, but if something big goes wrong, we call . . .' and she stopped dead.

'Yes?' I said encouragingly. I was totally bored with the conversation until the woman so obviously remembered she wasn't supposed to be having it.

'Nothing. Here I am, going on and on. I haven't even found out what you need.'

Angel and I were both well dressed that day, since I thought that'd be reassuring to an old lady like Alicia Manigault. I was wearing a little suit with a white jacket and a navy skirt, and Angel had on tailored black slacks and a sapphire blue blouse with a gold chain and earrings. So it wasn't out of the question for Angel to claim we were from the Metairie Senior Citizens' Association, which she promptly did.

'Oh,' the woman said. 'I never heard of that. But that's nice.'

'And you're Mrs—?' Angel said pointedly.

The woman reached for an eyedropper by a bottle of medicine on a table jammed into one end of the living room. She squeezed what was in it into the little dog's mouth. It swallowed obediently.

'Coleman,' she said, looking down at the animal. 'Lanelda Coleman.'

'So Mrs Manigault doesn't need transportation services to and from the center?' Angel asked.

'No, she's just here a few weeks a year,' Lanelda Coleman told us.

I was totally at sea.

I opened my mouth to ask where she was the rest of the year, but my cohort kicked me in the ankle.

'Then we'll just go, I can tell you've got your hands full,' Angel said sympathetically.

'Oh,' Lanelda said, 'I do. We're just terrified Kickapoo is hurt bad. We've about decided to take him to the vet. It's so expensive!'

I moved restlessly. They adored the dog but hadn't taken him to the vet?

'It sure is,' Angel agreed.

'Carl and I just were up all night with this little thing,' Lanelda said abstractedly, her attention on the dog.

'The man who kicked him should pay for the vet visit,' Angel said.

I turned to stare at her.

Lanelda's face looked suddenly determined. 'You know, lady, you're right,' she said. 'I'm gonna call him the minute Carl gets home.'

'Good luck,' I said, and we left.

We conferred by the car.

'We need to ask some questions,' I said.

'But not of her. She's been told not to talk about the arrangements for that house by someone, someone she's scared of. We don't want her calling whoever it is and telling them we've been asking questions.'

'So what do we do?'

'We move the car,' Angel said slowly. 'Then we go from house to house. Her curtains are closed, and she's busy with the dog. She may not notice. Our cover story is that we're canvassing old people in the neighborhood about the need for a community center with hot meals and transportation to and from this center every day. I just hope Metairie doesn't have one already. Ask questions about the old ladies who own Number Twenty-one.'

I looked up at Angel admiringly. 'Good idea.'

I wasn't so enthusiastic an hour later. I'd never knocked on strangers' doors before. We'd waited until after five o'clock so people would be home; most of the mothers here would be working mothers.

This was an experience that I later wanted to forget. I was never intended to be a private detective; I was too thin-skinned. The old people were suspicious, the younger people were too busy at this time of day to give much thought to my questions, or could think of no good reason why they should spend time talking to a stranger. I actually had a door or two shut in my face.

One woman in her sixties, Betty Lynn Sistrump, did remember the sisters when they were in residence, and had known them superficially.

'I was amazed when Alicia told me Melba had moved out,' Mrs Sistrump said. She was wearing a bathrobe and a lot of makeup for a woman her age – or any age. 'They were like Siamese twins or somethin'. Always together, though they sure fought sometimes.'

'So you don't think Mrs Totino lives anywhere in Metairie?' I asked, to keep up the fiction. 'We need to contact her about the center, if she does.'

'Alicia said she was going back up to someplace up north – Georgia, I think – to live with her daughter.'

'Do you remember about when that was?' I managed to say. I'd been struck almost speechless at the thought of Georgia being far north to this woman. Georgia, north! If my hair had been shorter, it would've bristled.

When Mrs Sistrump opined it'd been about five years, more or less, since she'd talked to Alicia – though she'd caught glimpses of her since then going into and out of the house – she admitted it had caused her no grief, not seeing the sisters. And that was the impression I'd gotten from all the people on the street who would actually talk to me.

Flattened by the whole experience, I returned to the rental car to find Angel leaning against it staring off into space. Angel had a great quality of repose.

'Carl's home,' she said. 'It must be him. He went in without knocking.'

It took me a few seconds to track that down mentally.

'Okay,' I said cautiously.

'Lanelda said,' Angel reminded me, 'that when Carl came home, she would talk to him about calling the man who'd kicked their dog. And that's the man who must know where Alicia Manigault is.'

'So what do we do?' I asked uncertainly.

'I can try to creep in there under the windows and listen,' Angel said dubiously. 'Or we can just wait to see if the man comes. He'd have to to give them the money for the vet visit, wouldn't he?'

'Sounds pretty iffy. What if the dog died this afternoon? What if the man says he won't give a dime?'

'Got a better idea?'

Well, we could go back to our luxurious hotel and order a great meal. But that wasn't why we were here, I told myself.

It was still light, but fading fast. While we waited for it to get darker, so Angel could gauge if she could risk her creep, we drove to the nearest fast-food place. While we dealt with French fries and chicken sandwiches in the rental car, we exchanged stories about our block canvass.

Of the people Angel had talked to, only two householders remembered the sisters. The other people had moved in since Alicia had rented the house. The two accounts Angel had pieced together basically matched Betty Lynn Sistrump's. About six years before, Alicia had told people who cared enough to inquire that her sister had gone to live with her daughter. Soon after that, Alicia had rented the house and had only appeared from time to time since then. One alert woman, confined to a wheelchair and dependent on neighborhood happenings for her entertainment, remembered a police car visiting the house about then – an occurrence so unusual that she'd asked Alicia about it, the next time she'd seen her.

'And got my head bit off for asking,' she'd told Angel. 'I guess I was just being nosy, but wouldn't you be? I mean, what if she'd had a robbery or a prowler? Those are things other people in the same neighborhood need to know about, aren't they?'

'And she never asked you why a do-gooder trying to find out if Alicia Manigault needed a ride to a senior citizens' center would need to know that?'

'Nope,' Angel said, simply. 'She just wanted someone to talk to. And she wanted to know if the bus that would take them was equipped to handle wheelchairs. I had to tell her the whole thing was still pretty much up in the air. She was disappointed.'

We looked away from each other, off into the distance. Angel drank the last of her Coke. Spenser and Hawk we weren't; not even Elvis Cole and Joe Pyke.

'What do you think, is it dark enough?' I asked.

'Yep. But I've been looking at that yard, and I don't think there's a single place I could get that I wouldn't be visible from at least four other houses.'

'Um. You're right.'

'So we better just watch for a while. Maybe he'll come. Whoever he is.'

In the short time it had taken to collect our food, return, and eat, the character of the neighborhood had changed. More cars were home; the little street was jammed with people who'd had to park at the curb. The streetlights had come on in the deep dusk and cast sharp-contrast shadows. There were some children outside playing. Angel was right, creeping around that little property was out of the question in a neighborhood as congested as this one. It was hard to see how we could sit and observe, even. How did police stake out places like this? Surely, if we started moving and kept driving by, someone would eventually get suspicious.

We left for a minute, and pulled in down the street a little, in front of a house that was still dark and had no vehicles in the driveway. We looked at our watches and shook our heads; pantomime of people waiting impatiently. Then Angel watched in the rear-view mirror and I watched the side mirror.

'I thought you were used to this, Angel,' I said.

'How come?'

'You used to be a bodyguard.'

'Then, I was watching out for people like me. I was trying to find anyone waiting for my employer. I never waited for anyone.'

'Oh. What happened to your last client? Martin never told me.'

Angel diverted her eyes from the mirror to look at me directly. 'And for good reason,' she said. 'Believe me, you don't want to know.'

I had a feeling she was right.

Sooner than we had any right to expect, our vigil was rewarded. Carl must have been persuasive or righteous over the phone. A pickup squealed up, a white one with a fancy pattern of fuchsia and green flames painted trailing down the side.

'Don't know where he can park,' Angel muttered. 'There's only one spot left on the whole street, and that's right in front of us . . . Shit, was I stupid! Get down!' The pickup did indeed maneuver into the space against the curb ahead of our rental car. The driver would have to walk right past us.

I dove down onto the floorboard and compressed myself into as tiny a ball as possible. Angel, as usual, had had her hair pulled back in a ponytail; now she yanked out the band that held it, fluffed her hair quickly, and unfolded our New Orleans map with hasty fingers. She held the map up, partially obscuring her face, where the bruises were fading and there were only a few scabs left.

I heard the pickup door slam and heavy steps pass quickly by the car.

'Is he going to their house?' I whispered.

'Shut up! Yes!'

After a long moment, Angel said, 'Okay, you can sit up. He's inside.'

'Did you get a good look at him?'

'Yeah.' She had the strangest expression as she gathered up her hair and bound it back into her customary ponytail.

'So?'

'It was the man who tried to kill us.'

The ax-man, somehow in league with Melba Totino and her sister Alicia? So he wasn't in any way involved with my husband's Latin American ventures; we could safely have called the police when he attacked us. We could be on the right side of the law, instead of Martin's side.

'So. We follow him?' Angel asked.

'I guess so,' I said. 'Can you figure this out?'

Angel shook her head. But she wasn't unconcerned; her mouth was compressed into an even thinner line. Her hands gripped the steering wheel until her knuckles turned white. She hadn't liked being beaten, she hadn't liked having been so close to losing her client, she hadn't liked having to tell Martin or her husband about what had happened, and on a personal level, I suspected she really hadn't liked having her face messed up.

From being basically indifferent about what she considered a personal obsession of mine, Angel had graduated to being vitally interested in the Julius case. So we both watched eagerly for the man's emergence from the little house.

'We better not be here when he comes out again,' Angel said, and she started the car. We drove around the block until we were positioned on a cross street so that when he came out, we would be able to fall in behind him unless he did something crazy, like attempting a U-turn on the narrow, crowded street.

I was able to see him for the first time when he shut the door of Alicia Manigault's house behind him. He was tall and muscular, and he looked younger than I'd remembered him. He wore jeans and a work shirt, with the sleeves rolled up. His hair was dark and curly, and he was clean-shaven; Angel and I had been good witnesses. It was hard to square this all-American blue-collar hunk with the maniac waving an ax who'd so nearly mowed me down a few days before.

'He's walking a little stiff,' Angel said happily. 'I think we banged him around some.'

'I hope so.'

He strode to his lurid pickup truck and started it up.

We drove out of Metairie and across the Huey P. Long Bridge and went south steadily. After at least twenty miles, he turned right, and we followed him. He didn't seem to be looking out for cars following him, or for anything else.

'An amateur,' Angel muttered. I couldn't tell if she was pleased by our attacker's amateurism, or disgusted, or enraged. If it was difficult following him at night, she didn't say so.

Now we were on a narrow road with a bayou on one side, houses on the other. There were boats lining the bayou, with signs for swamp tours, promising alligators and abundant wildlife. Most of the signs featured the word 'Cajun'. The lighting wasn't good, but the white truck with the bright blazes painted on the side was fairly easy to spot. Finally it slowed and turned into one of the narrow driveways. We had to drive on past, and I stared as hard as I could in the dark to see a sort of cabin with a screened-in front porch. Ax-man had parked the truck under a carport, which the truck shared with a battered blue Chevy Nova and a tarp-covered boat.

'That's the car he was driving in Georgia,' Angel said.

We drove on until we came to a juke joint, where Angel pulled in and parked. We looked at each other questioningly.

Neither of us knew what to do next.

'We could watch all night, or we could come back tomorrow, or we could call Shelby from a pay phone in there.' Angel nodded her head towards the bar, from which came loud zydeco music and a fairly constant flow of in-and-out traffic. I wasn't about to go in there.

'Let's find out more before we call Shelby,' I said. 'I want to know who lives in that house.'

Chapter Sixteen

It rained the next morning, steamy relentless rain that made the inside of the rental car damp and sticky despite the air conditioner. We went from the Hyatt Regency in urban New Orleans to the cabin in rural south Louisiana, a sort of cultural leap that sat better with Angel than it did with me. By the time we got there, the truck was gone, but the old Nova was still parked where it had been the night before.

There were neighbors close to this cabin; lots facing the bayou were as valuable as waterfront property anywhere, especially since most of the people along this stretch of road apparently made their living giving tourists swamp tours. On the other hand, since tourists were common, we didn't stick out as obviously as we might have. A tiny souvenir shop sitting cheek-by-jowl with a boat tour departure site was already open. The man inside, dressed in camouflage greens and browns, his rough black hair in tousled waves, looked like a refugee from a Rambo movie. Angel put on some lipstick and slid from the car. 'He's more my type,' she told me. 'I'll see what I can find out.' The rain had settled down to a very light drizzle.

She'd left her elastic band off this morning, and her blond hair fluffed prettily around her narrow face. In a pair of tight jeans, a sleeveless T-shirt, and sneakers, she could stop traffic if she chose, and this morning, she did choose. She sauntered up to the service window of the little shack, rested her elbows on the sill, and within a minute was deep in conversation with the dark-haired man, whose white teeth flashed in a constant grin. Angel was smiling, shrugging, tossing back her hair, and in general behaving atypically. But it seemed to be quite effective. When she started back to the car, she turned around several times to call back, as he extended the conversation.

'Whoo,' she said in relief, as she slid into her seat. 'Talk about Cajun! He had an accent so thick you could cut it, and could charm the birds from the trees, too.'

'What did he say?'

'I told him this long story . . . I'd met this guy in a bar last night, and I didn't know his name, but he had this really distinctive truck and lived somewhere right about here. And then I said I'd lost the napkin with his name and phone number, but I was trying to track him down before he called me, because I suspected he was married. And I wanted to know for sure before I went out with him.'

'And?'

'This guy in the souvenir booth wanted me to forget about the man I'd met last night and go out with him instead, but I told him I'd promised the man I'd meet him tonight, though I'd shove him off if he was married.' Angel made a circular sweep with her hand to indicate how long this badinage had taken her. 'What it all boils down to – the ax-man is renting this cabin, has been for a couple of years now. No one owns a house along this road that isn't Cajun, by the way, because of some law that the houses go to family members and no one ever sells, but this particular house, the only son is in the Army right now and just wants someone to live in it until he comes back from his tour of duty – or something like that.'

'Did you get a name?'

'The name is apparently Dumont, or something like that. He works at the lumber yard not five minutes from here. And he is married; or at least there's a woman in residence, and Rene said he's heard she's pretty ferocious. He advised me to keep clear.'

'I don't know what to do now,' I observed, after we'd looked at each other other for a moment or two. 'Why would a man named Dumont attack us with an ax? Why is he the rent collector for Alicia Manigault? Where is she? She can't be dead, if she appears for a few weeks each year and crams herself into that house with the Colemans and the dog.'

'And what does it all have to do with the bodies on the roof of your house, as long as we're asking questions?' Angel added. 'All I know to do is ask someone who might know the answer.'

I thought long and hard to find a way around that, but it did seem as if that was the only way to do it. At least the ax-man was gone, and maybe we could find out something in his absence that would explain his attack on us. What we were going to do about it once we discovered the reason, I hadn't the faintest notion.

'Someone comes running at me with an ax, I want to know why,' Angel said. She was looking at me sideways, sensing my hesitation.

This was a point of pride for Angel.

'Let's go knock on the door,' I said.

We reconnoitered briefly. There were no cars at the houses on either side of the cabin. We looked at each other and shrugged.

I pulled boldly into the driveway. I was driving, with Angel crouched on the floorboards. I parked as close as possible behind the old car, so the passenger door was not as visible from the front window. As soon as I'd gone inside with the woman, providing as much distraction as possible, Angel was to slip from the car and snake around back. There were enough bushes in the yard to provide cover. If the air conditioner wasn't already on, maybe there'd be a window open so Angel could hear if I got into trouble.

This was pretty close to having no plan at all.

My palms were sweating as I got out of the rental car. It was still raining enough to keep the tourists away, and the Bayou Cajun Boat Tour place across the road was deserted. I clamped my purse under one arm as if it were a friend, and I marched up to the cabin, creaked across the screened-in porch, and rang the doorbell.

I was prepared for the woman who answered the door to be

tough, perhaps cheap-looking and foul-mouthed. Though very nervous, I was braced.

But I was not ready for the door to be answered by a dead woman.

'Yes?' said Charity Julius.

She thought much more quickly than I, no doubt about it.

The expression on my face and the gasp I gave left no doubt in her mind that she was recognized. She didn't know who the hell I was, but she knew I recognized her.

About the time Angel was gliding around the side of the house on her way to the back, Charity Julius punched me in the stomach hard enough to double me over, and while I was bent, she brought her clenched fists down in a vicious blow to the back of my neck. By the time Angel was at the kitchen window listening, Charity Julius was dragging me to the bedroom and locking me into a closet where I suppose the owner ordinarily kept his guns; it was equipped with a very high outside padlock. At about the moment Angel began to be concerned at not hearing my voice, Charity was calling the ax-man at his job, and he was tearing home in his flashy truck.

I was sore but conscious in the dark closet, which seemed to be full of hard, lumpy things. I hauled myself to my feet, slowly and reluctantly, and waved my hand around above my head. I was rewarded with the feel of the string of the closet light. I gave it a tug, and looked around me in the sudden glare.

There were out-of-season clothes pushed to one side, and the other was occupied with fishing gear. The floor was covered with boots, from lace-up steel-toe leather ones to thigh-high waders.

I hoped Angel would come soon, but something might have happened to her, too. I had better find a weapon of some kind. The fishing poles refused to break into a usable length until I found an old bamboo one. With some effort, I shortened it to about a yard. The thick end was quite heavy, and I thought that if I had room to swing it, I could cause some harm.

'What are you doing in there?' Charity Julius asked from the other side of the door. It seemed prudent not to answer.

'We're going to take care of you, whoever you are,' she said raggedly. 'No one's found us in all this time, and we'll get the money in four more months. We haven't waited all these years for nothing.'

I leaned against the door. 'Who's on the roof instead of you?' I asked. I was too curious not to.

'They found them?' It was Charity's turn to be shocked. 'Oh, no,' she said, so quietly I could barely catch the words.

I wondered why Mrs Totino hadn't called her granddaughter. She had to know Charity was alive; her live-in lover's presence in the life of Alicia Manigault proved that. So why hadn't Charity known?

I shifted uncomfortably in the cramped space. What was taking Angel so long? A glance at my watch said fifteen minutes had crawled by.

I had a feeling things weren't going my way when I heard the male voice outside.

'Harley! She's in the closet,' Charity Julius said, and another piece dropped into place. Harley Dimmoch only wanted his family to call at a certain time because then he, and not Charity, could be sure to answer the phone. He didn't let them come visit without lots of notice because she would have to stay somewhere else.

'Let's see who it is,' he was saying, and then I had only the quick rattle of the key in the lock to warn me. I raised the fishing rod and launched myself out of the closet, which almost got me shot dead. The young dark-haired man was holding a no-nonsense revolver in his hands, and at my appearance he fired. Fortunately for me, the fishing rod caught him in the stomach and the shot went high, but at least it settled matters for Angel, who came through the unlocked back door like gangbusters.

The small bedroom was full of shouting, moving bodies, and the fear of the gun.

Charity was so busy trying to grab me that she missed Angel's appearance until Angel justified all her martial-arts training by kicking Charity in the side of the knee, a decisive move, since Charity shrieked and folded instantly, and thereafter lay on the floor moaning.

Harley Dimmoch had grabbed my arm with his free hand and was trying to aim the gun with the other when Charity shrieked. He saw her go down, and I watched his face twist with desperation. He had begun to swing his arm to fire at Angel when she seized it, twisted his wrist clockwise with a curiously delicate grip of her fingers, slid closer to him and under his arm, and then with his arm twisted and extended in what must have been an excruciatingly painful position, kicked one leg out from under him and kept on raising his arm while he was falling until his shoulder dislocated – or perhaps his arm broke.

He screamed and fainted.

The gun was lying on the floor beside his useless arm. With the end of the fishing rod, I poked it into the closet where I'd been imprisoned and shut the door. Angel and I looked at each other and panted and grinned.

'Idiot,' she said, 'if the gun hadn't gone off, I'd still be out there wondering what was happening.'

'Idiot,' I said, 'if you'd known he'd come home, you could have jumped him out in the driveway and then he wouldn't have had a chance to pull a gun on me.'

'What the hell happened to you? I didn't hear a thing after I got around back!'

'She punched me in the stomach and then the neck,' I explained, pointing to the young woman clutching her knee on the floor. 'That's Charity Julius.'

For one second Angel's face reflected the shock I'd felt.

'So the ax-man,' she said, 'must be Harley Dimmoch?'

'Yep.'

Charity tried to get up, gripping one of the cheap pine night tables, but she collapsed back on the floor with a white face and sobs of pain. I was far from wanting to comfort her, and she would have been glad if I'd been in her place, but still, I felt uncomfortable, to say the least.

Angel left the room for a minute and reappeared with some heavy, silvery duct tape and a pair of scissors. She used the tape efficiently on Harley Dimmoch's ankles and Charity Julius's wrists. I held Charity up while Angel worked, shrinking from touching her but having to.

The gunshot had attracted no attention, apparently. No one pulled up, or called, or knocked on the door. We three women gradually calmed down. Charity regained control of herself. Her wide dark eyes stared at us assessingly.

'What now?' she asked.

'We're thinking,' Angel answered. I was glad she had. I had no idea what would come next. But obeying an irresistible impulse, I leaned forward and looked into her face and asked, 'Who is the third body?'

She closed her eyes for a minute. She must be twenty-one now; she looked older.

'My grandmother,' she said.

'Then who is the woman living in Lawrenceton?'

'My great-aunt, Alicia.'

'Tell me,' I said intently. 'Tell me what happened that day.' Finally, finally, first among all the people who had wondered, I would be the one who knew. It was almost like being the only one to discover Jack the Ripper's true identity, or getting the opportunity to be a fly on the wall on a hot, hot day in Fall River, Massachusetts, in 1892.

'My aunt was visiting. She was staying over in Grandmother's apartment with Grandmother.'

'How did she get there?'

'She came by bus. My dad picked her up in Atlanta. She had been there three days.'

'How come nobody knew?'

'Who was to know? Who was to care? We didn't have many visitors, mostly because Mom was so sick. I didn't talk about it at school. Why would I? And Daddy had been working on the roof for three days, trying to get it finished. Going to pick her up was a pain in the butt, an interruption, but since Mother and Grandmother wanted her to be there, he did it.

'Harley had come to visit me and to help Daddy. I said I was sick and stayed home from school. I don't think they believed me, but they knew how much I missed Harley and they were willing to give me a little slack.'

Her face was flinty when she said this. She was willing herself not to feel, as she'd been willing herself not to for all these years.

'Harley – lady, do you think he's okay? He looks awful bad; you should call an ambulance.' She had asked Angel, not me.

'He's okay. He's breathing,' Angel said with apparent unconcern. But I noticed she was taking his pulse when Charity looked away.

'Harley was up on the roof with Daddy, hammering away. It was the day the patio was going to be poured; they'd spent the morning building the form. Daddy just insisted Harley help him, and Harley didn't really mind, but he had come to see me, and he was going to have to go back home without having talked to me very much. Daddy just didn't seem to understand, it was like when we lived close to Harley and Harley would help Daddy all the time, but then we could go out on a date and be away from them. But up on the roof, Daddy starts this heavy churchy stuff, about how Harley was going to have to stop drinking and learn how to control his temper if he was going to marry me, which was what Harley and I wanted. And he reminded Harley, all this Bible stuff, about keeping his hands off me until we were married, was what it boiled down to.' She sighed deeply, shifted to try to make herself more comfortable. 'Listen, can't you get me a pillow, or something?'

Angel got a pillow from the bed and eased it under Charity's shoulders. Charity was as striking as the newspaper picture had suggested, but even stronger looking, with the large dark eyes and the jawline giving her face character. What kind of character, I was finding out.

'So,' she resumed, 'Harley decides that up on the roof with my dad is a good time and place to tell him we've already slept together.' She rolled her eyes, the very portrait of an exasperated teenager. Silly old Harley. 'My dad went nuts. He was yelling and screaming and swinging his hammer around, and said Harley had to leave and not see me anymore. Harley got scared and mad, and he swung his hammer, and it hit my dad in the head, and he died. Right up there on the roof.'

I closed my eyes.

'Then Harley climbed down and told me. Mama had been over visiting with Grandmama and Alicia in the apartment, and she hadn't heard anything.'

Her face twisted with pain, and I felt another pang of guilt. What were we going to do with these people? But she rallied and plowed on, and I could tell she was feeling a certain degree of relief in the telling.

'I knew that Mama would tell. And Harley would go to jail. I'd never see him again. So I told Harley to go back up on the roof, and when Mama came back I told her to go up to the bedroom, lean out the window, Daddy and Harley had something they wanted her to see. So when she leaned out the window, Harley hit her, too.' She must have read something in my face, because she said, 'Mama was really sick, anyway, she was going to die.'

And no traces of the murders had been found in the house, because they had actually taken place on the roof.

'What about your grandmother?' Angel said.

'Well, I knew she would tell about Mama,' Charity said pettishly. 'It just seemed to grow and grow. I'd always felt closer to Alicia, anyway. Me and Harley couldn't think of what to do, so I told Great-aunt Alicia what had happened. She and my grandmother had never gotten along good, and sharing that house in Metairie had just made it worse. They had hardly any money, and they didn't have many friends, and she had forged Grandmother's name before, once or twice, and not gotten caught. She said people couldn't tell old women apart anyway. What she told us to do – she thought about the money right away – she said we might as well get it and have a life, rather than going to jail, that Mama and Daddy wouldn't have wanted me to go to jail. So she called Grandmama, and told her Mama was up in her bedroom and was feeling very bad, and Grandmama hurried up those stairs, and when she was in the bedroom looking around, I sort of wrapped my arms around her and stuck her head out the window, and Harley . . . took care of her.'

My stomach lurched.

I would just as soon not have heard more, but by then I couldn't have stopped her.

'We sat down in the kitchen and talked. Harley was kind of crazy by that time. We couldn't decide what to do with the bodies, or what to tell Mr Engle, who was coming to pour the concrete in two hours. Then we thought . . . just leave them where they are. Harley said we should cover them with lime, that's what his dad did when the family dog died and they didn't want other animals coming in the yard to dig at the grave. And up on the roof, we'd get turkey buzzards if we didn't do it . . . So he went into Atlanta and bought the lime and a gray tarp . . . He had gotten some blood on his clothes so he borrowed some of my daddy's. Harley got back and fixed them up on the roof, and then he waited.

'Alicia had realized by then that no one knew she was there, so she could pretend to be Grandmama. And she said if I put on Mama's wig, Mr Engel wouldn't know from a distance it wasn't Mama. And he had to see me as me, too. We'd just tell him Daddy had had to go off on an errand. So Harley drove the truck around behind the garage and hid it while Mr Engle was there, and I went out and talked to him, and then I ran upstairs and put on Mama's Sunday wig, because she was wearing the other one.' For a second the toughness cracked in Charity Julius's face and I could see the horror underneath. 'And I went and rattled round in the kitchen so Mr Engle could see me, and Alicia pretended to be Grandmama.'

I had wondered all along why Hope Julius had been wearing her Sunday wig when Parnell had seen her working in her kitchen, yet it had been on the wig stand when Sally had been shown through the house the next day. And I had seen the everyday wig, its synthetic hair fluttering in the breeze on the roof.

'How did you vanish?' I asked.

'It was my great-aunt who realized I had to. We sat down that night and figured it out. Harley had to go home like nothing was wrong. I had washed and dried his clothes by then, and he put them back on and we just put the ones of Daddy's he'd been wearing in a garbage bag . . . Harley's hairs might be on them or something. And I got in the car with him, not taking hardly anything of mine, just one change of clothes, because Alicia said it had to look like I'd just been taken without notice. I put Mama's wig back on the wig form; my hair was enough like Mama's that I didn't figure it would matter if they found one of my hairs in it. Then Harley, on his way back home, dropped me off at a bus station. I had the key to the house in Metairie. We used all the cash Mama had in her purse to buy the ticket.'

'The police checked all the bus stations within a reasonable radius,' I said.

'I wore an old pair of Mama's glasses, and I put a pillow in my front like I was pregnant,' Charity said rather proudly. 'That about knocked Harley over, he really laughed.'

For the first time, I met Angel's eyes. She was looking as sick as I felt. I had completely lost my taste for this insider information.

But she went on talking, though Harley was now stirring and moaning. She'd stayed in the Metairie house for a couple of days, eating only what was in the pantry and not going outside. On the third night, she'd slipped out of the house very late, gone to a pay phone at a convenience store a few blocks away, and called her great-aunt, asking her to get a message to Harley. Harley's parents might question a young woman calling their house. Harley could join her as soon as the investigation died down, maybe in a month, they figured.

'I couldn't stay in the house that long, someone would see me, I knew,' Charity said. 'I was going crazy.'

I was willing to bet that was true: shut in a house, forced to remain invisible, with her last memories of her family closed in that house with her.

'So what did you do?'

'Aunt Alicia cashed one of my grandmother's checks and snuck out and mailed it to General Delivery, Metairie, and after I picked it up, I went to New Orleans and rented a room and found a job. I'd never done any of that before.' She sounded rather proud. 'I gave them Harley's name and Social Security number. I figured girls could be named Harley, too. And it was a real Social Security number. I had it written in my billfold. I knew everything about Harley.'

'And he came down when he figured it was safe?' Angel wanted to cut this true confession short. She (and Harley) were shifting restlessly.

'And got a job at the lumber place. And then we rented this cabin. And here we've been for all this time. Until you found us. Who the hell are you two?'

'I own the Julius house,' I said.

'Oh, you're the one Alicia called about. The one Harley was supposed to get rid of. The one who was asking so many questions, with too much time on her hands.'

I could have done without Angel's cocked eyebrow.

'But he said he screwed it up. And he was too scared, being back in that area where someone might recognize him, to try again. He was so mad . . . Listen, I'll bet you don't care, but really I'm in awful pain.'

'Why didn't your great-aunt just sell her house and drop the phone number?' It was the last question I really wanted an answer to.

'She and Grandmother both had to be there for a house closing; they owned it jointly. And if Alicia cut off the phone, where was she supposed to be? People did call her from time to time . . . and she had to get her mail somehow. So she got the idea of renting it to that tub of lard, her cousin's daughter, so she could get some money to live on till the estate was probated . . . four months! We almost made it!'

And her confessional mood changed suddenly to hatred, all directed at me. She actually managed to heave herself at me, despite the broken knee, despite bound hands. I found myself wondering if it were true that Harley had wielded the hammer in all three murders.

'I've had a thought,' Angel said, unmoved by Charity's desperation. 'If the forensic anthropologist examined those bones the day after you found them, he knew that one skeleton wasn't Charity. He must have told them it was an old woman. So who are the police going to question first?'

'The woman they think is Mrs Totino.'

'Right. So why hasn't she called down here to warn these two? Why didn't she tell them the bodies had been found?'

I could tell from Charity's face she was asking herself the same thing. I was regretting not calling Sally Allison. I would have known so much more. I could have called the police anonymously, if I had figured out Charity Julius was alive; I wouldn't have been so shocked by a confrontation with a woman I thought was dead these past six years. And now we wouldn't be in the strange fix we were in now.

'They've got her in custody, or they're watching her so closely she thinks they're tapping her phone calls,' I said. 'I bet she never called these two from her own phone anyway.'

'Think Alicia will break?'

'I bet she will. Not because she's fragile, but because she'll want company, someone to blame the actual murders on. Yeah . . . once they actually question her identity, she can't keep up the pretense that she's Melba Totino, at least not for long.'

'This is going to be awfully hard to explain,' Angel commented.

That was an understatement.

'I have to go to a hospital,' said Harley clearly.

He was badly hurt, and so was Charity, and damned if I knew what to do with them.

'Shelby's not gonna like it if I get arrested for assault,' Angel said. I hardly thought Martin would enjoy my arrest either.

'Here's what we're gonna do,' Angel told her two white-faced victims. 'We're gonna leave, and we'll call the police from a pay phone.'

'What fucking good is that going to do us?' Harley asked.

'For one thing, you ungrateful moron, they'll take you to the hospital. Now, I'd like to point out that we could just leave you here to rot, or we could kill you, and I guarantee no one would miss you.'

I turned away so the two killers couldn't see the shock on my face.

'We'll tell them you did this,' Charity spat. 'You'll do jail time.'

'No I won't, and I'll tell you why,' Angel said calmly. 'Because we're not gonna tell the police about Harley trying to kill us. And we're both alive to tell about it, and positively identify him, too. But the minute you tell the cops about us, we tell them about you. At least this way you'll only stand trial on some old charges, with no evidence left to collect or eyewitnesses.'

It wasn't much, but it was something, and in the end they agreed. What choice did they have? We wiped my fingerprints off the fishing rod and anything else I might have touched in the closet, and Angel, I saw with some amazement, was wearing plastic gloves. I was feeling uncomfortably like a criminal myself.

They didn't ask why we hadn't told the police about Harley's first attack, thank goodness.

We left the house and didn't speak to each other until after we'd stopped at the next convenience store. Angel was driving again, and she parked rather over to one side so the rental car wasn't readily visible from the clerk's counter. She got out and used the phone. I waited numbly, slumped in my seat.

We negotiated the rest of the drive still in the same silence. When we were once more in our Hyatt room, light-years away from the cabin by the bayou, Angel said she was *very* hungry, and I realized I was, too. Wastefully, we ordered room service, and while we waited for our food, we took turns in the shower and changing clothes as though we could wash away the morning.

I was depressed and tired and it was just noon. Angel, on the contrary, seemed to have a blaze of triumph about her. For her, I thought, the morning had been a vindication. She had protected my life successfully and proved her worth, her effectiveness. But that triumph was offset by watching the suffering of the nasty couple from whom she'd rescued me; she wasn't cold enough to be indifferent.

When our food came, we were ravenous.

'Think they'll tell?' Angel asked as we swapped bites of our desserts.

'Don't know,' I said. 'It's a toss-up. Let's go home.'

'Good idea. I'll call the airline after I finish this cake.'

Within an hour we were on our way to the airport.

Chapter Seventeen

We couldn't escape rain that day. It was pouring in Atlanta. Shelby had maneuvered close to the door somehow, and we loaded in our luggage and got into the car – Martin's Mercedes – with a minimum of fuss. Angel and Shelby were very glad to see each other. Shelby passed a paper over the seat to me; I was buckled in in the back. It was a copy of today's *Lawrenceton Sentinel* and the headline did not pack the punch it would have this time yesterday.

'Autopsy Results Surprising,' read the headline, an understatement if I'd ever seen one. In a low voice, Angel began telling Shelby what we had seen and done that morning. I read between the lines of the story Sally Allison had written so carefully. The forensic anthropologist, faced with what seemed a straightforward job of identification, had been surprised (and perhaps rather pleased) to find his job was more complicated than he'd thought. I would like to have seen Jack Burns's face, and Lynn's, when they found the third body was not Charity Julius. It was apparently Lynn who'd gone to Peachtree Leisure Apartments to find if the purported Mrs Totino had any ideas about the identity of the third corpse. Ever since the bones had been brought down from the roof, this must have been the moment the old woman had been dreading. Lynn had not allowed Duncan, the security guard, to call ahead, but Alicia must have been watching the closed-circuit TV channel and must have recognized Lynn as the police officer who'd come by before to tell her the bodies had been found. She'd opened her window and jumped.

'How much would they have realized from the murders?' Shelby asked.

'Huh? Oh. The purchase price of the house, the money that Mr

Julius had accumulated to start his own business, and I guess whatever money was due from life insurance policies. I suppose the company has to pay up if the missing person is declared dead. If they just could have gone four more months without the bodies being discovered, the three of them could have scattered to the four winds once the money was in their hands.'

'You think she would have given Harley and Charity their share?' Angel asked as we changed highways to go northeast to Lawrenceton.

'I think so. She'd seen Harley in action.'

'It must have been galling, to have been so strapped for money all those years – the old woman, I mean.'

'Yes, for her. It may not have made much difference to Harley and Charity. They didn't kill the people they killed for money; the money was Alicia Manigault's idea, first and foremost.'

A teenage romance that went wrong; the Ballad of Charity and Harley.

I wondered what the Louisiana police were making of the two.

As we entered my hometown, I had a hard time believing I had questioned a seriously injured young woman as intensely as I had. I also had a hard time believing she'd hit me in the stomach hard enough to cause the deep bruise even now developing in the soft tissue around my navel.

I hadn't heard from Martin in two days. I wondered how things were going for him in Guatemala. I missed him, abruptly and passionately. Tears began to well up in my eyes, and I took off my glasses to dab at them with a Kleenex.

'Martin called,' Shelby said out of the blue. We were turning on the road out of Lawrenceton that led to the house. 'He tried your hotel room but found you'd checked out. I have to go back to the airport tonight to pick him up.'

'I'll let you, rather than going myself,' I told him. I was too tired to face the airport more than once that day, and I would rather be warm and rested and in bed when he came home than tired and wrinkled and public at the airport.

We pulled into the driveway, Shelby trying to tell me about the security systems he'd been investigating while we were gone, me not giving a damn.

'Are you afraid of going in?' Angel asked. The rain was coming down in earnest as we got the bags out of the trunk. We crossed the garage to open the side door and take the covered walkway to the kitchen door. Madeleine sat regally, tail wrapped around her, by her food dish.

'No,' I said, and realized it was true, 'I'm not afraid of this house. There aren't any ghosts here. The people who would have become ghosts are the ones who are still alive, down in Louisiana. The people who died were too nice to be ghosts.'

Now, this babble gives you some idea of my exhaustion, and the look Shelby and Angel gave me simultaneously told me I was becoming weird. But the house didn't scare me; I felt happy to be in it again. I breathed a sigh of relief when the Youngbloods left to go up to their apartment for their own reunion, after I'd refused Shelby's offer to carry my bags up to my bedroom.

The light on the answering machine was blinking. I pressed the 'Play' button to hear my messages.

My mother: 'We're back, and we had a wonderful time! The message you left saying you were going to New Orleans was kind of confusing, Aurora. Is Martin with you or not? Is this thing about the bodies upsetting you? Call me when you're home.'

Emily Kaye: 'Roe, I'm sorry to be such a pest, but we really do need help on the Altar Guild. Please call me at home when you get back from wherever you are. Oh, by the way! Aubrey and I are engaged!'

Aubrey: 'Roe, if you're upset about the discovery at your house, please call me. I want to help if I can. And I wanted you to know, first: Emily says she'll marry me.'

I made a face into the reflective glass of the clock.

My mother: 'You know, Aurora, I really wish you had left the name of your hotel with Patty at my office. It's very aggravating not being able to get in touch with you, to make sure you're all right. My understanding from calling Martin's office is that he is not with you. So what are you doing in New Orleans?'

I hoped the antique earrings would soothe her.

The other messages, in order: Sally Allison, Sally Allison, and Sally Allison.

I headed up the stairs, looking at my beautiful house with pleasure, glad to be home. Later my husband would be home; we would talk; everything would be all right.

But when I entered our bedroom, I had a sudden picture of a dark-haired girl seizing an elderly woman and forcibly shoving the gray head through the window so it could be stove in with a hammer.

I banished that vision firmly.

This was my house.